D0434997

Paradigm

A Novel

Also by Robert Taylor

OPStime: The Secret to Perfect Timing for Success

Paradigm

A Novel

Robert D. Taylor

SB

Savas Beatie

Cataloging-in-Publication Data is available from the Library of Congress.

First Savas Beatie edition, March 2006

ISBN 1-932714-16-2

SB

Published by
Savas Beatie LLC
521 Fifth Avenue, Suite 3400
New York, NY 10175
Phone: 610-853-9131

Savas Beatie titles are available at special discounts for bulk purchases in the United States by corporations, institutions, and other organizations. For more details, please contact Special Sales, P.O. Box 4527, El Dorado Hills, CA 95762, or you may e-mail us at sales@savasbeatie.com, or visit our website at www.savasbeatie.com for additional information.

To Carrie, my wife and best friend,
for her never ending encouragement and support

Acknowledgements

Life appears to be divided into segments, seemingly independent, each defining one's accomplishments. Certain individuals lend a hand and provide clarity.

To Lynn McGill, who worked with me tirelessly to the end. I applaud you. The research, ideas, and descriptions for this book wouldn't have been possible without you.

I thank Dusty Rhoades for his excellent advice. I would also like to thank Dr. Robert W. Bass, who spent years of hard work writing the programs that now do what seemed before impossible, and Dr. George W. Masters, Jr., For incorporating the programs into Xyber9.

Thanks are also due: Suzanne Thompson for interjecting artistic prose; Jim Agnew, for providing encouragement and direction; Jim Loy, for recommending the proper hieroglyphs; and Hikmat Faraj, for offering his expertise in Middle Eastern affairs.

I also extend warm thanks to the members of my family for their continuing love and enthusiasm.

And finally to my publisher. I would like to thank Theodore P. Savas, who had the vision to see *Paradigm* as it is—the Genuine Article.

Truth

The science uncovered in this novel is real.

In March of 2000, world renowned scholars and scientists signed a petition to nominate my discovery, *The Taylor Effect,* for the Nobel Memorial Prize in Economics. I will empirically prove in this book why and how stock market movements are *not random*, and explain to the reader exactly how to predict the stock market for years in advance.

The names of the organizations, places, things, and theorems mentioned in *Paradigm* are historically accurate. Architecture, art, antiquities, designs, and clothing exist in actuality.

Fiction

Where is the line between reality and fiction? This novel blends both. *Paradigm* is my vehicle of choice for publishing my discovery. I embellish only the plot line in order to hopefully provide you, the reader, with a compelling story. Some of the people mentioned in *Paradigm* actually exist, though most do not except within these pages.

The challenge of finding out just what is truly real and what is not is now up to you.

Prologue

Many prominent financiers, industrialists, and politicians the world over had passed beneath the carved crest on the lintel of Leviticus' library. Precious few understood its true significance. Not that anyone would believe the mysterious legacy that had been passed down through generations, a secret Leviticus' family had been sworn to protect since time immemorial.

Seated behind his huge desk in a mahogany wing chair, Leviticus hunched over a pile of papers, struggling to concentrate on the task at hand. It had been a very long day, and his one glass of whiskey had nearly put him to sleep. The letters on the page at the top of the pile wavered back and forth. He squinted and rubbed his eyes deeply with the balls of his fists. Leviticus' long, thin facial features were still handsome, despite his thick mane of white hair, but his once sharp coal black eyes were not as strong as they had once been. And today, they were heavy with fatigue. He closed them for a moment and sat absolutely still, listening to the pleasant sound of the fire crackling a few feet away across the room.

Without warning, a sharp pain erupted behind his sternum. With a labored intake of breath, he clutched his chest and slumped over on the desk. He struggled to catch his breath as he felt the choking sensation that had become all too familiar of late. With his right hand he clutched his blood soaked handkerchief, which he used to cover his mouth as his body was racked with uncontrollable coughing. As he coughed and wheezed, the library door swung silently open. His guest stood in the entry way, grim faced and inwardly shocked at the old man's deteriorating condition.

Randolph watched, his hand frozen on the ornate bronze doorknob, while his father choked out gobs of bloody spittle into his handkerchief. His thoughts turned dark. The old man's tuberculosis was rapidly draining away his life. My God, he thought, struggling to keep his emotions in check. He had no idea the disease had progressed so quickly. The reason behind the sudden and cryptic demand for his return from Europe was now clear. The dutiful son politely waited, refusing to enter the library until the coughing fit subsided. The last thing Randolph wanted was to embarrass his father.

After one last deep wet gasp, Leviticus wiped off his mouth and slumped back in the chair. He wondered how long it would take to die, and prayed the end would come quickly. The last thing he wanted to do was rot away on a bed, choking to death and losing his dignity.

"Ahem."

The old man straightened up with some effort and turned his head toward the door. "Randolph!" Even in pain Leviticus managed a broad smile. Stuffing his handkerchief in his pocket, he reached for his cane and lifted himself out of his chair. He would greet his son standing. "I am pleased you made such good time on the crossing. How's Catherine? Is London's weather still giving her fits? And my grandson, tell me, how is Bernard doing?"

Randolph smiled broadly in return as he crossed the richly carpeted room and walked around the grand desk to give his father a careful, though heartfelt, hug. As he did so, he bit his lip in horror. His father was nothing but skin and bones. He pulled back and looked him in the eye. "She and the little man are fine, you need not worry about them. What do the doctors say about your condition?"

"To hell with the doctors! What do they know anyway?" Leviticus growled in return, swinging his hand as if swatting a fly. He escorted Randolph around the front of his desk to the fireplace, where both men settled down into a pair of plush chairs facing the roaring hearth. "I enjoy the solitude and warmth of this fireplace more and more each day," whispered Leviticus.

"I noticed our investments are giving you a bit of enjoyment too, given the stock markets' dilemma." Randolph replied following with an amused laugh. As always, the old man was at the top of his game, despite the brave indifference regarding his health.

"Did you secure our interest in Europe?" Leviticus asked, raising his eyebrows as he always did when he asked a serious question.

"Yes, father, and just in the nick of time, considering current events." Randolph chuckled softly. "I have to admit, though, you sure do cut things close."

Leviticus joined him in the soft laugher that quickly ended in another coughing spell. Randolph jumped up to help the old man, who waved back his son with one hand while covering his mouth with the other.

"*Damn this disease*," thought Randolph as he stood helplessly by, twisting his hands together in frustration. He also knew he was vulnerable in the face of his father's limited future. When the coughing subsided, he took a step and leaned down, placing a firm hand on his father's shoulder. "You don't need to worry about our European partners or our investments there, although things were a little tight until the events of the last seven days. You had many of the family members scratching their heads."

"Let them scratch themselves bald!" Leviticus shot back with a grim smile. He put away the stained handkerchief a second time and straightened his shoulders. "Have a seat." His voice took a sudden, serious turn. "It's time I complete your training, son. Tomorrow you will take over our empire."

Randolph felt his stomach tighten with excitement as he sat next to Leviticus. At last, he thought with relief. He had finally reached the end of his apprenticeship, as had his father and the fathers before him. This final passing of the torch was not without its sadness for it had been hastened along by Leviticus' impending demise. Randolph remained quiet while his father rallied his strength and began to speak.

Slowly and methodically, Leviticus spelled out the recent events that he had anticipated and engineered. The results were in the books, undeniable, real. The stock market had crashed. In just four trading days, its value had plummeted more than 39%. The worst was yet to come.

His father's plans before the crash had been simply ingenious. In the months leading up to October 24, 1929, the Group's bankers in both the United States and Europe transferred their personal cash into a Swiss bank account. J. P Morgan's bank secured the American holdings by following the same procedure. The family and other close associates were instructed to follow Leviticus' orders to the letter. Other prominent financial players followed suit. Joseph Kennedy liquidated his stock positions and the entire Group's real estate holdings, with the exception of their main business locations and immediate family homes.

J. P. Morgan's brokerage firm sold the members' securities while the markets were setting new highs. Selling into the market allowed easy fills for their sell orders and drew little attention from either the market makers or the press. By the time the stock market began to collapse on October 24th, Leviticus had done the impossible. He had converted into cash and precious metals nearly seventy-two billion dollars of his own personal holdings, the holdings of his family, and the wealthiest members of his organization. Every penny was safely secured outside the reach of any government.

With obvious glee, Leviticus continued to detail the events of the crash. As the minutes ticked past, Randolph watched and listened in rapt awe as his father found strength he did not know he still had, his words gaining strength, his voice now strong and steady. To Leviticus, the crash was spectacular by any measure.

On Thursday, October 24, the market opened at 9:30 a.m. Mayhem broke loose on the floor within hours of the opening bell. The ticker tape machine fell behind by an hour and a half, leaving investors frantically scrambling to place sell orders for their investments without even knowing the current bid/ask prices. Within a short time, utter panic entrenched itself on the floor. As word spread of the selling frenzy, thousands of frantic investors gathered outside the stock exchanges and brokerages firms. Police were dispatched to insure the safety of the traders. As the trading day wore on it became more difficult to separate fact from fiction. Rumors had reached epidemic levels.

Shortly before noon, the Chicago and Buffalo Exchanges had to close down. The New York Times was abuzz with the rumor that eleven well-known speculators had committed suicide. The New York Stock Exchange closed the visitor's gallery to keep the desperate scenes below from spreading additional panic.

In the span of a few hours a record eight million shares traded hands. The pits were filled to capacity with traders and locals. Runners ran madly from one firm's trader to another. Jackets were shed, ties left to dangle, and the floor was covered with unfilled orders. To the right of the podium, the seven-story windows admitted the sparkle of sunlight, but to the frantic traders bustling about below, bedlam had set in, carrying with it a fear none had ever known before.

An American Red Cross flag hung incongruously across from the big board. It was an eerie sight for the men gathered on the floor, caught as they were in a cyclone of events as terrible as any catastrophic crisis they could imagine. Searching for answers, their eyes were drawn to the empty podium for an announcement that would end their agony.

On that day, Leviticus' time had come. Standing in J. P. Morgan's office, he put his lucrative plans into action. It began with a well-placed leak to reporters that an unprecedented meeting was taking place at the office of J. P. Morgan and Company. This meeting involved the most important men in finance and banking. Once the leak was set, Leviticus instructed Thomas Lamont, a senior partner at Morgan, to make the following statement to newspaper reporters: "There has been a little distress selling on the Stock Exchange due to a technical condition of the market," and that things were "susceptible to betterment."

As planned, the bankers jumped to assure their investors, trying desperately not to expose their already neutral market positions. Within a short time the market began moving up in response to Lamont's statement, but its climb was short-lived. Leviticus watched in anticipation as the market began to roll over.

It was at that point Leviticus' first hurdle presented itself. Richard Whitney, a partner to Morgan and vice-president of the NYSE, called Morgan and begged him to act as quickly as possible to shore up the market. Morgan explained the request to Leviticus. Furious, Leviticus demanded that the turncoat Whitney return to the bank. Whitney was disobeying his orders.

Visibly shaking, Morgan relayed the directive, listened for a few moments to Whitney's reply, and looked at Leviticus in stunned disbelief. "Go ahead and hang yourself if you want to!" he shouted into the phone, "but the bank is not going to back you!" With that, Morgan slammed down the phone and stared at Leviticus. "The man has lost his mind. Dick Whitney just told me that he would turn this around even if he had to use his own personal holdings!"

Leviticus shrugged and offered a smug smile. "It won't do any good, you know, the market is cooked!" Both men looked at the clock. It was 1:30 p.m.

Richard Whitney, meanwhile, walked onto the exchange floor. The silence was deafening, you could hear a pin drop. No one could have imagined what was about to take place. The press and just about everyone else had expected someone to take to the podium and announce that the NYSE would close. Instead, Whitney held up his hands palms in, and yelled out a 205 buy order for 10,000 shares of U.S. Steel. The current asking price was 195 which sent a clear message no trader could ignore. Fear no longer gripped the traders. As history would later record, an insatiable greed permeated all those present. No one wanted to miss the new bull market! The floor erupted in a fury of both buy and sell orders.

Whitney wasn't finished yet. He continued shouting similar orders for another ten minutes, stirring the traders' fury for a dozen more blue chip stocks. Frantic buying and selling continued for the rest of the day, but by the time the bell finally rang, the market was still down more than 20%. Leviticus nodded knowingly as he smiled at Morgan. It was as he expected.

The next day, Friday the 25th, the market traded flat to sideways as it entered the weekend. But when it opened on Monday the 28th, the market broke and ended down another 13%.

Randolph sat transfixed, his mouth slightly open as he stared into Leviticus' glowing eyes. "And by the end of Tuesday," concluded the old man, "the market tumbled another 11%."

The damage was done.

ꝑ

Both men sat quietly for a few minutes. Only the fire spoke. Now that his story was finished, the vigor that had suddenly flowed into Leviticus' withered body left it just as quickly.

"It is time. Help me up, son."

Together, father and son exited the library and walked down a short hallway to an adjoining room. Randolph pushed open the large double oak doors. In the middle of the room was a matching oak library table. Sitting squarely in the center was an object Randolph would come to understand better than anything else in his life.

It was an ancient Egyptian box. Many years ago, his grandfather Benjamin had told him the story of its origins and travels. After the genius of its engineering and humble beginnings, the ornately carved wooden box with a granite top had made its way to Egypt in 2585 BC, where it was used by Pharaoh Khufu to build Egypt's Great Pyramid. According to legend, it was stolen from Gaza by the magician Djedi and eventually came under the control of the cult of Isis around 1300 BC. After the fall of Alexandria, the box was secreted away to Rome by Ptolomy I, a Greek general in Macedonian service. There, the box's capabilities were utilized in ways unimaginable to those who had come before.

Today, October 29, 1929, its awesome power would be transferred to Randolph.

Leviticus took Randolph's hand and placed it on the granite lid. Randolph could almost feel the incredible supremacy contained within. "The empire is now yours, my son," whispered the old man. "I'll give you my last instructions now."

With that, Leviticus turned slowly around and sat down in a chair. A relaxed, almost relieved look, spilled over him. The torch had been passed. The short coughing fit that swept through his body ended almost as soon as it began. He swallowed with some difficulty and then, finally, began. Randolph bent low to hear his father's voice, which had been growing weaker and softer by the second. By now it was barely audible.

The old man pointed to the dials on the right side of the box and spelled out his instructions carefully. First, Randolph would convert 60% of the group's cash to buy DOW blue chips stocks by the middle of the next month, November 1929. Leviticus had a pen in his hand and wrote out his instructions on a pad of paper he always carried with him in his jacket pocket. "You will have no problem executing the positions. The market makers and locals will be more than glad to fill your orders. The remaining balance of the money should be left safely in cash." He paused and looked carefully at Randolph. "Is that clear?"

"Yes, completely."

Leviticus nodded and cleared his throat. "Next, during the middle of the month of April 1930, you must not only liquidate your positions to cash during the market rally, but in addition, sell-short the same blue chip stocks with 100% of the group's capital. However," Leviticus carefully cautioned Randolph, "be forewarned that the Group will protest mightily. Ignore them. My closest associates will stand by your decision."

He stopped again to make sure Randolph understood. Only after his son nodded in agreement did he continue. "Your next move is to close all your short-sell positions in the middle of October 1932 and take the profits to safe holdings." He was done writing. His spidery hand was still, his final command to his closest associates issued.

Randolph was now in charge.

ℬ

Leviticus was laid to rest long before the final results of the 1929 stock market crash were written. The market moved down to the middle of November 1929 just as he expected. Though down nearly 40%, the market gained back half its losses by the middle of April 1930, delivering to Randolph and the Group an extraordinary profit. And then the market began its long journey down until October 1932, by which time it had lost 89% of its value. The profits envisioned by Leviticus were fully realized and topped one hundred and thirty-seven billion dollars by the time Randolph closed their positions.

The coffin was finally nailed shut on the market, ensuring Randolph a victory of astounding proportion. His handling of the crash, an honor his father had enjoyed during the 1907 market collapse, sealed his position as head of the Group.

Fall 1932

Randolph leaned over his father's sprawling mahogany desk, delighted with the legacy the old man had left him. Shortly after Leviticus' death, he and Catherine had moved into the house overlooking Central Park. The home echoed with children's laughter and scampering feet.

Randolph was thinking about how much he missed Leviticus when his son raced through the pocket doors to the library with a nanny in close pursuit. Smiling, Randolph scooped up the fleeing Bernard in his arms.

"Now, where were you going in such a rush?" he teased, tussling the youngster's hair as he waved the girl off. He sat Bernard down on the desk and gazed thoughtfully at his son.

History, he knew, would repeat itself. Will he be ready when his time comes?

Chapter 1

December 2003

 The bright afternoon sun pierced long shards of light through the slats of the blinds and abruptly shook Nicholas Shepard from his work. He was supposed to meet his wife Cassandra for lunch. He breathed a sigh of relief when he realized he had a leisurely twenty minutes to make it across the quadrangle from White Hall to the Café Antiqo in the Michael Carlos Museum. That left him plenty of time to save recent changes to his PowerPoint presentation and leave a note on the office door for his graduate assistant, Lev Foust.

It took only a short time into his first quarter as a visiting professor for Emory University students to begin extolling his Economics courses. He attributed their enthusiasm to the novelty of having a new face on the faculty, but it was Nicholas' imaginative approach to simplifying econo-physics that captivated their young and eager minds. Even undergraduates not majoring in Economics were eager to sign up for his classes. To the chagrin of tenured faculty, he was already mentoring several doctoral candidates.

Stepping out into the sunlight, Nicholas was amazed, as always, at the warmth of the afternoon. Atlanta's December temperatures were balmy compared to winters in the mountains of Asheville, North Carolina. He had only reluctantly accepted Emory's teaching offer, for it meant that Cassandra had to give up her position at the Biltmore Estate. However, once university officials discovered that eminent art historian Dr. Cassandra Shepard was part of the package, they jumped at the opportunity to offer her a position as well. Flattered, she agreed to work part-time and then signed up for additional history courses. As she informed a stunned curator, "You can never have too many degrees!"

Nicholas steered clear of the elevator and took the steps two at a time, arriving breathless at the third floor café. He immediately spotted his wife at a table tucked deeply into a quiet corner.

"Must you run up all the stairwells?" Cassandra sighed dramatically as Nicholas approached with a broad smile on his face.

"It's the only exercise I get. You don't want me ending up with a middle-aged spread, do you?"

His wife shook her head in mock despair. Since high school, Nicholas had sustained the same 190-pound, six-foot-two-inch frame. Cassandra was no different. Women around the world would have killed for the ability to eat rich gourmet food without gaining a pound.

"Certainly not, my darling," she answered cheerfully, "which is why I've ordered for both of us."

Nicholas was about to give her a pained look when a student server approached with a pair of steaming cappuccinos and set them down on the table. "Well, this looks like a good start. I can always use more caffeine." He dropped into the chair opposite his wife.

"How is the presentation coming?" she asked, taking a small sip of the hot bitter liquid.

"Better than I was expecting. These kids today are so much smarter than we were at their age. I really have to keep on my toes." He raised his small cup in a salute and smiled. "Thanks."

Cassandra returned the warmth. "They adore your lectures, silly. You shouldn't angst so much over them. You are such a natural in front of a class." She looked over the rim of the cup at him and smiled to herself. Moving to Atlanta had been good for the both of them. "Oh, I nearly forgot," she said suddenly, breaking into a wide grin. "Gabriel called this morning. He's invited us to Biltmore for a party next weekend."

Nicholas' face lit up. "That's great! We haven't seen him since we moved here. Will Alex and Francesca be coming?"

"Are you kidding? It's a costume ball. They wouldn't miss it for the world! Francesca will stitch up some exquisite dress that'll make her look like a Rosetti painting!" They both laughed at the mental picture.

"And you, my dear? What will you dress as, Madame X?"

The server returned, this time with two bowls of homemade vegetable noodle soup. Cassandra slowly leaned back in her chair as he carefully set the bowls on the table in front of them. "We all have to go in costume, chum," she winked at her husband. "How about a ruthless industrialist and his society wife, say roughly 1896?"

"Well, if Alex agrees to dress up, I suppose I can as well," Nicholas sighed. Once his wife and his sister-in-law made up their minds to do something, the men were at their mercy.

"Perfect." She said, clapping her hands enthusiastically. "We shall do the Vanderbilts proud. It will be so beautiful with all the Christmas decorations. Maybe it will snow!"

Nicholas shook his head in amusement. Here was a Smith graduate in a traditional high-neck white blouse, lunching in the midst of remnants of ancient civilizations, as ecstatic as his six-year old niece at the prospect of a snowy weekend.

Nicholas studied his wife while she picked up her spoon, filled it with soup, and moved it slowly to her mouth. She pursed her lips to blow on the hot liquid. His eyes lifted and took in her long dark hair, conservatively arranged on the top of her head. Black glasses hung from a thin chain around her neck. He stole a quick glance over the edge of the table. Peeking discretely out from the hem of her dark navy slacks were a pair of red stiletto heels. He would never admit it, but he found her academic persona incredibly sexy.

"Do you miss the Mansion?" He asked the question suddenly, pointedly. Although he loved Emory University and Atlanta, his fear was that she might quickly grow tired of her new life.

"Miss it? No," she answered, shaking her dark curls at his worried expression. "I don't miss it *that* way, Nicholas. It's always fun to have the gang together again, though. I miss Gabe a bit." Nicholas nodded in agreement. He missed him, too. He picked up his spoon and tried the soup. It was better than he expected.

Nicholas had first met Gabriel von Stuyvesant when they were graduate students at Yale. He introduced Gabriel to his twin brother, Alex, who was working on a Ph.D. in aerospace engineering at MIT. The three quickly became friends. Although Nicholas had stayed on to acquire doctoral degrees in both mathematics and statistics from Yale, the three men had kept close ties over the years, even after the two brothers married and developed more complex, separate lives. Coincidentally, Gabriel ended up taking a position in the twins' hometown of Asheville as the estate manager for the Vanderbilt mansion. It seemed like an odd choice for the descendant of one of America's foremost banking families, but the position was perfect for Gabriel, who had written a doctoral dissertation on the global redistribution of wealth. Aside from threats to disown him over the dissertation's disloyal claims, his father could do nothing about the generous trust fund set up by Gabriel's grandmother. The von Stuyvesant family had ties to the Vanderbilts by marriage several generations ago. His job allowed him to dabble in his love for antiquities, exercise his concern for responsible land management, and distribute his wealth through a wide variety of community projects.

Nicholas looked across the crowded dining room and nodded a greeting to an attractive young student standing by the caryatid replicas from the Parthenon which flanked the hallway entrance. Cassandra swivelled her head and followed her husband's gaze until her own eyes fell upon the young woman with an armful of books and a warm bright smile. She was stunningly beautiful.

"Heavens, who is that?" she whispered. "She looks just like a Vigée-Le Brun painting."

Nicholas arched one eyebrow and worked hard to hold it in place until she burst out laughing. "Marie Louise Elisabeth Vigée-Le Brun. You've seen her paintings of Marie Antoinette and Madame Du Barry. She painted quite a few of the French aristocracy before leaving France during the French Revolution."

"Oh, right." French painters held little interest for him.

"Seriously, Nicholas, who is she?"

"That," he replied in a haughty, deep, but quiet voice, shaking his head as if afflicted with a mild palsy, "is Mademoiselle Felicia Theobald, a brilliant economics historian specializing in European trade routes in antiquity, a graduate of the Sorbonne and . . . drum roll please . . . my new graduate assistant, courtesy of Lev."

Cassandra's eyes widened. "*She* is Lev's girlfriend?"

Nicholas nodded. "They make a charming couple, don't they?"

The corners of Cassandra's mouth turned downward in an ugly grimace. Lev made her uncomfortable. The graduate assistant was outgoing, brilliant, and boasted an uncanny grasp of economic theory and application. But he was also arrogant and too clever by half. There was something ever so slightly wrong with him. For lack of a better word,

Cassandra thought he was shifty, and she had told her husband as much. Nicholas shrugged off her concerns. His guarded manner has a lot to do with his upbringing, he had explained. Lev's father was a prominent New York financier and his clients demanded absolute discretion. How would you act if you had grown up in a high-powered family chin-deep in the world of corporate intrigue and wealth, he had asked his wife. His attempt at rationalization had failed to convince her.

"I assume she can hold her own," Cassandra wryly replied, "but I think Lev would just as soon eat you for dinner as look at you." She watched as the walking piece of artwork strolled away and melted into a swirl of students and faculty.

"That's ridiculous." Her husband laughed softly. "I know you don't like Lev much, but we should have them over to the apartment for dinner some evening. It's the right thing to do." With that, Nicholas heaved a sigh and rose from his chair. "I have to get back." He leaned over and gave his cynical wife a lingering kiss on the forehead. "I love those red heels," he whispered in her ear.

Nicholas' warm breath sent a tingle through her body and she shivered and pushed him away with a laugh. "I've got my eye on you."

"I've got my eye on you," was a little joke the two had shared since they heard it in a smoky little blues club on a visit to New Orleans many years earlier. If Nicholas looked out his office window and leaned to the right, he could see the Post-Modern building that architect Michael Graves had so adeptly renovated to blend in with the Beaux-Arts buildings on campus. Although he couldn't see her office, he liked knowing his wife was so close.

When he got back to his office, Nicholas pulled up his PowerPoint presentation and reached for his notes. He groaned aloud when he remembered his notes were buried away in his filing cabinet across the room. Not having things readily available was a real pet peeve. Considering how other professors fared, he knew he was privileged to have an office large enough to accommodate both of his graduate students and all his papers and books. Generally he got on well with his office mates, although once he had an argument with Lev that nearly came to blows over something as mundane as scattered papers on a desk. Nicholas subscribed to the floor-stacking filing method of organization. Lev detested clutter of any sort and was compulsive about keeping the office meticulously tidy. Since they collaborated well professionally, Nicholas tolerated his obsession. The downside was that he was completely dependent upon his student whenever he needed to find something. And deciphering Lev's filing system was not unlike decoding the Rosetta Stone.

Chapter 2

Driving through North Carolina brought back powerful memories for Nicholas. As boys, he and Alex had traveled many of the state's back roads with their father, who owned several tobacco farms in the region. They often accompanied him as he journeyed from one to the other, overseeing production of the aromatic weed. As far back as 1765, the Shepard family managed acres of tobacco farms in North Carolina after their ancestor, Daniel Shepard, received a large land grant from King George III. Ten years later, when Shepard joined the patriot cause, the money from his tobacco was used to purchase much needed supplies in Europe.

When the twins were older their father sold the family farms. The Surgeon General, he explained, had finally reached the same conclusion England's King James had reached nearly four centuries earlier when he published his "Counterblast to Tobacco." In 1604, the monarch announced that smoking was *"loathsome to the eye, hatefull to the Nose, harmfull to the brain, [and] dangerous to the lungs."* Divested of the valuable acreage, their father invested in the stock market and changed the family business forever.

Nicholas had fond memories of the huge old barns with the creased brown tobacco leaves hanging on rods from the rafters. Painted black, with sides engineered to open and shut like huge window blinds allowing the tobacco to cure properly, the barns released a warm woodsy smell. He inhaled slowly and could still smell the musky scent. When the car hit a bump in the road he glanced over at Cassandra, who was leaning back in her seat with her eyes closed.

"Almost there?" she asked dreamily.

"Another fifteen minutes or so," answered Nicholas. Soon they were threading their way through the busy environs of Asheville. "Are you resting up for a late evening of Nineteenth Century frolic?" he teased.

"Yes. No . . . well, maybe." She opened her eyes and offered her husband a warm smile. "I know we just saw Alex and Francesca in Charleston for Thanksgiving, but I miss them. I wish the kids were coming, too."

"Oh, yeah? I bet you and Francesca would just love to dress poor Harrison and Rosemary up as little Vanderbilt children, complete with velvet knickers and petit fours."

"That's petticoats, you silly man," laughed Cassandra. "You would never have made Mrs. Astor's infamous Four Hundred list!" she continued. Cassandra was referring to Caroline Astor who, in an effort to snub the *nouveau riche*, adhered to a guest list of those who met three standards: they were a third generation millionaire; had a million dollars in disposable cash, and had never worked a day in their lives. It was said that The Four Hundred equated with the number of people who could fit in the ballroom of the Astor's New York mansion.

Pulling up to the main entrance into the Estate, Nicholas turned to his wife with a grin. "I know enough about The Four Hundred to recall that Mrs. Astor thought Commodore Vanderbilt was uncouth and swore too much."

"And the Commodore didn't care—but his children did! Things all changed by the time his grandson, George Washington Vanderbilt, came along. Besides, the Vanderbilts were richer than the Astors."

"Well, not paying income tax helped. I doubt G. W. Vanderbilt could have built the Biltmore mansion in today's financial climate. By the way," continued Nicholas, "speaking of the little heirs, who's taking care of my precocious niece and nephew this weekend?"

"With your parents spending the winter in Arizona, Francesca asked Galen to baby-sit." Cassandra turned to catch the look of surprise on her husband's face.

Father Galen Abbott was one of the twins' oldest friends, having grown up next door to them in Asheville. When Galen decided to go to seminary in Texas, the boys drove him out west in one long last fling of a road trip. Galen returned with a clerical collar, a doctorate in psychology, and a Stetson hat and alligator boots. His parishioners loved his patient ear and easygoing manner as much as the diocese cringed at his cowboy boots, Harley-Davidson, and barbed wit. As Nicholas thought about it, he imagined that Harrison and Rosemary were probably having a lot more fun with Father Galen, as they called him, than they would have with their over-protective grandparents.

Gabriel had sent them tickets to get in the gate because they would be arriving in the middle of the afternoon when the Estate was still open to tourists. They drove through the wooded approach to the house and Cassandra opened her window to take a deep breath of fresh air scented with pine. Nicholas stopped the car for a long moment in front of the house and they looked across the great lawn toward the mansion.

"I never get tired of looking at it," she sighed.

"Sort of an American Versailles isn't it?" said Nicholas.

"An American Chateau de Blois, to be exact," Cassandra corrected. "The architects drew on that chateau and others in the Loire Valley as well as Waddesdon Manor in Buckinghamshire in England. Eleven million bricks later, they wound up with a pretty spectacular creation."

They drove on past the main house to the farmhouse where Gabriel lived. There were people everywhere taking advantage of the warm December day to walk the grounds. Nicholas slowed the car to a cautious crawl as they rounded the tulip garden. He hated to admit it, but he was looking forward to the evening ball. And yes, it was even going to be fun dressing in period costume.

Gabriel was sitting on the porch of Brick House as his friends pulled up the drive. Cassandra marveled at his appearance. As he aged, Gabe was looking more and more like the Biltmore's original occupant, George Washington Vanderbilt. The resemblance was enhanced by his recent addition of a full mustache.

"Welcome!" he called out as they joined him on the wide veranda. "Alex is in the house changing, and Francesca has taken over my kitchen. I haven't a clue what she is doing, since we are dining at the house. But, you know her—once a chef, always a chef!"

Cassandra gave their host a warm squeeze and sped off toward the kitchen. As she entered, she spied Francesca stirring a huge copper pot on Gabriel's new six-burner stove. "Hey, you," she said, spreading her arms open to receive a strong hug from her sister-in-law. "What smells so heavenly?"

"Gabriel had some boar meat, so I'm making *scottiglia di cinghiale*," she said, turning back to the simmering concoction.

Cassandra leaned back on the granite counter and decided that she would rather not know why Gabriel just happened to have boar meat on hand. The last time she had seen the kitchen, he had just ripped out most of the old cabinets, replacing them with the rich glow of natural maple. He had also taken out the old wood stove and put in a gorgeous stone fireplace, which was now giving off the delightful scent of smoldering apple wood. The huge andirons for the fireplace had finally arrived from France and were now proudly on display.

A hesitant cook herself, Cassandra had always enjoyed watching her sister-in-law in the kitchen. She had once asked her if all Italians were good cooks, to which Francesca had tossed those glorious Titian red curls of hers and laughed. "All Italians love to eat, and every family has members who can cook and those who can eat! I was lucky to have a family of many cooks." At the moment, however, Cassandra had other things on her mind. Crossing her arms, she cleared her throat theatrically. "Well, what I really must know is what you brought us to wear?"

Francesca grinned and turned down the stove. "That took all of ten seconds!" Both women laughed. "Come on, let's run upstairs and I will show you. The guys are already getting dressed. We better also." The domestic Francesca was not only an expert with a whisk, but wielded a wicked sewing needle as well. It was a foregone conclusion when Gabriel invited them that she would design both of their frocks.

When she reached the first bedroom at the top of the landing, Francesca drew out of her closet a russet-colored Empire silk gown that included a voluminous cape. The color was perfect for her hair and highlighted her piercing emerald eyes. She also reached in and pulled out her sister-in-law's dress. When Francesca held it out Cassandra gasped. "Where did you get the pattern for that?"

"Do you recognize it?" asked Francesca

"Of course I do!" Cassandra was stunned. "Nicholas even teased me about coming dressed as the infamous Madame X."

"No, no, you are perfect for this! It's going to look fantastic on you, Cassandra."

Cassandra took the gown and laid it out on the bed to admire. John Singer Sargent's portrait of the mysterious Virginie Gautreau had shocked Parisians when it was shown in 1884 as "Portrait de Mme ***". Mademoiselle Gautreau and her mother had fled New Orleans during the Civil War when her father was killed at the Battle of Shiloh. Once in France, the charming Creole became well known in all the best salons in Paris. When Sargent hung the painting in a gallery, French society was so scandalized at its public sexuality that the artist fled Paris and never returned. The painting, which now hangs in New York's Metropolitan Museum of Art, was one of Cassandra's favorites—not so much for the daring black gown with its tiny straps and tight waist, but for the audacious woman inside it.

"Try it on, silly," Francesca said with an affectionate smile.

Cassandra hurriedly shed her clothes, slipped on the gown, and zipped it up, pulling the rhinestone straps over her shoulders. She turned to look at herself in a tall mirror by the door. Bands of black silk chiffon crisscrossed from bodice to bustle and showed off her narrow waist.

"Francesca," she breathed, "it is so beautiful. I think I'm going to be cold, though," she said with a little shiver.

"No problem," replied Francesca as she pulled out a glittering beaded shawl and draped it around Cassandra's neck. It was perfect.

When the women entered the living room, the three men were standing around the fireplace holding glasses of single-malt scotch. Nicholas lifted his glass with one hand and fidgeted with the collar of his tuxedo with the other, looking into a wall mirror until he got it just right. He held the fine scotch under his nose, swirled the pear-shaped snifter, and drank, breathing deeply as the whiskey warmed his mouth and throat.

"Lovely, Gabe," he said, complimenting him on his selection. "What is it?"

"Glad you approve. It's Aberlour," answered the host. "It's sweeter than most ten-year old single malts and velvety smooth without the smoky taste." His answer prompted Nicholas to pull the bottle closer and study its ivory label. "Hmm. I don't believe I have ever had it."

"You are never at a loss for good scotch!" Alex agreed. "Heh, are these new glasses, too?" he asked. The name of the scotch was etched into the side.

Gabriel nodded, his own glass already half empty. "Aberlour is a highland sherry-cask scotch. It's rapidly becoming my favorite." He smacked his lips. "I got a set of glasses the last time I was in the UK at Banffshire. The Speyside distillery tour is quite amazing, really. I highly recommend it."

As they debated the merits of good scotch, the men failed to notice the two stunning women standing in the doorway. Cassandra stretched out her hand to stop Francesca and together they stood for a few moments admiring the gentlemen in their timeless white ties and tuxedos. Alex spotted them first and his mouth dropped open. His brother followed his stunned gaze and when his eyes settled into place, the twins simultaneously mouthed the word, "Wow!"

Keeping control of both his faculties and his manners, Gabe set his glass down and walked quickly across the room, hands extended. "You will be the belles of the ball," he said graciously drawing them over to the fire.

"I wish we could dress like this all the time," blurted out Cassandra as she approached her husband.

"You are ever the romantic," he whispered nuzzling the nape of her exposed neck with his lips.

Francesca took the arms of both Alex and Gabriel. "Come on, let's go. I am starving!"

Gabriel escorted his guests to the front of the house where an estate carriage drawn by two Percherons stood patiently in the drive. "Your pumpkin awaits!" he said jokingly as he bundled his Cinderellas and their princes into the coach.

Snuggling beneath warm throws they set off, the *clip-clop* of hooves making it easy to envision an earlier, simpler time when the young family who had built the estate would have been enjoying the season in much the same way. The carriage rumbled down curving roads, along woodlands laced by tall loblolly pines, huge spruce trees, and the sere lacework of hardwoods against the twilight sky.

The carriage drew up to the main entrance and they disembarked, much to the admiring glances of the other arriving guests who were being let off by more modern conveyances. "The coach will come back for us in the morning," said Gabriel.

The couples were astonished. "We get to spend the night *here*?" asked Francesca.

Gabriel admitted that even he had never done that, and so had to buy sheets for their beds. They would be staying in a recently restored set of rooms on the third floor connected by a common room. "Please don't mention it to any of the other guests," he cautioned in a whisper as they made their way into the conservatory.

Before long an exquisite string quartet, flickering candles, and lavish costumes swept them all into the Gilded Age. Nicholas was pleased to see that Cassandra's gown caused a quiet stir among the other guests, many of whom represented the elite in Asheville society. It was a pleasant distraction from the academic backbiting of the Economics Department at Emory. As they danced and chatted with other couples, the stress of the preceding months fell away. Utterly relaxed, he was surprised at how at home he felt.

He leaned over and kissed Cassandra lightly on the check, whispering in her ear, "I could quickly get used to being a gentleman of means and leisure."

Chapter 3

When the clock struck midnight, the organizers of the charity ball firmly escorted the last of the revelers out into the chilly night. Gabriel pulled the Shepard couples aside and whispered, "Let's let the catering staff clean up. I have a surprise for you."

He pulled back the pocket doors leading into the breakfast room and gave a slight bow. "In keeping with the era, I thought you would like a light midnight supper before retiring."

The oval table literally shimmered with cut crystal glasses, Minton china, Francis I silver, and snowy white Irish linens. Alex walked in first, taking in the Adamsesque fireplace with its Wedgwood-style jasperware surround and blazing fire. He looked up at gold Florentine ceiling, down the leather-embossed walls, and finally to cut-velvet armchairs. Turning to his brother he shook his head in amazement, "This is all a little too much for an aeronautical engineer and a wannabe restaurateur," he said, motioning toward his bride.

"Speak for yourself," said Francesca, a small pout on her face. She tilted her head and looked at him. "I could become very comfortable living like this."

Alex nodded in agreement as the party settled into their places around the table. "I think we've quite a ways to go before we can live like this, but I sure wouldn't turn it down if someone offered!" He grinned at his double.

Nicholas put his napkin in his lap. "Say Alex, how is the aviation business these days?"

"You're the economist, you know the world market better than I do."

"Yes. Well, if the Dow hadn't been dead in the water for three years, we'd be at 20,000."

Gabe gave a mock shudder, "If my great-grandfather heard you say that, he'd climb out of his grave and invest the cache of gold coins I found behind a wall over here not too long ago. When the market crashed in '29, it had barely cracked 350!"

"What would that be in today's market?" asked Cassandra.

Nicholas was uncomfortable guessing at an exact number, but he wanted to provide his wife with some reasonable answer. Leaning forward he gestured with his fork as if it were a pen, and he was standing in front of a group of graduate students. "First, you must appreciate that most people today wouldn't understand the difference between market value and true value." When Alex gave him a blank stare, he paused a moment and decided to come at it from another direction. "Look, it is fairly simple, really. The market value is determined by the available money waiting to be invested in the stock market, plus money already invested. True market value, on the other hand, is money that is already invested. When you take out commodities, currency, bond investments, and so on, we are looking at more than three hundred billion in real dollars in 1929."

Francesca cut in, "Are you kidding? That much, back then?"

"Yeah," answered Nicholas. "Today, using that same formula, we are talking about nearly one hundred *trillion* dollars. That's the result of all those baby boomers reaching their top earning potential."

"Alright Professor," Cassandra spoke up, grabbing his flailing fork hand, "what about the Dow breaking 10,000 yesterday?"

"I can answer that," Alex offered. "It means that this particular economic downturn might be over, but even if this is a bull market, it probably still won't be a full recovery for all those people who lost half or three-quarters of their portfolios over the last three years. If you ask me, it's going to take ten more years to get back to that." Alex smiled at his brother. "Can't you apply the 'random walk down Wall Street' theory to this?"

Nicholas lifted a goblet of the estate's best red table wine. "Hmm. I don't know about that," he answered slowly. "I'm wondering about the relationship of chaos theory to the markets. If there is an order in what appears to us to be random, why shouldn't there be an order to the markets? We just don't discern it. Perhaps we could if we had a formula to distinguish it."

Francesca, who had been quietly admiring the presentation of the supper Gabriel had so thoughtfully arranged, suddenly looked up from her plate. "Hold on, you guys, what is this 'random walk theory' Alex referred to?"

"It's a concept proposed in the book *A Random Walk Down Wall Street*, which was written in the 1970s by Burton Malkiel, a Princeton University professor of economics," explained Nicholas. "Malkiel claimed that if you look at the stock market's historical data, its results will render future trends both unpredictable and independent of one another. Therefore—"

"Therefore," cut in Alex, "it's impossible to forecast future movement through historical trends."

Nicholas tilted his head. "Very nicely stated, brother." He turned back to Francesca. "I wish I could provide a better rationale. Not many people challenge that theory, and it is pretty well accepted as gospel."

Gabriel gave a deep sigh, "Despite my estrangement from my father, I keep up with things on the business end. They have a financial partner who has produced a return of better than twelve percent every year for the past three years."

"That's a decent rate of return when you realize that the various markets have lost between 30 and 85 percent of their value over the same time period. I wonder if they put their assets into energy, transportation, or bond funds."

"No, they have it in the Atlantic Trade Partnership."

"I know someone who works for them," said Alex. "I mean, I *used* to know someone named Mika Hunter. Atlantic Trade Partnership is a mega company, and she told me it tracks every nuance of the market. She encouraged me to invest some money with them a long time ago. I guess I should have." He chuckled to himself.

"I hope they continue to keep up the good work," continued Gabriel. His face immediately flushed red. "I mean, for all my family's conspicuous consumption, they have done huge amounts of philanthropic work over the last century. Much of it is based upon our market return, so I would hate to discontinue the work I've been able to do in this community."

Alex enjoyed a large swallow of wine. "You have certainly done a bang-up job with the vineyards, Gabe. It must be really difficult to know that your branch of the family didn't get to keep the house."

Trying to save their friend from further embarrassment, Nicholas shot his brother a searing look and changed the subject to economic issues facing the nation—including the impact of the Iraq War on the markets and the current political situation.

Nicholas was a great supporter of President Bush's tax cuts even though he knew that temporarily, the country's surplus revenues would evaporate. His colleagues at the university often challenged his views. Most were on the other side of the political spectrum, and as far as he was concerned, unable to understand the complexities of viable economics in a capitalistic system. Nicholas loved to refer to Reaganomics as the perfect plan to spur economic growth, and he often did so just to watch their faces steam with rage. He actively supported any tax referendum, and had even written to the chairman of the Federal Reserve suggesting that a better preemptive interest rate reduction would catapult the economy to the levels needed to support future growth.

Correctly sensing that his discussion of modern economics was losing its audience, Nicholas tactfully suggested, "Perhaps we should retire to the drawing room."

"An excellent idea, Professor," answered Cassandra, who was relieved they wouldn't have to endure another one of Nicholas' long lectures. "But which one? I think the library would be more suitable, don't you Gabe?"

The group wandered back toward the conservatory, which was now deserted of caterers, charity organizers, and estate employees. The room yielded quietly to darkness as Francesca blew out the candles, their lingering smoke exuding a smell of fresh bayberry.

Cassandra leisurely made her way down the 90-foot paneled hallway, taking in the familiar paintings and Belgium tapestries. Francesca trailed behind her, feeling as if she was floating down the elegant hallway with its tall candelabras glittering like the beads on Cassandra's shawl. "Just the ghosts and us," she whispered softly. Alex took her arm and led her down the hall in a slow waltz.

Cassandra's eyes danced down the stunning hallway. The long passage had once served as a sitting area for the Vanderbilt family. As the others chatted she remained quiet, thinking about Alex's tactless remark in the Breakfast Room. Ever since they were young boys Nicholas had been the reserved and thoughtful one, with Alex playing the role of the impetuous and often reckless twin. He had given his mother plenty of gray hairs by climbing tall trees at a young age. When he later took up mountain climbing, he liked to joke about his mother's hair turning completely white. Cassandra knew Gabriel was not insulted by Alex's remark. He had known the twins for a long time, and part of Alex's charm was his relaxed regard for civility.

Gabriel's family had their own claim to wealth. When his great-aunt had married into the Vanderbilt family, the dowry was only a fraction of the Vanderbilts' worth. As extended family, they had visiting rights to the mansion, but few of the von Stuyvesants had ever spent much time at the Biltmore except for Gabriel's father. Cassandra was still not certain what his particular relationship was to today's Vanderbilt family, and she was reluctant to ask Gabe too much about his parents. She only knew that if she had the smallest right to this home, she would never give it up.

The soaring library, more than two stories tall, took up the entire southern end of the mansion. The thousands of volumes lining the shelves came from around the world—Europe, Egypt, Constantinople—in container shipments the size of boxcars. Many were priceless first editions, some dating back to the 1500s. World globes from the 17th century stood at hand in convenient places, and huge refectory tables from the 16th century served as reading tables. The massive fireplace of elegant carved black marble offered a roaring fire. The soothing heat from the blaze enveloped them as soon as they entered the cavernous room. Cassandra lifted the hem on her dress and headed straight for the wrought iron and red velvet bench in front of the hearth and dropped her shawl, basking in the warmth of the flames. "This is my favorite room. Look at the ceiling, Francesca. Pelligrini's *Chariot of Aurora*, from the Pisani Palace in Venice."

Francesca frowned. "It should be sent back. We Italians miss it."

"I am afraid there are quite of lot of things in this house purchased in Europe," Gabriel explained. "But at least they are well taken care of. Many of Giovanni Antonio Pellegrini's works were destroyed during the World Wars."

Francesca shrugged as she settled next to Cassandra in front of the fire. "In that case, it must have been providence that they were brought here. But, such a fortune to spend," she sighed, "I can't imagine."

Cassandra glanced over her shoulder at Gabriel. "Tell Francesca about the library's secret room!" She was doing her best to lighten the mood.

"There's no secret room, Cassandra, but there is a hidden passageway beside the fireplace that leads to the second floor. Is that what you mean?"

"Yes, that's it! But I've never seen it." Cassandra put her shawl back on, stood up, and walked quickly to the foot of the spiral staircase leading to the wrought-iron balcony encircling the library. She passed Nicholas and Alex, who were busy examining an ancient Greek bible. A disbelieving Francesca, meanwhile, watched as Cassandra scurried up the winding stairs and began examining the bookcase panels on either side of the mantel. "It's here somewhere, isn't it?" she called down.

"This is completely creepy!" exclaimed Francesca, narrowing her eyes and staring at Gabriel. "You two are serious!" She shivered as a chill edged up her arms. "All we need is Vincent Price to step out and lead us into a dungeon."

Gabriel laughed. "There is indeed a passageway. I was in it once, many years ago. Nothing fancy at all. It just leads to a small stairway up to the next floor. And there's a key around here somewhere in one of these desks, Cassandra. The keyhole is behind one of the books up there, down near the floor, if I remember correctly, but I don't recall which one."

By this time the brothers had shifted their attention from the Greek script to Cassandra's investigation. While she explored they searched the room. After several minutes Nicholas triumphantly reached into the back of a drawer and pulled out a long brass key.

"Ah ha! Here it is, Cassandra!" he exclaimed.

Francesca reached out and plucked the key from his hand. She was about to rush up the stairs when the words Nicholas spoke stopped her in her tracks.

"Where's Cassandra?"

Francesca looked up and spun around, searching the second floor for her sister-in-law. Cassandra had vanished.

Chapter 4

"Cassandra!" yelled Nicholas. The three syllables echoed inside the library. There was no response.

Nicholas took the steps two at a time up to the balcony and began frantically pushing on the various walnut panels—just as his wife had. "I'm sure she's alright," puffed Gabriel, who had run up behind him. "The panel just shut behind her. Where is the key?"

Francesca had scurried up the stairs behind Gabriel, as fast as her gown would allow. "I have it. Here, take it," she said, handing the key to him. As Nicholas continued to poke and prod at the walnut panels, Gabriel dropped to his hands and knees and began examining the books lining the lower shelves, pulling them off in twos and threes and looking behind them for the keyhole. Alex bent down beside him to help. "We need a flashlight, Gabe."

"Indeed we do. Stay here." Gabriel dashed down the winding staircase and out into the hallway to a concealed utility cabinet, drew out a flashlight, and ran back into the library. Without a word he tossed it up to Alex, who was leaning over the railing. "Got it!"

It took a few minutes and scores of displaced tomes until Gabriel spotted the darkened indentation on the back wall. "Here it is!" he announced. He inserted the bronze key and turned it. A loud click filled their ears.

Nothing happened.

Everyone looked at one another in surprise. "What does the key do?" asked Francesca.

"I don't know," answered Gabe. "I've never personally used it. I guess the panel leading to the passageway is supposed to open, but it didn't." He turned the key back and forth, wiggling it in the hole.

"Wait! Do that again, Gabe!" shouted Nicholas, who had been keenly eyeing the walnut panel on the left side of the mantel. "There! This seam just opened about an inch!"

Nicholas took a step forward and pried back the tall bookcase. Behind it was a dark narrow hallway leading into blackness. Alex handed his brother the flashlight and, together with Francesca and Gabriel, crowded behind him to peer into the musty gloom. The beam of light played on the cobweb-strewn air and revealed nothing but dirty walnut panels lining a narrow hallway leading to a wooden stairway a few yards inside.

"Cassandra!" Nicholas shouted. Silence. "Quiet everyone!" he hissed.

For a few moments there was no sound except their irregular breathing. "Wait . . . I heard something," whispered Francesca. "It's like a muffled voice from inside the fireplace wall. Cassandra!"

"She must be behind the wall," replied Gabriel.

"How did she get there, Gabe, and how do we get her out?" asked Nicholas.

"I don't know," he answered with a puzzled look on his face, his palms turned upright. "I knew there was this passage, but there must also be some sort of compartment or space behind the fireplace itself. The stairs lead only to the bedrooms on the next floor, which have not yet been restored. No one goes there any more, especially this way. We haven't used it for years."

"Great." Nicholas started knocking on the panels. "Cassandra!" He pounded the wall three times and listened. "Cassandra!" he shouted again, pounding three more times. When he reached the staircase, he mounted the first two steps and stopped to pound yet again. This time everyone heard a responding knock, like sharp knuckles on the wall. "Nicholas! The steps!" shouted Alex. The bottom riser was slowly sinking.

Nicholas was too stunned to say anything, and before he could jump off, a hidden door in the hallway paneling near the foot of the stairs slid open and a disheveled Cassandra tumbled out. She was breathing heavily and utterly terrified, her eyes wide and her mouth opening and closing like a fish gasping for water.

"Cassandra! My God, how did you get in here?" Nicholas asked as she collapsed into him.

"I don't know! I pushed something that popped open this passageway and I stepped inside. I remember walking up a step and standing there for a few seconds but it was dark, and I tripped on my dress hem, lost my balance, and rolled into total blackness. I don't remember anything except standing up and hearing you guys shouting and pounding the walls."

Nicholas aimed the flashlight into the space that only seconds earlier had held his wife. "What do you see?" asked Francesca, her voice shaking with a genuine mixture of fear and excitement. "Now I really *am* worried Vincent Price might walk out of there!" Everyone joined in with some nervous laughter that helped break the palpable tension.

Nicholas gave a low whistle. "Hmm. It's not a small compartment," he announced. "It's a room." He moved the flashlight in a broad arc, taking in the size and shape of the discovery. "To quote Lord Carnarvon when he discovered King Tut's tomb, 'I see many things, wonderful things.' Gabe, you better take a look."

Alex groaned as Gabe moved forward. "Tut's tomb came with a big curse, as I recall." More nervous laughter.

Nicholas handed Gabriel the flashlight, and he aimed the beam along the walls for a few seconds. "We might not need this." He stepped a few feet into the room and flipped a light switch. Dark old-fashioned brass sconces softly illuminated the room and cast shadows over the dusty contents. Inside were a jumble of exquisite chests, furniture, chairs, crates, stacks of paper, books, and even a few stuffed hunting trophies, all of it reeking of dust and time.

The group slowly entered, marveling at their extraordinary find. "This is amazing, truly amazing," breathed Gabriel. "I cannot believe no one here at the mansion knows about this room!"

"It is something else," agreed Alex. "Look up there! There's a grate of some sort," he said, pointing up near the ceiling. "It must lead back into the flue."

"That might explain this room," replied Gabriel. "Perhaps it was originally built to service the flue, but for some reason was walled up along with all these boxes and miscellaneous items during an early renovation. I still can't believe this."

"I don't think so, Gabe," said Nicholas. "Somebody went to a lot of trouble to conceal this place. I mean come on, sliding panels? Sinking steps? This is straight out of Hollywood! And why leave all this stuff inside if you are abandoning the room? Even a bunch of completely incompetent workmen wouldn't have done that in any era."

Francesca and Cassandra were much more excited about what was in the chests and boxes than why the room was hidden away. "What shall we look at first?" asked Francesca impatiently. "How about this huge chest? It looks Italian!"

"It is called a *cassone*," Cassandra said. "My guess is Fifteenth Century—probably Florence. See how the simple lines carved in the walnut are not as ornate as the Venetian ceiling in the library? Definitely Florence."

"You are amazing, Cassandra, and you are probably right, too," agreed Gabriel, who was still looking around in shocked bewilderment. "I don't recall anything in this room being in any of the catalogues and I've certainly never indexed any of it." Finding out he had somehow missed an entire room in the mansion was particularly annoying. "This is going to take me a long time to inventory and catalog," he sighed. "Perhaps you can help me, Cassandra?"

"Gladly." Cassandra was already moving to clear the *cassone* from its jumble of surrounding objects. The chest was coffin-shaped, with bracket feet and carved acanthus leaf uprights supporting the top. Egg-and-dart decorations surrounded the front panel, which featured a painting of a river flowing through a city. "I think that's the Arno going through Florence," she said thoughtfully. "It looks remarkably like one that belonged to the Strozzi family I saw in a book for one of my classes. Let's see what's inside!"

In their excitement no one seemed to notice that the lid lifted with little resistance. The *cassone* was full of papers. "Ahh," muttered Alex. "That's damn anticlimactic. All this old stuff is probably accounting ledgers or something equally exciting."

"I don't think so, Alex," whispered Cassandra as she looked more carefully at the items filling the chest. "Some of these are scrolls . . . old scrolls . . . made of parchment." She reached in and gently lifted one out.

"Here's one made of papyrus! It's Egyptian!" Although the piece in her hand was little more than a large fragment a few inches square, it was covered with beautifully-drawn hieroglyphics. Gabriel nearly knocked her over to look at it. He had a fondness for the ancient world, and was something of an amateur scholar of the era. Nicholas and Alex exchanged amused looks and Francesca drew up a delicate Louis XVI chair and sat in front of the chest, admiring its gilt work and the surprisingly bright painting. Cassandra gingerly set the fragment on a table while Gabriel peered into the chest and carefully removed the rest of the papers.

"There's something else in here." Gabriel's voice was muffled because his head was well down into the *cassone*. Everyone peered over his shoulder. "Well, what have we here? Take a look."

At the bottom of the chest was a box. The historians were both silent. "What is it?" asked Nicholas. No one replied. "You mean neither of you can even hazard a guess?"

"I have no idea," answered Cassandra with a shake of her head.

Gabriel and Nicholas reached in and gripped it by the ends, lifted it out, and set it on the floor. "For its size, it sure is heavy," said Gabriel.

The hand-sculptured box had a solid granite top carved to fit its rectangular design, which included four protruding ends of the wooden box. The polished granite was a dusty light brown. Gabriel ran his hand over the smooth polished surface. "You know," he said, reflectively, "when I first saw this in the bottom of the chest, in the shadows, I thought it was carved out of ebony. But now that I see it in the light, this wood is definitely cypress."

Cassandra agreed. "Cypress trees were abundant in western Asia during the time of the ancient Egyptians." She looked at the others as she tried to explain its significance. "Cypress was the preferred wood of the sculptors employed by the Pharaohs and other influential persons in antiquity. It's hard, fragrant, and very durable. It was especially prized for sculpting mourning and funereal items. Cypress sculptures of that time period can be found on display at Egyptian museums and the Pergamon Museum in Berlin."

"Do you mind?" asked Gabriel suddenly, as he drew a micro recorder from his pocket. "I am going to have to inventory this anyway."

Everyone remained silent while Gabe began speaking, describing the box in detail. "The relic is approximately eight inches high, twenty inches long, and ten inches deep. It appears to be constructed of carved cypress wood, with a polished granite lid. The bottom of the box is raised approximately an inch above the surface with hand-carved scallops along the bottom edge. It rests on four gold lions' feet, which extend beyond the edge of the sides roughly one-half inch."

Gabriel switched off the recorder and with some effort lifted the box to examine the carved wooden relief on the front. "That's odd," he said, pointing to four arrowhead-shaped hands. They resembled markers. "This type of indicator—for lack of a better description—is similar to what you might find on an old—but modern, compared to this box—pharmaceutical scale. The other three sides of the box have similar indicators but no sculptured carvings. They simply have grooves scored in the wood to separate each indicator. The left side of the box as you face the front also contains four indicators."

Nicholas drew closer to see what Gabriel was pointing out. He cocked his head as he studied the carvings. "He's right. The back of the box has twenty indicators while the right side of the box has twelve. They have hands like you see on an ornate pocket watch."

"What are the hands pointing at?" asked Alex, trying to see over his brother's shoulder.

Gabriel began speaking into his recorder again. "The hands are pointing to elongated wooden bars. Each of these is approximately three inches high, positioned vertically. They are similar to the lines on a map or globe except they appear to have corresponding symbols, perhaps even numerical values. At the top of each side are hieroglyphic characters representing words. . . "

"Words?" Francesca broke in for the first time during their examination of the box. "The Egyptians used hieroglyphics to show pictures, right?"

Gabriel clicked off the recorder and shook his head in puzzlement, "No, they were words, but we don't know any of the vowels or exactly how sentences were strung together. Written language didn't really have practicality for the masses until the Greeks started adding vowels to create sentence structure. On brief examination of these dials, however, I couldn't tell you if these indicators are just ornamental, or whether they originally served some purpose."

"They must have performed some function at one time," insisted Alex, "but God only knows what it was." He reached over and tried to move the tiny hands on the indicators, but Gabriel grabbed his hand. "Let's wait until we find out what this is. Remember, it is extraordinarily old, and we should not even be touching it as we are now. My God, we are not even wearing gloves."

Cassandra, who was now examining some of the papers, tapped her sister-in-law on the shoulder. "This is written in Italian. Can you read this, Francesca?"

Francesca took the paper, but shook her head. "It looks like some sort of financial record, but I'm not much good at figuring out people's handwriting." She handed it to Nicholas. "Numbers are numbers to me. You're the economist in the family. Why don't you give it a go?"

"My Italian is a little rusty!" he laughed. "But they look like records of shipments received and exported. Beyond that, I'd need more information. Why would papers like this be here with papers from ancient Egypt?"

"I sure don't know," answered Cassandra, "but maybe if we figure out what this box is all about, or where it came from, these papers will make sense." She pointed to several pages. "Take a look at these. They all look like balance sheets." She shot a smile at Alex, who rolled his eyes and nodded even before she spoke. "Seems you were right after all. The chest does hold accounting ledgers!" She turned back to the stack of papers. "They represent a number of different eras. Look, here are accounts from the 1900s! Here's one from 1946 . . . and another from the 1930s. Everything from precious metals to other commodities, such as wheat and . . ." Cassandra stopped in mid-sentence. "Nicholas, look at this." She handed him a spreadsheet dated 1935.

He looked at it for several seconds before answering. "Well, this can't be right!" he exclaimed. "This report shows enormous profits from blue chip companies listed on the Dow, from treasury bonds, and world currencies. All in 1935!"

"What's so odd about that?" asked Gabriel.

Nicholas shot him a surprised look. "Gabe, 1935? It was during the depths of the Great Depression! Companies were not making money, and neither were investors in the stock market."

"Of course, sorry. So why are these things hidden away with this box in a secret room?" he asked.

Nicholas did not immediately answer. Instead, he focused his eyes on the hands on the indicators. They did not move, but he had the curious feeling that if he watched them long enough, they would. Cassandra, meanwhile, with Alex and Francesca helping her, organized the papers by material type—parchment, papyrus, wooden tablet, or plain paper.

Gabriel muttered something under his breath and clicked on his recorder again. "There are carved lions on the front of the box. Each lion is centered between the middle of the front and the end, and face each other. They are not rampant, but sit with their heads held high, teeth and tongue exposed. Their manes start at the top of their heads and transform into golden wings with each section of feathers overlapping to rest on the lions' backs. The wings are obviously made of beaten gold and are as ornate as anything I have ever seen."

Gabriel rewound his tape recorder a short distance and played it back to make sure it was recording properly. "The tails are long," he continued, "and they look like flames shooting along the ground, and then they circle up a few inches behind the lions and encompass half a human skull—part of which is inside the left lion's tail and the other part is inside the right lion's tail. They appear to have been split in half equally. Both of these skulls are encircled with what appears to be a grapevine. Positioned exactly between the heads of the two lions are four embossed vertical wooden bars surrounded by a gold ring that resembles, for lack of a better word, a dial."

Nicholas' head snapped up and he stared at Gabriel. "Gabe, are you following what you're saying?"

Gabriel clicked off his recorder and shot his friend a puzzled look. "What do you mean?"

"Your description of the carvings on the box. You're describing some sort of measuring system."

Gabe looked at the indicators and mused, "Something that goes up and down. I am fairly certain that the box is Egyptian because of the hieroglyphics and other symbols. Perhaps the sun god, Ra?" *Click* went his recorder, and the corners of Nicholas' mouth began turning up. He waited for Gabriel to finish.

"Along the top vertical bars inside the circle are the same hieroglyphic markings as on the other three sides. The sides of the box have gold indicators, but they don't have the gold rings. Symmetry appears to have been discarded for the purpose of defining difference from one side to the other. The bottom of the box is made of solid wood with nothing exceptional carved on it except for a cartouche with three hieroglyphic characters incised."

"It's a barometer!" exclaimed Alex.

"Some sort of weather or wind measurement?" asked Francesca.

"Nope," said Nicholas, "but I think I know what it might be. But it *can't* be. But I really think it is."

"What?" asked all the others simultaneously.

Nicholas calmly stretched his hands over his head, as though to bless what he was about to say. "I think our mystery box measures gravity."

Chapter 5

 Gabriel almost dropped his recorder. "What did you say? Did you say gravity?"

"He's joking, Gabe!" laughed Francesca.

Nicholas, however, was not even smiling. Instead, his mind was spinning with possibilities.

Gabriel cleared his throat. "Actually, I think he's serious. You put a new fact in your head, Nicholas, everything jiggles around and poof!—you have a stroke of genius."

"He's always been able to figure out puzzles and brainteasers," admitted Alex. "But this one's got me stumped. How are you figuring this, brother?"

Nicholas clicked his tongue thoughtfully. "It's not so far-fetched, Alex. Let's just theorize for a moment. What was one of the most important things to the Egyptians besides their obsession with the afterlife?

"The flooding of the Nile," Cassandra blurted out.

"Yes, exactly. The Nile, the river that allowed ancient Egypt to thrive. The river without which there would have been no Egypt. The Egyptians developed a complicated system to figure out when the Nile would flood. They built slabs, pillars, and a series of steps to calibrate the lowest and highest point of undulations."

"Didn't the Nile flood every year?" asked Francesca.

Cassandra offered the answer. "Yes. It has to do with the summer rains in the Ethiopian highlands. It happened every summer, between June and September, a bit like our hurricane season."

"So, why did they need to measure it?" Ever since moving to Charleston, South Carolina, Francesca had become very much aware of the threat of hurricanes.

"It would be the equivalent of our hurricane hunters," replied Nicholas, referring to the U.S. Air Force planes that went into the storms while they were still offshore to predict their intensity and area of landfall. "The Egyptians invented a water clock accurate to one day within 1,500 years. However, they were about six hours off on their calculations of one year, so subsequent calculations became more and more imprecise. Sometimes the floods would occur in the wrong season. It drove them crazy, so they kept trying to invent devices to predict the flooding more accurately."

"Let's go back to the Ethiopian rain theory," prompted Alex, his face screwed up in thought. "Wouldn't that have been the obvious precursor to a flood?"

"For the elite of Egypt, I suspect, though I have no real proof of that. Certainly it would have been the priests who held that information. No doubt they used it to maintain their power," replied Gabriel.

"Yes, and preserve the Pharaoh's supreme power over the masses," Cassandra said wryly.

"What else could they do to predict floods?" asked Francesca, who was now sitting on the edge of her seat.

Cassandra grinned. "Build pyramids! There's some evidence now that the structures at Giza are star guides. The flooding took place every year when the star we call Sirius rose. They found this a much more reliable system for predictions, and built all sorts of mythologies around the goddess Sopdet. They could measure all they wanted, but the amount of water coming couldn't be predicted, so they put this in the hands of the gods, most specifically the Nile god, Hapi."

"I am not sure I follow the point of this discussion," said Francesca. "What's does all this have to do with this box?"

"Maybe nothing at all," answered Gabriel. "But, if it's a measuring instrument, and it was invented by the ancient Egyptians, then perhaps it is a very sophisticated way to determine the rise and fall of the Nile. Few people know that the Egyptians really did have a measurement tool like that called a Nileometer. We just don't know today what it looked like."

Gabriel continued. "If they figured out how to measure gravity accurately, maybe they could predict the amount of rain. With enough measurements over a long enough time span—decades or even centuries—I suspect they could."

"But why were they measuring gravity?" asked Cassandra as she pulled out a chair similar to Francesca's, eased off her heels, and plopped herself down. "All I know about gravity is that it's keeping me on this chair and it made Newton's apple fall straight to earth."

Her husband smiled at her fondly, "Don't feel ignorant. That is about all most people know. Simply put, it is the force of attraction between all large masses in the universe—especially the attraction of the earth's mass for other large bodies nearby, such as the moon and the sun. Obviously, the more remote the body is, the less the gravitational effects are felt."

"He has a way of making you feel as if you are back in high school science class, doesn't he?" joked Alex.

Nicholas ignored him. "Albert Einstein said that gravity can't be held responsible for people falling in love, though it is responsible for how our universe operates. Today, even the fields of quantum mechanics and theoretical astrophysics concentrate a good bit on gravity, whereas the ancients merely accepted that there was a distinct balance and relationship between the sun, the moon, and the earth. That was before we knew the earth wasn't even at the center of the universe."

"It was at the center of *their* universe," interjected Cassandra. "But, seriously Nicholas, didn't Newton measure gravity in the 1600s? That was long after the Pharaohs."

"Cavendish made the first device that could measure gravity, but it was cumbersome. No one since has been able to improve upon it except for miniaturizing it. Recently, scientists developed a gravimeter they place on ocean bottoms, but the thing will only measure gravity for a specific second in time."

"Why do they put it at the bottom of the ocean?" asked Gabriel.

Alex, who had been studying some of the papers from the chest while listening to the conversation, weighed in. "This isn't exactly my field, but I just read an interesting article about this in *Discover* magazine. Gravity affects everything, most notably here on earth the movement of the seas. They are the closest we can get to measuring how gravity expresses itself. Science can't measure the force itself because it is not particulate. It just *is*."

"But Alex," Nicholas cut in, "couldn't you take continuous measurements for hundreds of years and come up with a model that would offer a pretty good prediction?"

"The Egyptians did!" Gabriel interjected. "They were excellent mathematicians and engineers. Imhotep, the architect who designed the step pyramids at Sakkara five thousand years ago, used geometry. Forty-five hundred years ago, Ahmose the scribe wrote *Directions for Attaining Knowledge of All Dark Things*, which included equations for figuring things like volumes and areas. The Egyptians kept amazing records. When the Greeks became aware of some of them, they used them as well."

"He's right," interjected Cassandra. "In fact, a Greek astronomer named Posidonius, around 74 BC, wrote on this subject and correlated gravity with ocean tidal fluctuations."

Alex snorted skeptically. "Well, let's hold on a moment. This is becoming a bit ridiculous. How could this little box, as pretty as it is, effectively measure gravity? Why would it be concealed in this forgotten little room on the Biltmore Estate, and what is the deal with this stack of old financial records?" All eyes settled on Nicholas.

"Well, suppose—just suppose," began Nicholas, thinking aloud while staring at the side of the box. "Let's assume this box really is Egyptian, and it really does measure—somehow—gravitational effects. Then perhaps the Egyptians used that information to predict other things."

"What other things?" asked his frowning brother.

Nicholas' eyes were bright as he turned to his friends. "Imagine that it gave them a kind of unique knowledge—an edge, so to speak—over their neighbors. Life was a great deal less complicated in those times. If you could forecast a natural disaster and predict large floods and even small ones, you might be able to predict trade and commerce patterns as well. Much of the trade was conducted by flimsy sea vessels, and so was often dependent on the seasons and the weather. Perhaps this," he said, pointing to the box, "is why Egypt was able to sustain itself for so long as the most powerful country in the ancient world?"

A silence fell over the room. For a long moment they seemed to hold their collective breaths. The room itself seemed to be waiting for something to happen.

Cassandra finally broke the silence. "Well, this is all a bit far-fetched, but I think we need to take a good close look at these documents. If fortunes were made with the help of this box, then somebody in the past stumbled upon something inconceivably enormous."

Alex gave a sharp laugh. "The fact that gravity affects everything, including the oceans and seas, does not explain how this little box could effectively measure it. Nor does it explain what in the world measuring gravity has to do with making money."

Nicholas looked at the box and then at Gabriel. "I propose we open it."

"I propose we take the box and some of these documents down to the library," cut in Cassandra as she pulled her thin shawl tightly about herself. "I've had a long night, I'm cold, and there's brandy sitting on one of the tables!"

"Yes, but is there good scotch?" chided Alex as he shot a sideways glance at Gabriel.

"Of course there is!" answered Gabriel with a smile. "But can you find it?"

Nicholas carefully lifted the box off the floor and moved slowly toward the door. Alex, who had made sure the door was propped open when they came in, held the panel firmly in place as everyone passed by on the way out of the secret room. "Leave that open," instructed Gabriel. "I am going down into the library for a cardboard box we can use to more carefully transport the papers."

With that, everyone slowly descended the spiral staircase in silence. Francesca led the way and reached the bottom first. When she turned to watch her friends wind their way down, she felt a shiver creep up her spine and caress her neck. Everyone was stepping in unison as though performing an ancient ritual.

Chapter 6

Nicholas set the box on the large refectory table, pushing an enormous floral arrangement out of the way. Cassandra and Francesca both made straight for the fireplace and the wide bench in front of the giant andirons, where the large room was the warmest. "How odd," Cassandra said, holding her hands out to the blaze. "I thought the fire would be out by now. Is there a mystery there, too, Gabe?"

Gabriel and Alex had just returned from the secret room with the box full of old papers. Gabriel carefully placed it the table close to the ornate granite and cypress box. "Oh, probably one of my staff hung around and kept it going before leaving," he answered. "Alex, would you kindly move about ten paces directly behind you and reach between those two oversize atlases."

Puzzled, Alex did as he was told and withdrew an unopened bottle of Aberlour, Gabe's favorite single-malt scotch. "That's why we love you so much, Gabe."

"It's good to be needed," he replied, pouring two snifters of Napoleon brandy for Francesca and Cassandra. Cracking open the scotch, he poured three glasses with three fingers each and passed one to Nicholas and the other to Alex.

Nicholas lifted his high. "To old friends and even older mysteries." Each glass clinked softly.

Alex moved to the table and stood over the wooden box, examining its sides. "Let's crack this thing open and find out what makes it tick. Maybe then we can see if it really does tie in with the financial documents."

Everyone looked to their host, who appeared a little hesitant. Gabriel exhaled loudly and nodded his agreement. "I have a feeling I could get into very deep trouble for what we're doing tonight, so let me open the box." Biltmore and its contents were his responsibility, after all. He was also better accustomed to handling priceless antiquities, and had made enough mistakes over the years to make him wary. Gabriel took a long swallow of scotch and ran his fingers gently along the smooth edge of the stone that cantilevered just a few centimeters over the wooden edge. He carefully tried to lift it, but the top refused to budge. He tried again, using a bit more force, with the same result. Sweat broke out in beads on his furrowed forehead.

"Hmm," was all he said. As his friends watched with rapt attention, Gabriel took his forefinger and slowly but carefully felt beneath the overhang. "There seems to be another curved edge near the top of the wood frame up under the lid." He had not noticed this part of the structure before, but now realized that the edges on the top beneath the lid were serrated.

He slowly moved his fingernails along the edge and found several places where there appeared to be a gap, or slight indentation. Suspecting that the inside upper edge of the carved wooden box might be the key for removing the lid, he asked Nicholas to retrieve the flashlight they had used to examine the hidden upstairs passageway.

Gabriel switched it on and peered up under the lid. At first he couldn't see the gaps that he had felt with his fingers. Then he moved the box sideways across the top of the table and shined the light up against the edge.

"Aha," he said. "These edges give the optical illusion of being perfectly uniform, but with the shadowing of the flashlight, and at the right angle, I can see three gaps."

He turned the box around to examine all four sides and found the serrated edges on three. "Now, what is this slightly sticky substance?" he asked no one in particular. He suspected wax, which would have been logical because Egyptians commonly used beeswax to seal compartments holding important documents, but how could wax have lasted so long? Unless . . . "Salt!" he exclaimed suddenly. "Salt sealed the beeswax to protect it from weather, bugs, and the test of time. It helped to maintain the soft texture as a sealing agent while making it impervious to erosion from the elements. On the surface of the wax there's also a thin coating of silver, thin enough for the wax to still be sticky but not too thin to afford protection."

Alex gave him a worried look. "Be careful there, Gabe. Silver is commonly used today to coat piezo elements in electrical circuits that use barium as one of their components. Certain types of barium are extremely toxic to touch. This may not be safe."

"That's easy," Gabriel grinned, reaching into his pocket. "Nowadays we have a unique invention that circumnavigates deadly poisons." He pulled out a Swiss Army knife from his pocket. "This thing has all the bells and whistles one could ever need," he said smugly, "but we only need the blade." Gabe very carefully inserted the blade and lifted gently upward. The lid lifted with it.

Together, they peered inside and, after a few seconds, looked at one another in bewilderment.

"What is it?" Francesca asked.

"I have no idea," answered Alex, "but I think those are diamonds."

"I do," said Nicholas. "That's a nested tetrahedron . . ."

Francesca looked puzzled. "A what?"

"A tetrahedron. It's the most sacred design discovered in history. It's the very basis for numbers, pattern, and structure in all sciences. It is one spectacular arrangement of what appears to be diamonds in their natural crystalline form."

Alex gave a low whistle. "The Egyptians knew a lot about those! After all, the most common tetrahedron is a pyramid whose base and three sides are equilateral triangles. But, the nested tetrahedron is multiple pyramids, each one placed inside the other, forming a perfect geometric structure. It defines ultimate power."

Francesca drew herself back as she shot a look at Nicholas, who was nodding his head in response to Alex's words. She looked back at her husband in amazement as he continued, his enthusiasm evident in his words. "A typical nested tetrahedron is formed by just two pyramids enclosed inside each other. This nested tetrahedron clearly shows forty protruding points instead of the usual eight—in other words, ten pyramids making up the structure."

Alex tapped his lips with his forefinger, deep in thought. "Each triangular surface of the nested tetrahedron, when measured, is the differential coefficient of the mathematical value 1.61803, which is considered by sacred geometry scholars to be the 'Creator's Fingerprint.'"

Nicholas stopped him. "What? You mean *phi*?"

"Yes," Alex replied. "An irrational number believed to have the most aesthetically pleasing qualities."

He was about to continue when Cassandra interrupted him. "Wait a second. Even I recall from high school math that *pi* has a value of 3.14 and it goes on forever."

Nicholas shook his head. "Alex is not referring to *pi*, which is the ratio of the circumference of a circle to its diameter. He is referring to *Phi*, spelled p-h-I."

Cassandra frowned. "Oh, sorry. I've never heard of that. Go on."

Francesca jumped into the conversation. "Alex, *phi* or *pi*, I didn't think you believed any of this."

"Nothing to believe, love. This is fact. The Greeks were obsessed with measurements, just like the Egyptians. The Egyptians worked with the triangle in all its dimensions, and arrived at geometrical proportions that the Greeks took up with great enthusiasm. They not only found that phi—expressed as the number 1.618—was the core number, but when multiplied by any other number it formed the basis for every single geometric figure they could think of. They called it 'The Golden Section,' and the Renaissance artists later dubbed it the 'Divine Proportion.'"

This time Gabriel did the interrupting. "Of course! Phidias used it to design the ancient Greek Parthenon. Architects employed it to construct many of the government buildings in Washington, D.C."

"In addition," interjected Nicholas, "it is found in the structure of Saturn's rings and even the theorized shape of the universe. Because of its universal applicability, it was referred to as the divine Proportion, although things got a little out of hand when the mystics started using it."

Cassandra smiled, "I know it best as Leonardo Da Vinci's Vitruvian Man."

"Yes, yes, but back to the box," said Gabriel impatiently. He continued to study the mechanism with an intensity that showed in his sparkling eyes. "Look how each point of this tetrahedron is connected to a clear hollow crystal tube leading to the extremities of the separate inside sides of the box."

While the three men examined the layout of the interior, Francesca asked, "Cassandra, why is he called the Vitruvian man?"

"Because Leonardo based his drawing—the famous one of a man in a circle—on the proportion provided by the number 1.618, which was used by the first century B.C. architect Vitruvius. You know the drawing, the one that shows the proportions of the body." With that, Cassandra finished her last swallow of brandy and reached over to pour another glass.

"It looks like on the front inside of the box we've got four cylinders, each one connected to four points on the tetrahedron," explained Gabriel. Four pairs of eyes followed his finger closely. "Look at this," he went on. "On the inside end of the cylinder tops there's a little metal lever. It appears as if it is connected to the outside gold rings through those vertical slots cut into the box's structure. The cylinder must have some kind of piston-type device inside it, designed to move up or down."

The crystal structure itself appeared to be filled with a murky liquid. Connecting crystal tubes and cylinders attached to the inside of the box were filled with the same liquid, giving the impression that the center of the structure was interconnected by its points to each indicator for a purpose. *But what function did the indicators serve?*

"It almost reminds me of mercury, expanding and contracting in a thermometer," Gabriel mused, "but this liquid is not mercury. Mercury wasn't discovered until much later."

Alex had studied the properties of liquids with qualities similar to those of mercury. "Maybe we've got salt water mixed with some other liquid or maybe even a solid element," said Alex. "If the mixture included a compound like ferrite, it might perform certain functions without being affected by weather conditions like humidity and temperature. When heated it wouldn't expand, and when cooled it would not contract or freeze."

Everyone turned to him as he continued. "Ferrite is an almost pure metallic iron element mined in the Middle East, but it didn't have many uses until electricity came along in the Nineteenth Century. Then it was used in core windings for power generation. When subjected to frequency resonance and electromagnetic energy, the mixture presents fascinating properties. When heated, for example, it has a tendency to cool down. When cooled, its tendency is to heat up.

"Alex, what exactly does this mean to a lay person?" asked Cassandra.

"It's simple, really. Theoretically, ferrite could be used to keep this tetrahedron's liquid center impervious to temperature changes."

Alex thought for a moment, recalling that a scientist from Austin, Texas, named Scott Brittle had observed this effect. Brittle found that when used in a generator core, ferrite caused the core to decrease in weight when it was measured during high power generation. His observations were considered controversial. But that conversation was for a later date.

"The point is," Alex continued, "if this liquid was intended to expand and contract according to temperature, then it had to have other proprieties to operate. The only way the liquid could move the gold indicators up and down would be to exert pressure inside the crystal pistons. Energy had to be transferred from the tetrahedron to each crystal piston, and vice-versa."

The more he talked his way through it, the more it made sense to Alex that this old wooden box with the granite top really was measuring gravitational forces.

Nicholas took over. "We know that all physical bodies, including bodies of water, are affected by the gravitational forces caused by the position of the earth in relation to the moon and sun. These forces pull at the earth and can normally be measured for only a single point in time. But, this box appears to be measuring gravity constantly." By now Alex was nodding in agreement

"So you *do* believe all this?" Francesca shook her head in amazement. Clearly she did not.

"And, as a reaction to the constant measurements," continued Nicholas, "the fluid inside the nested tetrahedron appears to be ever so slightly causing a change in the other gold indicator positions at each side of the box."

As Nicholas and Alex discussed the finer scientific points, Gabriel inspected more closely the markings on the outside of the box, especially those above the top of the elongated bars. He was familiar with the glyphs. "These really are quite amazing, and they make more sense to me now," he began, explaining to the others what each symbol stood for.

For example, the symbol ≈ at the top of the bars represented water. Others glyphs represented the earth (⊤⊤), the moon (⟩—⟨( ), and the sun (⌒⊙). The front of the box at the very top had a symbol that represented days (⊡⟩⊙) The first marking appeared to suggest two highs (⟩⟩) and two lows (||⌒⟩⟩). Nothing else on the front of the ancient box referred to anything other than these readings.

The left side of the box also had four indicators, but the inscription carved above the bars made reference to the lunar month (★⊙) Gabriel speculated that this side of the box measured two highs and two lows also, one for each of the four weeks of the month. The right side of the box's markings made reference to the sun's orbit (⟩⌒⟩)

His friends duly impressed, Gabriel continued with his explanation of the other glyphs carved into the box.

At the top of the right side of the box was a symbol (★⊙) that represented the Egyptian word for month. The right side of the old box also contained twelve gold indicators, each appearing to point at different levels with respect to their positions on each bar. When examined as a whole, these indicators seemed to be arranged in a *sine* wave formation. The inscriptions at the top of each bar were numerical values, meaning that the first bar was the number 1 (|) , and the last bar was the number 12 (∩||)

Thus the Egyptians had cleverly made reference to the twelve months of the year. Each gold indicator was pointing to a maximum or minimum (or somewhere in between), thus creating the *sine* wave appearance over the twelve bars.

When he was done explaining the meaning of the glyphs, Nicholas lifted an eyebrow and suggested the obvious: "Gravitational highs and lows for each month of the year, right?"

Gabriel nodded his agreement and continued with his inspection, speaking aloud for everyone to hear. "The back of the box has twenty bars with gold indicators adjacent to each. The inscriptions are again numerical signs from one through twenty. Above the vertical bars is a single inscription (⌠ ⌡) which I translate to mean 'years.'"

"These bars, if Nicholas is correct," continued Gabriel, "recorded gravitational highs and lows for each year."

Curious, Cassandra tilted her head and asked if Egyptian astronomers had decided whether the earth orbited the sun or vice-versa.

Gabriel shook his head. "Galileo made that discovery. He was sentenced to house arrest in Florence by the Church, but maintained that the earth wasn't the center of the universe and that earth orbited the sun."

Francesca walked over and laid her head on her husband's shoulder, smiling faintly. "No Gabriel, you are wrong. I am one of Galileo's daughters through my papa. And, as much as I would like to claim that he made that discovery, he did not. Copernicus did in 1530, but Galileo believed it. Unfortunately, he paid dearly for those beliefs. He was forced to his knees at a trial before the high inquisitor in 1633 and made to renounce every Copernican idea."

"And things haven't really changed much," sighed Alex, stroking his wife's hair, "we geniuses are still mocked to this day."

Cassandra shook her head fiercely. "This was a little more serious Alex. Remember the Catholic Church monitored such radical thinking. It wasn't until the Reformation and the Enlightenment in the Eighteenth Century that the Church's views were rebuffed somewhat, and science was allowed to march on more or less unimpeded."

She paused and studied the box. "Still, the Church would probably have liked to have had this box—especially if it helped line its coffers. In fact, in the Twelfth Century the Pope decreed that priests should not marry so they would leave their real estate to the Church. Today, the Church owns more land than any other entity in the world."

"Spoken like a true believer," laughed Nicholas. He and his brother and their wives were all practicing Catholics. His wife responded by sticking out her tongue.

Gabriel, who was still inspecting the box, cleared his throat. That was always his way of telling people he was about to speak. "Okay. Let's assume Nicholas is correct and the front side appears to be measuring the gravitational high and low for each day. The left side registers where the gravitational highs and lows will be for the month. The right side appears to be indicating highs and lows for each month of the year. The back of the box appears to be indicating the gravitational highs and lows for twenty years. But what good would this information be, other than to mark in time the obvious?"

Nicholas froze. "Wait a minute. Twenty years? Why twenty? Why not five or ten—or fifty?"

"Twenty must indicate some kind of cycle," answered Alex.

"Yes, exactly. They were measuring a sequence of events, such as highs for the Nile River floods, or perhaps some celestial occurrence. But Gabe is right. Why take the time to build a complex system like this to track something for twenty years that has already occurred? That is information they would already have known." Nicholas stopped for a few seconds to let the import of his words sink in. "I don't think this was just to mark time."

"Well then what was it measuring?" asked Alex.

Nicholas stood up and paced back and forth, stopping every now and again to look at the mysterious box. "This is going to sound a bit out there, but I think . . . these are the gravitational highs and lows in the *future*."

Cassandra, who had settled into one of the red brocade chairs, had been listening to Nicholas and scanning one of the documents that they had carried down. She sat up suddenly in utter amazement. "Oh, my God!" she cried out.

Nicholas spun around. "Well, why couldn't that be what it is?"

"No, no, you're right. You are right! Look at this last entry made in 1986. It looks like a long-term yearly forecast schedule. Listen to these entries: high 1987, low 1988, high 1992, low 1993, high 1996, low 1997, high 2000, low 2002, and high 2004!"

"That was recorded in 1986?" asked Gabriel, his mouth wide open in disbelief.

"Yes!"

"You're kidding. That can't be real!" interjected Nicholas as Cassandra handed him the document. "If this was really written in 1986, it describes the tops and bottoms of the Dow Jones Average up to and through . . . today!" He paused for a moment, his face flushed with excitement. "And that's exactly what happened! The market tanked in 1988, hit 11,000 in 2000, and then tanked again. Now we're above 10,000 again. But this is impossible. And yet these balance sheets total in the *trillions* of dollars." He shot a look at the box, cast a glance in the direction of his wife and friends, and then ran his hands through his hair as he began pacing anew.

By now Alex was also walking the room, exhibiting the same wild-eyed expression as his brother. They looked like two twin dervishes darting about the library.

"So how did it work?" asked Francesca. "But please explain it in a way I can understand."

Alex answered her in an excited voice each of them knew he was fighting to keep as calm as possible. "As in thermal dynamics, the gravitational pull, registered daily, transfers the energy to the nested tetrahedron, which was transferred back and forth to each cylinder—but would never be lost or incapacitated for any reason. The four cylinders inside the box's front measure the high and low gravitational extremities each day, causing the indicators to register the results."

He paused to see if everyone understood what he was trying to explain. Not everyone did. Francesca shrugged and wiggled her outstretched hand from side to side, as if to say, "sort of." Cassandra was nodding, but her face reflected uncertainty.

Alex continued: "The cylinders exact the correct force, pulling at the core of the nested tetrahedron, which through this rather complicated lattice work of crystals, affect the other cylinders. The result is a complex system that accurately measures gravity four times a day, and then calculates four times a month *in advance*, and twelve times a year *in advance,* and then each yearly high and low for twenty years *into the future.*"

"Oh yeah, this sounds plausible." Francesca was chuckling softly. "I think we are all sharing the same dream, or we have all consumed way too much alcohol tonight—"

"Stop for a moment!" Nicholas' voice was sharp and sterner than usual. "Let's take a breath and think about this. Certainly this is only theory and nothing has been tested," he began, staring in turn at each of them. "The box, though, is obviously ancient, amazingly complex, and mysterious inside and out. Think about it. Someone went to great lengths to hide it inside a secret room behind a hidden panel with a trick staircase! And look at the documents we found with it. One from 1936—at the height of the worst depression this country has ever experienced— showing fortunes being made in the stock market? And now another predicting market highs and lows nearly two decades into the future?"

Nicholas stopped to clear his throat and sip from his glass of Aberlour. The smooth amber liquid warmed his tongue and coated his throat. "If this ancient miracle of engineering is indeed used to measure gravity, it will change the world! We might have discovered 'The Keys to the Kingdom,' so to speak."

"I don't think that was the kingdom they were talking about," Francesca shot back, still a bit miffed at the way Nicholas had cut her off.

"Oh, sorry," Nicholas smiled at her. "Keys to an earthly one, anyway."

Cassandra spoke next, the serious look on her face reflected in her voice. "I think it already has changed the world—for someone." She tapped the pages in her lap. "Somebody left that box there. Someone *hid* that thing away. How far into the future does it go, anyway?"

Gabriel turned the box around and he and Alex studied the indicators on the back from left to right while counting the exact years. "If the first bar is 2003," Alex said, "we should see a high in 2004."

He continued reading the bottoms and tops: "There should be a low in 2006 . . . a high in 2009 . . . a low in 2010 . . . a high in 2013 . . . a low in 2014 . . . a high in 2018 . . . a low in 2019 . . ."

Alex looked at his twin as he ticked off the year of the last indicator. "The last bar represents a high . . . in 2022."

Astounded, Nicholas shook his head as it began spinning with the possibilities. "That would seem to indicate a correlation between the new reading on the box and where the documents that Cassandra found left off."

"Then if what we are looking at is true," concluded Gabriel, "we have just discovered where the market will be moving for the next twenty years."

Chapter 7

Gabriel offered his four stunned guests another round of drinks. No one declined. Francesca thanked him, hesitated a few moments, and then asked the question everyone was wondering: "So whose box is this?"

The room suddenly felt very cold. Gabriel crossed quickly to the fireplace and stoked the dying embers, though only half-heartedly. His voice sounded brittle, almost old. "The box had to get here somehow, and obviously someone was using it as late as 1986. I was in Europe then, so that was before my time here. The Estate has been open to the public since the 1930s, but members of the family have been active in its restoration and management throughout that period. Even father was here often. I'll have to look into that." He yawned and looked at his watch. It was 3:22 a.m. "But in the meantime—here we've got these great restored bedrooms for us to sleep in, and we're not in them! The house opens at 10:00 a.m. tomorrow morning, and we all have to be out of here and back at my house by then. I will take care of the box and the documents. Just leave them here for now and I will lock them into the safe."

"We need to study it," Alex insisted. "At length."

"I'll take care of it, I said." Gabriel was getting irritable. It had been one hell of a day for everyone. "Let's just call it a night."

"Since when are you not up for an all-nighter?" teased Cassandra, recalling the stories Nicholas had shared with her of their college days. The men grimaced simultaneously; there were many grad school parties they would just as soon forget, and several their wives would not appreciate hearing about.

"Since I grew up and got a job!" Gabriel motioned to the doorway. Outside the fog swirled around the tall north windows, the cold breath of winter depositing a thin layer of crystalline lace on the glass. The group moved quietly down the corridors; they would have to go all the way back to the elevator to reach the third floor, where eight of the guest rooms had been recently restored. The house was still, quiet, sleeping.

Cassandra admitted to being spooked. "It's almost like *we're* the ghosts now. I wonder what the Vanderbilts would think of a 5,000- year-old box that predicts the stock market."

"I still can't believe what we've found," Francesca sighed as she took hold of Alex's outstretched arm. "My forefather Galileo would have been really interested in it. Hey, maybe he even knew about it!"

"I would guess that the box would have been one of the best-kept secrets of the Renaissance," reflected Cassandra.

"You bet," her husband agreed. "If you owned it, you would have had a big advantage over everyone else."

"What do you mean?" asked Francesca.

"People are made up of more than seventy-five percent water. They respond to gravitational pulls just as planets do. If you knew when the lows were and understood what that meant, you could stand aside for the downturns and buy goods and merchandise—or stocks, in our case—for the projected upturns. That is a foolproof formula for profit."

"Buy low and sell high," Alex murmured dreamily.

Mulling this prospect, they arrived at the elevator and stepped inside. Since it had been designed to hold six, they all fit comfortably. Cassandra however, was not fond of elevators, having been in one that fell six stories when she was in graduate school. The lift lurched upward, and she held tightly to her husband's hand. The ride was mercifully short, as the small ornate compartment traveled quickly up the shaft.

While much of the third floor had not been renovated, their sleeping accommodations were in a newly completed section comprised of a long common room and four adjacent suites. "I've put Alex and Francesca in the South Tower room, Nicholas and Cassandra in the North Tower Room, and I'll be in the Raphael room," Gabriel announced. "I think that you will find everything you need. The bathrooms were renovated as well."

"Ooooh, William Morris wallpaper!" exclaimed Francesca. "At last something in this house that feels like home!" She circled their large round bedroom, furnished in the Neoclassical style with a half-canopy bed and Hepplewhite tables and chairs. She stopped at the foot of the bed and held herself back from collapsing into the center. Perching herself on the edge, she stifled a yawn and threw a little wave to Nicholas and Cassandra, "Good night, fellow treasure hunters!" They smiled wearily and followed Gabriel down the hallway.

Gabriel stopped. "I'm in here, and you're one room over. See you in the morning."

Nicholas thought that he sounded a little brusque, but he shrugged it off and opened the door to their room. It was a pleasant oval shape with an enormous four-poster bed, its head tucked into a curtained niche. "Definitely English Regency," observed Cassandra. "So dignified. What are we going to wear to bed? Oh, look! That Gabe!"

On the bed lay a pair of silk men's pajamas, a robe from the estate's inn, and an ivory silk peignoir. "I don't think we're going to need these," Nicholas said reaching out to push them off the bed.

"Maybe for just a minute . . ." Cassandra snatched up the lacy nightgown and was about to head toward the bathroom door when Nicholas turned his head suddenly toward the front of the room. "What's that?"

"What?"

"Shhhh," he whispered, pressing his forefinger to his lips. "Someone's out in the hall."

The light in the hallway cast a pair of shadows beneath the door. He tip-toed to the door, cracked it open, and looked toward the South Tower room just in time to see a slight blonde girl darting toward Gabriel's door. He started to chuckle. "The mystery of the blazing library fire is revealed. No wonder Gabe wanted to get to his room. His 'staff' person is a pretty little blonde." He turned back toward his wife. "Now, Madame X, or whoever you are, let me help you with all those hooks and eyes."

ᛒ

The next day's dawn had scarcely broken when they heard a sharp knock on the door. Nicholas swung his feet over the side of the bed and pulled on the robe. He looked over at Cassandra, whose long dark hair spread out like thick tumbling smoke over the pillow. She snored, though delicately. Nicholas shook her shoulder. "It's tomorrow in the mansion," he said. "Things are starting to hum."

A long groan escaped her lips. "We need a vacation so we can sleep in," Cassandra grumbled sleepily. She pulled the covers over her head and groaned a second time. Nicholas opened the door to find an overnight bag in the hallway with a suitable change of clothes. Gabriel popped his head out of the room next door. "No showers until later," he said. "Please make the bed up so no one will know you've been here."

Cassandra was awake now, sitting cross-legged in bed pinning up her hair. "You mean people are going to be parading through this room where we've—"

Nicholas just grinned wolfishly. Gathering their dignity they made the bed, dressed, and stuffed their unworn nightclothes into the bag. They found Alex and Francesca leaving the South Tower clutching their own overnight bag. Alex was wearing the same impish smile as Nicholas. The two women just shook their heads. "I just hope no one stops us and asks us any questions," giggled Francesca.

"Somehow I don't think that's going to be a problem," Nicholas said with a smile. "Gabriel has a way with things."

When they got off the elevator, Gabriel smiled warmly and urged them to pick up the pace. "Hurry now. Your chariot awaits."

Fortunately, they didn't see a soul on their way out to the carriage. The Percherons snorted and shivered, their nostrils sending spouts of steam into the early morning air. The fog had thinned some, but still hung like wraiths around the trees. It gave the winter grounds an eerie feel. "I feel like I am on the Scottish moors," sighed Cassandra.

"And I feel like I need a double latte," grumbled Francesca, gazing into the light vapor that promised to cloak their journey.

"Well, Gabe, you're in good spirits this morning," Nicholas said to his friend. "Get lots of . . . sleep?"

"Enough," Gabriel said evenly. His face revealed nothing. Nicholas decided that he probably wasn't keen on anyone finding out. Somehow, sleeping with the staff didn't seem like something Gabriel would do lightly. He wondered fleetingly if there was something serious going on.

Cassandra rubbed her hands together to ward off the chill, "I am starving. I'd give anything for a big breakfast."

"I'd give anything to see that box again," Alex said glancing over at Gabriel.

"Everything in good time," Gabriel said with smile, pulling back one of the furry carriage robes to reveal the box and a stack of the documents wrapped inside a heavy plastic bag and tucked neatly inside a second container. Alex let out an unintentional "Hurrah!" and the driver twisted around to see what the commotion was. They all grinned back at him and waved, feeling like teenagers caught kissing on a hay ride. Once the carriage pulled into Gabriel's driveway, he stepped out carefully with the box, still concealed beneath the woolly blanket.

Francesca and Cassandra headed for the kitchen to rustle up some much-needed coffee and a substantial breakfast. "Come down to breakfast when you're ready," suggested Cassandra as she ran her hand down her husband's whiskers.

"Guess that's our cue," Nicholas grinned, socking his brother on the shoulder. "I got dibs on the shower."

℘

Gabriel just shook his head. He was an only child, and the closeness of some siblings, particularly these twins, had always bewildered him. It made him feel both envious and a little uncomfortable. Certainly it was nothing he would ever be able to experience himself.

Climbing the stairs, he retreated to the comfort zone of his office. Though the room was large, it had the low ceilings common to Carolina farmhouses built in the Nineteenth Century. It was a good solid room with graceful windows, heart-of-pine floors, and a brick fireplace, which he tended to now, trying not to think about what had happened the night before. He put a long match to a piece of fat lighter beneath hickory logs and watched, rocking back on his heels as the fire caught. Frowning, he went back over to his office chair and whirled around in it a couple of times. Then he stopped and turned on the computers. A wall full of blue screens flickered at him. He had grown tired of trying to manage farms, the estate, his personal finances, the environmental conservancy, shops, and the winery on one machine. Now he had one for each venture. He could move back and forth between companies quickly, examining reports, creating memos, and making quick decisions on a myriad of issues. *Gotta keep all the balls in the air at once*, he thought.

He checked each screen and found nothing except a Mad Cow Disease scare on the West Coast, then turned his attention to the mail. The Georgia Pacific Company wanted him to sit on their board; he sent off a quick e-mail turning the invitation down. He had decided a long time ago against being one of those executives who make an easy salary sitting on corporate boards. He considered it a waste of time and money. Corporate waste, in general, infuriated him. He had seen it up-close and personal in his own family. Huge amounts of money were spent on his father's self-aggrandizing projects that did little actual good for the charities they sponsored.

Despite his best efforts, thoughts of last night's discovery intruded in the midst of his daily routine. "How could they not?" he asked himself. He pulled his recorder from his pocket and rewound it. He listened for a while, reliving the experience. He didn't say it to his friends last night, but one overriding thought troubled him: *Is this how my family made all its money? With an ancient box? Even if I'm willing to buy into this crazy theory of the nested tetrahedron, it doesn't explain how the family lost all that money around 1900. Was it bad luck—or were we being punished for something?*

Alex and Nicholas did well for themselves financially, but were not wealthy by any means. He smiled, remembering Cassandra and Francesca's dresses and their fantasies about being rich. *They really don't know what a burden it is,* he thought, *and how responsible you become for the livelihood of those who work for you.* His doctoral thesis had called for redistributing wealth on a global basis, and he could see that happening, a movement in its infancy. American companies were beginning to out source services to the Indian subcontinent, and within the next decade, wealth would begin to flatten out as countries such those in the Pacific Rim and China became their own consumer societies.

He moved to the conservancy screen and downloaded reports on arctic drilling and reforestation projects. Try as he might, he was unable to keep his mind focused on the tasks at hand.

Should we have taken the box?

What's my responsibility with this thing?

They're so eager, trying to figure it out, matching numbers, pairing profits and studying the data. What if they really figure out how to use this thing? Should I let them do that?

He spun around in the chair a few more times, contemplating his course of action. It took him several minutes, but once his decision was made he exhaled deeply and placed a call to New York.

"Hi," he said. "How are you?"

"I'm surprised to hear from you," the voice on the other end answered cautiously, "I never talk to you any more."

"I'm glad to hear your voice, too, Mother. I need to get some information about something I found in the mansion."

"Since when do you need someone else to tell you something about that house?" his mother laughed.

"Since I found a room I didn't know was there. Behind the library fireplace next to the staircase leading to the second floor—"

"You found what?" his mother interrupted.

"A hidden room. It's full of things that have evidently never been catalogued, including a pile of documents and lots of other things. I need to know what you want me to do with them."

"I'll get your father," she said abruptly, putting the phone down.

"Figures," Gabriel said to himself.

His father came on the line and wasted no time on pleasantries. "I am aware of that room. Nothing in there is worth anything to anybody, and after all these years who even knows where it all came from or who owns it. Just close the door and forget it. Just a bunch of junk in there."

The response was right out of left field and caught Gabriel off-guard. "Yes, sir. But I—."

"But nothing! Did you hear me, Gabriel? This is not a discussion or a committee meeting. Seal up the room, tell no one about it, and forget it!"

"Yes, sir." He pulled the phone away from his ear when the dial tone ended the conversation. *Just a bunch of junk? Tell no one about it?*

Gabriel cradled the phone in his hand for more than a minute before finally hanging up. Something was terribly wrong. Otherwise, his father would have demanded a full inventory of the room's contents. He had sensed something in his father's voice.

Was it fear?

"Forget about it? I don't think so," Gabriel muttered aloud.

He shut down the computers, retrieved the box from under his bed, and walked to the top of the stairs. He could see the twins seated in the living room.

"How would you guys like to take all this stuff with you? I just talked to my father. He said nothing in the sealed room was worth anything. If he doesn't want it, neither do I. Take it. It's yours."

Chapter 8

A pair of mouths dropped opened in astonishment. "How could he say that?" Nicholas demanded, rising to his feet. "This box and those documents are valuable antiques. They might also make us wealthy— incredibly wealthy—once we figure out how to use it."

"I agree," broke in Alex, "and from what I've heard of your father, he's certainly has no reluctance when it comes to making more money."

"Maybe he doesn't need it to make money," Gabriel shrugged indifferently as he reached the bottom of the stairs and placed the box on the table next to the twins. "His money earns more no matter what. Up, down, in the middle, he makes money."

Francesca and Cassandra entered with a big tray of biscuits, ham, marmalade, and lattes. "Just to warn you, they don't foam the milk in Italy, so I don't do it here," laughed Francesca. "If I did, I'd have to call it espresso with American foam, and charge you an arm and a leg."

Cassandra chuckled until Nicholas told her Gabriel's father had turned over the box to them.

She stopped in her tracks and frowned. "Well, maybe last night was all just fantasy. Perhaps it has no value at all."

"Oh, it has value all right. Look at this." Nicholas sat down in front of the box and pointed to the four indicators. "The first indicator has moved nearly to the top of the bar, and the third indicator has moved up 60 percent of the way. The second indicator, however, has dipped to about 20 percent of its bar, while the fourth indicator is at about the same level."

Alex attributed this to having moved the box. "Let's eat our breakfast and let a few hours pass, and then study this thing."

Cassandra agreed, adding, "We also need to carefully examine the documents from the *cassone* before we can come to any real conclusions."

The group exhausted the remainder of the day surfing the Web at Gabriel's house and rummaging through the mansion's vast library. This was one of the busiest times of the year on the Estate, and they found themselves acting as *ad hoc* tour guides for the many of the guests. Nicholas shook his head and finally gave up trying to count the number of poinsettias being brought in by the staff. Cassandra kept an eye out for Gabriel's mysterious blonde visitor. Nicholas had described her in some detail the evening before, but no one matching her description made an appearance. Besides being tremendously curious, she also believed Gabriel needed a stable female influence in his life. For all the years they had known Gabriel, there was still a great deal in his life that remained closed to them. He threw up a wall of privacy any time anyone brought up certain subjects—particularly if they related to his childhood. If he was seeing someone, he was certainly being secretive about her identity.

After spending Sunday morning pouring over their notes and discussing the mysterious find, the twins headed up to Gabriel's office, where they found him tapping away on his computers. Francesca and Cassandra, meanwhile, settled themselves in front of the fire in the living room, where they carried on their own conversation about the granite and cypress artifact.

"Cassandra," began Francesca, who was flipping thorough a recipe book she had picked up in one of the mansion's many gift shops. "I've been thinking . . . if the Egyptians knew about astronomy, giant pyramid construction, and accurate calendars, why couldn't they figure out the relationship between the earth, the sun, and the moon?"

Cassandra let the words sink in for a few moments before answering. "Good question. All the pictorial evidence I have seen has them depicting the earth as a flat disk with the starry body of the goddess Nut arching over it." She shrugged. "I think they regarded the earth as flat—the sun and moon, too. Stars revolved around it, not the other way around."

"There's actually an active flat-earth society today," Alex announced as he entered the room and fell into the comfortable chair by the fireplace. "The Greek Eratosthenes used the angles of the sun's rays to compute the diameter and circumference of the earth in 230 B.C., but I guess some of those ancient beliefs are hard to let go of. Science doesn't always shake off those old superstitions."

"Unfortunately, the Church doesn't either." Cassandra grimaced. "Consider this, Francesca. When your countryman Columbus set sail for the New World, the earth's roundness was still being debated in many societies."

"Yeah, and since Eratosthenes' calculations had been lost by that time, the ones who did believe thought the earth was much smaller than it really is," said Alex.

"Ah," said Francesca, turning back to the recipes. "Well then, in honor of Cristobal Columbus, how about *ribollita* for tonight? It's a kind of country dish with lots of veggies."

"What would we do without you?" Alex laughed, smiling at her enthusiasm.

"Starve." She gave him a quick kiss. "I'm going to run to the market. I'll be back in ten minutes," she announced, grabbing her purse and keys as she flew out the door.

A few minutes later Nicholas, who had heard her departure, came thumping down the stairs two at a time and sank into a chair by the glass coffee table directly in front of the box. Gabriel followed him down at a more leisurely pace, dressed in a pair of slacks and a red and black pullover sweater. He sank to the floor with his back against the wall. "So how did they do this?" he asked softly to no one in particular. "I'll take my answer on the air, please, but I only have a few minutes before I have to leave." Everyone chucked at the joke.

"It's rather baffling, I'll admit that," said Alex as he stared at the box. "They apparently understood the gravitational relationship between the earth, the moon, and the sun, and yet *did not* understand motion? How could they make a device to measure the one thing that eluded mankind and, indeed, every scientist until Newton?"

"Maybe they didn't need motion," Nicholas replied. "They only needed gravitational force, which gave them the ability to predict the actual height of the waters. In all likelihood, that's all they thought the box did."

Alex snapped his fingers. "Of course, Nicholas! Newton's equations could solve it."

"Solve what?"

"Look," Alex began, his voice rising in pitch and excitement. "Gravity holds the entire universe together—every galaxy, solar system, planet, and all other celestial particles, gases, and solids. The sheer fact that these heavenly bodies produce gravitational forces throughout our solar system made it impossible for Newton to calculate at any point in time what the sum would be of all gravitational forces at work on the earth. Even looking at our moon and sun, the other eight planets, meteoroids, comets and interplanetary dust—it's impossible to calculate as a measurement the effect of gravity on Earth. What makes the box so incredible is it measures the gravitational effects on itself collectively instead of a mathematical calculated sequence."

"What the hell does that mean?" Gabriel, who had been quiet up until now, had a confused look on his face. Alex did not immediately answer, his eyes fixed squarely on the box. Gabriel turned his gaze to Nicholas. "Professor?" Cassandra looked up from the stack of reference books, her full attention now riveted on conversation.

Nicholas was about to answer when Alex stood up, pressed both of his palms together, and rested the sides of his forefingers against his mouth. "To put it simply," he said, speaking quietly through his fingers, "the box is measuring gravity simply by suffering the effects of gravity *on itself.*"

Cassandra smiled. "Even I can understand that," she teased.

Alex nodded eagerly. "It's just like the oceans and seas or any other body of water. Even cows. They all measure the effects of gravity collectively."

"Cows?" asked Cassandra.

"Think about this for a second," continued her brother-in-law. "Haven't you been driving and noticed how cows seem to all sleep at the same time in the field—as far as the eye can see? It's like my secretary, who always goes to the vending machine around three in the afternoon to get a candy bar. All living creatures experience what is called circadian rhythms."

"That's true," said Nicholas. "I read a short but fascinating book about that not too long ago. Circadian rhythms are a powerful internal clock. I don't recall the author connecting them to gravity, however."

"Find that book for me," said Alex. "I'm sure it's in your library at home. Sounds interesting. Anyway, harmonic stations throughout the world measure the effect of gravity on the oceans. An algorithm produces these harmonic measurements."

"Err, an Al Gore what?" Cassandra looked up from her documents.

"Not *Al Gore*!" laughed Alex. "An a-l-g-o-r-i-t-h-m, a method of solving a problem through a sequence of very precisely defined steps. Algorithms can be extremely accurate. When Francesca comes back, for example, she is going to perform an algorithm."

"Boy, is she going to be excited about that!" said Cassandra. "You know what she thinks about all this math and chemistry!"

"She does it every time she follows a recipe," said Alex. "Different algorithms may complete the same task with a different set of instructions in more or less time, space, or effort than others. Take two different recipes for making potato salad, for example. One may have you peel the potatoes before boiling, while the other wants you to peel them after you boil them. Even though the steps are in the reverse order, they both call for these steps to be repeated for every potato and end when the potato salad is ready to eat."

"That's a good example, Alex," Nicholas added. "But remember, correctly performing an algorithm will not solve a problem if the algorithm itself is flawed, or not appropriate to the problem."

"Yes, that's exactly right," answered Alex. "Let's use the potato salad example again. The potato salad algorithm will fail if there are no potatoes present, even if all the motions of preparing the salad are performed as if the potatoes were there."

Alex looked up as Francesca entered with two sacks of groceries. "I didn't have to go far," she said. "There were caterers at the mansion who gave me all sorts of things, and I even got some fresh herbs from the green house. I can see how this place operated in the Nineteenth Century—talk about self-sufficient!"

"Francesca!" Alex greeted her teasingly. "You're going to do an algorithm!" The tone of his voice implied something provocative.

"I am not," answered Francesca without missing a beat as she strode toward the kitchen. "It's a *ribollita*." The twins laughed as Cassandra shook her finger at them and rose to follow her sister-in-law.

Gabriel checked his watch and excused himself. "I hate to leave my beloved guests, but as you all know, I have another dinner engagement I am unable to cancel. Save some of that algorithm for me," he quipped as he walked out the door.

"See ya, Gabe," said Alex. Nicholas nodded goodbye. "Come on, he's leaving," he said in mock seriousness. "Let's hit the scotch!" They could hear Gabriel's deep laughter as they helped themselves to a fresh bottle of Aberlour. Once the amber liquid was poured the conversation quickly returned to the only topic that mattered to them. The brothers always enjoyed debating scientific concepts, but the idea that the box somehow held the key to unlocking the world's financial markets naturally intrigued them.

Nicholas brought up the concept of *electro magnetic radiation* coming from the center of the universe as the glue holding all the galaxies, solar systems, and planets in place. "It's too radical a theory and makes no sense," argued Alex. "Only two percent of scientists believe it, and I think they're all charter members of the Flat-Earth Society. I just don't see how that could apply to our little box here at all."

Nicholas laughed. "Okay," he said, "but how about the *Schumann Resonance* theory?"

Alex bit his lower lip for a few seconds and furrowed his brow in thought. "Let's see, electro magnetic standing waves, like in a microwave oven, that fill the earth's ionosphere cavity and have a natural frequency, with concurrent harmonics, of ten cycles per second. . ."

"Yes. An atomic bomb explosion shifts the frequencies of these waves, but then they return to normal according to the geometry of the space between two concentric spheres."

"And how does this relate to the markets and the box?" asked Alex.

"The human brain's alpha-rhythms are almost identical in frequency to the Schumann Resonances."

Alex nodded gently and lifted his glass to his lips. "I'll grant you that the theory has credibility, but it's measured in cycles of a tenth of a second. We can't apply that to stock market cycles. You and other economists claim the stock markets have six to nine *daily* cycles and three to four *yearly* cycles. Now are you trying to tell me those cycles have nothing to do with quarterly earnings reports and what the 20-something-year-old 'experts' say on cable news, and everything to do with gravitational motion?"

Nicholas shrugged, spilling a trickle of scotch down the outside of his glass and over his fingers. After making sure Cassandra was not watching, he licked the Scotch whiskey away without looking for a napkin. "Let's just say for theory's sake that's what I am saying. The cycles have little or nothing to do with earnings reports and all the rest. Even great scientists like J. M. Hurst and Dr. Claude E. Cleeton plotted the cyclicity of the market and found undeniably that markets followed a quasi-periodical *sine* wave of just those periods, but they cannot explain when, where, or why."

Alex exhaled slowly before setting down his glass and turning to face the wooden box. He carefully turned the artifact around to reveal the *sine* wave. Nicholas stared at it for a long while. "So, brother," whispered Alex. "Taking into consideration the documents found with this box, and what they represent, is it fair to say you are claiming that instead of measuring gravitational fluctuations, this box *predicts* them?"

"Yes, I guess that is what I am saying."

Alex heard his own voice catch as he said, "If you are right, we can use the information it provides to invest in stocks knowing in advance what direction the market will take." He shook his head as if to clear it.

Nicholas smiled in response, holding out the bottle of scotch. "I think you need another drink. I know I do."

Chapter 9

 Ernest Gabriel von Stuyvesant, Sr., stood rigidly at attention as he gazed out of the living room's expansive windows. It was beginning to snow, and his view of the Hudson River was fast becoming cloaked in a pristine white blanket.

The old man exhaled noisily as he turned around. His bushy eyebrows gathered into a scowl that only deepened when his eyes took in the room his wife's nauseating interior designer had just finished. The large room was built for entertaining. Now it was divided up into multiple seating areas dripping in hues of yellow and blue. It was too damn cheerful for his taste, and he hated every one of the floral silk pillows that dotted the furniture. He walked slowly, methodically, around the room turning off the lamps so he could sit and look out over the city lights. He sat for a very long while, nursing a gin and tonic and pondering the twists of life. When his wife finally emerged from her office across the hall, she almost missed seeing him sitting alone in the gathering darkness.

Even in her sixties, Lilly von Stuyvesant was arrestingly beautiful. Her long neck and silver hair, which she kept short and swept back, were both eye-catching, and her aquiline nose below a patrician forehead gave her the look of a Dutch Renaissance portrait. She spent a lot of money to maintain her looks, and she expected people to notice her when she walked into a room. They always did.

"Gabby?" She walked over and tapped his shoulder. He jumped slightly at the touch. "You're still thinking about him, aren't you?" she said softly.

"I thought that damn box was buried forever. I should have destroyed it. Now the worst person in the world has it!"

"What a thing to say about your own child!" she scolded. "What could he possibly do with it? Yes, I agree you should have just gotten rid of it years ago if you didn't want anyone to find it."

He sighed, lifted his glass, and then lowered it without drinking. "How could I destroy something that has that much history?" he whispered. "Our son's passion for antiquities mirrors my own. I'm just worried he'll be able to figure it out."

"What if he does? Frankly, I cannot imagine that it would interest him." She joined her husband on the sofa and patted his arm. "After all," she said dryly, "he's not into making money. He's into spending ours."

The elder von Stuyvesant stood up slowly and moved about the room, this time turning the lights back on, illuminating the valuable porcelains, tapestries, bronzes and Chihuily glass that he had made the hated decorator put back in the room. "I don't like it."

"Maybe you should talk to Malachi," she suggested.

"Malachi." He almost spit out the name. "He thinks he is so damn perfect, but he set up a Swiss entity for one of the offshore investments that might come back to haunt us. The Feds have noticed these loopholes, and I don't need another battle with them right now. The family couldn't take the heat."

His wife crossed her legs, smoothed her skirt, and twisted her jewel-encrusted gold rings, thinking how best to answer him. She remained quiet for a few moments, hesitant to bring up an unpleasant subject. "He has done a good job shoring up our financial life. After all, you said his company managed to get us a thirty-four percent return while everybody else was losing money. I really don't think you should ignore him for too long, dear. You know what happened when your great-grandfather—"

"I don't need reminding!" snapped von Stuyvesant, his eyes blazing in anger. "They deliberately made poor investments. Nearly killed us, Lilly! Some times I can't stand Malachi or his ancestry. He has too much damned control."

"Give it up, Gabby," she whispered in return. "We are in his computers forever." She rose and held out her hand, "Come along now, it's time to dress for dinner." He murmured something she did not fully hear and followed his wife upstairs.

Outside, the snow drifted and swayed in the wind, the flakes swooping and dancing as they fell earthward.

Chapter 10

Nicholas tried to maintain a somber, philosophical outlook, but the tension was getting to him. His jaw hurt from clenching his teeth too tightly and his stomach churned with anxiety. He tried to appear relaxed, standing with his drink in one hand and the other awkwardly resting on the carved marble fireplace mantle that Gabriel had found in Savannah, Georgia. He knew his brother could see through the charade.

"I get it now. The box, the documents, the wealth—everything." Alex's voice was low, but he was finding it difficult to keep his excitement in check. "It's our turn, Nicholas! It is our turn!"

One set of unblinking blue eyes drilled into another matching set. Neither brother looked away. In the corner of the dining room, a Lomax of Blackburn grandfather clock, dressed in Mahogany with a burnished brass face, ticked off the seconds. Each click seemed louder than the last.

"What?" Alex demanded at last. He could see his brother's hesitancy plainly etched on his face. When he failed to answer, Alex sighed deeply. "Alright, let's stop and think." He pulled out a chair and sat down. "We've just rendered every economic theory in existence useless. Can you imagine watching CNBC now? While the experts are predicting what's going to happen next quarter, we'll actually *know*."

The soft chatter of their wives in the kitchen filtered into the room. The scotch helped muffle the tones. Nicholas turned and looked out the picture window. It was starting to snow, and huge wet flakes were sliding down the window. Except for the clock, it was very quiet.

Alex broke the lingering silence. "What if someone else knows? I mean, assuming we soon can prove all this, these documents establish that someone else was using the box in the recent past. What if he or they are still alive?"

Nicholas sank down into the chair, rubbing his face while pushing his fingertips deep into his eyes. "I've thought about that too, Alex. The box and documents have been hidden away in a secret room for many years. And now Gabe's father tells him it's all worthless. Maybe whoever used the box in the past didn't figure out all the answers? Maybe they only got part of it and then abandoned it? Maybe the documents were speculation and they never realized how close they were to breaking the key?"

"It's just been sitting there waiting for someone who knows what he's doing," offered Alex.

"And you do? We do?" asked Nicholas, running his hand through his hair. He cleared his throat and nodded for the scotch. Alex reached over and poured him a healthy shot. "Let's assume all this theorizing is something approaching the truth. We have to come up with a simple, leveraged trading strategy that takes full advantage of our discovery. But first things first. We need to plot when the indicators mark the up and down periods, and then superimpose those findings on the actual Dow Jones Industrial Average real-time charts back as far as the data is available. . . ."

"Wait. Go back to 'leveraged' and explain what you mean in more detail," interjected Alex.

"Hold that thought for a second," Nicholas answered. "Is it possible you could find sophisticated astronomical software that might give us more precise measurements than the box?"

"Maybe," Alex answered slowly.

"Maybe? Well if 'maybe' turns out to be absolutely, then once you figure out which software to use, and if I'm right about this, we need to decide on an amount to invest to try it. How about fifty grand? Can you swing that?"

Alex leaned back in his chair for a moment, thinking. "Software . . . the National Oceanic Atmospheric Administration would have the most accurate astronomical measurements for distances between the sun, moon, and earth. If we used their algorithm, we could exactly correlate specific times, such as minutes, hours, days, months, and even years with the indicators on the box. We should be able to produce a column of numbers that should give us better measurements as to where the stock market will be heading than the box can. We could also use a liquid dynamic algorithm that should precisely match astronomical measurements relating to the orbits of the sun, moon, and earth. These measurements would tell us even the minutest gravitational fluctuations."

Alex paused for a moment, thinking about what he had just said. He opened his mouth in astonishment. "Do you realize that with modern astronomical measurements, we don't even really need the box?"

"Of course, now you've got it!" Nicholas practically shouted. His outburst prompted Cassandra to pop her head out of the kitchen to see what the commotion was all about. "Whoever hid the box in the room at the Biltmore must have figured this out as well! That explains why Gabriel's father said it was worthless." Nicholas shook his head and let loose with a grim cackle. "He—or whoever owned the box—has probably already automated the system."

"So what's stopping us from doing the same thing?" Both men turned around to see Cassandra standing in the doorway. "Dinner's ready," she said, "and I have a feeling that this is going to be an interesting meal."

Francesca entered the dining room from the kitchen and stopped in her tracks. She nearly dropped the basket of warm bread she was carrying, "What's wrong?" she asked, looking at their faces.

"Darling, I think we are all going to become very rich!" Alex exclaimed, jumping up to grab his wife and twirl both her and the bread about the room.

As they all took their places, Nicholas reached over to fill their wine glasses. Francesca folded her hands in her lap and gave a small sigh. Cassandra turned to her, "What is it Francesca? Are you alright?"

"I know there is only one thing you two have been talking about in there, and before you tell me what your plan is, I need to ask a question." Francesca looked at both of them in turn. "Are you certain you are doing the right thing?" Her voice sounded small and hesitant. "I don't want to burst anyone's bubble, but is all of this moral or legal—or even meant to be?"

The question caught Alex off guard and his mouth dropped open in surprise. Nicholas quickly reassured her. "Well, nothing has been scientifically proven, so we may be completely wrong. But if we are correct, think of it as using whatever information is available. This is nothing like insider trading, Francesca. It's just gravity. The Egyptians who built the box figured out that much. All creatures, including human beings, are subject to the effects of planetary motion. We are influenced by gravity in everything we do including, what appears to be obvious, financial decisions. Now we have to find out how much—and how little."

Francesca tore off a chunk of Italian country-style bread and nodded her head slowly. "So, the Egyptians thought that the rise and fall of tides was the origin of the cycles, but it wasn't. It was really planetary relationships that caused the ebb and flow."

"Right," said Nicholas.

"But how do we know the box affects U.S. stock markets today?"

Alex answered the question. "Well, the box does not directly *affect* the market. It simply measures gravitational fluctuations wherever the box happens to be. And don't forget about the spreadsheet documentation we found with the box."

"I know," Francesca replied, sipping some merlot from her glass. "If it was not for the paperwork and the circumstances of how the box was found, I would think you two had utterly lost your minds."

"It sounds amazing, but it makes sense if you think about it," urged Alex. "Whenever someone sits down to make a trade, his decision is influenced by the gravitational pulls that influence emotions such as euphoria, greed, and fear."

"Wow," said Cassandra. "Can you imagine? If that's true, it would make the irrationality of Wall Street kind of logical after all."

"Wall Street runs on emotion," said Nicholas. "I heard a great segment on CNBC once. They interviewed half a dozen traders in a Manhattan bar, and asked each one why the stock market had behaved the way it did that day. They got five completely different answers and one 'I don't have the foggiest.' The guy who said that gave the only honest answer."

Francesca seemed relieved. "Well, as long as you guys aren't doing anything illegal."

"I have a question." Cassandra cocked her head inquisitively. "Just how rich can this thing make us?" A faint smiled broke out on her face.

Alex and Nicholas looked at one another and Alex nodded toward his brother. "You're the economics guru, but I bet we can double fifty grand in a month or two."

"No way!" said Francesca. "If you're right, you have to help me start a restaurant."

"Don't start looking for locations yet," warned Cassandra. "I don't have a lot of faith in these guys—even if we did marry them!"

The conversation gradually turned to other things, and by the time Francesca brought out her homemade apple-cinnamon cheesecake, she and Cassandra were actively discussing the heavy snowfall, Christmas plans, and a documentary that was coming on later that evening. Alex could barely keep himself in place for dessert. He wanted to get upstairs to commandeer one of Gabriel's computers and look for the astronomical software. When they were finally done eating, he grabbed his coffee and gave his brother a wink. "Let's get outta here before they make us clean up the kitchen."

Nicholas was fast on Alex's heels as they climbed the stairs. "What about the fifty grand?" Alex asked once they were settled in Gabriel's office.

"I'll put up half," Nicholas answered.

Alex looked at his brother skeptically and began expertly navigating the keyboard. "You know, I can't believe someone didn't think of this sooner. Human behavior is the lifeblood of markets. Markets are publicly auctioned entities. Even the computer-generated programs used for large institutions are ultimately determined by people, and people are influenced by gravity. Nobody but us and the original owners of the box know that!

Alex continued. "I read about a group in Santa Fe. I believe they were called the Predictors, or Prediction Company, or something like that. Anyway, these guys started with the idea that because they were so brilliant, they could produce a software program that would predict the stock market. Long story short, they failed after exhausting a huge amount of money, something like $200 million. They had more than forty physicists and mathematicians working full-time, and they never had better than 40 percent forecast accuracy. I think they finally ended up producing an automated trading machine that's used now at the Chicago Board of Trade for making continuous financial guesses based on technical indicators."

"They just needed somebody to tell them about gravity," Nicholas chortled, feeling slightly giddy. The wine and scotch mixed surprisingly well.

"Maybe they forgot to hire somebody in quantum mechanics! Hey, now I know where I saw that program—Matlab. But I'll have to check it out later." Alex went straight to a search engine on Gabriel's computer to look for tide and ocean current programs that published algorithms forecasting tidal fluctuations utilized at harmonic stations all over the world. The measurements were used in shipping and navigation software for merchant vessels and private ships. He found 315,000 related Internet sites, but the one with the most hits was a company called Nobeltec.

"I'm sure this is a simple question," Nicholas asked as they navigated the site, "but you're the one with astronomical background. Is it the moon or is it the sun that is influencing us the most?"

Alex had spent many hours studying the physical phenomena of space. His livelihood depended on mathematics, but he also needed to understand theories defining space and gravity so he could write system and parameter identification programs used in the space program.

"The moon has the greatest individual effect, but the collective effect felt from both the moon and the sun creates the actual highest gravitational forces. That's because of something called the *ratio of the closest*. It explains the gravitational effect felt from the moon as compared to the collective effect felt from the moon and sun."

"Because the moon follows an elliptic orbit around the earth, which means it's closest to earth at a predictable time during its monthly orbit," offered Nicholas.

"Yes, but to be precise, it is a 29.53-day orbit. It's called the *perigee*. During that period when the moon is the closest, the effect of gravitational force should be felt the most. The *apogee* is the farthest point to the moon in its orbit around the earth, and at this time the gravitational force from the moon should be felt the least."

Cassandra walked in and set down two cups of coffee, both black and steaming hot. "Freshly ground and strong, as you both like it, courtesy of your lovely wife, Alex." She kissed Nicholas on the forehead. "Lots to clean up downstairs, so I won't stay and bother you."

"Thanks Cassandra," said Nicholas. He turned back to his brother. "Keep going, Alex."

"Like the moon, the earth also travels a predictable elliptic orbit around the sun. Where the earth is closest to the sun, it's called the *perihelion*, and during this period you'd have the greatest gravitational force from the sun. The *aphelion* marks the point of greatest distance from the earth to the sun, and at this point the gravitational force from the sun should be felt the least."

"Sounds Greek to me," cracked Nicholas.

"Very funny," said his brother evenly without cracking a smile. "I believe that at a certain point during the year, the moon is in close proximity to the earth at the same time the earth is in close proximity to the sun. However, the sun's gravitational forces have a slightly less effect on earth, and probably also on the stock market. What's really interesting is that the combination effect of the two bodies should exert the greatest gravitational pull. Here, I'll draw you a picture."

Alex pulled out a legal pad and spent a couple minutes sketching out a simple formula for Nicholas:

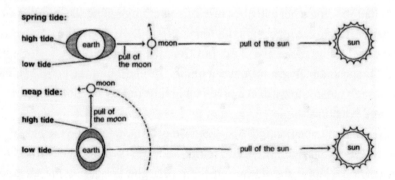

"That's helpful," Nicholas said. "But when is it exactly during the year that we have the highest and lowest gravitational forces?"

"The answer to that question is a little more difficult to understand. This diagram explains the greatest and the least gravitational forces on earth. We have high and low gravitational forces daily, but only two times each month and two times each year do we experience the total effects of gravity at its maxima and minima. During the equinoxes, March/April (*vernal equinox*) and September/October (*autumn equinox*) we suffer the greatest forces, with the *autumn equinox* being the greater of the two. During the December-January winter solstice and the June-July summer solstice, we suffer the least forces, with the summer solstice being the least of the two."

Nicholas' hands were wrapped around the warm cup sitting on the desk, and he pulled them away as if they had been scalded. "Wait a minute!" he interrupted. "If I understand you correctly, the markets, according to our market tops with low gravitational forces, and market bottoms with high gravitational forces theory, should move up at the solstices and down at the equinoxes, right?"

Alex nodded in agreement. He could see where Nicholas was going with his thinking.

Nicholas continued. "Couldn't we just buy the markets during the autumn equinox and sell during the winter solstice, and buy again during the vernal equinox and sell during the summer solstice? That would be so damn easy and besides, the logic absolutely follows conventional wisdom surrounding the market seasonality theory."

Alex shook his head in disagreement. "That would be wonderful, but it's a lot more complicated than that. We still need to complete the research." Alex tapped the drawing and continued. "You're right about one thing, though. The reality is obvious. There is a measurable effect. In our case the effects may well create a fortune for us. In the box's case, the effects just cause the indicators to move up and down. We still need to discern exactly when to buy and sell during the appropriate months."

Alex paused and took a sip of coffee before continuing. "Now comes the hard part. When the moon is directly overhead, the gravitational pull is at its maximum for that day, while nearly the same effect is felt 180 degrees around the world, but inversely."

Nicholas let the words sink in and groaned. "Of course."

"When the moon is straight overhead it pulls the earth and water upward," Alex continued. "At the exact opposite side of the world, the earth is being pulled inward toward its center. This makes the waters appear to rise, but in reality the earth and everything else is getting pulled inward."

Footsteps on the staircase interrupted the conversation. "Hi guys." Gabriel slouched in the doorway with an amused smile on his face. "Enjoying my scotch and my private domain?" He looked at the internet site they were studying. "Whoa. That's not my domain," he gave a low whistle. "What's going on?"

"Quantum physics, at least for the moment," said Nicholas glancing at his brother with a wide smile.

Chapter 11

"This should help." Alex sat impatiently as a copy of a current essay on quantum physics rolled out of the laser printer.

Seated at one of Gabriel's other computers, Nicholas scrolled through a National Oceanic and Atmospheric Administration web site that had a lunar perigee and apogee calculator. For any given year, the calculator was able to print out each month's perigee, perihelion, apogee, and aphelion points. More importantly, the graph pointed out the date in the month where the gravitational forces are at their maximum and the date where they are at their minimum. He typed in the year 2004. Running his finger down the screen, he felt himself growing more and more excited.

"Yes!" he exclaimed, throwing his arms into the air with clenched fists. He sat back with a grin and ceremoniously as he clicked the print button. Gabriel and Alex jumped at the outburst and spun around to look in his direction. Nicholas smiled at them. "You are not going to believe this!" The HP printer whirred. "Wait a second," Nicholas said as he bent over to check the pages of figures from 1950 to 2010 beginning to pile up in the tray. "This will take a few minutes." Gabriel and Alex turned back to the article they had been discussing, which in turn led them to search and print out additional material.

With a cup of coffee in one hand and a black ink pen in the other, Nicholas carefully went through each year, marking the month in the perigee columns that exhibited the maximum gravitational forces, and also marking the month in the apogee columns that showed the minimum gravitational forces. When he finished, he entered each distance, measured in kilometers for each column, onto an Excel spreadsheet.

Nicholas picked up the spreadsheet and examined the results, mumbling under this breath every few seconds. Alex looked up from the quantum physics article and noticed that his brother's eyes were beginning to dilate with excitement. "Speak up, Nicholas! We can't wait forever. Besides, Gabe is getting bored with all this talk of physics." Gabriel nudged his elbow into Alex's ribs.

"Ok, look at this." Nicholas leaned out of the way so they could better see the computer monitor, and pointed at the screen. "A recent history lesson. Remember when the stock 'bubble' burst in 2000 and the market bottomed out in 2002?" He looked up to see if Alex was following him. He was. "2004 shows a high and 2005 a low and a high. 2007 shows a low. 2009 shows a high and 2010 ends with a low."

"And what does all this mean?" asked Gabriel.

"Haven't you been keeping up with current affairs?" chided Nicholas. "We had a high in 2000 with a bottom in 2002, and now we are back up to a top again at the end of 2003. These gravitational numbers predict where, in a general sense, the market will go into 2010! The astronomical numbers are matching up with the historical market."

"Here, let me prove my point this way." Nicholas pulled up www.BigCharts.com on the internet and showed Alex a graph that proved his point.

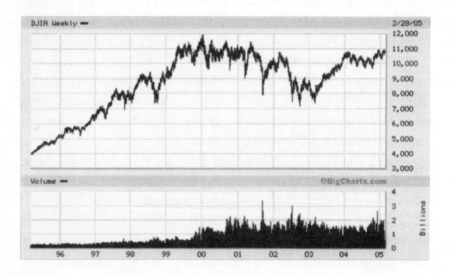

Alex looked at the screen. "Why do you suppose some of the years in the lunar perigee and apogee calculator have both a high and a low in the same year?"

"I'm not sure yet." Nicholas leaned back in his chair and looked over at his brother. What do you think? How do we treat them?"

Alex hesitated. He looked again at the spreadsheet Nicholas was holding. "Well, notice that a low always follows a high and vice-versa. Let's just assume those highs and lows in the same year would simply follow the previous sequence. If the preceding year was a high, we would be looking for a low in the year in question, right?"

He paused and looked up, "No, what am I thinking? Why don't we just look at exactly how the perigee and apogee graph checks out against the historical record of the market?"

Nicholas felt his stomach lurch. That would be the key. To Alex's delight and Nicholas' relief, the lines on the graph correlated with the low gravitational forces, and were a *precise* match to the highs in the markets. Market lows paralleled the high gravitational forces.

As the brothers sat in silence, Gabriel spoke up. "So the lower the gravitational pull, the higher the stock market goes, and higher gravity means a lower market?" Nicholas nodded. Alex did not react at all.

Stunned to silence, they weren't even aware when Cassandra and Francesca walked into the room carrying a large wooden tray with mugs of fresh coffee and a plate of warm fudge walnut brownies. All three men jumped when Francesca spoke. "It sure is quiet in here. I thought if you guys are going to stay up half the night figuring this stuff out, you'd need some sustenance." She looked around for a spot to put the tray, but the room was awash in spreadsheets, crumpled calculations, piles of articles, and scattered charts. "What in the world have you been doing? It looks like a hurricane hit!"

"I wouldn't feel any more astonished if an actual hurricane had sped through the house," answered Alex.

"That good, huh?" replied Cassandra, who leaned down and looked at the chart in front of Nicholas. "So which one affects people positively? The highs or the lows? Am I asking that correctly?"

"Wouldn't gravity work like a pressure cooker?" asked Francesca. "The more pressure you exert on a chicken, for example, the faster it falls apart. Right?"

Alex beamed at her. "Darling, you are a genius! The data indicate pretty conclusively that the greater the gravitational force, the lower the market will go. Gravity's effect on the human body's internal pressure appears to make people act more impulsively, irrationally, maybe even disastrously in terms of their investments. The opposite probably holds true. Less gravitational pressure makes people feel content and have a more positive outlook. So they invest or remained invested."

"I'll bet the bar tabs are higher, too," said Francesca, "This could help me with my restaurant."

"Hmmm," answered her husband noncommittally, looking at the screen in front of him.

Francesca glared at Alex. "I'm going to open a restaurant with or without your help!"

"I don't know," Nicholas interceded. "Maybe she's right. Maybe this information could be good for marketing. After all, Francesca's food is—what do they call it?" Everyone looked at him and Francesca crossed her arms, waiting for the answer.

"Yeah," he said suddenly. "*Comfort* food. Feeling low? Lost a bundle in the stock market? Eat Italian!" Everyone laughed, including Francesca.

Cassandra stood and stretched. "Are y'all going to get this finished tonight?" She had on a thick woolly sweater and was rubbing her hands together. "This Southern girl just peeked outside and the snow is really coming down!"

"I doubt if we will finish tonight," said Alex, picking up a mug of hot coffee. He turned to Nicholas. "When you get a chance, can you find a website that has a historical stock market database? While you're doing that, let me try and figure out the astronomical variables."

Alex was particularly interested in an effect called the process of lunar declination, or the tilt of the moon. "Based on my studies, even if everything else was in alignment—perigee-perihelion and apogee-aphelion—if the moon's inclination is not just right, you won't see the full gravitational impact on oceans or people."

"Why is that?" asked Gabriel, who had kicked off his shoes and lifted his feet onto the desk in front of him.

Alex elaborated: "It appears that the inclination (or declination) of the moon—the way it is tilted—affects water or substances made up of water like the liquid in the box." Everyone nodded, though not everyone understood. "The charts we are calculating from don't take into consideration the measurements for inclination or declination. They are just calculating the distance from the earth to the moon and the sun. Then too, there is also the matter of wobble."

"Excuse me?" Cassandra said, biting into one of Francesca's rich brownies. "I am still trying to figure out how the tilt of the moon affects anything. What is wobble all about?"

"The earth and moon tend to wobble during their respective elliptical orbits, as do other planets."

"The earth wobbles?" she asked, licking fudge from her fingers.

"Sure does." Alex smiled patiently. "The rotation and the density of the earth and moon aren't exactly balanced. Both heavenly bodies spin with a little wobble on their axes during their expanding and contracting elliptical orbits. This effect can cause gravitational forces to slightly increase or decrease, regardless of the astronomical measurements."

Nicholas interrupted him, "So, what you are saying is the measurements might be off?

"No," said Alex. "The distance measurements are almost perfect. It's the wobble that isn't. Albert Einstein's discovery of general relativity led to his alternate theories on gravity."

"I am not familiar with Einstein's work with gravity," replied Gabriel. "Please explain it in a way I will understand." Francesca and Cassandra chimed in to agree.

Alex stood up and faced the group, using his arm and hands as a conductor would during a symphony piece. "Ok, I will make this as painless as possible. But you have to listen carefully and ask questions if you need to. According to Einstein, 'gravity is the fabric of the cosmos.' He deduced that space was not just a vacuum, but a solid membrane, a special fabric, connecting the separations between all matter. Each particle in the solar systems, the galaxies including the universe, has an effect on all other substances by means of the connection by this spatial fabric. For this very reason, our mystery box gave the original owners an 'owner's manual' on how to accurately measure the *total* gravitational effects felt from the cosmos. The combination of all these heavenly bodies orbiting causes increases and decreases in gravitational forces felt by us humans." He paused. "Questions?"

"How do we measure the effect if we can't depend on just the astronomical measurement between the earth, moon, and sun? Plus you are now adding Einstein's theories, which certainly challenge the imagination," Nicholas added.

Alex smiled. "The oceans!"

"The oceans what?" asked Gabriel.

"The box will never be wrong because it measures the effects of gravity by suffering those same effects. So do the oceans. We, on the other hand, need to find a nautical software program that measures ocean fluctuations. These measurements will give us the necessary adjustment for the moon's inclination and declination, and the earth and moons wobbling effect because of the accurate harmonic measuring stations located around the world. They'll be more precise for what they are measuring than just planetary distances."

"Ah!" exclaimed Nicholas, his lips pursed in thought. "Ok. I saw something earlier. . ." He punched in a search string into Google and pulled up a website. "Here's just what we need."

Nicholas pulled out his credit card, completed an order form, and submitted his request. After printing out the confirmation, he turned around with a satisfied sigh. "Nobeltec is going to overnight the Tides and Currents edition. It includes data for the East and West Coast of North America. This will confirm our understanding of the astronomical calculations, and we can compare the results to the nautical program measurements."

"Overnight?" Cassandra didn't even try to stifle her yawn. "Does that mean we can go to bed now?"

"Go right ahead, darling. We're going to do a bit of research into live stock market data feeds," her husband answered. "We'll call it a night in a few hours. Yikes!" His search turned up more than 1.2 million Web pages offering something to do with real-time stock market data.

Cassandra and Francesca exchanged exhausted glances.

Nicholas wracked his brain for the name of the data source a day-trader friend of his used. TradeStation—that was it. His friend had tried to get Nicholas to day trade with him, but Nicholas didn't have the time or inclination. *Or declination*, he laughed to himself. "That's about to change," he said aloud.

"What's about to change?" asked Alex.

Nicholas was already keying in "TradeStation." He looked up. "Nothing. Just talking to myself. There," he said, clicking the enter button.

As Nicholas quickly discovered, the site not only showed all the major markets in real time, but also offered a trading platform included with the subscription.

"All right!" he exclaimed eagerly. "In TradeStation, we can write our own programs to interact with the software, *and* make trading transactions in the same program!"

"Now that will be helpful," replied Alex. "Hit that 'add to my cart' button." This time they didn't have to wait for a package to be delivered. As soon as the credit card was accepted, the download process began.

Cassandra, Francesca, and Gabriel had been quiet for some time, trying to keep up with the twins and their scientific theories without feeling ignored. "So," joked Gabriel quietly, "this is how it feels to be a football widow?"

"Some women are sports widows," laughed Cassandra lightly, "I take comfort in knowing that this is more brain than brawn."

"Would you ladies like to go horseback riding in the morning?" offered Gabriel as he helped Francesca pile the empty mugs and plates back onto the tray.

"That sounds like a lot of fun, sure!" Francesca sounded ecstatic.

Cassandra, on the other hand, looked doubtful. "Well, it's been a long time since I've climbed up on a horse."

"No problem," he assured her. "The horses are calm and know what to do. And it will be fun in the snow."

"Think of it as a cushion for your fall!" Nicholas teased, giving his wife a playful pat on her behind.

"Just for that, I *will* go!" Cassandra wriggled her hips and skipped just out of his reach as the three left for the kitchen.

"You know, Nicholas, we need to pull up the Dow Jones Industrial average and see how far back we can plot the data," explained Alex, his head resting on his chin. He was beginning to look a little tired. "Then, we should be able to compare the real-time data with the astronomical calculator results."

With a tool in TradeStation they located the weekly data all the way back to 1920. The information presented a perfect visual picture of the world's financial history. Alex picked up the spreadsheet on which he had marked the years with "High" for high gravitational forces, and "Low" for low gravitational forces and began drawing lines from the highs to the lows.

In years that had both a high and a low, he simply followed the rule that a low would always follow a high and the reverse. It took a while to do this. Nicholas was mesmerized with how easily Alex maneuvered the

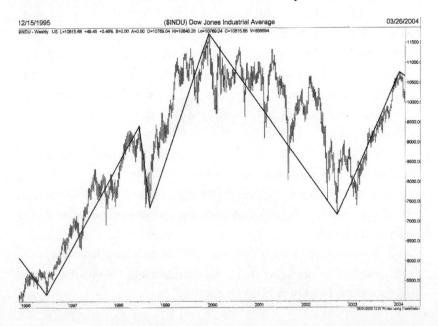

drawing tools provided in the program. When Alex finished, he held it out for his brother to examine. The results were stunning.

Both took in long breaths, grinned deeply, and looked at the graphs once again. The market highs correlated with low gravitational forces, and the lows in the markets appeared to correspond with high gravitational forces. It was an amazing discovery.

"Well, brother," began Nicholas. "Nothing like creating a theorem and proving it." He leaned back in the chair and put his feet up on Gabriel's recently-vacated desk, his hands clasped comfortably behind his head.

"Not so fast," Alex replied. Nicholas looked at his brother sideways, but did not move. "The years where the high and low values are the same are still somewhat of a problem."

"We'll compare the nautical values to see if the oceans tell the true story just like the good old box did. Let's wait and see what the Nobeltec charts say.

"Is there anything else we can do tonight?" yawned Alex. "As exciting as this is, I am really fading fast."

"No," replied Nicholas. "I'm just going to dream about the house I'm going to build. Make that *houses*."

"Any Ferraris in those dreams?"

"No, more like a Lamborghini. What will you dream about?"

"For the last few years I've been working on an alternative energy project. I now have certified results that prove my discovery. It would be nice to have the funding to take the project from research to reality."

"Alternative energy?"

"Yeah," Alex yawned again. "I think it is going to be a little controversial. But, I am too whipped to talk about it now."

With that, the twins stood up, stretched, and made their way toward their bedrooms as quietly as they could. "Goodnight," whispered Alex as he slipped into the corner room where Francesca was already sound asleep. He quickly shucked his clothes and crawled between the warm sheets. He was asleep by the time his head hit the pillow.

Nicholas, on the other hand, sank down fully clothed into an armchair by the window. Outside lamps illuminated the snow, which was still falling. Despite the stillness of the night, his mind was racing. He knew he was not ready to sleep, and the last thing he wanted to do was wake Cassandra, who was softly snoring a few feet away.

He clicked off the small bedside lamp and stared out the window into the forbidding blackness. *"Is it moral?"* Francesca's query rang in his ears.

"What exactly are we dealing with?" he asked himself, tilting his forehead into his hand. If their thesis is correct, could five people keep the discovery of a lifetime secret? If it got out, how many wealthy and powerful people and corporations would be ruined?

"Is it moral?"

He jerked his head up with a start. Had he been dozing?

Nicholas sighed deeply and stared out the window again. After a few seconds his eyes settled onto a small copse of dark trees, their branches stretching into the cloudy sky like ancient bony fingers. The wind blew the limbs to and fro, giving the knobby hands the appearance of life. The image sent a shiver down his spine.

It was a long time before he was able to fall asleep.

Chapter 12

The storm exhausted its fury by morning, leaving layers of powdery snowdrifts several feet deep against the sides of the house. In the storm's wake a large caucus of the Estate's avian population appeared, gathered about on the white carpet surrounding the mansion.

By the time Francesca opened her eyes, the sun was well up. It took her a few moments to gather her senses in the strange bedroom. The quilt was warm and soft, and Alex's breathing steady and deep. She smiled and lay still for several minutes, listening to the birds' chatter and singing. When she remembered the snowstorm, she threw back the covers and shivered as she walked to the window. As far as she could see the snowy tops of trees dominated the horizon. Everything was engulfed in a blanket of pristine white. The scene was indescribably beautiful.

This trip to Asheville had evolved into an amazing journey into a world she had never completely understood. She was familiar with the chemistry of cooking and of love. Why or how something worked never concerned her. Either it did or it didn't. Francesca was the very model of a practical romantic, if such a combination existed. Her own simple childhood romping through the Tuscan hills with a never-ending supply of cousins was something she would dearly love to give her own children someday, but her American family would quickly grow bored with such capriciousness. Her solution was to fuse her mama's good sense with a dash of 21st Century indulgences.

Not that she was a stupid woman; indeed, far from it. But she had made the decision a long time ago that, unlike her sister-in-law, Francesca's career was her family. She fulfilled her creative urges with cooking, sewing, interior design, and performing volunteer work as a patron for several Charleston art galleries. Unlike so many women she knew, she was happy—*truly happy*.

Francesca eased back into bed and ran her hand up Alex's warm, well-muscled back. He gave a little shiver and responded by pulling the pillow over his head with a groan. As a morning person married to a night person, she knew one central fact about their break-of-day conversations: there weren't any. Francesca leaned over and kissed his ear. "See you downstairs, sleepy." Dressing quickly in heavy winter clothes, she gathered up the furry hooded cape she had brought from home and stepped out into the hall. Cassandra was already there. "I heard you stirring about and waited," she said. "Let's get some coffee and let these aging scientists sleep."

Despite their best efforts to be quiet, the old hallway creaked as they walked downstairs. Francesca pulled out the grinder and dumped in a large double handful of Starbucks Breakfast Blend beans. She ground them for two or three seconds, stopped, and jiggled open the lid. Sticking her nose over the grinder, she inhaled deeply. "Ah . . . God, I love that smell."

"That makes two of us," replied Cassandra as she began heating a pan of croissants. She listened to the whizzing blades whip the beans into a finely ground powder. For a few minutes neither woman spoke. When the coffee was ready, Francesca poured two large mugs and passed one to Cassandra.

"It is such a relief to get out," Francesca said, looking at her sister-in-law through the steam rising from her coffee. "After we go riding this morning, we should go into town and do some Christmas shopping. I am really behind. Again."

"Me too," answered Cassandra. "It is nearly impossible to go shopping with Nicholas, because he gets impatient with long lines. I think he does all his shopping on the Internet."

"Alex loves to go shopping! I'm the one reining him in. He just goes nuts picking out extravagant presents for the kids."

Cassandra smiled, picked up her mug, and walked to the sink. She stood there for a few seconds with her back to her sister-in-law. "When you asked the question last night at dinner about morality, what did you mean, exactly?"

The question caught Francesca off-guard. Cassandra heard a deep sigh behind her and turned around to see Francesca's head drop. "I'm not sure." Her long red hair covered her face and her words were muffled, distant. "I guess I am . . . concerned . . . about the original owners of the box," she said softly. "Aren't you?" she asked.

"You mean Gabe's family?"

"This is going to sound silly, but I have a strange feeling about the box, Cassandra. A bad feeling. I mean, if whoever owned this didn't want anyone to find it, why didn't they just destroy it? The guys said once they figured out a working formula, they wouldn't even need the box any more. But they do need the box, don't they?" Francesca lifted her head and Cassandra was shocked to see the look in her eyes. Her sister-in-law was frightened.

"What are you trying to say?"

"Maybe it's my upbringing or something," she shrugged. "Too many folk tales and way too much Catholicism." She offered a weak smile. "It's as if the box was destined to be found, to be out in the light of day for someone to use it to fulfill . . . I don't know . . . some purpose." Cassandra stared at her, trying to understand what she was thinking.

"It's as if it meant us to find it," Francesca blurted out.

Neither woman spoke for several seconds. Cassandra gathered her thoughts and absorbed Francesca's troubled expression. "Have you said anything to Alex about this?" she asked.

Francesca shook her head.

Cassandra took a deep breath and sat down at the table, taking Francesca's cold hands into her own. This time, Cassandra gave her a stern look. "Francesca, this is foolish to worry about. I admit the box appears to have a very long and . . . rather mysterious . . . history. The documents we found in the *cassone* are certainly evidence of that. But, you are giving the box a life of its own. It has no control over who uses it and how. It is just a box. A *thing*." She tilted her head and smiled reassuringly. "Whoever put it in that room didn't want it to be found. Maybe he or they forgot about it," she offered unconvincingly and then bit her tongue. *How could anyone forget about something like that?* Cassandra tried again. "If they are using a computer, then they are off making money and are probably too busy to care about it anymore. And then we stumbled upon it. That's all it is. Dumb luck."

Francesca remained unconvinced. "There is something inherently creepy about that thing. I don't like it. Just promise me that you will finish up your research on the documents you found. I would feel a little better knowing its history."

Cassandra nodded. "I promise. Now, if we are going to go riding, we need to see if Gabe has the horses ready."

"I hope he brings those Percherons back," Francesca's face softened into a smile. "What were their names?"

"Traveller and Dixie. Weren't they noble? Did you know that breed was developed during the Crusades to carry knights in heavy armor? I hope they are not too big for us to ride. I don't think I could get my legs around one of them!"

Francesca gave a little mock snort in reply.

As if on cue, Gabriel appeared at the door. "It's mighty cold. Bundle up!" he said, his frosty breath emphasizing his words. Cassandra pulled on a hooded down jacket and heavy gloves. As he led them to the large horses, Cassandra asked if he had given all the horses names associated with the Civil War. "Yes. Guess I wanted to get my old man's goat," replied Gabriel as he helped them mount the two horses.

For Cassandra, it was a long way up. She looked very small atop Traveller with her cape billowing out over his palomino-colored flanks. Francesca, model-tall and thin, swooped one leg over Dixie's back and took the reins with the expertise of one who had spent time in a saddle.

"Aren't you coming with us, Gabe?" Cassandra reached down and patted Traveller's neck. "I'm not sure we should be wandering around the Estate without an escort!" Her real worry was getting lost on the vast grounds or having problems with the horses.

"I've got my faithful Beauregard over there," replied Gabriel, motioning toward the small corral where he sometimes exercised the horses. "If you're gone too long, I'll come after you. If you get lost, just follow the hoof prints in the snow back home!"

"Sure you don't want us to take along some breadcrumbs?" Cassandra laughed.

"I hear from some of the guests that there is a witch's house in the woods!" countered Gabriel. "If you find it don't tell my father. He will charge her rent!"

With that the women gently kicked their horses into a walk. Their misty breaths formed small moving clouds as the animals gently swayed beneath them.

"What a comfortable ride," said Cassandra. "It was a good idea to get out." She paused for a moment and then turned around and looked at Francesca. "I really don't want you to worry about the box."

Francesca's face was beet red, though whether from the cold or from embarrassment, Cassandra was unsure. "It was silly, really." Francesca reached down and patted her horse. "Alex says I am the consummate worrier. You've been such a good friend. No, actually you are more like the sister I never had."

"Well, I have three sisters and two brothers, and you're actually better than a sister because there's no sibling rivalry."

"Alex and Nicholas don't seem to suffer from that, do they?" asked Francesca.

"They did when they were kids," Cassandra replied frankly. "They were so competitive it became a family joke. It finally got better when they grew up and realized they could both excel in their own professions. Gosh, imagine if they had picked the same field! I think it's so interesting that even identical twins can be so different. Nicholas laughs at the whole psychic connection, but I've seen it."

"Alex feels the same way! But, that's probably because it doesn't sound macho. Oh, look!"

An all-too familiar Fed-Ex truck was slipping and sliding its way slowly down the road leading to Gabriel's house. The orange, white, and blue letters seemed almost obscene in contrast to the pristine white landscape surrounding them.

"That would be their new toy—you know, the software? They'll be at it all day. We might as well go shopping this afternoon. And by the way, why aren't we on the road, too?" Cassandra looked almost longingly at the plowed surface paralleling their route twenty yards distant.

"Oh, the path is so much more adventurous," said Francesca. "Plus, I think it leads down to the vineyards, and I've been waiting for years to see those. Papa is thinking about buying some vineyards back home. He wants to make an estate-bottled Chianti Classico."

Cassandra kept quiet for a moment as the horses clomped softly down the snowy path. "Francesca," she asked at last, "if the guys put all that money into the stock market, there is going so be some real damage to our wallets if they lose it. The stock markets are governed by gravity and astronomical software? I almost don't care what the documents prove or what the inclination or phi or whatever else they have discovered says about all this. I don't care bout the hidden room. Out here today, in the daylight, riding in the cold air—it all sounds ridiculous!"

"Well, they've gotten this far," Francesca sighed in resignation. "They aren't going to stop until they test their theory. And what if they are really onto something? There's an old culinary saying that the proof of the pudding is in the eating! But I hope they don't invest too much!"

Traveller snorted. Cassandra patted his neck. Dixie whinnied in return. "Thanks for the editorial comment, Dix."

Francesca threw her hood back, letting her hair loose as she kicked Dixie into a smooth rolling canter, passing Cassandra on the right. Traveller followed suit without Cassandra having to do a thing. "Oh, here we go!" she shouted as the riders bounced along with the horses' rhythm. They rode at that pace for several minutes before Francesca finally reined in her mount in a small clearing and waited for Cassandra to do the same. "That was fun," she said when Traveller finally pulled up next to Dixie. "We can't beat our husbands on science," explained Francesca, "so how's this adage: the proof of the theory is in the application. That," she continued with a grin, "is something Alex got from Stephen Hawking."

"Alex keeps good company," Cassandra smiled back. "Hawking has inspired many people, but I wonder if he would be willing to put his money where his mouth is. It makes a big, big difference when it's your own money on the line."

"You don't really think they would bet everything right off the bat, do you? Our very own conservative dress-down twin scientists?"

Cassandra sucked at her lower lip, picking at the chapped skin with her teeth. "I guess I wasn't brought up to take chances with my money. My family was not as well off as the Shepards. But I will say this: Nicholas has closely studied the stock market for many years, noodling around with various theories and such. I have never seen him so excited. He's wanted to prove for a long time that the market isn't random. Maybe now he will."

"Hey, if it works, maybe I can really open a restaurant! I have joked about this so many times, but it is something I really want to do."

"How are you going to do that and raise two kids?"

The statement surprised Francesca. "Isn't that a little sexist?" Her eyes widened in disbelief.

"I guess I'm being Old South," Cassandra apologized. "But, would you still want to run a restaurant, even if you had tons of money?"

"Absolutely. But, honestly, do you really think what they are planning will be that lucrative?"

Cassandra smiled a slow smile, "You know by now that Nicholas and Alex don't do things halfway. It's fun to think about, isn't it?"

"You bet it is. So, what would you do if you had more money than you could ever spend?"

Cassandra thought for a moment and gently kicked Traveller into a slow walk. "Not being able to have children has been hard, so we would just indulge each other. You know I love my work, but I can do that anywhere. Just being with Nicholas is what counts. I would like to travel more, though."

"It would be fun to . . . ." Francesca stopped in mid-sentence when a deer with an enormous rack of antlers leapt across the path and disappeared beyond the vineyard. Cassandra twisted in her saddle to get a better look at it. Her motion, along with her inexperience, caused her let go of the reins. Spooked by the deer's appearance, Traveller recoiled when the reins flipped against his left eye and Cassandra suddenly felt the horse rising beneath her. She desperately grabbed onto the pommel and let out a little screech of panic.

Francesca swiftly reined in Dixie, pressing her heels into the horse's side as she pulled up her reins sharply. Dixie stopped dead in the middle of the path.

"Let go of the pommel and roll out of the way," Francesca shouted. "Now!"

Cassandra did as she was told, hit the soft ground, and rolled away as far and fast as she could. Snorting and bucking, Traveller galloped off down the path.

ॐ

"This should do just fine!" exclaimed Alex as he installed the new Nobeltec nautical software. "Let's see how fast I can throw a learning curve ball." It never took Alex long to learn anything, and this exercise was no exception. Within an hour he had mastered the new programs.

The first problem was deciding which of the many harmonic stations should provide the readings. "There are hundreds of these stations worldwide," Alex explained to Nicholas.

He nodded in agreement, adding wryly, "And when was the last time Nobeltec fielded technical support questions about how to use their programs to predict the stock market?" He paused for a moment. "Maybe we should use a harmonic station at the New York City Harbor. It might make sense to use one close to the New York Stock Exchange!"

Alex nodded slowly in agreement, but interjected a new problem. "That does make sense, Nicholas, but there are many other exchanges that set markets around the world. Should we take readings at every station close to each of those exchanges?"

Nicholas shook his head. "No. The world's economic stability depends on the United States. You know, the whole dog-and-tail effect."

"You mean the U.S. stock exchanges are the dog, and the rest of the world is the tail?" confirmed Alex with a snicker.

"Yep, and the dog always wags the tail!"

"What if the dog gets sick?" shot back Alex.

"The rest of the world catches a cold," responded Nicholas without missing a beat. "Does Gabe have an atlas around here?"

Alex dug around the room and found a world map buried deep in the piles of books stacked along the walls of Gabriel's office. After some discussion, the twins agreed to find the latitude and longitude running as close to New York City as possible, but also encompass the majority of people around the world who trade the financial markets.

"The closest longitude line to New York is 75 degrees west," Alex lisped through the pencil stuck between his teeth. "The latitude isn't close enough for me to eyeball it, but I can make a calculation." He worked for a minute before announcing, "The exact latitude reading of New York is . . . 40 degrees north, and the exact longitude is . . . 74 degrees west."

The longitude reading of 74 degrees seemed perfect, since it ran down the populous East Coast of the United States. The latitude reading of 40 degrees was not as tightly on target. A majority of the world's population lives between 30 and 45 degrees latitude, but there were many harmonic stations working between those two lines.

Nicholas suggested they try finding a harmonic station between 30 and 45 degrees that exhibited enough of a tidal fluctuation to be significant to the scientific programs he wanted to incorporate. Alex opened the "Select location for new tide" window and clicked on the Mid-Atlantic Area. He scrolled down the different coastal city locations, trying to find a station that fit the bill. "Okay," he said suddenly. "Here's a coastal city called Reedy Point, with latitude of 39.33 degrees north and longitude of 75 degrees west. That's pretty damn close both ways. Let's try this one first."

With Nicholas nodding in agreement, Alex opened the tide window for Reedy Point. He moved through the program and clicked on "Search" and then on the "Event Search" button. He was looking for high tides with the greatest values for the years 1920 through 2020. They would only need to look at the yearly values. Nicholas set the program to search days Monday through Friday during the hours between 9:30 a.m. and 4:00 p.m., when the NYSE is open.

"Here we go," Nicholas said, punching enter on the keyboard.

Alex took a sip of coffee and watched as the printer hummed and the report spilled out into the tray. He leaned over his brother's shoulder and pointed a finger at the spreadsheet. "There's your *sine* wave. You were right, the yearly values move up and down."

"Hmm. Yes, so it would appear. But it's infrequent," murmured Nicholas. "It suggests that the lengths of the ups and downs vary in duration. Let's test our original theory—that the years with the lowest high tides represent the lowest gravitational forces and correlate to the highs in the market."

"Okay." Alex replied, reaching for the astronomical chart that they had printed off earlier. "These highs should correlate." By hand he marked a "high" at each of the high values with the lowest number. "Look at this, Nicholas!" he said with growing excitement. "In *every* case, the market high values are between four and five years apart, suggesting some common cycle." An even greater surprise was awaiting them. When they compared the column of numbers, they discovered that the lowest of the yearly values indicated the tops of the Dow average *almost perfectly*.

Alex chuckled quietly and shook his head. "I still don't believe this is happening. It can't be happening—can it?"

Nicholas shot him a sideways glance and raised his eyebrows up. "Oh yeah, it's happening and it's real. It is becoming exceptionally clear that coincidence has nothing to do with what we are discovering about the market highs and lows."

The brothers remained quiet for the next minute, contemplating the enormity of what they were dealing with. Alex leaned over the charts and reviewed the results a third time.

Nicholas rose from his chair and walked to the tall window. Sunlight beat down on the bluish-white icicles lining the edge of the roof. It had warmed up considerably during the past couple of hours, and the steady tap . . . tap . . . tap of the water dripping against a copper downspout just below the eves. He had the answer they had been seeking. The readings confirmed their theory that when the gravitational force was at its weakest, humans acted in a positive way.

"But is it moral?"

Nicholas turned back to face Alex. "What are you looking at now?" he asked.

"From what I'm seeing, the highest gravitational values correlate with the bottoms of the Dow average." Alex turned back to the nautical program. "I want to compare the low tides with the lowest values for the same time period."

"Okay, and this time don't specify the time of day or day of the week," Nicholas suggested, returning to his chair. "I want to allow for the overnight trading session that continues around the world after our own exchanges close."

Alex printed out the spreadsheet and began to mark the yearly lows. "Damn!" He stared at the spreadsheet in front of him. "This is really remarkable." He waved the page in front of Nicholas' face. Nicholas grabbed the spreadsheet and ran his finger down the columns, comparing the numbers to the yearly historical Dow data. The lowest values mirrored the lows in the market. By going back and forth from the high tide column of numbers to the low tide column of numbers, they could plot the Dow's *exact* highs and lows by drawing a straight line between the maxima and minima on the Dow graph.

Alex's elation was tempered a bit when he realized that during some years, the tidal charts exhibited identical values. "Look at this!" he groaned, stabbing at the chart with the point of his pencil. "How do we decide which year will be the exact bottom or top?"

Hunched over the desk, Nicholas looked at his brother for a moment, his forehead wrinkled in thought. After a few seconds he straightened up and smiled. "Don't sweat it, Alex. The program probably averages out the values. I think if you look for shorter time periods, like months or days, you could zero in on the actual low and highs for the exact year you want." Alex absorbed Nicholas' observation for a few seconds and nodded in agreement.

"Let's stop for a moment and think about what we have concluded," suggested Nicholas. "Maximum highs in the high charts and maximum lows in the low charts correlate to the lows in the market. Moreover, look at the inverse: the minimum highs in the high charts and the minimum lows in the low charts correlate to the highs in the Dow Industrial Average graph. This is exactly what we expected, and hoped, to find." He stood and stretched his arms above his head before pushing away the chair to walk around the room.

"Now," he continued, "look at the spots where the highest yearly tides are at their lowest value—that is, the least gravitational forces. It's amazing. It really appears as though low gravity creates an environment where people feel *bullish* about the market. They want to invest, do invest, and remain invested during these periods."

"So the reverse would also be true," Alex pointed out. "When the differences between the *yearly* values in the tidal fluctuations were greatest—the most gravitational forces—an environment is produced where humans felt *bearish*—they feel as though the market is not going to do well, and sell their positions." He grinned at his brother. "That proves that the box does absolutely measure gravity continuously and with no less accuracy than the astronomical software."

Nicholas drew in a long breath, held it for several seconds, and exhaled. "We've proven our theory, certainly, and in addition made an astonishing discovery." He looked up at the ceiling for a moment to gather his thoughts before continuing. "This astronomical software, combined with the nautical program, defines the movement of the American stock market as far back as data exists. It also means that whoever owned this box in the past—even without the technical tools we're working with—was still able to use it to make a fortune."

"Or fortunes," added Alex. "And, this would explain why the box was no longer being used and was locked away in a secret room in the mansion."

"Yes, I think that's right," replied Nicholas. "If we can figure this out, they certainly could have done the same thing—and possibly even wrote a program that replaced the need for the box. Obviously, if they went public with this information, we would have seen the results in fund journals with extraordinary annual returns. We have not."

"Do you remember the yearly highs and lows of the last accounting balance sheets that Cassandra found in the documents back at the mansion?" asked Alex.

"Yes, I have them here in a folder," said Nicholas, who walked to the desk and picked up the sheets in question.

"Good. Let's double-check those forward-looking results against what we know happened in the market," said Alex.

Nicholas read aloud the yearly high and lows for the last entry: "1987 high . . . 1988 low . . . 1991 high . . .1992 low . . . 1996 high." He took a breath and continued. "1997 low . . . 2000 high . . . 2002 low . . . 2004 high . . . 2006 low . . . 2009 high . . . 2010 low . . . 2013 high . . . 2014 low . . . 2018 high . . . 2019 low."

When he stopped, the twins looked at each other and smiled. "It's all right here," whispered Alex. They checked and rechecked the new nautical charts. Except for the 2002 market low, the actual highs and lows in the market matched the document exactly. The brothers checked and rechecked the astronomical calculator charts and again found nearly the same results. Whoever had owned the box was able to combine the astronomical data in their analysis to make a final determination for their decisions as to whether the market was going up or going down.

"My head hurts," said Nicholas, rubbing his temples, "but I can't wait to tell Cassandra." The enormity of their discovery suddenly had him jumping to his feet. "We should celebrate tonight."

"Celebrate what?" During all the cheering and clapping, the twins had not seen Gabriel standing in the doorway. They quickly brought him up to speed, pointing out how the tidal charts, astronomical information, and documents from the box all matched.

Gabriel's eyes widened in disbelief. The proof was there in black and white for anyone willing to examine it. "I had convinced myself this morning that all of this was rather ridiculous," he told them. "I guess I was wrong." Gabriel laid down the documents and looked at Nicholas. "So what do we do now?"

"We make more money than we ever imagined was possible!" Nicholas exclaimed.

Gabriel lowered his voice. "No, I mean what will it do to financial markets?" Nicholas and Alex looked at one another and then back at Gabriel.

"Is it moral?" Francesca's words echoed inside Nicholas' head.

Nicholas shrugged. "It won't do anything. It will just make us rich. The market is so vast that even if we were to trade millions of dollars daily, we would not even nudge the price one way or the other. The market encompasses billions of trades daily. No one would notice."

"But this could make the whole world rich," replied Gabriel. "Every Tom, Dick, Harry, and Esmeralda could retire with enough money to make old age a playground. You should open a public fund that anyone could invest in."

Nicholas chose his words carefully. "I don't know if . . . that would be possible, Gabe." When Gabriel responded with a quizzical look, Nicholas continued. "If everyone knows about how the markets rise and fall, and then invest accordingly . . ." He paused and looked at Alex, who looked away. "Well, look, this is all quite new, and—."

I'm sure there are ways around all this," blurted out Alex. "Maybe we could fund a research center?"

"Surely a worthy cause," replied Gabriel. "But a fund would make you money—along with everybody else, of course."

Nicholas rubbed his face anxiously. "This discovery is so profound I can hardly breathe, and you two are already marketing it! We have to take this one step at a time. There is a lot of work to be done. Alex has a system identification program in his laptop that he might be able to use to make forecasts, but he will need some time to input data and test a few theories. And, of course, we still need to develop a trading strategy."

"Is it moral?"

Nicholas began pacing again as he spoke. "Gabe, your question about what this discovery might do to the markets is important and worth thinking about. If everybody in the world believed and used this discovery, world markets would suffer greatly or even collapse altogether. The market is a zero sum game."

Gabriel blinked several times and swallowed hard. "I am not liking what I am hearing."

Nicholas put his hand on Gabriel's shoulder. "We have to face reality. There has to be a buyer for every sell order and seller for every buy order. That's the way the system works. If everyone put in the same buy or sell order at the same time, then no transaction would take place. Nobody would be able to manage the fallout."

"There would probably be panic and collapse," said Alex.

"There would indeed be panic. As for the collapse, I cannot say," answered Nicholas. "On the other hand, in the proper hands this discovery could be used to manage markets in a pro-active way instead of a reactive one. The Federal Reserve, for example, could use long-range forecasts to smooth out the tops and bottoms of market cycles— providing they had the nerve and political will to do so."

Alex and Gabriel listened intently as Nicholas thought aloud. His voice was getting stronger and his face was breaking into a smile as the implications expanded inside his economist's mind. "You remember when Alan Greenspan made his 'irrational exuberance' speech in 1996, saying the market was becoming overvalued?" Alex nodded his head; Gabriel shook his. "Remember it shocked the market for a couple of days? If he wasn't already taking steps to be cautious about what he says publicly, that sure taught him a lesson. I just read a quote in the paper this morning from a speech Greenspan made last week. He said that instead of taking 'drastic action' to control market cycles like the big "bubble" of 2000, it was better to wait and 'mitigate the fallout'—those were his own words—once a bubble pops. If he had the information we have, he could have done a lot more than sit on the sideline and wait to repair the damage."

And then Nicholas' grin turned into a frown. "On the other hand, terrorists could use this knowledge to completely sabotage the markets of the free world. Remember the reports about the Saudis shorting the markets prior to the 9-11 attacks? They made huge profits when the market fell."

"What are you trying to say, Nicholas?" asked Gabriel.

"I guess what I am saying is that we are going to have to be very careful—and very quiet. And take one small step at a time."

"I agree," replied Alex as he rubbed his mid-section. "Maybe that first step should be something to eat. Where are Cassandra and Francesca? I'd hate for them to miss lunch."

Nicholas laughed. "You mean you'd hate for them to miss *fixing* you lunch." Everyone laughed, knowing that was exactly was Alex had in mind.

"They're still out riding," chuckled Gabriel. "They've been gone for hours, but I thought they'd be back by now. They were heading to the vineyards. It's not that far."

Alex groaned. "Francesca and vineyards? Not a combination for a quick return, even with all the new snow on the ground."

"I'll saddle up Beauregard and go look for them," Gabriel offered. "In the meantime, you guys can rustle up whatever's in the refrigerator."

The brothers visibly sagged. "Never mind," said Gabriel with a wave of a hand. "I'll go fetch the ladies and you two can sit here in the office and go hungry a while longer."

ॐ

"Come on, boy," Gabriel whispered to Beauregard, pulling down tightly on his goose-down vest with gloved fingers. "We have to discuss the future of the world." He yanked the cinch on the saddle tight, placed his foot in the stirrup, and hauled himself up into the saddle. As horse and rider approached the gate, he reached down in one deft move to unlock it. Once Beauregard walked through the opening, he swung around and just as smoothly locked the gate.

Gabriel's temples were pounding from the blood flow and his stomach felt light, almost nauseated. The more he thought about the remarkable discoveries the twins had made, the more troubled he became. Surely his father knew the purpose of the box?

Had it been a mistake to call him?

The speed with which Alex and Nicholas had figured out how to use the box was simply breathtaking. Could he stop them from using it now that they knew what it was for?

"No," he said aloud. "I gave them the box. It's not the von Stuyvesant's secret anymore." He pulled his reins tight and Beauregard jerked to a stop. "My God, I hope I haven't put them in danger!" he whispered. The horse whinnied and stamped a front hoof into the snow, half turning its head to look at Gabriel.

I have to make sure they keep their experiment quiet.

Gabriel clucked the big steed into a trot and headed to the vineyard. As his mind raced with the possibilities, Traveller came around the bend in a gallop heading straight toward the barn.

"Whoa, boy. Traveller!"

The beast slowed to a canter and then a trot, allowing Gabriel to ease Beauregard alongside and take hold of the horse's bridle. He gently talked to Traveller as both horses came to a stop.

"Cassandra! . . . Francesca!" he shouted. Only the sound of the wind whipping past reached his ears.

With Traveller calmed down and trotting along behind him, Gabriel set off toward the edge of the woods. He reached it with a sick feeling in his stomach.

Chapter 13

Gabriel found Francesca and Cassandra at the edge of the vineyard. Dixie was tethered to a tree, nervously pacing back and forth while Francesca was holding onto Cassandra with one hand and frantically trying to make her cell phone work with the other. He spurred Beauregard forward and pulled up next to the two women.

"Oh, thank God," gasped Francesca.

"What happened?" asked Gabe, jumping from the horse while leaving the reins hanging loose above the ground.

Cassandra's face was pale and she looked dizzy. "Gabe?" She looked up at him as a trace of a smile broke out across her face. "Took you . . . long enough."

"I was trying to call you," explained Francesca, speaking so quickly her words slurred together. "Cassandra fell off her horse a few minutes ago when a deer spooked Traveller." As she spoke, a large buck bounded from the woods just a handful of yards away. Startled, Francesca and Gabriel watched as it ran out into the open field beyond. A loud "pop," like a powerful firecracker, echoed back and forth among the trees.

"Oh!" Gabriel blurted out in surprise, grabbing at his left shoulder. He slumped quickly to his knees. A slowly spreading pool of blood appeared where his heavy flannel sleeve emerged from beneath the vest. Beauregard gave a little jump, spooked by the noise and his master's response. Despite his dancing hoofs, Francesca was able to grab his bridle just above the bit and steady him; it was the only method she knew to stop the horse in its tracks, but it could have had disastrous consequences.

"Damn poachers!" Gabriel swore. A dazed and angry look was plastered his face. He struggled to stand, squinting into the sun as his eyes scanned the tree line for the shooter.

Francesca had not yet realized her friend had been injured until she saw the crimson-stained snow. It took a few seconds to realize that the blood was next to Gabriel. She forced her eyes to wander up his body until they settled on his bloody shirt sleeve. "Gabe! You've been shot! Oh my God, where is my cell phone? I need to call 9-1-1!" She gave herself a scattered pat down until she located the pocket holding the phone.

"No!" Gabe shouted, reaching for Francesca. "Look! It's OK. " He turned to fully expose his shoulder and arm. "See? It's just a flesh wound from a poacher's rifle. The bullet didn't lodge in my arm; it only grazed it. Nothing a good glass of scotch won't cure." He grinned weakly. "Let's help Cassandra. She could be seriously hurt. I'm OK."

The pair turned their attention back to Cassandra, whose color was slowly returning. She was struggling to stand. They rushed to her side, where each took an arm to steady her. "I'm okay . . . I'm alright," she said, more in an attempt to convince herself than her friends. She moved her limbs about and performed a full body check to make sure reality matched her pronouncement. "I agree, Gabe. I think I can use a glass of that scotch as well." She looked over at the huge Percherons now peacefully pawing the ground beneath the snow looking for grass to munch on.

"We're too far out for either of us to walk back in our condition," observed Gabriel. "Cassandra, do you feel up to riding back?"

Still dazed, Cassandra rubbed her right temple with the palm of her hand. "Sure, I think so. Yes."

"Francesca, help us up on to the horses, please," he directed. "I will have to send my vineyard manager out to find the poacher, but he won't know what to do with him if he does catch the guy. I have to file a report, too. Help me back up on Beauregard."

"Gabe, you are still bleeding. You need a tourniquet," said Francesca.

Cassandra unraveled her cashmere scarf and held it out. "Here Francesca, use this."

Francesca took the scarf and tied it tightly as close to the shoulder as she could, just above where the bullet had dug out a furrow of flesh. "That should stop the bleeding. Keep your arm up on the way back if you can." Gabriel was dubious about the necessity of the tourniquet, but he acquiesced gracefully.

Francesca grabbed Beauregard's reins and held the bridle. "Cassandra, if you can hold these, I'll help Gabe up." She made a cup with her hands and launched Gabriel onto the horse. Her great heave nearly threw him over the animal, but he grabbed the pommel with his right hand. "You don't know your own strength, girl!"

Francesca helped Cassandra up onto Traveller with a bit more finesse, and the trio rode largely in silence back to the house. The woods were ominously quiet. Not a bird could be heard, though a lone hawk circled against the midday sun. Melting snow made the path mushy but the footing for the animals was still solid. Pulling her jacket collar closer, Francesca's thoughts jumped from the mysterious granite-topped box to the theories about how to use it, from Cassandra's hard spill to Gabriel's accidental wounding.

They dismounted when they reached the corral. Gabriel called out for one of his staff to take care of the horses while they walked to the house, one blood-smeared and all three dispirited.

The twins were still up in Gabriel's office, hunched over his computers. "Why don't we follow the same procedure with the nautical program and type in the monthly highs and lows for each month, starting in 1920 and running through 2004?" Nicholas was saying. "We should be able to forecast for the shorter term."

Except to ask about lunch, the brothers did not bother to turn around and acknowledge the trio's arrival.

"Nicholas! Alex! Will you look at us?" demanded Cassandra.

The twins spun around and immediately jumped from their chairs to help their host. "Jesus, Gabe! Your whole arm is bloody. We need to take your shirt off," commanded Alex. Gabriel did as he was told, clenching his teeth a couple times as the brothers lifted his arm and as gently as possible removed his vest and shirt.

"What happened?" asked Nicholas.

"A poacher after a large buck missed and got me instead," he hissed through clenched teeth. "I guess I'm lucky. A few inches in a different direction and my balding head would be mounted in someone's cheesy den against cheap Home Depot wood paneling."

Nicholas laughed out loud. "Actually, Gabe, that was pretty funny."

Gabriel closed one eye and nodded in an effort to keep from revealing just how painful the injury was. His shoulder muscles were beginning to lock up, and his upper arm was throbbing like it had its own heart just under the skin. "Cassandra took a tumble from Traveller, Nicholas. She hit pretty hard. Better take a look."

Nicholas shot a glance at his wife, who shook her head and waved her open hands in front of her. "I am fine, honey. Really. I was shaken up, but I'm just fine. Two Tylenols and a brandy will right all that is wrong with me." She tilted her head toward Gabriel, adding, "This guy is the only walking wounded here."

"Please just let me go get washed up," winced Gabriel. "We'll go from there. Speaking of brandy, would one of you be so kind as to pour me a scotch?"

"You need to see a doctor, Gabe. And you will definitely need stitches," Francesca said as she examined the damage from the bullet. "You were right, though. It is a flesh wound and not very deep at all. But it sure did bleed a lot. How's it feel?"

"Hurts like hell," admitted Gabriel. "Where's the scotch? The customer service in this joint is abysmal."

"Shoot the guy and all the jokes start," Alex smiled.

Cassandra left the room and returned a few minutes later with a bowl of hot water and towels to apply a hot compress. When she cleaned the area with rubbing alcohol, the patient yelped with pain. "You aren't good about things like this, are you?" she joked as gently as possible. "I think you might need stitches, but I'm no doctor. We better go now."

"What, instead of shopping?" Francesca said in mock alarm. "Maybe they can stitch fast. But I do think we'll need to stay an extra day or two, just to make sure Gabe is okay. I'll call Galen and see if he can keep the kids."

"Bah, humbug," Gabe said gratefully, shooting a glance at the twins. *Just stay until I can figure out what the hell is going on with that box, he thought to himself.* He clenched his good fist and tried not to reveal the alarm he felt rising inside. He eased down into one of his club chairs while Cassandra bandaged his arm and Alex hunted up another shirt. Francesca disappeared to fix lunch. Now that everything seemed under control, Alex brought the other two up to date.

"I take it your morning went better than ours?" asked Francesca.

"Actually, we had an amazing morning. We've nailed the yearly forecasts," Alex said excitedly. "Now we are going for nearer-term market trends. We see a good correlation to the data, but the monthly high and low values aren't as easy to understand as the yearly charts, at least by visual observation."

"We need to be able to understand how this works on a monthly, then weekly, then daily basis," concluded Nicholas.

"Ok, ok, that's enough!" said Francesca, placing her hands over her ears. "I just can't switch gears that fast."

"Looks like it's you two who'll need a couple of extra days," Gabriel said wryly. "My computers are yours for the taking."

"Thanks, Gabe. It would probably be easy enough to take everything back to Charleston," said Alex. "Nicholas probably has to get back to school in Atlanta, anyway."

"Well, I do at that," replied his brother. "But I'll call Lev and ask him to get someone to cover my classes for a few days. The holiday break is right on us anyway. I just need someone to administer semester exams. Actually, I'll call Lev and ask him to do it himself." Nicholas grinned. "Lev will love that. He enjoys lording over the undergrads." With that out of the way he returned his focus to the project at hand. "We should be able to start trading right after the New Year—that is, if Alex can construct his programs by then."

"Already working it out in my mind," Alex said with complete confidence. "I never miss a deadline."

"We'll run some empirical tests on past performance with blind trials to build a statistical study," continued his brother. He held his hand over his growling stomach. "Let us know when lunch is ready, would you?"

"Ok, we're dismissed!" said Cassandra, leaping up. She took Gabriel's good hand and helped him stand. "We'll go play downstairs, eat a bite, and run Gabe to the emergency room." She kissed the back of her husband's head. "Maybe drop off this scarf to the cleaners, eh?" she said to Gabriel on the way out.

Gabriel excused himself and followed her into the hallway. "I need to investigate the damn poacher and file a report. Unfortunately, poaching is more common on these grounds than anyone cares to admit."

"Why can't you just put a stop to it?" asked Cassandra.

Gabriel assumed a sheepish look. "I suppose I could if I really wanted to," he admitted, "but I put up with it because some of the locals don't have enough to eat, and the Estate abounds with game."

"We are still getting you to a doctor to look at that wound, Gabe, so don't be long—understand?"

Nicholas frowned as he listened to Cassandra scold his friend. He tried to concentrate on the data on the computer screen, but his train of thought was elsewhere. Gabriel ran a pretty tight ship on the Estate. Allowing poachers on the land ran contrary with Estate security procedures. Then again, it was consistent with his friend's overall philosophy of life.

He shook his head. Gabriel was a mass of contradictions.

Chapter 14

Francesca and Cassandra were busy fixing lunch when Gabriel slipped out the kitchen door and walked down the freshly shoveled path to the garage. It was lunchtime, and he knew where he could find Gerard. He checked his watch, eased into his pickup truck, and with his left arm hanging limply at his side, gripped the cold steering wheel with his right hand and drove toward the winery.

Located in what was once the Estate's dairy barn, the winery's Tasting and Bottling Rooms were a popular stop for Biltmore visitors. The man responsible for the care of more than seventy acres of grapes was seated alone at a white-capped picnic table outside the winery in the warming sunlight. He was wearing a worn green goose-down jacket, which made his small and wiry frame look heavier than it was. His red knit hat was pulled down tightly over his brow, and a thin curl of smoke from the Frenchman's gauloise lingered in the air around his head.

"Bonjour, je peux s'asseoir ici?" Gabe asked, motioning to the vacant bench across from his employee.

Gerard squinted at Gabriel through the rising cigarette smoke and simply shrugged in response.

Gabriel sighed inwardly. The man knew more about grapes, wine, and wine-making than anyone he had ever met, but sometimes his Gallic mannerisms were irritating. Most frustrating was that Gerard usually spoke in his mother tongue, despite having lived in the States for more than twenty years. Gabriel suspected he knew more English than he let on. After all, his wife and seven children all conversed freely in the language.

Despite the sun, the air was still chilly, and Gabriel quickly tucked his hands into his pocket, wincing at the sharp pain that ran up his arm until it exploded in his shoulder. He clenched his teeth and smiled tightly. "Did you see anything strange when you made your visit to the vineyard this morning?" he asked in impeccable French.

Gerard looked up at his boss and frowned. "Non."

"Two of my house guests were riding in the vineyard and believe they spotted a poacher." Gerard lifted an eyebrow but said nothing. "There was a gunshot," Gabriel said firmly.

The Frenchman threw his cigarette down onto the swept pavement and ground it out with his boot heel, but remained seated. "Gunshots, monsieur?" He cocked his head and pinched his face in disbelief.

Gabe nodded. "Oui. But you don't believe me." Gabriel sat down on the freezing wood and unzipped his vest, gently slipping it and his shirt a few inches down to reveal the top of his bandaged upper left arm. "Does this prove it to you, Gerard?"

The Frenchman's pale blue eyes widened in astonishment. "Shot?" Gerard stood up quickly, licked his lips, and glanced around him as if expecting to spot a likely suspect among the group boarding a tour bus in the parking lot.

"It is only a light flesh wound, so I was quite lucky," Gabriel assured him. "But I want you to go down to the western slopes and look around. Maybe you can find some tracks before the snow melts."

"What about the police?" he asked.

"Did I say anything about calling the police? I just want you to see if you can find something out of the ordinary." If this was anything more than an errant poacher, Gabriel didn't want the police involved. The publicity would be anything but helpful.

He rose from the cold bench and began walking away, but stopped after a few steps and turned around. He looked Gerard squarely in the eye and held his gaze for several seconds. "One more thing. Don't mention this to anyone. I want you to look by yourself, and then talk to me about what you find. Only me. Do you understand?"

With a bored shrug of his shoulders, Gerard grunted his assent and lit another cigarette. He knew Gabriel hated the smell of tobacco, particularly the vile smelling French cigarettes the little winemaker enjoyed smoking.

ॐ

"This is damn frustrating."

Nicholas pushed back his chair and stood up, stretching his back with his hands on his hips until several cracks and pops eased his stiffness. He twisted gently to the right and then to the left, trying to loosen his body. Sitting for long periods of time tended to lock up his muscles, and if he did not stretch and walk often, he always paid the price the next day.

"I agree," nodded Alex. "We seem to be going in circles now on this one issue. It's quite maddening."

The twins were frustrated by the results they were getting from the nautical program. Its measurements illustrated monthly tidal highs and monthly tidal lows, in feet. But the program produced similar values for multiple months in a row, which made it difficult to understand *which* month they could expect to be the true high and which month would be the true low.

They tried to filter out the problem by looking at days in the month in order to pick the highest, or lowest, month—the same strategy they had used to pick the highest and lowest years. This strategy produced better answers, although they were not as clear-cut as they wanted. Once again, they printed out the spreadsheets and marked *High* for the highs and *Low* for the lows. When compared to the Dow data, they found a substantial correlation. Still, the monthly trends weren't nearly as perfect as the yearly results.

They performed the same procedure with individual days instead of months. This produced high and low tides for each day for each year from 1980 through 2004. Alex was about to go back to 1920, but remembered that the intra-day, real-time data only went back to 1980, which rendered the nautical data worthless for comparison before then.

Again the same problem haunted them. Not only did they find the same values for several days in a row, but the tidal highs and lows also appeared to suffer a phase inversion. In other words, the tidal highs correlated with lows in the market data, but then over a period of time, the tidal highs correlated with market highs.

"I'm totally confused," Alex grumbled. "How can the yearly trends be dead on, the monthly trends mostly on, and the daily trends on and off? There must be some logic to it, but damned if I can construct a model to describe it. Yet, that is." He grinned at his brother, who though frustrated with elements of their work, was still ecstatic with the yearly and monthly success.

"Agreed, but think about how huge this is!" marveled the economist. "Knowing the market direction in advance is the most critical part of everything. If the Federal Reserve had this information, they could proactively prevent recessions or depressions by simply raising or lowering the interest rates *in advance*. They could also decrease or increase the value of the dollar to help stabilize international markets. All they can do now is react—usually ten to twelve months too late—and then try to catch up. That's what we just saw in 2000. The Feds lowered the rates eleven times, but it was still too late to prevent the slide that wiped out trillions of invested dollars."

"However," Alex countered, "if we can't figure out why the data for the dailies seems opposite what it should be, it's possible the longer trends could suffer similarly, right? We've got to figure this out before we get surprised later on."

Nicholas rubbed the sharp two-day growth of whiskers on his face. "Agreed. And we will. We just haven't hit on what is making everything tick yet."

Alex bent over and opened a carrying case he had retrieved a short time earlier from his bedroom. He unclipped the fasteners and withdrew a new Dell laptop. "I've been working on system identification software programs designed to be autonomous in their usage," he explained. I brought this thinking I might have some downtime. I guess right about *now* it might come in handy!"

Nicholas reached out and slapped Alex on the shoulder. "I should say so! This could save us days or even weeks of work, Alex!"

Alex plugged in the computer and clicked it on. "I'm sure I can fairly easily redesign the programs to accept exogenous input that would adapt and catch the phase inversions before they happen. . . ."

Nicholas cut him off. "Whoa! In English, please."

Alex scratched his forehead. "Sorry. Exogenous simply means information from another source. So in this case, I would use information other than stock market data that I can then insert into my program as a leading indicator to test our theories. This assumes the gravity data we have collected really drives human behavior." Alex paused, thought a moment, and then continued.

"I also think we have a noise problem. It's the most promising theory rattling around in my brain"

Nicholas turned his head from the laptop to his brother, eyebrows in the locked and upright position. "Continue."

"I think it is quite possible that all the talking heads who report real-time events around the clock, twenty-four/seven, you know, earning reports, the normal ongoing daily news, the running ticker numbers, newsmaker interviews, and so on, keep the daily trends from working *naturally*."

"Hmm. Hadn't thought of that," replied Nicholas as he mulled the theory. He used his hand to beckon Alex to continue.

"In aerospace matters we often encounter 'noise' that interferes with normal conditions, but we can identify it by filtering it out. Simply put, we can get rid of the noise in order to see what's important and what isn't. If the markets are predestined to go in a certain direction, like we see in the yearly trends, then perhaps the 'noise,' as I just defined it, is keeping the daily market from responding correctly."

"Brother, you are one smart guy. Keep at it."

"I intend to," smiled Alex, rubbing his hands together in anticipation over the keyboard.

"I need a break, and I will be more in the way than helpful with your programming, so I think I will head downstairs and see if I still have a wife," said Nicholas. "

"Yeah, ok," mumbled Alex, already deeply focused on the task at hand.

Alex worked all afternoon, writing and adapting computer code for his programs, scarcely noticing when Nicholas popped in to look over his shoulder every so often. Lunch was a blur, but it was delicious. How the plate ended up next to his elbow he was unsure, and he did not even realize he was eating until he absentmindedly caught himself nibbling on the *panforte di Siena*, rich Tuscan honey, Sienese *Pecorino* cheese, and *finocchiona* that had been in the recent care package sent by Francesca's parents. Alex was so wrapped up in his coding equations that he barely noticed the tangy, earthy flavors.

ॐ

Gabriel parked the truck but left the motor running, replaying in his mind the odd conversation with Gerard. The Frenchman who doubled as a chimney sweep was hiding something—Gabriel was sure of it. But what?

He might have been too far away to hear the gunshots, but why was he not more surprised when he learned about the careless poacher and Gabriel's wounding? Gerard's blasé indifference to the whole thing was confounding.

Gabriel leaned forward until his head rested on the steering wheel. He exhaled loudly and tried to shake the thoughts from his mind. There was something else nagging at him, pawing at his consciousness. "No," he thought. No, that could not be possible.

He reached over and turned off the key, stepped from the cab, and made his way to the house, where he greeted Francesca and Cassandra with a warm broad smile.

"That food smells heavenly! And I am as hungry as a bull."

ॐ

Alex was determined to redesign one of his programs to do the impossible. He spent considerable time and effort calculating what components to use. After about an hour of manipulating the figures, he began punching in the formulas. He kept up a running dialog with himself, as if he was conversing with a fellow engineer.

"Oh, I see," he said to the empty room. "In FDP, one is in effect 'dividing the cross-correlation of the input and the output by the auto-correlation of the input, to get the frequency response' of a linearized model of the system." By the time he began entering the stock data into his Matlab program, he was getting hoarse. If anyone else had been listening they might have thought he was muttering gibberish, but Alex knew exactly what he was doing.

He began to calculate the necessary dimension for a test run of all the data they collected. Based on the number of frequencies in the astronomical data, he computed the most likely dimension to be $n = 73$. He shook his head, not believing his calculations. He did the numbers again and came up with the same dimension: $n = 73$. "Well," he sighed. "Anything over a dimension of five is going to be difficult and, at best, unreliable." With a pencil clenched between his teeth he forged ahead, entering the number 73 into the formula. He set the program to forecast ten days into the future. He hesitated, exhaled loudly, and pressed enter.

It took nearly fifteen minutes for the computer to process a matrix of that size. When the answer was finally revealed, it appeared as a simple *sine* wave, suggesting a forecast of the Dow moving up for five days, and then moving down from there. For some reason, the program, which he half expected would crash, remained completely stable.

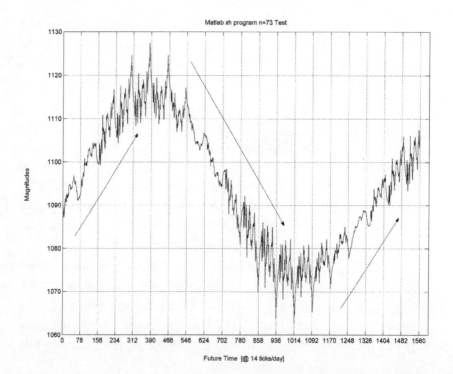

Alex set TradeStation to go back one month and cut off the data at that point. This time he knew what the future would be, but the computer did not. "Ok," he said under his breath. "Now let's see how reliable this is." He pushed enter.

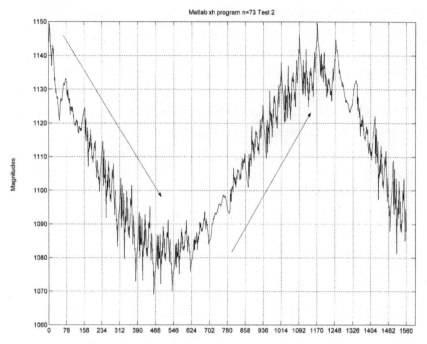

Several minutes later his program printed out a picture of a *sine* wave graph forecasting the Dow would move down for seven days, and then turn up. He immediately turned to historical data in TradeStation and compared the results. What he found made him jump up and run out the door to the top of the stairs.

"Nicholas get up here!" he shouted. No answer. He drew another breath to shout again when he spotted a piece of paper taped to the wall near the stairs. A message was scrawled on it in black magic marker: "Brother, I am accompanying the ladies around Biltmore Village. I tried to get your attention—impossible! Check your back. Nicholas."

"Check my back?" said Alex aloud. He stepped into his bedroom and turned sideways, looking into a mirror. He reached his hand over his shoulder, felt around, and removed a yellow sticky page: "Can't say we didn't try to take you with us! N."

Alex laughed out loud as he headed back to his computer inside Gabriel's office. They would have to wait to find out what he had just discovered: the forecast was perfect . . . to the day!

Alex spent the next few hours moving through historical data, recreating the same procedure, and printing out the answers. Most of the forecasts were correct and matched historical market movement, but a few did not. This, he decided, was probably due to the "noise" factor of reports and anomalies he had described to Nicholas. Of course, it could also be the wrong dimension to make the forecast. Another thought entered his mind. Was he using enough historical days, or maybe too many days, to consistently get a correct answer?

Alex recalled a book titled *The Dilemma of Dimensionality,* which described the frustration engineers experience when they try to find a dimension that would give stable answers. Alex decided to write another program that would go through the process of testing each dimension from n=2 through n=73 to find the one that had the least fitting error measured by the Kalman filter. Could this cut out the noise factor?

He called the new program *pragdimx* because it relied on a pragmatic answer for the program to score itself. He tested the program and found that it worked better to select the correct dimensions on an individual basis for it consistently gave stable answers. As it turned out, using the dimension of 73 wasn't always the best one to use.

Alex was perplexed with the second problem. There was no way for him to know how many days of historical data to utilize. There had to be something better than just plugging in fifteen days to make the forecast. Fewer than fifteen days would certainly be too few, but somewhere between fifteen and thirty might supply the best answer. He quickly wrote a second program dubbed *tdp22*. This program would start with fifteen days in history, and then sequentially move back one day at a time until it reached thirty days. He programmed it to continue making pragmatic tests on itself until it confirmed the best day in history to start from.

His confidence grew once he began studying the results. The final step was to compile all three programs into one.

The last program he titled *Xyber9*.

Chapter 15

The Biltmore Village was a charming shopping area located near the entrance to the Biltmore Estate. Originally designed by George Vanderbilt for the talented artisans and craftspeople brought in to complete the mansion, the quaint little neighborhood was now home to distinctive shops, galleries, and restaurants. The storybook cottages were especially enchanting at Christmas.

As a reward for her "courage under fire," Cassandra decided to spend some of Nicholas' potential wealth on a deep purple-blue Tanzanite and diamond ring. Francesca wondered aloud if perhaps her sister-in-law might have hit her head when she tumbled off the horse, but admitted that the ring was certainly beautiful when she held it up to the light to admire its fiery cobalt flash. Amused, Gabriel tried to remind them that the first rule of all successful financial moguls was not to spend it before it is deposited in the bank.

Perhaps it was Cassandra's enthusiasm over the ring, or Nicholas' confidence in the box's potential. It might have been his self-imposed guilt over the shooting incident. Something however, prompted Gabriel to pull the sales clerk aside as he withdrew his wallet from his pocket and handed her his own debit card.

"You can pay me back when your ship comes in," he said to Cassandra with a wink and light kiss on the cheek.

॰

It was late in the afternoon by the time Nicholas, Gabriel, Cassandra, and Francesca arrived home. As the women unraveled their scarves and Gabriel stoked the fire, Nicholas climbed the stairs two at a time to rejoin Alex in the office. He noticed the note was gone from the wall. Alex was sitting in the growing shadows, staring at his computer screen.

"I know you have been out of the chair at least once. My sign is down," began Nicholas. When his brother didn't answer, Nicholas leaned over his shoulder and looked at the monitor. "What is this?"

"This," Alex said with delight, "is *Xyber9*!"

"It looks impressive. Tell me more."

Alex spent the next several minutes explaining how he created the *Xyber9* program. An occasional glaze fell across Nicholas' eyes when his brother waded too deeply into the technical aspects, but Alex continued explaining until a look of realization slowly washed over his brother's face.

"I don't know what to say," Nicholas admitted as he sifted through the printed results. He pulled a chair alongside the computer and sat down. "The forecasts are perfect to the day."

"Pretty amazing, eh? I could use some help from you now. I need to back-test the *Xyber9* program using real-time S&P 500 data." Nicholas did as he was instructed, and within minutes he was looking at 100 percent accurate yearly forecasts using Alex's *Xyber9*.

"You can use the box and astronomical measurements too," pointed out Alex, "but I believe *Xyber9* will replace them both. And," he emphasized, "*Xyber9* is more adaptive. I've been able to come up with monthly forecasts that were 99.7 percent accurate." Alex's fingers flew over the individual keys. "Here, Nicholas, let me demonstrate something for you."

Alex set *Xyber9* to forecast the year 2003. He selected September 30, 2002 as the starting date of the forecast and pushed enter. Once Nicholas compared the Matlab print-out with real-time data, he leaned back in astonishment. *Xyber9* identified the monthly tops and bottoms of the market perfectly.

"What are you waiting for?" asked Nicholas.

"What do you mean what am I waiting for?" Alex retorted.

"Make a 2004 forecast!" Nicholas pronounced. "Don't you want to know the future?"

Alex's face lit up and he turned back to the computer and reloaded the appropriate data into *Xyber9*. "You know of course," he said solemnly as the computer crunched the data, "this is the real acid test."

"Of course it is, but unfortunately we will have to wait for the rest of the year to see if the forecast if correct."

Alex drew the lines, calculated the correct dates, and printed the results. He then held it up. "Damn," he exclaimed and handed it to Nicholas. "Looks like a wild ride."

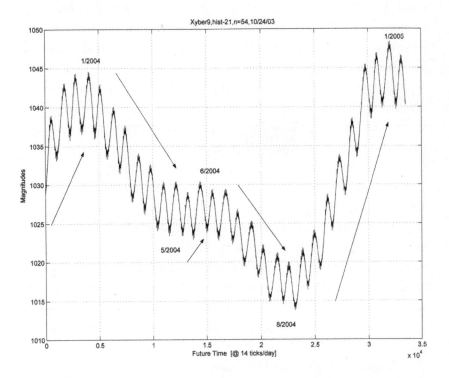

"Damn is right!" Nicholas replied as he studied the prices along the axis of the graph. "Does this show amplitudes?"

"No, the program will just give us the direction and duration, but let's face it, that's all we really need to know."

"I'll go along with that," agreed Nicholas with a broad smile. "Now what about running a couple of years we can actually compare to the Dow. Say, 2001 and 2002?"

Alex downloaded S&P data for November 2000 from TradeStation. He set *Xyber9* to forecast 2001 and began. Once again, the results matched absolutely with the historical data. 2002 was no different.

"My God," Nicholas shook his head in amazement. "I don't know if I am more impressed by the numbers, or by you!"

"I am pretty good," Alex admitted. "But, the numbers are awesome. *Xyber9* produces very accurate weekly forecasts as well."

Nicholas leaned back in his chair with a satisfied smile. "So this is proof. Events such as wars, political upheaval, international problems, geopolitical events, terrorists or even Alan Greenspan's handling of the Federal Reserve does not affect *yearly* forecasts. *Monthly* forecasts, on the other hand, are affected only slightly by anomalies."

"Correct. And by using the adaptive abilities of *Xyber9*, we can produce continuing forecasts that precede the kinds of anomalies you just mentioned. The program will adapt and redraw graphs to forewarn us if the market is moving deeper or higher, or for a longer duration of time."

"These forecasts were produced using historical data, but the computer had no idea of the future—which made the empirical tests bullet-proof. Right?"

"Absolutely," replied Alex, rubbing his eyes with the palms of hands. He was beginning to look very tired. "The anomalies affecting the monthly forecasts usually don't knock the market off course long enough to matter. The markers seem to reestablish their predestined direction before the end of the trend." He yawned for several seconds. "Just to make sure, we can run the program every week, which should adapt to any short-term anomalies and plot out an updated correct answer."

Nicholas nodded. "The noise factor."

"Yup," said Alex, stifling another yawn. "The weekly forecasts are more problematic because of the continuing bombardment of reports and announcements—"

Nicholas jumped in. "Things like unemployment, the Consumer Price Index, the Producer Price Index, Michigan sentiment, consumer confidence, corporate earnings reports, geopolitical events, Mad Cow disease, Fed meetings, you name it. All of this information must have some short-term effect on the market."

"I think these events might shock the stock market temporarily," replied Alex cautiously, "sometimes enough to cause the short-term trend to be wrong. *Xyber9* did its best to adapt to the shocks, although not enough to provide 100 percent accurate weekly forecasts."

Nicholas examined the spreadsheets again. "The weekly forecasts may not be 100 percent accurate, but they're certainly good enough to trade with—and make a hell of a lot of money!"

Chapter 16

The brothers were still seated when their wives darkened the doorway of the office. "Come on, you two! Enough!" Cassandra ordered as she and Francesca physically tried to pull their husbands away from the computers. "Gabe needs to get some work done, and you both need a breather from all this!"

The brothers dug their heels in. "We don't have time," Nicholas said flatly. "This is far too important . . ."

His wife cut him off in mid-sentence, responding just as firmly but much more forcefully. "You will just have to make time!" Gabriel slipped into the room and squeezed past the squabbling couples. He stopped next to Alex and offered a bow. "May I?" he asked, nodding toward his PC.

Alex groaned aloud, but moved his laptop off to the side before getting up.

"Ok, Gabe," chimed in Nicholas, "we will leave you alone for a few hours."

"Where can we go?" Alex asked in a tone that sounded too much like a whine.

"We're going into Asheville to an art gallery," answered Francesca, "and then to dinner at the Grove Park Inn." She bounced on her toes in anticipation. "It happens to have one of the best collections of Arts and Crafts in the United States, along with lots of fabrics and wallpapers by William Morris."

"I should have known," groaned Alex a second time, looking longingly at the computer Gabriel had already reclaimed. "Don't even think about it," whispered Francesca in his ear.

Once back in their room to change and freshen up, Nicholas asked Cassandra whether she was going to wear the Madame X dress.

"Too formal," she said, wrinkling up her nose as she picked through her suitcase. "But I do want something to match my new ring!" she exclaimed, slipping it on her finger and holding her hand out to admire its sheen.

Nicholas reached over from his easy chair and gave her palm a kiss and began working his way up her arm. She bent over and offered the nape of her neck, which he nibbled as she climbed into his lap and gave him a long kiss. "How much time do we have?"

"Enough," he answered. He was about to kiss her again when he stopped suddenly and asked, "How's your head? Are you ok?"

"It's about time you asked!" she laughed. Nicholas was often so deeply involved in his work he forgot everything else. She was used to it by now. "Only a few bruises and a slight headache, darling," she assured him as she planted her mouth firmly back on his.

Down the hall, Alex was on the phone to Father Galen while Francesca was changing. "Sure," the priest was saying. "I'll be happy to stay with the kids a few more days. They miss you, though. Isn't Harrison's birthday coming up? What would he like?"

"Don't worry about buying anything, Father," answered Alex. "We'll be back in time for his birthday. But now that you mention it, I think I will get him a telescope. In fact," he mused, "I wouldn't mind having one myself."

"So who would this telescope be for?" joked Father Galen. "But, seriously Alex, how does Francesca manage ballet lessons, music lessons, soccer, and all the rest of it? These kids wear me out."

"Mommy magic," he offered. "There's no substitute. But there is a list of acceptable sitters on the fridge if you need a break."

"Thanks," said Father Galen. "I will take you up on that. It's time I made my rounds to the nursing homes and convents."

"Do what you need to," said Alex. "We'll be back on Wednesday. "And wait until we tell you what we found out here!"

"Looks like I'll have to wait. Here comes Miss Rosemary with a puppet show."

Francesca smiled and popped an earring off as she walked to the phone to tell the children goodnight. She hung up with a sad look on her face. She missed the kids.

"Ok," Francesca said as she rummaged about in her huge suitcase. "How about this?" She pulled out a rose-pink sleeveless shift and a silk jacket hand-painted with tropical birds and orchids.

"That's perfect," said her husband automatically. He knew how the game was played. Alex watched her as the clothes started to come off. She lifted her eyebrows as he ran his eyes over her.

She pushed him down on the bed, climbed on top of him, and held his arms against the comforter. "Tell me again how rich we are going to be," she whispered, nibbling on his ear lobe.

ॐ

It was late when they finally left the house, both couples grinning sheepishly at each other but utterly relaxed and ready for a fun evening. They opted to use Gabriel's Land Rover for the drive to town. "Classical or jazz?" asked Nicholas, looking through Gabriel's CDs. "How about we drive in to Brubeck and back to Beethoven?"

"I'm game for anything," Cassandra said, sinking back into her furry coat. "You guys get everything squared away with Father Galen and the kids?"

"Yes, we left our children with a renegade priest," laughed Francesca.

"Is that what he's doing these days? Being a renegade?"

"Sort of," said Alex. "He's always been on the cutting edge. He has become a kind of traveling counseling center, going from one parish to another to rescue priests and families in trouble. He is finally getting an opportunity to put all those psychology degrees to good use."

Nicholas glanced in the rearview mirror at his brother, remembering their raucous adventure when the three of them drove across country. He and Alex exchanged smiles. There were some things better kept between the guys.

"Definitely not your typical priest," Alex announced with a grin. "Father Dempsey would just as soon whack your knuckles when we were growing up. Galen *talks* to his parishioners."

"Yeah, well, Father Dempsey was eighty years old. Galen holds very little sacred, and his answer to everything is 'it depends,'" replied Nicholas with a grimace, remembering the old priest's penchant for swinging long rulers.

"Depends on what?" asked Cassandra.

"The situation," Alex answered. "He's one of the founding fathers of situational ethics."

"You mean where there aren't any rules but the ones you make up for yourself? Doesn't Mother Church have an issue with him over that?"

Nicholas spoke up. "He's so reality-based, and so well-known that he gets away with it. The legions of people he has helped would never let the Church get rid of him, but they don't give him a parish, either. I believe he's perfectly happy this way, being the peripatetic angel flying in with the save. Sometimes he can't help, though."

"What do you mean?" asked Francesca.

"There was a priest in Atlanta who was cross-addicted to food, alcohol, and little boys. The guy was such a mess they had to institutionalize him. Galen couldn't do much for the guy, but he worked with the parish to help them get through it. He likes to work behind the scenes, finding the right people to fill the right positions."

Francesca snuggled closer to her husband, "I keep meaning to ask him what he thinks about all this recent scandal. In Europe, things happen all the time, and it just gets swept under the carpet."

"Really? How terrible!" gasped Cassandra.

Francesca shrugged her shoulders. "It depends!" she said, echoing Galen's philosophy. "Europeans are very different from Americans when it comes to sex. We just do it, we don't analyze it afterward. Puritan morality. Such hypocrisy!"

"It's a little more complicated than that, but I will admit that we can be somewhat prudish, although when it comes to predators abusing a child, that's a different story," Alex said, putting his arm around her shoulders.

"So, Alex," Cassandra said teasingly, "where do you stand on mistresses? The Americans and British have had their share of scandals and yet, Europeans are always shocked that we make such a big deal of it."

"My husband is not *that* continental!" exclaimed Francesca from the back seat.

"You are treading into dangerous territory," warned Alex, who never seemed to mind engaging anyone in mind-bending conversations about wormholes or quantum physics, but cringed at sexual banter.

"Here we are," said Nicholas, "one of Cassandra's favorite places." He navigated the Land Rover into a parking spot in front of the Blue Spiral 1.

"This is one of the best little galleries in the Southeast. Artists from all over the region submit their work for showing here." Cassandra said excitedly, "I can't wait for you to see it, Francesca."

"Did you realize that Asheville didn't go bankrupt in the Great Depression like so many municipalities?" Alex suddenly announced to no one in particular. "Instead, it insisted on paying off all its debts—even though it took until the 1980s to do it."

"Didn't Gabriel's family help out with that?" inquired Francesca.

"Quite the contrary. His family lost a lot of money in bad investments before the Depression, and it took them awhile to recover."

"It must have been dreadful," Cassandra grimaced as she accepted Nicholas' help getting out of the car. The cold was stiffening her injured arm.

"There were a few families who didn't suffer at all during the Depression," said Nicholas. "Take the Kennedys, for example. Old man Joe got completely out of the stock market just before the 1929 crash. Wonder what kind of insider information he had?"

Cassandra stopped before a large white bear sculpture just inside the gallery. "That's very interesting."

"The bear?" asked Nicholas. "I think it's ugly."

"Not the bear." Cassandra turned and looked sharply at Nicholas. "Kennedy. It sounds like some people were forewarned about the crash, doesn't it?"

ॐ

Gabriel waited until he saw the taillights of the Land Rover disappear into the woods before picking up the phone. "It's safe, you can come now."

He busied himself catching up with e-mails until he heard a car pull into the drive. Rushing to the top of the stairs, he saw the front door swing open and his face relaxed into an easy smile. It had been too long.

Phoebe Snow looked up and smiled broadly, climbing the steps as Gabriel waited at the top. She kissed him lightly on the lips. "Hi," she said in the perky voice he loved so much. It matched her looks. Her hair was a bubble of frizzies from a cheap perm, and her nails had been recently painted a bright Pepto pink. Phoebe peeled off her winter jacket, purchased some years ago from a local thrift store, revealing her starched staff uniform. Once in the office she tossed the jacket onto the back of a chair and curled up in another. "I'll let you finish," she said as her eyes wandered from screen to screen.

"Thanks," he said, typing as fast as his stubby fingers allowed, but not as fast as he would have liked. "Just a couple more minutes."

"Would you like me to do that for you?"

"Yes, please! My arm is killing me. I guess you heard about what happened. Gerard will probably call in a minute to tell me he has no idea how a poacher came onto the property, shot me, and slipped away with such ease. At least I think it was a poacher."

"Who else would it be?" She uncurled her thin legs and walked over to him. He put his arm around her hip and buried his face into her stomach right below her breasts.

"A shot across my bow."

"A what? I don't know what you mean," she said, massaging his temples with her fingertips.

He sighed and shut his eyes. The rubbing felt wonderful. "I know you don't, and I love you for it. Suffice it to say that I never know what my father is likely to do."

"Your father? He would shoot you?" Phoebe gently slipped her hands down to his cheeks and turned his head to face her. "Gabriel?"

He did not meet her gaze. "Well, no, but he might hire somebody who would. My father's disconnect is almost total. He doesn't like me, and that's putting it mildly."

"Then why do you work for him?" Phoebe moved back a little, regarding him with her deep doe eyes.

"Because my family gives me access to great wealth, which I am working hard to distribute to the people here in Asheville."

"And my family is grateful," she said, caressing his face. "Especially me. You were wonderful to let me learn all the things I'm capable of—all the responsibility you've let me take on."

Gabriel had a well-earned reputation for encouraging talent. His hands-on management approach helped him recognize it, and he often gave more responsibility to his "student" managers. Phoebe's gift for organization and unprepossessing people skills helped her rise quickly among the staff, and no one denied her abilities. Gabriel never intended to fall in love with the hired help. Becoming personally involved with one of them was strictly against his—and his father's—rules. He and Phoebe had resisted the attraction with great effort for many weeks, and used the same effort to hide their emotions behind a mask of professionalism. So far it seemed to be working.

Gabriel took her hand. "One of these days we'll have to let people know about our relationship, but I'm just not ready to do that yet."

"And I don't understand your relationship with your family," Phoebe answered. Her unwavering stare made him uncomfortable. Despite their differences, he occasionally did some work for his father. It was not something he was proud of, and he had only recently admitted it to Phoebe. It was too complicated to explain, and he had not shared this with Nicholas and Alex because he was certain they would never understand.

Phoebe bit her lower lip. The last thing she wanted to do tonight was upset him. Gabriel seemed tired and stressed. It was time to let it go. "Actually, I think I understand." She looked at him sweetly. "I trust you."

A relieved Gabriel gracefully changed the subject. "Let's go down and find some dinner. One of my house guests is an Italian and cooks like one."

For now, for this moment, everything was all right. Gabriel avoided thinking about the future. If he took this lovely young thing, so completely without guile or etiquette, to New York to meet his parents, they would eat her alive and disown him in the bargain. Not doing so was filling him with guilt, but he was not yet ready to fight that battle.

ॐ

"Francesca!" Alex stopped his wife at the entrance to the inn. "We'll go to eat at Horizons, but you have to promise you won't stomp into the kitchen and give the chef a hard time."

Francesca hung her head in exaggerated shame.

Cassandra burst out laughing. "You don't still do that, do you?"

Alex put his arm around her shoulders. "We do not want to relive that adventure at the Four Seasons in New York, do we?"

Nicholas' laugh was so loud strangers turned to stare in his direction. "As I recall that was just breakfast, wasn't it, Francesca?" She stuck out her tongue in reply.

The twins and their wives walked into the lobby, which immediately changed Francesca's attitude. Though huge, it was warm and intimate, thanks to the enormous fireplace with its roaring oak and hickory-log fire. They took turns riding the tiny elevator inside the fireplace wall, viewed the room where F. Scott Fitzgerald stayed when he visited Zelda, peered over the edge of the balcony where a mysterious young lady had apparently committed suicide, and listened to Nicholas tell Francesca about her ghost. Once in the restaurant they were shown to a window table. The starlit mountains glimmered in the distance.

"*Carpaccio* for the appetizer. I'm daring them to do it better than I can." Francesca looked coyly over the menu at her husband.

"As long as you do it *silently*," shot back Alex without raising his eyes.

Cassandra ordered the Muscovy duck breast and the men settled on steaks. When the waiter left Nicholas appeared especially quiet. He was staring out the window, obviously deep in thought. Cassandra reached over and poked him gently. "Hey. What is it?"

"Phase inversions," he answered, still peering out the window as though wishing to see the solution written in large letters across the horizon. He turned back to the table. "We can do this, Alex. I know we can. If we can solve that one problem, we'll have every answer we need to start trading."

Chapter 17

When the twins and their wives returned from dinner, they found a note from Gabriel telling them he had gone into town. The brothers were pleasantly full and tired. Normally they would have headed straight for bed, but a desire to return to their spreadsheets and programs was stronger than their need for sleep. Cassandra shook her head and exchanged glances with Francesca as Nicholas and Alex mumbled excuses and heading up to the office. "Come on, Francesca," laughed Cassandra. "We'll have a nightcap *alone* before retiring."

Alex and Nicholas took up where they had left off, with Nicholas studying the spreadsheets and Alex back-testing the data. "These damn phase inversions!" Alex exclaimed after a few minutes of work. "The short-term weekly trends are inconsistent: the tidal values are either perfectly in phase with the market, or 180 degrees out of phase."

Nicholas frowned. "The highs in the tidal charts should be lows in the market, and the lows in the tidal chart should be highs in the market."

The data, however, was not as clear. Without warning, the inverse would show up, where the highs in the tidal charts correlated with highs in the market, and the tidal lows matched market lows over long periods of time.

Alex sighed and leaned back in his chair. "I am missing something. I can't figure out why the short-term trend inverts, but the longer-term monthly trends do not, nor do the longest yearly trends, which stretch back as far as eighty-four years. *Xyber9* catches the inversion, but usually only after taking a loss. Glad this is just paper trading and not real money."

Alex hopped onto the Web and looked for research on phase inversions, knowing that several scientists had worked on this problem in areas related to economic time issues. Alex recalled that J. M. Hurst, for example, had had a similar problem with phase-inversions and market cycles, but Hurst could never figure out a solution. Dr. Claude E. Cleeton had also encountered a phase-inversion phenomenon. "If scientists as smart as this couldn't figure it out, how are we going to do it?" Alex muttered.

Nicholas shook his head. "We are not exactly uneducated, Alex. Let's keep our focus and think about this. We have some data and insight they didn't have."

Alex tapped his pencil on the desktop as he thought out loud. "The only thing I can figure out is that there must be some connection to the aerospace version of phase inversion."

"What do you mean?" asked Nicholas.

"In my field," answered Alex, "it is not unusual to have an astronaut's instruments go 180 degrees out of phase. In physics, this is called *Covariance of Theta*, and electrical engineers describe it as when the instruments go from a positive reality to a negative reality. Those same engineers wrote a program to correct the problem." Alex closed his eyes and thought hard for a minute.

"What about the box?" Nicholas said, jarring Alex out of his thoughts.

"You're right!" he said, opening his eyes and sitting up straight. "Maybe it has something to do with the earth-moon relationship. Maybe the sun too. The moon orbits the earth once every twenty-nine days. The earth is rotating counter-clockwise at a speed many times faster than the moon's orbit, which makes it look like the moon is coming up in the East and setting in the West. In reality it's the opposite, because the moon is orbiting the earth counter-clockwise." Alex stopped for a few seconds, nodded to himself, and continued. "If you were standing in the same place on earth for roughly twenty-nine days, the moon would complete one orbit when it passed you on that final day, although you would have seen the moon rise and set twenty-nine times while waiting for one rotation."

"Where are we going with this?" Nicholas asked.

"Give me a second. I think I'm onto something. While the moon has the greatest effect on the earth's gravitational field, the sun also adds to the effect. During the summer solstice when the earth is farthest from the sun, the gravitational effects of the sun are felt the most in the Northern Hemisphere, which we will consider 'positive.' During March and September, the sun is located exactly on the equator, which we will consider 'zero.' During the winter solstice, when the earth is closest to the sun, the gravitational effects of the sun are most felt in the Southern Hemisphere, which we will consider 'negative.' Phase inversion takes place when the gravitational effects of the sun move from positive to negative, and vise versa."

"Hmm. I think I follow you," Nicholas answered slowly. "So if an astronaut's instruments suffer this effect, then maybe the weekly trends do as well. Is that it?

"Yes, that makes complete sense, don't you think?"

"Let's give it a test."

The twins printed out the daily tidal values for the past five years, back to 1998. They started from the beginning and followed the high-to-low sequence. The phase inversion phenomenon appeared first in March of 1998, and then again in September 1998, and followed the same pattern every year thereafter. As they expected, the lows in the tidal data matched highs in the market, and the highs in the tidal data matched lows in the market. That is, until the inversion took place, when the lows in the tidal data matched the lows in the market, and the tidal highs matched market highs.

Now it was Nicholas' turn to surf the Net, which he did until he discovered a lecture on astronomy from a Dr. David Rhoads of Atlanta's Fernbank Science Center. From it, the twins deduced the inversions could only happen during the new or full moon in the months of March and September.

"That's it! It explains everything!" Nicholas looked relieved and exhausted at the same time. "It's only during these moon phases at Vernal Equinox and Autumn Equinox. How is that for incredible? No wonder it all looked so random to begin with!" He raised his hands in the air like a preacher and shouted, "Hallelujah!"

Nicholas stopped himself and looked at Alex. "The funny thing, though, is that most economists refer to the radical movements in the markets as 'seasonality.' Down during the summer—you know, they call it the "summer doldrums"—and up around the first of the year. They all say the same thing, blaming it on third quarter earnings reports for the lows in the summer. Then, of course, it's the portfolio managers re-positioning their clients' accounts at the end of the year that causes the markets to rally." Nicholas spun his chair around and faced Alex, grabbing both of his shoulders and squeezing them tightly. "This is truly incredible, Alex! Jesus, we have just proven that gravity causes '*market seasonality!*' This provides us with a perfect road map for making a fortune!"

For once Alex was speechless. He sat perfectly still and looked into his brother's eyes. Instead of the uncontrollable excitement Nicholas was expecting, Alex's face assumed a somber look. "Do you think the owners of the box figured out the phase inversion problem?"

The question took Nicholas completely by surprise. "Well, no, I doubt it." He let go of Alex's shoulders. "Why?"

"I don't think so either," replied Alex. "If they were somehow aware of the aerospace phase inversion problem, maybe, but most likely they hired mechanical engineers to write their programs, not aerospace scientists. I'm using both *time domain* and *frequency domain* processes in my program, not to mention astronomical measurements. Most scientists would not have thought of that. My guess is that they lost track of the market cycles twice a year, and probably lost a lot of money in the process during that time."

Nonplused, Nicholas shrugged, "So what? That's their problem."

"Yes, I suppose you are right. I'm just a little tired." Alex smiled wearily. "Now, where were we?"

"Let's see," began Nicholas as he stood up to pace the room. "Of course, we need to think about the practice of investing for the short-term. It's funny, I've spent most of my adult life preaching the benefits of the good old buy-and-hold theory, but now the teacher is the student. Now *that* is a paradigm shift. We have to indoctrinate ourselves in a whole new theory: no one should *ever* just buy and hold, because as of this minute, the market's inevitable highs and lows are absolutely predictable."

"That's what's known as a pre-set condition," offered Alex, "a stable-state space vector in which the future has been predetermined."

"More aerospace language!" His brother laughed, "I am learning a lot this weekend." Nicholas sat down and pulled out a clean sheet of paper. "How about if we just buy on an up yearly trend, go to cash at the top, bank the interest with the account balance, then buy back at the next yearly bottom? We would make good money. However," he continued, "if we bought at the bottom of each *monthly* trend and went to cash at the top, we would definitely make much *more* money."

Alex took out a calculator and figured out the difference. Looking at the TradeStation chart in front of him, he saw the Dow data with the trends drawn from bottom to top, and then to bottom again over the entire market data. He started punching in the numbers on a spreadsheet.

"Say we sold on this Dow high, January 16, 2003, which was 8,869.29, and bought back in March at a price of 7,416.64. We would have saved a 16 percent decline in our stock value." He looked up to make sure Nicholas was following him.

"Alright, then if we would buy back and ride the trend up until June," continued Alex, "which on this nautical chart and *Xyber9* forecasts is a high, we would have made 26 percent in that move alone. We could again be in cash during the next down trend, which shows here to be August, and we will have saved four percent. Buying back in again then, and up we go to December 31, where we would sell again with a 16 percent gain. I have to figure the additional shares we would own in the process because we would have been able to buy more shares at the bottom of each of these trends."

He calculated the answer and smiled at Nicholas. "Here's the bottom line, Nicholas. We start with a 1,000 shares of the Dow, which of course are called Diamonds. In January, the account would be worth $88,690, and now in cash, because we sold our shares pending the next predicted down trend to March. In March, we buy back the Dow, but we will own another additional 195 shares because of the new lower price. Our stock is now worth $88,621. We sell at the top in June at $93.52, which brings our stock value up to $111,764. Is my math right?"

Nicholas was leaning over a desk punching the numbers himself on a calculator. "Yes, dead on."

"We stand aside again until August and buy back the stock at a another lower price of $89.97, giving us an additional 47 shares and bringing the total number of shares up to 1,242, which we sell again December 31 for $104.62 per share. Our account value is now up to $129,938—*up 46 percent*—and we have generated an additional 242 shares to top it off. Of course, we'll have to pay some tax on those short-term capital gains, but what the hell." Alex stopped and smiled.

Nicholas clicked a few more keys, looked at his brother and nodded in reply. "I would be happy to write that check to Uncle Sam."

"On the other hand," continued Alex, lifting his hand and shaking a finger, "if we simply bought on January 1 and sold on December 31, we would have made just 18 percent. True, that is considered a strong return, and we would have to pay less tax since it would be a long-term capital gain, but that wouldn't make much difference. We're definitely much better off timing our investments."

"A timing method!" Nicholas almost spat the words under his breath. "They say you can't time the market! The fact is, they can't time the market, but they all do!"

"How's that?" Alex asked.

"I don't know why I didn't think of this before!" Nicholas began pacing anew, back and forth as if lecturing his class at Emory.

"When a financial company upgrades or downgrades a stock, they are timing the market. When your brokers calls you and tells you to buy this or sell that, or even shift more money into cash or bonds, what's he doing?"

"Ah, timing the market?" replied Alex with a set of raised eyebrows.

Nicholas ignored the sarcasm. "As a matter of fact, there is not a single time when the financial advisors aren't timing the market, one way or the other, with their advice. They just want you to *believe* they aren't playing a timing game. Alex, they don't have a *clue* as to where the market is really going. They use the buy and hold theory just to keep everyone's money in the brokerage firm to get their annual fees, because whether you win or lose, they get paid."

"Plus any other fees that the regulators let them get away with." Alex interrupted.

Nicholas stopped and turned to face his twin. "I knew the buy and hold theory was just a marketing ploy. Sure, the statistics show a long term positive gain by holding, but try telling that to all those people who lost their shirt in the 2000 bust. But never mind the damn brokers. I'll attend to them with the essay I plan to write later about market timing and the 'random walk' theory. They—hey! I just thought of something else."

"What's that?"

"Here's the deal, Alex. If we just buy the stocks for the up trends and use a simple hedge on the down trends, we can add the same number of shares and make the same profits, but this time we won't be subject to taxes."

"What are you talking about?"

"We'll never sell our shares," Nicholas explained. "We'll only sell stock futures on the down trends, which will keep our stock position from losing money, otherwise called market neutral. At the end of the downtrend, we take the profits from selling the futures and buy additional shares for the up trend. If we keep doing that throughout the year, we would have made all the profits, all 46 percent, but because we don't sell any of our shares of stock, we won't have to pay taxes until we cash out."

"Don't the futures profits count as short term capital gains?" argued Alex.

"Not if we use IRA accounts for the hedge," Nicholas assured him with a smile.

"Talk about wily business tactics," Alex exclaimed. "The Vanderbilts have nothing on you, brother. And just think, we could be Wall Street tycoons by the time we're finished."

Chapter 18

Francesca woke up to a bright room full of early morning sunshine. Even after her shower Alex was still sound asleep, curled up in a tight ball on his side and breathing deeply. She pulled on her warm wool pants and a long chenille sweater. Grabbing her little Italian leather boots, she carried them into the hall and walked softly downstairs.

The kitchen counter was a mess. Gabriel! "Bachelors," she sighed despairingly. Gabe really needed a woman in his life. There was no way she could start breakfast until the mess was cleaned up. As she moved to turn on the faucet she bumped a porcelain serving plate that fell to the floor and exploded in a hundred shards.

"Oh, darn it!" Francesca gritted her teeth, as she dropped to her knees to begin picking up the pieces. Once she had finished, she ran the hot water and began stacking the plates and silverware for washing. A few seconds of soft footsteps behind her and Cassandra appeared, yawning and gathering her soft curls into a clip.

She leaned forward and kissed Francesca on the cheek. "Good morning," she mumbled. "A whole six hours of sleep, on vacation no less." She, too, was wearing heavy wool pants but had wrapped herself in a thick fleecy robe before coming downstairs.

"Cassandra, I'm sorry. I didn't mean to wake you," replied Francesca.

"That's all right, Francesca. Just show me the coffee."

"I still have to make it. Give me a few minutes."

It was then that Cassandra realized her sister-in-law was washing dishes. "Whoa there, my friend. Just how many wine glasses are you washing?"

Francesca shot her a puzzled look. "Two." Then she stopped to think about it. "Two," she repeated more slowly, delighted at the revelation.

"Two glasses. No wonder the leftovers disappeared! Our Gabriel had company last night while we were gone!"

"I wonder if it was the blonde woman Nicholas saw at the mansion the other night," smiled Cassandra as she busied herself setting the breakfast table with the sturdy earthenware Gabriel stored in the Welch cupboard lining one of the walls. "I would so like for him to settle down with someone."

"So would I, but maybe he doesn't want to," observed her sister-in-law as she poured coffee beans into a grinder and closed the lid. "He seems quite happy with what he does and how he lives. He can go anywhere at the drop of a hat, he can buy anything he wants, study antiquities and orchids at his leisure . . ."

"It might seem nice to you, tied down with two kids and no time for yourself," teased Cassandra. "But, I suspect we're both victims of the 'grass is greener' syndrome. Which is pretty absurd, given that our lives are close to perfect."

With the coffee brewing and the dishes washed, Francesca began whisking a Hollandaise sauce. "You have your choice of eggs Florentine or Benedict. You're right. I wouldn't change anything, though a little more money wouldn't hurt."

"If the boys succeed, that won't be a problem! Let me help. Can I cut up this fruit?"

Francesca nodded. "How are the bruises on your arm?"

"Better." Cassandra flexed it for her and hid a grimace beneath clenched lips. "It is a bit tight. I hope Gabe's ok this morning. I am worried about infection, but we cleaned his arm pretty well and it wasn't deep."

"Well, he is stubborn like a bachelor, isn't he?" laughed Francesca. "Anyone in their right mind would have at least had a doctor look at it, but not Gabe!"

Cassandra nodded in agreement. "Let's see what today brings. I need to get back to those documents. They really intrigue me. They are so old and some of them are beautifully written. Do you want to help?"

"Siena has probably not changed much since some of those documents were written!" laughed Francesca. "Sure I'll help with your research." Francesca was bustling about the kitchen now, sautéing string potatoes to a crispy turn, checking on the eggs Florentine baking in the oven, arranging the fruit on the plates. "Now! Where are those men?" She walked to the bottom of the stairs and called out their names.

A few minutes later both brothers appeared in their bathrobes, unshaven and with their hair uncombed. "I am glad you boys dress up well because you aren't much to look at in the morning. Anyone seen Gabe?"

"He's not in his room, or at least he's not answering my knock. Must be out and about already." Alex made a beeline for the coffeepot and poured a full mug of dark French Roast. He wrapped his hands around the cup and absorbed its warmth as he inhaled its rich scent. "God, that smells good."

Just as they settled in for the mini-feast, someone rapped softly at the door. Cassandra answered it. It was Gerard, from the Winery. He seemed embarrassed to find them in the middle of a meal.

"*Non, non, non*," said Cassandra, leading him into the kitchen to an empty chair. "*S'asseoir, et mange avec nous.*"

Gerard had a startled look on his face and was twisting his cap in his hands. He took a deep breath and broke into rapid French.

"I understood the word 'police'," said Alex with his mouth full of eggs.

Cassandra interpreted for the others. "He said, 'I followed footprints to the eastern border. I found strange holes on either side of the electric fence and figured that someone had placed a ladder over it, and climbed onto the property. On the road outside, I found tire marks. Do you want to contact the police?' *Attendez,* Monsieur Gerard," Cassandra motioned to the chair.

Gerard sat down warily and glanced at their plates. Francesca poured him a cup of coffee and set a plate of food in front of him. Before long he was chatting away with Cassandra as though they were old friends. Nicholas understood French well, but Alex and Francesca were only able to pick up a few words here and there. They were all relieved when Gabriel's boots were heard stomping off snow on the back porch. He stepped through the door and a look of surprise shaded his face when he saw his vineyard keeper eating breakfast with his friends. Gerard stared to rise but Gabriel waved him back to his seat.

Gerard repeated his report while Gabriel helped himself to breakfast. He would have preferred talking with Gerard in private. "*Bon travail, Gerard. Merci. Revenez* à *votre travail, s'il vous plait,*" he replied rather brusquely. Gerard nodded silently and took his leave.

"Why don't you want to call the police?" asked Nicholas warily, his brow deeply furrowed.

Gabriel was eating and did not look up. "It's complicated." The answer was unconvincing.

"But you could have been killed!" Alex exclaimed, thinking about how he would feel if it had been Francesca or Cassandra who had taken the bullet.

Gabriel sighed, wiping his mouth with a napkin. "But I wasn't. Look, it has to do with the relationship of the estate to the town. Occasionally, people hunt this property, but only out of necessity. If they really need the food and are brave enough to risk being caught, I don't mind sacrificing a couple of deer here and there. I don't appreciate getting shot, but I'm fine." Gabriel's tone of voice was hard, as if spoken by a stranger.

Alex was beginning to look angry. "Why can't they go hunting in the forests that ring the estate? This entire region is woods, Gabe."

Gabriel carefully put his fork down on the napkin and straightened it out before speaking. "All the land is owned by the government or by private investors." His voice was tense. He was holding back his anger. "The government people only lease a small amount of land to be hunted. It's over now."

An uncomfortable silence descended over the breakfast table. None of them had ever heard Gabriel speak with that tone of voice. It was a side of him they had never seen before. Everyone looked down at their food as Gabriel shoved down the last of his breakfast, stood up without a word, and practically threw his plate into the sink.

Cassandra frowned at his departing back. "Guess now is not the time to ask about his dinner guest," she whispered into Francesca's ear.

Francesca, always the bridge-builder, hated tension more than anything. She reached over and tousled her husband's hair. "Gabe's right. He's fine and Cassandra only has a couple of bruises. Help me knead some bread?"

"Damn odd," said Alex between clenched teeth as he stood to help his wife.

Nicholas glanced at his watch. "My class!" he said as he pulled out his cell phone and punched in a number. "Lev? . . . Dr. Shepard. How is everything going? . . . Great . . . Listen, I am tied up with something in Asheville, and I need you to cover me for the undergraduate exams tomorrow . . . Thanks. I'm going to e-mail you some information I want you to start working on. We've made a huge discovery here, one with incredible implications. It's a timing method to predict the movement of the stock markets. I need you to . . . Lev?" Nicholas put his hand over the speaker. "I think he dropped the phone!" he laughed. "Lev? . . . Oh, there you are. No. Really! We did! We found . . . wait a second."

Without warning Gabriel burst into the kitchen, his face pale and his eyes wild. He was gesturing furiously with both hands. "Don't say anything about the box!" he whispered loudly. "You can say anything you want, but do not under any circumstance mention that box!"

Nicholas nodded quickly to let Gabriel know he understood. "Sorry, Lev. I've got some excited people here. I, uh, want you to do some back-testing on the material I'm going to send you, then start researching how we can set up a fund as a vehicle to trade. When I get back, we'll start looking at rolling stocks, the ones that always follow the direction of the market, to see if they correlate with the patterns we discovered. I have a theory that I can pick under-priced solid stocks and play them along with the forecasted trends. We'll look at bonds, too, since they usually move in the opposite direction of the stock indexes. I'm working on a long-term strategy of buying stocks on the up trends and bonds on the down . . . What? Yes! I told you it wasn't a 'random walk!' Now we've proven it! Oh, might as well look at currencies, too—chart them against the other two . . . No, not necessarily, but as quickly as you can. I'll help you when I get back."

He hung up the phone and looked at Gabriel. "What the hell is this all about, Gabe?" Alex, who was standing by the counter, pushed aside

Francesca's attempts to put an apron over his head so he could help with the bread dough. "Well, Gabe? What's the game?"

Gabriel massaged his temples with his fingertips. "I've just got a bad feeling about this whole thing. A really bad feeling. My father, who would never say anything ancient was worthless, said this box was worth nothing. And yet, it was sealed away in a secret room even I didn't know about."

Francesca let out a small groan and sank into a chair. No one but Cassandra noticed her ashen face.

Gabriel continued, his voice gravelly and low. "The documents seem to chronicle massive amounts of money made over centuries from a box that measures gravity. Somebody out there has this proprietary knowledge. Do you really think they want their game interfered with?" When no one answered, Gabriel caught and held Nicholas' gaze. "Put the programs on disks, Nicholas, and scrub my hard drive completely clean before you leave."

"Why?" Nicholas narrowed his eyes and squinted at his friend. "Who do you think is going to be digging into your computers?"

"I don't know who," shot back Gabriel, "but I am not going to take any chances. I have seen up-close and personal what money—lots of money—does to people." He lowered his voice. "And what people are willing to do to keep it."

"What about the box?" Nicholas inquired.

"Take the box and the documents, but please don't go around talking about the connections. Keep all this close to your vest until you find out everything you need to know."

Alex walked over and dropped himself down on the chair next to Nicholas, who was nervously tapping his foot on the floor. "Could we be sued or something?"

"It's the 'or something' I'm worried about," sighed Gabriel. "Lawsuits—who knows? You can be sued for walking outside these days. Technically and legally, the box belongs to the estate. As far as I know, everything here was legitimately purchased at some point in time. There is probably a sales receipt for it, or at least there should be." He fell silent and thought for a moment. "Alex, can you take the box out to have it appraised? There are several very reputable antique dealers in Charleston, and I am sure there is someone who deals in antiquities there. After all, it's my job to know the value of all the stuff in the mansion. Nobody will object to that. Just tell them you are doing it on my behalf. What do you think?"

"Ok," shrugged Alex. "Why?"

"It's important to me, and I would like it done."

"Sure, Gabe. I'll take it with me when I go home," Alex assured him. "What harm can come from it?"

℘

After Alex agreed to take the box with him back to Charleston, Gabriel left by the back door. The twins, still mystified by his behavior, headed upstairs to the office. Cassandra and Francesca were left alone in the kitchen. "Still want to make bread, or do you want to help me with those documents?" Cassandra asked, refilling her coffee.

Francesca bit her lip and rubbed her finger across the top of the old worn kitchen table Gabe had found in Ireland. She was remembering the first time she had met Alex. Even then, she knew that Alex liked living on the edge. The more time they spent together, the closer to the edge she found herself sliding, and she *liked* it. But, that was before they had children to think about. Nicholas and Cassandra would never let Alex get too far ahead of himself. Gabriel was probably just overreacting; he always did when it came to his father.

"No," she finally said with forced calm. "You work on the documents. I promised Gabe I would do some baking."

"Ok." Cassandra knew cooking was like therapy for her sister-in-law. Maybe she just wanted some time alone.

Cassandra carried her coffee into the living room, where she lit a fire. Sitting on the floor, she began sorting through the papers, placing the oldest-looking pages in a pile and arranged them in a chronological line that eventually stretched around much of the room. She had made copies in Gabe's office of the most fragile documents so she could avoid handling the originals.

She was looking at a copy of a fragment of papyrus when Gabriel walked into the room. "Hi Gabe," she said with a smile, trying to judge his state of mind. He looked more relaxed, and almost embarrassed. "Hello Cassandra. What are you doing?"

"I am digging through copies of these old documents we found in the room. I could sure use some help. Can you tell me what this is?" she asked, handing him a page.

"Sure, happy to oblige." He pulled off his wire-rimmed glasses and stuck them on top of his head. "Hmm." The original papyrus had obviously been part of a larger scroll at one time, as many of the hieroglyphs were only partially visible. Dominating it, however, was the glyph for Isis: 𓊨𓏏𓆇 Revered as the ancient Egyptian mother goddess, Isis was the feminine counterpart to Osiris, her husband.

"This fragment is about the cult of Isis," he explained. "She is still worshiped today. From the way this is written, I'd say it hails from about 560 BC, when the Isis mystery cults were at their height. The birth of Horus, her son, was celebrated on what we now call December 25. Another son, Aion, was born on January 6, which is Christmas for the Orthodox Church. In fact, they had many practices, such as baptism by water, which were later blended into Judeo-Christian beliefs. I always found this aspect of ancient Egypt quite fascinating. Wait a moment, I think I have something that might help you." Gabriel walked over to one of his tall bookshelves, quickly ran his finger along the spines of dozens of books, and finally pulled out a worn copy of *Biblical Archaeology Review*. He spent a few seconds thumbing through the pages until he found what he was looking for.

"Here is an interesting article by David Ulansy, "Solving the Mithraic Mysteries." As he was introducing the article to Cassandra, Nicholas and Alex walked downstairs quietly debating a programming question. When they heard Gabriel talking they skirted the old papers on the floor and found seats on the sofa behind Cassandra. No one interrupted Gabriel when he was in his element.

"Many scholars now accept that the early Christian church absorbed some of the Isis beliefs, such as resurrecting Osiris in three days. In fact, there were many Egyptian temples that had been originally dedicated to

Isis that the Church rededicated to Mary when Christianity swept across Egypt during the first century." Gabriel ignored Nicholas' snort of disapproval. "Now this part is interesting," he continued. "Look at this." He handed the page to Cassandra and pointed to a symbol:

"I've never seen this before, have you?" asked Gabriel.

Cassandra pondered the ellipse Gabriel indicated. It appeared to be a cartouche-style symbol. "No, I've never seen anything quite like this before," she admitted. "Aren't these cartouche symbols used as family crests?"

"I think sometimes, sure," he answered. "This one looks like an amalgamation of the glyphs for the sun, moon, and earth. Considering the secrecy of the mystery cults, it wouldn't surprise me if they had constructed their own set of symbols. It looks a bit like a scarab, which was also used by the early Christians as a resurrection symbol."

"How do you think this ties into our research?" She asked.

"Well, if some of the documents you are examining are associated with mystery cults, it means the trail you need to follow leads to Mithraism. You will then need to study whatever comes after them. I'm not too up on this, but you will be." He smiled and handed the journal to Cassandra. "It's my theory that we'd all be Mithraists if it weren't for its being such a secretive cult. Christianity was available to everybody, and eventually won out. However, the two have a lot in common. In fact, if I had been standing on the Palatine Hill in Rome two thousand years ago, I'd have put my money on the Mithraists."

"By the look of these documents," broke in Alex, "you'd be putting your money where the power moved through the ages. I'll make a copy of this article." Cassandra handed him the periodical and he climbed back up the stairs to Gabriel's office.

When he returned a few minutes later, he was holding an elaborate parchment written in Latin. "Oh, God!" Cassandra exclaimed. "I completely forgot I had left that up there."

Alex squatted on the floor next to her and pointed to the bottom of the parchment. "Look at this," he said, pointing near the bottom of the page. Cassandra gasped aloud. Nicholas leaned over get a better view. It was the same symbol Gabriel had pointed out on the more ancient parchment, small and faint, but unmistakably the same. "Let's see if we can find this same thing on other documents," suggested Alex as he reached for one of the piles. Nicholas and Cassandra joined him. Gabriel nodded approvingly as he stepped across the room and lifted a bottle of Aberlour from the shelf. "Anyone care to join me?" he asked. When his friends, deep in their search, shook their collective heads, Gabriel poured himself a glassful of the Speyside single-malt, drank deeply, capped the bottle, and put it away.

Within a short time they found the identical symbol on nearly every one of the ancient documents—and even some of the more modern ones. After the turn of the 20th century, when the documents were typed, the symbol took the form of a stamp before disappearing altogether. "They probably didn't have any way to print it, so they reverted to a stamp," conjectured Cassandra. "Somewhere along the line the stamp must have gotten lost or something. I can't find any trace of it after the early 1950s."

The news excited Cassandra and Gabriel almost as much as the project Alex and Nicholas were working on. "If we discover who the last owners were, maybe we'll be able to figure out how well they did in the markets," Alex offered with a glance at his brother.

"It's obvious from the documents somebody out there is already doing what you guys are going to do," Cassandra agreed, looking over at Gabriel, whose face had suddenly grown pensive.

"Well, there ought to be room for a couple more players," Nicholas said with a sly grin. "After all, we don't plan to take over the markets. We'll just take our little part and . . . buy a Lamborghini?" He smiled again and waited for Cassandra to respond.

"What? One of those Italian zoomsters that only belong on the Autobahn? You think you're going to drive that around Atlanta, the traffic capital of the world? Lot of fun that will be."

"I can drive it on 285," he responded.

"Okay, you can do that. It's a parking lot six hours every day anyway. You can drive in rush hour." She smiled at him. "How about putting it up on blocks and selling it in thirty years as a boutique item?"

"You got a ring. Already!"

"The ring won't kill me unless I choke on it. And it didn't cost . . . how much does a Lamborghini cost?"

"Well, it depends on which one you want. I want a Diablo Roadster."

"How much?"

The others were quiet, watching the couple banter. She stared at him until he finally cleared his throat and croaked, "Two-hundred and fifty thousand dollars, but lots more in *lire*," he added hastily.

"You are not suddenly going to become ostentatious new money," she said firmly. "You can reset a few priorities, but that's a little much. If you want a new car, I'd go for a Mercedes ML500 SUV. Something practical."

Alex muttered something about gas mileage and the men laughed loud enough to draw Francesca in to see what was going on. *Here's my rescue*, thought Nicholas. "Say, how would you like to drive around in a red Lamborghini this spring?"

"About as much as I'd like to open a restaurant specializing in fast food," Francesca answered without missing a beat. "You really shouldn't ask a liberated woman about a phallic-symbol car."

Alex roared with laughter so hard that tears rolled down his cheeks. Gabriel did the same, wiping scotch off his chin as he searched about for a napkin. "How about at least a test drive?" jibed Alex.

"How about helping me finish this bread," she poked back at him. Alex dutifully followed her into the kitchen, filling her in on the strange symbols they found on the documents.

Cassandra began carefully piling up the documents. "We should be getting out of your hair, Gabe. Have you got something I can put these in?"

Chapter 19

By the middle of the afternoon the suitcases were packed and standing on the porch. Alex had scrubbed Gabriel's hard drive and made CD backups for his laptop. "What's next?" he asked Nicholas as they stood on the shoveled porch, basking in the bright sunshine.

Nicholas shaded his eyes with his hand to keep down the glare reflecting from the shimmering fresh snow. "Why don't you test the rest of the phase inversion data when you get home—just to make sure we have it right. We can e-mail our stock strategies back and forth, and maybe I can drive up to Charleston this weekend after I finish out the semester. If we think we have it, we can start investing some money."

The couples loaded their belongings between Nicholas' Saab and Alex's ancient Subaru station wagon. Gabriel brought out the box last. He had wrapped it tightly inside a clean blanket and slipped it inside a heavy cardboard box, which he then carefully taped shut with a roll gun. Alex helped him load it into the back of the wagon. After a round of warm hugs they pulled out of Gabriel's driveway and wound their way out of the Biltmore Estate.

Gabriel waved until they were out of sight. "Goodbye, box," he whispered, leaning his head against a column. "Go in peace."

ঽ

"My," Cassandra sighed as they left the Asheville area and headed back toward Atlanta, "that ranked right up there with the 'most exciting weekend getaway' I have ever had. What about you, sailor?"

Nicholas kept his eye on the road and nodded thoughtfully. "I spent far too much time away from you, my dear, but it looks like these past few days might have been the most potentially profitable we have ever had." He shifted his eyes quickly into the back seat and spotted the atlas.

"Honey, can you grab the map for me? How about driving down in the mountains through Cashiers?" They had taken this route before, but never in the middle of the winter.

"Can you focus on driving that road? You won't chatter on about market trends?"

"I'll concentrate, I promise. I feel like I need to clear my head of all this."

She nodded in agreement. "This has certainly been one amazing weekend. A little veg time sounds good to me, too."

Ignoring the easier North Carolina Highway 25, which would have taken them on a smoother route through Greenville, they made for some of the highest peaks in the Smoky Mountains and then through the Nantahala National Forest. Traffic was almost non-existent—and they soon discovered why.

"Nicholas, the last time we came this way, it was summer. Don't they close some of the passes this time of year?"

"Oh, you're right! They might. It has warmed up a lot, so maybe they are still open," hoped Nicholas.

His wife tightened her seat belt. The two-lane road began to hairpin and she found herself mesmerized by the turns. The higher they climbed the colder the mountain air became. Cassandra shivered and turned up the heater. The narrow road seemed little more than a small ledge chopped out of bedrock. Huge icicles, many longer and wider than the car, clung stubbornly to the sides of the shady bands. Above them were snow-capped peaks, and just a few feet to the right was a 3,000-foot drop that often felt as though it was only inches from their wheels. At Cassandra's insistence Nicholas drove slower than usual, which was a good thing because patches of black ice had formed on the pavement.

Just after they passed a large rock outcropping, a grumbling dull roar flooded the car. "What the hell is that?" shouted Nicholas. He looked into the rear-view mirror and instinctively hit the gas pedal.

"Holy Christ! The mountain is coming down!" Cassandra screamed.

The mountain was not coming down, but a large piece of it was. The rock and snow slide completely buried the road immediately behind them. Cassandra watched as boulders as large as small houses bounced off the mountainside, crashed onto the road, and fell thousands of feet to the valley floor below. The avalanche missed the car by only a few yards. With his heart pounding in his throat, Nicholas pulled into a turnout and they both climbed out to look back at the damage.

"Maybe this wasn't such a great idea," said Cassandra, shivering as the wind howled through the ridgeline. "Nicholas, we were only a few seconds away from being killed."

"Hard to disagree with that," he said, stomping his feet to keep the cold away. "You're the one with the name of a Greek prophetess. Are we headed for greater danger?" he asked.

She stood there for a moment, rocking back and forth on her boots, heel to toe. "We shouldn't be doing this."

"I remain unconvinced."

"That is something Alex would say," she shot back, adding, "Nobody believed my namesake, either."

As they turned to go back to their car, a siren echoed through the peaks, a haunting mechanical sound completely out of place in the wilderness. Its rise and fall swept closer with each passing second. It was hard to tell which side of the rockslide the siren was on. As they opened the doors, a North Carolina state trooper pulled around the bend and rolled to a stop next to them. He took in the rockslide for a few seconds before turning his reflective shades in their direction.

"You folks sure picked the wrong time for a scenic drive," he said with some sarcasm in his voice. "These roads will kill you. You drove right by a 'road closed' sign just a quarter-mile back."

"We're sorry, officer. We didn't see any sign," Cassandra said with a confidence that she didn't feel. "The road seemed ok. . ."

The trooper gave her an impatient look, "Oh, they are fine—if you are accustomed to driving around rock slides every day." He motioned toward the tumble of boulders that littered the road behind her. "This ain't no rally race. We've got unstable places like this all up and down this stretch of road, what with the weather acting so strange, temperatures in the 60s one day and 20s the next. Y'all had better follow me down through the next few passes."

Nicholas reluctantly did as he was told. He could not help but think how well a Diablo Roadster might have handled this terrain. He turned to his wife with his eyes twinkling. "Let's find someplace in Highlands to spend the night. You think the High Hampton Inn is open?"

"You never miss the opportunity to get me in one of those feather beds, do you?"

Nicholas flashed her a devilish grin. She stared at him for a moment in thought. "I don't think so, but if I can get Ann Austin, she might be able to find a cabin for us."

Cassandra pulled out her cell phone. "And I have reception!" she exclaimed. "Might be a good sign." She punched in the number for her old friend, whose real estate company specialized in luxury mountain rentals. Ann's great-great-great-grandparents had been one of the first pioneer families to move into the Cashiers' area, and her firm was helping to make it possible for modern day families to enjoy the beautiful mountains.

Ann was happy to hear from Cassandra, and after a few seconds of chit-chat booked them in a guest cabin across the road from the venerable High Hampton Inn. By the time they parted ways with the State Trooper, a fog was settling in. They inched toward Cashiers. "This is worse than the black ice and rock slides," Nicholas complained. "This fog is so thick I can't see the windshield wipers."

"Just keep your eyes on the road." Cassandra's hand gripped the armrest so hard the whiteness of her knuckles matched her diamond rings.

"I'm trying!" Nicholas practically shouted, moving forward to the crunch of gravel, feeling his way along. In the other lane, huge headlights came into view and quickly went out again. They saw the word Greyhound glide by them in the mist. Finally, they reached the driveway to the guest cottage and crept up to the parking pad. Ann had come ahead of them to turn on the heat and light the gas fireplace. "There is nothing— *nothing*—like an old friend," Cassandra sighed before heading off for a long hot shower.

Mesmerized by the fire, Nicholas gazed into the flickering red and yellow flames. Now that he was warm and safe, his thoughts were drawn inexorably back to the box. He hadn't said anything to Alex, but he wished he had the artifact with him. Shortly before dawn earlier that day, while everyone else was still fast asleep, he had slipped quietly into Gabriel's office to sit and stare at the granite-topped mystery. Antiquities were Cassandra's and Gabriel's field, but even he could see that this box was more than just a tool. Its shadowy history was a seductive force. The box had occupied his thoughts, rousing him from a deep sleep, and luring him out of a warm bed into a dark office. The financial records Cassandra had examined so carefully in Gabriel's living room told something of the human side of the story. Real people had used this box and profited from its secrets. It was bizarre to think that he and his brother were about to join this unique fellowship.

"Is it moral?"

Francesca's question rang inside his head. He felt somewhat bemused by his reaction to the whole thing. His first response was to simply face empirical challenges like the scientist that he was—and leave any underlying consequences to others.

"Is it moral?"

He shivered even though his shirt was toasty hot and his forehead was sweating. He felt—*knew*—deep down that a large mantle of responsibility had been placed on his shoulders. His own hands had placed it there. It was all too easy to fantasize about buying a sports car and getting rich beyond his wildest dreams, but it was something else altogether to fully grasp the magnitude of the journey they had embarked upon—and the potential consequences of their actions.

Is . . .

Nicholas closed his eyes for a moment and thought about his brother. Neither of them would ever admit it, but he knew Alex was thinking the same thing.

it . . .

He could *feel* his brother's excitement in his own veins, but he was experiencing one thing that Alex was not. His twin was excited and challenged by the mystery and science of their discovery. He, on the other hand, was a little frightened, but he could not pinpoint exactly why.

. . . moral?

Nicholas did his best to shrug off his unease. There was a lot of work to do before they could start counting money. He rose, stretched in front of the crackling wood, and yawned deeply.

Cassandra was right. It had indeed been one hell of a weekend.

Chapter 20

When Nicholas walked into his office Tuesday morning, he stopped for a moment to witness academic bliss unfold before his eyes. The enigmatic Lev Foust and the beautiful Felicia Theobald were bent over a stack of spreadsheets, which was not unusual except for the entangled romantic embrace. When Lev looked up and spotted his boss standing in the doorway, his mouth fell open with a gasp.

"Don't move, you are just fine where you are," said Nicholas with a straight face, stifling the laughter welling up inside. A crimson stain spread across Felicia's face as she slowly slid her chair away from Lev's.

Nicholas tossed his L. L. Bean canvas briefcase onto his immaculate desk. "Been at it again, huh Lev?" he asked, raising an eyebrow and shaking his head. "Always cleaning up after me. He'll clean up after you, too," he nodded toward Felicia.

"He already does," she said in a low, heavy Parisian accent.

"Thanks for babysitting for final exams," Nicholas said as he eased into his desk chair.

By now Lev had collected himself sufficiently to muster a response. "Sure, it was a piece of cake."

Nicholas opened his briefcase, rummaged about inside for a moment, and then leaned over and flipped through his in-basket. The amount of paperwork generated within the university system was staggering. Whoever claimed the personal computer would make the world a paperless place should be shot, he thought. "You know, Lev, Cassandra and I were thinking that maybe we should pick an evening over the holidays when you can come over for dinner." He paused for a second and looked at both Lev and Felicia, adding, "Both of you of course. My wife loves to exercise her French, and we should celebrate our findings."

"Thanks, Dr. Shepard. That's very nice of you." Lev looked at Felicia, who nodded her assent. "Ah, just what have you found?" Lev leaned forward curiously.

Nicholas tried to remain calm and forthright, but the excitement pressing inside was almost irresistible. The more he spoke, explaining the long weekend at the Biltmore Estate, the more animated he became. "We just stumbled onto this secret room," he told them, his assistants' eyes opening with excitement and, in Lev's case, at least a tad of skepticism. "We never expected to find something that would change our lives. But we sure did." Nicholas stopped for a few seconds to add a touch of drama to the moment.

"What?" they both demanded.

In the excitement of the moment Nicholas forgot Gabriel's warning, and the words tumbled out of him. "This sounds crazy, I know, but we found what turned out to be an ancient Egyptian box! We think it was a Nileometer."

"A what?" interjected Lev.

"A tool that measured the highs and lows of the Nile." He stopped to see whether his assistant understood.

Lev shot a puzzled look at Felicia as if to ask, "*Is he serious or just crazy?*"

Nicholas continued. "Anyway, inside it there's a crystal structure, the mechanical algorithm that predicted how much the Nile would rise and fall. We figured out that this box actually measures gravity, so it could tell whoever knew how to use it how to predict when the Nile would flood, which, as you might guess, was an important thing for them to know.

Felicia was looking down at the floor when Lev attempted to cut in again. "Ah, Dr. Shepard, boxes don't measure. . ."

"Wait, Lev. There's more," Nicholas cut him off, nearly breathless in his excitement. He slid his chair back and stood up, gesturing with his hands. "We also found some old financial documents in the same room—reams of them—which are ledgers of the money the box's former owners made using it!"

Speechless, Lev and Felicia sat there unsure how to respond, their eyes wide open, though whether in disbelief or outright shock, it was difficult to know. Nicholas nodded his head. "I know, this sounds nuts. Just hear me out, ok?"

Lev shrugged. "Sure, Dr. Shepard. We're listening—and you're right, it is a bit out there." *This can't be true*, thought Lev. *This better not be true.*

Nicholas cleared his throat and continued from behind his chair, his hands gripping the back hard enough to turn his knuckles white. "Alex and I decided to match its predictive ability with the American stock markets cycles. It matched . . . perfectly!"

"What!" Lev shouted as his body tensed in his seat. "What matched perfectly?"

"The gravitational effects on earth and the highs and lows of the financial markets," responded Nicholas. "We're developing a trading method to capitalize on the market's direction, whether up, down, long-term or short-term. We plan to start by trading weekly trends with futures contracts, and then hopefully, with your help, we can add security positions to the mix."

Lev's dark eyes were glued on Nicholas' face. The assistant sat motionless like a coiled snake, tightly wound and ready to spring. "This is impossible! You might have found an old box, but no one has ever been able to predict the stock market," he maintained hoarsely. "What are you doing that no one else can?"

Nicholas rubbed his hands together in glee. "Over the weekend, Alex and I completed a systems check using this discovery and a program he had already created. We got yearly stock market forecasts that were one hundred percent accurate and monthly forecasts that were nearly one hundred percent accurate. Our weekly forecasts weren't originally that great, but Alex's system identification program, which he calls *Xyber9*, projects nearly perfect market forecasts to trade by. *That's* what we're doing that no one else can do, and with a little more research, there's no limit to what we can do."

Felicia was sitting quietly, knowing the discussion was really between the professor and the student. She was merely a fortunate observer. Lev exhaled loudly, stood up, and walked to the window, trying to restore his deferential student persona. He leaned his forehead against the chilly glass and closed his eyes. Inside he was whirling in panic. *If this is true*, he thought, *this cannot be good.*

"Amazing, isn't it?" asked Nicholas, who was surprised Lev was not jumping up and down in excitement. "Aren't you excited?"

"Yes . . . of course I am. Yes," replied Lev unconvincingly. He managed a small but forced smile. *Just stay calm*, he thought. "It is all a bit—well, overwhelming, don't you think?" He nervously licked his lips and forced a smile. "Dr. Shepard, just let us know what else you want us to do. We've already found some good rolling stocks and plotted the bond markets back to about 1980, like you asked."

Felicia nodded and decided to speak. "We've looked at currencies, and you're right—the Fed does interfere with the dollar, but we found it follows somewhat of a distinct pattern. The dollar usually moves opposite the market."

Both the graduate students knew as well as Nicholas that the Federal Reserve and strategists from foreign countries manipulate currencies. Lev, however, was aware that some of the world's financial leaders did much the same thing—but he was not about to tip his hand. Drawing a breath and collecting himself, he started gathering up the scattered documents on the table in front of him. It was a nervous gesture, but since Lev was always straightening up, no one noticed that his hands were shaking. "So what else can we do?" he asked again, doing his level best to keep his voice from cracking.

"I'm going to give you some charts and graphs and some predictions for the short term over the next few weeks. I want you to plot the foreign markets as you did for the Dow, the NASDAQ and the S&P 500, and calculate the lag time between the American market moves and the Asian and European markets. I want to see if the dog wags its tail like I think it does."

Felicia tipped her head to one side, looking confused. "Americans have as many idioms as the French! What does that one mean?" She turned her deep blue eyes toward her professor.

"Sorry," smiled Nicholas. "It just means that when the American markets move, the world markets will follow. I want to know the delay time and if the percentage of movement correlates."

When she nodded in understanding, Nicholas continued. "Next, we're going to do some test trading in real time. We'll buy the S&P 500 index—the Spiders—and on the downtrends we'll sell S&P futures contracts as a hedge. Alex and I figure we can make between 25 and 40 percent on a yearly basis—to begin with! However, that percentage will eventually become exponential because at the end of every downtrend, we'll take the profits from the futures and buy more shares of the S&P 500, which will give us extra earnings when the market ticks upward again. As an extra benefit, our gains will be tax-free because we're not selling any shares of the stock index."

Lev looked like a freight train had just hit him. "I know, Lev, it is brilliant," grinned Nicholas. "You guys get to work on the foreign markets, and I'll work on setting up the trading methods."

Felicia nodded as she finished taking notes in her expensive leather notebook. Lev pursed his lips and returned a slow nod and an encouraging smile, but his heart was beating so fast and loud he could feel the blood pumping in his ears. He breathed a sigh of relief when Nicholas excused himself in search of the department's ancient secretary, so she could decipher her spidery scrawl on a pink phone message sheet.

Lev walked over to the small refrigerator in the corner, opened the door, and withdrew a cold can of Coke. He popped the top and took a long draw. His head was spinning and he felt light-headed, clammy, and feverish all at once. He wondered if he was going to throw up.

"Lev, this is the most exciting thing I have ever heard!" exclaimed Felicia, who could barely keep from jumping up and down like a small child in a candy store. Her face was flush with excitement. "I can't believe this is really happening!"

"Me either," he said dourly.

His tone surprised her. "What's wrong? Something is wrong."

Taking her small hand in his, he gave it a little squeeze and a smile. My god, he thought, she was so beautiful and so smart. She was going to make the perfect wife. For a change, his father would be delighted with his choice.

"No, everything is fine. I am just trying to digest Dr. Shepard's discovery," Lev sighed. He tapped her notes with a long thin finger. "We'd better divide this up. You take the Western European markets, and I'll take the Asian ones."

He decided he was in no hurry to call his father.

Chapter 21

 After getting Lev and Felicia started on their assignments, Nicholas finished a stack of departmental paperwork and left early for the day. He kicked himself several times for revealing so much of their find to his grad students.

How could he have been so careless? *Neither presents the sort of threat Gabriel worried about,* he thought as he negotiated his car out of the tight faculty parking lot. He just felt bad that he had ignored Gabriel's warning. By the time he was sitting at the first stoplight, he decided it was best to work on the project from his home office. After all, anything he put on the university computer was fair game to any number of people.

Nicholas put on his cell phone headset and called his brother from the car. "You ready to start? Got the money?"

Pause. "Nicholas?" asked Alex

"Your twenty-five grand and mine should be a decent entrée. We'll just open a securities and futures account with TradeStation Securities. I am on my way home now."

The brothers would still have to sign the securities and other documents required by the trading firm to confirm their partnership, which would give each the right to call in or electronically trade the account individually. The money would be wired to the securities bank used by the firm, and it would take a few days before the go-ahead to start trading would arrive.

Alex was making pancakes for the kids when Nicholas called. "And good morning to you too," Alex laughed.

"And to you, dear brother," laughed Nicholas. "Now we have to make the hard decision. We have to agree that whatever the outcome is for any trade we make, we should always trust the forecasted trend and take the win or loss."

Alex took a long breath. "I know. I have been thinking about that. There will be many times the forecast will disagree with what everyone else is saying, and what our gut believes is right." Static interfered with the call for a couple seconds. "Nicholas? Still there? I agree. We give up control and trust the statistics, which tell us we should succeed at least 83 percent of the time."

The voice on the other end did not respond. "Come on Nicholas, if we are going to do it let's go for the gold! What do you think about calling it the 'Let it Ride Account?'"

That bit of humor drew a laugh from the twin. "That's good, Alex. Ok, done. But," and there was another long pause. "Did I tell you what happened to this guy at work?"

"No, what?"

"He made a small fortune in the market."

"How?"

"He started with a large one!" Nicholas guffawed at the old chestnut as his brother groaned. "Don't worry Alex, our trading strategy will hold up so long as the box holds water. Or whatever that liquid is!"

The brothers were ready and the plan was in place. After several long late night phone calls, both agreed Nicholas would do all the trading to start with. Now that they had familiarized themselves with Trade-Station's ordering procedures, the whole issue of trading in the markets did not appear as complex. The order bar platform was simple: either of them could just enter the symbol they wanted to trade, the number of contracts, and the buy or sell order. In the event neither of them was at a computer, a simple phone call to a floor trader at the Chicago Mercantile Exchange could complete any transaction they wanted to make. The idea of leveraged futures positions really excited them. "It takes less money to enter the market, and we can leverage ten times the investment," explained Nicholas. "If we follow the simple *Xyber9* forecast, the odds are in favor of large gains and small losses."

ॐ

School was winding down for the Christmas holidays and Nicholas was busy closing out the semester. He was not too busy, however, to notice that both his graduate students were champing at the bit to get their holidays started. Lev had apparently invited Felicia to go to New York City to meet his family, and she was anxious to make a good impression. Their anxiety was palpable, which Nicholas found amusing in a rather tender way. He recalled announcing his involvement with Cassandra to his parents. Even though the pair had been best friends since grammar school, it had been enough to make both of them goofy with nerves. His parents had just chuckled and told them they had known this was going to happen for years, and would have been more surprised if it had not!

Lost in the memory, Nicholas walked down the hall for the teachers' lounge, where the free coffee beckoned. He was unaware Cassandra was heading for his office.

Although Cassandra and Nicolas were going to spend Christmas in Charleston, she was determined to put up a tree and decorate their condo. Unbeknownst to him, Cassandra had decided to kidnap her husband that afternoon and go pick out a fresh tree.

She was about to open office door when she realized it was ajar and voices insider were raised in a heated discussion. She froze, her hand gripping the doorknob. She carefully uncurled her fingers and listened. The male voice was Lev's, of that she was sure. The other voice was a female's, and when it broke into angry French she guessed her identity as well.

"I don't understand what your father has to do with any of this!" the woman said.

"You don't have to understand," he replied hotly. "It isn't for you to understand!"

"I need to know, I need to understand if you want me to go through with this!" *A stubborn woman,* thought Cassandra admiringly.

"It will only take a moment," Lev explained, his voice taking on a softer tone as he began pleading with her.

"No! Not unless you tell me why." *You go, girl.* Cassandra's smile was erased in a heartbeat and was nearly replaced with a scream when she felt a firm tap on her shoulder, followed by a soft voice in her ear, "Learning anything?"

She turned, startled and embarrassed to be caught eavesdropping outside her husband's office door. Before she could respond, Nicholas laughed and guided her into the office while holding firmly onto her elbow. "Hey, look who I found skulking about in the hallway. You know Lev," he said, nodding in the direction of his assistant, "and this is Felicia Theobald."

Cassandra quickly regained her composure and smiled warmly at both. Felicia, who had been standing stiffly by the window, extended her hand. "Bonjour, Madame Shepard." Her voice was lovely, her manner polite but without warmth.

Cassandra answered in French and watched as Felicia started to relax. To Cassandra's secret satisfaction, Lev appeared uncomfortable, and she wondered if he suspected that she had overheard their conversation. *Good,* she thought. *Keep him on his toes.* Nicholas, of course, noticed none of this.

"I've come to kidnap you, darling," Cassandra announced blithely, grabbing her husband's leather jacket.

He looked up, his computer glasses suspended on the end of his nose. For a moment Cassandra thought he looked young and sweet. *Ah, the Christmas spirit,* she thought. It certainly brought out the excessive sentiment hiding within her. "Come along, dear. We are going to go get a tree. Today."

"Oh . . . fine." Nicholas allowed her to drag him off in search of the perfect Christmas tree, leaving his assistants alone in his office. As soon as the door swung shut, the tension that had only lingered in the air bloomed anew. Refusing to look Lev in the eye, Felicia gathered up her work and reached for her coat.

"I'm sorry," Lev whispered softly.

She turned to find him sitting with his head bowed. A part of her wanted to walk out the door, but she needed answers. Maybe now she could get them.

She took a deep breath and began. "Just tell me why you wanted me to ask my friend to hack into Dr. Shepard's computer. His encrypted files are none of our business, and they are certainly none of your father's business." She could feel the anger boiling up inside her all over again.

"I can't fully explain it," Lev protested.

"I need a better answer than that."

He lifted his head and looked at her. A lock of dark hair fell over his forehead and for a brief moment she swore he looked as though he might break out in tears. Instead, he shook his head angrily and snapped at her, "This project of Dr. Shepard's could present a danger to my father and his clients! Not a random walk!" he hissed sarcastically. "Felicia, don't you see the effect his theory, or discovery—or whatever you want to call it!—might have on the market if someone with Dr. Shepard's reputation makes this sort of claim?"

Lev rose from his chair and banged his fist down on the table. "My God! What if he actually makes money? What then? What if he proves his claims to be scientifically empirical?"

Felicia's eyes widened in disbelief. "What then, indeed? That would be a good thing! I think you are making too much of this." Lev glared at her as she approached him, softly putting her hand on his arm. "This isn't going to happen overnight. And, what if it isn't a 'random walk?' This is an incredible discovery, and we are here to play a part in it!" She made an effort to smile. "Your loyalty to your father and his clients is admirable, but don't you owe Dr. Shepard some loyalty as well?"

She was right, of course. So far, this all just seemed like dumb luck with an unproven theory attached to it. Nicholas Shepard was a very smart man, but he was no Malachi Foust. For now, decided Lev, he would wait and see what happened. Shepard wasn't going to run out and advertise his discovery, and so far only a few people even knew about the box. He and his brother hadn't even made any money yet. Maybe Felicia was right; he was overreacting. He gave her a small smile in return.

His father would know what to do.

ঽ

Cassandra was seated cross-legged on the floor in the midst of tumbled Christmas boxes. "It's so festive and so sad at the same time. I miss my parents and yours always spend the holidays in the sunny Southwest." She looked up into the limbs of the huge Noble Fir they had managed to drag into the elevator up to the third floor and sighed dreamily.

"Look, here's Dad's favorite ornament!" Nicholas held up a miniature tobacco leaf dipped in gold, a remnant of the days when the boys traveled around to his tobacco farms. Nicholas smiled reminiscently. "You know, we had some good Christmases, but my mom was always worried about spending so much money needlessly. Christmas being so commercial and all. I am not sure what they would say if they knew what we were up to."

"Well, for starters, I'm not sure they'd believe it," she pointed out, handing him a box of jewel-toned balls. Cassandra rose to adjust a silver bell that was bending the branch. "By the way, Nicholas, how many people have you talked to about this? I mean, what exactly did you tell Lev and Felicia?"

Nicholas shrugged. "I mentioned something to the Chair, of course, although he definitely doesn't believe me." He grinned. The Chairman of the Economics Department was so close to retirement that he rarely kept up with what the faculty was doing. "He's just counting the days and abiding by the 'don't rock the boat' philosophy."

"And your grad students?" Nicholas' eyes gave it all away. She recognized that look of guilt a mile away. "Please tell me that you didn't say anything about the box. We all heard Gabe ask you not to tell anyone."

"Ok, I did say a *little* something about the box." He was not telling the complete truth and he knew Cassandra knew it too.

"Nicholas! How could you!" She shook her head at his sheepish grimace and clenched her jaw tight. Cassandra was genuinely angry.

"I *know*. I guess I was just so excited it slipped out," he tried to explain. Nicholas picked up a box of colored icicles. "Honestly, honey, I don't think it matters. Remember, they are each a dissertation away from being my colleagues. If they are going to help me with my research, I had to give them all the information."

She looked doubtful and shook her head. Nicholas crawled across the floor and took her in his arms. "You worry too much, my love. Be of good cheer, tis' the season, trust your fellow man, and all that," he said teasingly.

She had been debating whether to tell Nicholas about the conversation she had overheard in the office, but it seemed silly now. Besides, she was not even sure what the argument was about. "You're probably right," she sighed, snuggling into his warm embrace.

"How many of those sterling silver ornaments do we have?" he asked suddenly, looking over her shoulder at the crowded tree.

"Lots. I guess I was sort of a compulsive collector there for a few years, but I haven't bought any for awhile."

"Tell me about it," he moaned, feigning a painful memory. "I was the one who drove you to all those after-Christmas sales!"

"That's as close as I ever got to being one of those mad women diving for bargains and knocking people out of the way," Cassandra laughed.

Nicholas drew her down beside him on the sofa and pushed yet another box of ornaments to the side. "It's all right. I love the way you decorate. Everything looks so festive, so warm."

"You are a dear. With a big mouth . . . but a dear no less," she whispered, reaching down and pulling out a small box tucked beneath the sofa. "Merry Christmas."

"Uh, oh." He sat up and eyed her warily. "And what is this?"

"I think you are supposed to open it," she replied.

He unwrapped it slowly and peered under the lid of the box as if the box would explode if he lifted it too quickly. Inside was a perfect replica of a Lamborghini Diablo Roadster. He laughed out loud, delighted with her joke.

"Why don't you open one?" he said, knowing full well she could not wait to open the presents. Cassandra was worse than a six-year-old when it came to opening gifts. He handed her one so beautifully wrapped she knew he hadn't done it himself. Nicholas could not wrap a gift with straight corners if his life depended on it.

She tore into it to reveal a diamond and tanzanite necklace to match the ring she bought in Asheville.

"Oh my God, it is lovely!" she shrieked, grabbing his face and kissing him hard on the mouth. She broke away with a flushed look on her face. "Let's open all the presents!" she cried out.

With a half-decorated tree standing before them, they ripped open all of the gifts they had purchased for one another. Cassandra held her breath as Nicholas opened the hand-tailored linen shirts and gold cuff links she had picked out. He sat with a wide grin on his face while she laughed gaily.

Later, while sipping champagne and nibbling on the goodies they had picked up from EatZies, they snuggled into each other's arms beneath the glow of their tree, enjoying its pungent scent.

It was an altogether perfect world.

Chapter 22

With a nod, Malachi Foust greeted his son. His interest was drawn to the slender woman at his side. "Dad, this is Felicia Theobald."

Felicia shook his bony hand firmly and looked straight into his eyes. She was stunned by his vigor and youthful appearance. *He must be in his late sixties*, she thought, but he was in excellent shape—trim, muscular, fit. His closely cut iron gray hair and the fine wrinkles around his blue eyes only added to his charm. Lev was handsome in his own right, but he lacked his father's subtle sophistication. Felicia took a deep breath and smiled.

Though startled, Malachi did not outwardly display any emotion beyond a soft, pleasant smile. She was far more attractive than he had expected. It was apparent from her expensive clothing and posture that she was not at all like the other girls with whom his son had become enamored. She was quick to shake his hand, and her gaze never wavered. Even her smile appeared genuine. Malachi decided to like her. He would of course investigate her background, but she passed the initial test with flying colors.

The three were standing in the round domed foyer of a Park Avenue apartment. Above them, hanging from the richly finished walls, hung huge garlands of evergreens. In the center of the cream-colored marble floor was a fragrant Christmas tree studded with gold balls, gold ribbon, and tiny gold ornaments. Felicia examined the tree closely and saw that even the lights had gold globes. The tree looked as if King Midas himself had blessed it. *And*, she thought, looking at Lev's father, *perhaps he had!*

Felicia took Malachi's proffered arm and he led her into the living room. One of the servants made a timely appearance. "Take these suitcases into adjoining guestrooms," Lev demanded, his voice sharp and unpleasant. Without waiting for a reply he turned on his heels and walked briskly after his father and Felicia.

Lev knew that the little golden tree was just a tease for the real thing. He watched Felicia's face as she took in the living room's fifteen-foot ceilings, its pair of immense Baccarat chandeliers illuminating the exquisite walls Malachi, all of which he had imported from France. The wall panels were entirely gilded, with finely cut pilasters filling the spaces between panels boasting Romanesque paintings. Stunning Lapis lazuli fireplaces anchored each end of the room. Scrutinizing her from every side of the room were a dozen family portraits. The floor-to-ceiling windows, hung with gold silk draperies in a formal Empire Revival style, overlooked Central Park. Even the ceiling itself was remarkable, covered with paintings attributed to Simon Vouet, circa 1637, which had been carefully removed from the ceiling of a Paris mansion, shipped across the Atlantic Ocean, and installed here, on Park Avenue.

Under their feet was a magnificent floor with herringbone patterns in walnut duplicated from Louis XIV's court at Versailles. The furniture, although not antique, was hand-crafted to fit the room and its modern-day occupants. Rich silks and cut-velvet upholstery covered the comfortable sofas and chairs that made up four separate seating areas by the windows and close to the fireplaces.

The *pièce de résistance* was not one but six huge Christmas trees, strategically placed around the room. Lev watched as his father closely studied Felicia's reaction to the ornately decorated trees. Each represented a different country, and all of them were surrounded by packages whose wrappings matched the theme of their respective evergreen. To her credit, Felicia focused on twin *buffets a deux corps* filled with Sevres porcelains. "I feel quite at home here already!" she announced to Malachi's delight.

For Lev, however, the most precious thing in the room was the woman in the wheelchair by the windows. "Mother," he said simply when his eyes fell upon her, crossing the room quickly to lay a gentle kiss on her cheek.

She smiled warmly. "My son, how are you?" She turned her gaze to the stunningly lovely young woman standing next to her husband. "And who did you bring with you?" She held her hand out to Felicia. "I am Constantina Foust."

She spoke with the barest hint of a Greek accent, and as Felicia drew near she could see where Lev had gotten his dark eyes and hair. She was somewhat surprised that Lev had not told her that his mother was confined to a wheelchair, and hoped Mrs. Foust had not noticed her initial shock.

Constantina took her small, fine hand in both of hers and gave her a deep smile. The handshake lasted several seconds as she held Felicia's gaze. *She is sizing me up*, Felicia thought with a start, *and not even trying to hide it. Mon dieu,* Felicia realized, this is a formidable woman, and her handicap has done nothing to diminish her.

"Oh, I almost forgot," added Lev with a bored flip of his hand. "This is Mika Hunter, one of my father's colleagues." Felicia gently removed her hand from Constantina's grip and turned to see a Japanese woman in a black Prada suit enter the room. Mika took her hand. "We are so pleased you are here," she said, bowing to Felicia.

Felicia bowed just slightly deeper. "It is my honor to meet you."

"Please, everyone sit down," said Malachi, motioning them toward one of the expansive sofas overlooking the park. Lev pushed his mother's wheelchair next to the end of the sofa, close enough so he could hold her hand while he sat. Malachi remained standing next to one of the fireplaces. A manservant entered with a tray of small aperitifs while Constantina asked Felicia about their trip to New York. The conversation turned to other polite topics, such as the weather and the view of the Park. Everything was proper and cordial. The reception was not cold, but it was not altogether warm, either.

"This room is simply stunning," Felicia said to Constantina. It was Malachi who answered. He explained how he had been present at the destruction of a Paris mansion to make way for Les Halles' reconstruction some years before, and had rescued the interior architecture. "It was rather remarkable," he said, leaning on the mantle and looking around the room. "It was almost as if this room had been born to receive it. Everything fit almost perfectly. If you look closely enough, you might see where the craftsmen had to add a little here and there, but essentially it is a Parisian room of the 17th century."

As far as Felicia was concerned, French treasures belonged in France, but she just smiled politely at the man she hoped one day to make her father-in-law. His movements were smooth and effortless. His eyes flickered about the room, taking in the occupants as he explained how the room came to be. It suddenly dawned on her that she was staring at the man, her eyes drawn in his direction; it was difficult to turn away. She darted quick looks at the others, hoping no one had noticed. They hadn't. Lev was in a quiet conversation with his mother, and Mika was listening politely as Malachi spoke.

Why had Lev been so reluctant to introduce her to his father? He was perfectly charming, thought Felicia. It became clear very quickly, however, that someone else thought so, too. Mika wasn't just looking at Malachi. Her gaze was fixated on him. Indeed, it never left him. She's a very exotic and beautiful woman, thought Felicia. Was there something going on between them? It was obvious Lev didn't care for her very much, and Constantina paid her no attention at all.

A servant, this time a tall woman, interrupted the civilized and somewhat stilted conversation to announce dinner. Once again, Malachi took Felicia's arm and escorted her into the dining room, which was decorated in the distinctive blond and ebony woods of the Viennese Beidermeier furniture. A huge 18th Century Florentine chandelier made up of dozens of quartz crystals bathed the table with light from real candles. The glow sparkled on the Baccarat goblets, the ornately patterned Sevres china, and the exquisite dinner silver.

Felicia was seated with Mika to her left and Malachi at the end of the table on her right. Lev sat next to his father and there was a space for Constantina's wheelchair to slip in next to her son. Felicia hoped this would give her an opportunity to speak with Lev's mother now that she was seated across from her. Unfortunately, the conversation took a sudden and unpleasant turn.

"How are your studies progressing, Lev?" asked Malachi.

Lev turned away from his mother and held his father's gaze for a few seconds. "Rather dull, really, and not very challenging. Thankfully, I have only my dissertation left to finish." He turned back to his mother.

"Dull?" blurted out Felicia without thinking. "Lev, how can you call the stock market prediction research we are doing for Professor Shepard dull? His discovery—." Felecia quickly lifted her hand to her mouth before pulling it away just as swiftly. Lev's mouth fell open as he shot a sharp glance at Felicia and closed his eyes tightly.

A fork of orange-glazed carrots stopped a few inches from Malachi's mouth. He held it there for a moment before inserting the food, chewing thoughtfully, and swallowing. The sound of the silver being set down on his plate echoed in the silent room.

"Stock market prediction research? Discovery?" The father's icy blue stare settled on Lev. "That sounds quite interesting. Perhaps someone should fill me in?"

Chapter 23

Francesca loved going over the top during Christmas. She didn't care that their house had more lights, wreaths, and bows than any other along the Battery, Charleston, South Carolina's scenic and historic waterfront, or that a handful of the town's snobbier class commented about it in sarcastic whispers each year.

Despite his pleas, Alex spent days each year standing precariously on an extended aluminum ladder stringing strands of lights along the 200-year-old home's long porches, windows, and roof lines. Nearly every room glowed with a luminous freshly cut tree, resplendent with bright holiday decorations. Rosemary had a little tree in her bedroom, which she decorated with tiny glass ballerinas her parents had purchased in Czechoslovakia. Harrison preferred his super hero tree, which this year featured a wide assortment of items from the red and black Spiderman franchise. Even the kitchen boasted an evergreen, adorned with German glass fruits and vegetables, dried fruits, and baby's breath.

The lights and trees were just the tip of Francesca's Christmas iceberg. Replicas of 18th Century Italian angels hung from ceilings, cranberry ropes laced the walls, and glass balls atop candle holders created magnificent centerpieces. She delighted in crafting garlands of real fruit and greenery, Magnolia leaves with dried flowers, holly, and pine boughs. The wreaths infused the house with a particularly festive scent, although it was nothing compared to the aroma of cookies baking and the vat of wassail on the back of the stove, with its warm smell of apple, cinnamon, and nutmeg.

This year Alex had something else to decorate. To Francesca's amusement, he placed a big red bow on top of the Egyptian box. His work desk was a contemporary affair of blackened ash, and the box made a splendid addition.

"Not too hard to spot, is it?" remarked Nicholas, as he and Cassandra drove slowly past the house near twilight. They parked around the corner on Meeting Street. When she got out of the car, Cassandra took a long breath, held it, and slowly exhaled. "I always feel like we're about to experience Christmas on steroids." Nicholas laughed, offered his arm, and together they approached the house. Harrison spotted them first and bounded off the porch to greet them.

"Aunt Cassandra! Uncle Nicholas! I'm going to get a puppy!" he shouted, grabbing their arms and pulling them toward the house. Without stopping, Nicholas offered his sister-in-law a smile and hug as he headed up to see Alex. She and Cassandra just exchanged looks.

"Well, anyway, welcome! Merry Christmas!" Francesca chuckled. "Who's more excited this year—Harrison about his puppy, or Nicholas about the box?"

Her kitchen looked like a cookie factory, with cooling trays of sugar cookies covered with red and green sprinkles spread across the counters. She took off her green and red apron and twisted her hair into a knot on her head. "Come on upstairs and we'll get you settled in. Harrison Shepard! Do you see *any* evidence of a Labrador puppy around here? Santa hasn't made up his mind yet."

"There *is* no Santa!" Harrison announced dramatically. His little sister, coming into the room with a just-completed drawing of a reindeer, stood shocked in the doorway.

Francesca swept both of them up, saying, "Of *course* there's a Santa Claus. He's the spirit of love at Christmas, and your uncle is named after him. He has presents for everybody!" She glanced back over her shoulder and winked at Cassandra. "Now, my little Christmas mice, scamper upstairs and get ready for dinner."

Cassandra shook her head. "How do you come up with things like that?"

"I speak only the truth," Francesca said, as she walked to the top of the polished wooden staircase and cracked opened the door to Alex's study. Cassandra followed her in and gave her brother-in-law a kiss on top of his lightly graying head. He smiled in absentminded acknowledgment.

Cassandra looked over at her husband, "Were you planning to bring in our luggage?"

"I will." Nicholas smiled distractedly, and turned back to Alex. The twins were in the middle of a conversation. "I'm re-thinking this idea of pyramid trading with the futures contracts," explained Alex. "The math just doesn't add up if we take a big loss. Every time we buy or sell contracts and make a profit, the money is added to the account and then we will buy or sell additional contracts the next time we make a trade. That is right, right?"

"Right," Nicholas replied, "and I agree it's pretty risky."

Alex continued, thinking out loud. "If we keep adding to the number of futures contracts after each successful trade and then take a big loss, we could lose seventy-five percent of the total amount of the account balance! The higher the pyramid gets, the greater the loss is if the trend is wrong. It's too much risk for the average trader," he said, shaking his head, "and it certainly is in our case."

Nicholas hitched his eyebrows at his brother. "I knew a trader at the Chicago Board of Trade who always used to say, 'Never make a trade unless you have an edge.'"

"What was his edge?"

"Inside information."

"Lucky guy," his brother smiled. "I think we'll stick to the inside-the-box method. That should keep us out of prison!" The brothers shared a conspiratorial glance while their wives groaned and backed out of the room.

"I think I've heard more than I want to know," Francesca said with a mock shiver.

"Say, can we get a couple of those trading jackets they wear? What's the deal with those things, anyway?" Alex said, hardly noticing their departure.

"Well," Nicholas explained, "traders in the pits originally wore them during the open outcry sessions to keep cigarette ashes from burning their shirts or skin. Now the exchanges don't allow smoking on the floors or in the pits, but the jackets still remain as a tradition, especially at the Chicago Board of Trade.

"They sure are gaudy," remarked Alex.

"That's so the member brokers outside the pit can spot their trader inside the pit and flash their trade orders by hand. It's all those hand signals that amaze me," said Nicholas, leaning forward in an effort to demonstrate what he was describing. "When a broker wants to *buy* contracts, he holds up one or both hands, backs turned outward, and indicates the number of contracts with his fingers. The trader in the pit sees the signal from his broker and flashes the same sign to the other traders in the pit. They, in turn, flash back a sell signal for as many of the contracts as they have available for sale. If the broker outside the pit wants to *sell* contracts, he holds his hands up palm out."

"Huh. I never knew that," replied Alex. "Sounds like it would be pretty easy to screw up."

"They get many trades wrong," continued his brother. "It is so common, in fact, that every morning they set up booths in the lobby to settle differences with the traders. It's been working that way since the opening of the exchange. It's something like you've never seen. I've taken students to the CBOT to watch the open outcry sessions on field trips. They love to watch the action. When a brokerage firm or bank flashes a big trade to their trader in the pit, all the independent traders start jumping and yelling to get a piece of the action. If they get a piece, they ride it just long enough to make a good profit, then close their position and get out."

Taking quick profits, Alex thought. "That's interesting and probably pretty smart considering the volatility."

"I agree," replied Nicholas. "There is a movement going now to get the exchange to go completely electronic, but we'll have to wait and see if this long-held tradition bites the dust. Either way, we will be trading electronically so it won't really matter to us, but it might to the other 12,000 traders in the pits."

Nicholas remembered an interview he had once heard between a radio reporter and one of the independent traders, and explained it to Alex. "This was in July, and the reporter asked the trader if he would hold his futures position until it expired in September, which is one of the four times a year when futures contracts expire. The trader answered, 'If I'm in the market longer than five minutes, I'd be crazy!' Then he laughed like a maniac. I don't think the reporter understood what was so funny, but the fact is that most futures traders might as well be betting the horses at Churchill Downs. They get in, hopefully make a profit, and get out again—then look for the next chance. These futures traders *play* the market; they don't invest in it."

"Do we know enough about futures to get involved?" Alex asked.

"I suggest we trade every weekly trend that agrees with the monthly up/down bias, which should give us the monthly 99.7 percent accuracy edge. If the shorter-term trend happens to be wrong, we can just hang in with the trade until the market eventually turns back in the direction of the forecasted monthly trend. That way the trade will turn out to be profitable."

Alex pondered the logic and nodded in agreement. "That sounds logical. But you know what? I want to put a little mathematical true grit into the equation by adding the exponential factor. Shall we try some of this pyramiding? I know it's risky, but during the back testing, the wrong trends were either flat or just slightly wrong, so the profits from the winning trends would definitely outweigh the losses."

"I don't know," said Nicholas shaking his head at the idea. "Who's going to sit around and watch the computer tick up and down all day? I don't have time to do that, and neither do you."

"We won't have to sit around and watch the computer monitor. We just buy futures contracts on the first day of a weekly up trend, then sell them and reverse our positions on the last day of the weekly trend," answered Alex. "This way, we only have to pay attention every six days or so. We can take turns. When one of us can't be at his computer for the trade, the other one can cover."

"So take the profits at the end of each trend, reverse our position by buying or selling more contracts, and watch the pyramid of contracts grow?" asked Nicholas.

"That's it, yes!" replied the enthusiastic twin.

"Well, I must say, that's going for broke. And if it works, it'll sure prove the genius of our discovery in a hurry. But remember," he cautioned, "the longer-term hedge strategy we first came up with was pretty good, too. It will produce more conservative profits at first, but with few or no tax consequences, they also grow exponentially because of the compounding profits. And it's much safer."

Both brothers smiled when they heard Harrison yelling outside the door and Francesca ordering him to drop a candy cane. "Okay, why don't we do this," continued Alex. "Let's use the conservative trading strategy to safeguard our savings accounts and IRAs. This will give us total security and investment privacy, since we'll be investing in one of the largest indexes in the world, where no one will notice us—the S&P 500 and its futures."

"And then we'll trade weekly trends with our 'mad money'," added Nicholas.

"Right," said Alex. He sighed deeply, "Our wives will disapprove, but we should be able to ease their anxiety soon enough. Look at this trading spreadsheet in Excel," he said, reaching over and turning the computer monitor so his brother could get a better view. "I've included all the macros that will do the math for us following our entries for each trade. It will show at a glance each buy or sell trade, the profits and the percentages of profits on a continuous basis. In this column, I've incorporated percentages for the year compared to the S&P 500. I included this column because every other fund manager compares their fund results to this index."

"These macros are great," replied Nicholas, "but you know me. I like good hand-drawn visuals. Let's shoot over to an office supply store and get some blank calendar charts and erasable markers. I can fill in the dates, and also the trend direction in the appropriate days."

Both brothers stood to leave, only to find their way blocked by Francesca. "Going somewhere, boys?" she asked in her best Mae West voice.

"Yes, downstairs for dinner, my dear," Alex shot back in a perfect W. C. Fields retort.

"Good guess, Mr. Fields. Leave your hat and your bottle of whiskey at the door."

Chapter 24

 All eyes turned expectantly to Lev. He would have preferred to speak to his father alone. He especially didn't want to talk about this in front of Mika Hunter.

Lev cleared his throat and offered his father a weak smile. "It seems that Nicholas Shepard has constructed a new trading method for the stock markets, with which he claims he can forecast the direction of the market with one hundred percent accuracy for yearly trends and over eighty-two percent on weekly trends."

His father held up his wine glass in a mock salute. "More power to him! I thought you really admired this Shepard fellow. You certainly don't seem impressed." He pursed his lips. "I am disappointed." Unsure how to respond, Lev looked down at his plate and remained quiet.

"Lev, tell your father about the box!" Felicia suggested, gaining confidence in Malachi's initial warm response. Her voice was sharp, her point clear.

Malachi's upheld glass tipped slightly, spilling a few drops of red wine onto the table. He took no notice of it as his eyes narrowed. "Box? What is she talking about, Lev?" His voice was hard, level, and cold.

"Oh, yes," Lev struggled to respond. He managed a small chuckle and shrugged it off as unimportant. "I forgot. Apparently, he attended a party at the Biltmore Estate and found a box he claims measures gravity. Can you believe it? Gravity? He seems to believe he can use it to predict stock market trends." When Malachi did not even blink in response, Lev felt compelled to add, "It is completely foolish. Nonsense, really."

Felicia knew Lev was oversimplifying what Dr. Shepard had told them, and was about to say something when she realized the cold turn of the room. No one was laughing at the foolish Dr. Shepard. Lev lowered his eyes and picked away at his food while Malachi, Constantina, and Mika Hunter stared in his direction. Lev's mother leaned back in her wheelchair and looked at Malachi, trying to catch his eye. It was Mika

Hunter, however, who spoke next. "This Nicholas Shepard . . . would you happen to know if his brother's name is Alex?"

Lev lifted his eyes in surprise. "Yes. They're identical twins."

Malachi's gaze shifted to his colleague though his head remained absolutely still. Mika's usually enigmatic expression was gone. In its place was a positively shaken exterior. Malachi's expression never wavered. He inquired, "Mika, do you know the Shepard brothers?"

Mika's almond-shaped eyes remained locked on Lev as she answered. "I know only Alex. He was a . . . business associate of mine some years ago. I lost track of him until recently, when I received a query from him asking for particulars about one of the funds we manage."

"Ah, well then," began Malachi, raising his glass of Bordeaux, which had been quickly refilled by a waiting servant. "Let us toast to the Shepards' financial success!" His perfect teeth blazed a brilliant white smile. Lev, Mika, and Constantina complied. Felecia lifted her glass to toast with the others, knowing full well that something was not quite right.

"Lev," continued Malachi, his smile still wide and obviously insincere. "Perhaps I should come down to Atlanta and meet your Dr. Shepard?" It was not a question, and Lev did not misunderstand the thrust of the words. He swallowed hard and nodded. Felicia sucked quietly on her lower lip and tried to catch his eye, but Lev refused to look in her direction.

Constantina gave the young girl an understanding smile. "Come now," she said smoothly. "Dinner is no time to discuss business. We don't get to see Lev enough as it is. Tell us, Felicia, how did you two meet?"

Throwing her a thankful smile, Felicia began chatting with Lev's parents and sharing amusing stories about her childhood in France and her adjustment to life in Atlanta. Before long, Lev found himself relaxing a bit. Even his father was laughing politely, although he was certain that inside, Malachi was burning to know more about Nicholas Shepard's supposed discovery.

The next thirty minutes passed at a painfully slow pace. After the dishes were cleared, Constantina rolled her chair back from the table with practiced ease. "Felicia, my dear, perhaps you would let me give you a guided tour of our home, and we can freshen up. The gentlemen would probably like to enjoy brandy and cigars in the library."

Mika also rose. "If I may," she said to her hostess, "I'll join the gentlemen. I believe we have some business to discuss." She bowed to Felicia, who responded with a lower bow in deference to Mika's culture. It was a gesture Malachi had caught the first time around. Knowledge of other cultures was important to his business and his family, and indicated an educated, cultured woman from a good family.

Mika followed Lev and his father into the library, where a servant was pouring Napoleon brandy into oversize crystal snifters. Malachi waved the proffered cigars away. "Thank you, Brent. We'll pass on the cigars. Leave us."

"As you wish, sir." Brent exited quietly. The arched mahogany doors closed with a soft *click*.

"Alright, Leviticus," Malachi said, using his son's full name. His voice was stern and his face as warm as a block of uncut marble. "Do you want to tell me what the hell is going on?"

Lev opened his mouth to speak, but the words froze in his throat when Malachi slammed his fist down on the leather arm of the sofa. "How in God's name could he have found that box! Jesus Christ Almighty! That room was a complete secret, unknown even to the estate's god-damned caretakers!" Malachi downed his drink in one gulp and closed his eyes. Both Lev and Mika were smart enough to keep still. Malachi's eyes opened slowly. He rose from his chair and crossed the antique silk Sarouk carpet to refill his glass. His voice was lower, calmer. "How did they find it? What were they doing there, anyway?"

"I don't know, sir," answered Lev truthfully. "But I can probably find out pretty easily."

"You will indeed! Yes, sir, you will do so—quickly." Malachi looked at Mika with a scowl carved into this face. "I wonder if Ernest von Stuyvesant is aware of this breech."

Mika sipped softly from her glass of brandy. "Malachi, why don't we wait and see what Nicholas Shepard really thinks he has? The only way to establish control is to find out everything we can first."

"No!" He was nearly shouting now. "I want you to call von Stuyvesant first thing in the morning and see what he knows!" Malachi's mouth narrowed in anger. "He has a lot to account for. That damn box was his responsibility!"

Mika nodded, drained her brandy, and rose to her feet. "I think I will take my leave now." She gave Lev a thin smile. "Your girlfriend is quite lovely." Lev merely nodded. He didn't give a damn what Mika Hunter thought. "Thank you for the lovely dinner, Malachi," she said.

Tossing back his second brandy, Malachi growled in return. "I want that box back! Tomorrow you will bring me a plan."

"I know, Malachi, but we can't just go and ask for it, can we?" Her smile had a faint malevolence to it. "I am sure Lev will help us get it back, won't you, dear?"

Chapter 25

Alex plopped down in front of the computer with a fresh mug of coffee. "Here goes," he said to himself. It was January 1. "Happy New Year," he sang to himself, his tune tainted with the theme song from Barney and a smattering of the Sesame Street jingle thrown in for good measure. So much had happened during the preceding few weeks it was hard to believe almost a month had passed since they had stumbled into the hidden room at the Biltmore and found the box.

He loaded the S&P five-minute stock data ending December 31 into the *Xyber9* program. The forecast showed the market moving up until January 16, and then down from there. Alex was reassured that the forecast was so in sync with the current business news—unemployment, orders for durable goods, and better-than-expected holiday retail sales. The brothers had decided that this would be a good trend to begin trading with.

Michelangelo, Harrison's ten-week-old black Labrador puppy, bounded into the room and skidded to a stop at Alex's feet. He chuckled as his mind shifted instantly back to Christmas. The idea of putting a puppy in a stocking on Christmas morning had been a good one—in theory, at least. The event had not gone as smoothly as Francesca had hoped. She had placed Michelangelo gently inside the stocking the first two times before stuffing him inside in frustration the third. Wiggling free, he had scampered into the kitchen, where he yelped so loud after puddling on the floor that he woke up the children earlier than anticipated. Harrison sprinted downstairs screaming "a dog, a dog!" at the top of his lungs. When he finally spotted the pup, he hugged the Labrador so hard he almost crushed him. Still, seeing the excitement in his face had made the effort worth it.

Francesca was delighted when Harrison named the dog after her favorite Renaissance painter. Alex didn't have the heart to tell her that a

Teenage Mutant Ninja Turtle also shared the name. Now, the curious puppy was struggling to climb onto the low coffee table, where Nicholas' calendar pages were spread out. "Come on, buddy," he coaxed, scooping up the puppy in his arms. He dumped the dog gently back into the hallway and closed the door tightly behind him. With another interruption removed, he sat back at his desk to resume working.

He and Nicholas had bought a big cork board, along with push pins, erasable markers, calendar charts, and reams of printing paper—all so they could keep the forecasts posted on the wall in front of their eyes. They had initially wanted to simply tape the sheets to the wall, but Francesca nipped that idea in the bud. Painters had charged them a small fortune to produce the *faux* Moroccan leather, and she wasn't about to allow them to tamper with her walls.

On the charts, Nicholas had marked a blue *H* for each trend top on the date of the last up day, which indicated where they needed to close their "buy" contracts and reverse their position. He also put a red *L* for the bottom of the trend on the date of the last day down, indicating when to reverse course. Their $50,000 deposit allowed them to control twenty-five S&P futures contracts for their first up move. Each contract required $2,000 to cover the margin in the event the market moved against their position.

And so it began.

The following afternoon, Alex bought twenty-five S&P E-mini at 1,103.50 and luckily caught the bottom of the day. On January 16, he reversed his position and sold forty-seven contracts short, betting the market would move down until January 26. The profit from the first trade astounded the twins, but also allowed them to control the extra contracts for the downtrend.

He called Nicholas and provided a blow-by-blow report. "Are you hearing me?" he said excitedly. "That is a profit of $44,375! Can you believe it? Eighty-nine percent right off the bat!"

Although Nicholas had hoped for this result, just hearing it took his breath away. He tried to get his head around the opening success. Although he wanted to shout out loud, he instead offered a calm "Alright,

Alex. That is really good work." The new money allowed them to add extra contracts, which in turn began their pyramid strategy.

The next trade wasn't as profitable because the market remained generally flat, although they did gain one point. Now they were controlling forty-eight contracts for the next uptrend, just one day, to the 27th of January. The one-day trend seemed odd since Alex expected to see a six-to nine-day cycle, but he nevertheless reversed his position and bought forty-eight contracts for the one-day up trend, planning to go short the next day. The market rocked up through the 27th and provided them with a $38,400 profit and control of an additional nineteen contracts for the downtrend, or a total of sixty-seven contracts. After reversing his position and selling short, by the 29th he was already up another $94,638, with a net asset value for the account now at $191,363.00—a 382-percent gain in a single month of trading.

Although January closed out an amazing month of trading, it had not been easy for the twins. It was nearly impossible to resist the temptation to take a profit too quickly or, even more difficult, to suffer the heat when the market went against them. Their strategy demanded they make their trades and then, in effect, turn off the computer until the end of the forecasted trend. By the end of January Nicholas had had enough. He called his brother.

"Alex, there's only one remedy for my shot nerves. We're going to have to take a vacation."

"A . . . what?" stuttered Alex.

"See?" insisted Nicholas. "The word's not even in your vocabulary. How long has it been since you and Francesca actually went somewhere for a few days just to relax?"

Alex thought hard for a moment. "We were at the Biltmore less than two months ago!"

"That was hardly a vacation!" shot back his twin. "That is where this all started. Besides, don't you think it's time we let the girls in on our success?" Thus far, Nicholas and Alex had not been entirely truthful with their wives about their earnings. Part of it was simply superstition. Both brothers were worried they might jinx their success if they told Cassandra and Francesca how much money they had made. All the girls knew was that the guys were making "some money," but were still working out "bugs that plagued the system."

"Come on," Nicholas coaxed. "I can't think of a better way to tell them. Let's find a place in the islands we can all go. Why don't we make it for Valentine's Day?"

Alex reluctantly agreed. "Alright, but you make the plans."

They decided to surprise their wives by slipping the airline tickets into their purses with a card and seeing how long it took them to find them. Naturally, both women found the tickets right away and instead of calling their husbands, they called each other.

"What do you think?" Francesca asked, sitting at her kitchen table in semi-shock.

"I think I need either a new bathing suit," Cassandra laughed, "or a new body."

Francesca laughed at the joke. "Well, you have less than two weeks. Might be easier to just get a new suit!" Her voice turned more serious now. "Cassandra, is this too good to be true? I mean, shouldn't we put this money in a savings account or something?"

Alex was right, Cassandra smiled to herself. Francesca was the consummate worrier! "Come on," she said gently. "The boys certainly seem to have everything under control and what's a little vacation? They've both been working hard and it would be nice to spend some time together."

Alex was so excited and pleased with their success that Francesca decided not to mention her unease. Everything was falling nicely into place. Nicholas has the trip planned, and Galen, who lived in a dormitory-like room, was more than happy to move into the house and stay with the kids. She decided to just go with the flow.

Nicholas arranged for Dr. Tony Faraj, a friend and colleague at Emory, to cover his classes. For his graduate students, he left a series of research assignments. During the entire month of January, both Lev and Felicia had seemed distracted, distant. When Nicholas had asked them about their visit to New York, neither seemed completely forthcoming and their responses were mixed and confused.

Initially, Felicia had shrugged and told him it had been a nice break from Atlanta. When pressed for more detail, however, she had turned on a dime and went on and on about how nice Lev's parents had been— particularly his father. The entire conversation felt palpably contrived. Lev had been reluctant to even comment about the holiday except to say, "it went well."

Something else was bothering Nicholas. Lev's eagerness to help with the new project was gratifying, but Nicholas was rapidly losing patience with the graduate student's persistent curiosity about the box. He initially welcomed Lev's questions since they seemed to evince a healthy professional interest in the project. The interest, however, rapidly took the form of a barely veiled inquisition. Every other sentence was a question, and regardless of the answer Nicholas provided, Lev probed deeper.

"How did you find the room?"

"Were you looking for it?"

"How did you figure out the box had something to do with gravity?"

"How did you determine it could track the stock market?"

"Had you ever heard about the box before you found it?"

"Forget the box, Lev!" he had told him one day in early January. "Let's focus on the data I need from you. You know more about how we found it now than I do!"

When questions moved into the realm of his personal life, a red flag went off in Nicholas's head. Lev was deeply interested in the project, but there was something else—something deeply troubling—behind his lines of inquiry. Nicholas was glad he had decided to keep the trading information on his home computer.

Sitting in his office, Nicholas wrote out his last instruction memo and double checked to make sure everything was in order before he left for the Bahamas. He casually glanced across the room at his graduate students. They had both been particularly quiet that afternoon. "So, what are you two doing for Valentine's Day?"

Felicia smiled, lifted her eyebrows as if she was sharing a secret, and looked at Lev. Nicholas realized that she was probably hoping for an engagement ring, but Lev seemed preoccupied. "I don't know . . . dinner, I guess." Felicia's face fell.

"Hey," Lev said suddenly looking up from his laptop, "speaking of dinner, Dr. Shepard, didn't you say you wanted to have us over after the holidays?"

Felicia groaned to herself at Lev's clumsy attempt to extract an invitation. Ever since they had gotten back from New York, he had been dropping small hints to Dr. Shepard about meeting for dinner. The clues had not gone unnoticed, but his growing discomfort with Lev had made Nicholas leery of inviting him over. However, he thought, perhaps that is why Lev had been acting so odd. After all, he had extended an invitation to Lev many weeks earlier but had not followed up on the offer. Now Lev was asking him directly. Avoiding the issue had become impossible.

"Sure, Lev," Nicholas answered carefully. "We would love to have you over. Let's plan something right after we get back from our trip." That seemed to satisfy him, because he smiled in reply and dove into his work. *Hopefully, the Bahamas would make Cassandra more amenable to having the couple over,* thought Nicholas.

He stood and stretched at his desk. He had just one more thing to do before they left.

ॐ

The phone rang just as Gabriel walked into the house after a brief riding trip to the vineyard. Since the shooting incident, he had been riding Beauregard nearly every day on that part of the estate. Whether he thought he might find some evidence Gerard had overlooked, or even incite the shooter to strike again, he could not say. There were moments when he felt certain his father had something to do with the shooting, but deep inside he realized how ridiculous that sounded.

He grabbed the receiver off the kitchen wall on the third ring. "Hello?"

"Gabe!"

He was surprised to hear Nicholas' voice on the line. "Hey, how is the New Year treating you?" he asked, curious to hear how their project was coming along.

"All I can say is that it works, Gabe—it works very well! Are you sure you don't want to take advantage of this?

"No, I think my family already has . . . I mean, already has enough money. But I am glad to hear that someone else is benefitting."

"Listen, Gabe, I was wondering . . ." Nicholas hesitated. The last thing he wanted to do was upset his friend. "Did you ever find out anything about your mysterious poacher?"

Gabriel pulled out a kitchen chair and sat down with a sigh. "No. Whoever it was is long gone."

"Ok, well I was just asking. But, that isn't really why I called." Nicholas held his breath.

"Oh?"

Nicholas decided to just come out with it. "I don't suppose you've heard from your father, have you? I mean, he hasn't called to ask for the box back, has he?"

"No, of course not," answered Gabriel quickly. "Why are you asking?"

"I guess I am feeling a little jumpy, Gabe," replied Nicholas. "Alex and I have not been completely forthcoming with Cassandra and Francesca about the amount of money we've made. It's happening so fast, and I guess we just didn't want to believe it ourselves. Anyway, we've decided to take them to the Bahamas for Valentine's Day and come clean."

"How much have you made?"

"More than two hundred thousand dollars."

"Wow!" Gabe gave a low whistle. "That will be some kind of a surprise!"

"Yeah, well, I guess I just wanted to make sure that before we told them the good news, we weren't going to get sued by your Dad or anything crazy like that."

Nicholas thought he heard Gabe let out a huge sigh. "No. I can honestly tell you that my father has not asked for the box back or even mentioned it." *Although he did try pretty hard to get me to go to Germany next month, like he was trying to get me out of the country to . . .* Gabe put that thought on the back burner.

"Alright, fine. Well, we are off to the sunny islands. We should try and get together after we get back."

"Absolutely!" said Gabe in a voice that sounded much happier than he felt. "Have a good time and give my best to everyone. Nicholas, make sure before you leave that all of your documentation is left someplace—safe."

Nicholas hesitated. Why would he say that? "Sure, no problem, Gabe. Thanks for the advice."

Gabriel pushed the disconnect button and sat there for a long time holding the phone and thinking. His father's offer of travel abroad had come at an unlikely time—especially since he never invited his son anywhere, ever. Could he have an ulterior motive? *Why would he want me out of the country?* Wondered Gabriel. He scoffed at the idea that entered his mind. Ernest von Stuyvesant was greedy, but that was the extent of his wickedness. He didn't want to pay anyone to do the inventory on the medieval castle he had just purchased. He was a miserly penny-pincher and a terrible father, but he was not an evil man.

Gabriel walked to the refrigerator and poured himself a glass of water. He lifted it to drink but lowered it before it reached his lips. His heart was racing, and his mind was troubled. He was afraid of his father's associates—and what they were capable of without his father's knowledge.

He was frightened that Nicholas was going to start asking questions he wasn't prepared to answer. *My God*, Gabe closed his eyes for a moment. *I should have just closed the lid on that damn cassone and been done with it. If something bad happens I could never forgive myself.*

ॐ

The next day Nicholas, Alex, and their wives flew to Marsh Harbor in the Abaco Islands and jumped on a ferry to Elbow Cay and the small village of Hope Town. He and Nicholas had agreed not to worry about their trading and had simply turned off their computers. Not that they could do anything anyway, because the rule was no cable, no Internet, no newspapers, no magazines—nothing. Alex felt naked leaving the house without his laptop and Palm Pilot.

When they arrived on Elbow Cay, a man named Don picked them up at the north dock in his small SUV, an American-made vehicle of which he was extremely proud. The locals used golf carts to get around, but even these were prohibited within the "city" limits. The tiny island was only three miles long and about a quarter-mile wide.

"I am beginning to think this was a really good idea," whispered Francesca to Cassandra as they stood in front of their rental cottage and soaked in the ocean view and warm tropical breeze. They both loved the British Colonial look inside the bungalow. The dark rattan and wicker furniture graced a mahogany floor gleaming with a thick fresh coat of wax, which offset the stark white walls.

"This is marvelous, and it smells so fresh!" Cassandra sighed as she walked into their bedroom with its wide-open windows and mosquito netting blowing softly in the breeze. Francesca however, was drawn into the open kitchen with colorful cabinets and a stunning view of the blue sea just a handful of yards beyond.

The two couples spent the week on the beach and in the water. It was a break they all desperately needed. On their last evening, they decided to return to a restaurant that had served up the best grouper any of them had ever eaten. Alex ordered a bottle of expensive champagne and was speechless when Francesca ordered the same dish she had eaten every night since they arrived. This was something Alex had never seen her do before in all their years of marriage. It was a good sign. Things had been more than hectic for everyone after the trip to the Biltmore, so he was glad to see her relax and enjoy herself. "Would this be a great place to live happily ever after, or what?" he mused aloud.

"I wonder how long it would take you to get bored," asked his wife.

"About twenty-three seconds if we actually had to *live* here," Cassandra answered, grinning at Nicholas, who laughed in agreement.

"No, really." Alex grew serious. "Maybe Francesca is right, sometimes I work too hard."

"Sometimes?" Francesca replied sardonically.

Alex looked hurt. He reached out and took her hand. "I've been doing a lot of thinking sitting out there on the beach. It suddenly struck me as—." He paused, searching for the right words. "It struck me as terribly sad. Nicholas had to practically twist my arm to get me to take my wife on a vacation."

Francesca was speechless. The others knew better than to say anything. Cassandra just took Nicholas' hand and squeezed it.

"To the most patient woman I know." Alex held up his glass.

"Hear, hear!" Nicholas agreed as they all raised their glasses and toasted Francesca.

As they were leaving the island, Nicholas pulled Alex aside in the airport as they prepared to board the plane. "Look," he said, "I'm the economist in the family, why don't you let me play the market for a while?"

Alex gave him a knowing nod and smile. "You don't need to be an economist to buy and sell when told, brother, but I get your point. I need to spend more time with my family, don't I?"

"Yes—at least long enough to get that dog housetrained!" shot back Nicholas with a tanned grin.

ॐ

Within a few minutes of arriving back at the Battery in Charleston, Alex e-mailed Nicholas the forecast. Then he shut down his computer and locked the office door. *At least I've made a good show of it,* he thought. He hated not being in control.

The forecast showed the market trading upward for three days and then down from there. Nicholas opened up TradeStation only to find his Internet connection was down. A call to BellSouth's tech support caused him to groan aloud: he would likely be without the data for the rest of the day. He would have to call the floor at the Chicago Mercantile Exchange to place an order to buy his futures contracts. The market had seen a big sell-off the day before, and was still dropping pretty fast when he made the call. He told the trader that he wanted to buy 243 ES E-mini June contracts.

"What?" asked the trader, who surprised Nicholas by shouting back, "Buy? Are you kidding? That's like stepping in front of a freight train!"

Nicholas hesitated, wondering what the trader knew that he didn't. It was then he realized the man didn't know anything except for the ever-changing numbers on the big board. He asked the trader where the market was at that second, and as soon as the trader answered, he asked again. This time the trader's answer indicated a slight up-tick. That was all he needed to know. He placed his buy order and hung up.

For the first time Nicholas understood what might actually happen if he told the world that there was a way to predict the stock market. Cassandra was right: no one would believe him. No trader would dare stand in front of a freight train headed south and put in that buy order. If Nicholas waved his arms and shouted, "But wait! I know for certain the market's going to turn," who would find his announcement believable?

On the other hand, he fully realized the trader's warning had almost worked. He had hesitated, questioned himself, and nearly flinched. It would be easy to let some "expert" derail their plans. *Here we've been in the market for six weeks, made more money than we ever thought possible, and I'm letting some bozo at the CME put pins in me!*

He got up and stretched, placed his open palms on his hips, and turned first one way and then the other, listening as his vertebrae popped and twisted. "That was a great learning experience," he said out loud. "That is the last time I let that happen."

Chapter 26

 It only lasted two days. Unable to sleep, Alex slipped out of bed and down the hall to his office. It was the middle of the night, and he was checking the direction of the market on his computer.

He sat there for more than an hour, scrolling through financial reports before he heard a noise behind him. He turned to see tightly robed Francesca standing in the doorway, a bemused look on her face. "Couldn't stay away, could you?"

"I'm sorry honey." He hung his head.

"Alex, this is who you are. I know you trust Nicholas, but you like managing things. Don't you know that's why I love you?" He looked up and tried to understand. "Darling," she sighed softly, crossing the room to reach him. "I love the fact that you take care of us. You can fix a leaky faucet and help the kids with their homework. You finally got that silly puppy to stop chewing Harrison's action figures." She stroked his hair. "It's alright if you want to have another go with this stuff."

"Really?"

"Sure, if you promise to take off three weeks during the summer so we can take the kids to visit my family in Italy!"

"Can I think about it first?" he asked. Both of them laughed.

๗

A few days later Alex discovered an interesting intra-day trend. He was planning an 11:30 a.m. buy and was carefully watching the time. Just before 11:00, one of his co-workers appeared in his doorway. "Let's get a quick bite to eat."

"Okay, Mel," he answered, glancing at his watch. "Just so long as it's quick."

When they returned, Alex invited his fellow engineer to come in and have a look at the trading charts. He checked his computer and found that the market had indeed dropped down another 15 points before turning up at exactly thirty minutes before noon. He placed his buy order and explained to his friend that they had just eaten a $169,500 lunch.

Mel lurched in his seat, white as a sheet. "What? You lost that much money in a couple of hours? What the hell are you doing?"

Alex laughed heartily. "I didn't actually lose a penny, but I did miss out on that hundred and sixty-nine thousand I *could have made* during lunch. But not to worry, I just now placed my order, and the market has another five days to move up to the end of this trend. We'll still make a killing."

"My God, you scared me. Alex," his friend laughed. "Don't take this the wrong way, but we've all been a little concerned. You seem obsessed with the stock market, dude. We just don't want to see you get into any trouble. Please don't fool around with the mortgage money, ok?"

"Hey, don't worry." Alex replied nonchalantly, "I've got everything under control. Just think of it as a science project."

২

Nicholas unlocked the door of their condo. He was only seconds away from having to tell Cassandra that Felicia and Lev were coming to dinner on Saturday, and he wasn't looking forward to her response. She had decided the first time she met Lev that she didn't trust him—and that was not about to change any time soon.

He took a breath and walked into the second bedroom, which she had made into a study. It was a cheerful room, lined from floor to ceiling with art history, architecture, and interior design books. She had indulged in a Ralph Lauren writer's chair and ottoman. Curled up reading *Mansions of Paris*, she lifted her head when he entered and smiled warmly. He spotted an opening and moved in quickly. "Wouldn't you like to talk to Felicia about those mansions? She's probably been to all of them."

She peered at him over her reading glasses and studied his face. "Why do I think you're about to say something I won't like?"

He broke the news, plain and simple.

She uncurled herself and placed a marker inside without shutting the book. "I don't believe we should socialize with your students. That's the first thing. Second, I think that guy's an oil slick."

"I think they're going to be married," he answered, grasping at straws. "It's only three or four hours out of our day."

"What about the food? Is it going to appear by magic? You know I'm no Francesca in the kitchen."

"I'll go pick up something. How about Everybody's Pizza?" he suggested, knowing she would find his idea absurd.

She wrinkled her nose. "I bet you've already invited them, haven't you? Okay, I guess I can be nice for one evening. I'll be the perfect Southern Belle."

"Your prettiest hypocritical face?" The words jumped out before he could stop it.

She snorted rudely and slammed the book shut. "For your information, mister, it will take every bit of good old Southern charm to get me through that dinner!"

Saturday arrived all too quickly. The anticipated leisurely morning, however, fell apart when the toilet flooded and the car battery died. When the afternoon arrived Cassandra was so far behind schedule she was nearly frantic. By the time the doorbell chimed she was trying hard not to scream at her husband, and he was trying hard to keep his mouth closed. Several glasses of scotch helped.

"You answer the door," she directed Nicholas in a curt voice. "I'll put the last touches on these hors d'oeuvres." Nicholas had forgotten to pick up appetizers, prompting an angry Cassandra to thaw frozen scallops, wrap them in bacon, and broil them in the oven. The first batch had burned when Nicholas ignored the timer. This time she wasn't going to let them out of her sight.

Cassandra heard Nicholas offer to take their coats just as the timer rang. She opened the oven and peered inside. This time the scallops were perfect. She arranged them carefully on a silver tray, took a deep breath, glued a smile on her face, and walked into the living room.

As a passive-aggressive protest, she wore her second-best little black dress. When she saw Felicia, Cassandra's smile intensified. Thank God she had decided to adorn herself with the diamond necklace Nicholas had given her for Christmas. The graduate student was wearing what was obviously her own very best little black dress, a darling strapless Versace silk with a chiffon stole. Her ears sparkled with several carats of diamonds in chandelier earrings, and she wore a necklace studded with diamond slides. *My god, the little goddess looks like a walking jewelry store! I'm so far out of my league*, thought Cassandra as she offered Felicia her hand. "*Bonjour, Mademoiselle. Comment ca va ce soir?*"

"*Je vais bien, madame,*" Felecia answered politely.

"Nicholas, would you get me a neat Scotch?" Cassandra asked as she shook Lev's hand.

Felicia selected a Chardonnay while Lev and Nicholas both followed Cassandra's example. "Honey, I think you have had enough," Cassandra whispered in his ear. Nicholas waved her off and disappeared to make the drinks and the students slipped some of the scallops onto the small Wedgwood plates Cassandra offered them. They both perched themselves on the edges of their chairs and looked around the room. "These are delicious, Mrs. Shepard," said Lev, pointing to the scallops.

"Thank you."

Lev's eyes settled on the collection of Murano glass. "Have you been collecting long?" he asked.

"Yes," admitted Cassandra. "We flew to Venice on our honeymoon and went to the island to see the glassblowing factories. We've been collecting reproductions of the classical designs, but lately they're promoting the work of some very famous contemporary glassmakers."

"What did you like most about Venice?" Felicia asked. Mrs. Shepard was polite, she thought, but seemed very stiff. She wondered if the couple had quarreled before they arrived.

"We loved the little squares where the tourists don't go much. People sitting out enjoying the night air, eating, drinking, talking."

A lull in the conversation ensued, but Nicholas appeared just in time and handed Cassandra her scotch. She looked into the glass, wanting to throw it back in a single gulp, but her manners held. They discussed travel in Italy for awhile and after a refill Cassandra began feeling more relaxed. "Perhaps we should start our meal," she said. "We will be having boeuf bourguignonne, chunks of beef, bacon, onions, and mushroom caps, simmered in a red wine sauce. It will be accompanied by a chilled lentil salad with hard sausage in a Dijon vinaigrette, and a warm crisp baguette."

"It sounds perfect and smells delicious," complimented Felicia.

"Well, that's just little 'ole me in the kitchen," joked Cassandra, which prompted a snort of laughter from Nicholas.

"Now, just so you know," she continued, "I told Nicholas that y'all are not discussing any business or research tonight."

At that, Lev made a strange noise and they all turned to look at him. Flashing what he hoped was a melancholy look, he shook his head slowly, "Oh, I had hoped Dr. Shepard could tell us how he was doing with his project!"

Felicia laughed. "Oh, come on Lev, tell them the truth. You just want to see the box they found."

Cassandra felt herself go rigid and she shot a glance at Nicholas, who answered very quickly and louder than necessary. "Sorry Lev, but you're out of luck. The box is at my brother's house in Charleston."

Lev shrugged in feigned disinterest. "I just thought if you had it handy. It sounds like an interesting antiquity."

"Oh, it is definitely that all right!" answered Nicholas as they took their seats around the dinning room table. He struggled for a few moments opening a bottle of wine as Lev watched, wondering whether he should offer to assist. When the cork finally slid out, Nicholas continued. "You should have seen the chest we found it in . . . what was that called, darling? A callone?"

"A *cassone*," Cassandra answered flatly as her husband filled the wine glasses. When he poured hers, she threw him a sharp look he failed to notice. This conversation had gone on far enough. She really wished he had not told anyone about that damn box.

"Again with the Italian," replied Lev, forcing a smile.

"My sister-in-law is from Italy," Cassandra explained, hoping to steer the conversation into a safer zone.

"And, you? Where is your family from?" Felicia asked.

"I'm Welsh," answered Cassandra. "Nicholas is a mixed breed."

"The name Shepard is interesting," said Lev. "Mix the letters a bit and your name would be Sephard, which stems from the Jewish Sephardim in Spain at the time of the Inquisition."

Cassandra cocked her head. "Hmm—that is fascinating! I might have to dig into that." Perhaps this will be a passable evening, she thought. The Napa Valley Pinot Noir was certainly excellent. She was about to ask for a refill when her husband began speaking.

"I think you have enough to do digging into your current accounting project, Cassandra," he chided.

"Oh, what are you working on, Mrs. Shepard?" asked Felecia. "I didn't know you're an accountant!" Lev looked on with interest, waiting for her to answer.

"I'm not an accountant," explained Cassandra shaking her head. "I am just, ah, helping Nicholas on something—a project."

No one said anything for a few seconds, until Lev asked the obvious question. "Is this the same stock market project we are working on for Dr. Shepard at school?" When neither Nicholas nor Cassandra immediately responded, Lev had his answer.

Nicholas finally blurted out, "We have some old documents we found with the box, that's all. Cassandra is studying them."

Lev's eyes nearly bulged out of his head while Cassandra contemplated throwing a loaded fork at her husband. It was one thing to mention the box; it was another to talk about the ancient documents. She drained her glass.

"Documents? Really? There were documents with it?" Lev was doing his best to pry out more information.

Cassandra looked Lev squarely in the eyes and carefully set her goblet on the table. They were dark, impenetrable pools. Alarms were going off in her head and she felt as if her throat was closing up. "Why are you so interested?" she choked with more intensity than she intended.

Lev began some artful backfilling. "Forgive me if I sounded over enthusiastic, Mrs. Shepard. The whole discovery is so extraordinary, and we're hard at work on many components of the trading strategies." He stopped and offered a smile. "But you said we would not discuss business. I'm sorry." Lev turned to Felicia and skillfully redirected the conversation. "Now, here is the person with the genealogy. Felicia's family has a history as long as your arm!"

Relieved, Nicholas quickly asked Felicia to enlighten them. Cassandra reached out and filled her own wine glass.

"At one time," Felicia began, "my family owned a chateau in the Loire Valley. They were quite well-off."

Lev pushed her along. "She's being extremely modest. My Felicia is actually a Merovingian."

Cassandra's eyes widened. "Really! How fascinating. Is it true that they can actually trace their history back to Mary Magdalene?"

Felicia was a little embarrassed to find herself as the center of attention. She rarely told people about her background for that very reason. She had no way of knowing Lev was trying desperately to shift Cassandra's attention.

Nicholas reached over and filled Lev's glass with more wine. Felicia shook her head and mouthed the words "No, thank you," when he moved the bottle in her direction. "If you don't mind telling us about it, you've really piqued my interest," said Nicholas. "I am not as informed as my wife about the . . . Mer . . . what did you call them?"

Warming to her professor's genuine curiosity, Felicia fell into the story. "A friend of my father's, J. R. Church, wrote a book called *Guardians of the Grail* in the late 1980s. Even though I was only thirteen at the time, I practically memorized it! The book explained how the Merovingian dynasty ruled France for three hundred years—from the fifth to the eighth centuries A.D. Most of Europe's monarchs have come from Merovingian lineage, from the Middle Ages even until the present day." Felicia paused and this time allowed Nicholas to top off her goblet. "Church has a lot to say about the so-called 'heresy' that the Merovingian bloodline sprang from Jesus Christ and Mary Magdalene," she continued. "He encouraged more research into ancient history—especially into the migration of nomadic tribes. Church was particularly interested in the Germanic Franks, ruled over by King Merovee, whose name sounds like the French word for 'mother'—*mere*—as well as both the French and Latin words for 'sea,' from which this legend arose."

Felicia settled back in her chair, twirling her glass of wine thoughtfully as she leaned forward slightly to relish its bouquet. After the little tale, Cassandra viewed her guest in a different light, impressed by Felicia's ability to seamlessly translate from her native French into near-perfect English. Her young face beamed with the emotion of the story and captivated her listeners.

"According to the legend, right before Merovee was born his expectant mother, who was the wife of Clodio, King of the Franks, went swimming one day in the Mediterranean Sea. She was attacked by a dreadful sea creature, which impregnated her with a divine seed. Therefore, legend has it that in Merovee's veins flowed a co-mingling of two different bloods—the blood of a Frankish ruler, and the blood of the mysterious creature. Of course, we know that's not possible, but the iconography of the story suggests the sea creature may have been merely a symbolic representation of the legend that Merovee was the offspring of Mary Magdalene."

Nicholas was fascinated by the story. "I have never heard any of this," he admitted.

"Most people know nothing about this. Even today," Felicia went on, "the Provençals believe that Lazarus and his two sisters, Mary Magdalene and Martha, emigrated to their lands when the three sailed across the Mediterranean to France—or what was then Gaul—to escape the Roman destruction of Jerusalem in 70 A.D. So the belief that the mother of the Merovingian dynasty came from the Mediterranean Sea, or from across the sea, may be represented in this symbolic fairy tale. Mary Magdalene is still considered today, by those who subscribe to the belief in the 'holy bloodline,' to be the progenitor of Merovee—four hundred years removed." Felicia laughed lightly and sipped her wine. "Frankly, this link seems weak to me."

She looked at her hosts as her eyes widened. "I think the Merovingian story has more to do with shifting patterns of wealth and power. To me, this aspect is more interesting than the legends. This is something that may be possible to prove. I have always believed, as has my father, that this line of power and wealth may well be traceable to many of today's richest and most powerful families in the Western world. I just haven't found the trail. I would love to do something on this for my dissertation."

Lev reached over to stroke her arm. "No business, remember dear?" He looked over at Cassandra, who was listening so hard she sat absolutely motionless in her chair. "Mrs. Shepard?" he asked.

"No, no, I love this," Cassandra whispered. "Please do go on."

For the first time that evening, a genuine smile spread across Felicia's face. "In 1653, when the tomb of Childeric I, son of Merovee, king of the Salian Franks, and the father of Clovis I, was discovered and opened in Tournai, they found three hundred miniature bees made of solid gold. Napoleon had these golden bees sewn onto his coronation robe when he crowned himself Emperor of France in 1804. When he married Marie-Louise Hapsburg of Austria, she wore a royal robe with the bees woven throughout. The bees may well represent an important clue as to the lineage of the Merovingian dynasty."

Nicholas turned to Cassandra. "Have you ever heard about this?"

"She nodded in reply. "Yes, but it has been many years. Please Felicia, continue."

"Most people have no interest in such matters," explained Felicia. "I am glad you do, Mrs. and Dr. Shepard." This time she reached for her water goblet, drank deeply, cleared her throat, and continued. "There also may be a clue in ancient Norse mythology. Merovee claimed to be descended from Odin, the primary god of the Teutonic people of northern Europe. Another twist is the speculation that the second syllable of Odin is just another way of spelling Dan, the famous lost tribe of Israel."

"Why would they want to claim that lineage?" asked Cassandra.

"It may have to do with divine power. The . . . *q'est que le mot?* . . . special property of kings throughout the ages always touches the divine. Who can really tell? Don't forget there were many groups from the Mediterranean people who moved about Europe engaged in warfare, commerce, or both. As they mixed with the European tribes, their myths and legends merged. While the Jews kept both their history and their religion fairly intact during their numerous migrations, everyone else's history got somewhat confused. I don't notice many Jews claiming to be Merovingians. Even Dr. Church could do no more than speculate on their origins, and he had the most access to ancient documents of anyone I know."

Nicholas weighed in. "The ancient Egyptians saw their pharaohs as gods. It isn't a far stretch to equate the two throughout history—though I'm not sure that does justice to the divine. By the way, you sound a lot like our friend, Gabriel. He knows just about everything there is to know about antiquities in general, and ancient Egypt in particular. He helped us out quite a bit with . . ."

"Nicholas, dear!" Cassandra interrupted with a thin-lipped smile. "Would you fetch another bottle of wine?" She deftly turned back to Felicia. "But the Church has been going right along with the program for two thousand years. Is there a difference between pope and king?"

"Ah, well, France is nearly ninety percent Catholic," Felicia pointed out, "and just about the same percentage no longer attends church. Our cathedrals are in ruins outside of tourist venues, but if they were asked, every Frenchman would swear allegiance to the pope before the government."

With that, the hosts removed the dinner plates and went into the kitchen to get the last course, a selection of French cheeses, grapes and pineapple intended to complement the after-dinner drinks. "Nicholas!" Cassandra had enjoyed Felicia's tale, but her female antennae were once again erect and vibrating. She whispered *sotto voce*, "You must *not* tell them anything else. Nothing. Zero. Nada. Zip. Something's going on here that isn't right."

"You're just being paranoid," Nicholas complained without attempting to conceal his annoyance. "You have no reason to suspect him of anything. They are both charming."

"Felicia is definitely enchanting," she said, placing the cheeses on a plate as Nicholas fumbled with the Irish coffee. "And *you* have had more than enough to drink." With the cheeses and fruits properly arranged, she turned to her husband and assumed coffee-making duties. "I cannot wait for them to leave. Not because of that, but something Felicia said. I'll tell you when they go. I think it is very exciting, but I know you missed it!"

She was ebullient now, reflecting on her little secret. With a smile she picked up the plate and sailed into the dining room.

Felicia sighed happily. "Thank you for being so attentive to my country's way of eating. I am so often puzzled by the way Americans eat."

"You can thank our favorite chef," Nicholas blurted out, to Cassandra's immediate chagrin.

Felicia's face blanched. She felt her mouth drop open in horror. *They served takeout?*

"We're used to European cuisine," said Cassandra a little too stridently. "Nicholas' brother Alex is married to an incredible Italian cook. I'm afraid I don't have her skills in the kitchen."

"Ah," responded Felicia with an apologetic smile. "I am sure you underrate yourself, Mrs. Shepard. Oh, I nearly forgot, Lev said you wanted to know something about the mansions of Paris? I am afraid I do not live in one."

Cassandra had forgotten the whole conversation about the French mansions and had to think a moment before responding. "Oh, yes, the mansions! We've never been to one. Can you recommend any to visit?"

"Yes, several of them. I could make a list. Are you planning a trip?"

"Not at the moment. But maybe this summer after Nicholas finishes with school."

They chatted on for another hour while drinking strong coffee, the pace and tone of the conversation much more comfortable than it had been when the evening began. Cassandra's mood had lightened to the point of buoyancy. She could not wait to talk to Nicholas in private. She even shook Lev's hand when they left, and gave Felicia a little hug. When the door clicked shut, she did a little dance through the living room.

Nicholas was amused and intrigued. "What's gotten into you?"

"Something Felicia said." She peeked through the curtains to make sure they were gone. "Come on, follow me into the kitchen and we can clean up as we talk. Do you remember when she was in a trance telling us the Merovingian story, talking about the patterns of wealth and power shifting all over Europe, and how she couldn't find the trail? Darling, that trail is right here in our house! The documents I have been studying for nearly two months trace it!"

It took several moments for what she said to sink in. "Are you serious? How do they do that?"

"Do you remember that little Egyptian cartouche that we found on the documents, the one that is on nearly every piece of paper?" When Nicholas nodded in reply, she continued. "I am *certain* it is an important clue to learning more about the people who owned the box. They all came from times of enormous wealth, from families that wielded great power. That is exactly what Felicia was talking about, Nicholas! I admit I would feel a lot better about all this if I had some idea of what was going on. I know Francesca feels that way, too."

Nicholas shrugged indifferently and kissed the top of her head. "That's really fascinating, honey. I guess it would be interesting to know." He inserted the last of the dinner dishes into the dishwasher and pushed the start button. "It sounds like Felicia would love to get her hands on those documents for her dissertation."

"Well for God's sake, Nicholas. Don't tell her what is in the documents! In fact, next time someone asks you about the box or the documents just change the subject!"

"I still think you're overdoing it, honestly," said Nicholas. "But, after all, those documents are only borrowed, right?"

"Right," she repeated. He turned and started walking out of the kitchen. "Nicholas?"

"Yes?" He stopped and turned to face her.

She smiled. "You forgot to put soap in the dishwasher."

Chapter 27

Lev eased his little Mercedes convertible out of the parking slot and swung toward the exit gate of his professor's condo complex. Though the complex was gated, condos like these were fairly ubiquitous, somewhere between Georgian and modern in the $350,000 range. Solidly middle class, nicely maintained, and well landscaped.

"Want the top down?"

"Sure. It's a beautiful night."

It was, in fact, a night only the South can deliver in late March, on the verge of spring and ready to blossom into full azalea and dogwood splendor. "If all the poets in the world could come to one place for heaven, it would be the South in the spring," sighed Felicia. "It's as beautiful as the Lavender Roads—though I hate to admit it!"

Lev rolled on down the byway toward Felicia's house. She lived in Morningside in a meticulously groomed vernacular Tudor bungalow purchased by her father for her sojourn at Emory. "That's quite a compliment," he said. "I've never heard you give America so much distinction."

"Well, I think it's true. Give me credit for being a lover of beauty rather than just being French!" She turned her head toward him. "Mrs. Shepard seemed to go from heavy to light during dinner. I wonder what was going on."

He shook his head. "I can't figure her out. I don't think she likes me."

"She doesn't," said Felicia matter-of-factly. "But why? Have you ever done anything to annoy her?"

"That's just it," replied Lev. "I've been incredibly deferential and polite every time I've been around her. I have gone out of my way to be friendly. We first met at a party for the graduate students before you came. My father handpicked Dr. Shepard, so I was prepared to become close to him and his wife. But she seemed cold even as we shook hands."

Nearly a full minute passed before Felicia asked, "Lev, has Dr. Shepard told you how much money he's made?"

"No. But I have a feeling it is quite a bit."

"Well, I would have thought they could afford to buy a house by now. And Dr. Shepard is still driving that mousetrap of a car."

"That's a rat trap." Lev let out a loud laugh.

"I don't care what you call it; they seem to have good taste. They need to at least hire a cook." Felicia was still appalled that dinner had come in disposable cartons. Not that she would have ever guessed, but once she knew it, it seemed so . . . proletariat. She shivered and turned to Lev. "I would certainly like to know why she was acting so oddly. Even Dr. Shepard seemed on edge. I found it all rather confusing."

Lev had a pretty good idea why they were behaving oddly. He reached over and rubbed the back of her neck. "Don't try to make too much of it. We were just all awkward and anxious."

"You? Awkward? You were smooth . . . just like your father."

He smiled. "You haven't known us long enough. We're just as human as anybody else, and if we seem suave and debonair, it is because it is just the good genes. I think they live there and don't have servants because they're American middle class and don't know what to do with money. We know because we were born to it."

He turned into her driveway. "Want to come in?" she asked coyly. "I have some new etchings."

They laughed. She actually had some exquisite etchings from the Renaissance and had invited him in on that pretext on their first date. "Darling, you do have some delightful etchings but I've got a paper to finish." He kissed her, slowly, several times.

She groaned. "You're right. I'll see you tomorrow." She swung her long slim legs out, and Lev watched her stride briskly to the front door. *Lovely*, he thought as she practically floated over the flagstone walk. She brushed her long hair back, unlocked her door, and waved goodbye. He stayed long enough to see the lights go on before backing out on to Morningside Drive. Instead of going home, a mere block away, he headed back toward the Emory campus. It was 10:30 p.m., and the air was soft and sweet. He regretted not staying at Felicia's, but he knew if his father didn't hear from him, he would catch hell.

He knew that Felicia was expecting this relationship to become something more permanent. He was falling in love, but until this current situation was taken care of, he wasn't ready to commit to anything. The family secrets were too dark, too complex, and too dangerous. And no one was about to let her in on the secret. *Power and wealth*, he thought scornfully. *If you only knew, my sweet*. He wasn't sure what Felicia would think if she knew he was following generations of Fousts sworn to uphold an ancient tradition. No, unlike his mother—whose discovery had led to disastrous consequences—his wife would remain in blissful ignorance.

Lev pulled into the empty parking lot outside the Economics Department, deep in thought. He had not lied to Felicia when he told her that Constantina had lost the use of her legs in a car accident. He knew she was dismayed that he had not forewarned her about the disability, but he still found it difficult to talk about. He was only nine years old and away at school when the call came. By all rights she should not have survived the fiery crash. But she had been thrown from the little Aston Martin before it made its tumbling decent down the rocky cliff. It wasn't until he was much older that his father told him the truth of that terrible day.

Suspecting that his father was having an affair, which he probably was, his mother had broken the lock on Malachi's desk with her nail file and read through his records. Shocked and disoriented, she left the house and headed up the coast in the little car he had given her for her birthday. She drove for hours. It was raining and somewhere along the jagged shoreline of Maine she lost control. After that, she changed. Not to Lev, who she loved more than life, but to Malachi. Constantina became what in Japan is known as a 'formal wife.' It was a power marriage after the accident, packed with a mutual and wary respect for each other, but emotionally uninvolved.

The building was stone-quiet. Lev walked slowly through the darkened hallway, listening to his footsteps echo off the walls. He used his key to unlock Nicholas' office. Before he turned the lights on he shut the blinds. *The usual mess,* he thought as he shifted papers. When he moved a rubber-banded stack covering the mouse, the monitor flashed on. Lev entered the usual passwords and started searching his professor's files. *Damn*, he thought. *He must have the trading files on his computer at home.* He kept digging through the directories in search of something, anything.

"Bingo," he said out loud after just a few short minutes. Alex Shepard's resumé popped into view.

Lev printed out a copy and left the office.

א

His own house in Morningside was not much bigger than Felicia's, but his father, frustrated architect that he was, had hired an expert to reconfigure the warren of original rooms into a reasonable facsimile of a loft. The new design removed the ceiling and curved all the walls, giving each "room" a sinuous, flowing feeling. The only space with any privacy was the bedroom, into which Lev went to change from his dress clothes to pajamas and a wine-colored bathrobe—a nice contrast to the stark white and charcoal interiors.

He grabbed a Coke from the kitchen and threw himself down on the dark gray sectional sofa. Fidgeting, he turned on CNN, but didn't watch it. Instead he stared at the telephone. He got up and retrieved the resumé from his coat pocket, sat down, and returned to staring at the phone. When it rang, he nearly jumped out of his skin.

"Jesus!" He leaned over and picked up the black handset and held it to his ear.

"Tell me."

"I was about to call you." He stopped and cleared his throat. "You beat me to it, father. I just got home. It was atrocious. Everyone was on edge. Mrs. Shepard was unfathomable and even Felicia couldn't make anyone comfortable . . ."

"I do not care about any of that!" snapped Malachi.

"I have news you will want to hear," began Lev anew. "I just stopped by the office, where I hoped to get into the trading files, but it looks like they must all be on his home computer." He knew he was talking too fast, so he forced himself to take a deep breath and slow down, or his father would immediately think something was wrong.

"Does he suspect something?"

"No, I don't think so. But Mrs. Shepard might. She's very protective of him, and has a certain . . . sense . . . about her. And she doesn't like me."

"Why?" laughed Malachi. "She senses your duplicity, your secret life? That Machiavelli was an ancestor?"

"She has a powerful intuition," Lev said more meekly than he intended or desired. "People like that can be dangerous. They intuit too much and then make assumptions based on those feelings—"

"So what did you learn that I want to hear?" interrupted Malachi again.

Lev smiled to himself. "I got my hands on Alex Shepard's resume. Someone had to design the system identification programs, and Nicholas was being coy about it. I am sure it was Alex."

Malachi coughed. "What else?"

"There is something else that might interest you . . ." Lev smiled vindictively, anticipating his father's reaction.

"Yes, what?"

Lev took a swig of his Coke and muted CNN. "Apparently, they found documents—lots of them, I think—along with the box." He held the phone out from his ear awaiting Malachi's response.

"*What?*" screamed Malachi, whose breathing became suddenly heavy and irregular. "They found those, too? How the hell can this be happening? Things are going from bad to worse—quickly."

Lev did not interrupt the long pause that followed. "Tell me something." His father's voice was strained but much calmer now. He was back in control again. "Just what did you say to the wife to make her so suspicious of you?"

Damn. Lev rolled his eyes and winced. "Forgive me, father. I'm not as smooth as you are. I might have seemed too . . . interested."

"You have your mother's lack of decorum," he replied nastily.

"Anyway, I have Alex's resume."

"What do you think I am, an idiot? I also have it! My secretary could have found it on the internet in five minutes. Mika also had a copy—a few years old, but the information has not changed significantly. There's nothing on there but a lot of advanced degrees and overblown credentials."

"Did you realize the Shepards were born in Asheville?"

"Who the hell cares about that?" Malachi's voice was rising again, but just as quickly he saw the connection and throttled down again. "Hmm . . . yes. That is rather ironic and interesting. The Biltmore Estate just happens to be there, doesn't it?"

"Do you know if there is someone there named Gabriel? They apparently showed him the box or he was with them when they found it—something like that."

"Gabriel? Of course! That's Ernest von Stuyvesant's liberal do-gooder son. What a good-for-nothing little bastard," Malachi cursed loudly. "Well, son I think you just redeemed yourself. This little scheme would suit him perfectly. He probably delivered them the box with a dozen roses and chocolates on the whimsical notion that they'll make the whole world rich and divide the undividable evenly."

"They're certainly making themselves rich."

"I'll have Mika check on that in the morning. Now, where is the box, and where are those documents?"

"Well, I am not exactly sure, but Dr. Shepard claims the box is in Charleston, South Carolina, with the brother. They really did not say where the documents are."

"Alright, let's assume that is so and everything is in Charleston. How are you going to get them?"

Lev nearly fell off the sofa. "Me . . . me?" he stuttered. *So this is what comes with the legacy.* He swallowed loudly and asked, "Do you have any suggestions?"

Malachi thought about it, gazing at the mahogany paneling in his study as though he might read the answers on the wall. "I'm coming to Atlanta. Suggest to Dr. Shepard that I would like to see the box. Maybe I can arrange a trip to Charleston, the other Shepard can come down, or perhaps he will FedEx it over."

"Wouldn't it be easier to simply fabricate a robbery at the house in Charleston?"

"I'd like this to remain reasonably civilized, if possible," replied Malachi, "though of course if it comes to that we can arrange it. Mika talked me out of calling Ernest von Stuyvesant, damn her, but I think we need to have a little chat—even though I don't think he talks to his son very often."

"Lucky son." quipped Lev irreverently.

"Yes," Malachi chuckled dryly. "He is even harder to get along with than I am. Expect me the day after tomorrow. You've done moderately good work."

Lev breathed a sigh of relief. He was back in his father's good graces.

৯

Malachi eased the phone softly back into its cradle. A solitary lamp burning on his desk finished the room with a warm womb of rich color. He moved over to the silk coral-and-melon-striped draperies and looked out over the twinkling square of Central Park and on out to the city spread out below him.

It's mine, he thought with pride. *I control this city, the markets here, and all over the world. And some stupid economist discovers secrets of incalculable value—by accident!*

He hated these little inconveniences. Especially ones with nasty outcomes.

৯

The morning after the discussion with Lev, Malachi arrived at his Manhattan office at 6:30 a.m. He had a mountain of paperwork waiting for him. The month of March had been a disastrous one for his investments, and the firm had lost several billion dollars. He still could not comprehend why, periodically, the markets bucked the predicted trends. Nor could he anticipate when it would happen. But when it did, it was very expensive. Despite pushing Mika Hunter for answers, she was only able to confirm what he already knew: the market sometimes reversed itself in the winter and the summer. The patterns, she reported to his dismay, seemed random and unexplainable.

Once seated at his desk, Malachi barked into his speaker phone to his secretary, "Get me Ernest von Stuyvesant."

"Yes, Mr. Foust. Right away, sir." When Malachi worked early, so did she.

When Ernest finally answered, Malachi wasted no time. "Where's the box?"

The quick strike surprised Ernest, who cleared his throat nervously. He knew quite well what Malachi was referring to, but had no idea why he would be asking him. "At the Biltmore, of course!"

"No, damn it, it's not!" Malachi's voice had a steel edge, as it always did when he was angry. He stood up and leaned forward onto his desk. "It's in Charleston along with, as far as I know, its centuries of impeccable credentials!" he shouted into the speaker.

Ernest's throat went dry. "Malachi . . . I don't understand."

"Well I do! Have you spoken with your son lately?"

"Yes." Ernest folded. He could never stand up to Malachi. "Gabriel told me he had found the room and the box accidentally. Naturally I did not tell him a thing. Instead, I told him the box wasn't worth a damn— which it isn't anymore. We have all the information we need from it—"

Malachi jumped in, his voice calm, flat. Cold. "Where is Gabriel now?"

Ernest closed his eyes and squirmed uncomfortably in his seat. He clenched his teeth and drew in a sharp breath. He was all too familiar with that tone of voice. "I sent him to Germany. He will be there for quite a while."

Malachi digested the answer for a few seconds before continuing. "The box may not be worth anything to us, Ernest, but your damn fool of a son gave it to his two friends!"

Ernest gasped aloud. "He *gave* them the box?"

"Why shouldn't he?" Malachi was shouting again. "You told him it wasn't worth anything! How stupid can you be? In my book, that's a license to give the damn thing to the Salvation Army, for Christ's sake!

You know the genes in that boy of yours are haywire! How about some more good news?" Sneered Malachi. "His buddies have figured out how to use the goddamn thing to predict the markets!"

"I am sure we can get it back . . ." began Ernest. He sounded as though he were choking.

Malachi was not about to let him off the hook easily. "The cat could be out of the bag! Serious harm has been done! We have to prevent them from finding out the rest, because if they figure it out, our credibility will be completely shot. And the media—never mind the courts!—will hang us in public. Here's an idea for you. How about a new reality T.V. series where they walk us to the top of the Empire State Building and throw us off?"

"How do we fix it?" Despite the early hour, Ernest was already unscrewing a bottle of bourbon. His hand was shaking so hard he had to put the bottle down to avoid spilling it.

"We? *We?* We are not going to fix anything!" Malachi went silent, turned around, and looked out his window. The city skyline was cut against a wall of heavy clouds. It was going to rain. He turned back to the desk and slumped into his chair. "I will deal with it, Ernest. You should have called me. I could have prevented this."

"I know, Malachi. I am . . . sorry."

"You will do nothing from this point forward—except tighten your belt. Some of your investments are going for a ride!" He slammed the phone down. "Get in here!" he barked into his private intercom.

Ten seconds later Mika walked into Malachi's office. She was dressed in a skintight black leather suit and red silk blouse.

"Well?" he asked. There would be no pleasantries this morning.

Her face betrayed her puzzlement as she deposited a sheaf of spreadsheets onto his desk. "I returned the call to my former colleague, Alex Shepard, and offered our service. He thanked me for calling back, but declined. He does his own trading."

Malachi laughed out loud, but not out of amusement. "Oh he does, does he? I'm sure he's lost his shirt just like everybody else in this upside-down market."

Mika spun the spreadsheets around so they faced Malachi. "I called a friend at the Chicago Mercantile Exchange. He sent me these figures."

Malachi pulled the papers closer and scrutinized them. His expression of smug indifference faded quickly. Rising from his chair, he looked across his desk at Mika in complete disbelief. According to the spreadsheets, the Shepards had begun with an investment of $50,000, and in three months amassed a total net gain of $2,080,000—a profit of 4,060 percent.

"How is this possible?" Malachi sputtered. "It can't be possible—that's the answer!"

"I double-checked with my contact," Mika said quietly. "These spreadsheets and every figure on them are accurate to the penny."

Sweat broke out on Malachi's forehead and he reached into his pocket to pull out a handkerchief. He dabbed his skin lightly as he shook his head, shifting his gaze from the papers to Mika and back again. He finally turned around and looked outside. Large soft raindrops were hitting the window and running down the pane. "What do they know that we don't know?" he whispered.

"I don't know, Malachi."

"Then why the hell do I pay you?" he snarled angrily. "Isn't it clear? The honorable Shepard brothers have managed the unmanageable. They have cracked the secret of the phase-inversion phenomenon! While we were losing all that money during the month of March, the Shepard brothers never missed a trend!" He picked up the spreadsheets and threw them across the room.

Malachi eyed Mika coldly while the papers fluttered softly onto the carpeted floor. "I am on my way to Atlanta. I may need you to bring some experts to help us with this."

Mika's throat tightened. "Experts?"

"You know very well what I mean."

Chapter 28

Striding across the Emory campus, Nicholas attached the earpiece to his cell phone and rang up his brother. "Alex, a couple things before I lose you. The battery in this phone is low. First, we should lock down all of our technology information and store it somewhere safe. Our program source codes could be hacked by any amateur on the Internet."

"Good idea," agreed Alex. "We can use a memory key—a miniature hard drive about two inches long and one-half inch wide. It will easily hold everything."

"Why don't you pick up a couple of those?" suggested Nicholas. "We'll plug them into our laptops and back up everything permanently. I don't mean to sound paranoid, but I've heard it from both Cassandra and Gabriel. Keeping everything on a hard drive is really asking for trouble. Maybe we should pay attention."

"I'll get on it this afternoon. What's the second thing?"

"This one is a bit more . . . odd," continued Nicholas. "You know Lev, my graduate student? His father is coming to Atlanta this afternoon and wants to meet with me. He's incredibly wealthy. I mean *incredibly* wealthy. Guess what he wants to talk about?"

Alex groaned. "You have got to be kidding."

"Nope," replied Nicholas, nodding his head and smiling at a former student as he passed. "He wants to talk about our project. Malachi Foust is particularly interested in the box. I'm glad, frankly, that I don't have it here. I don't think we should be showing it around, you know? What do you think?"

"Geez, Nicholas. You sound pretty calm about all this," said Alex. "How did he find out about all this? Your student?"

"I think it's safe to assume Lev mentioned it when he told his father about working with me on our trading strategies."

"We should not be marching that box around in public, I agree—especially to a complete stranger. Besides, we don't even own the damn thing." Alex thought for a moment and then asked, "Why is he so interested?"

"He's a rich guy and I suppose he has an interest in everything related to the financial markets. Everyone wants a hot stock tip!" Both brothers laughed. "Really, all I know for sure is that I am taking them out to dinner without Cassandra. She said she fulfilled her duty by entertaining Lev and his girlfriend the other night." Nicholas whistled. "Oh, man."

"What?" asked Alex.

"Here comes a limo the size of a yacht. I've never seen this thing on campus. Must be him. Gotta go, Alex. Talk with you later."

Looking entirely out of place, a white Mercedes stretch limousine rolled up to the front of the administration building. Feeling self-conscious, Nicholas adjusted his tie and smoothed out his hair on the sides. He had a feeling he was going to be glad Cassandra insisted that he buy a new suit and expensive linen shirts. He stuck his hands in his pockets and watched with amused curiosity as a uniformed driver stepped carefully out of the car and circled around to open the rear passenger door.

Malachi Foust slid out of the car. He wore a charcoal pinstriped Versace suit with a claret shirt and tie in the latest monochromatic fashion. The driver handed him a slim Italian leather briefcase and touched the brim of his hat before returning to the driver's seat.

When Nicholas caught his eye, Malachi stepped in his direction. "Dr. Nicholas Shepard?"

"Yes," smiled Nicholas, "and I have no doubt you must be Malachi Foust. Good to meet you, sir."

The men exchanged a firm handshake and Malachi managed a reasonably genuine smile. Nicholas looked into a cold set of blue eyes and tried to return a grin. *This man exudes power*, he thought. *He makes me feel like some dumb hillbilly.* Nicholas' only advantage was his height: Malachi's skinny 5'10" was no match for his own more powerfully-built 6'2" frame.

"And it is a pleasure to meet you. I have followed your career with much interest."

"Thank you. But . . . why would that be?" Nicholas lifted his hand and steered the older man down the quadrangle toward his office.

"Because it's very seldom that I meet a university professor who isn't misguided by liberalism," said Malachi with a chuckle. "It appears that you have the rare ability to make complicated economic theories comprehensible. I was most interested in your paper clarifying and extending Robert Mundell's analysis of fixed and pegged exchange rates, as well as your essay defending the debt implications of current supply-side economics."

Nicholas nearly fell over. This man knew exactly how to impress a total stranger. "We have come a long way since every Roman Emperor creating his own coin of the realm, haven't we?" *Flattery will get you everywhere*, thought Nicholas as he quickly warmed to Lev's father. "Mundell's writing is very much to the point, I believe, and I was delighted when he won the Nobel Prize in 1999. He's one of the most forward-looking thinkers of our day."

"What are you working on now?" asked Malachi.

"I'm researching a second paper on the current state of supply-side economics and its effects on fixed exchange rates. For the moment, however, I've had to put that aside to work on . . . on another project, which I'm sure Lev has told you about in detail. For a financier, you seem well-versed in economic theory." Nicholas caught himself and backtracked. "I don't mean that to be insulting. It's just that most of the financiers I know are not much for the subject."

Malachi nodded and laughed. "No need to apologize and no insult taken. We must know the same bankers! But I'm fortunate to have some extremely capable colleagues—like Mika Hunter—who allow me my 'think tank' time." He watched Nicholas' face as they walked along. Would the name elicit any response? It didn't. "Perhaps there's a place to have coffee nearby?"

Nicholas led the way to Café Antico in the Carlos Museum. Both men ordered a double espresso. They sat outside in the spring sunshine and talked pleasantly about former presidents and their impact on the country's economy. Nicholas found much to admire in Malachi's assessments. "It was a good thing Mundell came along when he did," observed Malachi. "Reagan's people were ready for economic conditions favorable for cutting taxes to encourage capital growth. And grow it did. Never looked back."

"Unless you count the savings and loan fiasco, and lately the dot-bomb . . . excuse me . . . dot-com bubble," Nicholas replied. "My research shows that most recessions only last nine to eleven months. This last downturn really wasn't a recession, in my estimation; just a single-sector anomaly brought on by exuberance, just like the Federal Reserve warned. This administration's debt is simply a function of absorbing defense costs, along with lower tax revenues stemming from market value losses. The funny thing is," continued Nicholas, pausing for a few seconds to sip from his espresso, "most people give Clinton credit for paying down the debt, when in actuality it was Reaganomics still at work, along with some shifty tax-the-rich policies."

"Clinton raised taxes, which almost always cuts the throat of the economy," responded Malachi.

"Enchanting metaphor," Nicholas smiled.

Malachi did not return the smile. Instead, he leaned forward, his fine well manicured hands encircling the tiny espresso cup. He locked his ice blue eyes firmly onto Nicholas' and did not let go. "I am going to be blunt, Dr. Shepard." There was no longer an ounce of warmth or friendliness in his voice. "I believe you have it in your power to change macroeconomics on a global basis. If my information is correct—and it always is correct—you have solved the phase-inversion problem." Nicholas blinked his eyes several times, unsure he was really hearing what he was hearing. Malachi's eyes remained open and unblinking. "Your discovery would literally change the world. You must be very, *very* careful how you use it, doctor. If it falls into the wrong hands, nine-eleven might seem like a picnic in the park."

He knows about the phase-inversion problem!

Nicholas stared open-mouthed at Malachi, shocked beyond belief at the sudden turn in their discussion. He had expected more general questions about Lev's progress, their discovery—perhaps even inquiries about their trading strategies. Instead, Malachi was three steps ahead of him. Was there also an implied *personal* threat in his words?

Nicholas swallowed deeply. He wanted to drink more of his espresso but he was unsure whether he could lift the tiny cup without spilling it. "I only intend to use this technology for the benefit of my family," he replied quietly.

Francesca's question uttered so long ago reverberated once again inside his head. *"Is it moral?"* Now he understood even what she, perhaps, had not fully grasped. How would this discovery impact the rest of the world?

Malachi merely folded his hands on the table, his face resembling chiseled granite. He looked as though he was angry, but Nicholas couldn't be sure. "Have you given any serious thought about what could happen if your . . . your discoveries . . . were brought to the attention of the Federal Reserve?"

Nicholas frowned and did not answer. Malachi pressed him further. "What if you showed it to people who could use the knowledge to create a prosperous global economy in which poverty ceased to exist? Or, what if scientists used the knowledge to predict human behavior? What about scholars who could apply it for the benefit of all humankind?"

"Most of this has crossed my mind, Mr. Foust, but I admit I have not thought it through perhaps as thoroughly as you have."

"Dr. Shepard—may I call you Nicholas?" He voice had once again warmed. His eyes softened as his smile grew. "I believe you. I believe you are like most other men who only want to provide for their families and make money, make their lives easier, acquire fine things. But perhaps you should do more. Have you thought about sharing your knowledge with a think tank? Perhaps the Bilderberg Group?"

Nicholas furrowed his brow in thought. "I've heard of the Bilderberg Group," he acknowledged. "I really don't know much about it. I can't quite see the connection of the group to what we are talking about."

"My friend, you have much to learn. And please do not take that as an insult," added Malachi quickly. "I would like you to come to New York—as my guest, of course—to discuss the possibility of hiring you to consult with my firm."

So that was it. For a moment his mind flashed to the long white limousine, uniformed driver, the thin expensive watch on Malachi's wrist, the expensive tailored suits. Would I ever fit in a world like that? He was about to respond when the sudden appearance of Lev and Felicia interrupted his reverie. Malachi did not stand up. Instead, he turned and greeted the young people with a short nod before refocusing his gaze intently on Nicholas.

If he is waiting for an answer, thought Nicholas, *he will have to wait a little longer*. He rose and smiled at his graduate students. "Mr. Foust, why don't you let me show you around our beautiful campus?" The offer did not please the financier, but he offered a curt dip of his head in reply.

Seated comfortably on the plush leather of Lev's Mercedes, the four of them drove over to Virginia-Highlands and ate outdoors at one of the neighborhood's trendy restaurants overlooking Piedmont Park. Malachi was visibly bored throughout. Once coffee and dessert were served, he broached the subject Nicholas had avoided earlier, albeit in a more roundabout fashion. "Lev, I have invited Dr. Shepard to come and be a consultant with our firm. What do you think?"

"I think that is a wonderful idea, father!" his son dutifully responded. *He knew this was coming*, thought Nicholas.

Felicia, however, looked genuinely surprised. "What an opportunity, Dr. Shepard! But wouldn't you miss teaching?"

"Naturally I would encourage you to maintain your academic connections," Malachi interjected.

"Absolutely," Lev agreed. "I'd love to continue working with you after I've finished my dissertation, Dr. Shepard. I should warn you, though, father—he's incredibly messy!"

"We can deal with just about anything," Malachi countered. He was beginning to relax, but he wasn't about to take any chances. It was time to sweeten the pot and set the hook. "Perhaps I could arrange for you to address the Bilderberg Group at our annual meeting next month," he said, carefully choosing his words. "Your discovery is of potential Nobel Prize value, don't you think Dr. Shepard?"

Nicholas was barely able to stifle a cry of delight. "I really hadn't thought in those terms," he replied slowly and softly, though he felt himself being drawn like a moth into Malachi's flame. "Do you really believe the Nobel Committee would be interested in our findings?"

Malachi smiled but remained silent.

"I . . . well, I'll have to think about all this." Nicholas felt his head spin as the espresso and sudden turn of events kicked his adrenaline into overdrive. It was all he could do to contain himself. "Would you mind if I get back to you in a few days?"

"Please take your time," answered Malachi. "Ah, I see my ride has arrived." The stretch limo glided into view and Malachi stood to make his departure. He faced Nicholas and edged closer to him. His proximity made the professor feel a bit uneasy, almost violated. "I know you will make the right decision, Dr. Shepard," whispered Malachi. "You are a very bright man. I shall await your positive response." The two men shook hands and Malachi patted Nicholas' shoulder with his left hand. "Can we drop you at your home?"

"Thank you, no. My wife is just down the street at a previous engagement, and we planned to meet up afterwards. I'll just get another cup of coffee and wait for her to call."

এ

The driver dropped Felicia off at her home. As soon as the father and son were alone, Lev exclaimed, "Father! What are you doing? We only make money when the market spikes up and down. If Dr. Shepard makes his discovery public, it could ultimately flatten the markets. It could cause worldwide financial chaos! What would we do then?"

Malachi picked at a pointed well-manicured fingernail and looked absentmindedly into the distance. "How long have you known me? Apparently not long enough. When we get the phase-inversion information from the good doctor, we'll use it to our own advantage. I have no intention of offering it to the world. I have no intention of even offering it to the Group."

Lev frowned. "I'm sorry, but I do not fully understand."

"Of course you don't! You're not me, are you?"

"But if he presents his discovery to the Group—"

"He will indeed present his findings." A wicked look enveloped Malachi's feature and settled in his eyes. "But with my help, the Group will find our professor and his theories absurd. I am afraid no matter how much he enjoys teaching, he'll be lucky to find a job tutoring high school economics when I am finished with him."

Lev clapped his hands twice in delight and shook his head in admiration. "My father—a true Machiavelli!"

"Just call me the Prince—but never in public." His father was smiling now as he looked out the window. "My God, how does any civilized person live here?"

Lev looked distressed. "I don't see how Dr. Shepard and his brother are going to sit by and let you undermine their theories."

"Well son, life teaches us so many lessons. Unfortunate things do happen in this world." His smile faded.

"May I get my dissertation completed first?"

"I'd advise you to hurry."

The limo pulled up to Lev's house, where the son climbed out after a brief, emotionless handshake. Malachi continued on to Peachtree-Dekalb airport, where his private jet was waiting to fly him back to New York.

ঽ

Alone, Nicholas nursed a cup of coffee. His ankle bobbed restlessly on his knee as his mind replayed the meeting with Malachi. It wasn't just the caffeine that was making his heart beating like a tightly-wound snare drum. He really had not given much thought beyond trading strategies, beyond making money. What would their discovery mean to the global economy? Sure, he and Alex had discussed it, but only in passing. He certainly hadn't considered what their discovery could mean to his professional career.

A Nobel Prize?

Fear and excitement roiled in his gut. He pulled his cell phone out of a pocket and dialed a number. "I need a chauffeur," he said to his wife.

"I'm around the corner at 20th Century Antiques. Want to walk down here?"

He was already beginning to feel calmer when he spotted Cassandra contemplating a Fortuny silk lamp. He offered her a tender kiss and asked quietly, "How would you like it if I won the Nobel Prize?"

For a brief moment Cassandra's eyes glowed, but the excitement turned to skepticism just as quickly. "Is that what Lev's father is baiting you with? How could he—or should I say, how *will* he—arrange that?"

"Will you be wanting the lamp then?" inquired the clerk.

"Yes, please, and would you carefully wrap it for me?" asked Cassandra, who followed a few steps behind the clerk as she carried the lamp toward the front of the store.

Nicholas walked alongside Cassandra. "With ease, apparently." He told her about his conversation with Malachi and the job offer. She listened without interrupting while they waited. After she paid for her purchase, they walked to the car.

"You are not saying anything, honey."

"I don't know what to say," answered Cassandra. "This is all rather a shock to the 'ole system."

"It would mean I would have to deal with Malachi's people on a regular—and social—basis," continued her husband. "Be a New York type. Sweetheart, this is really major."

She nodded. "It's hard to disagree with that!"

He could read the doubt on her face, "How about we go to Charleston this weekend and talk it over with Alex and Francesca?"

She smiled, partially relieved. "I was hoping you'd say that. After all, this is partly Alex's discovery too."

"This could be a great opportunity for us, Cassandra. Who knows where it might lead?"

Chapter 29

Alex hung up the phone and grabbed his wife by the shoulders. Francesca listened as Alex excitedly told her about Malachi Foust's offer to Nicholas. "Can you imagine, a Nobel Prize?" he said in awe.

"No, I can't imagine that," smiled Francesca as she wiggled free of his grasp and popped open the oven to check the bread baking inside. *Something is not right*, she thought. "Of course, I don't know anything about that subject or who is worthy and who is not."

"The discovery is really a quantum leap in economic theory," offered Alex. "I suspect it might be worthy of a prize like that."

Francesca grimaced before plastering a smile on her face and turning to her husband. "I think I might invite Father Galen over to share in the good news. Do you mind?" *If anyone could talk some sense into the twins it would be Galen Abbott,* Francesca thought.

"No, that's a great idea. We should call Gabriel as well."

২

Comfortably ensconced in Francesca's newly redecorated living room, the priest, the twins, and their wives sipped coffee and admired the newly installed wall coverings recently arrived from England. Only Gabriel was missing. Repeated calls had produced no response. Michelangelo, who had just spent a great deal of time at obedience school, was resting quietly in front of the fireplace. The children were asleep.

"I'll take some credit for that dog's behavior," boomed Father Galen. "While you folks were on vacation, I gently allowed the fear of God to come to him." When Cassandra raised her eyebrows, he lifted his index finger and waved it slowly back and forth. "I said *gently*, Cassandra."

Nicholas wasted little time beginning the conversation. He briefly outlined his conversation with Malachi and the wealthy man's offer. "I have to say that neither Alex nor I seriously considered the full *intellectual* significance of our discovery, or the wide range of its implications. The excitement of the discovery and the idea of making more money than we could ever spend pushed everything else aside. Malachi certainly made the ramifications very real to me. I mean, a Nobel Prize opens up some possibilities that could make our lives pretty exciting. Not to say that we would win it, but, really, the notion is pretty exhilarating!" He offered a wide smile at his captive audience. "Cassandra and I wanted to talk to you all about it before we, I mean I, got too enthusiastic."

His wife offered him a polite elbow and smile. Inside she was as troubled as Francesca. Both the women could sense there was something more going on here than met the eye. Francesca turned to Nicholas with a challenge in her eyes. "I've heard the Nobel Prize is a political football. Does Malachi think he can lure both of you with it by dangling it like bait?"

Galen stepped in with his dependable voice of reason. "Hold on there. We'll get nowhere fast with that kind of negativity. But as long as we are on the subject, what are the drawbacks?"

They all talked at once except for Nicholas, who thought he knew what was bothering his wife. Cassandra would hate spending a lot of time in New York socializing with people she did not respect and whose company she would not enjoy. He sat and listened to everyone's objections.

Francesca wanted to know what Alex's part was in all this, and why he wasn't being given as much credit as he deserved. After all, Malachi had not invited Alex to consult with his New York firm. Alex brushed aside her concerns and focused on the Bilderberg Group, which he thought was too shadowy and sinister to be involved with.

"What is the Bilderberg Group, anyway?" Francesca asked.

"It depends on who you speak with. To many people it's a think tank," Alex began, "a very secret group made up of powerful Western financial and political leaders. Conspiracy theorists think it is an organization seeking world domination by a single global government."

Galen turned toward a grim-faced Cassandra. "What are you thinking?"

"I'm thinking I'm a conspiracy theorist," she responded flatly.

"This is just ridiculous," Nicholas replied emphatically, lifting his hands and slapping his thighs. "If these guys were out to rule the world, they'd be doing it. I researched the group. It is a loose assemblage of about 120 people from all over the world who get together once a year in the spring to discuss everything from bioengineering to politics. Security is tight, but that is because the members are very wealthy and influential people. You know, people like the Rockefellers. They don't allow the press in their meetings, but they don't make any secret about scheduling the conferences, either."

He looked about the room. Except for Alex, the faces were impassive. "Why are the three of you acting like this? You are essentially denying us a shot at the Nobel Prize. Of course Alex and I would share it, Francesca. I would never accept it if it was offered only to me. This is a great opportunity for both of us—all of us!" he continued, his voice growing louder with his word. "Sure, we'd be rich, but we would be making history as well." A startled Michelangelo looked up and barked at Nicholas' tone.

After a long moment, Galen spoke. "I don't think any of us would deny you that glory, Nicholas. I think we really just want to know the best course to follow. For example, what would Alex have to do with your consulting? Wasn't he responsible for quantifying the discovery?"

"Sure he was. I didn't really get into it with Malachi about who did what."

"Does he think you did it all?" Galen almost whispered the question.

Nicholas raised his eyebrows. It was a legitimate inquiry. "I think all he knows is what Lev has told him, and all Lev sees is me trading and working on quantifying the discovery. I don't think he knows about Alex or what his part has been in all this. But I would certainly tell him that we shared in the discovery and both developed the trading programs. I'd make sure he knew that the discovery is as much Alex's as it is mine."

Alex went over and sat down next to the puppy, rubbing his velvety-soft floppy ears. "I think Mika Hunter works with Malachi Foust."

"Who?" asked everyone in unison.

Alex cleared his throat. "Mika Hunter. She works with the Atlantic Trade Partnership and, I think, Malachi Foust."

Nicholas frowned. He had heard that name before. Malachi had mentioned it. Nicholas snapped his fingers when he recalled the financier's words. "When I had lunch with Foust earlier today, he mentioned a Mika Hunter. He said something about how capable she is, and her expertise allowed him—I think he referred to it as, 'think tank' time."

Alex was still stroking Michelangelo's ears when he spoke up. "Mika is an extremely competitive woman. We've met on several—for lack of a better word—battlefields, in the aeronautics arena. I have to admit she usually won. Her academic and professional background is a lot like mine. Frankly, I don't trust her. Under no circumstances do I want her near the software programs we've developed—especially the phase-inversion information. Given her competitive nature and capabilities—and the power of Malachi's firm—I'm afraid she would take it away from us."

The answer surprised everyone, including Nicholas. "You think she could reverse-engineer your programs?"

"Definitely," Alex said, nodding his head. He was holding his knees now, slowly rocking back and forth.

Nicholas lifted his arms and turned his hands palm up. "Well, I guess that answers some other questions I had. We are seriously limited in the information we can share with Malachi's firm. Plus, it leaves New York out of the question for you, right?"

"Absolutely, assuming you plan to work with his company," answered Alex. "I'd rather remain the silent partner and keep doing what I'm doing. Francesca and I have a great life here with our kids and"— Michelangelo got up and waddled across the room sniffing the carpet— "this dog, who is about to pee on our floor!" Alex scrambled across the oak planks, lifted the lab in his arms, and carried him toward the kitchen.

Francesca beat him to the door. "I'll do it," she volunteered. "I need some air."

Nicholas could feel the energy level in the room deflating and tried hard to pump it up again when Alex turned around.

"You wouldn't give up a chance to win a Nobel Prize, would you, Alex? That's the ultimate reward for a couple of scientists like us. It seems to me it would be worth the effort—maybe even worth a little discomfort."

Galen drummed his long fingers on the sofa's arm and spoke before Alex could muster a response. "Nicholas, your portrait of Malachi is of a charming, extremely wealthy financier. In other words, you don't know anything about him. People don't climb that high in life through altruism and piety. Everyone . . . even me," he laughed, "has a dark side and a few skeletons in the closet." Galen's voice had assumed a serious tone. "A man like this carefully plans his every move. His kind looks at life as nothing more than a giant chess board, and I can guarantee you he is always thinking several moves ahead."

"So what are his motives?" Cassandra cut in.

Galen nodded in agreement. "I think that is the fundamental question before us."

"I haven't even met him," replied Alex, "but anybody who would hire Mika Hunter would have to be both ruthless and unscrupulous, given what I know of her. And if he's a member of the Bilderberg Group, you have to figure he's all about power and control—probably including the control of everyone around him."

"That's a pretty good shot-in-the-dark analysis," said Galen. "I think absolute control is likely a key motive behind his actions. There are many issues at stake here, but you must carefully consider this as well: how much do you value your independence and privacy?"

"You know with me it's damn near paramount," Nicholas responded. "It's why I don't like being tied down in a tenured position. I like it on the edge, where I have to think to survive, and endure, and prevail—to misquote Faulkner."

"How independent will you be under Malachi's thumb?"

Nicholas brooded about that for a moment. "Well, if it is only consulting, then I can still teach and we wouldn't have to live in New York."

"Well, thank God for that," blurted out Cassandra. "but I know you, Nicholas. You'll go to New York and attach to all that excitement like glue to paper. We'll end up with a commuter marriage because"—her mind suddenly made itself up—"I can't, and I won't, go with you." She lowered her eyes and stared at the floor. Tears crawled down her red cheeks.

The words stunned Nicholas into silence as the blood drained from his face. "Cassandra," he whispered, leaning in close and moving her hair away from her forehead. "Sweetheart, I would never do anything that would come between us. Ever. We've been together since we were children. Nothing will change that."

"I love the way things are now," Cassandra choked out. "Oh, God, I can't believe I am blubbering like this!" Galen produced a handkerchief and she smiled as she took it, wiping her eyes and blowing her nose. "I don't like anything about what is happening right now."

Francesca had returned to the room a few minutes earlier. Tears were welling up in her eyes, too. Embarrassed, Alex noisily cleared his throat.

Galen leaned back in his seat. "There's one more important thing you probably should consider. It sounds like Malachi is offering to buy your entry into the Nobel Committee. If you accept his offer, would that bother you—living with the knowledge that you had this guy's help in winning the prize?"

"That's right." Francesca nodded vigorously in agreement. "You don't even own the box. Someone else knows its secrets and has been using it. You can't claim you did it all yourselves."

Nicholas stood and walked slowly to the front window. Charleston was beautiful this time of year. Bright azalea bushes lined the front veranda and the weather was warm, though without the humidity that would soon arrive.

"The perfection of the discovery *is* our work," he began. "It deserves recognition in its own right. We're not even sure anyone is currently using the box's secret. Maybe that information was lost many years ago."

He turned and looked at his brother. "Alex, you know as well as I do that when you develop a theorem and perfect it, even if you're standing on the shoulders of the people who've come before, you're entitled to the recognition. We would know if someone else had taken this idea as far as we have. We've charted new territory here."

"We are further along," agreed Alex.

"Yes, exactly," replied Nicholas. "Leaving Malachi out of it for the moment, though, is there any reason why we can't make our findings public if we choose to?" Nicholas held out his hands in a plea. "Alex, what if *we* choose the time and the place to share this with the world? Maybe I can put off answering Malachi until we sort this out."

"Have you considered what the consequences would be if you turned Malachi Foust down?" asked Galen.

Michelangelo bounded back into the room and sat at Cassandra's feet. She reached down, picked him up, and placed him on her lap. "I have," she announced. "Nobody turns down Malachi Foust. He probably rules the world."

Nicholas turned back to the window. It was a windswept day, and the smell of the sea was heavy in the air. He could taste it on his lips. "Well, he doesn't rule me. Or us. We have to do what's right and decline his offer."

Cassandra shifted the puppy to Galen's lap and walked slowly to where Nicholas was standing. She placed her hand on his cheek and turned his head toward her. "I know how disappointed you are, but in the end you will have kept your integrity—and your independence."

He hugged her and offered a tortured smile. "I'll take your word for it."

Alex jumped up and thumped his brother's back. "If you hadn't made that decision, I would have made it for you! Now we can get back to trading. I am ready to go on another vacation!"

Everyone laughed. The tension in the room was rapidly thawing. A very relieved Francesca grabbed Galen by the forearm and led him into the kitchen with her. "My official taster," she explained to the others.

Galen gave an exaggerated shrug. "If I must. . . ." More laughter. Alex followed, knowing that Cassandra and Nicholas needed to be alone.

Nicholas took his wife's hand and they went out of the house to walk along the water. "I am relieved," said Cassandra, wrapping both hands around her husband's arm, "but I am a little worried about how Malachi Foust might respond. What are you going to say to him?"

"I'll just tell him I'm not ready. And I'm not. There may be a day in the future when we'll change our minds, but it isn't today." He looked out at the dark green water. The day's last light was fading, and a half-moon was rising against red-rimmed clouds. "Red sky at night, sailor's delight." They leaned against each other and enjoyed the beauty of the moment.

"Will you ever publish your discovery?"

"I guess when I think the world is ready for it," he answered. "You know, you all made Malachi Foust out to be the devil, but I have to say I *liked* him. He might come in handy one day. We should find out more about his organization. It's like what they say about the market: a stock is only worth its performance over time. Let's treat Malachi like a stock."

By the time they returned Francesca was serving pork tenderloin marinated in dark rum, lime juice, brown sugar, tarragon, and garlic. The house smelled divine, and Cassandra realized that all the anxiety of the day had made her tremendously hungry. Dinner was relaxed and cheerful, though Nicholas couldn't quite dismiss the vision of himself standing at the Nobel podium. Still, he knew that he could not do it without Cassandra's support.

Galen left early Sunday morning. He was opening counseling centers in Virginia and Pennsylvania. The priest was relieved that he had been of some help, but was still worried about Nicholas. It wasn't like him to be so impulsive—ready to jump into the water with sharks. Nicholas was the brother with the steady head; it was usually Alex who went off half-cocked. Galen made a promise to himself to call Nicholas next week.

It was late Sunday morning before Nicholas and Cassandra woke. Francesca had packed them a picnic lunch with leftover pork sandwiches on homemade focaccia bread. Cassandra gave her a tight hug. "Thanks for the weekend," she whispered.

Nicholas winked at his brother and started backing out of the drive. Before they reached the street the car made a horrible grinding sound and stopped cold. They hadn't gone ten feet. The engine was running, but the transmission was out.

"Damn! I thought I noticed some slippage the last few weeks and on the way here, but I've been putting off getting it checked. Now can I get a Lamborghini?" he joked, turning to face his wife.

Cassandra was not amused. "I have an eight o'clock class tomorrow morning." Nicholas did, too.

Alex leaned his head in the window, "Ah, you know you could fly. We do have an airport here in Charleston, and I am fairly certain you have the money." He offered to drive them to the airport and assured his brother he would see that the car was fixed. "Can't leave an old junk heap like that sitting in my driveway."

ঽ

The morning after the late flight back to Atlanta, Cassandra dropped Nicholas outside his office just in time to grab his lecture notes and hurry off to class. "Maybe we should think about a new car for you," she conceded, "but *not* a Lamborghini!"

Lev was waiting for him when he returned from class. "Good morning, Dr. Shepard."

"Good morning, Lev."

"I hope you enjoyed meeting my father. He's really looking forward to having you move to New York."

Nicholas had to admire the boy's eagerness, but he was unable to disguise the look on his own face, which told the tale plainly enough. Lev sat down heavily in his office chair, his mouth slightly ajar.

"I'm sorry, Lev. It's a wonderful offer, a splendid opportunity, but right now just isn't the time." Nicholas sat down in his own chair and began picking through his stack of mail.

Lev's face blanched and his mouth twisted into a worried grimace. "My father thought he had a deal with you. He was sure you would accept his offer, Dr. Shepard. He'll see this as an insult, I'm afraid."

Nicholas twisted his head to look at Lev. "He can see it any way he wants, but I assure you it was a family decision. I am really not ready to make a career change right now."

"Does that mean you might change your mind?" he asked hopefully.

The professor shrugged. "The world changes. Sometimes we seize opportunity. Other times we wait. That's all. I'll call him. Nothing will change between you and me as a result of this, so don't worry about that."

Lev excused himself, mumbling something about getting coffee. He liked Nicholas Shepard. He knew in his heart he could never be as ruthless as his father, but right now, he would not want to be in the professor's shoes. Malachi Foust would never let a negative response stand in the way of getting what he wanted. Lev knew his father would blame him when he learned Nicholas was declining the offer. Perhaps he could redeem himself if he could retrieve the box. But how he was going to do that, he hadn't a clue.

Disoriented and unsure what to do next, Lev stood in line in the cafeteria waiting for coffee. How could Dr. Shepard say no to money and fame? Even if his father had Dr. Shepard fired, he could still finish his dissertation—but what then? A move back to New York, a position at Atlantic Trade, and an office next to the cunning Mika Hunter? A lifetime of keeping secrets from Felicia? Lev shuddered. Daily competition with his father's bloodthirsty Ms. Hunter was a deplorable prospect. If he were half the man his father was, he would think of a way to get rid of her. But, for now, he was surprised to realize that he was actually worried about what might happen to Nicholas Shepard.

Nicholas waited until he heard the elevator doors close. He didn't really want to talk to Malachi while Lev was around. He closed the door to his office, swung around in his office chair, and picked up the telephone. The twin emotions of fear and excitement that had so recently stirred within him settled into a nagging disappointment. He was about to say no to Malachi Foust, and it was not the answer he truly wanted to give. Still, it was the right decision and he knew it.

Sighing, he keyed in the number on the business card in front of him. "May I tell him who's calling?" asked the secretary who answered.

Malachi was on the line within five seconds. "I'm ready to welcome you to my firm, Dr. Shepard."

"Thank you," Nicholas said, drawing a deep breath. "Unfortunately, I have to decline your generous offer." He paused and heard only silence on the other end of the line. Unsure whether to proceed, he carefully worked his way through an explanation of how he reached his decision.

"So it's half your brother's discovery? I didn't realize that. Of course I would be willing to nominate both of you for the Nobel Prize and hire you both on as consultants—expensive consultants."

"To tell you the truth Mr. Foust, my brother isn't interested at all. I'm the one who appreciates your offer, and regret having to turn it down."

Malachi listened carefully as Nicholas explained his decision. There was indeed a genuine sense of regret in his voice. "You don't sound completely convinced, my friend," replied the financier. "Are you saying that you would like to leave this door open?"

Nicholas paused, looking out his window at the quadrangle—the boisterous students, the lovely old trees, the warm spring air. "If it were simply up to me," he said, selecting his words very carefully, "I would be there tomorrow—tonight! But it is not just up to me, and my obligation to my family is my first priority."

"That means there is still a possibility, then," Malachi said, a flat and humorless smile spreading thinly over his perfect teeth. "I will take your refusal as a 'maybe,' and keep in touch with you."

Before Nicholas could respond the phone line went dead. He let his breath out in a long, relieved sigh. "That's as close as I can get to no consequences," he said to himself. He called Cassandra to tell her the conversation had gone well, and that everyone had worried for nothing.

ৠ

In New York, Malachi folded his hands over his flat stomach, leaned back in his chair, and contemplated the half-million dollars of wormy chestnut paneling that formed the skin of his office. He had had it hand-planed on site, and finished with French wax to retain its color. His architect had recreated, to scale, pilasters found in the Doge's palace in Venice for the bookcase divisions, and coffered the ceiling with wormy chestnut-boxed beams. One wall of the paneling hid a bank of large computer screens. Malachi pushed a button on the underside of his desk and the paneling disappeared like pocket doors. He studied the screens for a moment before barking into his private intercom, "Get in here!"

Mika appeared immediately through one of the panels opposite the wall of monitors. When she entered, Malachi was standing at the bar pouring himself a brandy. He shot her a nasty look, set his snifter down on the coffee table in front of his big plasma television, and turned on CNBC. "Stocks are down moderately in heavy trading," intoned the announcer. "Analysts blame the worse-than-expected unemployment report . . ." He clicked it off.

"We know why the stocks are down!" he yelled at the television, throwing the remote control at the screen. "And it has nothing to do with the god damn unemployment report!" He motioned for Mika to join him on the big leather Chesterfield sofa. She chose instead a wing chair, perched on the edge, and waited for him to speak.

"He turned me down. The arrogant bastard turned me down." A stunned Mika held her tongue as Malachi repeated what Nicholas had told him. "It was his brother who solved the phase-inversion problem."

Mika slowly nodded her head. "I might have known it was Alex." She shifted back into her seat and crossed her legs. "It is therefore him that we want, and not Nicholas?"

"Alex, Nicholas, it doesn't matter a tinker's damn!" Malachi spit through clenched teeth. "We get neither of them. According to his brother, Alex is not interested in anything I have to offer. Nicholas, however, is interested, but his family appears to have nixed the idea. No doubt that wretched wife of his stuck a dagger in the deal. Lev did not trust her from the get-go."

He tossed back his brandy, leaned his head against the sofa cushion, and closed his eyes. "Now they have the box *and* enough documentary evidence to destroy us—if they ever put two and two together. It's only a matter of time before they discover the whole story."

"Perhaps not," offered Mika. "Perhaps they will keep it to themselves. Isn't that what Dr. Shepard told you?"

Malachi grimaced. "I have never believed words are honorable, as your culture does. And neither do you!" he spat. "Words are for going back on. I must have the box, the documents, and whatever information they have—including the phase-inversion solution—in *my* hands."

"And what would you like me to do?" she asked

Malachi leaned forward and narrowed his eyes. "Lev is way out of his league. He couldn't clean a dog kennel with a shovel and a fire hose." He looked at Mika and smiled.

She picked up where his thoughts left off. "This family seems to visit one another frequently. Perhaps when they're together again, we can . . . work something out." She sipped from a tumbler of mineral water and continued. "That way, perhaps they will have everything in one place."

"That would be the best solution," agreed Malachi. "But we don't actually know where the documents are—maybe in several places, maybe in a safety deposit box. Hell, we are not even sure Alex has the box; we have only the other brother's statement to that effect. But you're right—if all the people are together, our chances are more favorable."

Mika put her glass down and shifted again in the chair, resting both hands calmly on the arms. "I am hearing you say that we need Alex's programs and talents, and not Nicholas."

"Nicholas is expendable," Malachi replied, waving one arm in the air as if he was shooing a fly away from his head.

"Should I call the messenger service?"

He shook his head. "Not so quickly. I dislike extremes when they're unnecessary. I'm giving Lev one more chance to get the box and the documents."

Mika rose, bowed, and quietly exited through the secret panel to her office next door. She was surprised Malachi was so willing to allow his son to flounder. Lev would never get what they needed. She knew that. Malachi, she thought, also knew it. It was his one shortcoming. She smiled. *Sooner or later, Lev would make one too many mistakes.*

Chapter 30

 Alex called Nicholas on Friday morning. "Hey," he said playfully, thinking about how much he should tease his brother about his car. "Your jalopy's fixed."

"What was it?"

"You needed a new transmission. And you could use a valve job, a change of spark plugs, new brakes, and new rings. Shall I continue?"

"Ouch! Too bad it's not under warranty."

"Why are you . . . never mind. A penny saved and so on. Are you taking the commuter or will you come in Cassandra's car?"

"We'll fly up tomorrow. I never thought I would be saying that. We never just hopped on airplanes when we could drive."

"Yeah, well, get used to it."

Nicholas chuckled softly before turning pensive. "Alex, do you think if we told this story, anybody would believe us? For my part, as an economist, being able to tell the financial future is an incredible discovery—but it might be *too* incredible. Everyone we know will think we are crackpots. We'll rank right up there with cures for baldness and companies selling erection pills."

Alex exhale noisily. "Yeah, you're probably right, except for one thing."

"What?"

"Our bank account and our trading records. Together, they offer verifiable proof of our success, not to mention a simple plot of tidal undulation patters that correlate with the DOW perfectly. Besides, your friend Malachi believes that we can predict the stock market, and he is no dummy."

"Boy, that situation cooled down," replied Nicholas. "I called him Monday morning to decline the position, and now Lev won't even look me in the eye."

"All for the best, if you ask me. I am glad last weekend is behind us. A little too much drama for me."

"That's saying a lot," Nicholas joked. "But seriously," he continued, "Thanks for suggesting we put everything on those little hard drives."

"It's amazing how much data they can hold, isn't it?"

"It's not that. I just feel better having it in my pocket. Do you know what I mean?"

"Sure I do," responded Alex. "I carry mine with me all the time, too. We're just paranoid, you know? Hey, I have a call I have to take, e-mail me your flight info and I will pick you up at the airport."

"Plan on it. See you then. Give Francesca and the kids a hug and a kiss."

"Right back at you, brother."

২

The next morning, Nicholas and Cassandra hopped on a Delta flight to Charleston International Airport. Flying time from Atlanta was less than an hour. Despite its impressive name, the airport in Charleston was small and easy to navigate. Within ten minutes of touch-down they were at the curb with their carry-on luggage.

"You e-mailed Alex with our itinerary, right?" Cassandra asked, looking around in a vain attempt to spot her brother-in-law. It was unseasonably warm, and she couldn't wait to get to the beach.

"Yeah," replied Nicholas. "He probably ran into some traffic."

After another ten minutes of waiting he called Alex's cell phone, got his voice mail, and left a message. Five minutes later he tried again with the same result. A call to their home triggered the answering machine.

Cassandra re-adjusted the strap of her bag for the tenth time. "I wouldn't be surprised if he was holed up in his office on the Internet."

Nicholas lifted his arm and hailed a cab.

"What are you doing?" asked Cassandra. A taxi quickly pulled over and when Nicholas bolted for the door, she ran after him. "Nicholas!"

Rather than answer, her husband tossed their bags into the trunk and gave the driver Alex's address. His face was white as a sheet and his lips had gone blue, like someone in shock. "Jesus, Nicholas," she said, "you are scaring me! What is the matter with you?"

"Something's wrong, Cassandra. Don't ask me how I know, call it twin intuition—I don't care. Something is definitely wrong. I can *feel* it." Cassandra bit her lip and looked out the window. She had never seen him like this. *God*, she prayed, *please let him be wrong.*

The drive through the crowded downtown area was torturously slow. Tourists were everywhere, and out-of-state cars were driving slowly, their occupants gawking at the shops, the restaurants, and other tourists. As they closed on the Battery, traffic was diverted several blocks, apparently because of an accident. When they finally pulled onto Alex's street Cassandra choked back a scream. Nicholas looked on in stunned silence.

Two police cruisers, their blue lights flashing, were parked in front of the house. As the taxi rolled to a stop, they watched, horrified, as Francesca collapsed into the arms of one of the officers on the porch. Nicholas jumped from the moving cab and ran down the street toward his brother's wife, tears rolling down his cheeks.

He already knew.

ॐ

The hawk's silent approach ended when it dive-bombed toward the church steps, its wings silently beating the hot air. With an expertise born of experience, the bird snatched its prey off the far step, clutching it tightly in its talons as it took flight again. The episode triggered several short gasps from the assembled funeral party. Straight up it climbed, its great wings moving regularly, slowly, majestically. A shiver went down Nicholas' spine when the bird's triumphant shriek coursed through the yard as it swooped over the church steeple in search of a suitable place to enjoy its meal.

Startled like everyone else, Cassandra looked up at the predatory bird in amazement as it circled the church twice before vanishing behind the towering live oak trees dripping Spanish moss. Father Galen, dressed in his best ecumenical robes, caught her eye before bowing his head.

The priest picked up where he had left off. "We have come together here to witness the miracle of death, and its liberation from these, our mortal bodily vessels." The group turned back and listened to his rich but solemn voice. "We are but dust, and to dust we shall return, but our souls will continue on to eternity. Amen."

"Amen," echoed those in attendance.

Cassandra squeezed Nicholas' hand tightly. She knew he despised the service—which Alex himself would have hated. The traditional Catholic ceremony was more for their parents. She looked over at the elder Shepards standing next to Francesca and the children. The twins' parents had been suffering from a variety of health problems the past few years. Today they looked small and shriveled. The death of their son would only hasten their own ends. *How was Francesca able to stand this?* wondered Cassandra.

She inched closer to Nicholas, whose big frame stooped slightly as he reached out to put his arm around her shoulders. Cassandra knew they looked dreadful, their faces drawn, creased with sorrow and the accumulation of several sleepless nights. The emotional burden was nearly unbearable. Nicholas eyed the priest, his left eyebrow cocked. The two men looked at each other and Cassandra knew that something passed between the two old friends, but she was too exhausted to care what it was.

The Spanish moss draping the cemetery's oaks swayed in the soft April sea breeze. The mourners drew closer in the chill. They made an odd knot, there in the centuries-old graveyard filled with Charleston's earliest settlers. Francesca had chosen the early-morning service and burial because it was Alex's favorite time of day, with the sun slanting over the cherub and gargoyle gravestones, illuminating them as only spring light can, while the shadows of the trees and moss danced as if an invisible hand was tossing them about. To Nicholas, it seemed an unpardonable offense for the day to be so bright.

"Alex would love this day," Cassandra murmured.

Nicholas groaned lightly and looked at her, his golden, leonine eyes brimming with tears. He thought he had cried himself dry, but he could feel the spigots opening again. "Don't," he begged as he wiped fresh tears away from his cheek with the back of his hand. "Please don't do that." She pulled his hand around her shoulder and leaned against him.

"*Requiem eternum*," intoned the priest.

Alex's children, Harrison and Rosemary, walked slowly to grave and placed two red roses on top of the shiny maple wood casket. The gesture drew a muted cry and anguished sob from Francesca. Harrison leaned over and placed his two small hands on the polished wood and rubbed it tenderly. "Daddy," he murmured in a low, papery voice. Father Galen put his hand on the boy's shoulder and gently grasped little Rosemary's tiny hand. He signaled to the rest of the mourners that it was time to leave. They slowly drifted away singly and in knots of two and three. None of them wanted to see the casket lowered into the ground. That much finality would have pushed several mourners over the edge.

As they moved back toward the church, Nicholas cast his eyes to the sky as though looking for the hawk's return. He shot one last look back at the grave. Out of the corner of his eye, he thought he saw someone move quickly into the shadows. Damn tourists, he thought, feeling the urge to go after the interloper and beat him to a bloody pulp.

A small hand tugged on his sleeve and distracted him from his thoughts. Harrison, a miniature double of his father and uncle, was looking up at him. "Uncle Nicholas, my mom wants to talk to you." Nicholas looked over to Francesca, who was hanging on to Rosemary a few feet from the casket. For a moment he imagined her flinging herself into the open grave onto his brother's coffin, her screams echoing in the churchyard like the cry of the hawk.

My God, he thought, his gut tightening, *how are they going to get through this?*

Chapter 31

Nicholas took a deep breath and walked over to his sister-in-law. She cut a striking figure in her simple black dress, her auburn curls backlit by the morning sunlight. The perfect wife and soul mate for Alex. Now she was simply his widow. Rosemary leaned up against her, clutching her mother's hand tightly.

Francesca looked away from him and stared into the distance. "Tell Uncle Nicholas what you saw, Rosemary." Her voice was flat and without emotion.

Puzzled, Nicholas knelt beside his niece and took her small hand in his own. "What did you see, honey? It's okay to tell me."

She frowned and looked down at the ground. "It's about your car."

His brow furrowed, Nicholas looked up at Francesca, who refused to catch his eye. "What about my car?" he asked, slowly, gently.

When tears welled up in the child's eyes, her mother reassured her. "It's okay, Rosemary. Tell Uncle Nicholas."

Rosemary steeled herself and looked straight into her uncle's eyes. "I was on the sidewalk next door, playing with Nicole," she said, referring to the other six-year-old who was her constant companion. "A stranger rode by on a bicycle, and then he turned around and rode by again. He was looking at our house. The second time, he rode by he got off his bike and crawled up under the front of your car with something in his hand. But when he stood up again, he didn't have anything in his hand. Then he rode off." Rosemary's chin began to quiver and she lifted her arms, begging her mother to pick her up. Francesca held the child tightly, nestling Rosemary's head against her shoulder.

Nicholas stood and rubbed her back. "Honey, are you sure?" he asked. "Very sure?"

The girl nodded her head vigorously. "He put something under your car."

Rosemary buried her face in her mother's dress and began to cry. Both adults comforted her, but Nicholas was so distracted by her revelation he could only stroke his niece's head absentmindedly while his brain danced in several directions simultaneously.

"He put something under your car."

Francesca lifted her eyes and looked at Nicholas over the top of Rosemary's head. Her face was pale and taut with grief. Wordlessly, he accompanied Francesca and the children away from the grave toward the church. Patting her arm clumsily, he left her with a group of mourners and entered the sanctuary alone. The sudden shift from sunlight to gloom momentarily blinded him. With a sigh he lowered himself down slowly into a back pew. Once his eyes adjusted to the shadows, he looked up at the exquisite fan vaulting. Alex had loved this church, particularly its craftsmanship and the engineering it took to create the Perpendicular Gothic traceries in the vaulted ceiling. It was built in the 1700s when Charleston was a bustling colonial harbor, inspired by King Henry VIII's Chapel at Westminster Abbey.

"He put something under your car."

Nicholas closed his eyes as the emotional pain of losing his twin wracked his body. Rosemary's words ricocheted inside his brain while his mind's eye redrew—over and over again in brilliant colors—the inferno that had once been his car. By the time he and Cassandra had arrived at the scene it was evident no one could have survived the crash and that little would be left of his beloved brother. Several witnesses to the accident told the police the exact same story: the car suddenly careened around the curve in the road and went straight into the sea wall at high speed. "It just exploded!" remembered an onlooker.

It was all Nicholas could do to keep Cassandra from collapsing onto the pavement as they looked on with horror at the burning wreckage. The overwhelming grief threatened to consume them all. As hard as it was to look at Francesca, it was much harder making the call to his parents in Scottsdale. Afterward, once the police had left, he climbed the stairs and sat alone in Alex's office. As an identical twin they had shared more than simply physical features. Part of Nicholas' own soul had been charred into ash that day.

Rosemary's story only confirmed what he had already suspected: that Alex's death was not an accident. The high speed crash into the sea wall made some sense now. Whatever the man had placed under the car triggered the accident and killed his brother. The fire incinerated everything inside. There was no evidence to sift through, no clues to find. It was almost a perfect crime.

But why would someone want to kill Alex?

Nicholas' stomach tightened into a knot. Did it have something to do with their trading discovery? Could it be the box? He fingered the miniature hard disk in his pocket before drawing it out and holding it up. Alex had bought them this unprepossessing piece of technology so they could keep their discovery backed up and close at hand. It had no meaning or value unless it was inserted into a computer and examined. Nicholas held it up to the thin light pouring through the huge stained glass windows. Could the information stored on this tiny object have been the cause of Alex's death? If someone was willing to kill Alex, were they all in danger? And if so, who wanted them dead?

Suddenly it struck him and he understood. He pounded the pew in front of him and moaned aloud. "It was me they wanted!" he nearly shouted. "They wanted to kill me!"

The door behind him burst open. He stood up and turned around quickly, suspicious of anything and everyone. Francesca's red hair was a beacon in the sunlight. Nicholas drew a deep breath and slowly exhaled. "Where are the children?" he asked softly.

"With your parents and Cassandra on the way to the house," Francesca sighed, falling back into the same pew a few feet away. Nicholas followed her lead and slumped down. "Rosemary is just beside herself. She thinks she caused her daddy's death."

"Why?" asked Nicholas, startled. "Why would she think that?"

"After she saw the man ride off, she thought maybe she had imagined the thing in his hand. She and her friend went back to playing with their dolls. Later, after Alex got into your car and pulled out of the drive, she decided to come and tell me." Francesca looked down so that a veil of hair hid her face. She uttered the next few words very slowly, and it was obvious to Nicholas they caused her considerable pain. "I . . . didn't believe her. Like most children, she has a vivid imagination." Francesca lifted her head and continued, tears welling in her eyes, "Alex had decided to take your car to pick you up at the airport and I was fixing lunch. Rosemary kept pulling on my arm trying to get my attention. I could see she was really upset. I . . . I told her to go play so I could finish lunch."

Francesca stood slowly and walked toward the altar, biting her bottom lip in agitation. "Why would anybody do that to Alex, Nicholas? I don't get it." When she reached the front pew she clutched at the carved-angel post. Grief often comes in waves, and a powerful one shook her now. Her body quivered with sobs and a low moaning wail filled the church. Nicholas stood up and ran up the aisle to her, holding her close as they both cried.

After several minutes she dabbed his eyes with a Kleenex she pulled from her purse, wiped her nose, and pushed herself away from him. Standing back several feet, she stared at Nicholas and whispered, "I saw your face when Rosemary told you. The police may never buy it, but we both know Alex was murdered." She paused and then asked, "Do you know anything about this that I don't? Level with me, Nicholas."

"Francesca, I don't know what I know," he said in a low voice. "If what happened wasn't an accident, then I don't believe Alex was their intended victim."

She looked at him and shook her head. "I don't know what you mean."

"Francesca, think about it. It was *my* car."

Francesca threw her hand to her mouth and gasped back a sob. "Oh my God! No!" Nicholas thought she was going to begin crying again. Instead, she suddenly found her equilibrium. Her voice was steady now, firmer. "It's the box we found. The documents, the stock trading . . . the discovery. That's why Alex is dead." She laughed softly, grimly. "I knew it was a terrible idea. This is all about power and money, isn't it?"

Nicholas took a stab at rationality. "Alex and I never thought that we were doing anything wrong, Francesca. We thought we could make money for our families, and then publish our findings. That's all."

Her face turned an ugly red and her nose wrinkled in disgust as she spat out the word: "Money!"

Nicholas drew back as she snarled at him. "Don't you think I would trade it all for Alex to be sitting there in that pew? He always made plenty of money. What did we need with more?"

He held out his arms in an effort to encircle her, but she pushed him away and lashed out at him. "Why couldn't they have killed you?" She flailed against his chest with the heels of her hands until Nicholas grabbed her wrists and held them tightly. She stopped suddenly and sobbed quietly. "I'm sorry, Nicholas . . . I didn't mean that . . ."

"I know, Francesca," he said, pulling her close once more. "He was my brother, and I loved him, too." Neither said a word for a full minute as they listened to muffled voices as mourners passed by outside the windows. "I don't know exactly what's going on, but I promise when I finish, we'll know everything," Nicholas assured her. "He won't have died for nothing."

"No, Nicholas," she said firmly and with conviction. "I don't want anyone else hurt. If someone wants the damn box, give it to them before I smash it and throw it into the sea."

A quiet clearing of the throat startled them, and they turned to see Father Galen standing a few feet away. Neither had heard him enter through the sacristy door. "Ah, here you both are. Most of the others are on their way to the wake." He looked for a moment at Francesca and smiled softly. "Are you all right, dear?"

"No Galen," she answered. "I will never be all right again as long as I live. I had better head over now."

When she was gone, Nicholas turned to Galen. "You might be able to help me." He moved back up the aisle to make sure the doors were solidly shut. "I want to be sure nobody can hear us."

Galen raised his eyebrows. "Except for the fellow upstairs, we're the only ones here." He swung a cowboy-booted foot onto the pew, which struck Nicholas as a bit sacrilegious. Galen followed his gaze as he took in the odd combination of apparel. "I know what you are thinking. Why don't I just shuck these fancy boots?" he remarked. "I don't want to say anything blasphemous while wearing them."

For the first time that day—for the first time in several days—Nicholas found himself laughing, even though it was very softly. It still felt good, and he knew Alex would approve—even on the day of his burial. When Nicholas seemed hesitant to speak, Galen spoke for him. "Come on, follow me," he said, leading his friend into a small room at the rear of the church, where Nicholas watched as he carefully removed his vestments and hung them up in a closet.

"I know this may be an odd time for this question, but I had intended to call you last week," Galen continued. "What happened with Malachi and the job offer?"

Nicholas tried to clear his throat, but it took several attempts before he was satisfied with the result. "He seemed to understand, but now I believe we have another problem."

"What do you mean?" asked the priest.

"I think Alex was murdered, Galen, and I don't think they will stop with just him." Nicholas sighed. That was easier than he thought it would be.

Galen's eyebrows arched up quickly and his mouth opened before it closed again in a tight-lipped expression. "Tell me," was all he said.

And so Nicholas did, beginning with his conversation with Malachi and ending with Rosemary's revelation about the man on the bicycle. "But I think it was all a mistake, Galen."

The priest's green eyes lit up. "A mistake? How so?"

"Alex was driving my car."

"Oh my God," he uttered, stringing the three words together as if they were one. "I guess that explains why Francesca was so mad at you."

"Yes. She told me she wished they had gotten me instead of Alex."

Galen reached out and patted his friend's shoulder. "Of course she would say that. It was her husband. She would do or say anything to have him back. It is merely her way of coping with a loss that is almost too much for one person to bear." Galen rubbed his own red eyes. "I nearly broke down during the service," he admitted. "She knows she must stay strong—for her children if not for herself. She will get over this." He hesitated a moment. "It is you, Nicholas, for whom I worry."

"Me?" asked Nicholas in surprise.

"Yes, you. I worry what you might be planning to do. We don't need any more funerals. If you seriously suspect foul play, you had better go to the police."

Nicholas shook his head. "I can't do that! Tell them what—that my six-year-old niece saw a man put something under her Uncle Nicholas' car, and her daddy's death wasn't an accident?"

"Well, yes," replied Galen.

"Even the police who believed O. J. Simpson wouldn't buy that."

Galen shrugged. "They might. You won't know until you try. I believe this might be the only clue you have."

"Galen, I admit I am not a detective. I'm an economics professor, a scientist. I have a hard time believing anything beyond what I can see, hear, feel, smell, touch, or prove with an equation. I don't know," he said, sighing loudly and running his hand through his hair. "Maybe I'm just being paranoid."

"No," Galen shook his head. "Neither one of us thinks you're imagining this and you're hardly the paranoid type. But I don't understand . . . what purpose would it serve to kill you? Certainly you don't think it was Malachi, just because you turned down his job offer?"

Nicholas shrugged. "When you put it that way, it does sound pretty ridiculous. To tell you the truth, I don't know who the enemy is. But I think we somehow stirred up a hornet's nest by talking about what we are doing, and they—whoever *they* are—found out that we have *their* box and documents."

Galen cocked his head quizzically. "And, who do you think *they* would be?"

"Whoever owns the stuff, is my guess."

Galen looked at his watch and tapped its face. "Ah! Come."

As the priest led Nicholas back into the sanctuary, he stopped to look down at his feet. "These boots look great, but they hurt like hell," he said, tugging at his heels.

Nicholas clenched the brass handrail leading up the altar steps. "What did I do, Galen? We just wanted to use the information for ourselves. It was supposed to be future financial security for us and the children. That seemed like the right thing to do."

"What, you don't know that one of the seven deadly sins is greed?" Galen looked archly at his friend. "Your parents didn't do as good a job on you as I thought."

"Bunk," spat out Nicholas. "All that archaic stuff was just to keep the peasants in line. Make poverty a virtue. I have never been into that—no insult intended, Father."

Galen took Nicholas' arm. "None taken, old friend. Let's talk about this later. We are going to be missed if we don't get over to the wake."

Chapter 32

Francesca closed the sacristy door and walked down the narrow, shadowed passageway leading to Archdale Street. The steady clicking of her heels on the stone pavers echoed in her ears, as did a myriad of thoughts and emotions. The hundred-foot walk did little to amend her mood. She was still angry.

Once she reached Archdale, Francesca turned left and continued down Queen toward Meeting, completely ignoring the crowds of people jostling their way along the sidewalk.

Charleston reaches a peak of Southern beauty in the spring, with banks of azaleas, flowering cherry and pear trees, and daffodils and tulips blazing in every small patch of earth. Tourists love the old city, with its 18th century buildings and upscale shops. Today they were out in force. Masses of visitors bustled along the sidewalks and crossed streets wherever they wanted, paying little or no attention to traffic laws they sensed would not be enforced anyway. Dressed in black and clearly distraught, Francesca stood out among them as she made her way through the tourist throng.

As she was about to cross Meeting Street she mumbled to herself, "Alex, Alex, please help me. I can't go on without you." Another wave of grief washed over her. Without realizing it, she began crossing against the light but stopped suddenly in the middle of the street. Out of nowhere a bicyclist raced in her direction and the two collided in the middle of the intersection. The blow spun Francesca around, and the next thing she knew she was outstretched on the cobblestone street. The cyclist lost control and flipped over to the pavement, but sprang up just as quickly. Darting his eyes from side to side, he adjusted his helmet and sprinted a short distance down the street before ducking into an alleyway.

The stunned bystanders crowded around a dazed Francesca, talking all at once. "Are you alright?" "What can I get you?" "Can you stand up?" Someone offered her a glass of water from a nearby restaurant.

"What happened?" she wondered aloud.

"Some guy on a bicycle was riding pretty fast and just hit ya," replied a twenty-something woman with a Chicago twang in her voice. "There's his bike right there," she continued, pointing behind her. "You don't look so good. Are you OK? Should I call an ambulance or something?"

Francesca turned slowly and looked at the bicycle. It was not one of the cheap tourist bikes people rent to ride around the city. Sleek and professional looking, the cycle reminded her of something Lance Armstrong would ride in the *Tour de France*.

"Then that guy just left—just ran off," an older male onlooker explained to a burly young police officer who had just arrived to see what was holding up traffic.

The cop turned to Francesca: "Are you alright? You look a little shook up." When Francesca told him she was fine, he cleared his throat. "We have to get the bike out of the street, ma'am." He picked it up by the handlebars and walked it to the sidewalk.

Francesca followed, still a bit unsteady on her feet. "It's not my bike," she replied.

"It still needs to be off the street," explained the officer as he leaned it up against a storefront. He was looking down for the kickstand when he asked, "What's this?" A small tubular compartment was hanging loosely from the handlebars. He opened it. The vial contained a clear liquid. "Humph," he mumbled. "No wonder the guy took off. Probably drugs or something! I'll take this down to the station and see what we can find out about it." He unclipped the radio from his belt and called the station.

Feeling nauseous, Francesca turned to leave but the police officer stopped her. "Ma'am, you can't leave yet. I'll need some information from you."

He guided her to a nearby wrought-iron bench, where she sat down to wait. Her dress had been torn in the fall and her black hose were in shreds. She hung her head down over her knees as her emotions once again overcame her. All the policeman could see was a mass of curls shaking. "I'm sorry, ma'am," he said. "I'll need your name and address. Is there someone I can call for you? Are you hurt?"

She shook her head. "And I don't want to file any charges," she replied through the tears. "Please let me go, I need to be at my husband's wake."

"Francesca!"

Nicholas and Father Galen pushed their way through the curious crowd that had gathered around the accident scene. When they had spied Francesca's red hair they sprinted through as fast as possible. She looked up and saw them. "Galen? Nicholas? Oh, thank God."

"Are you alright?" they both asked breathlessly. "What happened?"

She answered them as best she could, with a few onlookers helping to fill in the gaps. The policeman had moved off to the side to take witness statements. Galen turned to Nicholas. "She's fine, Nicholas. Go to the wake and hold down the fort. We will be along in a few minutes."

Although he felt a twinge of guilt at leaving his brother's widow, Nicholas heeded Galen's advice and walked briskly to Alex's house, which was only a couple blocks away. The grand old Victorian was swarming with mourners. If it weren't for their dark sober clothing and grave expressions, he would have been cheered to see so many familiar faces. The last thing he wanted was to be inside his dead brother's home presiding over his wake.

Instead of going inside, Nicholas walked a short distance toward the Battery and sat on a bench facing the harbor. In the distance stood Fort Sumter, the old masonry fort that had witnessed the beginning of the Civil War. He found himself wishing he could go back in time before that fateful visit to the Biltmore Estate. The thrill of the discovery, working closely with his brother on the project, all that money they'd made. . . None of it meant a damn thing now without his brother to share it with. More than anything else he wanted his old life back, his sweet Cassandra, a sense of normalcy. That, he realized with a chill, was probably gone forever.

Nicholas punched in the number for information on his cell phone. "Charleston, South Carolina. Police Department . . . No, it's not an emergency. Yes, please connect me." When the duty officer answered, Nicholas identified himself and asked to speak to the officer who had done the paperwork for Alex's accident. Two full minutes passed.

"Officer Thompson speaking."

At the risk of sounding like a lunatic Nicholas plunged in, explaining what his niece had witnessed before the accident, but skipping all the other details that fleshed out the likely motive behind the death of his brother.

The officer listened politely. "That is interesting information, Dr. Shepard. Unfortunately, sir, your car was completely incinerated. I seriously doubt we will find *anything* left under the front bumper. I promise you, though, I will personally go right now and inspect the car. Just one moment." Officer Thompson covered the phone with his hand and said something Nicholas could not make out. "Sorry, doctor. Can you give me a number where I can call you later?" Grateful for his interest, Nicholas replied with his cell number and thanked him for his trouble.

Squaring his shoulders, Nicholas rose from the bench and turned toward Alex's house. His place was with his family. Nodding somberly at the guests, he climbed the steps slowly, like a man mounting a gallows, and eased his way into the house.

"Cassandra? She's in Alex's office," replied his cousin Jeff, pointing up the wide stairway.

At first Cassandra didn't see her husband. When she was leaving the church Francesca had pulled her aside to tell her about what Rosemary had seen. The news left Cassandra cold and stunned. When Francesa left her to enter the church, Cassandra made a beeline for the house and Alex's office. And there Nicholas found her, surrounded by the mysterious documents, stacked in organized piles around her. She had them arranged according to their age in an effort to craft a sensible time line of the data.

"Jesus, Cassandra! What in the world are you doing?" Nicholas startled her. "Today of all days?"

"Nicholas—you scared me!" she gasped, jumping up as if embarrassed by what she was doing. "I thought I had locked the door." She sat back down and looked at him. "Don't you see?" she said, pushing her hair out of her eyes. "The answer—all the answers—are right here."

"Cassandra, it's Alex's wake. Come down—"

"No!" she shot out, shaking her head with determination. "Nicholas, just listen to me. This is where we pick up the trail."

"The trail? What trail?" He went down on one knee in front of her and tried to pry her fingers from one of the documents. "Cassandra, please come downstairs . . ."

"No!" she said again, more forcefully than before. "I get it now. *I understand*. This is where we find the murderer."

He drew back in shock as if his hand had touched a hot stove. "What are you saying, Cassandra? How do you know?"

Cassandra moved her arm off a piece of parchment and reached out to grasp Nicholas by the hand. "Francesca told me at the church."

Nicholas' mouth hung wide open. He felt as though he were drowning in guilt. "I still don't understand. What do these have to do with anything?" he finally asked.

"Oh come on, Nicholas! Think of what you two found, think of the money you have made, and think of what is going to happen to the financial world if your discovery is made public! Can you imagine what will happen on a global scale to the world's wealth?" She took his hands into her own. "Do you think Alex just accelerated his car into wall and it just happened to explode into a fireball?"

He shook his head. In a slow, halting voice, Nicholas recounted what Rosemary had witnessed. Cassandra leaned back, listening patiently; she knew Nicholas needed to find answers from somewhere. She closed her mouth tightly, remembering Francesca's version of the same story. Anger burned inside her eyes.

Nicholas rose and looked out the window for a moment before easing himself into Alex's desk chair. "There's more," he said. "Francesca was just run down by a bicyclist."

"What! She didn't tell me that!" Cassandra gasped and jumped to her feet.

"She's ok," he said quickly. "I don't think it was a coincidence. She was probably being followed and with the crowds, he just ran into her. One witness told me Francesca had been walking quickly, but stopped suddenly in the crosswalk. I don't know. Anyway, she's okay," he added in response to his wife's gasp. "Galen should be with her."

"Yes, he is . . . They both arrived together."

"We're all going to have to talk. I think we're in danger. All of us— you, me, Francesca, maybe even Gabriel. I called the police hoping they might turn up something."

"What did they say?"

"That they will investigate and get back with me."

Both of them glanced at Alex's credenza, where the box was sitting under a black satin sheet. "That damn box," Cassandra spat. "I think it has probably cursed everyone who has ever used it."

"I know," Nicholas sighed. "And we don't even need it anymore, now that we've got all its information computerized. But it's beginning to look like whoever owned that box wants it back, or at least wants the secret to remain, well . . . secret. I guess its obvious they will kill to get what they want."

Cassandra nodded in agreement. "People kill for money all the time, Nicholas. I imagine they will also kill to keep it."

Nicholas' cell phone rang, startling them both. "Hello . . . Yes, this is Dr. Shepard." He listened carefully and hung up.

"Who was that?" Cassandra asked.

"Officer Thompson with the Charleston police. He didn't find anything under the front bumper, but said he would pass on the information to forensics. He did mention the air bags had deployed, which would probably have been some help, but because of the fire . . ." He choked up at the thought and was unable finish.

"No one will believe us," said an exasperated Cassandra. "What are we going to tell them? We have this box, see, and we found it in a secret room in this mansion, and it's ancient, and it measures gravity, and we figured out how to make millions of dollars in the stock market with it. There are people all over the world who might kill to get it back or learn its secrets—or protect their fortunes. Even I think this all sounds nuts, except I have seen our bank account." She rose with a determined look in her eye. "We have no evidence, Nicholas. It's up to us now."

"It's up to us for what? What exactly are you suggesting?"

"The only clues we have are in those documents," Cassandra replied, pointing to the pages stacked carefully on the coffee table. "I think we need to track down some of the families who owned the box. I have a feeling—and what I have been studying so far bears me out—that most of them are somehow connected to one another. If we can identify the last owner of the box, we will probably have a good lead on who killed Alex."

It all seemed a little farfetched to Nicholas, but he nodded slowly anyway. *Was such a thing even possible?*

"I know what you're thinking," she said bluntly, sizing up the indecision in his expression. "You underestimate yourself. You and Alex figured out how to use that damn box. You and I should be able to trace its lineage."

"How, exactly? By gallivanting around the globe, looking in old archives and libraries? Chasing up spooks in cemeteries?" He stopped suddenly. "Sorry. Didn't mean to say that last part. Can't we just do this over the Internet?"

Cassandra burst out laughing. It was such a cheerful, musical sound that it seemed to split the day in two—the first half dark in sorrow and despair, the second lit with possibility. "Ok, ok," he yielded, turning his palms toward her in submission. "We'll do this for Alex."

"Good. Come on," she said, grabbing his arm and moving toward the door. "Downstairs, professor. That is where we both belong now. With your parents, Francesca, and the kids."

જ

He watched them leave the office from inside a guest bedroom down the hall, the door cracked ajar just enough to hear fragments of their conversation and spot them when they left. When he was sure they had gone, Lev Foust stepped carefully out into the hallway, sprinted like a cat a few steps to the office, and silently slipped inside.

Lev rubbed his hands together in delight as his eyes shot around the high-ceilinged room. They had been talking about the box and the documents. Now, where were they? When a quick search of the closet did not turn up anything of interest, Lev's heart began to pound harder and he could feel the anxiety of the moment pressing in upon him. He knew his time was limited, and he could not leave empty-handed. He did a double-take and his heart skipped a beat when his eyes settled on a black sheet covering something on the credenza. Lev crept quickly to the door and cracked it open slightly, listening for a few seconds to make sure no one else was upstairs. Confident now, he made straight for the prize.

With a trembling hand he lifted a satin corner a few inches and sucked in a sharp breath. "I didn't expect you to be so beautiful," he whispered, running his fingers lightly over its carved sides and smooth granite top. *My father will be so proud of me.* Lev bent down to examine it more closely, his wiry frame forming a question mark.

"What are you doing?"

Lev straightened with a start and spun around. With a sinking heart he saw that the office door had slowly eased its way open by at least three feet.

He had not shut it all the way!

Silhouetted in the doorway was Harrison Shepard, holding his squirming dog by the collar.

Lev smiled as he slowly lowered the sheet back into place. "Hi. I'm, ah, I work with your uncle, Dr. Shepard. You must be Harrison?"

The boy nodded slowly as he looked warily at Lev. "Why are you in my dad's office?"

"Oh, I'm just looking for your uncle. I need to speak with him. Have you seen him?"

Harrison's face relaxed. "Yes, he's downstairs with my mom. I came up to get Michelangelo. He is always getting into trouble."

"That's a nice dog. I love the name," smiled Lev as he eased past the boy and descended the elegant stairway. *Damn*, he thought to himself. *Of all the luck!* Coming up the steps as he made his way down was Nicholas Shepard.

"Dr. Shepard, everyone was waiting for you downstairs," Lev sputtered nervously, stumbling over his words and speaking more quickly than usual. "When I didn't see you, I thought you might be upstairs, so I went up to find you."

Nicholas stopped a few steps below him. "Hmm. I've been downstairs for a while now, Lev," he answered quietly. Nicholas leaned to the side and looked past his graduate student. "Have you seen Harrison?"

"Yes, he's upstairs with his dog." Lev licked his lips nervously.

Cassandra was watching the exchange from across the great room. *What was Lev doing upstairs?* With a drink in hand she walked purposefully to the bottom of the steps. The men were turning now and coming down. Lev smoothed his thick black hair and readjusted his small oval glasses on his hooked nose. A line from the musical *My Fair Lady* suddenly popped into her head: *Oozing charm from every pore, he oiled his way about the floor.*

"Harrison's in the house. He's upstairs," Nicholas told her. He took her elbow and beckoned her to follow him into the living room. As she walked away, Cassandra turned and looked up at Lev, who had stopped three steps short of the bottom. A brief staring contest ensued. He reminded her of a cobra watching its prey.

Galen sat on a sofa next to Francesca while her mother perched on the edge of a chair, her dark red-rimmed eyes taking in the sadness that filled the once-vibrant and happy home. Cassandra pulled shut the living room's sliding pocket doors behind her. She had always thought of this as Francesca's room. For years, Francesca had been collecting bits and pieces of William Morris reproduction fabrics and designs, but since they had started making money she could now afford the real thing.

Francesca rose slowly, unsteadily, and walked toward the couple. Bruises were clearly visible on her arms, and the side of her face was starting to show some redness. Francesca took Nicholas by his arm and squeezed it firmly. "I'm sorry for my behavior earlier. You know I didn't mean it." She had changed out of her torn clothing into a pair of silk black pants and a dark gray sleeveless blouse. Although she looked more comfortable, it was obvious from the dark circles under her eyes that she was mentally and physically exhausted.

Nicholas leaned down and kissed her gently on the forehead while Cassandra looked on. "I know. No need to apologize, Francesca. Nicholas told me about the spill you took. Are you sure you are all right?"

She nodded. "Galen has made some sense of all this for me and my mama agrees with him." Cassandra gave her a careful hug. The bruises looked painful. Nicholas threw a grateful glance at the good Father, who regarded him with a wry but concerned expression.

Francesca's mama, round and affable, nodded briskly. Her English was minimal, but her Italian good nature made up for it. "Everybody should be together," she said, holding up her hands to include them all. She launched into a story in Italian, leaving everyone but her daughter with blank faces.

"She's talking about her Uncle Marco," Francesca explained. "He had an argument with his wife and then went to take a nap. He never woke up, and the wife weeps about it to this day."

"*Si, si!,*" said Mama Gamba. Smiling, she joined Nicholas' hand with Francesca's. "*Mangiano!*" That, at least, was something they could all understand.

Although most people would have catered a wake for a hundred people, Francesca had been cooking nonstop for two days. Her homespun therapy included the best of low country cuisine. White wicker tables literally groaned with she-crab soup, crab fritters, Brunswick stew, barbecued chicken, mile-high biscuits, country ham and, of course, shrimp made every way Francesca could devise. Alex's death may have broken Francesca, but preparing and overseeing the food was solace for her soul.

Cassandra prepared a plate for Nicholas, and he gave her a grateful smile as she walked over to stay close to Francesca. Surprised at how hungry he was, he wolfed down the delicious fare, remembering it had been a whole day since he'd eaten anything. He watched while Harrison and Rosemary picked at their food and saw how anxious they became if their mother got up to receive a visitor or bid one goodbye. Mama Gamba took the children under her wing and led them off to a playroom upstairs. Francesca looked relieved. "They won't go anywhere with anyone except Mama," she said to Cassandra. "They even sleep with me. They're so confused." Her voice drifted off. "I am not going to cry," she told Cassandra. "I am done crying."

"Let's sit out on the porch," suggested Cassandra, who led the party outdoors. Francesca settled into one of the wicker chairs. "I was remembering our wedding . . ." she began, and a cluster of people gathered around to listen to the story.

Nicholas recalled it, too. It had been a five-day affair on the slopes of the Gamba's olive farm south of Siena in Tuscany. He and Cassandra reveled in the whole event, enjoying every minute of the festivities. There had even been an opera performed on the terraces leading away from the house, while they sat under a vine-covered pergola in front of the ancient homestead. Its double-tiered loggia provided spectacular views of nearby Sienna, with its medieval spires and deep-rooted history. Francesca and Alex had been introduced at a party in Charleston during the Spoleto Festival. Francesca was in Charleston to take courses at a culinary school; she had never meant to settle there. But then she met Alex. He was handsome, smart, and adventurous—and he never stood a chance. It only took one date for her intensity and love for life to sweep him away.

At the wedding, Cassandra hit it off immediately with Francesca's father, Vincenzio, who was thrilled to meet an American who knew and appreciated Italian art and culture. One evening when Papa Gamba was sharing a second bottle of Chianti with Cassandra, he let her in on the family secret. The surname Gamba could be traced back to Marina Gamba, Galileo's mistress.

"It is an honored name." Vincenzio spoke English much better than his wife, for he used it regularly in his export business.

Nicholas could not wait to tell Alex that his future children had a famous ancestor. Perhaps they will be great scientists. Alex laughed his deep chuckle when he learned about the family "secret."

Dusk idled over Charleston as the soft voices of Southern and Italian women melded in the twilight. Listening to Francesca now, Cassandra recalled a more recent occasion when they had discussed Francesca's family: the night at the Biltmore when she had stumbled into the hidden room.

Cassandra caught Nicholas' eye. He was hugging a column as he looked out toward Fort Sumter. She studied his fatigued face. What was he thinking? What would it feel like to lose a brother—an identical twin? A chill had slipped into the early evening air. Nicholas' mother walked onto the porch with a sweater and laid it over Francesca's shoulders, smiled softly at Cassandra, and stood by as mourners filed past to hug and kiss the widow and offer their final condolences.

In an effort to escape, Nicholas slipped down the porch and entered the house through a sliding door to seek out Galen. He found the priest in the great room, deep in an abstruse conversation with Lev about a mathematical topic in theoretical physics. Behind them was the empty and cold stone fireplace. "Excuse me Galen," interrupted Nicholas. "We need to have a family meeting upstairs after everyone is gone. Can you join us?"

"It's time for me to leave now, anyway," said Lev, who offered his condolences to Francesca before leaving.

Lev climbed into his rental car, started the engine, and drove off. He pulled over a few blocks away and punched a number into his cell phone.

"Yes?"

He could barely control the excitement welling up inside. "Father, I have seen and touched the box—and the documents are also here in Charleston."

ॐ

Once the house was again quiet, Francesca, Cassandra, Galen, and Nicholas gathered in Alex's study. Francesca announced that her mother wanted her to return to Italy and take the children with her.

"I'm all for it," Nicholas said approvingly. "You'll be safe there, surrounded by your family and friends."

"How do you know we're in danger?" asked Francesca. "We don't really know anything."

"That's true," Nicholas replied slowly. "But if Alex was . . . murdered . . . because of the box and what we have discovered, then we are all potential victims. At least whoever did this thing won't know where you've gone."

"Well, I'm not naive," said Cassandra, shivering and pulling a sweater close around her. "I don't understand what's happening or who's responsible, but I know enough. I don't see how we can keep this to ourselves and not at least try to get the authorities to help us."

"Come on, Cassandra! Even you agreed earlier that no one is going to believe us without proof!" Nicholas argued. "Alex and I haven't told anybody any real specifics about our trading account or the system identification programs—"

Galen interrupted. "Does the brokerage firm you've been trading through know anything about how you make your decisions for each trade?" When Nicholas shook his head, the priest tried again. "Is it possible somebody there could be connected with whoever it is that killed Alex?"

Nicholas shrugged. "I have no way of knowing the answer to that question, Galen, but it doesn't seem likely. It seems highly improbable that we picked a trading firm from the Internet, and someone there is involved somehow with whoever owns the box."

Galen nodded, conceding the point. "Still, Nicholas," he added, "it seems hard to escape the fact that someone knows what you and Alex are doing and does not like it."

"Malachi knows, Galen. He knew all about the phase-inversion solution. That's why he offered me that consulting job. But I never recall discussing the phase-inversion solution with anyone."

"Then how did Malachi know about this phase-inversion thing you keep talking about?" asked Galen.

Nicholas turned his palms over and shook his head. "I have no idea."

"Nicholas," broke in Cassandra, "who did you tell at Emory about your project, or the box, or anything having to do with the technology?"

He thought for a few seconds. "Well, I mentioned it in passing a few times to my colleagues," Nicholas recalled. "I told them I was onto something that would change the way economists view traditional methods of investing, but I never went into the particulars."

"Who else?" Galen asked.

"Only my grad students, Lev and Felicia. They helped a lot with the project while Alex and I set up the trading strategies. Then, of course, Lev told his father. But specifics I kept to myself." Nicholas ran his fingers through his hair in frustration. "So far our chief suspects are some unknown broker, two graduate students who don't really know that much, some mild-mannered professors heading toward retirement, and a businessman living in New York? I'm no Sherlock Holmes, but it's difficult for me to believe any of these people had anything to do with Alex's death. Lev is a brilliant student, and he's also the heir to a billion-dollar fortune. He doesn't need money. Neither does Malachi, who was rather enamored with all the positive good it could do for the world."

Francesca had been listening closely to the discussion and thought she had a solution. "Nicholas, what if you wrote an essay and published your findings? Wouldn't making the information public render it useless to whoever wants it back? They would never be able to keep it to themselves or stop people from exposing it."

"You mean like a witness to a crime, who goes public so there is no longer a motive for anyone to kill the messenger?" asked Galen.

"Yes, exactly," replied Francesca.

Nicholas got up and paced the room. "I guess you have a point, but I can't just whip something out in a week or two, Francesca. In order for it to be taken seriously and have the effect you suggest, I'd have to quantify everything, and it would take time to write something worthy of publication, and it would have to be peer reviewed. Besides . . ."

"You scientists!" Francesca threw her hands in the air. "It's always quantify this, quantify that! Just publish something and show a reporter your financial records! My husband is dead!"

"That's right," said Nicholas sternly. "Your husband—my brother—is dead. But just publishing our findings will do absolutely nothing to find out why he's dead or who killed him. I, for one, want to know those things, don't you?" When Francesca did not reply, he continued. "If we can get you and the children to a safe place, Cassandra and I can start piecing together the clues in those documents, which is beginning to look like our only chance to find out the truth."

"Hold on there!" Galen looked up suddenly. "What is all this about? How do you plan on doing that?"

Nicholas raised his eyebrows and turned to Cassandra, who spent the next few minutes explaining her theory about the documents and how they could be used to find the last owner or user of the box.

Francesca shook her head. "So the two of you are just going to get on an airplane and go poking around the globe dusting off genealogical charts?" She shot Cassandra a hard look and frowned. "Why wouldn't whoever killed Alex do the same to both of you? Or suppose you find who you're looking for. What are you going to do then? Accuse some Italian or Greek or English aristocrat of killing someone in South Carolina because . . . why?"

"I realize it doesn't sound all that rational," Cassandra sighed. "We should have investigated all the connections to this box a long time ago—before we began trading. We just got too swept up with the idea of making money." Francesca crossed her arms and looked ahead into space.

"Those are good questions, Francesca," Nicholas replied gently. "But knowledge is power, and whoever we have pissed off knows enough to not stop with Alex. But we have the box, and we have all the documents that go with it. I'm not sure what discovering the root of this evil will do for us, but I refuse to sit here defenseless and wait for some bastard to kill another one of us! I am bound by blood—you of all people understand that, Francesca—to find whoever did this and make sure they never do it again."

The room fell quiet. A tear ran down Francesca's face and Cassandra reached out to take her hand. "It will be alright," she said, squeezing her fingers. "We will all get through this together."

Francesca offered a small smile in reply and looked across the room at a recent photograph of Alex and the kids at a beach on Sullivan's Island. She began speaking in a low voice:

Lo duca e io per quell cammino ascoso
intrammo a ritorner nel chiaro mondo;
e sanza cura d'alcun riposo
salimmo su. El primo e io secondo,
tanto ch'I I' vidi delle cose belle
che porta 'l ciel, per un pertugio tondo;
e quindi uscimmo a riveder le stele.

When she finished, both Nicholas and Cassandra shot Galen a puzzled look. The priest nodded soberly. "Francesca, no one can promise to bring you into that light, but we will all do the best we can." He turned to Nicholas and Cassandra and explained. "It's the end of Dante's *Inferno*. His guide and Dante are emerging out of Hell and see the light of the stars and heaven."

"As I recall," replied Cassandra, "the next step is purgatory, isn't it? I have a feeling we're not out of Hell yet." She pointed to the documents stacked up carefully along a wall shelf. "We need to muster the strength and the will to go wherever those documents lead us. Someone must be watching us, waiting for our reaction."

Nicholas' eyes lit up and he snapped his fingers with a smile. "We have to fly beneath their radar!" he exclaimed, unclipping his cell phone and punching in a number.

"What are you talking about? Who are you calling?" asked Cassandra.

"Gabe. We need that little jet he has access to." In a heartbeat Nicholas' expression changed. He had not been able to get word to Gabriel about Alex's death. "Gabe will never forgive me," Nicholas whispered under his breath. "I hope this time he answers."

Galen stepped across the room and gripped Nicholas' shoulder with his massive hand. "You left messages on his phone and even tried sending a telegram," answered Galen. "Who knows where he is in Europe or if he is even getting messages. He will be shocked at first, Nicholas, but he won't hold it against you. He will understand your grief." Galen stepped away and met Cassandra' gaze. "Make the call Nicholas. It will be much more difficult for anyone to track your movements if you can use Gabe's jet."

"I'll start packing," said Cassandra, with more confidence than she felt.

Chapter 33

Nicholas took particular care that night to make sure the doors were locked and the alarm set. After everyone was in bed he walked through the rooms, picked up a few neglected wineglasses, and carried them back to the kitchen. He paused in each room, recalling this story or that memory. Now when he thought of Alex it brought a smile to his face instead of a tear to his eye. The heaviness in his heart, however, was a burden he knew he would carry forever.

By the time he finally headed upstairs, he was utterly exhausted. To his surprise Cassandra was still waiting up for him. He fell asleep while she was massaging his knotted back muscles.

Nicholas' eyes shot open and he sat up in bed with a gasp. It was still dark and it took him a moment to get his bearings and remember where he was. Something had shaken loose the grip of a deep sleep, but what? He looked at the clock and rubbed his eyes: 3:32 a.m. "Ohhh," he groaned, rolling over and pulling the covers tightly around him.

When he heard Michelangelo's vigorous barking a second later, he realized that was what had awakened him in the first place. He jumped out of bed and began searching for his robe. The dog's warning ended abruptly with a high-pitched yelp. Cassandra was still sleeping as he crept quietly to the bedroom door. The knob wouldn't turn: it had been locked from the hallway!

"Shit!" he cried as he fumbled for the light switch and clicked it. Nothing. The electricity had been cut off.

Nicholas reached the phone by his bed stand but he knew even before he lifted it to his ear there would be no dial tone. "Oh, God, be calm," he said to himself. "Think, think!"

"Nicholas?" mumbled his wife sleepily.

He turned to Cassandra and whispered, "Get up and get some clothes on." A heavy sleeper, she groaned and rolled over. "Cassandra!" he hissed, "Get up now!" When she finally rolled over, he stuck his face close to hers and whispered, "Intruders in the house!"

She nodded vigorously that she understood and jumped out of bed to get dressed.

Nicholas slid open a drawer on the night stand, grabbed a flashlight, and clicked it on. His brother, ever the engineer, not only kept such things handy but changed the batteries once a year.

"Do you have your cell phone? Call 9-1-1."

Edging quietly to the door, he listened but could not hear anything except his own heart and labored breathing. He flashed the beam along the frame and studied the antique pin hinges. With a grunt he shoved up on the end of one of the bolts with the butt of the flashlight and yanked it out. He repeated the process until all three bolts were on the floor.

"Stay here!" he instructed Cassandra.

Grasping the side of the door, he turned off his flashlight and carefully eased it open and stepped out into the hall. He was about to check on Francesca and the kids when he heard the creak of a floorboard behind him. He spun around and held his breath.

The house was so dark he could barely make out anything. Crouched low, he gripped the flashlight like a weapon and crept toward the stairway and Alex's office. He swallowed hard and flattened himself against the wall. Two figures dressed in black were standing just outside Alex's study. Nicholas had locked the door before going to bed, and the key was still in his pants' pocket. They were whispering to themselves, trying to figure out how to get in without waking the entire house.

"Hey!" he roared at the top of his lungs. He could have kicked himself. *Man, that was stupid!*

The two figures turned and ran down the stairs three at a time. Nicholas reached the top just as one of the intruders fired a handgun wildly in his direction. The bullet zipped past his ear and lodged in the wall. Nicholas fell to the floor. *What do I do now?*

Someone in one of the bedrooms was screaming, but he could not tell who it was. "Cassandra!" he shouted. "Use your cell and call the police! Francesca! Do the same thing! Hurry!"

When he heard the door downstairs leading to the porch slam shut, he ran down the steps and into the living room, groping for his own cell phone, which he had left on the coffee table. He punched in 9-1-1 and whispered the address into the phone: "Robbery in progress. Gunshots fired. We need help!"

When he reached the porch door he opened it slowly and crawled out on the verandah. Two men were climbing into a rental truck parked near the street at the end of the driveway. One of the intruders spotted him peeking around the corner of the porch and sent another bullet singing in his direction. He pulled his head in as the lead slug splintered the column next to him. With a roar the truck's engine turned over and the vehicle backed out of the drive, skidding to a stop in the street before the driver threw it into gear and disappeared up Meeting Street. Nicholas stood up and put the phone to his ear.

"Sir?" asked dispatcher. "Sir? Is there gunfire? Police are on the way."

"Nicholas!" screamed Cassandra from the top of the steps. "Nicholas, answer me!"

"I'm ok! They're gone," he shouted back as he ran back into the house. "Everything's ok." He turned and trotted up the stairs, using his flashlight to see so he did not break his neck. "Winston Churchill was right," he gasped breathlessly. "Nothing in life is so exhilarating as to be shot at without result!"

Cassandra grimaced at the quote. "Who were they? Did you see them?" He shook his head. "Francesca and the kids are upstairs screaming and pounding on their doors," his wife informed him with breathlessly.

"That's because they're locked," Nicholas replied. "Go see if you can get the lights on at the fuse box in the closet off the kitchen. I'll deal with the door locks."

Nicholas could hear a terrified Francesca screaming as he hurried up the stairs. "Everything's okay!" Nicholas shouted outside her door. "We'll have you out in a few minutes." The doors were fixed shut with a device similar to what car owners put on their steering wheels as a theft deterrent. When the lights flashed on, he breathed a deep sigh of relief.

Two squad cars, their blue lights flashing and sirens blaring, arrived a few minutes later. Nicholas explained what had happened and led a policeman upstairs while the others fanned out through the first floor and outside. "They definitely weren't after you or you would be dead right now," observed the officer. "Please don't touch those locks. We need to dust for prints, although this doesn't look like an amateur job. I will be surprised if we find much."

The officer carefully removed the device from a bedroom door. Francesca, together with her mother and children, emerged looking pale and shaken. "Where's Michelangelo?" Harrison asked, his voice quivering. As if on cue the puppy came galloping up the stairs with Cassandra on his heels.

"They muzzled him," she explained as Harrison fell to the floor with the dog gripped tightly in his arms. "Thank God that's all they did." A dazed and bereaved Francesca hoisted Rosemary onto her hip and held her close.

Once he made sure the women and children were all right, the officer freed Father Galen. "They were trying to get into the office, Galen, but I scared them off when I yelled at them," explained Nicholas. After retrieving the key from his pants, he led the group to the office and unlocked the door. It was as pristine as they had left it.

"Let's go downstairs. I'll make some coffee," offered Francesca. "Where's . . ." She stopped in mid-sentence, embarrassed and heartsick at the same time. Her hand went to her mouth and she ducked out of the room with a gulping sob, Rosemary still clutched to her bosom.

By 4:00 a.m. the smell of coffee filled the kitchen and a half dozen of Charleston's finest had arrived to dust for fingerprints and document the crime scene. They found the truck abandoned a few blocks away. There was nothing inside, explained an officer. "It looks like they didn't get away with anything." That was no surprise to anyone, but for the lieutenant's benefit, Francesca managed a believable sigh of relief.

"This was a very professional job," continued the lieutenant. "I doubt we will find anything that will help us, especially since the house was full of people today; prints, hair, and fiber samples are everywhere. Frankly, I wouldn't get your hopes up." He narrowed his eyes and looked carefully at Francesca. "Do you have any idea what they were looking for?"

She shook her head and turned away, sending the children back to bed with Mama Gamba, despite Harrison's howls of protest.

ॐ

Lev sat in a rental car two blocks from Alex's house. With shaking fingers, he pushed a speed dial number.

"What the hell is going on!"

"I guess you've heard by now." He held the phone a foot from his head and winced at the reply.

"I'm sorry, father. It wasn't my fault." His voice was weak, pitiful. "I have no idea what went wrong. I drew them a floor plan. I told them where the fuse box was. I even told them precisely where to find the box!"

"Of course it's not your fault! It's never your fault," snapped Malachi.

"Did the messengers get away?" he asked hopefully.

"Yes—empty-handed." Malachi cursed their ineptitude.

"Thank God for that, anyway," replied Lev, trying to calm him. "They must have wakened someone or tripped an alarm, because the police didn't waste any time getting there."

"You assumed the family would be exhausted after the funeral." Malachi spoke firmly but quietly. "I guess you underestimated your Dr. Shepard. According to one of the messengers, he was running around like James Bond. The idiots took a couple shots at him."

"Was Dr. Shepard hit?" asked Lev.

"Apparently not. Nothing has come across the police radios about anyone at the home being injured." Malachi cleared his throat. Lev could almost hear his father's mind churning. "It will be much more difficult now," he continued. "The family will be constantly on guard. You said the wife's mother was there for the funeral. Any chance she might take the kids home with her?"

Lev brightened at the thought. "Yes—I overheard them talking at the wake about travel arrangements to Italy. Someone said something about taking the kids."

"Good. I own Italy. What about Shepard and his wife?" asked Malachi.

"I don't know what their plans are. The police are still at the house. And there's a priest there named Galen Abbott. Do you know him?" asked Lev.

"Never heard of him," shot back Malachi. "That busybody Gabriel von Stuyvesant is in Germany. I don't think he even knows about the other Shepard's unfortunate death, or he would have been at the funeral. Let me know if someone mentions his name—particularly if he is coming home anytime soon."

Lev agreed, but before he could say anything else the line went dead. When he saw another squad car approaching he slipped down low in his seat and looked through the steering wheel. It was time to get back to Atlanta and work things from that end.

After all, Dr. Shepard had just lost a brother. He was going to need a friend.

ॐ

It was mid-morning before the police wrapped up their work and left the house. The detective who had been placed in charge of the case promised to let Francesca know if they found anything to report. An enervating lethargy settled over the disheveled group. No one seemed able to muster the strength to do much of anything.

Galen broke the silence. "I suspect that we are all too distressed and too exhausted to make good decisions right now, but we are dealing with people who play for keeps. If any of us harbored any doubts about what happened to Alex, tonight's activity would seem to confirm that he did not die accidently. At times like this, self-preservation is the best course of action."

Cassandra stifled a yawn. "I'm sorry, Galen. What did you just say?"

"It's time to vamoose, as my Texan brethren would say. Skedaddle." He looked at each of them in turn. "All of you need to get out of town. And not just out of town, but out of the country. We don't know who we are dealing with, but they seem to know a lot about you."

Nicholas nodded in agreement. "Galen's right. We can't just sit still and make it easy for them. They screwed up on the robbery and took a couple shots at me. I doubt this bunch will make the same mistake twice."

The course of the conversation energized everyone. "I didn't mean to scare you," Galen apologized quickly. "I'm just trying to instill some urgency here."

"Well, you did that." Nicholas rose from the table. "Any suggestions?" he asked, cocking an eyebrow in the priest's direction.

Galen nodded. "Francesca, take your mother and children and go to Siena. Pack lightly and hurry. I'll make reservations out of Atlanta for you tomorrow. I'll see to the house, though I might need to use the living room for a counseling center occasionally." He chuckled and fingered his collar. "Let's see them break and enter a house full of priests and nuns! That leaves you two," he said, looking at Nicholas and Cassandra. "Where can you go?"

Nicholas rubbed his chin and thought for a few moments before answering. "I have temporary faculty status, so it won't be any problem for me to take a leave of absence."

"Then this is probably as good a time as any to go to Europe and start tracking down the original owners of the box—that is, if we can ever get hold of Gabe!" exclaimed Cassandra. "We need access to his plane."

"Gabe!" Nicholas jumped up and snatched his cell phone off its clip. "I forgot! He left a message on my phone last night, and I spotted it right before the police got here. It slipped my mind completely." He looked at the phone, pressed a button, entered his password, and pressed it against his ear.

Cassandra turned toward Galen. "I have cousins in Paris. I'm sure whoever is behind all this knows nothing about them. They live in Croissy, just outside the city. If we can get there, we can hole up and figure out how to proceed. I could e-mail her this morning and tell her we are coming. It will take her by surprise, but I'm sure she'll help us."

"That sounds smart," Galen replied. "But make sure she doesn't call you, and under no circumstances should any of us use land line phones to talk about any of this. They may not be secure. We ought to get you out of here and into France as discreetly as possible. I hope Gabe can handle that."

Nicholas looked up, his cell phone still in his hand. "I guess we'll find out soon enough. Gabe called and left a number. God, if I had only been able to get hold of him sooner. He could have been with us." Nicholas took a deep breath and shook his head, thinking about his failed attempts to reach his friend in the hours and days following Alex's death, and how Francesca had refused to delay the funeral. "How in the world am I going to explain any of this to him?" he asked without expecting an answer.

He took a breath, dialed the number, and tapped his foot nervously while waiting for the overseas connection. "Gabe! Where are you? Oh, Lord. We're fine . . . well, no, were not fine . . ." Nicholas searched for the right words, but finding them was harder than he expected. "Can you . . . get back here . . . right away?" When his voice broke, he handed the phone to Galen.

The priest took the phone and in a low, calm voice, informed Gabriel about Alex's death and the attempted robbery. From the tone of the conversation, Nicholas knew Gabriel felt responsible, but Galen assured him it wasn't his fault. The talked for several long minutes.

"So the box and the documents are safe?" Gabriel finally asked.

"Yes," the priest assured him, "but we all need your help now."

"You know I will do anything I can."

"We need to use your private jet, Gabe. Let's just say a trip is in the works."

"Do you think they are up for a little smuggling?" he asked.

"If you are suggesting what I think you are suggesting," replied Galen, "I don't think they have any other choice."

Galen listened carefully while Gabriel outlined his plan. He would send his jet to Atlanta's Hartsfield-Jackson Airport the day after tomorrow. Directions to a private hangar would arrive via e-mail. His personal pilot would then fly them to Orly, France.

"Got it." Galen turned to Nicholas and Cassandra. "He said the pilot could land at Orly and drop you off at a private hangar, and continue on to Germany to pick him up. Can you arrange for your French connections to get a car for you there? Gabe will join you wherever you want him to show up."

"Tell him we can do all of that," answered Nicholas, "but I think he needs to come back home. Somehow, I think he will be of more use here, keeping his ear to the ground for us." Galen nodded, gave Gabriel the message, concluded the call, and hung up with a grim but satisfied look on his face.

Cassandra turned to her husband. "Nicholas, what about Lev and Felicia? You can't just leave them, right?" Nicholas groaned and rolled his eyes. "I have an idea," she continued. "Don't they need to prepare for their orals? Maybe you could cut them loose from their research project and tell them to spend their time preparing for them."

"Yes, that's a good idea," he nodded. Nicholas turned to Francesca. "I hate to bring up money, but this is important for you too, Francesca. Just so you know, our futures account is in a cash position right now, so we have plenty of money available to cover any expenses. I just wanted to make sure you did not worry about that."

"I don't know if you have thought of this, Nicholas, but you will have to be able come and go without worrying about being tracked," explained Galen. "I think you might need forged passports with another identity."

Everyone looked at the priest as if he was a complete stranger. He laughed, big and comfortably. "I watch a lot of spy movies, but I promise I'm not an undercover CIA agent. I have a contact from some years ago. I can get you new passports, new social security numbers, new names, bank accounts, whatever you need."

Nicholas was impressed. "Anything else we don't know about you?"

Galen looked slightly embarrassed and tried to explain. "I've occasionally helped the government with its witness protection program—you know, some of the counseling centers I set up employ people who are starting new lives."

After a brief back and forth, Nicholas decided they should keep their own passports, but if they needed to disappear or got in a pinch, Galen would be ready to provide them with whatever they needed. "It's understood," he added, "that nobody can know where we're going. Absolutely no one. Galen is right. Whoever we're dealing with has obviously outmaneuvered us so far. Let's not continue to underestimate them. We need to go quickly and quietly."

"What about your parents?' asked Cassandra suddenly, alarmed that she didn't think about them before.

"Thank God they stayed at the Planters Inn and not here!" Nicholas sighed. "Let's not mention last night's little adventure to them. They are leaving tonight, anyway. The less they know the better."

Galen agreed. "And don't worry; I'll take them to lunch this afternoon so you all can make your plans. By the way, have you thought about what you are going to do with that darn box?"

Nicholas shook his head. "We also have to store the programs and the documents in a safe place. Any suggestions?"

"How about a good old safe deposit box?" suggested Galen. "Give me the keys. They don't know me from Adam's house cat."

"I like that," said Cassandra. "I need to put some of the original documents in there, too. I have copies of most of them we made at Gabe's, but I didn't get all of them. If something were to happen to us, the documents won't matter anyway. Where should we put the box?"

"We'll take it to Italy with us," offered Francesca. Everyone looked at her in surprise. "I know what you're thinking, that box is probably the last thing I want to see right now." She gave a little shudder. "And, you would be right. But I don't think anyone would suspect that we'd be traveling with it. It would be too obvious."

Nicholas exhaled noisily. "I don't know about that. Now that we don't need it for our calculations I'm tempted to just get rid of it. However, speaking as a scientist, it's a critical piece of evidence we might need one day. I'd give it back to Gabe, but somehow I don't think it would ever get back into that secret room, and I wouldn't want to hang him with the responsibility."

"So I take it," repeated Francesca.

"I don't think you can, Francesca," answered Cassandra. "The new X-ray machines will spot that thing immediately. It's too oddly-shaped to be a typical travel thing, and the nested tetrahedron isn't likely to get the green light from a Customs inspector. He'd probably think it was a neutron bomb. I don't think we have much of a choice. We'll take it with us on Gabe's plane."

Galen agreed. "You'll be flying in as unregistered visitors, and it's unlikely you will be bothered by Customs in France. It would be easy for you to hide the box on the plane. That gets my vote. You can meet up with Francesca later and leave it at her parents' house if you want to."

"Ok, done," said Nicholas. "Let's help Francesca with breakfast and get moving."

༄

Nicholas called Felicia from Charleston that morning to break the news. Lev's heart skipped a beat when he returned to the office and she filled him. "What are we supposed to do?" he whined. "We need him!"

Felecia winced as if someone had yelled at her. Whining was not an attractive attribute in a potential husband. "Dr. Shepard said we should just study for our orals. He will be back in a couple weeks or so. He promised to keep in touch."

"But . . . but where are they going?" he demanded. "What about the research we are conducting for his discovery?"

"I don't know, Lev, and I didn't ask!" shot back Felecia. "His identical twin brother just died in a terrible car accident and left a widow with two young children. I am sure they just need some time." Felicia's heart ached for Dr. Shepard's wife. Family was so important to her. "It is such a tragedy," she said, blinking back tears.

Lev's face took on a glum appearance. "Yes, a terrible tragedy," he repeated. "Listen, I have to run to the library. I'll see you later."

Malachi's son had other things on his mind beside his professor's grief at the loss of his brother.

༄

While Galen lumbered off to take Nicholas' parents to lunch, everyone else pitched in to get Francesca and the children packed. The children were still exhausted from the night before, and after a quick snack fell sleep in the den watching a DVD. While they slept, Francesca packed two large suitcases with their belongings, taking extra time to put their favorite toys and stuffed animals into a carry-on bag for the long overseas flight.

A long and tearful goodbye took place the next morning. Harrison took Michelangelo for one last walk with Galen, who promised the boy he would take good care of the puppy as if "he were my very own." Everyone was quiet and pensive on the drive to the Atlanta airport. And then they were gone.

During the short trip back to their condo, Nicholas and Cassandra discussed the logistics of their own flight. "I am beginning to feel a bit paranoid," Nicholas admitted. "Every car I see in the mirror seems to be following us, and I imagine that every person we pass is staring at us!"

Cassandra confessed feeling the same way. "This all seems silly. I want to scream 'stop this!' and get off the ride. And yet, it's all very real."

Just in case someone was really following them, the couple decided on a little subterfuge for the morning's trip to the airport. They would split up. After they packed, Nicholas dropped his wife and the luggage off at the Atlanta's Hartsfield-Jackson Airport, where she settled herself outside the boarding area with a cup of coffee and a magazine. Once she was out of the car, he drove downtown to a parking garage and grabbed a cab back to the airport. The box was with him, buried away inside a large titanium photographer's case. They hooked up at a prearranged time and, their luggage in tow, took the escalator down to the baggage area and stepped quickly outside to catch a taxi that took them directly to the hangar where Gabriel's plane was waiting for them.

The plane was a Gulfstream IV-SP, a high-altitude twin turbofan jet outfitted with an apartment and a large hold suitable for transporting the antiquities Gabriel and his family routinely brought back from Europe. When they arrived, the pilot was inside the cockpit conducting a pre-flight safety check while the co-pilot walked slowly outside the aircraft, inspecting it before take-off. Smiling, he introduced himself and offered Cassandra a hand as she ascended the rollaway stairs. He offered to take the large camera case, but Nicholas declined politely and lugged it up and into the plane himself.

Neither Nicholas nor Cassandra had ever been aboard Gabriel's Gulfstream, and the elegance of the spacious interior surprised them both. "This is like the Ritz!" exclaimed Cassandra as Nicholas entered the main cabin. In addition to the comfortable gold damask-covered banquettes, highly lacquered burled wood appointments, and thick carpet were several tiny touches including fresh flowers, a full bar, and crisp white linen cloth on the dining table. There was also a small bedroom with Eve Delorme linens and a walk-in shower.

"I hope it takes a long time to get to Paris," she sighed, plopping down on one of the plush banquettes. She toyed with a remote and a screen slid back, revealing a plasma television and DVD storage.

Nicholas tucked the case with the box in a closet near the back of the plane. "If I had to choose a way to be stuck in a tube for hours on end, this would be my pick." He was finally beginning to feel relaxed.

The hatches banged shut and the co-pilot reappeared. "We'll be under way shortly, Dr. Shepard," he said. "I have to apologize in advance because there will not be a flight attendant to serve you. If you want anything to eat or drink, you'll find a fully stocked kitchen in the forward compartment. We should arrive at Orly at approximately 10:00 a.m. Paris time. Have a good flight, and let me know if you need anything."

Shortly thereafter, the engines roared to life and the jet began rolling out to the tarmac, where they waited for five minutes before gliding down the runway in a perfect, smooth takeoff. The passengers looked out the windows at the rapidly diminishing landscape of buildings, trees, and freeways. A left bank took them through a layer of puffy white cumulus clouds as the jet continued climbing to its cruising altitude. Nicholas put his arms around his wife and they enjoyed the gentle pressure of the G-force pushing them against their luxurious seats. At 30,000 feet, the plane leveled out at 547 mph. Nicholas looked over the DVD collection. "What are you in the mood for? Something fun like *Pirates of the Caribbean*? Or maybe something spooky like *Rear Window*?"

"How about *Pirates of the Caribbean*?"

"Why that one?"

"Because the good guys win!"

Chapter 34

Despite the wonderful amenities of the private jet, the thrill associated with the new experience wore off rather quickly. The crushing weight of Alex's death, coupled with the potential threat against their own lives, distracted Nicholas and Cassandra on a trip they would otherwise have immensely enjoyed.

Nicholas had picked up a book to read well before Johnny Depp's Captain Sparrow discovered the truth behind the ship's curse. Equally distracted, Cassandra decided to sleep. After tossing and turning for an hour she opened her eyes and sat up next to Nicholas, who was absentmindedly staring out the window. Wrapped in their memories of Alex, burdened by sorrow, anger, and apprehension, the couple remained quiet for long intervals. When they felt the plane begin its descent, Nicholas looked down at the coast of Normandy. *Please, God,* he thought, *let us find some answers here.*

They settled back into their seats as the plane executed a graceful landing. "It looks as though we are in the middle of nowhere," observed Nicholas. Orly is slightly more than seven miles south of Paris, and although not exactly in the countryside, its air traffic is substantially less than Charles de Gaulle Airport.

Cassandra's cousin Marie had been surprised and delighted to hear of their visit. Though it had been years since the two had seen one another, they exchanged occasional e-mails and cards at Christmas. Since Marie and Jacques Beaudrot both worked, their new American guests would necessarily be left on their own much of the time. The extra privacy suited them just fine. The French cousins had been told next to nothing about what had transpired in the States. Luckily, Jacques was a banker with Credit Suisse. "My hope," Cassandra had explained during the flight, "is that Jacques can get me into bank vaults so we can compare some of the accounting documents. I want to try and match the handwriting on ours with their copies from the same period. That way, even if there's no cartouche, we can establish a connection."

As the plane approached a small hangar, Cassandra spotted Marie standing next to the Beaudrot's station wagon. As soon as the pilot opened the door, Cassandra flew down the steps and into Marie's welcoming arms. Nicholas followed slowly, careful with the heavy case that held the box. He shook Jacques' hand warmly and exchanged hugs with Marie. The Beaudrots looked happy to see their guests, but it was obvious they were confused by the sudden visit.

"Thanks for meeting us on such short notice!" Cassandra said as she watched Nicholas hugging her cousin.

"We are of course very pleased you have come," responded Marie, "and in a private jet no less! Things must be good in America for you."

The pilot appeared at the top of the stairway with the luggage, and Jacques and Nicholas quickly moved to help him unload it. "Well, Nicholas had a chance to take a leave of absence," continued Cassandra, "and our friend Gabriel made his plane available, so we decided to take advantage of our luck and see your wonderful country."

Because the von Stuyvesants and their jet were regular guests of the Orly airport, Gabriel had assured the couple there would not be a problem with the Customs inspector, and he was right. The bored government worker took down the passport names and numbers on a sheet attached to a clipboard and waved them through without even matching the photo identifications to the people presenting them.

The two couples stuffed everything into the trunk of the small Euro-sized station wagon. "That was all very easy," said a relieved Nicholas. "Gabriel told us not to be nervous about doing it this way, and he was right. I think I might look into buying a Gulfstream myself." Jacques slammed the back door down and shot Nicholas an odd look. His wife's cousin was doing a lot better than he had remembered.

As Jacques drove toward a service road, Cassandra and Marie broke into steady conversation about everything from their recent flight to American politics. Her English was excellent, and much better than her husband's. Marie loved conversing in other languages as often as possible. Although she taught English, she also spoke German, Dutch,

Spanish, and a little Russian, which made traveling virtually anywhere on the globe much easier. Unlike his garrulous wife, Jacques preferred to sit back and observe. Although he understood a great deal more than most people realized, he was a little uncomfortable speaking in a foreign tongue.

At the moment, he was listening intently to his wife and her cousin chatter in the backseat. He could see Cassandra's face in the rear view mirror, and although she was dressed impeccably, there was weariness about her eyes, a false air of happiness in her voice. Something was very wrong.

Cassandra regarded her cousin with amazement. "You have not aged even a little bit!" she exclaimed. "Aren't we the same age? You certainly got all the good French genes from your mother!"

"And you would not believe how young *she* still looks!" Marie laughed gaily.

"How is she doing?"

Marie's laughter faded. "We still do not speak. She is quite crazy, you know. It has been nearly fifteen years since we had any correspondence, except when papa died. Then she only wanted to know how much money she would get. I had to write and tell her she would get nothing. My father's estate was subject to American taxes, and he had no other assets to speak of. I do not know that she believed me, but it was true, and I heard no more from her."

Cassandra shook her head sadly. It was a familiar story. Marie's uncle Roy, her mom's older brother, had married a French woman when he was stationed in Paris after World War II. After suffering through years of deprivations, more than one European girl jumped at the chance to marry a GI and start a new life in the States. Roy brought Jacquelyn home to live in Washington D.C., and in the beginning it was a dream come true. But he worked long hours, traveled often and, in truth, neglected her. They had two children by the time Roy was assigned back to Europe. After living on an Army base in England, Roy was ordered to Heidelberg, Germany. Moody and often depressed, Jacquelyn frequently took the train home to visit old friends in Paris for long weekends. Roy suspected she was visiting one friend in particular, but he never found out for sure. One day, Jacquelyn never returned.

When Marie was accepted at the Sorbonne, she was glad to be leaving that unhappy household. At the university she embraced a free life and met and fell in love with Jacques. For her, the two were synonymous. Jacques was in every way the opposite of her stiff and emotionally conflicted father. After twenty-five years, their marriage remained steady and strong. Marie often wondered how she had made such a healthy choice, given the rest of her family's dysfunction. Jacques' family, a riotous lot of merchants, scholars, and farmers scattered across Europe, remained connected to the family compound in the south of France, where many of them spent their summer holidays.

"We're going to drop Jacques off at his office on the rue Royale," Marie explained as they pulled around a slow-moving lorry. "We'll do some sightseeing and come back for him, then go to dinner. One night this week, we'll go to the Opera and see *Il Trovatore* with that sizzling Argentinean tenor Dario Volonte."

Jacques shook his head and rattled off something quickly to his wife, who turned to Cassandra as Jacques caught her eye in the mirror. "You both are very tired, yes? Perhaps we are planning too much on your first night? Maybe you would rather go straight to our home and relax? You both look exhausted, and I know my Jacques. He thinks there is something bothering both of you." The wise woman's eyes narrowed as she confronted her cousin. "I think perhaps so, as well." She smiled warmly, radiating empathy.

Nicholas broke in before Cassandra could answer. "Neither of us wants to lie to you, Marie," confessed Nicholas. "We are not here just for a vacation. Cassandra and I are in France to carry out some historical research related to a discovery I made in the field of . . . economics." He stopped, unsure how much to reveal, but knowing full well he could not endanger their lives by sharing the secret with them. "I'm sorry," he added when neither immediately responded, "but I can't tell you more than that. Think of it as a professional code of silence." Nicholas tried to smile, but the effort was half-hearted and wholly unconvincing. Neither cousin believed he was telling the full truth, especially since the modestly paid college professor had arrived in France in a multi-million-dollar jet and had casually mentioned buying one for himself.

Jacques and Marie exchanged glances. "There is something about historical research that is too . . . confidential . . . to share with us—or too dangerous?" asked Cassandra's cousin.

Nicholas turned around in the small front seat and looked at Marie. "We do not wish to endanger you. My discovery has upset certain moneyed interests who do not want my research to be made public." He turned back and looked out the windshield. "My brother Alex was involved. They killed him last week."

Marie let out a loud, anguished gasp. "Mon Dieu!" whispered Jacques, "Can this story get any more amazing? We are very, very sorry for you."

"How can we help you?" asked Marie.

"Thank you, that is so kind," replied Cassandra. "We have some old documents, many from France . . . accounting ledgers, banking records, and so on. We were hoping Jacques might be able to help us track other similar documents for us." Jacques' face tightened in thought, prompting Nicholas to add quickly, "There is nothing illegal about our activities, I assure you."

"I believe you," Marie declared firmly. "Both of you are good people."

Nicholas said carefully, "Cassandra and I wanted to come here because it's the only place we know of where we can be safe, where we can hide and make some plans, and hopefully research the background of some of our documents. Of course, there's some chance we're putting you at risk, and we completely understand if you don't want to take that chance. We just did not know who else to contact."

Jacques and Marie looked at each other, shrugged, and smiled. Marie squeezed her cousin's hand reassuringly. "You are always welcome at our house." Cassandra squeezed back in gratitude. "But, for now," Marie said, pointing out the window, "you are in Paris!"

Cassandra smiled widely. "And we've never been to a Paris production. I'm sure the opera will be spectacular."

"Did you bring something special to wear?" Nicholas asked.

"Of course, so don't think that will get you out of a night at the opera!" The excitement rose in her voice as she shared the story about her black dress and the Biltmore party with Marie and Jacques. As she recalled Alex and Francesca dancing down the corridor to the library, her voice cracked and she dissolved into tears. "I can see why people took the European grand tour to get over lost love affairs and the deaths of loved ones," she said, using her finger to wipe a tear away. "This is so incredibly difficult. But traveling makes such immediate demands on people that it doesn't leave much time for grief."

Nicholas looked out his side window, seeing but not fully appreciating the magnificent buildings slipping past on the Boulevard Haussmann. Alex and Francesca had spent a lot of time in Paris, including an entire year before they had children. Cassandra and Nicholas had flown over for one brief but memorable week. He would give anything to . . . Nicholas stopped himself. It was too hard to go back in time.

When at last the car pulled over to park near the Madeleine, Jacques turned to Nicholas with a sympathetic smile. "*Mon ami, c'est ici les bureaus de R. R. Donnelly.*"

"*Oui,*" said Marie. "You can go here to handle any personal financial matters. They have offices you can use, and translators. They are globally connected."

"Thank you," replied Nicholas. "I'm sure we'll need their services soon."

The French couple switched drivers, and Jacques waved goodbye as the car pulled back into traffic. As they made their way through the *Place de la Concorde* toward the Seine, Cassandra and Nicholas absorbed the Napoleonic grandeur of the *Place*, which formed the joyous end of the *Champs Elysees* and the beginning of the wonderful gardens of the Tuileries.

"It does give you a little shiver of pleasure just to be in Paris, doesn't it?" Cassandra dreamily asked.

Marie made a right turn and proceeded slowly, for a French driver, up the *Champs Elysees*. "Believe me," she said, as a driver behind her blew his horn, "sometimes it is better not to get in the car to begin with!"

"Paris has its own special magic, doesn't it?" Cassandra said with her nose virtually pressed against the car window. "In London, a lot of those bombed-out historic buildings from the blitz were replaced with modern edifices. Thank God the Germans didn't destroy Paris! And if I am not mistaken, it even looks cleaned up since we were here last!"

"Oh, pollution is such a dreadful thing. But they are persevering. All the buildings Haussmann designed in the 18th century now have the golden glow they had in the beginning. Wait until you see *Notre Dame de Paris*! They have finished cleaning the façade now, and all the scaffolding is *finally* down!"

"There must be scaffolding somewhere at Notre Dame, Marie," joked Nicholas. "I think the French put it up just so the Americans can't take pictures!"

Marie chuckled and took the bait. "It's our answer to freedom fries. We disappear behind our restoration platforms."

By this time they were at the *Arc de Triomphe*, and Marie drove them in a fast and tight circle around it to test their courage. They failed. Marie found a parking spot and the three of them climbed from the car. "Something else we have is the good sense to put tunnels underground so that visitors to the famous landmarks won't be killed, while the French can go about their business as fast as they care to."

The day was bright and sunny, and Cassandra put her hands on the cold stone and looked up. Marble florets marching along in a grid pattern crowned the inside of the Arc. "I know an Atlanta architect who copied that design and put it on the ceiling of a kitchen." Aghast at the thought, Marie walked over to the other side muttering that Americans should have their cameras taken away from them at customs.

They walked along the street looking through the shop windows. Marie could see they were still dazed and shocked from the cascade of events that had brought them there, so Marie led them a few blocks to a small café unpopulated with noisy tourists. They sipped espresso in the cool shade while Marie and Cassandra caught up on family gossip.

At the end of the day they dined at Le Grand Vefour for dinner, where Jacques had pulled strings for a good table. It was one of the most famous restaurants in all of Paris. Opened in 1784, it had entertained both famous and infamous, including Napoleon himself.

"I hope this evening's plans aren't too much for you," Marie whispered to Cassandra as they were shown to their table by the elegant maitre d'.

"It is perfectly wonderful, Marie. I don't know how we can begin to thank you," she replied. "We needed something like this." The table was in a quiet corner, where they could see much of the restaurant but converse without being overheard by other guests.

"Francesca would love dining here tonight if things were different," Nicholas sighed.

Cassandra smiled. "Do you think she would try to help the chef here?" She turned to Marie and Jacques. "She actually went into the kitchen at the Four Seasons in New York to scold the chef."

Marie put her hand to her chest in mock horror. "I do so love Francesca, but she would not, *n'est-ce pas?*

Nicholas laughed and Cassandra brightened at hearing his bass rumble. And though they tried to treat the Baroque 18th century appointments with casual Parisian aplomb, they soon found themselves gaping at the gilded and painted ceilings, the remarkable chandeliers, and decorative panels surrounding the room. Windows overlooked the Palais Royale and the fountain where people were catching the warmth of a lovely early Paris evening. Cassandra imagined it filled with people arguing politics several centuries ago and wondered how Napoleon had behaved here. Probably very badly, she thought.

"Just think, Victor Hugo ate here," she said out loud, "Alexandre Dumas, and Colette—not together, of course," she smiled at Nicholas. "George Sand came here to get over her affair in Mallorca with Chopin. It has an amazing history."

A server brought the drinks and the conversation turned to the subject of the documents. Cassandra explained, as far as she was willing and able, what they had in their possession and that they were seeking trace the lineage of the papers. Jacques pondered the problem as he sipped from a glass of Bordeaux. He offered his assistance in broken English. "My bank has many underground vaults with financial documents few people have ever seen," he said, nodding slowly while trying to choose his words carefully. "The vaults date back to days even before Haussmann reconstructed the inner city. There are some ancient incomplete maps and these vaults are mentioned in several old manuscripts, but I don't know anyone who really knows how many there are, or even who built them. They just exist. I have a friend at the bank who has some knowledge of these. Perhaps he can help us."

Cassandra's eyes grew wide with excitement. "That's more than we could ask for. Can this person be trusted?"

"We are bankers," Jacques assured her with a small smile and tip of his head. Nicholas lifted his glass and toasted, prompting the others to follow suit.

Cassandra leaned forward. "We are looking for documents bearing this symbol." She took a slip of paper from her handbag and drew the cartouche on it. "This is an ancient Egyptian glyph, and it is unique to the cult or group that used it."

Both Jacques and Marie studied it. Marie considered the drawing for a moment. "I have a friend, Claudette, who deals in antiquities and rare manuscripts. Her apartment is near here. Perhaps she has seen this and can help."

"Absolute discretion is essential," reminded Nicholas. "We have to be able to trust these people not to say a word. Powerful people are after us, Marie, and we don't know who might be in their network. We can't have people talking all over Paris about an American couple asking questions about ancient documents."

The French couple vouched for the trustworthiness of their contacts and promised to call them the next day for appointments. "But, now," Jacques said with a sweep of his hand, "we eat. I have requested that the chef prepare some very special dishes."

The first dish was tiny white cups filled with chilled soup of goat cheese and lobster. "This food is absolutely delicious," said Nicholas, relishing the epicurean paradise. Course after course arrived, each presented quietly on Limoges china accompanied with the correct wine. They indulged themselves on ravioli stuffed with *foie gras* and topped with truffles, lamb with a chocolate coffee sauce, lemon roasted turbot on a plate artfully decorated with baby vegetables. Desserts included *crème brulee* served with a milk-almond sorbet, chocolate mousse on a hazelnut pastry, and a white cheesecake with mangoes and coriander. The meal was as perfect as any Cassandra or Nicholas had ever enjoyed.

When the bill came, Nicholas snatched it from the table and paid in cash. The Beaudrots were appalled—not that he had paid, but at how he had done so. "You should not carry money like that," whispered Jacques. "It is not safe."

"Don't worry," replied Nicholas. "That was nearly all I had. We have to figure out how to get around without using credit cards. They leave a trail."

"I will arrange an account at my bank," offered Jacques. "You may use any name you wish."

"How about my middle name, Llewellyn?" suggested Cassandra.

One last sip of cognac and it was time to leave. "I am stuffed," sighed Cassandra, "but in a good way." She gave the beautiful old restaurant one last admiring look as they passed into the foyer. She froze when they reached one of the tall, ornately painted columns. On the lower right side was the cartouche symbol, emblazoned for all to see. "Nicholas," she whispered, tugging on his arm as Jacques and Marie continued on. He stopped and followed her pointing finger. His eyes widened in disbelief. What could it mean?

"May I help you?" The stiff maitre d' was standing behind them, a razor thin smile cut into his otherwise implacable face.

"Do you know what this means?" Cassandra asked breathlessly. "I am . . ."

Now it was Nicholas' turn to take her elbow and gently lead her away. "I'm sure he doesn't know what an Egyptian cartouche is doing on an 18th century painting, dear," he said in a voice intended to convince her to drop the matter then and there.

"Alas, Madame, your husband is correct. I do not. Perhaps it is a signature of some sort?"

"Thank you," said Nicholas, leading Cassandra toward their waiting hosts.

"What did I do?"

"You called attention to yourself in a public place where you know absolutely no one, and where anyone could be interested in what you know. Or what you want to know."

As soon as they were out the door, one of the Taittingers, an owner of the restaurant, quietly approached the maitre d' to ask what it was the Americans were so interested in. Christian pointed out the cartouche to his boss, who raised one eyebrow and looked after the departing couples. "Do you know them?"

"The Frenchman is Jacques Beaudrot, a banker at Credit Suisse. He has been here many times for lunch with some of his managers and clients."

He thought deeply for a moment before answering, "I will make a note of it."

Nicholas and Cassandra were both nearly asleep by the time Jacques pulled up into a small driveway in Croissy. The nearly century-old home had been erected on a corner lot. It was constructed in a much older style, with no lower windows looking out to the street, while those on the upper floor were heavily shuttered. To anyone passing by, the structure looked more like a right-angled wall than a home. It was not until the beginning of the 1700s that home builders began paying attention to street orientations. Before that time, homes were often looked upon as small forts to ward off thieves and ensure a family's safety and privacy.

Once inside, Marie directed Nicholas and Cassandra upstairs, where they would find good red wine and a feather bed. They complied sleepily, climbing the steep narrow stairs leading up to their bedroom. Their host had it stocked with down comforters, chenille bathrobes, and big white fluffy towels. Table lamps lit the richly polished wooden floor and iron canopy bed, which was hung with the sheerest white silk chiffon panels Marie could find. Jacques hauled their luggage upstairs, bid them good night, and left.

After quickly changing into their pajamas, Nicholas poured two small glasses of wine, and slipped into bed next to Cassandra, carefully handing her a glass. "We should call Francesca tomorrow," she said.

Nicholas agreed, stifling a yawn. "Where do you think we should begin the document search?"

"I think tomorrow we should really do some general historical research first," she answered, nibbling at her upper lip. "If we are going to do some time travel through the ages with the documents, I can think of no better place to start than with the Louvre." Nicholas nodded again, this time yawning deeply as he fluffed his pillow and dropped his head down in exhaustion. "A day or two after that, we can meet with the contacts Jacques and Marie mentioned. Does that sound good?" Cassandra took a last swallow of the wine, set the glass down, and snuggled under the warm covers.

"Sure," he murmured sleepily as he slipped over the edge of consciousness, the cartouche on the painting column dancing vividly in his mind. Why would someone paint the same Egyptian symbol there? He wished his brother were with him. "We will find out, Alex," he thought as he drifted to sleep.

২

They awoke well after sunrise and a full hour after their hosts had left for work. Marie had left directions on how to get to the Metro and suggested they buy a week's ticket. She also left good strong French coffee, fresh croissants, and sliced apples. Marie's kitchen was small but well organized. There was room for a tiny breakfast table and three chairs, but little else. She opted for counter space when they renovated, so there was plenty of that. Like Francesca, she loved to cook, and recipe books lined two shelves of cupboard space. Nicholas and Cassandra carried their breakfast out to the courtyard and sat in silence, soaking up the early morning sun. It was time to get ready for their trip into the city.

The upstairs bathroom was converted from a bedroom, with a big walk-in shower sparkling with aqua and turquoise tile. Cassandra cracked open the shuttered windows so she could see the sky and rooftops while showering. Nicholas recalled the last time they had been at Jacques' and Marie's. They had showered together with great slathers of soap, laughing and singing; most of the day had been spent in bed. Today was different. They took separate showers, dressed, and set off for Paris.

The hopped off at the Louvre Metro stop and Cassandra pulled Nicholas out into the sunlight to admire I. M. Pei's pyramid in the middle of the courtyard separating the Richelieu, Denon, and Sully wings of the Louvre. "I suppose I am in the minority," she sighed, "but I love the juxtaposition of the modern glass and those brooding dark statues that look down like knights of old."

"Don't say that too loudly," warned Nicholas with a smile. "You don't want some rabid Frenchman to hear you compliment the hated pyramid."

She chuckled as they headed for the line to buy their tickets. "Let's go through the Sully access," Cassandra suggested, reviewing the map in her hand, "I want to revisit the Medieval Louvre because it prepares me for what happens later." She turned and walked purposefully to the section containing the moat and dungeon, which were all that remained from the original building finished in 1202. The entrance was astonishingly plain, thought Nicholas, with bas-relief sculptures placed at strategic intervals along the walls. Lit by skylights set into the pavement in the courtyard above, the entry allowed visitors to clear their minds before stepping into the magnificent collections. A circular walkway around the medieval tower displayed the cut-stone achievement of the Masons of that era, which rivaled the work of the Incas who had labored in much the same manner on the other side of the world. Nicholas paused, marveling at the precision. "It's no wonder the masons' guilds were so elite," he said. "Are you in the mood now? What next?"

"Let's start with Egypt, since that's where the box began," answered Cassandra. They walked up a flight and made their way through the exhibits. It was overwhelming. The Carlos Museum in Atlanta was a fine exhibition, but where their Egyptian display had two head rests the Louvre offered hundreds, all perfectly presented in huge glass cases. They wandered into the Galerie Henri IV, where architectural remnants and colossal figures looked down upon statues of commoners and craftspeople. They strolled to the Old Kingdom galleries, where the earliest artifacts awaited them. "Look at this couple," said Cassandra. She studied an acacia wood statue of a pair of figures. The male, wigged and dressed in the classic linen skirt, held his companion's hand as they traveled toward a destination only they knew. "It's almost emotional," she said, deeply touched by the detail and beauty of the figures.

"Look at this pair over here," said Nicholas, motioning her toward the statue of Raherka and Meresankh. The carved limestone depicts the couple standing very close together, the male apparently pulling something as his hands grip two handles. The woman's elbow is bent and her hand is across the man's arm and torso in a classic demonstration of love and helpfulness. "I never noticed how women are depicted in this art," he said. "So many of these stelae and glyphs show war and conflict, but all around life goes forward in this amazing society. You see how love worked there, too." Temporarily forgetting why they were there, the couple began taking notice of the strong role women played in ancient Egyptian culture. Finally Nicholas brought them back to earth. "Hey," he whispered. "We forgot to look for the cartouche."

"I'm not sure we could find it in all these glyphs," Cassandra replied. "It's so much more obvious out of context, like the one we found last night at the restaurant. I don't know, Nicholas, there is so much to look for. We might need years to do what I suggested."

"Cassandra, years we don't have, but maybe we should just take a different approach," suggested her husband. "Let's draw a little map of the movement of wealth and power in Europe, beginning with the fall of Egypt to the Romans, and so on, and see where it takes us. Let's assume a Roman soldier or politician looted the box from Alexandria during the Ptolemaic period. Remember, Egypt fell to General Ptolemy nearly three centuries earlier, just after Alexander's conquests."

"What? Are you suddenly the historian?" Cassandra teased.

"No, it's written on that plaque over there. You forget I read French pretty well. I just wouldn't dare speak it—especially here."

She laughed. "So the glory that was Rome comes down to our box? Let's see. From Rome, power shifted to Florence and Venice. When Rome fell in 476 A.D., there was a period of chaos and then the Catholic Church began its long ascension. Power then bounced back and forth between Spain, Germany, France, and England for hundreds of years. If the box *was* the spoils of war, it probably wouldn't have all those documents attached to it. What if the box was a leader instead of a follower?"

"You mean that it preceded the power? I like that," mulled Nicholas. "What a fascinating philosophical issue. It would make history a lot less accidental."

"Maybe, maybe not," answered Cassandra. "What if some organization or group controlled the box, and whoever this group wanted to have the power got it."

Nicholas was not quite sure what she was saying, so he explored the thought a bit. "You mean like the Masons? Some secret cult?" Cassandra nodded in reply. "Didn't Gabe mention secret cults when we went through the documents before?" continued Nicholas. "That would tie back into the rather mysterious religious groups in ancient Egypt, and it all sort of passed down from whatever those evolved into. Is that what you are suggesting?"

"Yes, I think so," she said, rising from the bench. "Let's get some coffee first, and I really want to see the Mona Lisa. I think there's a restaurant just near her."

They found the restaurant, inhaled some French coffee and sandwiches, and proceeded down the corridors to Room 6 on the first floor of the Denon wing. "Damn!" she exclaimed. "The Mona Lisa room is closed for repairs!" She consulted her guidebook. "I guess while we're here we could look at Italian Renaissance paintings."

They passed into Room 76, the long gallery with its brilliant huge paintings by the Italian masters. "These are amazing," Cassandra murmured, as she stopped to admire the deep blues and scarlets of the oversized masterpieces.

They had been shuffling along the wall for several minutes when Nicholas froze in his tracks and leaned forward. His mouth slowly fell open. He had a hard time believing what he eyes were telling him. "Malachi!" he exclaimed.

Cassandra stopped in her tracks and turned around to face him. "What did you say?" She followed his gaze to the painting and froze.

"The box!"

Chapter 35

Mika Hunter's chauffeur opened the door for her in front of the Dakota. Built in 1884, and most notoriously the last home of slain Beatle John Lennon, the building's Edwardian cupolas and neo-Tudor decorations offered a sharp contrast to the young woman's ultra-contemporary look and demeanor.

Mika thought the building's façade hideous. She lived there because, like so many of the building's occupants, she appreciated the security and anonymity that came with the exorbitant cost. Nodding to the gatekeeper and service staff, she disappeared into an elevator and rose to the top floor. She turned the key in the latch and opened the front door.

No visitor could have been prepared for what lay inside, not that she ever had any visitors. Even Malachi had never been there. Alex Shepard, however, had. But that was one of those memories she fought hard to obliterate.

Mika removed her shoes and left them in the *genkan,* a stone entryway. She picked up a small bonsai tree from atop its cabinet perch and carried it to the door of the small roof-level garden where she raised the miniature flora. The garden's only Western feature was the automated overhead shoji screen that covered the area during the harsh months of winter. In fact, except for her clothing there was not a single Western object visible in the entire apartment. The floors were either stone or polished wood, adorned with traditional Tatami straw mats. The living room contained an alcove for seasonal displays, low benches for seating, and an arched entryway leading into the tea room. That room opened by shoji to a dining room, where the table sank into the floor and was surrounded by benches beneath the floor's surface. The kitchen contained Western conveniences, each carefully hidden behind wooden cabinetry. The whole effect was that of carefully cultivated, spare, and austere elegance.

Mika set the bonsai down and continued into her bedroom, separated from the living area by shoji screens and a curtain *noren* in the doorway. She removed the red Dior suit and chose her favorite kimono from an antique *iko* garment rack. Its design was scattered *aoi* and chrysanthemum crests, produced in an ancient craft called *maki-e*, on an aventurine ground. The kimono itself, a *koshimaki*, or outer robe, was embroidered with pine trees, plums, and the seven jewels of Buddhism. The long *obi* sash ended in a particularly lovely 18th-century wooden *netsuke* of two young boys and a frog.

She let out a deep relaxing sigh and entered the bathroom, which contained a luxurious *furo* tub she would enjoy later. At the moment, however, she was desperate to remove the remainder of her Western professional persona. Once the pins were removed, her hair cascaded like a veil of black silk over her shoulders. Washing her face each evening was pure pleasure. She hated wearing makeup, but compensated by having it specially made for her by a chemist in Switzerland.

Her ritual continued as she moved into the living room and then the garden, where she shaped the tiny branches of the *bonsai* and groomed the green foliage of any errant leaves or city detritus that had floated in during the day.

Service personnel delivered fresh flowers and food each day. Today's floral offering was peonies, some of which she arranged in a bamboo vase and set into the alcove. The rest she put into a 12th-century bronze *kine-no-ore*, intending to place it in the tea room's alcove. Removing a panel next to the raised platform, she revealed a shrine set with an ornate Buddha, incense, and votive candles. She lit these, along with a stick of floral incense. She wrote "Alexander Shepard" in Japanese on a slip of paper and held it over one of the votives. A gilded wooden tray held an incense burner along with the accoutrements of the ritual burning of the perfumed wooden sticks. The tray was from the *Edo* period, commissioned by Tokogawa Ieyasu, the first shogun and one of Mika Hunter's ancestors. She knelt and bowed low before the shrine, her lips moving in prayers as ancient as the Japanese people. She prayed that her grandparents would forgive their daughter for marrying an American, and herself for falling in love with one. She prayed that her father would understand her culture and people, and that his spirit would forgive her for torturing her mother. Finally, she prayed for Alex Shepard, although not without first asking for forgiveness. She held the slip of paper over an open votive and watched his name go up in smoke. Bowing low once more, Mika sank into a deep meditative trance that helped her clear her mind of the day's events. The votives had nearly burned themselves out by the time she finished. She snuffed them out and closed the shrine's panels.

With the flowers for the tea room in hand, Mika slid back the tiny entrance *shoji*. Her staff had assembled the tea ceremony for her earlier and had made sure the hearth was on. She crawled through the tiny opening, which was little more than two feet square. Since it symbolized equality and peace, even lords and samurai had to prostrate themselves to enter a tearoom. Participants in this ritual were required to discard pretension and status. Mika pushed the flowers through and crawled in, adjusting her robe in modesty even though she was alone. The room glowed from the electric illumination behind the screens forming the room's shell. Because it was an interior room, Mika had installed special illumination that recreated natural light. It allowed the intricate designs woven on the ceiling and cut into the screen frames to stand out equally. The space conformed to a standard 4 ½ tatami mat room, about nine feet by nine feet, a measurement sacred to Japanese architects. For thousands of years, room sizes in Japan have been designed around these mats. The space also contained a small alcove. Mika placed the flowers in it with great formality before turning to the electric brazier holding her tea water.

A formal tea ceremony is a deeply purposeful ritual. Every movement has meaning and purpose. Even turning the teapot has protocols. Mika had studied the ceremony at length and now the ancient movements seemed instinctive. She used antique implements, from the *kara-marutsubo* tea caddy and 16th century cinnabar trays to the encased tea scoop, *mushikui*. The simple yet exquisite shapes gave her pleasure as she handled their rough surfaces. She brought the cup of green tea to her lips with a long indrawn breath.

Emerging from her tearoom, she ate some of the sashimi and sushi that had been delivered along with the flowers. Japanese flute music filled the space—low tones spiraling into rapid high ones—and she ate without hurrying, tasting each morsel and taking comfort from the music. At last she felt completely Japanese, once again utterly connected to her ancestry. Mika cleared her table, put away the ceramic vessels, and turned out the lights.

In her bathroom, she filled the *furo* and removed her robe, lowering her sleek, well-toned body into the swirling water. Her muscles finally relaxed from the workout her trainer had put her through that morning, though she could look forward to another round early the next morning. After washing with cinnamon soap, she climbed out of the tub and into a soft cotton nightdress. Her bed, on an austere raised platform, was free of telephone, alarm clock, and radio. No television was present to distract her. She crawled into bed and almost immediately fell into a deep sleep.

The next morning, Mika was ready to face another Western workday. Her car picked her up promptly at 6:00 a.m. for her work out, and again at 7:30 a.m. for the short journey to the office, where she always arrived a few minutes before 8:00. She stepped out onto the curb and smiled to herself. *Enter Mika the barracuda.*

She knew most people naturally assumed her office décor reflected her tastes at home. Nothing was further from the truth. Like her home, it was rather Spartan, but there the similarity ended. Her office was stark, cold, and often put people on edge. All stainless steel, chrome, and leathers, it was dressed in mostly black, white, or shades of gray. The only bit of color was from the red roses she placed on her desk or the occasional red in her clothing. Since Alex's death, she had been wearing red every day. It was her quiet memorial to the only man who had ever really understood her. Today she was wearing a red brocade jacket over a black shift.

She picked up the stack of papers her assistant brought in and flipped through them. She raised her eyes and stared blankly at the opposite wall. Damn! *Why did they have to go there?* Mika gripped the report in her hand so hard one of her rose-red nails cut through it.

"This appeared on my desk this morning," she announced as she walked though the private door into Malachi's office.

He looked up and waited for her to continue.

"They are in Paris."

"Let me see." Malachi snatched the report of the Customs inspector at Orly Airport out of Mika's hand. Gabriel had no way of knowing just how thoroughly Malachi watched his clients—and his enemies. His network was vast, and its efficiency enviable.

Malachi lifted his eyes and looked at Mika. "It looks like they were dropped off in Paris on the plane's way to Frankfurt. That good-for-nothing Gabriel von Stuyvesant is in Germany, so I'm assuming the plane was to pick him up. Find out where he's going."

Mika was about to ask for the report back to study it more closely when Malachi continued. "And get somebody to go to Asheville, North Carolina, to find out everything about Nicholas and Alex Shepard. I want—. What the hell is the matter with you?"

Mika's knees nearly gave way when Malachi mentioned Alex's name. She steadied herself on the edge of Malachi's desk. "My personal trainer is destroying me." She straightened up and awaited further orders.

"Then fire him!" answered Malachi. "I want to know every living and dead relative, every public record, and any private ones you can steal or buy. Find out if they've made any credit card purchases in Paris, and whether they have set up any bank accounts. If they're stupid enough to travel under their own identities, there will be an easy paper trail to follow. Find it!" Malachi's eyes brightened in a simmering anger. He really hated Nicholas Shepard. "Are the box and documents with them?"

"I don't know," answered Mika. "There's nothing in the report about either."

Malachi stroked his chin as a wicked smile filled his face. Without looking, he reached into his humidor and withdrew a Vegas Robaina Don Alejandro. The thick hand-rolled Cuban inched its way below his nose as he inhaled its aroma deeply. "I may have them arrested for theft," he said as he lit the cigar, blowing out a thin stream of bluish smoke. "Get me the information about the box and those documents. They mean *everything*."

Mika bowed, turned, and left the room.

Chapter 36

Nicholas and Cassandra stood transfixed. At 22' x 32', Veronese's *The Marriage at Cana* is not the world's largest painting, but it was big enough so that neither could mistake its salient details.

"Look," whispered Nicholas. "Cassandra, *look!*"

He was pointing in the lower right-hand third of the painting to a man dressed in an embroidered garment much like a Cardinal's robe, decorated in a Florentine Renaissance design with gold figures on a black-and-white ground. He was holding a glass of wine, tasting Christ's first miracle, the changing of water into wine at a marriage in Cana.

Cassandra slowly, almost reluctantly, shifted her gaze to where her husband pointed. When she realized what he had seen, she brought her hand to her mouth as if to stifle a scream. "That's impossible," she breathed hoarsely. "My God, Nicholas, it looks exactly like Lev!"

"Yes, and he's a dead ringer for Malachi as well, only much younger." Nicholas edged a few inches closer to get a better look

"About 432 years younger," said Cassandra, consulting her guidebook. "This picture was painted for a Benedictine Convent to replace one by Titian that burned in a fire in 1562. It's Venetian," she added, catching Nicholas' gaze. "But that's not the most interesting thing Veronese painted, Nicholas," she said, grabbing his arm and moving a few feet to the left. She pointed to the exact center of the painting. "Look!"

Nicholas leaned over the felt rope protecting the painting and Cassandra had to catch him to prevent a complete tumble to the ground. Between musicians atop a table was a black box that seemed to have about the same dimensions of their box. Nicholas rubbed his eyes and blinked several times as they both stared long and hard at the remarkable canvas.

"The box?" he asked slowly. "Our box? Could it be?" He closed his eyes tightly and then opened them in an effort to refocus them. "What's in front of it?"

"I think it's a small hour glass," replied Cassandra. "Let me put on my art historian's hat for a minute." She studied the painting thoroughly: its vast scale, its perfect symmetry. The top half depicted a serene blue sky and Palladian architecture, while the lower half contained nearly 130 exquisitely drawn figures attending a wedding. The Veronese had all the sumptuous elements of a great city at the zenith of its power: colorfully plumed birds, eunuchs, gorgeous women, silks, velvets, and precious metals. The feast seemed to include every possible culinary delight and all served on heavy gold plates. The painting was also racially inclusive, with Africans, Middle Easterners, and Caucasians all engaged in lively conversation. The huge canvas encompassed the best life had to offer to the privileged class at the height of the Italian Renaissance, glittering with gold, jewels, and silver.

"This painting is divided into halves," she observed. "It seems appropriate to place an hour glass precisely in the middle. Oh, Jesus. I almost didn't see him." The miracle worker sat tucked into the middle of the lower third, dressed in a blue and red robe with a halo around his head. Cassandra gasped suddenly. "Look to Christ's left. Is that . . . is that . . .?" The figure next to Christ was also endowed with a halo, and was dressed in conservative grays and blues, with a dark head scarf on her head. "Maybe it's Mary, his mother."

"That guy who wrote *The Da Vinci Code* wants people to believe that's Mary Magdalene," said Nicholas. "What was his name? Don Brown?"

A man standing behind them overheard the question and corrected Nicholas. "Dan. It was Dan Brown," interjected a small elderly gentleman dressed in a three-piece suit, complete with pocket watch and silver-handled cane. By his accent, it was obvious the man was British. "Sorry, I did not mean to be eavesdropping. Have you read the book?" he asked.

"Sure," Nicholas replied. "Who hasn't? I even went to the website and looked at the picture of the Last Supper. That definitely looks like a woman next to Christ, but we went to a lecture from the Dean at our church, and he said there was no historical evidence one way or the other, either in the Bible or anywhere else. And, he said Leonardo was something of a trickster."

"What do you think now?" the man asked. They studied the painting and the Englishman smiled. "I wonder if Veronese was responding to Da Vinci. Or perhaps everybody back then just assumed she was Christ's companion. Da Vinci's "Last Supper" was painted in . . .""

"1498," said Cassandra. "This Veronese was done sixty-four years later."

A small knot of people overheard the discussion and clustered around them. One snagged a passing docent who was happy to answer their questions. "The figure here in the center, in yellow playing the viol, is Veronese himself. Tintorello, Bassano, and Titian are playing the other instruments. It is more than a Biblical story—it's a political and societal portrait as well," he replied in good English with a cultured French accent. He pointed out other figures of note: "There is Suleyman the Magnificent, emperor of the Ottoman Empire and a Muslim; Francis II of Spain, married to Mary Queen of Scots, also one of the guests. The writer Pietro Aretino is there. Elenore of Austria is over there," he pointed, "representing the Hapsburgs. The Marchesa di Pescara is present, you see, she has a toothpick in her mouth. She was a close friend of Michelangelo." There was general laughter from the group at this.

"Who is the wine taster? The Master of Ceremonies?" asked Nicholas.

The docent shook his head. "I am afraid I do not know who he is. All of the figures in the painting represent people Veronese knew, or knew of."

With that, the discussion petered to a close, the docent continued on his way and the crowd of a dozen people splintered off in several directions. Nicholas gave a polite nod to the curious Englishman and they continued down the long gallery, dumbstruck by what they had seen. Cassandra guided them into the museum store, where she purchased a print of the painting so they could study it in more detail. Cassandra made a mental note to visit the Biblioteque Nationale and search art books for more clues.

"Well," sighed Nicholas, "what does this do for our search? Why would the guy put the box in a painting if it were so secret? Assuming, of course, it is *the* box. And why would a guy who looks just like Malachi—it is such a striking resemblance he could have posed for it himself—be the central figure in such a painting?"

Cassandra admitted she had not a single answer. "I am as confused as you are. It looks like every great and/or royal family of Europe and the Middle East is represented in that painting," she marveled. "Perhaps that means all of these people somehow benefitted from the box? I wonder if we can connect the cartouche to these families . . . not to mention others, like the Borgias, Machiavelli, and a whole collection of Popes. We can ask Jacques' friend at the bank to help us find documents from these families, and Marie's friend, Claudette, too. The whole painting is such a fantasy."

Nicholas looked puzzled. "What do you mean, a fantasy?"

"It has Christ present, Nicholas! It should be set in first-century Cana. Instead, Veronese painted a scene straight from his own time to show off the wealth of Venice—and yet Christ appears. Did you notice how subdued Christ and his companion seem? They are not interacting with anyone."

"I never thought about it that way," he admitted. "Well, you're the art historian. I'm sure you'll figure that out, too. Where to next? We gave up on Egypt, and were headed to. . ."

"Rome," Cassandra finished his sentence. "If the box was taken there—let's just fantasize for argument's sake, to help flesh out the discussion, that it was taken there by Cleopatra when she married Marc Anthony—we might find some clues in Ptolemaic Egypt, Coptic Egypt, and the Roman galleries downstairs in this wing."

Nicholas laughed at the suggestion. "Cleopatra and Marc Antony? Ok, in for a penny in for a pound."

Their explorations through these galleries, however, simply increased their frustration at the magnitude of their search. When they found themselves standing in the front of a gallery containing hundreds of marble busts of Romans stretching as far as they could see, Cassandra threw up her hands. "I give up!" she moaned, plopping down on a marble bench.

Nicholas looked down at her, rubbed his temples, and then ran his hand through his thick hair. "Let's think about this for a minute, Cassandra. I think our effort is a bit out of focus. Our theory is that powerful families used the box to somehow gain and maintain wealth and power, right? And that a great many people benefitted from this knowledge over hundreds of years—maybe longer. What ties them all together?"

She looked up at him with a blank stare and shook her head. "I don't know. What?"

"Those to whom the box was . . . *given*," he answered, raising his eyebrows as he looked at her.

She let his words sink in for a few seconds. "Ahhh. I see where you are going with this," she said with a fresh excitement in her voice, leaping up beside him. "Hello! We aren't tracing families! We're tracing money managers! *They* were the ones in charge. Whoever they chose to be recipients got the money, while the managers got both money *and* power. I always had a hunch it was the bankers."

"I agree," said Nicholas. "But you can sit down again because I am tired as hell and my feet are killing me." He lowered himself down on the bench and slipped off a shoe. Cassandra joined him. "We need to concentrate on the bank documents, inventories, and other financial manuscripts," he continued, massaging a foot. "Man, these marble floors are tough on the feet."

"Remember the restaurant last night?" Cassandra asked. "We're supposed to go to the opera tonight, which was also built in Napoleon's time. Maybe we should look around there, too."

"Sure, why not? But in the meantime, let's take a look at Roman Egypt. I want to check into something."

Egypt under Roman rule witnessed the dissolution of the kingdom's former glory as it absorbed Greek and Roman influences. "What are you looking for?" asked Cassandra.

"Do you remember when Gabe told us how the Isis mystery cults merged with something called Mithraism?" asked Nicholas as he scrutinized the exhibits. "I'm looking for anything that has the bull-throwing iconography associated with Mithras, combined with images of Isis."

A question to a museum worker pointed them quickly in the right direction, and five minutes later they were standing in front of several examples, clearly cut into hieroglyphics of the period. "Gabe believed that if Mithraism hadn't been a mystery cult, it would have spread more quickly and smothered out Christianity as a world religion," mused Nicholas. "I think he may have been right. Not only did both believe in an ideology of cosmic transcendence, but they both attracted people who liked secrecy, and particularly relished being the power behind the throne, so to speak."

"Ok," answered Cassandra slowly. "I think I get it."

Nicholas lifted his finger to his pursed lips and rubbed it back and forth as he thought deeply about what he was saying. "Gabe thinks the cult of Isis handled the banking systems of Egypt's priestly class, and it's entirely possible that any number of these powerful men went on to Mithraism and from there to Christianity. Romans introduced the standard of coinage and credit for the whole Empire, which made it possible to hoard wealth. I'm guessing that a small but dedicated group of money managers kept the box under wraps until they figured out which way the wind was blowing, and then offered their services on the recommendations of families they had already helped. That could explain how the box and documents stayed together through all those centuries."

"That sounds logical given what we know," said Cassandra. She checked her watch. "But it's getting late. We have to meet Jacques."

ঽ

With reluctance they left the Louvre and walked to Jacques' office on the rue Royale, where all three caught the train for Croissy. Back at the house, Marie and Jacques were swept up in the excitement of the day's discoveries. Jacques particularly was intrigued by their power behind the money theory, though neither Nicholas or Cassandra had fully shared all the details of the box with them. "This makes a great deal of sense to me," he said. "I think that this will help you tomorrow when you meet with my friend." It was agreed Nicholas would go to the bank while Cassandra met with Marie's friend, Claudette.

"But, now," said Marie with a flourish, "it is time for a night at the opera!"

Cassandra went upstairs first and showered in the big bathroom. She almost wished that she had brought her Madame X gown; in Paris, who cares if you are over the top? She pulled out a black dress from the vacuum pack she used for storage and slipped it on. The front of the dress was conservative, with its neckline resting demurely across her collarbone. The back, however, was daringly cut in a "V." She arranged her hair in a sophisticated chignon and added her diamond chandelier earrings for a bit of sparkle. Grabbing the beaded shawl that she wore at Biltmore she hurried down the stairs.

Jacques gasped in exaggerated admiration. "Are you certain you are not French?"

"*Merci pour le compliment*," responded Cassandra. They chatted along in French as Nicholas put on his best black suit and tie.

Jacques offered his wife a wolfish whistle when she exited the master suite in a salmon and apricot silk dress cut in strips on the bias, tea-length and off the shoulder. She put a lavender pashmina with it, as Paris nights get chilly in April. After sampling glasses of wine from Jacques' brother's vineyard they set off into town, this time in Marie's new Mercedes.

At the opera they were joined by the other 2,196 elegantly dressed patrons lucky enough to have tickets to the evening's sold-out performance. Many arrived in limousines, the women sparkling with jewels and beaded dresses, the men in suits or tuxedos. Nicholas and Cassandra had never been inside this quintessential landmark with its neo-Baroque foyer, and they confessed to being impressed by the grandeur of its sweeping staircases and gilded vaulting. Velvet, gold leaf, nymphs and cherubs, and a six-ton crystal chandelier created a fabulously ornate atmosphere.

"You see before you nearly 120,000 square feet of loveliness," explained Marie, who was more than happy to act as a tour guide. "The auditorium takes up nearly half of it. The stage has accommodated horses, camels, and a variety of other animals. Emperor Napoleon commissioned the building in 1862, and Charles Garnier, who was only thirty-five years old at the time, designed it. Seven of the stories are below ground, and there's still a lake and spring down there that they built over."

"Please pardon me," Nicholas said, turning a full 360 degrees to examine the ceiling, "but I'm just going to flat-out gawk at all this for a couple minutes."

"You are excused," responded Marie. "Marc Chagall painted the ceiling in 1964."

"What is, 'gawk'?" asked Jacques.

"He means he will behave like a farmer from Lyon," said Marie, smiling widely.

"Ah, so," said her husband, who was doing the exact same thing as Nicholas. The wives prodded the men toward their seats, which were less than fifty feet from the stage.

"What's so fabulous about this Dario Volonte?" asked Nicholas as they settled into their seats.

"You will see," smiled Marie, who was an ardent admirer of the celebrated Argentinean tenor. "I read an interesting interview with him," she went on, fanning her program at Cassandra. "He was in the Falklands War in 1982 and spent thirty hours on a lifeboat waiting to be rescued. They say the experience changed him, so that he's able to give characters like Manrico even greater depth and passion. He says these characters face death on a spiritual level—as a higher level of love."

Nicholas studied Marie. She looked back at him with her large hazel eyes. "I want you so much to feel better about Alex," she said. "I thought that might help."

"Thank you, it does help," he answered, "and that's the best explanation I've ever heard for the motivations of operatic characters." He was genuinely thankful. "Ah, here's the conductor."

The lush romantic strains of Verdi's overture for the opera began, and as the curtain rose they could see this would be an event to remember. The set was huge, Manrico's entrance commanding. Combined with a Van Dyke beard, the black hair tumbling about his shoulders gave Dario Volonte a stunning presence, and his voice was a lyric tenor that in ten years would be dramatically *spinto*. When it was time for "Di Quella Pira," he held the high C perfectly, and even the jaded Parisians leaped to their feet with ear-splitting applause. The production halted briefly to allow him his well-earned bow.

It was during intermission when Jacques made the discovery of the evening: a cartouche in a display case exhibiting financial papers signed by Napoleon. Each of the four took turns peering at it in the dim light, their excited whispers attracting the attention of other patrons. Marie explained in French that her American cousins were excited to see Napoleon's signature, to which the Parisians responded by staring at Nicholas and Cassandra as though they were selling corn at the market.

"Did I look enough like a rube?" Nicholas asked Marie on the way back to their seats. She assured him that he would never look like one of those—in any language.

After the opera ended and they had climbed into the Mercedes for the trip back to Choissy, Cassandra exclaimed, "That was simply grand and exhilarating! An opera I shall never forget." She reached forward and patted Jacques on the shoulder. "Finding the cartouche was a special bonus, Jacques. I hope tomorrow we can begin to make some sense of it all."

Chapter 37

 Nicholas tossed and turned most of the night. In a sleepy huff, Cassandra finally abandoned him shortly after 2:30 a.m. and headed for the bedroom once occupied by the Beaudrot's eldest son.

"You were so restless last night, I thought you would sleep better if you had the bed to yourself," she explained when she crawled back into bed with him for a bit of snuggle time before they took their showers.

"Oh, man," he said holding her tightly. "I had the wildest dream. Veronese's *The Marriage at Cana* came to life, and there were scores of rich people at this huge party, speaking every language in the world." He chuckled softly. "Everyone from the Rothschilds to Donald Trump!"

"That's some dream!"

"Yeah. But here's the strange part." His voice grew softer. "Alex was playing the role of the wine taster in the painting. He had the box, and he was toasting everyone's financial success. The guests were kowtowing to him because they knew he could make or destroy their fortunes." He paused for a moment but Cassandra remained silent, waiting for him to finish. "I don't think they understood where he was getting the knowledge from; some seemed to think he had divine powers, and others thought he was demonic. He, on the other hand, thought it was all a good joke because he knew it was just science, and there was nothing mystical about that."

"That sounds like our Alex," she said softly, glad that her back was to Nicholas so he could not see the tears welling up in her eyes.

Hot showers, strong coffee, and a sense of excitement revived them quickly. Jacques took Nicholas to work with him, while Marie and Cassandra planned to visit Claudette and the Biblioteque Nationale.

Claudette's apartment, tucked on a side street near the American Cathedral and the rue Galilee, was a second-floor walk-up with three small rooms, two of which overlooked the street with tall casement windows and boxes of flowers. She had painted the oak floor in a black-and-cream checkerboard pattern for a border to edge the café au lait-colored sisal carpet. Her cream-color theme extended to the wool floor-to-ceiling window treatments and cotton velvet armchairs and sofa. The effect in the dazzling sunlight was that of being in a cozy cocoon. A petite woman with short, spiked blonde hair and vivid green eyes, Claudette was tending the colorful flower boxes when they arrived.

Proper introductions prompted a genuine smile from Claudette, who was relieved they could converse in French. On the way to a small table, Cassandra stopped to admire a small collection of early Greek vases. "Claudette is a dealer in antiquities and rare manuscripts," explained Marie. "She is an expert in this area—one of the best!"

Sipping on a glass of mineral water, Cassandra explained to Claudette that she and her husband were conducting research in financial transactions from different historical periods.

"Yes, I understand," she answered in her soft voice, though with a slightly perplexed look on her face. Few people sought her assistance on such mundane matters. "And what exactly are you seeking?"

"We need banking manuscripts from the period between Roman Egypt and the Renaissance, and perhaps as recent as the eighteenth century."

"Well of course there are thousands of these sorts of documents all around the world," she replied. "Perhaps you can be more precise?" She smiled warmly.

Cassandra pulled a small yellow Post-it pad from her purse and began drawing the cartouche with a pencil. "We are trying to solve a mystery of sorts, and we believe the answers might rest with this symbol." She turned the yellow paper around and pointed at it with the pencil lead. "Apparently, it belonged to some of the most powerful men in the world throughout the ages," continued Cassandra, hoping she was making sense.

Claudette licked her lips, which had suddenly gone dry, and wrung her petite hands together tightly. "I have seen this," she said slowly. "I know it because one of my clients collects historical papers that bear this cartouche."

"Really?" replied a stunned Cassandra. "You have seen this actually printed on documents you have collected?"

Claudette nodded and swallowed heavily. "I have a manuscript waiting for him now."

Cassandra's heart began beating faster. "You actually *have* one? Here? Please, may I see it?"

Claudette shrugged. "I can allow you to see, but I cannot sell it to you."

Barely able to contain herself, Cassandra followed Marie and Claudette into a bedroom, which was as dark as the other room was bright. Painted in a warm terra cotta, Claudette had enriched the room with a deep green velvet sofa in a Louis XVI style, a painted desk, and a Burgundian *chiffonnier*. These offset a contemporary platform bed, which was covered in a nubby apricot chenille spread. From a chest she pulled two sheets of vellum wrapped carefully in acid-free archival tissue and laid them out on the bed for viewing.

Cassandra leaned close and without thinking reached out a hand to touch them. "Please don't!" warned Claudette sharply in English.

Cassandra apologized as she pulled her hand back. Claudette also apologized profusely in French. "These documents are very old and extremely rare. They belonged to one of the early Knights Templar. It is an inventory of a palace in Italy." She watched Cassandra carefully, as if gauging her reaction.

Cassandra's stomach clenched. The cartouche was indeed there, carefully recreated near the bottom of the page. "To which of the Templar Knights did it belong?" she asked.

"There," pointed Claudette. "His signature. I believe it is Bertrand du Guesclin."

Cassandra's eyes widened as she recognized the signature. Her heart was beating so fast she put a hand over her chest in case the other two should see her excitement at finding a name she could actually research. "Thank you. I will convey this information to my family, who will be . . . quite interested." She scribbled down the name on another Post-it note.

Marie, who had been standing by the window watching this interchange, watched and listened carefully to the interplay between the two women. Claudette was usually a carefree spirit and never raised her voice. Today, however, she appeared nervous, her voice strained and anxious. In fact, she seemed almost frightened. There was something else that was also bothering her. She had expected that Claudette would have run across the symbol at some point during her many years of dealing with rare manuscripts, or at least would have heard about it. But what were the odds that she would actually *have* such a document in her possession—and on today of all days?

"Claudette, this client you mention," asked Marie carefully. "He must be someone with a great deal of money. Have you located many documents like this for him in the past?"

Claudette paled and offered a weak smile. "I really shouldn't say. He wishes to remain anonymous, and I should really respect his privacy." Marie frowned. She was not asking for the man's identify. Clearly she was avoiding the question.

"Oh, I certainly understand," Cassandra answered quickly. "I, too, am hoping that you will be extremely discreet regarding my inquiry. This . . . family mystery of ours is a very sensitive subject for us, and we can assume you will not speak of it?"

Claudette's demeanor Marie knew so well quickly returned. "But of course, *mon amie.* Your search is safe with me." She gave Marie a hug and saw them to the door, suggesting to her friend that they meet again soon for coffee or lunch.

Cassandra nearly skipped down the stairs. "Why didn't I think of that before?" she asked, turning to look at Marie. "The Knights Templar! Of course!"

"I've heard of them, but don't know much about them," Marie confessed, bemused at her cousin's antics but still concerned over Claudette's odd behavior. "Let's have lunch so you can tell me why you are so excited."

ৰ

Breathing a sigh of relief now that Marie and Cassandra had left, Claudette walked quickly to her living room and peered outside. She watched as Marie and Cassandra disappeared down the street. After re-wrapping the documents in archival paper, she slipped them into the chest, picked up her telephone, and dialed an international number.

"Allo? Yes. This is Claudette. I have another manuscript for you." She listened to the disembodied voice ask a question. "This one is very old. I know you will like it." Claudette hesitated, hating to betray a friend like Marie, but part of her financial arrangement with this client was to let him know if anyone else appeared interested in his collection. And his offer for the information was a lucrative cash bonus.

"You asked me to tell you if anyone else approached me about manuscripts bearing the Egyptian symbol," she continued. "It is curious that it happened so soon, but just a few minutes ago an American woman came to my apartment asking for similar documents. She knew of the cartouche."

A pause, followed by a simple question.

"Her name? Cassandra, that was the only name my friend Marie gave me."

Another question.

"Her full name? Marie . . . Beaudrot. Do you wish for me to send this the usual way? *Merci, monsieur.*"

Claudette hung up the phone, washed her hands over the kitchen sink, and returned to her window boxes.

⸬

Jacques was having trouble with his English. Nicholas put his hand on his friend's shoulder. "*Je comprends Francias, mais parle lentement, s'il te plait.*" Relieved, Jacques began to explain their search. "My bank building was constructed in 1981," he said, "but we own many small buildings throughout the city. We will visit one of these this morning in the 14th Arrondissement near the Palais, the *Jardin du Luxembourg* and the Montparnasse cemetery."

They were sitting near the rear of the Paris Metro train so that they could carry on a conversation without being overheard. When they reached the station, they walked quickly through the tunnels to catch a second train to the 14th Arrondissement, which had been the scene of much of the city's Bohemian life around the turn of the 20th century. Hemingway wrote and drank a great deal there, and the famous cemetery holds the graves of many international writers. Novelist and playwright Jean-Paul Sartre and philosopher Simone de Beauvoir shared a single grave, which Jacques found hugely entertaining. "The master of atheistic Existentialism sharing eternity with Simone," he chuckled. "*C'est macabre*!" He looked at Nicholas, whose eyes were cast down and seemed far away. "*Mon ami*," he said gently. "Today you may see some things that will be difficult for you at this point in your life. Are you certain you wish to do this?"

"Yes, I am fine. Thank you. Please, let us continue."

"I will warn you, Nicholas, it is not for the faint of heart."

They emerged from the station, blinking in the sunlight, and Jacques led him toward *Place Denfert-Rochereau*, which was presided over by a lion sculpted by Bartoldi, the same sculptor who created the Statue of Liberty. Jacques pointed out bistros and cafés where Marx and Lenin once worked out their lives' passions and argued their misguided philosophies. A few minutes later they arrived at a small structure with a colonnaded portico constructed of ancient limestone, decorated with simple Tuscan columns. The only adornment was the entablature, which contained a frieze with the ubiquitous Greek horses and warriors.

Nicholas paused and took in the ancient-looking door. The faded walnut was Gothic in style and strapped with hand-forged hinges. There were no windows anywhere.

Jacques held out his hand and they walked toward the doorway. "This building served as a bank for the neighborhood for many years, but it dates back to before the 1700s, when much of the Left Bank was quarried for the stones to build Haussman's projects on the other side of the Seine. I do not know how it escaped the stone masons in their search for usable stone. We always suspected it of being a small church. The French resistance found it useful during the war as an entrance to underground tunnels, which of course Paris is riddled with. We will meet with Monsieur Marshal, who has for many years taken it upon himself to care for the many thousands of manuscripts the bank owns."

Jacques tugged on the door, which swung open reluctantly with a groan. A gust of dusty air blew out as they stepped into a stone room with groin vaults lit by several 1970s-style chandeliers that seemed wholly out of place. Teller stands and other evidence of a working bank had been removed, and the space was bare except for a handful of wooden refectory tables and pigeonhole shelving. The holes were stuffed with rolls of old manuscripts.

A wizened old man was standing at the foot of one of the long tables. He looked up as they entered, and the light caught the glass in his spectacles just so. *He looks like a scholarly owl*, thought Nicholas. Bald and stooped, he nevertheless possessed a great deal of enthusiasm, for he smiled widely at Nicholas and Jacques, bobbing his head up in down as if excited to see them. Nicholas guessed he probably didn't get too many callers.

The old man was clearly suffering from sclerosis, and his twisted spine made it difficult for him to walk. He held out a thin-skinned wrinkled hand. Nicholas was surprised how warm and firm it was. His English, though heavily accented, was quite good.

"I understand you are interested in looking at some of my . . . the bank's . . . manuscripts. I have been their keeper for nearly fifty years, and I follow my father and his father before him," he explained with obvious pride. "Although they are the bank's property, my family has always felt an obligation to preserve them. I am afraid very few people are interested in them any longer." He shook his head sadly and continued, almost more for himself than for the benefit of his guests. "Sometimes a manager will request something from the later half of the eighteenth century, but no one is interested in anything too very old." His melancholy turned quickly into a smile as he chuckled, "Maybe because they are all dead! It is unfortunate for this is the true history of France and its financial resources. We have never been able to interest the Louvre in them. So, here they sit, and there are many thousands more below ground." He held his hands up in a helpless gesture, and smiled crookedly.

Nicholas pulled a drawing of the cartouche from his wallet and wordlessly handed it to Monsieur Marshal, who adjusted the pince-nez set on his Gallic nose and examined it. "Do you have documents bearing this symbol?" asked Nicholas.

The old man immediately stiffened and threw a sharp look at his visitors, first at Nicholas and then Jacques, and then back at Nicholas. "Why are you interested in this, Monsieur?"

There is anxiety in his voice, thought Nicholas. *Or was it alarm?* "I am an economist at Emory University in the United States, as I am sure my friend Jacques has explained to you. I am conducting research about financial transactions through the ages—"

His sentence was severed when the old man cut in, "Monsieur, you are traveling a dangerous road!"

Nicholas decided to tell him more of the truth than he had originally intended. "Monsieur Marshal, I think my brother was killed because of something to do with this symbol. It is extremely important to me and my family to understand why."

The archivist's eyes widened and he shot a brief glance at Jacques while calculating his response. His eyes settled back on Nicholas. "I am sorry about your loss. So you understand that this symbol is very important to powerful people, even today?"

Nicholas exhaled and nodded. "I appreciate the warning—yes. Still, I would like to exam everything you can find with this symbol, and I want to see every document that you have that relates to it and the people involved."

Monsieur Marshal closed his eyes and tapped his foot for several seconds. He did not look particularly happy. Jacques' presence was making it difficult for the little man to refuse him.

"Alright," the archivist finally nodded. "You have asked and you understand the ramifications of your request, so I will tell you all that I know. We will want to begin, then, with the Knights Templar, from whom I am directly descended. My ancestor was William Marshal, one of the first of the Warrior Knights."

Jacques gasped. "Monsieur, I had no idea!"

Nicholas scratched his chin thoughtfully. "If I recall from some material I read recently, at one time they controlled the banking for

Medieval Europe and basically invented international banking systems. Is that close to the truth?"

"Very good! You are correct. For nearly two hundred years the Templars were a powerful force over the money houses, as well as the leaders of Europe. They were the first monks who took vows of chastity, poverty, and obedience, and later followed the military vocation of knighthood in 1128. This superiority in their military order, secrecy, and banking eventually caused their downfall at the Council of Vienna on March 22, 1312. But by then they had become, with the Knights Hospitallers, Europe's primary defense against the invading Saracens from the Middle East. Over time, they had amassed incredible wealth."

Monsieur Marshal paused with a sigh and a shrug before continuing. "Alas, Philip the Fair wanted the money to fund his own projects in France, so he dissolved the order and burned as many as fifty-four Templars at the stake in a single day! It was a horrible time in the history of this noble order. Of course, there are vestiges of the Templars today, through the Sovereign Military Order of Malta, for example. The succession of Grand Masters remains unbroken."

The archivist rolled up the parchment he had laid out on the table and put it into one of the myriad document shelves lining the wall. "I do not have any of the manuscripts you seek on this level. We will have to go downstairs. You will follow me."

He went to a small door near the back of the room, where a sacristy might have stood at one time. Instead, it opened to a brass grille and an elevator. It was of a style still used in some of the older Parisian bed-and-breakfast hotels—a small cage without enclosing walls, usually made of highly polished brass and quite quaint. This brass elevator was neither polished nor quaint, and Nicholas shuddered as he squeezed himself inside. As soon as he stepped inside he wrinkled his nose in disgust: the odor in the elevator shaft was nauseating. He stifled a gag and forced himself to breathe through his mouth until he got used to the sickening smell.

Monsieur Marshal closed the grille and the car began its squeaky inch by inch descent as the wheels holding the ropes protested loudly with each revolution.

What if this guy works for whoever is looking for me? Nicholas asked himself. *What are the chances that I will ever ride up in this elevator?* Before the cage had descended even a few feet he was wishing he had never come. His feeling of dread was exacerbated a hundred-fold when they reached the bottom of the shaft. The odor was much worse now—fetid, sweet, and dense. Nicholas gagged again and turned to Jacques, who had pulled out a handkerchief and placed it against his nose.

When Monsieur Marshal found the light switch and clicked it on, Nicholas jumped back against the rear of the elevator. Bare bulbs hanging from electrical wire illuminated human bones. Not just a heap of bones, but *walls* of bones. The entire low–running corridor as far as he could see was constructed of bones stacked from floor to ceiling. Skulls offered macabre square smiles, hipbones made frames for arrangements of ribs. Small spotlights spaced unevenly along the floor contrasted with the light cast by the bare bulbs hanging overhead to create a nightmarish atmosphere. He had never seen anything like it in his life.

"Welcome to the catacombs, Monsieur Shepard," smiled the stooped Frenchman. "Please come with me."

Jacques looked at his friends, one calm and businesslike, the other blanched and looking as if he would vomit at any moment. "You have never heard of the catacombs of Paris, *mon ami*?"

Nicholas swallowed hard, wishing he had a glass of water to wash the bitter bile from his throat. "I've heard of them, yes, but never in my wildest dreams did I imagine they would look—or smell—quite like this. I was always under the impression that the Paris catacombs were simply old Roman sewers."

"No. The sewers are just that—*sewers*," replied his guide firmly. "These catacombs wind around for 157 miles, and are formed of quarry tunnels beneath the left bank. When Haussmann was constructing the most beautiful city in Europe, the left bank was in danger of collapsing, and the cemeteries outside the city were full of corpses that stank all the time, even more than the medieval slums the architect demolished to rebuild the city. Some fine thinker put the idea of corpses and tunnels together, and *voila!*—there we are. It took hundreds of workers several years to make these walls. They are really quite tidy and practical. They even named the streets. Look." Nicholas peered at a spot between a cranium and a femur. Sure enough, "Boulevard Haussmann" appeared on a small sign.

Following Monsieur's rolling gait they reached a door decorated with leg bones above a sign that read, *"Pensez le matin que vous n'irez peut-etre pas jusques au soir et au soir que vous n'irez pas jusques au matin."* Nicholas translated out loud: "'Think each morning you may not be alive in the evening, and each evening you may not be alive in the morning.' How cheerful."

Monsieur Marshal offered the American a wry smile and a bony shrug. "A sense of humor even in this loathsome place." He reached inside the doorway and switched the light on. Before them was a fully furnished room, but the walls and ceiling were decorated with bones. Several large desks were equipped with telephones, and wooden document bins and metal filing cabinets lined the walls.

"This was the headquarters of the French Resistance," Monsieur Marshal announced calmly. "I replaced several of the phone lines a few years ago." He held up one of the receivers, and the dial tone blared into the silence. "Now," he said hanging up the receiver and getting down to business, "I have not organized these documents by the appearance of your cartouche. They go instead chronologically. I have a few from the twelfth century, but many from the years of the Templars and Hospitallers. There are some from the Napoleonic era because Napoleon tried to collect all such documents in one place. Then, when his Empire fell, the documents became paper for farmers to wrap their produce in."

Nicholas gazed at the curious display of bones and phones as if he had fallen down the rabbit hole like Alice in a bizarre wonderland. "Let's look at the Templars," he suggested while doing his best to breathe as shallowly as possible. "If they controlled the money, their documents, I think, might lead us to where the power went next, whether it was Philip the Fair or someone in the Hospitallers. I am not as interested in the rulers as much as those who managed their finances."

"Yes, I understand what you mean," Monsieur Marshal brightened. "That will narrow the focus well enough."

The old man shuffled about the room, selecting parchments from one cabinet and vellum from another. The three men carefully unrolled the documents, some of them beautifully illuminated with gold, others simple inventories of royal treasuries or chateaus. To Nicholas' surprise and delight, in some form or another, the cartouche was clearly visible on many of the documents.

They buried themselves in the work, silent for long periods, taking note of what document belonged to which king or empire. With the archivist's permission, Nicholas withdrew a digital camera and snapped pictures of each document he considered important, intending to give these to Cassandra for handwriting comparisons. His repugnance at the ghoulish environment slowly ebbed. In its place grew an excited awareness that he was looking at the very foundation of international banking systems and the emergence of credit.

"The Templars charged interest!" he said out loud at one point.

Monsieur Marshal nodded. "Yes, against the specific rule of the Church, but it is how they made much of the money. Simply put, they arranged loans."

The hunt continued for hours as the three men prowled their way to 1300. The cartouche was found on a succession of documents from England, France, Spain, Portugal, and finally, Italy. Nicholas took special note of the Avignon Papacy, beginning in 1309 and lasting until 1378, during which two Popes ruled the Western world. The Black Plague, when Europe lost a third of its population between 1347 and 1353, temporarily stopped the flow of money and power, but the document trail quickly resumed. The cartouche bounced back and forth between countries, winding up in Florence about 1430, when the Borgias ruled supreme for nearly a century. Thereafter, the ancient Egyptian symbol shifted to Venice and England for the Age of Elizabeth. Nicholas carefully plotted each time the symbol appeared, in which country, and the name of the person the document represented. Several breaks, including a brief run to the surface for lunch, interrupted their work.

Late in the afternoon he seemed to reach a dead end. "Where are the documents for the Louis'?" he asked.

"Alas, those that survived the French Revolution are in glass cases in the palace at Versailles," replied Monsieur Marshal.

Nicholas took a deep breath and exhaled. The odor of the remains no longer bothered him after so many hours of working in the proximity of the dead. As he stood up and stretched, one of his hands bumped the end of a leg bone, which fell out of place and clattered to the stone floor. A few seconds later foul-smelling liquid dripped out of the gaping hole, threatening to spoil some of the documents. "Oh, God, I'm sorry," moaned Nicholas as he grabbed his notes and pushed a small pile of manuscripts out of the way. The dripping stopped almost as soon as it began. Monsieur Marshal waved away the accident.

Nicholas glanced at his watch. It was nearly evening. "I think I'd better call it a day," he said.

"As you wish," replied the old Frenchman. "I am happy to have been of service. You know where you can find me if you require additional research."

"You've been much more than that," Nicholas told him. "Your documents have provided critical clues for our research. I can't thank you enough." As Monsieur Marshal led them from the room, Nicholas thought of the cramped, perilous elevator. "Is there another way out of here?" he asked. He had already pushed his luck three times in that rickety old thing.

Jacques grinned. "You do not want to try finding a way out on your own," he said. "I remember reading about one man who tried that in the nineteenth century. They did not find him for nine years. He had become one with the catacombs, and they placed his bones in a special display."

"Back to the elevator," Nicholas said as all three men laughed. Nicholas ducked through the low door and bumped his head on the corridor ceiling when he stood up. "I do not like this place," he said to Jacques. "And you can congratulate me on my gift for understatement." When a puzzled look crossed his face Nicholas added, "Never mind, Jacques. Cassandra will translate the idiom."

They walked in silence back to the elevator, their footsteps echoing through the narrow halls of the cemetery. Once back at the shaft, the men squeezed inside the cage and ascended slowly to the world above. As they were leaving, Nicholas turned and looked at the archivist, who was already lost in thought, poring over some manuscript at the foot of a long table. They opened the door and practically sprang outside, sucking in deep gulps of fresh, moist air. A storm had come up while they were in the catacombs, and the sunny day they had left behind had been overtaken with damp and chill.

"Look there!" said Jacques, touching his friend on the arm and pointing across the street. Nicholas followed his gaze and was surprised and pleased to see their wives waving at them from under the awning of an outdoor bistro. They had planned to meet back in Croissy.

"We were worried about you, and couldn't reach you on your cell phones," chided Cassandra after they crossed the street and exchanged hugs. "Cassandra took a step backward and wrinkled her nose. "God, Nicholas, you smell awful!" Before he could explain she continued. "Marie told me where you two were going, so after we finished at the Biblioteque Nationale we shopped for a while, took in a few sights, and decided to wait for you here and got a bit damp in the process. We were beginning to think we had missed you!"

They settled into wrought-iron ice-cream chairs around a little table covered in checkered oilcloth, reviewing their day and warming up over hot coffee and pastry.

"So, tell!" said Cassandra excitedly. "Any luck?"

"Wait until you hear," began Nicholas as he slowly unraveled his incredible tale of the catacombs, documents, and the trail of the cartouche through the 14th and 15th centuries. Cassandra and Marie flooded him with questions.

Cassandra's morning meeting with Claudette seemed anti-climactic compared with Nicholas' adventure. He was initially excited when she described the manuscript, but when his face turned into a frown, Cassandra stopped mid-sentence. "What?"

"Where did she get it?" he asked.

"I . . . don't know. She just said she had a client who collected them. Why? I mean, I really didn't want to push her to reveal her sources. She was getting a bit paranoid, really. Do you think she might have gotten it from Monsieur Marshal?"

It was Marie who answered. "No, definitely not! Monsieur Marshal is a fanatic about his manuscripts. Frankly, I'm surprised he let Nicholas and Jacques touch them. Claudette is internationally known and could have many sources. Every time there's a regime change anywhere, documents disappear." Marie thought for a moment and cleared her throat. "I was surprised she actually had such a document in her possession, but now," she shrugged, "it sounds as though they are not quite as rare as I thought."

"Yes, that certainly seems to be the case," agreed Nicholas. "No one could blame these folks for loose accounting practices!"

He pulled out his notes from the document room in the catacombs and handed them to his wife. "Now, all you have to do is get to Versailles to check on the accounts of a few kings named Louis," he chuckled, "and find the names of every royal accountant for hundreds of years."

"Oh, thanks for giving me the easy part," said Cassandra with a smirk. "Your notes indicate that several power brokers may have known about the box at the same time. Do you think they used it to destabilize political situations? At the Biblioteque this afternoon, I found evidence that Suleyman the Magnificent funded the Protestant Reformation in order to create turmoil in the Church and destabilize Europe."

"Really?" asked a stunned Nicholas. "The Reformation funded by the Muslims? No kidding." He thought of Martin Luther nailing his "95 Theses" to the door of the Wittenberg Church in 1513—the reformer's high-minded, hammer-fisted attack on papal abuses, the sale of indulgences, and all the rest. To conceive of the Protestant Reformation as financed by the Ottoman Empire was one hell of a leap. "It would have happened anyway," he mused, "but funding never hurts."

Cassandra told her husband that she had not had any additional luck identifying the rest of the figures in Veronese's *The Marriage at Cana*. "No 'who's who' that we could find," she explained. "On the other hand, we know that every crowned head in Europe is there. So, we'll just have to find their accountants."

They gathered up their lists and paraphernalia, made plans to go to Versailles the next day, and headed for the metro. An hour later they arrived in tranquil Croissy and walked a few blocks to the house. The air was cold and damp, darkness was nearly upon them, and they were shivering by the time they arrived. Splinters of light were visible through the cracks in the shuttered upper-story windows.

"I know we didn't leave lights on," said Cassandra warily. "Is one of your sons home?"

"No," replied Jacques. "Lately there has been much crime here. We wired lamps to come on in the evening. It makes the house seem always occupied. There is also an alarm system in case anyone opens the gate." He pushed numbers on a keypad and the gate swung open. "Besides, I like to come home to a cheerful, well-lighted place."

Once inside, Nicholas excused himself and went upstairs, where he removed the disk from the camera and put it in a compartment inside the photographer's case that held the box and document copies Cassandra had made. The big case had two main compartments, one on the bottom for the box, and a second on top for the camera equipment—which included two digital cameras and a good Hasselblad 35mm film camera.

Nicholas set the case on a table in front of the door so he wouldn't forget it the next day and went immediately for his laptop. After writing a brief report of the day's activity, he plugged into a phone line and began surfing the Web to find whatever he could about the accountants and financial organizations of the various European courts. The Internet search proved fruitless, however, and he was happy to give it up when Cassandra called him down for supper. After a dessert of wonderful French cheeses and fruit, the two couples drank wine and chatted until they knew sleep would come easily.

"I'm finally beginning to feel safe and invisible from whoever is out there," Cassandra said when they crawled into bed. "I meant to call Francesca today and forgot. Remind me tomorrow. I had every intention of calling her sooner."

Nicholas mumbled his understanding, yawned, and slid beneath the covers. For the first time since Alex's death he fell asleep almost immediately.

Chapter 38

Low angry clouds hovered outside Mika's office window. She watched the rain pelt Central Park and the city surrounding it. She usually loved the gloomy beauty of a rainy day, but today the weather was like a festering wound. The memories were coming faster and clearer now, and she could feel the knife in her breast twisting with sorrow and remorse. Harder still was hiding it from Malachi.

The plan had gone terribly wrong. The recipient of the only love she had ever felt was dead. Lowering her head, she closed her eyes tightly against the feeling of utter wretchedness and despair. These were unfamiliar emotions for her, and she was ill-equipped to deal with them. My God, she thought, I cannot even properly mourn the man.

"I thought I had worked this all out of my system," she told herself quietly. She had been pushing herself and her personal trainer relentlessly these past few days. Restless, she tapped her long French-polished fingernails against the window glass. *But I guess not,* she thought, *because I would very much like to throw Malachi through his office window and watch him hit the concrete forty floors down.*

"Bring the Shepard files in here." Malachi's voice cut through her reverie like the polished steel edge of a Samurai sword.

She turned away from the window, slipped on her black Chanel jacket, and pulled out the files from a locked drawer. Dutifully arranging her face in the best geisha girl expression she could muster, Mika walked through the panel door and bowed her good morning. He nodded, barely noticing her subservient simper and accepted the file. He didn't even open it.

"Does the name Beaudrot appear in this file?" he snapped.

Mika was caught by surprise. "Yes," she replied. "Cassandra's cousin married a man by that name. They live in Croissy, outside of Paris. The address is listed separately in the back of the file along with anyone else of consequence. Cassandra's middle name is Llewellyn, and it was apparently a family name. I did not find anything under that name. I was primarily concerned with the Shepard's genealogy, however."

"I received a telephone call this afternoon from an antiques dealer in Paris who has a manuscript for me," began Malachi. "She told me an American woman had just been there with her friend Marie Beaudrot, looking for documents with the cartouche on them!" He slammed the palm of his hand down on the desk. "Do you know what this means?" he asked, rising from his chair to look out his window. "This tells me that they know what they are looking for. I have to admit, they are not stupid people." He spun around with his mouth twisted in a half smile. "They are hot on the trail, and I'd like to help make that trail hotter still. Burning hot, in fact."

Mika's stomach tensed. She knew what was coming. She only hoped he would not send her on another clean-up detail. It was one thing to be on the planning end, but quite another to execute it. The last time, it was a Federal prosecutor with damaging evidence in a fraud case against Malachi, and it was her job to make sure the fellow was properly disposed of and the evidence destroyed. The grisly affair had filled her with nightmares for weeks. "What do you have in mind?" she asked steadily, her almond eyes revealing nothing.

"I wish someone would rid me of these . . . problems," he answered calmly. "These people must be stopped before they discover what the documents reveal. They must be stopped from attaining any credibility in the public's mind. Burn the house in Croissy to the ground. Do it late Saturday night when they are all asleep, and make sure you inform me of the foolproof, French-proof method they will use, along with what time we can expect confirmation."

Mika's mind began spinning. "What about the phase-inversion information we need from Nicholas?" she asked, hoping it might give him pause.

The words seems to have the desired effect. Malachi scratched his ear as he reached into the humidor for a cigar. He was about to light it when he stopped and nodded. He had an answer. "If Shepard and his wife meet with an untimely death, it may still be possible to get that information from the widow, or maybe from that priest Lev told me about. In any case, my chief concern is to keep those people from finding out anything else about the documents. That could be the end of us." He shot her a hard stare. "Everything else is secondary. *Everything!*"

"Perhaps they have the box and documents with them," Mika suggested. "You are willing to give those up. Forever?"

"Yes," declared Malachi emphatically. He prided himself on his nearly infallible instincts. His eyes narrowed into tiny slits. "Are you playing devil's advocate, Mika, or are you suddenly getting squeamish on me?"

"Are those my only choices?" she asked, forcing a benign smile. "I only have the good of the company and our clients in mind. You know that."

"That's admirable," he replied, popping the unlit cigar into his mouth, sitting down in his chair, and hooking his hands behind his neck. "I thought I sensed . . . reluctance, perhaps?"

"I feel nothing," she stared straight ahead blankly. "I merely wanted to review all our options."

"You're very good. You are the only woman I've ever met whose mind I can't fully read. That must be why I keep you around." He handed the file back to her. "Get this organized."

She bowed and returned to her lair next door. After closing herself in, she took a deep breath to gird herself for the next task.

If I think about it too much I will falter.

Without taking a seat she picked up a secure line and made a transatlantic call. She gave the instructions in rapid-fire French. Afterward, she sat down, pushed a button on her desk, and waited for the four monitor screens to rise from their wells. The balance of the day she spent focused on trades and meetings. When the markets closed, she returned to Malachi's office.

"The French messengers have viewed the property and analyzed their approach. There are several alarms, and the house presents no opportunities for entrance from the street that wouldn't be detected. They are recommending the rather time-honored method of two Molotov cocktails pitched over the gate into the courtyard."

"Well, isn't that simple?" Malachi smirked. "Good terrorist tactics. Shouldn't leave any evidence, either. You might not have to go clean up."

"I will do whatever you wish," she replied, refusing to take his bait.

"I thought you would!" he laughed as she disappeared quietly through ther door.

Chapter 39

The voice on the other end of the line was clear and crisp, as if she were across town rather than in another country.

"Francesca? It's so good to hear your voice!" Happy tears rushed to Cassandra's eyes. "Yes, it's me! I'm sorry not to have called before this. How are Rosemary and Harrison?" She paused, listening to her sister-in-law. Cassandra covered the receiver with her hand and nodded to Nicholas. "She sounds good."

Removing her hand, she nodded again. "Oh, good, Francesca. Yes, we have been busy. This mystery is unraveling in a good way, and we wanted to have some good news for you before we called. Today is the first morning we really have a handle on where we are going with all this. She listened, said a few words in return, and covered the phone again before whispering to Nicholas, "Francesca found them a great nanny, a nun who takes them everywhere and is teaching them Italian!"

She returned to her conversation. "Oh, we're on our way to Versailles to track down more clues. I don't know when we'll get to Italy, but more and more evidence is leading us to documents that might be stored in your neck of the woods. Would we be safe in Siena, do you think?" She paused. "That's a great idea. Go ahead and take care of that when you can."

As soon as Cassandra hung up, Marie appeared in the garden with coffee, freshly squeezed orange juice, and buttery marzipan-filled croissants.

"What did you tell her to do?" Nicholas asked around a mouthful of delicious fat and sugar.

"She said she could get rooms ready for us at her parents' home, where we can go whenever we need to. Whenever that is," she added. "Except for Versailles, I think we've done about all we can do here in Paris. It looks like the trail points to Rome. Didn't somebody famous say that all roads lead there?" She smiled.

The sun was just peeping over the bougainvillea and splattering against the eastern wall of the courtyard garden. They both felt almost too content to leave, but they were anxious to get moving. Since nobody knew how long it would take to find the documents they were seeking—or even whether they would find them—they wanted to get to Versailles as soon as possible. As soon as the light breakfast was over, they piled into the car and drove off. The house in Croissy was not far from Ste. Germain-en-laye, the birthplace of Napoleon, and only about thirty minutes from Versailles. Nicholas and Cassandra had never laid eyes on the magnificent gilded palace, and were excited to finally have the opportunity.

"As I am sure you know," Marie said, "Versailles was the seat of government for several kings until 1789, when Louis XVI and Marie Antoinette were dragged off to Paris and ultimately to their executions." She went on to describe the glorious sprawling well-manicured grounds, the Grand Canal, fountains, paintings, sculptures, and the palace's seven hundred ornately detailed rooms. Just as she had been at the opera house, Marie proved a font of knowledge and an excellent tour guide.

"Seven hundred rooms?" Cassandra exclaimed. "How are we going to cover that much territory between four of us? And we only have three cameras."

"Oh, damn," said Nicholas softly. "He turned and looked at Cassandra seated behind him. I forgot the cameras."

"Oh, Nicholas," sighed Cassandra.

Jacques thought the same thing as he rolled his eyes and turned the car around. They were only ten minutes from the house, but nobody wanted to waste any of their precious time.

"Just grab the whole lot," suggested Cassandra. "And get your laptop, too. We can go back over your notes on the way."

Once they were back on the road, Nicholas pulled out a fistful of pages he had printed out from his search for financial advisors. The search yielded some information about the Sun King and his court. When Louis XIV began his reign as a child in 1651, France was the richest country in the known world. When he died in 1715, the country was near bankruptcy and seventy years away from the bloody French Revolution.

"It must have taken them that long to spend the money," Nicholas surmised.

"And you are about to see how they spent it," smiled Marie as they drove into the town of Versailles. Tree-shaded streets and pale limestone buildings sheathed in stucco heralded their arrival. As though in a time warp, they bumped along the cobbled streets in their metal chariot. Attention to detail was manifest everywhere. Not a single meter of space, it seemed, had been left untouched by a superb architect or craftsperson. They parked the car and climbed out.

"Look at that," marveled Cassandra as they walked down sunny streets. "Even the shutter latches are beautiful." She was studying one in the shape of a dolphin, whose tail held the green shutter open.

Marie and Jacques shared a chuckle. "As you say in the States," said Marie, "you ain't seen nothing yet." Everyone laughed heartily.

Marie's catalog of facts about the Versailles palace impressed Nicholas and Cassandra, but it had not prepared them for what they were about to see. They followed the cobbled pavement toward the central chateau until the vision that filled their eyes and senses brought them to an abrupt halt. They stood, mouths agape, as they stared in stunned silence at what many have proclaimed to be the most beautiful building in the world. All the glory of the Louvre disappeared in the face of this monument to art and architecture. Its craftsmanship was unparalleled on either side of the Atlantic.

At last they stood in the Marble Courtyard, where Moliere's *Tartuffe* debuted, and evening concerts by Lully entertained 17th century audiences. "I had no idea it would be so beautiful," Cassandra whispered, enthralled by the brick patterns in herringbones and plaids. Her husband sat down on the marble steps and withdrew several more pages of research material.

"Now I'm beginning to get a fix on the kind of power and wealth they were talking about," he said, his eye sweeping the data he was holding. "It's almost like this is what they invested in, instead of stock markets. Trade between countries had to have produced much of this wealth," he continued, oblivious for the moment of the great palace itself. "The gold for the gilt came from somewhere, as did the exotic woods, fabrics, flax, spices—everything. Everything came here to this opulent warehouse in the middle of France, presided over by the Bourbon kings."

He shuffled his papers and continued. "The London Stock Market, the oldest one of all, was formed around 1700, fifteen years before Louis XIV died. Before that, there was Versailles, the Vatican . . . ." He scanned his pages.

"So whose documents are we looking for?" asked Cassandra.

"I think we are looking for the records of Nicolas Fouquet," answered her husband without lifting his eyes from the page. He went on to explain why he had selected Fouquet. When no one responded, Nicholas looked up to discover he had been talking to the pigeons cooing in circles around him as they pecked the ground in search of food. The others were some distance away, absorbed by the fabulous architecture and marble busts perched on corbels all over the courtyard.

"Hey," he shouted to his little party, which elicited raised eyebrows and frowns from worshipful tourists. Gathering his little audience together, Nicholas held up a small portrait of Nicolas Fouquet, which he had printed out from the Internet.

"He looks a lot like you, minus the mustache," commented Cassandra.

"Holy cow!" responded Jacques in English.

"What?" asked Nicholas.

"Is it not an idiom from America?" asked Jacques.

"Yes, Jacques, you said it correctly and I know what it means," Nicholas said quickly. "But why did you say it?"

Jacques began talking rapidly for a few seconds before slowing down for Nicholas' benefit. "He is your missing link—Fouquet. I know of this man," said the Frenchman quickly. "He comes from a long line of very old money. He was the most aristocratic of all blue bloods of his time. It was people like him that the royal families depended on to loan them money."

Nicholas looked at Jacques. "Why do you call him the missing link?"

"Because during his tenure France prospered," Jacques said with a triumphant smile. "When Jean Baptiste Colbert, a descendant of wealthy merchant bankers and the snake who betrayed him, took over Fouquet's duties, France fell into a slow but certain decline."

"Colbert?" said Nicholas, thinking back through his recent research. "I think I have him here as well." He shuffled through several papers until he pulled one out and waved it around. "Colbert's policies as Louis XIV's finance minister essentially ruined France's own market economy, didn't they?"

"Yes, they did." answered Jacques.

"Tell us more, Jacques," urged Cassandra. "Tell us more about Fouquet."

"Certainly," he replied heartily. "Every educated Frenchman, especially those who work in the financial world or who study history, knows of Fouquet!" The story Jacques told was one of power, riches beyond belief, royal intrigue, and ultimately, betrayal and death.

Nicolas Fouquet was born in 1615 into a wealthy and powerful family. His own father, François Fouquet, was a trusted advisor to Cardinal Richelieu on maritime and commercial matters. In 1653, the 38-year old Nicolas was given the chance to essentially rescue a bankrupt France by being appointed King Louis XIV's finance secretary. Fouquet's personal fortune was used to guarantee his country's loans. At the same time, he employed two of the country's finest architects to design and build Château de Vaux le Vicomte thirty-five miles southeast of Paris. Today, many refer to it as the forerunner of the Palace at Versailles. Grand beyond compare, it was built with his father's legacy and money he inherited from his first wife. "Unfortunately," explained Jacques in slowly spoken French, "the jaw-dropping splendor of his creation helped bring about his downfall."

"His downfall," repeated Cassandra. "How?"

"The Chief Minister of France, Cardinal Mazarin, despised Fouquet and saw him only as a threat to his own power. He convinced the king that Fouquet was an embezzler who used state money to build his magnificent palace, and that his misuse of funds was crippling the country. Mazarin's private secretary was none other than Colbert, who continued the campaign of lies after Mazarin died. He whispered to the king that the finance secretary was an anti-Royalist—a threat to Louis XIV himself!

Fouquet foolishly ignored the growing storms brewing against him, and in 1661, threw the most impressive party France had ever witnessed—and invited the king! Can you imagine! How dense can a man be?" Jacques started laughing so hard he had to stop for a moment to collect himself. "The king's own fêtes did not hold a candle to the one Fouquet threw. Louis XIV, who was but 22 years old at the time, decided it was time to arrest Fouquet. As our own Voltaire later wrote, 'On 17 August 1661, at six in the evening, Fouquet was the King of France! At 2 in the morning, he was a nobody.' Or something like that," Jacques smiled.

"What happened to Fouquet?" asked Cassandra, leaning forward in anxious anticipation of the story's climax.

Jacques shrugged. "Fouquet came to an unfortunate end. He was tried and the court wanted to banish him—essentially an acquittal of the charges against him. Louis XIV overruled the court and sentenced him to life in prison. He was sent into the Alps to the citadel of Pignerol, where he lingered in a cell for almost twenty years before finally expiring."

"That's terrible!" exclaimed Cassandra.

"By locking away Fouquet and blocking his access to the outside world," continued Jacques, "the king was also hiding embarrassing state secrets, and Fouquet knew plenty of them. This is what some historians believe, at least. Fouquet is considered by many to have been 'The Man in the Iron Mask'—you have heard of this, yes?"

"Whoa!" cried out Nicholas. "The same man in the story by Alexandre Dumas?" Jacques nodded. Marie beamed.

"Nicholas!" cut in an excited Cassandra. "What if Fouquet had the box, and Colbert stole it, but perhaps never figured out how to use it because the instructions were passed down by word of mouth through generations and never written down? That would explain all the mistakes he made." She stopped suddenly, her face a bright red when she realized her mistake.

"What box?" Marie and Jacques asked simultaneously. Nicholas and Cassandra looked at each other but remained silent.

Marie softened her voice and spoke slowly, deliberately, as if to a child. "Since the day of your arrival, both Jacques and I have known there is something important you have not shared with us. You called it a professional code of silence, or something like that. Perhaps it is time?"

Cassandra and Nicholas reached the same conclusion without having to voice their thoughts. "We have not been fully forthcoming with you," Nicholas replied in a firm, clear voice. He sighed, as if shedding a tremendous weight. "There is an ancient box . . ."

Cassandra interrupted. "Start at the beginning," she urged. "Otherwise, none of it will make sense."

Nicholas looked around to make sure no one was within ear shot. He began with the Christmas party at the Biltmore Estate, describing for their hosts Cassandra's encounter with the secret room behind the fireplace, and how in rescuing her they found the Egyptian box and ancient documents stored with it. He did his best to not leave out any significant details.

Marie looked deeply interested from the beginning, but her husband looked on with a blank expression, his arms folded tightly across his chest. At one point, Marie interrupted Nicholas' narrative to exclaim, "Jacques said on the night of your arrival that he did not think your story could get any more interesting," exclaimed Marie, "but he was wrong!" She turned to her husband and repeated the story in French to make sure he fully understood. He nodded his understanding, shifted his legs to get more comfortable, and folded and unfolded his arms as if he was nervous.

"It gets even more bizarre," admitted Nicholas. "We discovered that this box measures gravity, and has been used through the centuries to— for lack of a better description, 'capture the market,' so to speak, on the world's finances. The documents fully support that theory." He paused and looked at his French cousins. Marie and Jacques were listening politely, but their expressions had quickly switched from interest to outright incredulity.

"Believe me, I *know* all this sounds crazy, and I am oversimplifying it or we would be here until nightfall," continued Nicholas, "but Alex and I used that hypothesis to create our own computer program that does the same thing. We've been using it to make a fortune in the stock market."

"Excuse me," Marie interjected with disbelief written on her face. "What could gravity possibly have to do with the stock market?" She looked at her husband and said something quickly in French neither Nicholas nor Cassandra fully understood. He shrugged and shook his head.

"Nicholas, let me," said Cassandra. She took a deep breath and began by explaining how human emotions were effected by gravitational pull. "Believe me," she said with a little laugh, "you don't want me to get too technical, but the guys have been able to predict the ebb and flow of the stock market by looking at oceanographic tidal charts."

Marie merely nodded without speaking and turned to translate once more for Jacques. By the look on his face he didn't believe it, either. Indeed, both now looked embarrassed and almost angry.

"Wait!" shot out Cassandra. "I can prove it." She dug for a few moments inside her purse and withdrew their most recent brokerage statement. "I stuffed this inside my wallet and forgot about it." She looked at Nicholas, who nodded in approval, and handed it to Marie. The statement showed an account worth more than $2,000,000, complete with trades, dates, and profits. Marie's mouth fell open as she studied the document. Nicholas helped drop it a bit more as he pointed out detail after detail.

The French couple sat in shocked silence. Jacques whispered a few words to his wife, who just as quietly whispered her reply. "This does show that you are both very wealthy," Marie said slowly. "It does not prove anything about this box or these documents, but you are both honest, good people. The story is, frankly, incredible, but we believe you are telling us the truth—especially given what we have both seen these past two days with our own eyes in your presence."

Both Nicholas and Cassandra heaved a sigh of relief. "What was supposed to create a nice little nest egg for our families has become a nightmare," Nicholas continued. "Someone, somewhere, has this information and isn't happy that we've been using it. I told you Alex had been killed. The automobile he was driving—it was my car—was tampered with, and this triggered the accident that took his life."

It was Jacques who finally spoke. "I am afraid to ask, but did this box accompany you to France?"

"Yes," confessed Nicholas. "It is in my large photographer's case."

Jacques looked at Nicholas exhibiting complete shock. "Can you show it to us?"

Nicholas looked at Cassandra, who nodded. "When we get back to your home I'll show you both how it works."

Jacques scratched his temple and turned to Marie to speak, but she held up her hand to silence him. "I think we understand, and we thank you for sharing this with us." She stood up. "It is a lovely day and we are at Versailles! How can we help you?"

ß

Nicholas turned to Cassandra. "You had a theory about Fouquet and Colbert. Can you explain it again?"

Cassandra struck a thoughtful pose. "Yes . . . sure. I was thinking out loud that perhaps Colbert stole the box but could not figure out how to use it, because instructions were not passed generation to generation in writing, but by word of mouth. That might explain all the mistakes he made after Fouquet's death."

"That is brilliant," Nicholas said. "Let's find a tour guide and see if we can dig up any documentation."

The Domain offers guides for private tours, and they found one easily enough. Lorraine was a big, square-shaped French woman who looked as though she had just come in from the country. As it turned out, she had. Her husband owned one of the farms that had supported the kitchens at Versailles for many generations, and she had been leading tours of the palace and grounds for nearly two decades. More than anything, she wanted to show them the various kitchens in the town of Versailles responsible for feeding thousands of courtiers and staff, and thus appeared disappointed when they asked for documents belonging to Fouquet.

"Fouquet, yes of course I know who he was," she replied, slightly miffed that anyone might suspect she could not identify one of King Louis XIV's finance ministers. "There are at least two documents on display that bear his handwriting and signature. They are on different floors, but on the same side of the complex."

She led them into the fabulous Hall of Mirrors, glittering with chandeliers both suspended from the ceiling and held up on pillars supported by sparkling nymphs and Grecian-inspired maidens. The chandeliers reflected into the mirrors, multiplying the grandeur and scale of the hall. On the right-hand side were the elaborate formal gardens designed by André le Nôtre. The French guide was in no hurry, and took her time to point out the ceiling paintings by Charles le Brun, chronicling Louis XIV's early years. "You will be interested to know that Monsieur le Brun was also the painter for your subject, Nicolas Fouquet, at Fouquet's palace Vaux-le-Vicomte. It was that estate, in fact, that inspired this one." Jacques turned to Cassandra and raised his eyebrows as if to say, "See, I told you so!"

"Ah, here we are," said Lorraine. She led them through an antechamber into the War Chamber, which was dominated by a huge marble medallion sculpture of Louis XIV riding to victory on a magnificent steed. More paintings by Le Brun celebrating the Sun King's victories adorned the ceiling.

Cassandra studied the paintings. "Did he ever do anything besides pose for portraits?" The rhetorical nature of the question was lost on the French guide, but Lorraine shot her a sour look nonetheless. Even if she didn't understand the question, she recognized the American brand of sarcasm. She gave Cassandra a little nudge in the direction of a small glass cabinet against one wall.

"Here is one of the documents written in Fouquet's own hand," said Lorraine with a sweep of her arm. "It is a contract for a loan of money to the young Louis XIV, in return for his good grace and favor—along with a small amount of interest to be paid over ten years!" She laughed. "Can you imagine—charging interest to a king who could take your head with the stroke of a pen?"

"May we take a picture of this?" inquired Marie shyly. She knew guides gossiped unmercifully about their subjects and often just walked away if their tourist-clients did something of which they disapproved. Lorraine hesitated before shrugging her hefty shoulders, thinking that if she acquiesced, they might give her a better tip.

Cassandra quickly held up her digital camera and recorded the image. She was almost certain the fine script matched one of the documents bearing a cartouche back at Croissy.

The next destination turned out to be the Chapel Royale. Constructed of blindingly white marble, it presented a startling contrast to the rest of the building. The only color was provided by ceiling paintings and red-marble patterns in the floor. Simultaneously Baroque and Gothic, its shape and form echoed medieval cathedrals in the lofty colonnaded floor plan, stained glass, gargoyles, and pointed roof. The columns, however, were typical of the early 1700s, as were the pillars and painted vaults.

"This building contained the largest sculpture studio in the early eighteenth century," Lorraine informed them. The altar amazed them with its gilded bronze bas-relief. Every inch of surface was carved or adorned in some manner. The guide gestured for them to follow her to a second-floor antechamber that bayed out over a courtyard. Here, ensconced in another glass case, was the other carefully preserved Fouquet document. This one was signed by both the Sun King himself and his minister, Jean Baptiste Colbert. It was the document sentencing Fouquet to life in prison. At the bottom of the page was the cartouche.

Marie gasped aloud and Lorraine looked at her. "What's the matter? Did you see a ghost? You would not be the first, you know."

"No ghosts," stammered Marie. "Just indigestion."

"Nicolas Fouquet should be better-known today," Jacques remarked to the guide. "We are hoping to make people more aware of his unique role in French history." Lorraine nodded her approval and shifted from one foot to the other. They had what they wanted, and it was time for her to leave. Jacques dug in his pocket and handed her a fifty-franc note, along with his profuse thanks. She beamed, wished the four of them well, and disappeared. Cassandra snapped three more shots of the document, shifting each time in an effort to avoid any glare that might obstruct the writing.

"That was just too easy," Nicholas beamed as they headed back out of the chapel. "You might be right, Cassandra. Colbert could have stolen the box when they imprisoned Fouquet!"

"This is such an amazing place," sighed Cassandra as they walked out into the sunshine. "No wonder the peasants revolted!"

Marie nodded soberly. "It is beautiful and obscene at the same time."

"Shall we make a day of it?" Jacques offered.

"We have found the information we were looking for. You and Marie have seen all this before," Cassandra protested.

"There's no telling when you will be able to come back," Marie answered simply, taking her cousin's arm and guiding her along.

This time, instead of a tour guide, they picked up headphones in their respective languages and followed the herd through the spectacular chateau. Once they had had their fill of gilding and portraiture, they went outside and queued up for the miniature train tour of the entire estate. They spent the afternoon exploring such venues as the Petit Trianon, where Marie Antoinette loved to play at being a peasant—to the everlasting distress of those who actually were. They ate dinner just outside the gates at Chapeau Gris, and returned to the estate for the *Grande Fête de Nuit*, a musical and fireworks display continuing a tradition begun by the Sun King himself. They sat out on the lawns, watching the twirls of skyrockets and exploding color reflected in the shimmering pools with a chamber orchestra playing early Baroque music in the background.

It was after midnight when they finally piled into the station wagon and started back to Croissy. Nicholas was pleased with their progress. *It's all there if someone bothered to look for it*, he thought. *Of course, without knowing the power of the box, and relating it to the documents, who would ever know to look?*

The short pamphlet they had picked up on what happened to the country after Colbert assumed Fouquet's duties was only superficially presented. "Marie, Jacques, can you tell me more specifically about France's course while Colbert's hand was on the tiller?" asked Nicholas.

Marie answered. "Colbert managed to keep the country solvent for a long time, but he made one *big* mistake."

Jacques jumped in to finish the answer. "Yes, he was very advanced with his balance of trade theories and expansion of commerce. It is called Colbertisme. Unfortunately, as you mentioned before, he was not as progressive on the home front, and this is where it ultimately counted. He implemented a very regressive tax system, which was especially disastrous for the peasants. Colbert tried to implement a handful of reforms later in his life, but it was, as you Americans say, too little too late. His policies, according to many French historians, were the root cause of the French Revolution in 1789."

"So we could say it was Colbert and his policies that brought the country down, not the box," mused Nicholas. "But what happened after the Revolution? Where did the power shift?"

"I can answer that," said Cassandra. "England. Maybe that's where we ought to go next."

Nicholas agreed. "In London, we can take a look at the infant stock markets being developed about the same time as Louis XIV's death."

They rode on in silence for awhile, savoring the events of the day. Soon after motoring into Croissy their Mercedes was forced onto the sidewalk by a screaming fire engine.

"It looks like a fire, perhaps in our own neighborhood!" said Marie worriedly. They followed the truck as it turned onto their street. "No!" screamed Marie. Red flames were shooting straight for the sky from the roof of the Beaudrot's home.

Chapter 40

Cassandra would remember Marie's sharp scream and that terrible moment for the rest of her life. A grim-faced Jacques held her tightly as she rocked back and forth in the front seat of the car with her hands over the lower half of her face. His own pale features glowed by the light of the flames as he watched the disintegration of his home where they had spent a quarter of a century raising their family.

The street was thronged with the fire brigade, gendarmes, and knots of neighbors gathered to watch and worry about houses close by. Unable to move the car in any direction, Jacques turned off the engine and the four of them sat and watched as the center of their host's life disappeared into the night sky. For several agonizing minutes none of them could move. They could feel the heat even where they sat. The fire was completely out of control. There was nothing that could be done to save the house or its contents. Ashen-faced and shaking, Nicholas and Cassandra reached for their cousins' shoulders simultaneously.

"Jacques," Nicholas hissed in his ear, "we must leave. We are in danger. We cannot stay here."

Without warning, Marie jumped out of the car and started running toward the house. Jacques took off after her, with the American couple close behind. Marie saw one of her neighbors and collapsed into his arms. When Jacques arrived, she moved into her husband's waiting embrace, sobbing hysterically.

"Jacques, I am so sorry," said the neighbor.

"What happened? Does anyone know? Is everyone else alright?" he asked.

"No one is certain, but I heard the police talking about an incendiary device. They think someone threw one into your courtyard. It might have been vandals. One of the police patrols saw two men running down the sidewalk shortly after midnight."

Jacques stiffened at this news and looked at Nicholas. *Will this never end?* Wondered Nicholas. *Everyone we involve in this mystery is punished.*

"Tell the police that my wife and I have been here, we are fine, that she is extremely distraught, and that we have gone to a hotel for the night. I will be in contact with them tomorrow." His neighbor nodded and started on his mission as the two couples returned to the car. Jacques put Marie in the back seat with Cassandra for comfort, and the two men sat up front.

"Thank God we have a line of credit and insurance," Jacques murmured putting the key in the ignition.

"Is that all you have to say?" Marie sobbed. "We raised our children in that house. All our things, our memories. Gone!"

Jacques had no reply. When a police car finally moved, he managed with some difficulty to turn the car around and head away from the orange glow of the fire.

Both Nicholas and Cassandra were acutely aware that the horrific event was their fault. "Jacques," began Nicholas.

"Do not speak of blame right now," his cousin-in-law said bluntly, swinging the car onto the highway. "We can spend the rest of our lives sorting that out. Right now we must go to a place of safety. If I ever doubted you, my American cousin, I am rapidly becoming a believer. Someone wants you dead."

"I don't know if there is such a thing as a safe place," Nicholas said softly.

Jacques stared straight ahead. "Sometimes Marie and I stop in Fontainebleau on our way to my parents' compound near Nice. We stay at what you Americans call a bed and breakfast. We are friends with the owner—though he will probably be shocked when we appear on his doorstep at three in the morning."

Marie's sobs eventually evolved into an exhausted stare. She rested her head on Cassandra's shoulder while her cousin looked out at the passing darkness with tears rolling down her cheeks. "Shouldn't we call ahead?" Cassandra asked between sniffles.

Nicholas almost smiled. "My wife has more manners than any one else on the planet," he said, and pulled his cell phone out of his pocket. He dialed the number Jacques gave him and handed him the phone.

"*Mon ami*, Jacques Beaudrot here. *Oui*, something *is* terribly wrong. Our house burned down tonight. No, no, we are fine, but we need a place for four to stay. Oh," he sighed, then listened another minute. "*Merci, mon ami*. Perhaps half an hour." He hung up. "The hotel is completely booked up, but he says we can stay in his own guest rooms at his house next door."

They continued in somber silence, pulling up at last before a charming 19th century inn done designed in a Norman Revival style with half-timbering filled in with brick. The house next door, dating to the same period, was built of native stone. A small covered porch formed a portico leading to stone steps and a short driveway made of two slate-paved tire lanes filled in with grass.

When they arrived, the inn's proprietors met them dressed in nightclothes and robes. Marie stumbled out of the car and fell into her friend's arms. "Jocelyn," she said, sobbing anew. Jocelyn, whose white hair was caught up in a disheveled bun, gathered Marie up and practically carried her into the house with Jacques just behind. Cassandra introduced herself and Nicholas to the man left behind.

He shook their hands. "I am Jocelyn's husband, Antoine. Please, follow me." He led them inside, where they found a crowded landing and a stairway leading to a second floor. Exhausted and numb to their surroundings, they followed him to an upstairs bedroom.

"We have put housecoats in your rooms," he said. "If you would like, leave your clothes out here in the hall. We will have them washed and dried for you."

"We are profoundly grateful," Cassandra replied, offering the innkeeper a thankful smile.

They entered the room to find that an enormous, hand-carved, walnut *lit clos* filled almost the entire space. It was so large that the armoire was out in the hall. Ordinarily, they would have enjoyed this quirkiness, but now they could only concentrate on getting out of their clothing and into the white cotton nightshirts provided by the thoughtful innkeepers.

Exhausted, frightened, and distraught by the sadness they had brought down onto Jacques and Marie, they sank into a fitful sleep.

ᛤ

"What do you have to report?" asked Malachi into the intercom.

Mika was looking out over Central Park when his voice erupted into her office. A low-pressure system had settled over the mid-Atlantic coast and the rain was starting to bore her. She blinked as a lightning flash lit the sky, followed a few seconds later by a clap of thunder that shook the windows. "Appropriate," she muttered, and stepped through the door. She took a grotesque satisfaction in what she was about to say.

"No requiems today," she announced as she entered the room, though without her traditional bow.

The news did not amuse Malachi. "They escaped? Who the hell was in charge of that fiasco—my son?"

"They were not there. According to the fire and police report, the house was empty of humans and animals. Our messenger service served up two packages into the courtyard, and apparently the gasoline bursts left the identifying marks of incendiary devices, so the police are looking for the usual suspects. But the area is now a crime scene. The police will attribute it to the rising pattern of crime in the area that has been fueled by religious tensions."

Malachi studied the tip of his gold Mont Blanc fountain pen. He felt like flinging it at her, but he resisted the childish response. "Am I going to have to fire the entire messenger service network?" he asked with a surprising calm and steadiness in his voice. "They haven't done anything right yet. Why didn't they watch the house to make sure the Shepard's were in there? Where the hell *were* they? Some day trip, I suppose—more research into our secrets. For your sake," he snarled, finally letting his emotion take hold, "I hope the hell they're not finding what they're looking for!"

"We do not know that yet. Nothing has appeared on any credit report, so we cannot track them with our usual methods. They don't have a place to stay now so they'll be making some kind of financial transaction soon, and we will pick that up."

He grimaced as though he had tasted something rotten. "Well, my dear, it appears that you are on clean-up duty now. I want you to take my jet to France and assume the guise of an insurance inspector. You know how to get the appropriate credentials. Find out where the hell they are!"

As I expected, she thought cheerlessly.

"What name will you travel under?"

She could see that he liked this part. Even powerful men enjoy games, she thought ruefully. She picked up the Mont Blanc and wrote it on the back of one of Malachi's business cards: Keiko Tokugawa.

He had never heard that name before. "An old family name?"

"I would prefer not to say." Her dark eyes, as usual, gave away nothing. *Mull that one over,* Mika thought irreverently.

Malachi had yet to succeed in crossing the bridge into her personal life, and it frustrated him to no end. He wasn't gaining any ground here, either.

As a sort of payback, he decided to give her detailed instructions on how to perform her job. He knew that would irk her. "Your job is to search the ruins of the house for the box and documents. The nested tetrahedron is crystal, and from what I have been led to believe, impervious to flame. You may find it intact. Parchment and vellum have fat in them, so the documents are gone unless they were somehow protected from the heat and fire. Get back to me the minute you're finished. If you find anything, I want it. Just remove it from the site and take care of any consequences. If you do not find anything. . . ."

She gritted her teeth and smiled prettily. "It will mean they still have the box with them or it is somewhere else."

Malachi's face changed and she recognized a new light in his eyes. The game playing was over. "I think I may have worthy, if bumbling, opponents," he began softly, rocking back in his chair. "They have been lucky, true, and we've been incompetent on a few occasions. But they have been clever enough to discover the nearly undiscoverable, and now travel abroad without leaving a paper trail. The wife having relatives in Paris was another damnable piece of luck. But let's face it: if it weren't for Claudette, we wouldn't have the slightest idea where they were." He paused for effect. "Now I think I will raise the bar." Malachi punched a button on his phone and looked back up at Mika. "I don't know why I didn't think of this before."

He smiled as he spoke into the phone. "Lev! Surely, our Professor Shepard left some contact information with his Department Chair? Get me that number! Oh, and what's the name of the priest there? Galen. Galen what?" Malachi scribbled the name on a yellow legal pad as he hung up the phone.

Mika pulled up a chair. Despite her personal entanglement in this particular case, she liked to watch Malachi rearrange the order of his universe. He was a good teacher. She sat back, carefully clasping her knees together. Her suede skirt was short, and she paid close attention to where her hem fell.

Malachi dialed the phone. "Galen Abbott, please. Good morning. This is Malachi Foust. I'm trying to get in touch with Nicholas Shepard. Oh, I see. I am a business associate of his and the father of one of his grad students. Yes, Lev Foust. You've met him? Thank you for the kind words. I am happy to hear he made such a good impression."

Malachi looked at Mika with a conspiratorial gleam in his eye. "I wanted to mention to Dr. Shepard that my company is putting together a world economics symposium for early summer in Paris, and we would like him to be the keynote speaker. Can you relay this information to him? Yes, I believe he has my number. Many thanks."

He hung up the phone and crossed his legs. "Have you figured it out?"

"You are going to call a symposium of the Bilderberg Group and have the members assail Professor Shepard's credibility?"

"If he lives that long, which I doubt," spat Malachi. "He'll never survive the professional disgrace I have in mind for him, that I can guarantee you. And afterward, if he tries to expose any of us with information from the documents, no one will believe him. It will be dismissed as an attempt to salvage his reputation."

Mika's bright red mouth curled slightly up at the corners. It was excellent sport, and Malachi was a master. His devotion to the game—to the art of the game—was almost Japanese in its purity. She would enjoy watching as he moved against this skilled and potentially dangerous foe. Malachi was the only man she had ever met more intelligent, more rational, more coolly calculating than she—the only man worthy of her own considerable talents.

And, of course, Malachi had not meant for Alex Shepard to die.

ß

Galen looked at the receiver as though it might bite him. "That fellow's smoother than the underbelly of a snake," he muttered to himself as he hung up. The priest mulled calling Nicholas directly but thought better of it, opting instead to send an e-mail. It would be safer than a telephone call to Paris.

Galen also typed a long letter to Francesca. He told her about a small roof leak he had fixed, asked her if she had heard from Nicholas and Cassandra and, because he wondered what she would think, mentioned Malachi's telephone call. The nanny she had found for Harrison and Rosemary was the last issue he addressed. "I understand she's a sister with the Poor Clares," he wrote. "I've set up quite a few counseling centers here in the states at Poor Clare monasteries. In fact, there are about 20,000 of these Franciscan nuns all over the world. The Vatican recognized them as the Poor Ladies of Assisi early in the 12th century. They're an interesting group, very cloistered and reflective, under strict vows of poverty, but they've done some remarkable work in the world. Let me hear from you soon!"

He hoped his letter didn't show it, but Galen was beginning to chafe at his house-sitting obligations. Accustomed to traveling about the country monitoring counseling centers, he was now administrating them mostly by e-mail. It was time to hire a housekeeper, he decided, even if it took a bite out of his budget. It was also past time to jump on his Harley for a brain-cleansing ride out to Middleton Place, an 18th century plantation on the banks of the nearby Ashley River.

ß

"Reserve the Coco Chanel suite at the Paris Ritz," Mika ordered her assistant, who promptly left to do as she bid. It was time to go home and pack.

Two hours later the car returned her to the office, where Mika rode the elevator up to the roof and boarded a helicopter for the short trip to JFK Airport. It was still raining, but the thunderstorms were finally moving out to sea. She enjoyed seeing New York spread out beneath her, glistening with raindrops backlit by the city's electric glow. The trip to France in Malachi's MD-11 consumed more than six hours of her precious time. Now, especially, she missed flying the Concorde. She spent the hours researching ideas relating to the phase inversion problem.

Because of its adaptive abilities, Mika was certain Alex had figured out the problem by working in the science of time-domain. She knew the system was not either linear or stationary, but working with dimensional theory would make it adaptive using astronomical measurements as an input type of modeling.

Mika had even contemplated the idea that frequency-domain methodology might have entered Alex's mind, where finding a state-dimension would be irrelevant. She quickly dismissed this idea because the frequency domain primarily dealt with cross-correlation of market data. She shook her head, thinking about how close other scientists had come to finding the answer to the predictability of market movements, only to fail because they never thought of an outside influence such as gravity.

She knew gravity was the outside driver that caused millions of investors worldwide to act the same. Her research showed that low frequencies such as yearly (and even monthly) trends did not suffer phase inversions, and that the phenomenon was limited to the short-term weekly trends.

But why?

Mika had yet to figure it out, and neither had any of the brilliant mathematicians she had hired to solve the problem. She sighed and closed her notes. Alex had figured it out. Now only Nicholas knew the answer.

Mika arrived at the Paris Ritz by private limousine early the next morning. Her suite was ready, and she took some time looking over the three rooms where the great designer, Coco Chanel, had spent thirty-seven years of her life. The interiors could not have been more different from Mika's own apartment. These rooms reflected the essence of French *couture* fashion in the great Jazz Age, with luxurious fabrics, Louis XV furniture, and Chinese lacquers. An art historian had restored or replaced every item in the suite, so that visitors could briefly enjoy the life of the fabulous Coco, looking out on the *Place Vendome*, sleeping on the silk sheets, and sampling the same cuisine offered by room service.

The great sweep of silk draperies enhancing the oddity of the architecture was one of Mika's favorite features. The walls slanted inward and upward to the ceilings, reflecting the exterior architecture, and Coco's designer had created window treatments to follow the angles from the ceiling, a technique that gave great definition to the rooms. Another thing Mika found endearing was the television set perched on a round table—so completely intrusive and out of place it was amusing. Mika was well aware Coco's coromandels and Chinese lacquered furniture, which were made primarily for the export markets, had none of the character of furniture designed for ancient Chinese emperors. She had her own collection of Chinese porcelains not intended for export, and Coco's pieces made her reflect on the integrity of the authentic work.

Mika changed quickly from the black silk suit she wore on the plane into a plain white Chanel shirt and tailored black slacks. With her laptop and briefcase in hand she walked briskly to the lift, rode it to the ground floor, and ordered the concierge to call a taxi. He remembered Mika quite well from her previous visits, and thought it odd that she asked for a taxi rather than a limousine.

Once the cab driver had the address in Croissy, Mika busied herself with her laptop. She looked up only when the taxi rolled to a stop in front of the burned-out shell that once had been home to the Beaudrots. Yellow crime-scene tape surrounded an L-shaped blackened area. A handful of beams and posts poked up through the blackened wreckage like fingers clawing skyward.

She climbed from the taxi and looked around. The street was deserted. "Return in one hour," she instructed the driver, who nodded and drove off. With a final glance up and down the street, Mika walked carefully into the rubble.

The sharp smell rising from the charred ruins was almost overpowering. With a long stick she began poking about, turning over pieces of debris in search of the box. She had no idea where it was when the house was fire-bombed. As thoroughly as an archaeologist working a grid for artifacts, she moved back and forth, foot by foot, turning over burned objects no longer identifiable as household items. After forty-five minutes of fruitless exploration, she discovered a bent metal tube buried under rubble in what had once been the kitchen. It was still capped at both ends. With some effort she managed to pry one end open. To her delight, the tube contained a piece of vellum. She unrolled it to discover an index of accounts in a 19th-century script and the cartouche as signature.

Looking up, she found herself staring into the curious eyes of a stiff gendarme. He looked her over. "Who are you, and what are you doing here?" he asked brusquely.

"I am an inspector for Jacques Beaudrot's insurance company," she replied matter-of-factly, pulling out her passport and company identity papers from the leather briefcase. He examined the papers, mumbled something, and handed them back.

"What do you intend to do with that," he asked, pointing at the tube in her hand.

"It is remarkable that this survived, no?" she answered in perfect French, smiling coquettishly. "I recognize this rare and valuable document from the inventory. We cannot just leave this here in the elements, can we? I shall deliver it at once to Monsieur Beaudrot."

The gendarme arched an eyebrow. "You know where Monsieur Beaudrot is located? We are looking for him and his wife. We found a neighbor who said he saw them briefly, and then they disappeared with their American friends into the night. All our efforts to find him have been useless. Where is he, mademoiselle?"

Mika smiled at him again. Her cheeks were starting to ache and she despised flirting but it could not be helped. "I have only just arrived from

New York. I am not sure exactly where he is at this moment. We got a call from him asking us to investigate the fire and to begin to prepare his claim."

"That doesn't sound like the Jacques Beaudrot I know," said the gendarme, pressing his advantage. "He would contact us first, I'm certain. Perhaps I should take the document with me."

"Ah, then perhaps this would persuade you that it will be perfectly safe with me," she responded coolly, pulling 500 Euros from her briefcase. The gendarme shrugged as he reached out and pocketed the money. When Jacques returned, he would tell him about this curious visit from the insurance lady.

He took down the pertinent information from Mika's papers and also noted the taxi's license plate number as it rolled up to collect her. He tipped his hat. "Good day, Mademoiselle Tokugawa."

Without acknowledging the gendarme's salutation, Mika stepped into the backseat of the taxi and sped toward Paris.

Chapter 41

 Nicholas felt as if the weight of the whole world was resting on his shoulders. *The burden of guilt*, he realized with sudden clarity. *There's a special place in hell for people like me.*

There was at least one thing he could do, he thought as he climbed over his sleeping wife to get out of bed. Cassandra grasped his hand and squeezed it as he sat on the edge of the *lit clos*, whispered "I love you," and tunneled back into the covers. He stepped to the door and looked out into the hall where his clothes, freshly washed and pressed, hung on a hall tree next to the armoire. Cassandra's were there too, smelling of fresh lavender. He took them back into the room, laid hers across the end of the bed, and made his way quietly into the bathroom.

It was not until he got downstairs that he realized it was the middle of the afternoon. He padded into the kitchen, where Jocelyn was sectioning oranges in the light from a mullioned window. It was a pleasant and well-organized, but cluttered, kitchen. An assortment of spices, dishes, baskets, and bottles filled the wire shelving that lined the walls. A huge blue stove dominated the room, and there was but little counter space. Still, Nicholas couldn't help but notice how wonderful it smelled. Jocelyn had made them a gruyere soufflé, paired with rosemary and garlic hearth bread and oranges. She took one look at him and poured him a huge mug of dark French coffee.

Jacques was sitting at the table lightly sampling the food while writing on a yellow legal pad in front of him. He did not look up as Nicholas sat down opposite him. The small kitchen table was covered by a bright yellow gingham cloth with a blue ceramic pitcher full of wild flowers in the center. It looked lovely, and for a moment it seemed as if last night's horror had not really happened. But of course it had, and Nicholas had reached a conclusion.

"Jacques, I thought of something I could do for you."

Jacques regarded him coolly, as if to say that Nicholas had done quite enough, thank you. Nicholas understood but persevered. "I can pay you whatever it would cost to rebuild your house in Croissy. I can write you a check today, or get the money wired to you. How much will you need?"

His cousin-in-law sat up straight in his chair. This was the last thing Jacques expected to hear today. "I have some insurance, and have already called them for an estimate," he explained, his voice warming up to the thought of actually being paid for his loss. "But there may be a problem with the circumstances. If my neighbor was right and there was some incendiary device used, the fire could be mistaken for terrorist activity." He winced. "Today, insurance companies find this a convenient excuse so they can avoid making payment altogether. I was making an inventory of the furnishings, just in case." His shoulders drooped as he thought of what he and Marie had lost in the inferno. "It is not a pleasant thing to do."

Marie walked over to where the men were sitting. Her eyes were puffy and she had a haggard look. Marie had been standing at the counter pouring a cup of coffee, and so overheard the conversation. "Thank you for your generous offer, Nicholas, but it's not just the house. It's all the years of memories and all those things like photographs, the children's drawings, my grandmother's jewelry—" She took a deep breath. "Everything is gone. I still cannot believe it."

"Nothing in the world can replace those things," Nicholas nodded, rising to give her his seat. "Certainly money cannot. But I'm offering you the price of the house so that you can move forward, and as quickly as possible."

Marie began to eat, slowly, her thoughts were obviously elsewhere. "This is probably not a good day to make such considerable decisions," she finally answered. "There are many options to weigh. I would feel better if we could go on to Jacques' family compound. I am feeling quite confused and disoriented right now." Marie withdrew the pencil from Jacques' hand and made a few additions to his list. He read what she wrote, looked at her, and nodded in reply. Nicholas turned his gaze away.

Jocelyn bustled around, pushing extra chairs up to the table while she supplied them with more coffee and bread. She didn't speak, but she was watching her friends carefully. What a ghastly thing, she kept thinking, praying to God to never experience such a loss. Mentally she crossed herself and forced a smile for her guests.

They had nearly finished eating when Cassandra appeared, her clothes starched and pressed, but a tangle of long hair half-covered her sleep-glazed eyes. The four of them ate, mostly in silence. Marie kept adding things to the list, and Jacques kept jotting down a value for each item.

Everyone helped Jocelyn clean up before disappearing upstairs to gather what few belongings they had. It was a somber and beleaguered foursome that gathered around the Beaudrots' station wagon to set out for southern France. They decided to drive to the compound first and then go shopping for clothes and other essentials after they had settled in. They drove most of the night, taking turns behind the wheel.

At one point when the Beaudrots were dozing in the back seat, Nicholas was driving with Cassandra leaning on his shoulder. "Let's come back," she whispered. "I can smell the lavender all around us, but you can barely see the fields in the moonlight."

He smiled and kissed the top of her head. "We'll take the back roads and stop in every little village if you want," he promised.

Both were trying to act as normal as possible under the circumstances. For now, however, they were speeding out of Aix-en-Provence down A8, a highway that bypassed most of the country's charm. They just wanted to get where they were going.

Cassandra took a quick peek in the back seat; it looked as though Jacques and Marie were asleep. "When we get to Cuers," she said softly, "we need to figure out what we have and what we don't have. We should have all of the copies of the documents in the camera case, and most of the originals, but I wonder if the few originals I was working on survived the fire. I put what I thought was the rarest one in a metal tube that is supposed to be fireproof. Do you think one of us could go back and look around?"

Nicholas checked his speed. It was easy to go too fast through the dark countryside, with so little traffic to compare against. "The documents couldn't possibly have survived," he replied. "Copies will have to do. I took good pictures in the catacombs. If we can match the handwriting on your copies to the ones I photographed, we'll be making progress."

Cassandra sat quietly in the darkness, thinking to herself. "Do you think it's possible that at some point the person or persons who had the box could have represented a number of families at once? Many European royal families were related to each other—as that Veronese painting illustrates. Even later in history. I mean, my God, look at all those descendants of Queen Victoria! Right now, our clues suggest that many royal families benefitted from whoever was controlling the money, but there are still so many gaps. We have to figure out some kind of lineage."

"And we have to do it fast," Nicholas replied. "You mentioned that some of the evidence might be in the Vatican. How are we going to get in there? And where would the documents be? The Vatican is huge—and basically impenetrable."

"Oh, if only we knew some outrageous Catholic priest . . . ."

Nicholas could feel Cassandra's smile in the dark, and his heart swelled with feeling for her. He shook his head and chuckled low. "I cannot believe you. We've caused your cousin's house to be burned to the ground, we have no clothes, we have hardly slept, we've been driving all night to God only knows where, and you've still got a sense of humor?"

"What else can I do? Some days you're the pigeon; other days the statue."

Nicholas coughed softly to avoid laughing too loud and waking up their passengers. "I must say, if I had to choose one person in the world to run all over Europe with on some impossible quest, you'd be the one. Oh, wait," he said, struggling to sit up higher in the seat. "I think that's the sign Jacques told me to look for. We're about to get to Brignotes."

The car suddenly jolted sideways. Nicholas grabbed the steering wheel with both hands to keep the Mercedes from swerving off the highway. "What the hell is that?" Cassandra braced herself against the dashboard. Out of nowhere the car was being whipped by a wind so powerful they thought they were in a tornado.

"Pull over!" Jacques ordered from the back seat, now totally awake and gripping Nicholas' headrest. Marie sat bolt upright, holding onto the seat in front of her. "It's the Mistral," said Jacques, as though that explained everything.

Nicholas slowed down and pulled off onto the shoulder. The gritty wind blew even harder, swaying the car back and forth. "Pull up into the lee off that abutment," Jacques commanded again. Nicholas managed to maneuver the car into the shelter of a large stone outcropping, and the four passengers finally exhaled in relief.

"What's a Mistral? French for tornado?" Nicholas asked, his adrenaline still pumping.

"No, it is a straight-line wind that blows, at times, at a force 10—about a hundred kilometers per hour. It clears the air," explained Marie.

"Seems to me it'll clear anything not nailed down," replied Nicholas dryly. It was about 6:00 a.m., and by this time several other vehicles had come to a rest in the same area. The wind continued to blow mercilessly. Dawn's first light arrived in shades of gray.

"We will soon be turning south down the D43, and will have the wind at our backs. My *maman* will make big jokes about what the Mistral blew in," Jacques said dryly. "Let me drive. I have driven in it many times before. It is nothing to underestimate." Jacques got behind the wheel and pulled slowly out on to the highway, with the other vehicles following him in single file. The Brignotes cut-off came up after a couple of slow, frightening miles, and the car itself seemed to breathe a sigh of relief as the mighty wind now pushed it from behind. The wind-whipped landscape looked as barren as the desert hills of Southern California.

"And what was it again that makes this region so wonderful and special?" asked Cassandra casually. "I seem to have forgotten."

"Just wait," said Jacques. "Tomorrow you will understand. Today you will see, but you can't go outside. The Mistral is an endurance test." Only minutes later, the landscape around them was covered with lush orchards and vineyards, but every tree and vine bent southward in the violent wind. "The Mistral teaches flexibility," said Jacques with a small smile. They passed through timeless hillside villages as the land began to make its descent to the Mediterranean. Everywhere, the houses were battened down against the blast.

"Isn't this the same wind in the movie *Chocolat*?" asked Cassandra. "The same wind Peter Mayle talks about in his books? I'm afraid I don't see why people have romanticized it."

"You will see when it is over, when the sky is a color you can find only in this part of the world," Marie said with a knowing nod, squeezing Jacques' hand tightly. "And you have closed the shutters and spent the night with a great lover." She and her husband exchanged glances and she sighed deeply. No matter what happens, their eyes said, they would have each other.

"We are not far from the Beaudrots' *mas*," Jacques said, turning onto a dirt road where stood a gatekeeper's cabin with a thatched roof and walls made of compressed clay and straw. There appeared to be little sign of life behind the tightly shuttered windows. As they twisted and turned among olive orchards and grape vineyards, the wind buffeted the car each time it strayed from its north-south line. Laurels and bougainvillea lining the road bent low under the force of the wind. Only the stone barns and warehouses seemed impervious to the gusts of air.

"Those are the factories where we produce the olive oil and wine," Marie pointed out. "Jacques' family makes oil for big manufacturers, and also a boutique oil, an estate-bottled oil, I think you would say in America. The wine we drink ourselves." They passed small garden plots already plowed for spring planting, and greenhouses where seeds sprouted before being planted.

At last they drove up to the *mas* itself. The construction was typical for the region. Five low farmhouses, all built at different periods, were attached to each other, with taller end wings bracketing the construction. All the roofs sloped gently, covered with canal roof tiling—*tuiles romaines*—after the Romans who invented the system. There were no windows on the north side because of the Mistral winds, but the front offered many windows and doors into the several "houses," thus creating the compound effect. Rough stone comprised the facing on several houses, rough brick on others, and a combination on the end wings. Pergolas attached to several houses boasted huge wisteria vines about to burst into a panorama of purple and white blooms. Six huge trees with white bark stood staunchly against the wind. Slate terraces bordered by herb and rose gardens completed the compound. Jacques drove around to the front of the *mas* and pulled up onto one of the terraces just in front of what was obviously a well-used door.

Cassandra opened her car door and immediately closed it again. Despite the howling, she was still unprepared for the wind's intensity. Here in the cloistered serenity of the gardens and house, the noise was constant and unearthly, as though thousands of banshees were screaming in the air. Jacques and Marie bravely emerged from the car and, crouching low, Jacques grabbed the photography case and followed Marie inside. Nicholas and Cassandra followed, dashing through the door and closing it quickly behind them.

They found themselves in a kitchen the likes of which the Americans had never seen. The room consumed the entire first level of this particular house. The brick-floored kitchen had blue-painted *buffets-a-deux-corps* lining some of the walls and beams as massive as trees girding the ceiling. Nearly everywhere they looked were glimmering copper pots and pans. Baskets hung from every conceivable place. Racks of bottles, jars of spices, huge breadboards, and jars of utensils were everywhere. Pottery jars stuffed with patês were stuck into a ground-trough near the north wall. Cassandra stood with her mouth open and promised to herself to one day bring Francesca here. In the middle of it all stood a tall slender woman stirring a copper pot on a massive stove that dominated the center of the area.

"Look what the Mistral blew in," she said in French without much of a smile. She leaned down for kisses from Marie and back up for Jacques, still stirring. "Béarnaise sauce," she announced as if that explained everything.

They all stood smiling at her until Marie remembered her manners and introduced Jacques' mother to the Shepards. "You are welcome here," she said. She glanced around them, puzzled. "Where is your luggage?" When she remembered, she added quickly, "I'm so sorry. Marie, please take the guests to their quarters, where they can relax before breakfast."

Marie led Nicholas and Cassandra toward the next house. Between the two structures was a massive fireplace, with several cooking pots hanging on chains. Cassandra marveled at the different ovens for breads and niches for various types of woods, each one intended for a particular type of cooking fire. A wooden ledge crossed the entire width of the house and was lined with fragile porcelain vases, baskets of dried flowers, and small figurines. A table with five place settings waited for them in front of it. They ducked through one of a pair of doors and a short tunnel through the stone firewall into the next house where they would be staying.

Living areas comprised the lower floor, and an enclosed staircase wound its way lazily upstairs. Cassandra followed her cousin up the narrow stairs to their guestroom. Though shuttered, its charm was everywhere; the wind's howl only added a certain enchantment to the entire experience. Polished wooden floors glowed beneath scattered flat-weave Oriental rugs, simple whitewashed plaster walls, and a lovely bed. The burled walnut sleigh, freshly made with blue and white toile linen, was the room's centerpiece. It sat cozily beneath a *baldachin*, from which cascaded yards and yards of the same toile, enveloping the bed in a curtained shield. A cherry wood *chiffonier* occupied one corner, and through a door she saw a stunning bathroom with burnt terra-cotta tiles and a huge marble empire bathtub. A wooden plaque set into the wall held spigots for hot and cold water. Sets of fluffy white towels and robes lay across a plain wooden table next to the marble tub.

"This is simply lovely. Oh, Marie," Cassandra exclaimed, turning to give her cousin a warm hug. The embrace lingered until tears began to fill Marie's eyes and splash down her cheeks. Cassandra's were only a few seconds behind. Sucking on his lower lip and deciding it best to avoid the scene altogether, Nicholas left in search of Jacques and the photography equipment.

He found the Frenchman downstairs searching for a book in the impressive library lining one entire wall. Painted a Provençal green with a blue underlay, the top sections contained books behind brass chicken-wire doors. "My father has many books," he said running his finger along the titles. "I am sure there is one here on appraisals for insurance."

Nicholas sat down in a wing chair covered in a persimmon and chocolate plaid. This room, on the other side of the massive kitchen fireplace, had beams like the kitchen but was paneled in a blonde cypress. Sisal rugs covered the wide-plank floor, and comfortable sofas covered in persimmon chenille made the room intimate and cozy. Even though it was May, a small fire burned in the fireplace. The wind brought cold air from the Pyrenees Mountains, and all of it seemed to be hitting the north wall.

After pulling out his laptop, Nicholas opened the photography case and removed the camera disks. One by one he loaded them into his computer. "I need to print these pictures out, Jacques," he said. "It's impossible to compare them like this. Where can we find a printer?"

Jacques stopped his search, thought for a moment, and motioned him to follow. "Come with me," he said, opening a door on the other side of the room. Nicholas was startled to find himself peering into a modern, very American-looking office, complete with a fax machine, multiple computers, two printers, and several storage systems. It seemed incongruous inside the ancient house, especially with an even more ancient wind howling outside.

Nicholas stared at the contemporary setting. "Where does the electricity come from? I didn't see any lines coming in here from the highway."

"We have several large generators on the property," Jacques explained. "We are very self-sustaining. It was a necessity in earlier years. Now Toulon is reaching out to make us a suburb. In a few years, we could have city plumbing! You will recall that we have several businesses here. We have an overseas market that is nearly global now for our boutique oil. It keeps my father traveling a lot. Right now he is in Hong Kong trying to convince the remaining British chefs there that oil is better than butter."

Nicholas laughed as he loaded the printer's software, plugged in the disks with the photographs he made in the catacombs, and began printing them out. Each one seemed to take forever. "You still have to wait for technology to perform its miracles," he observed, tapping his fingers on the glass and steel desk. Just then Marie appeared at the office door to announce that breakfast was ready. Leaving the documents to print, the two men walked to the kitchen and pulled up chairs at the table in front of the fireplace, where a small blaze cut through the chill of the morning.

"*Oeufs en Croustades* à *la Béarnaise*," announced Jacques' mother, serving them pastry shells filled with a mixture of mushrooms and poached eggs in a Béarnaise sauce. She also served hot fresh croissants, honey and butter from local farmers, and as much coffee as they dared to drink. They chose between orange and grapefruit juices and melons imported from southern Italy.

"*Maman,* we are so grateful for this," said Jacques between forkfuls of food. "Nicholas is printing some documents out. We have your permission to use papa's office for a little while?" She gave Jacques a quick nod. He thanked her and turned to Nicholas. "What is your plan, my friend?"

Nicholas took a bite of his eggs and began spreading honey on a croissant. "First, I'm going to wire you 750,000 Euros for your property in Croissy," he announced smoothly. Everyone stopped eating at once; the couple stared at him. Even the stern Madame Beaudrot appeared dumbfounded as she stood there wide-eyed, coffee mug in hand.

"I absolutely insist," he continued. "I can afford it, and you can use the money to re-build." He glanced at Cassandra, whose smile blessed his decision.

At last Jacques replied, "We . . . have for many years thought about retiring to a town close by and working with these vineyards and orchards. Marie wants to open a bed and breakfast much like Jocelyn's."

Marie slapped her palm down on the table. "We accept!" she said with finality, before her husband could finish. Startled, Jacques could only smile. For the first time in two days, Marie was back to her confident self. He would accept money from the devil himself to ensure her happiness.

Cassandra and Nicholas quickly finished their meal and excused themselves. They needed to get back to work. Hunched over the computer-generated images of the documents, Cassandra began putting them in chronological order and pairing those that seemed reasonably good matches.

Nicholas, meanwhile, logged into his Web mail account. "Damn!" he said loudly, making his wife jump. "Look at this, Cassandra. It's from Galen. Malachi wants me to speak at an international symposium on economics in June in Paris." He turned and looked at her. "He wants me to call him."

"It's a trick," Cassandra replied without hesitation. "I just knew he was the sort of man who couldn't take 'no' for an answer." Nicholas held a firm frown in place, his eyes glued to his computer screen. "What are you supposed to lecture about anyway?" asked Cassandra.

"Oh, I guess about our discovery. You know, how it works and its impact on the world market. He had mentioned this before."

"Aren't you worried about going public about this right now? I mean, is it safe? After what happened to Alex, then the break-in and now Marie's house?"

Nicholas shook his head. "No, of course it's not safe."

"Nicholas," she reached out and touched his shoulder, "how are you feeling about . . . about the discovery right now?"

"Look at this place we're in!" He stretched out his arms and turned to her enthusiastically. "Out somewhere in the wilds of Provence, Jacques' family is running a global business. It's happening. Right now my thought is that this discovery is too big to keep to ourselves." Her eyes widened as he continued. "I am going to e-mail Galen and ask him to call Malachi back and tell him if we get everything straightened out, I'll consider giving the speech."

The old Nicholas was talking. She smiled widely, "And while you're at it, why don't you ask Galen if he could manage a trip to the Vatican?"

For the moment everything seemed to be falling into place. Cassandra went back to arranging the images into separate stacks. "Here," she said, pointing to a gap between two stacks. "This is what we're missing—the era of the Borgia popes. I have paperwork before and after, but nothing from about 1450 to 1500, when the Medicis and the Borgias ruled Italy and much of the Western world. Except for the Veronese painting, we have no substantial documentation from Venice during that period, either. I don't have to tell you that a lot can happen in fifty years!"

Nicholas nodded in agreement. "Ok, we need to research and fill that gap."

"I meant what I said about Galen," continued Cassandra. "Why don't we ask him to go to Rome while we go to Venice and prowl around the archives in the Doges' palace? We'll have to have an Italian translator. Think Francesca would be up for that?"

"I'll e-mail them both and see if we can't get that plan to work," answered Nicholas, tapping away on his keyboard. "I bet Francesca would be more than happy to go with us. I'll see if she can meet us in Verona. Now, what year would we be up to in terms of chronology?"

"We're nearly to the end of the eighteenth century. There are also some gaps in England—the nineteenth century, too. I suspect I'll find those in London. At least we won't have all these language issues. Thank God all the numbers in here are Arabic!"

"Speaking of Arabic, what have you got on Suleyman? You think he might have had knowledge of the box in the fifteenth century? Would the fingerprints of current oil cartels stretch back that far?"

"I doubt it, but I don't really know," she sighed. "Thanks for piling on the work."

He hugged her. "It's one hell of a mission we're on."

"First things first. We've got to go buy some clothes," she reminded him. "Then we have to plan the trip. Let's see if Jacques can find us a place to stay in Venice under those assumed identities Galen got for us." She paused for a moment, realizing what she just said. "My God, I never thought I would be asking you this, but did you bring our fake passports, dear?"

Nicholas laughed and pulled a thick envelope out of the camera case. "I put everything that was valuable in here so it would all be in one place." He handed it to her with a flourish. "We are now David and Marjorie Kamen," he laughed, humming the theme song from Mission Impossible.

She giggled. "I wonder who those people really are . . . or were . . . or if Galen made them up. They sure have our pictures on them, don't they?

We have new social security cards, and . . . wait a minute . . . ." She dumped the whole packet onto the desk. "Nicholas! It's a bankcard! A debit card on an account in Atlanta in the names of these Kamen people! Thank you, Galen, for thinking about the small details. I was beginning to wonder how we were going to get any cash. How much do you guess is in there?"

He shrugged. "I'll write to Galen and ask. Maybe he does instant messaging. What time is it there? Seven in the morning? He should be up." He typed in the codes. "Ah, he's on line. He says to tell you hello." Nicholas typed for a few more seconds, pressed enter, and waited. "He also said to tell you that Francesca is doing well. He got our message and will contact Malachi's office. Let's see how he feels about taking a trip," said Nicholas, who typed in the question and dispatched it. A few seconds later he turned back to her with a grin. "He'll be happy to go to Rome. Sounds like he was going stir-crazy house sitting. He said he can be on the next available flight."

"That's our Galen!" Cassandra replied with a little shake of her head. "Hey, ask him about the money."

Nicholas typed a question. "There's not any money in the account to speak of," he told her after thirty seconds. "He says my broker will have to wire some." Nicholas started to answer back, "Okay. I'm telling Galen I'll get in touch with my broker. I guess I'll get 1,500,000 Euros and put half into the debit card account and the other half into Jacques and Marie's bank account. That should cover everything. Oh, and Galen wants to know what his mission in Rome will be. What should I tell him?"

"Tell him I want names and handwriting samples from financial documents of the Borgia popes that have the cartouche on them. I want to know who handled the finances."

Nicholas typed out exactly what Cassandra told him and sent the message. A few seconds later they got Galen's reply: "YOU WANT ME TO DO WHAT???"

"Uh-oh, all caps. He's hollering," said Nicholas. "Can you give him any more information?"

"Tell him I think he'll have to get into the Vatican's restricted archives."

Nicholas raised his eyebrows as he typed, and then sat back and waited for another electronic eruption. He was relieved when he saw a lower-case reply appear. "He says he knows somebody who knows somebody," Nicholas read. "He also says his knowledge of papal history during the period you are asking about is the length of an inch-worm. Can you recommend a few websites or books to orient him?"

"Tell him to hold on a few minutes," said Cassandra as she put down her images and pulled out her notebook. She quickly found several outstanding academic sites and gave the addresses to Nicholas, who fired them off to Galen.

"There you are, Father," chuckled Nicholas. "Off on a merry cyber jaunt through the latter half of the fifteenth century."

"He says he'll study up and be in Rome in a couple of days. He's found a housekeeper who can take care of things in Charleston." As soon as Galen signed off, Nicholas got a reply from his broker. "Oh, good," he said. "The money will be available first thing in the morning."

Cassandra was organizing her materials when a message from Francesca came in. She would be thrilled to meet them at the Roman arena in Verona. "She says we can't miss it," repeated Nicholas. "And she'll reserve a hotel suite. Verona is a few hundred kilometers away from her and a two-day trip for us if we push it. No time for smelling any roses."

"When are we coming back here again?"

"How about in the fall, after the symposium?" Nicholas raised his eyebrows after asking the question.

"So are you seriously thinking about doing it?" she asked.

"I'm giving myself until Venice to decide."

"Good. Let's take our time, then, because I don't like it at all."

He got up and went into the kitchen for more coffee. Jacques and Marie were still sitting at the table, making plans and figuring out how many hectares they could buy. He added to their enthusiasm with the news that they would have the money the next day. They made plans to go into Cuers, buy clothes, and arrange for a vehicle so that they could drive to Italy.

Jacques offered his car, but added, "It's possible that you could be hassled about your driver's license name not matching the car registration."

"There shouldn't be a problem with anyone checking your driver's license there," Marie put in. "The Toulon-La Seyne-Hyeres triangle is the coastal Mafia capital. The highest level politicians are in jail, and so are several of the neighboring town mayors. Corruption at its best." Always the tour guide, Marie gave them her expert advice. "Toulon is an ugly town full of post-war concrete buildings. No need for you to pause there. We'll give you maps to get you to Genoa, then cross-country to Verona. That will be the quickest way."

"That is what we want, the quickest way," replied Nicholas. "We are supposed to pick Francesca up in Verona at the arena."

"You can't miss it," Marie confirmed.

Nicholas and Cassandra spent the rest of the day exploring the nooks and crannies of the Beaudrot property. Despite the hodgepodge of architectural styles, Cassandra found it charming. She loved looking at the old family photographs, which were nearly everywhere. The Beaudrot family was large, and Jacques' mother could identify every face. Jacques explained that his family purchased the property early in the 18th century, and had farmed there ever since. There were Beaudrots all over Europe now.

"But you should be here at Christmas!" he said with a grin. "We gather on the terrace and eat oysters and mussels."

"Both cooked and raw, with a lot of our own white Provençal wine," Marie added.

"The children have a visit from St. Nicholas and we go hunting wild boar," boasted Jacques.

"Yes, and one year they actually shot one!" cut in Marie as she held her hand over her mouth, trying not to laugh. "No one knew how to field dress it! Fortunately, a local butcher came to their rescue. Unfortunately, they had to give him half the boar for the service!" Everyone laughed, even Jacques.

They spent their last evening together talking about everything but the fire. Outside the Mistral continued, but by now they had grown used to its roar.

It was nearly ten o'clock when they finally headed for bed. Cassandra lit candles and bathed in the exotic marble tub. Drying herself off with one of the big fluffy towels, she slid into bed next to Nicholas and winked at him. "Shall we see what Marie meant by the romance of the Mistral?"

Sometime during the night Cassandra awoke with a start. The wind had not died down, but had simply stopped altogether. Except for Nicholas' deep breathing, the room was utterly silent. She got up, opened the shutters, and stared into the brilliant night sky. She woke Nicholas so he could see it, too. Stars studded the sky like Pavé diamonds, and the air was so sharp it seemed they could see to the ends of the universe. They sat in awe, wrapped in their warm bedclothes. When they finally fell back into bed, sleep quickly found them.

In the morning, they walked outside into a clear and brilliantly sunny day. They took a long walk to visit the greenhouses and look at the olive-oil operations, then went into Cuers to buy clothes and anything else they thought they would need.

Cassandra was surprised to find a Prada store. She grinned at Marie and pulled her inside. "Come on," she said, "you need to splurge!" When they emerged they were burdened with hangars and boxes. Jacques and Nicholas had already filled most of the trunk with their own purchases.

Nicholas took care of the banking and arranged to rent a car while Cassandra and Marie went to buy some luggage. Since they planned to leave for Italy in the morning, Cassandra wanted to get back to pack all of their new clothes and plot out a route.

The next day dawned just as bright and clear. Cassandra woke early and lay in bed staring at the ceiling. Oh, Alex, she thought with a prick of sorrow. This was just the sort of adventure he would have liked: to assume a new identity and take off through Europe searching for the box's former masters.

She gave Nicholas a little shake. "Wake up, sleepy," she said softly. "Let's go meet Francesca!"

Chapter 42

Feeling alternatively fascinated and disgusted, Galen spent nearly every waking hour of the next two days reading through websites and digging into history books at the local diocese. By the time a faceless flight attendant announced that it was time to board his Rome-bound plane, Galen almost knew enough about the Borgia popes to write his own book. Much of what he learned was new to him, and most of it he found sickening. It was as if he had just spent two days watching R-rated soap operas.

Galen was grateful for the business-class seat Nicholas had reserved for him. Folding his large frame into coach for a trans-Atlantic flight would have been torture. He settled back into the new cradle seat, put the footrest up to accommodate his long legs, and clicked open his laptop. Since he couldn't search the internet, he opened his journal—an ongoing dialogue with himself and with his God.

"I know I'm not telling You more than You know," he wrote. "But what I want to know is why on earth did You let the Church get away with it? For two days I have investigated the life of Alexander VI, not only Your pope from 1492 to 1503, but also the money man behind half a century of greed, corruption, licentiousness, and brutality. It doesn't look like he received any earthly punishment from You, unless You count his burial."

According to his diarist Burchard, when Alexander VI died of a fever, the pope's son Cesare looted the Vatican and took everything his people could carry. Servants robbed the bedroom where the dead pope reposed, and palace guards drove away the priests guarding the body. The forever loyal Burchard had the body moved to the Sistine Chapel, where it lay in the August heat. The face turned a bluish purple with pronounced black and blue dots covering it, and his lips swelled to four times their normal size. When attendants finally got around to placing him in a coffin, the corpse was so bloated it wouldn't fit. After rolling him in a piece of carpeting, they beat and pushed on the outside until the dead pontiff was squeezed inside.

"I am not sure I want to see the glory that was Rome," Galen continued, somberly, "if that's what built it. For nearly forty years I have worked for You, carrying the message of the Church, which I thought was a righteous voice. But I see that for much of its history, the Church did not speak or act with Your thoughts in mind. But of course, 'No man can know the mind of God,' as the Good Book says in Romans 11:33-36." Galen stopped for a moment before continuing. "Pope John Paul II has tried to right some of these wrongs, but even he comes up short with respect to women's roles, marriage, and birth control . . . well, You know my list. Yes, I believe You have led me to happiness, hope, and salvation through all that I have learned and taught all these years, but why hasn't the rest of the Church followed Your example? And now, now I am going to the Vatican's Secret Archives to investigate the murder of my friend and one of Your children, and I am not yet prepared to face the fact that men who worked in Your name may hold the key to my friend's death."

Galen looked at the screen in horror. Had he really just written those last lines? He had not thought about it in this way before. Even reading through the history, he had not actually associated the names with the box. He leaned his head against the seat and grimaced. If he had been at the Biltmore Estate when his friends were figuring out the purpose of the box, would he have had the strength to back away, or would he too have been tempted?

Father Galen had spent his life counseling fellow priests and other members of the clergy because they led such conflicted lives. These pillars of the community, these vessels of the Lord, they carried a lot of baggage their congregations would never know about. The centers he founded were ecumenical, funded by many denominations, and even many religions. This was his calling, and he did it well. Hardliners saw him as a renegade, but his success was beyond dispute, so the Church quietly encouraged him even when it knew he was outside the pale.

Until now, Church history had not held much interest for him. After reading deeply of Alexander VI's escapades, however, he began to see the past in a more contemporary light. He knew firsthand how the Borgia children were raised to manipulate, cheat, lie, and steal because this was what Galen witnessed every day. But he hated to be reminded that the Church was equally as corrupt and unrepentant. To be honest, he was not happy to be dabbling in ancient Church history. He preferred dealing with human imperfections he could *do* something about, today. These wicked deeds of the past had no place in his ministration of hope and renewal.

So he harbored much trepidation when he pulled up in an Italian taxi at the small apartment not far from the Vatican. His friend, Carlo Sforzi, had made the rental arrangements and left a key beneath the doormat. Three flights up on the top floor, the apartment overlooked a crowded street lined with shop buildings and the same small apartments above them. His windows were tall and arched and, together with twelve-foot ceilings, made the small rooms appear rather grand. Antique-plastered white walls lent it a spare feeling, and a small altar with a wooden cross stood in one corner of the living room. Galen tossed his suitcase on the sofa, knelt at the altar, and said the office for Compline by heart. He meditated until he realized it was growing dark outside.

Galen switched on a lamp and walked about the little flat. Two rooms with a view. A miniature kitchen took up one wall of the living room, which also offered a well-worn armchair and a nondescript wooden desk with an equally plain table lamp. The bedroom was furnished with nothing but a metal bed and squat wooden bureau. Galen nodded in satisfaction. This was top notch—scrubbed clean and simple. He figured that in the days to come he would see enough opulence to last a lifetime. Coming home to this would be an absolute relief.

When he opened the small refrigerator he was delighted to find a fresh loaf of Italian peasant bread and some good salami. A reasonably good Chianti Classico waited for him on the counter, and he ate and drank with deep gratitude for his thoughtful friend.

Galen woke the next morning to the sound of traffic and bustling people in the street. He dressed quickly, donning a heavy unbleached linen robe with a hood. He was about to slip on his shoes when he realized he had nothing to wear but his alligator cowboy boots. Galen thought for a moment, shrugged, and pulled them on. At least no one in the Vatican would forget him! Sliding some guidebooks into his knapsack, he shot one more look around the austere rooms and took a deep breath. Time to go into the lion's den, he said to himself with a chuckle.

His friend Carlo had recommended he rent a Vespa motor scooter, which would be easy to navigate through the city's heavy traffic and even easier to park. He didn't take into account how ridiculous the large priest would look straddled on the tiny machine, especially with his robe flapping behind him. Galen didn't mind; every ounce of self-consciousness disappeared as the splendor of St. Peter's came into view. Stopping in the middle of the square, he drank in the golden color, the colonnaded cloisters, the incredible statuary and the dome, beneath which the apostle Peter is said to be buried. The sun was just rising over the plaza, drenching the old stones with its warm roseate rays. He lifted his eyes and turned in a slow circle, spellbound. Surrounding him was a circle of 140 statues, saints all, perched on top of the circular colonnades. It was as if he was at the pinnacle of thousands of years of history, a living presence around him. Inside, he felt as though he would soon have a role in that history, though he knew not what or how.

He sped down the *via di Porta Angelica* and turned left on *Viale Vaticano*. His route took him past the Leonine Walls, once a last defense against the Saracen invaders, and through the Gate of St. Anne. He traversed an arched road past the *Osservatore Romano* to the Belvedere Courtyard, where the Secret Archives are housed. Where to begin? He wondered. After parking the cycle, Galen entered the building and looked around for his guide. With more than two thousand rooms to negotiate, he would need a good one. A Swiss guard approached him and asked for his pass. He would have to show it three times to as many guards before he was finally introduced to his escort, Father Thomaso.

The Father shook his hand warmly. "We have heard of your work here," he said in impeccable English. Galen's eyes widened in pleasant surprise. "We are especially impressed by your work with America's troubled priests. Your humility and dedication pleases his Eminence."

Galen cleared his throat in embarrassment. He didn't want Thomaso to see that he was caught off guard. But, the pope! He was amazed the

Holy See had been monitoring his work—especially since, as Galen saw it, he had barely scratched the surface. He bowed his head and sent the pope his best wishes and sincere thanks for the blessing.

Thomaso's eyes twinkled. He had shocked this big hulk of a priest. He held out his hand in an invitation for Galen to follow him. The guide priest was as tall as Galen but as thin as a rail, his black robes swirling around his long legs as he walked. Galen thought they were probably the same age, but as he strolled along side he saw that the priest's face was deeply creased with fine lines. *That is what living in this place does to you,* he thought irreverently.

They approached a statue of the 3rd-century antipope Hippolytus, which Pope John XXIII had installed at the entrance to the Vatican Library. Galen walked slowly, taking in the architecture and painting. Every square inch of wall was adorned. The libraries and Secret Archives were housed in the Tower of the Winds and two long corridors. As they made their way down one of them, Galen took in the hundreds of tall units made of beautiful exotic woods and, behind them, sliding panels hiding thousands of books, manuscripts, and documents. The upper walls blazed with paintings of diplomatic history. The simultaneously impressive and intimidating building was casting its spell over Galen; everywhere he looked were the stories of humankind—its effort to live in peace set against its quest for power.

"This corridor leads to the Borgia apartments, which now house some of the Vatican's most beautiful art treasures," explained Thomaso, making a half-turn and lifting his thin arm to his right. "And here is what was once the Borgia Popes' private chapel," he continued, pointing to a painting on one wall. It was the infamous Lucrezia, Alexander VI's daughter, arguing with philosophers. She had blonde hair and looked like a nymph. *No wonder Alexander VI was able to marry her off three times*, Galen thought. He scoured the painting looking for the cartouche, but it was nowhere to be found.

The priests continued on, walking through a large room called the Hall of the Parchments, where thousands of documents relating to the rights of the papal state were housed. Beyond was a room holding inventories and indexes. Father Thomaso stopped, faced Galen, and smiled. "Now, Father Galen, what may I help you find?"

"I'm looking for financial documents from the papacy of Alexander VI," he answered as he contemplated the enormous, handwritten volumes. Some were so heavy it took two people to lift them.

Thomaso nodded as if the request was not out of the ordinary. "I will introduce you to the prelate who oversees all the libraries. He will need to give you special permission to access some of the ancient documents. Follow me."

The priest led Galen down a stairway to the ground floor. It was the most modern part of the archives, and lined with large steel bookshelves from America. Electric lights automatically clicked on and clicked off again as they moved through. The floating pools of light and endless corridors made Galen feel as if he was starring in a spy movie or perhaps an action thriller. His guide pointed out the records of the Consistory, an ecclesiastical senate of cardinals, and the seven thousand volumes of petitions requesting every kind of papal grace and favor. Archives of Roman families were here also, as were the records of the Sacred Rota, an ecclesiastical court. The priest showed Galen a great safe, whose drawers contained the most precious documents of all.

"Here is a bit of your English history," said Thomaso. He opened a drawer to reveal the last letter ever written by Mary Stuart—Mary Queen of Scots—addressed to Pope Sixtus V. It was inked in French just days before her head fell to Elizabeth's axe. The parchment conveyed her acceptance and defiance of her death sentence. "*I, born of kings, I alone have remained, of the blood of England and Scotland, to profess this faith . . . I must prepare myself to receive death . . . I commend to you my son. . . Bidding you my last adieu. . ."*

Caught up in its power, Galen's eyes poured over the remarkable document. "My eyes are not as good as they once were—may I, Father?" he asked, pulling out a small penlight from his pocket. Thomaso shrugged and nodded at the same time. At the bottom of the letter the handwriting became more irregular. "*Please take care that after my death the enemies of the Church do not calumniate me. . ."*

Galen shined the narrow beam on the paper and peered beneath the handwriting. *Oh my God!* he thought, swallowing hard as he gripped the narrow pen in his hand, fearful it would fall from his shaking fingers. Though faint, the cartouche was clearly evident. He felt a surge of adrenaline.

Should he tell his guide that that was what he was looking for, or should he keep quiet? He compromised. "Do you have more documents like this?"

The priest pursed his slender lips. "When you say 'like this,' I am not exactly sure what you mean," answered Thomaso as he walked a few steps to his left and carefully slid open several more drawers. Inside were the futile petitions of seventy-five English lords, under seventy-five wax seals the size of tea saucers, asking the Pope to give Henry VIII and Catherine of Aragon an annulment. Another drawer held love letters from King Henry to Ann Boleyn, so tender and sweet that Galen could not believe what he was reading. He had always thought of Henry as a self-serving lout; discovering another side of the infamous king was rather humbling. Galen scanned them all carefully, but there was nothing on them of interest.

Thomaso slid open another drawer, which yielded a letter from Thomas Howard, Third Duke of Norfolk and one of Henry VIII's Lords Treasurer. Galen bent over the parchment and scanned it quickly. Near the bottom right-hand corner was the cartouche, still bold and sharp after all these centuries. Galen took meticulous mental notes of whose papers bore the symbol.

Finally, Thomaso showed Galen the dogma of the Immaculate Conception, bound in pale blue velvet and illuminated in pale pastels. Galen was stunned to see it. He knew that the dogma arose out of the early Church's efforts to inculcate the belief that Christ is divine, a concept with which he himself had wrestled with for many years. Finally he had come to accept Christ's divinity, along with the Immaculate Conception, as essential to his own faith. Seeing the dogma with his own eyes sent a chill down his spine and his arms erupted with goose bumps. He didn't know how long he stared at it, lost in contemplation, before he remembered his mission.

They ascended a small twisting circular staircase to the oldest sections of the archives, which opened off the Tower of the Winds. The ancient tower had served as an astronomical observatory during the Baroque period. Here, in this almost inaccessible place, Paul V Borghese had set up the archives in the early 17th century. Here also lay the Miscellanea, which filled fifteen enormous closets.

Inside was the prelate. He was a very old man, completely bald and dressed in a white Benedictine monk's robe. When the two priests entered, he was busy studying an old piece of parchment. Thomaso introduced Galen to the prelate, who looked him over from head to foot with more than a touch of aloofness. Satisfied, he wrote down his special permission on his own letterhead, handed it to Galen without a word, and returned to his parchment. Galen thanked him as Thomaso led him back to the winding stair, which ascended to the top of the Tower before dumping them into the empty room of the Meridian. Galen had never seen anything like it. Frescoes of the winds as godlike figures in flowing garments adorned the walls. On the floor was a zodiacal diagram oriented to the sun's rays entering the room through a slit in the wall.

"It is here that the Gregorian calendar was worked out," Thomaso told him. Galen nodded slowly, listening to the room's history as he looked up at the ceiling. A moving pointer, ringed by dozens of flying cherubs and clouds, indicated the wind's direction. He could literally feel the movement of time in this room, and yet how difficult it must have been to figure out precisely how it worked.

"Below us, in the room where the prelate is working," continued Thomaso, "we have the document Galileo signed admitting his guilt to the inquisitors. The Church was wrong to accuse Galileo, and we are glad His Eminence has corrected the error." The thin priest offered a toothy smile that Galen happily returned. Thomaso touched Galen's arm gently. "Come, let us return to the Hall of the Parchments so you can continue your research."

As they retraced their steps to the Hall of the Parchments, the white-robed prelate lifted his eyes to watch Galen, who found it difficult to avoid his cold stare. The eyes remained locked on the younger priest in the Alligator boots until he was out of sight. Galen felt uneasy until they reached their destination. "Here you are, Father," said Thomaso. "I will return later to check up on you."

Galen thanked him profusely, but was happy to see him go. It was time to get to work. Since he was armed with a small digital camera, he was happy Thomaso had not insisted on remaining by his side. He walked along one wall, running his fingers along the spines of oversized books until he found the one he was seeking.

Sunlight spilled through the high windows and the angels painted on the ceiling hovered above him as he pulled the heavy book from its shelf and set it down carefully on a tabletop. He blew a cloud of dust from its leather binding. No one had thumbed through it in ages. After a quick check failed to reveal a surveillance camera, he carefully opened the book, which creaked and groaned as the hinges stretched open. Inside were Thomas Howard's letters.

These documents, as well as letters from Henry VIII, were stolen after Henry's death and taken to the Vatican as a weapon to combat England's break from the Mother Church. He snapped a few pictures even though none bore the telltale cartouche. Maybe Cassandra could use them somehow; certainly she would find them interesting.

After thumbing through the volume without success, he slipped it back on the shelf and continued his search. He was looking for Alexander VI's documents. After a few false starts, he hit a gold mine. *Looking up at him on document after document was the cartouche.*

For thirty-four years, between his uncle Callixtus' reign as Pope and his own, Rodrigo Borgia had managed the papacy's finances. He endured through four popes before managing to purchase the title for himself and selecting the name Alexander VI. It was a blatant act of simony, a practice he himself immediately outlawed upon his ascendancy in 1492. Galen paused and frowned. That was the year Spain's Queen Isabella and King Ferdinand commissioned Columbus to sail to the New World. Not long after Columbus left, the royal duo began throwing the Jews out of their country. The next step was the Inquisition. He growled softly to himself. Centuries have passed, and Spain is still trying to emerge from that unholy repression.

Did that exodus relate somehow to the search at hand? Galen pursed his lips and thought for a moment. Many of the Jews, intellectuals, and financiers who had made Spain a wealthy country migrated to Italy, France, England, and across the Byzantine Empire. Pope Rodrigo took advantage of the opportunity to establish the Jews from this diaspora as financial counselors for both himself and his family. The Sephardim, as they came to be called, imbued the rest of the high Renaissance with their culture and sophistication. Meanwhile, Alexander VI acquired a vast fortune. Power, wealth, and brutality marked the route of the papacy through the ages.

Looking around to make sure he was still alone, Galen began taking pictures of the parchments. All were written in Italian, and most were sealed with the cartouche. He flipped through them, one after the other, until he ran out of disk space. *Damn!* he thought to himself. *He had forgotten to bring along a second backup disk.* He could delete some pictures from memory, but he had no idea which documents were more important than others.

With his camera full, Galen carefully returned the books to their shelves and waited patiently for Thomaso to return, occupying himself with the beautiful illuminated manuscripts on reading stands placed about the room. He hoped the priest could not hear his heart pounding in his chest.

Footsteps echoed on the marble floor. "Would you like to see the Borgia apartments?" Thomaso asked, coming up behind him. Galen nodded enthusiastically.

"Many people spend years in these archives," his guide went on, "while others, like you, are here only for a day or two looking for specific documentation. You may not know this, but the 'secret' designation of these archives hearkens back to the days when 'secret' meant 'private'. The popes initiated the archives simply as church records, but they have now acquired their special status because we do not welcome the press or anyone only interested in . . . scandal."

Galen smiled at Thomaso. *Does he know of my search? Was there another meaning here beyond the words he uttered?* "The collection is so immense," Galen remarked, licking his dry lips. "Has anyone ever attempted a complete index of the holdings?"

"It is a work in progress," the tall priest assured him.

They walked down the Sistine Hall, groin-vaulted and colonnaded, lit by sunny windows, and completely painted with frescoes of various popes. A twist and several more turns led to the Borgia apartments, housing some of the most stunning art treasures in the world. Galen wandered and stared, ostensibly looking at the artwork, which Thomaso knew intimately and discoursed about at length. When Galen's brain could accommodate no more, he asked to see the Sistine Chapel.

"Of course," responded his guide. "Please follow me."

As they passed through a doorway, Galen looked up at the carved lintel crowning it and stopped dead in his tracks. His mouth fell open and his breathing grew shallow as his hands rose involuntarily until they covered both of his ample cheeks. "Oh . . . my!" he said out loud.

Thomaso turned and looked at him. "Father? Are you alright?"

Galen struggled to collect himself. "Yes, Father. I'm fine." He swallowed hard. "Fine," he repeated.

Thomaso retraced his steps. Once beside Galen, he followed the American priest's gaze to the carving above the doorway. "This lintel carving interests you?" he asked softly.

Galen nodded as they both took in the giant-sized cartouche. *The cartouche is the entire lintel! A picture is worth a thousand words*, Galen thought. *Too bad I can't take one.*

"Hmm," shrugged Thomaso. "Given all the splendor and beauty here, I never found it particularly appealing. But then, that is the wonder of art and its effect on each of us!"

At this hour the Sistine Chapel was closed to visitors, so Galen had it to himself except for a privately arranged tour group, which was preparing to leave as he and Thomaso entered. This famous chapel took his breath away. For once in his life Galen was speechless. The reaction did not surprise Thomaso, for the chapel had affected him the same way the first time he saw it. He backed out of the room to allow the American his privacy.

Galen spun around slowly, taking in Michelangelo's figures in all their glorious color. This was the most compelling reason for faith Galen had ever seen. The Bible's stories came to life on that ceiling. The rear altar wall was covered entirely with *The Last Judgment*. Galen fell to his knees before it. Four hundred figures in various stages of damnation radiated in circles from the central figure of a powerful, judging Christ.

"*Dies Irae*," said Galen out loud. "The wrath of God."

The artist's melted self-portrait in the hands of St. Bartholomew intrigued him, as did the resigned acceptance of the Virgin, floating with her hands crossed over her breast next to the Christ. He looked at the writhing bodies and faces heading for Charon's boat and the depths of Hell. Michelangelo's own religious struggles were captured here: the naked and the dead, without any of life's possessions and with souls in torment, facing the terror of eternity.

Galen didn't even notice that tears were running down his face until he touched his cheek. When he looked down at the tears on his fingers, he began to weep.

Chapter 43

 Malachi walked around his office holding the phone in one hand and waving his other hand in exasperation. Smoke from the cigar burning between his fingers swirled around him as he spoke.

"The box was obviously *not* in the burned house! You would have found some evidence of it otherwise," he said sharply. "That means they either have it with them or it is here. Or, it could even be in Italy. How is that for narrowing it down?"

Stretched out on Coco Chanel's silken bed wearing only a light robe and a sheer thong, Mika moved the phone away from her ear. "Malachi, we are . . ."

He angrily cut her off. "Where are the Beaudrots and Shepards now? I asked you that, and your answer was 'gone.' God damn it, 'gone' is not a good answer. Track them down!" He paused, collecting his thoughts. "And before you leave Paris, set up that conference. We will publicize it as the First Annual World Economics Symposium, and bill Dr. Shepard as a brilliant economist with a revolutionary theory on the stock market that will take the world by storm."

Mika had been working with Malachi too long to be upset by his outbursts. It amused her to think that he had no idea how she was dressed. She barely caught herself as a giggle broke free from her throat.

"What the hell was that?" asked Malachi.

"Nothing. A small cough," she answered. "I'll set it up, but what makes you think he will agree?"

Malachi hesitated. Was Mika laughing about all this? He steeled his voice. "Because I saw his face when I mentioned the Nobel Prize to him. Get a conference room at the Ritz for 250 people for the weekend of June 13, with all the bells and whistles. Make sure catering puts on its $200-a-head dinner. I want a free bar. Reserve 200 rooms. I want the

Ernest Hemingway Suite. When you get back, you can take care of the invitations, make the calls, and start the publicity."

She raised one leg into the air, studying its superb shape, flexing muscles and pointing her toes. "It will be done," she said simply and hung up the phone.

Mika had called her special escort service to let them know they would have a geisha available for the evening. She smiled serenely and began the elaborate ritual of transforming herself into the ancient Japanese female entertainer.

She paused for a moment in front of the mirror and frowned: *no, she wasn't going to think about Alex tonight.* This was a secret that she had kept even from him. He never knew that he was the only man who had ever made love to just Mika. It was as pure a thing as she had ever experienced. She had never felt so happy and so vulnerable. But she was spiraling out of control and knew that it was suicide to continue with him. He was hurt terribly when she broke it off. She made him swear never to tell anyone of their affair, and even threatened him if he did. Alex had stared at her in surprise, for he had never seen that side of her. His anger had faded quickly, and he just shook his head sadly.

"You take yourself too seriously, Mika," he said as he turned to leave. She hated him for his pity.

Given his own state of turmoil, Mika's veil of unruffled calm irritated Malachi more than usual. He had more to say, and *she* hung up the phone, ending the conversation? Something was wrong with his Japanese personal assistant. *But what?*

He bit down gently on the end of his Don Alejandro, which by this time had gone out. Striking a match, he lit the cigar and puffed it vigorously as he slid open his top drawer and began sifting for the hundredth time through Mika's file. His eyes fell upon what they had seen before: a double Ph.D., a stellar career in astrophysics and aeronautical engineering, and a triple-A credit report, along with the usual information from his federal sources. It annoyed him. There had to be something else. He placed a telephone call to an investigative service he had on retainer.

"Get me everything you can on Mika Hunter," he barked. "Set yourself up as the firm's official biographer. Interview her childhood friends and relatives—everybody she's ever talked to. Make sure she doesn't find out about it, or you've seen your last check in this country."

He hung up abruptly. It was time to do something a little more cheerful. He pulled up his address book on his computer and put in a call to Sir Andrew Willoughby Ninian Bertie in London.

"Bertie? Malachi Foust. How are you?"

"What? Malachi?" repeated the raspy-voiced Brit. "I'm as well as advancing age will let me be. How are you, you old sod?"

Malachi smiled. "I am fine. Have you chosen your successor yet?"

"Don't be impertinent, young man; I'm not in the grave yet am I?" Sir Bertie blew a wheezy sigh into the phone. "Funny you should ask, though. I was thinking on that very subject when you called. I suppose I will leave that decision to the Group. They have shown infinite wisdom since the twelfth century. Who am I to abrogate that tradition?" Both men joined in with a hearty laugh.

Malachi winced when the old man's laugh changed into a disgusting gurgling noise as the ninety-year-old cleared his throat. "What sort of troubles have you got us into with those American markets?"

The younger man sighed. "Everyone seems to think that I will actually make a mistake one day, but I am glad to report that the markets couldn't be better. We managed to capture the exact bottom last March, as the significant gains in your portfolio clearly demonstrate." Malachi paused for a second to let his response sink in before continuing. "We have an interesting development stirring in current econo-physics, Bertie."

"A development? Did you say development? And what is that?" asked the old man.

"It appears that a certain academician thinks that he has found the secret to predicting the stock market by using an exogenous input. Not only are his theories insulting to traditional economics, but they could be a threat to the stability of investor confidence on an international level."

Sir Bertie was silent for several seconds. "And what do you propose to do about this?"

"That's one of the reasons I'm calling," explained Malachi. "I want the Group to sponsor an economics symposium in Paris in June. We need to take a leadership position on our global expansion. I am engaging this academician as keynote speaker. Will you be able to attend?"

Sir Bertie offered a quavering sound that approached a thin laugh. "If I am above ground, old chap. Every new morning looks pretty good these days. What does this keynote speaker know that you do not?"

Malachi stiffened at the unintended insult. "Actually, nothing. I want to use him as a platform to launch the Group as the global leader on economic policies. If we can make him look like a lunatic, it will go a long way toward guaranteeing our own legitimacy, and any final resistance to our global expansion should melt away like snow in summer."

Malachi paused. It was time to unfold the rest of his plan—up to a point, anyway. "Sir Bertie, you know how well we succeeded in devastating the Asian markets and holding their collective heads in the toilet, so to speak. Well, based on the indications I've been getting from their leaders, now is the time to pull them back out and welcome them as new partners to the Group."

"Indeed?" Sir Bertie fairly chirped. Malachi could hear him fiddling with his hearing aid. "Are you saying the time has come to move?"

"I think so," Malachi replied. "After a thousand years of controlling the financial systems of the West, I believe the time has come to embrace our partners in Asia and the Pacific Rim. But let me make it clear: if the radical theorems of Dr. Shepard are given any credence, our expansion could be delayed indefinitely or destroyed forever. We must denounce him utterly. At the same time, we will have created a forum to advance our plans for the Asian introduction."

Malachi listened as the Englishman babbled on about world markets. Sir Bertie knew a lot about the operation, and he certainly grasped that there were huge profits to be reaped from the Asian expansion and the emergence of China. But he did not know everything. Malachi and Mika alone knew the secret to the technology that held trillions of dollars at their disposal. Of course, the old man did not know the upstart professor had zeroed in on this information, or that he posed a dire and direct threat to the Group's very existence.

Malachi closed his eyes as he enjoyed the stirring in his loins. No woman had ever excited him like raw power. The strength of the Group, which had been making and destroying kings, emperors, and presidents since the 12th century, was now in Malachi's iron grip. This ascendancy was his centuries-old inheritance. Control of the world's wealth was Malachi's destiny—a destiny now threatened by an obscure economist from a second-rate university. Bertie must never know how desperate Malachi was to crush Nicholas Shepard.

A slow smile crossed Malachi's face, as he interrupted the old man with his edict, "Sir Bertie, it is in the Group's best interest that we successfully destroy Nicholas Shepard."

Sir Bertie was quiet for a second. "I have heard of Dr. Shepard. In fact, I have even read some of his articles in the *Journal of Economic History*, and I know that he is well-respected, thought somewhat . . . *avant-garde*, as they say. We will have to call a meeting of the principals; this must be a Group decision."

"Excellent," responded Malachi gleefully. "We will meet here in my office next week."

Sir Bertie coughed gently several times. "The Order has a great deal of work to do in the Middle East," he said carefully.

"I can clear funding for those projects if you can help me persuade the others it is time to move." Malachi held the cards, of course, but it was always wiser to play the game out.

"Consider it done, old chap. Cheerio!" Sir Bertie rang off, satisfied that he had done his part.

Malachi sat with one hip on the side of his desk, contemplating the revised New York skyline. He missed those towers every day. In his mind, they had represented his own supremacy: tall, strong, prominent. And to think a pair of measly jet planes had brought them tumbling down in ruin. The work Bertie's Order was doing in the Middle East would provide sufficient salve for that wound. *If Bertie's on board, the rest will fall like dominoes*, he thought. The phone call was well worth the time.

A few keystrokes and a list of the committee members, headed by Sir Bertie, appeared on his screen. *Seventy-eighth Grandmaster of the Sovereign Military Order of Malta*, he read, scrolling down through the dossiers of Bertie and his seventy-seven predecessors.

He touched another key and brought up a history of the Order, which Malachi always enjoyed reading. It was the fourth oldest religious order of Christendom, preceded only by the Basilians, Augustinians, and Benedictines. The Sovereign Military Hospitaller Order of St. John of Jerusalem, Rhodes, and Malta traced its origins to Jerusalem before the first crusade. Known to most as the Hospitallers, the organization bonded early with the Knights Templar, a monastic order of knights founded in 1112 A.D. to provide protection for pilgrims traveling from Europe to Jerusalem. Together, the two formed a unified force for the defense of Christian states in the Levant against Muslim attacks. Their strength lay in their combination of military, chivalric, religious, and Hospitaller skills. When Philip the Fair of France dissolved the Templars, he executed many, but those who escaped took up the cause of the Hospitallers, to whom Philip granted much of the amassed wealth of the Templars. German Templars joined the Hospitallers as the Teutonic Knights. In Portugal, the Templars simply changed their name to the Knights of Christ. In Spain, France, and England, Templars joined similar military orders, or fled to Switzerland, where they once again put to use their talents at international banking.

"Today's Knights of Malta carry on the Hospitaller mission of the Order all over the world," Malachi read. As its financier, Malachi made no apology for the fact that the Order's good works depended on ill-gotten money. For him, the harmony of the world lay in doing evil and painting its face with the smile of charity. It made the game that much more interesting to play. He called his wife to let her know they would be entertaining the leaders of the Group the following week, and then punched in another number.

"Had enough?" he said into the telephone.

Ernest von Stuyvesant grunted. Thanks to Malachi, his investment portfolio had been decimated by fully 25 percent in a matter of a few weeks. He had been going to his office every day with a pale face and tight-pursed lips, and the only thing he would say to his accountants was that he expected better weather shortly.

"Perhaps I can loosen those screws," Malachi went on jovially. "Has the wife tossed you out yet?"

"You sound far too pleased with yourself, Malachi. You must want something," Ernest said sourly.

"A small favor. I would like to convince the Rockefeller Foundation that the time has come to complete our Eastern expansion."

"That'll cost you a full recovery of my portfolio's value."

Malachi hesitated. The markets had been moving according to forecast recently, and he really didn't want to mess them up to do any personal favors for Ernest. "I'll leverage you some futures contracts that should get you back to even in due time."

Ernest wasn't buying. "I want it all back—as of the day you started robbing me last quarter," he insisted, pushing his luck, but knowing the expansion into Asia was at the top of Malachi's agenda.

"Done," said Malachi graciously. "Now get to work." He heard a sigh of relief on the other end of the phone and smiled as he hung up.

ℬ

Within a few days, a small assemblage of world leaders arrived in New York. The financial press took little notice until a retired prominent British diplomat and the former American Secretary of Defense turned up at Malachi's office at the same time. Intrigued, a veteran investigative writer with *The Weekly Standard* begin digging into government travel logs only to discover that a former German Chancellor, France's previous ambassador to the United Nations, and several European princes were also visiting the same office building on successive days. Malachi was seeing each individually before the general meeting. He took advantage of the press' curiosity and directed Mika to publicize the upcoming conference.

The entire executive board of the Group met on Thursday in Malachi's conference room. The massive antique rosewood table would seat two dozen, but he managed to squeeze in several more.

"Ladies and Gentlemen," he began, his eyes meeting each of the attendees. "Thank you for coming on such short notice. To recapitulate briefly: we initiated our Asia plan in the early 1990s, and in the succeeding years we successfully destroyed their markets, as well as their economic confidence. We used our own wealth to short their international stock funds here at our exchanges and in the exchanges of their respective countries, and we doubled our investments in the process. We so severely manipulated their interest rates that Japan and other countries reduced their rate to zero in panicked reaction, trying desperately to shore up falling confidence. In the end, we managed to hold their markets flat. The effect destroyed their real estate values and reduced them to nearly third-world status."

He presented a brief smile and continued with barely a pause. "It is interesting to note that traditional economics is no match for our technical advances. It is only a matter of time before we can claim to have done the impossible—which is to conquer the financial world. The final Asian shoe will drop soon, and we will ride in on white horses as saviors of its financial future. Our dominance will be complete when we welcome our thankful Asian brothers to our table as members of the Group.

"It is with this vision in mind that I call your attention to a small but potentially significant problem. You are all aware that we have stifled all research in economic time series trying to find predictability in financial markets. Unfortunately . . . an economics professor from a Southern university claims to have discovered a formula that could afford market predictability to any economist. I have studied his theories, which I find radical to an absurd degree, but his arguments could nevertheless stimulate interest among our Asian friends. Worst case, their investigation of these theories could delay our expansion for months or even years, until they have exhausted their research and come back to us for help."

He paused and sipped quietly from a glass of water. He had their undivided attention. "I am suggesting we set up a forum in Paris in June in order to feature the work of this economist."

"Who is he?" asked one of the European princes.

"His name is Dr. Nicholas Shepard. Our real mission, with the aid of the willing and always pliant press, will be to disgrace the good doctor and expose his theories to public scorn and ridicule. The fallout will be that the world's economists will once again trumpet the infallibility of the 'random walk' theory."

"I should like to read up on this Dr. Shepard," said another member.

"My staff has all the pertinent material for you to review, and with no further delay I will proceed with the organization of the symposium and the initiation of our expansion into Asia."

Chapter 44

"Oh, no! Not again!" Cassandra moaned. She was hanging on to the arm rest for dear life as she dizzily peered over cliffs leading down to the blue waters of the Mediterranean. Nicholas was driving, zipping his way around several hairpin turns along highway N98, a scenic stretch of road that runs the length of the Coté d'Azur.

"At least there aren't any ice storms and rock slides," he replied cheerfully.

"It certainly is beautiful," she admitted, relaxing her grip on the door handle only slightly. "I've never seen so many flowers, and look at how those villages are just carved into hillsides. Oh, for heaven's sake, look down there. It's exactly like the picture in this guide book."

"Sorry," Nicholas replied. "I'm too busy wondering how James Bond drove so fast on these roads."

"He didn't, dummy. They sped up the film. They did the same thing for Indiana Jones under that truck in *Raiders of the Lost Ark*."

"There's no way to make good time this way. We have to go over more mountains outside of Genoa. I think we should fly to Verona." Nicholas strained his neck to look at a passing sign. "Well, we're already to Cannes." Suddenly the roadway was jammed with vehicles, many of them limousines. "I wonder what's going on?" he asked.

Cassandra consulted her guidebook. "Oops!" She gave him a baleful smile. "It's the Cannes Film Festival. Every rich and famous person on the planet is here for two weeks in May. Maybe we'll see some Hollywood stars."

"Don't count on it," Nicholas grumbled. "Besides, all we're going to see is the back of these limos. There's a sign for the A8. I'll get on that and bypass this place."

"You sound like we're back in Atlanta, complaining about rush-hour traffic instead of driving through one of the most scenic places on earth."

"You're right. Sorry. Any ideas about where we should put up for the night?"

"How about a bed and breakfast in Monaco?"

"Sounds good. See what you can find in your guidebooks. A8 takes us straight there."

Cassandra skimmed for a couple of minutes until she found just what she was looking for. "Oh, yes, yes, yes!" she hissed between clenched teeth through an exaggerated smile. "This is perfect. Le Chateau Eza-Eze, in the town of Eze, a five-star hotel with only ten rooms. It was the residence of the Swedish royal family between 1927 and 1957. It sits on top of a rock 1,300 feet above the sea. I'll give them a call and see if I can book it. The town itself is medieval. Take the Moyenne Corniche–RN 7. Eze is ten minutes west of Monaco."

A few minutes later they were on the narrow winding road leading to Eze, a town that seemed to exist in a completely different world from that of the grand and sophisticated resorts of the Coté d'Azur. The inn was actually a small castle that looked like it had erupted from the rock just above the town. Cassandra craned her neck to see up the tiny ancient cobblestone street.

The concierge welcomed them in Provençal, a quirky dialect Cassandra handled reasonably well. They checked in as Mr. and Mrs. Kamen, and the bellman took their luggage to a suite with a wide and deep balcony overlooking the sea. The bedroom featured one of the most exotic beds they had ever seen, with a canopy formed by rococo masses of wrought-iron tendrils, arches and curves. It was a beautiful room with high arched ceilings and massive rough-hewn wooden beams. Ancient tapestries lined the walls and fresh flowers enlivened every room. The opulent bath seemed to have been designed for Roman sybarites.

After demonstrating how to turn the lights off and on, the bellman opened a massive armoire on one side of the room to display a plasma television, which he clicked on. "CNN," he announced with evident pride. The couple stared. There was Daryn Kagen giving them the morning news.

"*Vous etes Americains, oui?*" he asked at their startled laughter.

Cassandra explained to him that they had not seen or heard American television for weeks, and it seemed strange and out of place. When he left, Nicholas picked up the remote and began flipping through the channels to find Fox News. After searching without success, he surfed back to CNN and fell into an antique *fauteuil*. Cassandra joined him in the matching armchair.

"In financial news," said Kagen, "Well-known New York financier Malachi Foust is entertaining some very high-powered friends this week. Let's go to Wall Street and check in with our reporter there. Andrea?"

"Jesus!" exploded Nicholas as he leapt to his feet. "They just mentioned Malachi!"

"Good morning, Daryn. Everybody who is anybody in the financial world is meeting this week with Mr. Foust, who says he is planning a world economics summit in Paris this summer. He won't reveal the identity of his keynote speaker, but promises he will shatter all our illusions about the stock markets." CNN switched to a clip from an interview with Malachi.

Cassandra leaned forward and pushed Nicholas to one side, her eyes glued to the screen. "So, *that's* the infamous Malachi Foust!"

"Shh!" He scolded, "we need to hear what he had to say."

"No, I'm sorry," said Malachi with a broad white-toothed smile and playful shake of his head. "I'm not prepared to give you the name of the speaker at this time. But I can assure you that his theories are extraordinary, and I am eager for him to share them with this esteemed audience."

Back in the studio, Daryn was talking with the reporter who had interviewed Malachi. "Andrea, just who is this esteemed audience he was referring to?"

"According to Mr. Foust, it's just a group of friends—but his friends include a former president, secretaries of defense, several European heads of state and princes, and many well-known Wall Street investors. This morning all of Mr. Foust's guests are meeting together for the first time that we know of, and I can tell you security is very, very tight around this building. They tell us we can't even enter, but someone will be out this afternoon to give us a statement. Back to you, Daryn."

"Thanks, Andrea," said Daryn. "We'll certainly get back to you when that statement is released. In other news . . ."

Nicholas switched the set to other news programs, but when nothing else on the subject appeared he turned it off and sat down with a scowl. "No wonder he won't say who the speaker is. I haven't agreed to do it yet. I wonder what he's up to, and why all those big shots are there." He looked at Cassandra. "What do you think?"

"I don't know what to think except that he is skinner and older than I thought, and looks like I imagine Lev will look in forty years," she said as she walked to a Louis Philippe dressing table, picked up a brush, and began running it through her hair. "I think you had better make up your mind, Nicholas. You have to decide whether to share your discovery with the world or keep it to yourself. And I don't think it matters whether people believe you. What matters is whether you believe it's the right thing to do." She stopped, thought a moment, and then said it: "What do you think Alex would do?" Cassandra walked over to the chair and began massaging his shoulders.

The half-empty feeling that immediately descended upon him was beginning to feel all too familiar. Nothing would ever fill that gap. "I wish he were here to tell me," he said with a sigh, reaching across his chest to take one of her hands.

She sat on the ottoman in front of him. "Don't you believe he's still with you? Isn't his soul right now trying to heal the sadness inside you? Maybe you should let go of your emptiness and sorrow, and let his goodness fill you."

Nicholas leaned over and took her head in his hands. "You sounded like Galen just now, but you are so right. I've been looking at this all wrong. Alex would make the presentation—and to hell with the consequences!" He gave her a weak, but genuine, smile. "And besides, going public might take the heat off of us."

"That-a-boy!" She answered, smiling back at him.

"Up for a little exploration?" he asked suddenly.

They wandered hand-in-hand for half an hour through the chateau, finding unexpected niches, alcoves, and antique treasures at every turn. The concierge found them in the gardens and announced dinner, so

Cassandra returned to the room. She put on a long flowing black chiffon skirt, twisted her hair up with a jeweled comb, and joined Nicholas in the salon. Dinner was delicious. They ate *salade Niçoise*, grilled scallops in a light garlicky cream sauce, locally grown vegetables, and a *mousse du chocolat* for dessert. The wine list contained more than 400 selections, so they let the maitre d' choose. He brought them a buttery local white burgundy, which they polished off as they watched the sun set over the sea.

The next morning, they allowed themselves time to explore the tiny medieval village, one of the hundreds of "perched villages" in the area. According to the owner of a small shop, the abrupt turns and stone gates along its narrow winding lanes were constructed as a defense against invaders. The tiny side entrances to the shops and houses had the same rationale, he explained, so that invaders would have to pass by the front of the building before they could do any damage, giving the owner the first shot.

"It is amazing that almost nothing in the town has changed since it was built centuries ago," marveled Nicholas. "In America, it would be torn down at least once a century."

The shop owner seemed to find this idea mildly puzzling. "Well, of course," he replied, "if something breaks down, we repair it. Otherwise, the town is completely satisfactory and has been for more than one thousand years."

His tiny establishment traded in local crafts, beautiful linens, and fine antique porcelain. Objects covered every inch of space except for the narrow aisle and the cash register, so it took Cassandra more than an hour to examine it all. Nicholas left her there and took a walk. He especially delighted in the small flower gardens he could see through courtyard gates. He tried to pay attention to every twist and turn, but soon discovered he was lost. He laughed to himself: if he and Cassandra hadn't had their cell phones, they might have wandered those ancient streets for a week in search of each other. Even so, when they finally met up, they still had to ask a local to point them toward the way out.

Back on the A8 later that morning, Nicholas again suggested flying to Verona.

"And what do we say if some security person asks us to explain the box, or worse yet, confiscates it?" asked Cassandra.

"You're right," nodded Nicholas. He shrugged. "Oh well, these roads aren't that bad, at least when the countryside isn't sheer cliff on one side and sheer drop off to the sea on the other! We'll manage."

Later that morning, they joined the queue at the border between France and Italy, where they waited anxiously for their turn at the checkpoint. At last the guards began a leisurely inspection of their recent purchases of clothes and luggage. Nicholas felt sweat seeping through his shirt when they came to the camera bags.

"Oh, here it is!" Cassandra said brightly, handing the guards a receipt for their purchases just when they were turning their attention to the camera equipment. When one of them asked if the camera equipment was new, Cassandra rattled on about the fire and how these were the only things they had left, and how terrible it was to have to start all over again. She was still at it when the guards gave up and waved them through.

"Whew," breathed Nicholas, still gripping the wheel tightly on the other side of the border. "That was quite a performance! Forget about the box. Our real papers are hidden in the bottom of that camera case. The game would have been over if they had found those. Thank God for your wagging tongue."

"Hey, you were looking at nerves of Jell-O back there," Cassandra laughed. "Luckily, being nervous makes me talk instead of sweat." She noticed her husband's soaked shirt. "You want to stop in Genoa and do a little more shopping?"

He shook his head. "I'll dry. Let's see how far we can get today. I'd like to bypass Genoa and get on toward Verona. We can stop in a little town somewhere for lunch. Call Francesca and find out when she wants to meet us."

Francesca gave them until noon the next day to get to Verona, so they took the time to visit Genoa, where Cassandra wanted to track down Columbus' childhood home. They wound their way up the A7E62 toward Allessandria and turned right on to A21 toward Piacenza. They decided to stop there for a late lunch at the beautiful 15th century palazzo and the *Antiqua Osterio de Teatro trattoria*. They began with *crostini*, followed by *tortelloni* stuffed with local cheeses and mushrooms. For dessert, they chose a *torta di limone*, the recipe for which Cassandra begged the trattoria owner to give her for Francesca. "I want to have that at least once a week when she opens *Mia Mama*," she said to Nicholas.

They drove on, catching the A21E70 to Cremona, where they looked around the Stradivarius museum and listened to a chamber concert of native son Monteverdi's music on the square of the Duomo, or cathedral, on *Piazza del Comune*. Invigorated, they drove on toward Brescia and turned right on the A4 toward Verona. When they arrived, they checked into the *Due Torri Hotel Baglioni*, a mansion built in the 13th century. Each room in the hotel was furnished in a different era. Theirs was an 18th-century Italian suite in which Mozart had composed one of his symphonies. It was not Mozart's heavenly music Nicholas was contemplating, however, when he carefully sat down in one of the Louis Philippe chairs intended for someone about half his size. For the sake of both himself and the chair, he moved to the bed, where he scrolled through the numbers stored in his phone until he found the one he wanted.

He announced himself and the assistant immediately put him through to Malachi, whose voice sounded warm and effusive.

"Nicholas, my friend! How are you? Where are you? I haven't heard from you in ages."

"We're fine, Malachi," he replied. "Just doing a bit of traveling in South America. Always wanted to see Machu Picchu and Lima, and now is as good a time as any."

That bastard is lying to me without so much as a single syllable stutter, thought Malachi. "South America? Wonderful place, though you must watch yourself because it can be quite dangerous—especially for Americans. Hold on a second, Nicholas." Malachi pressed the hold button and hissed into the intercom: "Do you have it?"

A male voice answered: "Yes, keep him on the line."

"Sorry, Nicholas. You were saying?" continued Malachi.

"I was saying thank you for your concern and yes, I have been *very* careful of late."

Malachi caught the implication, but was unsure whether he intended it as such. "Nicholas, have you been watching the news lately?"

"As a matter of fact, that was one of the reasons I was calling," Nicholas explained. "I caught your off-the-cuff press release on CNN."

"Ah, so you have heard of our little summit?" answered Malachi, blowing a cloud of rich Cuban smoke into the air. "And did you catch the news about our excellent keynote speaker?"

"I made the connection," Nicholas replied with a chuckle. He couldn't help but catch Malachi's enthusiasm.

"Excellent. When can you come to New York to discuss the details? Perhaps let me answer any questions you have about the summit?"

"I'm taking a little time for my family right now. But I might be able to make it before too long."

You mean you need more time to complete your damn search in Europe, Malachi thought to himself, his jaws clenched in impotent frustration. "Of course," he managed to say brightly. "We have until early June to take care of things. You are doing well? And your lovely wife?"

"We are as well as could be expected, thank you for asking. I'll call you in a couple of weeks about the final preparations. In the meantime, feel free to use my appearance however you think necessary in marketing the event."

"Oh, yes, we will certainly do that!" Malachi said as enthusiastically as he could. "You know, I was thinking . . ."

"I have to go, Malachi. We will speak again soon." The line went dead.

"Did you get it?" Malachi shouted into the intercom. "Well?"

The system chattered with light static. "Sorry Mr. Foust. He was not on long enough. But he is definitely in Western Europe and not South America."

"Damn it!" he shouted, slamming an open palm onto his desk. "I know that already!"

ϐ

Nicholas twirled the phone in his hand as a meditative frown settled on his face. Cassandra noticed the expression and queried him about it. "I just don't have a good feeling about this conference," he replied.

"Start writing the lecture. You always feel better after a couple of drafts."

"No, that's not it." He smiled at her and got up off the bed. "But I'd feel better with a full stomach. Let's go eat."

The next day brought bright sunshine along with the happy expectation of seeing Francesca again. They hopped in the car just before noon, assured by the concierge that the arena was only five minutes away, and that they could not miss it. Fifteen minutes later Nicholas was telling Cassandra, "I think we missed it."

She buried her nose in a map. "*Stradone Porta Paulo* changes names to *Corsco Cavour*. We should be able to turn right on *Via Oberdan* and go right to the piazza."

Sure enough, one minute later they rolled into an enormous plaza containing a 1st-century Roman arena. In American fashion, Nicholas drove around it looking for Francesca instead of getting out and walking. Cassandra finally spied her sister-in-law's burnished hair gleaming like a red flame in the sunlight. They parked and ran for her. Nicholas grabbed her and swung her around. When he finally let her down, Francesca wrapped her arms around Cassandra and held her tightly. Tears of joy and sorrow mingled in their greeting.

"Come," Francesca finally commanded, leading them off down the *Via Mazzini*. "We'll go to the *Piazza Erbe* and buy some roast suckling pig sandwiches for lunch."

A block away was the city's marketplace, in business for more than 2,000 years. "Where Francesca is, food is also," Nicholas teased.

"Isn't this wonderful?" Francesca laughed. "Look!" Hundreds of umbrellas and carts dotted the piazza, which was filled with genial farmers and their wives selling plain and fancy mushrooms, local produce, fish, fowl, cheese, and meat. The roasting pigs, turning on spits in huge steel drums, filled the air with their succulent aroma.

"Nicholas, wouldn't you like to live here?" said Cassandra. "How could it get any better than this? Come to this market every day, live in a sixteenth-century palazzo, travel all over the place. Where's the real estate office?"

Nicholas' laugh boomed out. "Are you serious? Just like that?"

"Totally," she replied. "Look at this place."

At the north end of the square was the baroque 17th-century Maffei palace, in front of which rose the Venetian lion declaring Verona's absorption into the Venetian Empire in 1405. The 14th-century fountain, almost overshadowed by the vendors' umbrellas, filled the space the sound of splashing water and muffled the conversations taking place all around it.

"Romeo and Juliet lived in Verona," she added breathlessly.

Nicholas peered at her doubtfully. "Fictional characters who committed suicide lived here?"

"Luigi da Porto wrote about them in the 1520s, and Shakespeare picked up the story," Cassandra informed him with a smug grin. "Also, our painter Veronese was born here."

Francesca tugged at Cassandra's sleeve. "If you think Verona is magnificent, you haven't seen anything yet! Wait until you get to Venice."

She shook her head reluctantly. "If you say so. But this gets a big gold star on my list of places to come back to and see again. Besides, as you may recall, we went to Venice on our honeymoon."

They wandered around munching on their sandwiches, picked up fresh fruit and gelato for dessert, and finished it off with a cup of hot fresh espresso. In one of the shops Cassandra found some antique filigreed silver bowls and baskets that she was dying to buy. Nicholas pointed out that they had a little research journey to complete, and that Francesca had to fit into the car. Cassandra argued that she could rearrange the luggage to fit everything and promised that Francesca would not have to ride on top. Francesca offered to drive, both her guests thought a capital notion, and off they went to Venice. Cassandra put a note in her guidebook next to Padua when her companions refused to stop because of the time they would lose.

"Honey, we didn't get to Padua on our honeymoon, either. I guess we're doomed to miss it every time."

"We would have gotten to Padua if you hadn't lingered so long in Venice."

Cassandra blushed as she told Francesca about their last night there, when she'd worn a little leopard-patterned outfit and made so much noise the people upstairs banged on the floor.

Francesca laughed. "Our honeymoon was just heaven. We didn't get out of bed for four days, except for room service and long hot baths."

"I think that's more than I wanted to know," said Nicholas. "Where did you get us rooms?"

"At the *Hotel Saturnia*," replied Francesca.

"On our honeymoon we stayed at the *Luna Hotel Baglioni*. You could see San Giorgio's island from there, and we had a room with a terrace overlooking the Grand Canal."

"I looked into that hotel, but I think you'll like this one, and it's on the *Piazza San Marco* side of the canal, only a few meters from the square. The restaurant is owned by a friend of mine."

They all began to smell the briny sea air wafting in over the rolling hills, which were gradually flattening out to form the giant estuary of the northern Italian coastline.

"Why would I think that the restaurant influenced your choice of hotel?" Nicholas joked.

"Because it did!" Francesca responded, taking him literally. "Venice is the ultimate cook's school for seafood—and that includes fishing for it, raising it, cooking it, and eating it! The restaurant is *La Caravella*. Look it up in one of your guidebooks."

Cassandra looked up both the hotel and its amenities. "Good choice, Francesca! It looks delightful." She continued thumbing through the pages. "Do you think we might have time to take a little side trip to the *Baglioni*?"

"Please tell me you don't want to re-visit the room," said Nicholas. "They probably still remember us."

"Not as Mr. and Mrs. Kamen, they won't. But anyway, the reason I want to go back there is because of this note about it. It was once a hotel for the Knights Templar, and then for the Hospitallers, who got their money after Philip the Fair dissolved them. A lot of our documents seem to be connected to those groups, Nicholas. We might find some information there."

"I don't remember any of that," he said.

His wife just looked at him. "Maybe that's because you had other things on your mind at the time?"

Francesca turned off the A4. "Would you rather park the car in Mestre, where we can park for free, or go on to the car park at the *Piazzale Roma*, where we will need to rent a space?" They voted for going to the terminal in Venice, and from there took a private water taxi to the hotel.

The three were in agreement that nothing on earth quite equaled a beautiful day motoring down the Grand Canal in Venice. The majestic island city rose on each side as they passed under the ancient bridges connecting it. With the wind and salt air whipping their hair, they linked arms in the boat's seats and gave themselves up to the sights of the city on the water. In a quick twenty minutes they were at the *Piazza San Marco*, and they took in the sight of the Doges' Palace and San Marco. The taxi turned into the small canal on which the hotel sat and left them off at an unprepossessing door with *Saturnia* written over it. This was the rear of the building, but the easiest to get to during high tide. They walked toward the front to get to the desk.

"I would love to spend a lot of time here, too," said Cassandra, adoring the beamed ceilings typical of the 14hth-century architecture.

"Welcome," exclaimed Signor Alberto Serandrei, the great-grandson of the original owners. The family established the hotel in 1908, which explained the early 20th-century antiques furnishing the grand salon. A porter showed them to their adjoining suites, explaining on the way that the palace had belonged to the Pisani family in the 14th century.

"Vettor Pisani," he elaborated, "was appointed Admiral of the Venetian fleet during the war with Genoa over who would control merchant trading in the Mediterranean. We won!" he said proudly, opening the door to the Shepards' room, which overlooked the *campo* on which the hotel stood.

"Good for you," observed Nicholas in English. "Genoa's on the other side of the country."

He tipped the porter, who went next door with Francesca. While Cassandra unpacked, Nicholas locked the door and took the box out of the photo case. When he examined the indicators on each side, he was startled to find readings markedly different from those he knew by heart from his work back in the States. This was a puzzle, so he plugged the laptop into the hotel's data port. He was soon completely absorbed.

"Ok, I know you have been dying to check out the markets for days. I'm going to look in on Francesca," Cassandra told him before knocking on the door connecting the suites. "Hey," she said gently. "How are you doing?" Francesca invited her in and Cassandra closed the door behind her.

Francesca pulled some sleeveless linen dresses in lime and orange from her suitcase and paired them with contrasting cut-velvet shawls. She hung them up in the armoire. "I don't cry any more, Cassandra," she began. "Time doesn't heal everything, believe me, but I can see now I have to live with it. I *can* live with it. I guess that's progress. It helps to be here in Italy, where all my family lives—except for you and Nicholas. Who knows? Maybe sometime in the future you could move to Verona."

Cassandra flopped down on the bed. "I'm afraid I've wanted to live every place we've stopped. It's an amazing time in our lives, straddled between beauty and grief."

"Isn't it? It was hard for me to look at Nicholas. Every time I do it brings up so many memories." Francesca sighed heavily and sat down next to Cassandra. "Life may go on, but it sure isn't the life I wanted." She paused and stroked her sister-in-law's arm. "Even though I feel at home in Siena, and my children are changing and becoming Italian right in front of my eyes, I can only see all this as an interim. I just don't know what's on the other side of this bowl I'm in."

"Nicholas is on the other side of this wall, working on his computer trying to figure out the odd readings on the box. I'm actually glad for that. He's been grieving hard, but I think he's reached another level—beyond denial, anyway."

Francesca blew her nose and shook her head. "Not there yet. Let's go down to *La Caravella* and talk to my friend, Paulo. Do you need to tell Nicholas?"

"No. He can come find us."

They trooped downstairs to the lobby, where a man was waxing wooden floors set in a herringbone pattern resembling the brickwork at Versailles. He gave them directions to the restaurant, where they found Signor Serandrei putting the final touches on the table settings in the adjacent plant-filled courtyard.

Cassandra delighted in the architecture of *La Caravella*, which was designed to look like the interior of an ancient sailing ship. While she explored, Francesca went to get Paolo and returned with the chef and some good coffee. Since Venice introduced coffee to the western world through its trade with Turkey, Cassandra knew how wonderful a cup of Venetian coffee could be. She inhaled the espresso's distinctive aroma and sipped its dark mysterious flavors while Francesca and Paolo talked about cuttlefish and pumpkin ravioli with shrimp sauce and *gnocchetti ai calamaretti*. She had an inkling that a feast would appear at their tables tonight, and she basked in the late-afternoon sun dancing about the courtyard. She finally left them immersed in conversation and went back upstairs to research their itinerary for the next day. The *Baglioni* was definitely on the list, as was the Doges' palace, the home of the elected chief magistrate of the former Venetian republic. *Those will take up the whole day*, she thought. She found Nicholas in the half-dark room still tapping at his keyboard.

"Did you go somewhere?" he asked without looking up.

"I sat in the courtyard on the *campo* drinking espresso."

That stopped him. "Why didn't you come get me? What time is it? Do you know what I've found here?"

"You were busy. It's just after five. What did you find?"

"The Adriatic is virtually a closed sea, but its tidal fluctuations are enormous because of the gravitational pulls at this latitude and longitude and the combination of winds from Syria, called the *sirocco*, and the *bora*, a wind from the Hungarian steppes. When everything is in place, all these cause an *acqua alta*, which means that the city flooded In 1966, San Marco found itself under four feet of water. In the fifteenth century, people would have absolutely worshiped this box here since it could predict gravitational fluctuations and thus changes in water level. No wonder Veronese put it in a painting!"

"Really! I'm impressed," replied Cassandra. "We were right to come here, then." She consulted her guidebooks as Nicholas continued reading. "That all makes sense. Venice fell to Napoleon in 1797, and the last elected chief magistrate of Venice, or Doge, Ludovico Manin, proposed that the Great Council dissolve itself to make way for a new government with protection from France. He and a couple of hundred noblemen dispatched the Republic of Venice in a little ceremony, and stole away into the night before the French troops arrived. Now, my question would be this: Did they take the box with them, or leave it here for Napoleon to find? You remember we originally thought he might have found it in Egypt? Now I really doubt it. If the Italians took it with them, where did they go?"

"I have no idea," Nicholas murmured. "But I do know I need some coffee. Want some more?"

"No, I'm fine," she said, sitting down at his laptop. It was time for her to do a little work, too.

When they left Cassandra ran a history of Napoleon's conquests and came up with some critical details for their search. Nicholas returned an hour later with Francesca, who was flushed and happy from a turn in the kitchen making them a special appetizer. "What are you researching?" she asked.

"Things are coming together," she said excitedly. "Let's go have dinner and I'll tell you about it."

Francesca changed into her lime-green dress and a peach sorbet-colored stole, while Cassandra wore a sleek oyster-hued silk dress with a mandarin collar and strappy sandals she had purchased in France. Nicholas took one woman on each arm and they strolled down to dinner, where the anticipated feast began.

Paolo himself brought out Francesca's appetizer, *scampi crudi al prosecco*. Cassandra's hand jumped to her throat when she looked at the dish.

"Francesca," she whispered, "these shrimp just moved on my plate!"

Francesca doubted it. "I peeled them and they've been chilling for an hour. They're fresh, but not wiggling. I hope." She examined her own plate, where the shrimp moved not at all. "Here," she said, trading plates with Cassandra just to be sure. She speared a shrimp, which still had its head, and bit off the tail. "There," she said. "That's the way to eat this."

The Shepards shot a glance at one another, dutifully nibbled the fare, and then gladly helped themselves to seconds.

"In Venice, gluttony is an art form," said Francesca. "*Mangiano!*"

During a succession of dishes and wines, including *tegame di coniglio e farona con barba dif rate e polenta* and *trippa rissa con sale grosso*, Cassandra explained her theory about Napoleon.

"Napoleon had a spy network that rivaled or even exceeded Frederick the Great's—or Osama bin Laden's. Historian Thomas Petlowany, an expert on this subject, has written about Napoleon's *'bureau des affaires secretes'*. It was headed up by the great spy Landrieux, who succeeded by distributing bribes to an important network of local revolutionary agitators. One of these was Giuseppe Giovanelli, who was born to a patrician family in 1759. Landrieux gave him 124,000 francs—nearly two million dollars—to bring Italian towns under French rule without bloodshed." Cassandra stopped and eyed them both. "Would either of you like to guess who Giovanelli's grandfather was?" Her companions looked at her and shook their heads. Cassandra turned to another page of material. "Ludovico Manin!" she hit the tablecloth with her palm in excitement. "Isn't that amazing?"

Francesca and Nicholas looked at each other blankly, and then back at her.

"Who was Ludovico Manin?" asked Nicholas.

"Oh, I am sorry. The last Doge!"

"Ahh," said her companions, though neither fully understood the importance of Cassandra's revelation.

Cassandra rolled her eyes to the beamed ceiling. "So this is the deal. Think about it in light of everything we have learned—and yes I still have to prove this theory, but I think I can. Giovanelli is a spy. He knows about the box because of his grandfather, and because someone in his family stole it before the French Revolution in 1789 and took it to Venice, where many people thought it belonged, anyway. Giovanelli convinces Napoleon that he can rule the world with it. Napoleon gives him more money to steal the box and take it back to France. It looks to me like he did just that, so now we can place the box in France early in the 19th century. I think from there it went to England after the British defeated Napoleon at the Battle of Waterloo in 1815 and sent him to rot on St. Helena."

"Hold on, I want to make sure I follow you," interrupted Nicholas. "Somebody steals the box and takes it to the English side because someone there has a plan to use it?" Cassandra nodded. "Who would be a good candidate for that?" asked her husband.

She sank back in her chair. "I think we'll need to go to England to track that down. The last Doges' papers, believe it or not, are in the Library of London. Tracking down Giovanelli will take some genealogical work, but it shouldn't be that difficult. I'll keep at it."

"Nice work," admired Nicholas, nodding happily. "You really are good at this."

Cassandra smiled. "Maybe there's a connection between the Hospitallers and all this. They were a powerful force here for hundreds of years. Tomorrow we'll go to the *Baglioni* and the Palace and look for evidence of the cartouche."

After dinner they sauntered down the side streets of the *campo* to walk off the rich food, and then retired early. The next day, Cassandra and Nicholas left Francesca at the hotel and went to the *Baglioni*. They took a gondola through the Grand Canal, remembering how fresh and new and young they had felt fifteen years before.

"Rocking on the water didn't bother us at all," recalled Cassandra. "Now when I get off the boat, my sea legs seem to stick with me." She patted her hips a couple times and added, "So have the six pounds I've put on eating all this food!"

Nicholas laughed as the gondola pulled up to the dock. He steadied his wife as they climbed out and entered the hotel. The grand lobby still featured the largest Oriental rug they had ever seen, and the Marco Polo Lounge was adorned with huge 18th-century frescoes from the Gianbattista Tiepolos School.

"You'd never know this place was once a convent, never mind a hostelry for Knights Templar and Hospitallers," Nicholas grumbled. "It's been renovated so many times we'll never find anything from the twelfth century."

Cassandra went to the concierge while Nicholas wandered the lobby. He glanced over and saw the concierge shaking her head, listening, and then nodding. "She told me that there's still part of the twelfth-century hotel left up on the upper floors," Cassandra told him when he joined her, "but she didn't know if there were any documents up there. She said that during the last renovation, they found lots of documents, but sold them to a guy named Luciano Filippi, who sells reproductions of old Venetian texts. His shop is near San Marco. Do you want to go search the attic rooms?"

"I don't think so. People have been going over this place with a fine-tooth comb for centuries. Let's go collect Francesca and head over to San Marco."

The San Marco Plaza was an established seaport long before the first Doge appeared around 700 A.D. Its reputation grew into legend after two merchants stole the corpse and relics of St. John the Evangelist and brought them to the lagoon in 828. Less than 200 years later, Venice emerged as a city with a stable form of government and the perfect location to become the hub of the Adriatic Sea's fast-growing commerce.

The three took a gondola over to the famous plaza and walked around in admiration of the Gothic, Oriental, and Moorish architecture, which had all been blended in a distinctive fashion. They proceeded to the shop of Signor Filippi, where they found a delightful proprietor eager to help them search for documents.

"We are looking for documents belonging to the Knights Templar and the Hospitallers up until about the time of Napoleon," Cassandra explained as Francesca translated into Italian. "Were any of the Doges connected to these groups? And do you have any documents establishing the connection?"

Signor Filippi listened carefully, asked Francesca to clarify a few things, and then scratched his head. "I make reproduction copies, and often sell the originals to collectors. I do not get a request for what you are asking about very often, but I recently acquired some during the renovation of a hotel here. Would you like to see them?"

He retreated to the back of his shop and returned with several large books. "I put them in these books to flatten out the parchments when they are rolled," he said.

They turned through the books carefully, with an increasing sense of excitement. It took less than ten minutes to find the first cartouche. Nicholas lifted his eyes and locked them with Cassandra's. She smiled faintly. Several more documents bearing the symbol followed in quick succession.

"Are these documents for sale?" she asked Filippi. In Italy, everything is for sale. After fifteen minutes of bargaining, yelling, and nearly walking out of the store, they closed the deal. When they finally emerged from the shop, they felt as though they were carrying out the crown jewels. Filippi was just as pleased, counting and recounting the large amount of cash the Americans had been willing to spend.

"These Hospitallers really got around," said Cassandra. "And they used the cartouche! We have the proof! They may be our connecting link, but we still don't know for sure. Let me put these documents together with the ones we have and see how many connections I can make."

They explored the Doges' Palace. Cassandra wanted to view the Doges' private chambers, convinced she would find something there. They went through the magnificent rooms occupying the mezzanine and ascended the Golden Staircase to the second floor. The Doges had lived in a suite of rooms overlooking the square, probably the only part of the palace that remained much as it was in the 1570s. The rooms were rather spare, given all Nicholas and Cassandra had seen of late, with beautifully carved ceilings and the severe classical style of the early Renaissance. However, the few documents they managed to find did not bear a single Egyptian cartouche. Their visit to the Chamber of the Council of Ten, however, was far more successful.

The Chamber had been the center of power for Venice for a number of centuries and contained numerous paintings by Veronese. Cassandra stood in the center of the room with her mouth hanging open. "Look," she pointed. "The cartouche was carved into the lintels of each door leading into the room."

"This is really unbelievable," exclaimed Nicholas with a shake of his head. "I feel the same way I did when we discovered the box in Veronese's painting. The trail seems so damn obvious, but I guess we know exactly what we are looking for. We just have to keep following it."

"Easier said than done, though I admit we have been more fortunate than I was really expecting," remarked Cassandra, taking out her camera for a few snapshots. She took one picture with Francesca standing under the lintel with the largest example of the carving.

"So this is what you have been up to." Francesca laughed, "What a treasure hunt. I hope that Galen is having as much success."

"I hope so as well," Nicholas remarked. "Remind me to power up the laptop this evening and see if he's written us yet."

"I imagine he is in heaven just *visiting* the Vatican," Cassandra replied.

That night, they celebrated their new discoveries and made plans to return to Siena. Nicholas signed on to his e-mail provider and found a message from Galen.

"He didn't write much," Nicholas explained to the girls, "but he did say his research went well, he just arrived in Siena, and has interesting things for us to look at."

Cassandra, who was expertly placing acid-free tissue between the parchment documents, looked up and grinned. She couldn't wait to see him. "Tell him we're on our way."

Chapter 45

The late afternoon sunlight shimmered through the wispy clouds over the roads to Siena. The golden light illuminated the gently rounded hills covered in vineyards and green spring wheat. With the car's windows yawning wide, Nicholas, Cassandra, and Francesca wound slowly through the countryside, breathing deeply of the still-cool May air. Rounding the top of one of the little hillocks, they spied the large farmhouse perched on a hill a few kilometers away.

"Oh, it looks so welcoming and beautiful," murmured Cassandra. "The cypress trees have really grown up, haven't they? I can't wait to see what our architects did after your wedding!" Once Alex was married, he and Nicholas had presented Francesca's parents with the services of two American architects, who collaborated to renovate the thousand-year-old structure into a more livable habitat.

Francesca drove up into the cobbled courtyard and they tumbled out, happy to stretch their legs after the long drive from Venice. Cassandra scurried about the courtyard, marveling at how wonderful the loggia looked and how amazing it was that the renovation had not harmed the wisteria on the pergola over the terrace.

"Wait until you see inside!" Francesca said happily.

As soon as they heard Cassandra's voice, Harrison and Rosemary came running out of the doorway. They were as brown as acorns, their hair beached nearly white by the Italian sun. Francesca knelt down with her arms open to embrace them tightly.

When Cassandra turned to smile at Nicholas she discovered him standing by the car, staring at the children with tears running down his face. She felt her knees grow weak and it took all her strength to turn and walk slowly back to him. He looked down and away, wiping his face with the back of his hand as she reached out and wrapped her arms around him.

These two little kids will never see their father again, Nicholas thought. *How can I ever make up that loss?* Nicholas clung to Cassandra and for a few seconds hid his face in her hair. He didn't want the children to see him crying.

"Children recover," Cassandra comforted him. "Francesca says they are doing well. We will all survive this together—as a family."

Mama Gamba had walked briskly out of the house on the heels of the children, but when she saw Nicholas nearly collapsing in the arms of his wife, she quickly herded Francesca and the children into the house with their grandfather and the new nanny following in their wake.

A large shadow approached the car and both Cassandra and Nicholas looked up in surprise. "Come on, now," he said, gently pulling both of them into a strong bear hug. It was Galen.

Cassandra smiled through her own tears and hugged him back. "Galen, am I ever glad to see you!"

"Me too," admitted Nicholas, blowing his nose into the handkerchief the padre handed him.

"We can't just stand out here. Let's go inside." Galen eased them gently toward the doorway. "The kids will think something is wrong otherwise, and they have been so looking forward to seeing you."

They followed Galen into the cucina, or kitchen. "Uncle Nicholas! Aunt Cassandra!" shouted both kids as they ran to greet them. The adults dropped to their knees to embrace and kiss the children.

Mama Gamba threw out her hands, grumbling something in Italian that made Francesca laugh so hard that tears welled up. "My mama says dealing with all of you is like herding cats!" she finally managed to explain. Nicholas and Cassandra were surprised to discover the nanny, Sister Angelica, barely looked twenty. According to Francesca, the nanny was wonderful with the children, who obviously adored her, and that is all that counted.

Italian and English mingled through the kitchen as everyone spoke at once. The architects had left the ancient raised hearth, with its several ovens and racks for roasting, and installed a stone hood over it with wine racks stretching to the floor. The stone walls feathered into white tile at the doorways, so that the walls converged at the corners in white tile and feathered back out again at the next opening. Glass doors had been installed that led to the loggia, and marble columns divided the kitchen and dining spaces that overlooked it. They had even managed to build in a huge sub-zero freezer in a work triangle, along with double ovens and a microwave. Mama Gamba made an island out of a massive farmhouse table they had found on the property when they bought it. Now it was covered with pasta dough, mounds of fresh baby spinach, bowls of fruit, onions, garlic, and shallots.

Francesca rolled up her sleeves to help her mother with the food, said goodnight to the nanny, and asked Rosemary to show Nicholas and Cassandra their room.

Rosemary took Cassandra's hand and pulled her up the wide wooden staircase. "*Come va?*" she said to them. Cassandra congratulated her on learning Italian so quickly.

"*Grazie,*" she said, pulling open a heavy wooden door with a pointed Gothic arch at the top. "*Io imparo . . .* um, um, *fast!*" she improvised.

Cassandra gave her a hug, and the little girl climbed onto the canopied bed, twining her arms around the massive posts supporting the canopy. She stared deeply at Nicholas as if in a trance. Rosemary was seeing her dead father.

Nicholas walked slowly to her and picked her up. She clung to his neck, his warm embrace triggering a flood of tears. He was carrying her downstairs to her mother when Galen intervened at the bottom step. The priest lifted her from Nicholas, set her on his knee, and let her have her cry.

"Hey, little one," he said gruffly. "Those tears just came out from hiding, didn't they? Have you got any more lurking in there? Let me see." He tugged on her eyebrows and made her giggle through her tears. "It's okay for you to feel sad," he said, "as long as you also know you won't be that way forever." She hugged him and ran off to the kitchen.

"You'd make a great dad," observed Nicholas. Galen flashed him a look that told him not to go there, so he changed the subject. "What did you bring us?" The men slid over to a sitting area and sat in two armchairs, facing one another.

"Pictures worth at least a few dozen words," replied Galen. "The one worth a thousand words I found after I ran out of disk space. Unfortunately, I wasn't alone, so I couldn't take any time to delete a picture to restore disk space. Otherwise, I would have had a shot of the most unbelievable lintel I have ever seen."

"Lintel? Is that what you said?" Nicholas asked. "Let me guess. The cartouche was carved into it, right?"

Galen tilted his head and scratched his big neck. "I guess you're one step ahead of me," he said, and described what he had seen in the Vatican.

Nicholas listened carefully, nodding as he spoke. "This is all *very* interesting, Galen. We found the symbol on the lintels at the Doges' palace, but they were small and carved into the design. The one you saw at the Vatican was essentially the whole thing over the door. Let's see the disks."

Galen and Nicholas trotted up the steps to the bedroom, passing Cassandra on her way down. "Don't be too long up there now, Nicholas. We just got here."

Nicholas opened his laptop, hooked up a small printer Francesca had brought with her, and clicked it on. Once it was fired up, Galen loaded the disk holding the pictures he had taken in the Vatican's Hall of Parchments. Just then, Francesca shouted up to announce dinner. Both men groaned and headed downstairs to join the family gathered around the table. Since it was still too chilly to eat outdoors, they enjoyed the last rays of a pink and deep rose sunset through the glass wall of the dining area.

Francesca and Mama Gamba brought out antipasti made with ingredients purchased in Venice. Shrimp, scallops, cuttlefish eggs, baby octopus, tuna marinated in balsamic vinegar, and simmered spider crabs vied for attention with locally grown olives, celery, carrots and a fresh goat cheese. Bowls of steaming bean soup with leeks and ham arrived, followed by duck breast with apple and sides of spinach and risotto. Happy to be together again, they talked and translated for hours, sharing stories of Alex, wiping away tears, and wondering how they were going to put together all the clues they had to lead them to the owner of the box. Nicholas complied when Francesca suggested he show the box to the

Gambas, but they seemed more apprehensive than interested in the artifact. They even refused to touch it, as if it held some ancient evil. Mama Gamba asked Nicholas to take it back upstairs.

It was approaching midnight when Nicholas, Cassandra, Francesca, and Galen gathered on the terrace to look at the magnificent stars rolling away into infinity. It was strikingly beautiful, but too cold to stay out long. Exhausted from traveling, they decided to call it a night.

When they woke the next morning it was pouring rain. Great curtains of it swept over the distant hills and splattered the windows. They watched from the comfort of the glass-walled loggia, and after an Italian-style breakfast of ham, eggs baked in tomato cream, and fresh bread with toasted rosemary and sun-dried tomato, they put their heads together and went over all the information they had gathered.

Galen described at length the manuscripts from Mary Stuart to the Pope and those of Thomas Howard, finishing with the story of the lintel in the Borgia apartments.

Cassandra, meanwhile, listened to their conversation while sifting through the printed photos Galen had taken at the Vatican. The documents were primarily in Italian, so she handed them to Francesca to translate and made notes in the margins. Nicholas set up a master list of the obvious connections on his laptop.

"Let's do this chronologically," Cassandra suggested. "Let's match handwriting and names where we have them, and see where it leads us."

"Ok, that sounds reasonable," answered Nicholas. "Beginning with the little piece of papyrus and moving forward, what have we got before the year 1000?"

Cassandra looked from her notebook to the stacks of copies neatly arranged along one wall, and back to her notebook. "Primarily, we have Roman documents with inventories of palaces, and several trading agreements between Rome and Egypt," she answered. "We have a few written in Latin," she announced, handing them to Galen to read.

"What?" exclaimed Galen, knitting his eyebrows together "You want me, a Catholic priest, to read Latin?" In fact, his four years in seminary had made him quite competent in the language.

"The history gets much more complicated after 1100," observed Nicholas. "Here's one signed and dated by someone named Gerard Tenc in 1120. Look at the large cartouche stamped at the bottom. It looks like it was made yesterday."

He handed the document to Cassandra, who studied it closely for a few moments. She set it by her elbow and keyed the name into the laptop to search the Internet. "Ah, Gerard Tenc was indeed someone special. It says here he was a Grand Master of the Knights Hospitaller."

"I'm glad I got that Internet connection set up in time for your visit," said Francesca. "Otherwise, this would have been impossible to do here. Ok, sister-in-law, tell me again about Grand Master something or other. I find it a bit confusing."

"So do I sometimes," answered Cassandra, "and I have been reading this carefully for weeks. The Knights Hospitaller, or Order of Knights of the Hospital of St. John of Jerusalem was a militant monastic Christian group started in the 11th Century. It was originally based in Jerusalem, and its purpose was the care and defense of pilgrims traveling to and from Europe to the Holy Lands."

"Oh, I get it now," Francesca said. "Hospitaller . . . hospitality . . . taking care of people. So how did they get powerful, or tied in with powerful people?"

"It's a long story, but a fascinating one. Let me sort of sum it up," replied Cassandra, reaching for her notebook. "In 1020, Italian merchants wanted to erect a safe house, a welcoming hospice, in Jerusalem, for Christian pilgrims traveling from Europe to see the birthplace of Jesus. Building something like that required permission from Egypt's Caliph, or leader, and this permission was granted. The hospice was built in the name of Saint John Almoner and eventually dedicated to Saint John the Baptist." Cassandra paused and took a mouthful of coffee.

"The monastic order itself was founded after the First Crusade by our very own Gerard Tenc, whose position and authority was blessed by Pope Pashal II in 1113. Gerard was very aggressive, and he acquired land and money for his group even beyond the borders of the Kingdom of Jerusalem. The first semi-permanent Hospitaller hospice was built near the Church of the Holy Sepulcher in Jerusalem. At first, the Order fed and clothed and cared for the traveling pilgrims, but before long it was also escorting them to offer protection. It was dangerous to travel in those times—especially as Christians in the Muslim world. Before long, the Order was a small army and, with the Knights Templar, became a very powerful force."

"The Papacy backed the Hospitallers to the hilt," observed Nicholas.

"Oh, absolutely," continued Cassandra. "There was strong incentive to remain a religious Order because the men were granted special privileges by the Pope. The Order answered only to his authority, had its own religious buildings, and did not have to pay any taxes. The order was eventually expelled from the Middle East and North Africa, though its military role against Muslim armies trying to invade Europe continued for centuries."

Cassandra was just finishing when Mama Gamba arrived with a fresh pot of coffee. She poured more of the strong, steaming brew into their mugs, smiling to each in turn. Leaning over the table to fill Cassandra's cup, she stared intently at the Gerard Tenc document next to the laptop. Reaching into her apron, she removed a pair of reading glasses and slipped them onto her nose. She jerked back suddenly, spilling coffee out of the pot and onto the floor. "I'm sorry, I'm sorry!" she exclaimed, setting the pot down on a trivet and wiping up the spill with a small towel she carried with her. Something had traumatized her.

"Mama, what's wrong?" asked Francesca.

With her hands shaking and her body trembling, Mama Gamba began speaking in torrent of rapid-fire Italian. Every few seconds she animated her account with an emotional wave of her arms. The Americans stared, uncomprehending, and looked at Francesca who seemed both amused and fascinated by her mother's tale.

After she told her story, Mama Gamba shouted for Sister Angelica to look at the documents. The young nun appeared a few moments later with the children in tow. When Mama Gamba showed her the cartouche, the nun uttered a loud gasp and crossed her hands in front of her body, shaking her head as she retreated from the room. Mama Gamba turned to the others and bobbed her head once, sharply, as if to say, "See? Do you believe me now?" Finished, she peered breathlessly at her daughter over her square reading glasses.

"*Grazie, mama*," said Francesca, patting her on the shoulder and rubbing her cheek. She exhaled loudly and faced her friends. "Well, it seems that my little mama has seen this symbol. She says there are many illustrated manuscripts in the library at the Duomo in Siena, and that the cartouche can be found there."

Nicholas turned his palms up and held out his hands. "It took her that long and agitated her that much just to tell us that the city's cathedral has manuscripts like these?"

"No, there's more." A coy smile lit Francesca's face. "The rest was a brief history of the family members who have passed down what they knew or heard about the cartouche. According to Mama, this symbol has long been associated with people of great power who were known to abuse their positions. My family—and many of the families in this region—regards such people as evil, and she is upset that this symbol might have something to do with Alex's death. She is also upset we have brought it into her house. It is bad luck."

"What was Sister Angelica's reaction to this?" asked Cassandra. "It looked like about the same thing."

"She sure was shocked when she saw the symbol," Galen answered. "Although keep in mind that she is a Poor Clare committed to the bonds of poverty and mercy. So it makes sense that she would be frightened of it if, to her, it represents the misuse of power." He paused. "You know, until now none of us have ever considered the cartouche as a symbol of evil."

That observation produced a moment of unsettling quiet. It was Nicholas who broke the silence. "Wealth and power aren't inherently evil. They can just as easily be used for the public good and often are. But maybe you're saying that the public good might be an accidental side effect—or maybe an intentional cover—for implementing evil?"

"I haven't really given it any thought yet, Nicholas, but I guess we should consider that," responded Galen with a deep sigh. "Obviously the people after you are willing to kill for it, right? That's evil in anyone's book. Well, we don't have any hard evidence connecting the cartouche with whoever killed Alex—do we?"

"No," answered Nicholas.

Cassandra rolled her shoulders in slow circles to get the crick out of her neck. "Now we have more clues than we know what to do with, and we've added 'evil' to the mix. We have so many clues we are clueless. Clueless in Siena." Her companions rolled their overworked eyes at the lame joke and tried to focus once more on the bewildering mass of documents.

Cassandra had a better idea. "How about we split up? Francesca and Nicholas can go into Siena and browse around the Duomo, while we stay here plowing through and organizing these documents."

Nicholas and Francesca practically leapt out of their chairs, ecstatic to be relieved of paper shuffling duties. "Ok, I guess we should go right now," suggested Nicholas. Francesca agreed.

ℬ

The pair jumped into the car and drove north. It only took a few minutes before the medieval city dominated by the Duomo, one of Italy's most spectacular cathedrals, hove into view.

"The city's site is so ancient no one really knows its origins," explained Francesca. "It was evidently named by the Romans after a famous Etruscan family. Look, there's the city's symbol, a she-wolf suckling twins. Legend has it the city was founded by Remus' twin sons, Senius and Ascius, who fled to Tuscany to escape the murderous schemes of their Uncle Romulus—who you might remember founded Rome with Remus after being raised by wolves. Different story, same as the original legend, I guess." She wound through the narrow streets with the expertise of a taxi driver, finally rolling up at the *Via Francigena*, which was surrounded by fortress-like residences that had belonged to feudal families seeking safety there on the hilltop that commanded the region.

Had it been completed, the Duomo would have been one of the largest cathedrals in Europe. However, the plague of 1348 reduced the city's population by half, killing off the expertise and financial base necessary to finish the job. Behind the grand Romanesque-Gothic façade was a large courtyard where the nave would have been. The completed part alone was enough to please even the most jaded traveler. Nicholas stood in awe of the luminous striped columns, floor mosaics, and bronze angels on the altar. He already looked forward to the day when he could come back with Cassandra.

Francesca headed straight for a door off the north aisle. Nicholas followed a few steps but stopped in his tracks to examine the colossal 3rd-century statues of the Three Graces. When he realized he was alone, he hurried after Francesca. The library was commissioned in the 15th century by Pope Pius III to memorialize the achievements of his uncle, Pope Pius II, who was born Enea Silvio Piccolomini in Siena. Twelve huge frescoes telling the story of the Sienese Pope's life adorned the room. Below these, exquisite glass cases displayed manuscripts both sacred and secular from the city's history.

With Francesca at one end and Nicholas on the other, they began searching the face of the documents. The second parchment Nicholas laid his eyes on confirmed Mama Gamba's story. "Francesca," he whispered, motioning with his head. She walked over and looked down where he was pointing.

"There it is," she nodded. "Our favorite Egyptian symbol—a bit faint, but present nonetheless."

"What does the document say?" asked Nicholas.

Francesca took a minute to study it closely before answering. "I am not entirely sure, but it seems to be a report of some sort relating to Siena's bloody relationship with Florence."

They eased their way along the case and stopped. There it was again, this time on papers relating to the annexation of Siena to the Medici State in the mid-16th century. They filed past dozens of additional documents, but the cartouche did not appear again. Whatever powers in Siena had knowledge of the cartouche, Nicholas concluded, must have been swallowed up into the Medici kingdom. He took pictures of the ones they found and walked over to Francesca, who was sitting in front of the altar. A frown creased her face.

"I do not enjoy the splendor exhibited by these popes," she said. "My disapproval is genetic—a result of the Church's dubious past and especially what they did to my forefather Galileo. I admit Galen has been doing a sales job on me lately, and he might eventually win me back. But never my parents. Blood runs deep here in Italy."

They returned to the Gamba hilltop villa through cloud-filled valleys of rain. Nicholas took a turn at the wheel and Francesca leaned back in the seat, looking out at the hills she loved so deeply. When they arrived home, Nicholas let the car roll slowly to a stop and turned off the engine.

"You think your parents would let us leave the box here, considering how they feel about it?" asked Nicholas. "I have to go to New York next week to talk to Malachi about the symposium, and Cassandra wants to go to England. I've asked Galen to go with her because I am worried about her traveling alone."

"That's a good idea," Francesca agreed. "Leave the box. Just stick it under your bed, Nicholas. Nobody will know it's there and I guarantee you nobody is going to clean under there before you get back. Since you have copies, you might as well leave the original documents, too. 'll be the guardian for you."

"That's a load off my mind, Francesca. Thanks. I've got to get to work on my speech. I would love for you to come to Paris to hear it. Can you?"

She cocked her head, a little puzzled. "I must admit, I am surprised that you've agreed to give it."

Puzzled, Nicholas looked at his sister-in-law. "Why?"

She avoided his stare and shrugged. "When we talked about all this in Charleston, I was under the impression you had changed your mind about working with Malachi."

"Francesca," Nicholas spoke softly. "I understand your surprise. The events of the last week have been so hectic I completely forgot your disconnection from them." Nicholas paused for a minute and studied her face to see if he was reaching her.

"After the fire," he continued, "we began to realize that the only way to guarantee our safety, and I mean the safety of *all* of us, Francesca, was to make the discovery public—including the box and the documents. I believe if I present it properly in Paris, there will be no reason for anyone to harm us." Nicholas was unsure how to put it into words. "I guess," he began slowly, "I guess I am doing it . . . for Alex."

He paused again with a warm, reassuring smile. "Once I make sure we're safe, we will have the time and the peace of mind to thoroughly research the true owners of the box. With any luck, we will find out who killed him."

"I trust you Nicholas," she finally answered. Her voice was soft, but steady and confident. "I think you are right about this." She caught and held his eyes. "So this means you are thinking about moving to New York and working for Malachi?" Her question confirmed her deepest concern.

"To tell you the truth, Francesca," he answered softly, "I don't think I could ever go back to a regular job. Not now. These past weeks . . ." He interrupted himself and looked out at the rain. A warm hand slipped into his own. "There are so many more important things in life, and we no longer have to worry about money."

"I know," she said reassuringly. "I would be happy to come to Paris, but I'll leave the children here with my parents and Angelica." He smiled as she released his hand. "Alex would be very proud of you, Nicholas. You know that, don't you?"

Nicholas inhaled deeply. "I do know that. Say, did you bring Alex's laptop over here with you?" It had occurred to him earlier in the day that he would need his brother's notes. He hoped he wouldn't have to go to Charleston to retrieve them.

"Yes, it's here. I thought you might need it." She flashed him a side ways smile. "You two were very alike, you know, but I liked the way Alex could do detail."

"I depended on that gift all my life," he replied. "I feel so bereft of it now. Come on, let's get inside."

Opening the doors, they dashed into the house, where Nicholas found Cassandra right where he had left her. Galen had given up and gone to the kitchen.

"Hey, honey," she said over her shoulder. "Do you recall if our document guy among the bones in Paris told you what happened to the Knights Templar after it was dissolved in 1312? The reason I ask is that the cartouche appears on lots of documents belonging to Scottish, Portuguese, and Swiss bankers after that date. This whole stack," she said, pointing at a mound of papers, "belongs to that group."

"Of course!" he exclaimed, hitting his forehead with the palm of his hand. "Now *that* makes sense!"

"What makes sense?"

"The Templars who were able to escape execution went to Switzerland and set up the banking system in that region that is still famous today! Where has my mind been?" He paused to think about it. "You'd never be able to get in there, though. That society is so closed, the smell doesn't leak out when somebody dies in a vault. You remember that huge scandal over Swiss bankers keeping Jewish gold and currency after the Holocaust?"

"Nicholas, I think you're on to something," Cassandra agreed. "I think the banks had to give some of it back to the families—but too little and too late. Maybe I'd be better off tracing the English, Scottish, or Welsh Knights. They look more accessible."

When Cassandra reappeared twenty minutes later she erupted with a shout: "Galen! Pack your bags. We're off to Rosslyn Chapel!"

Chapter 46

Confident that he was still operating beneath his pursuer's radar, Nicholas booked a flight to New York and a room at the Plaza Hotel under his new identity. He did the same for Cassandra, who would be flying to London with Galen. Arrangements had been made for them at the Savoy in Covent Garden, one of Cassandra's favorite places. Knowing the priest was with her gave him the strength he needed to fly to New York and meet with Malachi.

When he called up the Paris Ritz on the Internet to reserve his room for the conference, Nicholas was dismayed to find that the entire hotel was booked already full for that weekend. *Surely Malachi already booked us a room?* But if he had, thought Nicholas, it would have been under his real name. Since he would be publicized as the keynote speaker, he would have to shed his new identity anyway once he arrived at the conference. That would make him completely vulnerable to whoever was after him. Maybe he would bring the point up with Malachi. There was little use worrying about that now.

Nicholas logged off the Internet and looked under the bed, which sat a good three feet off the floor. Cassandra had to use a small step-stool just to get into it. A heavy linen bed skirt surrounded it, and the space behind it was dark and musty. He slid the box and original documents into a suitcase and tucked it in deep, up against the headboard wall. Even a vacuum would not reach that far back, he thought. After dusting off his hands, he slipped their original identity papers into a padded envelope and addressed it to himself at the Plaza.

Wonderful smells wafted up from downstairs, and he followed his nose to the kitchen. Tonight would be their last meal together, perhaps for several weeks, and they wanted it to be memorable. He watched Francesca and her mother work in tandem, scurrying about the big kitchen, missing each other by inches at full speed. Cassandra allowed him to wash spinach and tomatoes, which she then dropped into a pot of boiling water, left them to bubble for a few seconds, and then took them out with big tongs. Nicholas peeled and seeded them, and finally handed the huge bowl of tomato extract to Mama Gamba. Francesca's father brought in Bellavista, a sparkling white wine from Franciaporte, together with a Ricci Curbastro to have with the antipasti.

The dinner was fit for a king. It began with some artisan-made Balsamic vinegar drizzled over little chunks of Parmigiano-Reggiano cheese, followed by *caprino fresco con erbe a spieze*, with a *Graziano Pra Soave* Classico white wine. The first course was *tagliarini con cariofi, Parmigiano e limone*, which paired artichokes with *prosciutto di Parma*, followed by *zuppa di Maria Lembi,* a soup of sweet squash, faro and beans. For the main course, Papa Gamba cooked a butterflied leg of lamb, *cosciotto d'Agnello arrosto*, on the terrace grill. He had marinated the meat all day in red wine, olive oil, fresh rosemary, and garlic, cooked it to pink perfection, and served it with a *Barberra d'Asti* red wine. Grilled fresh vegetables accompanied the lamb, with a thick tomato sauce Francesca made from the peeled tomatoes.

"I'm utterly full," announced Nicholas as he pushed his plate back. "But what's for dessert?"

Francesca laughed and got up from the table, heading for the kitchen. "*Torte alle prugne con crosta alla mandorle*," she said, somewhat tipsy from the grand march of wines. "It's a plum and ricotta tart in an almond crust." Cassandra helped her bring out the plates. Mama Gamba made coffee. "I told you gluttony was an art form here," joked Francesca. She gave them heavy pottery plates colored with the same sunny apricot color the sky turned on May evenings.

"I'm coming to understand how Europeans can eat and drink for hours on end and never get fat," Cassandra said, mentally reviewing the cavalcade of delicacies they had consumed. "They don't eat very much of any one thing, and space it out just enough to become ravenously hungry for the next course."

"Easy for you to say," Nicholas said, helping himself to a double serving of the tart.

"Say," said Galen, sipping a glass of *Albana di Romagna Passita,* which complemented the plum and ricotta tart perfectly. "Did you hear the one about . . ."

"Uh, oh. Galen must be toasted. It's joke time," laughed Nicholas. "He has his hat and boots on—watch out!" When Galen shot him a playful glare, Nicholas surrendered. "Okay, let's hear one. *One!*" Nicholas raised his glass to his friend.

Galen continued in mid-sentence: ". . . about René Descartes walking into a bar? He had a couple of drinks, and soon it was closing time. The bartender came over and asked him if he wanted another. Descartes said, 'I think not,' and poof! He disappeared."

Cassandra immediately burst out laughing, but it took the other Americans a few seconds before they chucked at Galen's humor. The Italians, who never favored French philosophers, needed a considerable amount of explanation before they understood. None of them even smiled. Everyone took their coffee out to the terrace, and then went for a walk in the Tuscan moonlight.

The next day, slightly hung over and going their separate ways, they split up at the airport in Florence for their flights to London and New York. Cassandra and Nicholas said goodbye with their eyes from several gates apart. Galen waved as they walked away, turning Cassandra around several times to keep her on course as they walked toward their gate. Nicholas stood still, smiling each time his wife threw a glance in his direction, until Cassandra and the priest vanished into a faceless crowd of travelers.

When they finally disappeared, he sat down at his own gate and pondered his meeting with Malachi.

ℬ

Nicholas arrived in New York disheveled from twelve hours on an airplane. Even first-class accommodations could not mitigate the discomfort of being cooped up in a long silver tube with artificial air for half a day. Desperate by this point for a shave and fresh clothes, he fumed in the slow traffic from JFK and arrived at the Plaza in a sour mood. The room overlooked Central Park, and was plush with damask furnishings in pale gold. Recalling the character and imagination of the European beds they had slept in on their recent journeys did not improve his disposition; Cassandra's absence further darkened his mood.

He tried to sleep for an hour, but was unable to. Rubbing his eyes, he sat on the edge of the king-sized bed and dialed Malachi's number.

"Delighted to hear from you, my friend," Malachi said through clenched teeth. *At least now I know where this trusting fool is.* "When can we get together? Today?"

"Well, I really am exhausted—jet lag and all."

"Well, jet lag hits all of use sometimes," answered the financier sympathetically. "How about tomorrow after lunch at my office?"

"Yes, that sounds fine. I have your address and will see you then," answered Nicholas.

"Good! I look forward to seeing you." When he was sure Nicholas had hung up, Malachi slammed the phone down in its cradle so hard that he had to pick it back up to see if he had cracked the plastic casing. "Why isn't there a good way to trace cell calls?" he fumed. "I could have known where that man was the whole time, and now I still don't know. Mika!"

She heard him through the wall and dutifully appeared. "Nicholas Shepard will be here tomorrow at one o'clock. I want you here as well. Give me fifteen minutes or so with him, and I'll call you. In the meantime," he said with a humorless grin, "could you please invent a system that actually works that will identify the locations of cell phone calls globally?"

"Of course," she said without smiling, her stomach twisting at the prospect of meeting Alex's brother. As she turned to leave she said, "Oh, and about the cell phone trace . . . I'll set one up on the Group's private satellite." She smiled prettily. Sometimes it felt good to twist the knife. "I did not know you wanted one, or I would have set it up earlier."

"I thought I hired you to read my mind," he snapped. He abruptly returned his attention to the computer screens monitoring the markets. He wasn't watching as she bowed and backed out of his office.

 broken

Nicholas shaved, showered, reserved a massage for later that afternoon, and called room service for dinner. Refreshed and invigorated, he opened up his own and his brother's laptops, clicked them on, and waited for them to boot up.

Using Alex's computer, he scrolled down the list of directories, looking for the Matlab programs Alex had written for their stock market research. He found the file titled "Matlab" and opened it up to look at the sub-folders. He was searching for the *Xyber9* program, along with any others he recognized from Alex's work on the system identification processes. He quickly located the *Xyber9* programs, but his eyes continued down the column.

He noticed another Matlab file called *Over Unity*, which listed several sub-files with names like *Electron Charger*, *Electron Accelerator*, and *Aetheric Energy*. They apparently had to do with alternative atomic energy. Alex had mentioned this new project, but not in any great detail. He was familiar with some of Alex's engineering projects with NASA but this was a different field.

Curious, he opened the file called *Electron Accelerator* and started reading some of Alex's notes. The text discussed in great detail a new device that could produce more energy than it used. Nicholas frowned. According to the laws of physics, the entire concept of "over unity" was impossible. As far as he knew, no one had been able to produce power from nothing. Still, he was fascinated, impressed, and a little guilty about reading his dead brother's files. He was also annoyed with himself for procrastinating, so he closed that file and went back to the Matlab file titled *Xyber9* and opened it.

As he read through the source codes, with Alex's notes conveniently highlighted in green, he came to a sentence followed by the author's name. It wasn't Alex's. The credit was given to Robert W. Bass. Nicholas had heard of Dr. Bass and assumed he had collaborated with Alex in the early development of the system identification program. He was positive this was one of the programs Alex adapted to fit the exogenous astronomical measurement input for their own work. He read further and found one other name under different sub-programs: George W. Masters.

Who were these men? wondered Nicholas. He entered Robert W. Bass into Google: Robert W. Bass holds a B.A. in physics from Johns Hopkins University, an M.A. Oxon in Mathematics from Oxford University, where he was a Rhodes Scholar, and a Ph.D. in Mathematics from Johns Hopkins, after which he did post-doctoral studies at Princeton University. He served as a Professor of Physics & Astronomy at BYU, 1971-78, and holds patents on thermonuclear-fusion plasma- confinement techniques.

"He and Alex were colleagues," Nicholas said softly. "Now, let's see about you, Mr. Masters."

Nicholas typed in Dr. George W. Masters: George W. Masters holds a B.S. in physics from MIT, an MS in Electrical Engineering from MIT, and a Ph.D. in electrical engineering from the University of Florida.

It was obvious to Nicholas that, unlike his own career, Alex's had bordered on genius. He couldn't help but feel a little hurt that there was so much his brother had never shared with him. Alex had been a deep and quiet thinker, at times so focused on his work that even Francesca complained about his absence. Still, it was unsettling that only now, after his death, was he catching glimpses into the other side of his brother's life. In any case, it was obvious these men had had much to do with Alex's finished system identification programs, and Nicholas decided it would be appropriate to include them in his presentation.

Dusk fell over the city and the hum of its nightlife began. Refreshed by a massage and a supper of salad and a flaky cod baked in cream with shallots, Nicholas sat down to begin penning out his speech: *First, I would like to thank those people whose foundational work in this area helped make possible our subsequent discovery . . .*

A wonderful burst of concentrated energy enveloped him, and he wrote for nearly two hours without looking up. When he finally hit a stumbling block he stood, rubbed the tightness out of his neck, and opened the mini-bar. He poured himself a scotch from the tiny bottle, unwrapped some shortbread, and sat back down to work. The scotch was awful, and he found himself wishing he had a bottle of Gabe's Aberlour handy. Still, it was scotch. Nicholas dropped in a few more ice cubes and nursed the drink while hunched over the computers. After another two hours he closed the laptops. It had been a productive evening but he was exhausted. With a deep yawn he crawled into bed and fell asleep without even turning off the lamp.

After he shaved and showered the next morning, Nicholas realized the stylish clothes he had bought in Cuers would not fit in with the subtler elegance preferred by corporate New York. He wolfed down a quick breakfast and hopped a cab to Barney's, where an impeccably dressed sales assistant sold him enough off-the-rack Armani to get him through his meeting with Malachi and any others that might follow. He bought a set of tanzanite and gold cufflinks to remind him of Cassandra.

He looked himself over in the full-length mirror. The banker's dark-gray three-piece suit, salmon-hued shirt, smart tie, and handmade Italian shoes offered a look he figured would stand up next to Malachi or any of his associates. He could use a haircut, but that would have to wait. Ten minutes later he was in the back of a taxi on the way to Malachi's office, where a private elevator carried him to the fortieth floor. He felt slightly nauseated when the door closed and the box began shooting skyward. *At least its not the smelly catacombs of Paris*, he thought.

The elevator doors slid open to reveal an enormous lobby slick with dark gray marble tiles that reflected tiny spots of light from the hundreds of halogen bulbs inset in the ceiling above. He felt immediately humbled, and realized that this was exactly what the designer had intended. He smiled to himself. He wasn't about to let this intimidate him. Squaring his shoulders, Nicholas walked confidently forward. More strategically placed lights illuminated pieces of art he recognized as works by Todd Murphy, a contemporary artist. Walking past the enormous, somber pieces made him think of old fairy tales when the prince had to pass through the evil forest to complete his quest. The artist's subjects, waif- and ghost-like, floated against black backgrounds as if calling out a warning to all those who passed into Malachi's lair. *Wow*, he thought, *that jet lag is sure giving me strange thoughts. And after what I had just seen in Europe, this stuff just doesn't impress.*

A tall angular woman with jet-black hair cut in a short Prince-Valiant style greeted him at the end of the lobby. The Keeper of the Gate. "You are Dr. Shepard," she stated flatly.

He immediately recognized the steely voice as that of Malachi's assistant. "Yes, I have an appointment with Malachi Foust."

"Follow me." Her voice was as cold as the marble floors.

She walked down a hallway and opened a set of double doors, motioning for him to enter. Nicholas took a step back, adjusting to the change in temperature. The lobby and hallway were cold and gray, but Malachi's office radiated gracious warmth. He could feel himself relaxing in its womb-like embrace. He swallowed and entered.

The financier rose from behind his huge desk and greeted Nicholas warmly, his handshake firm and friendly. "Nicholas, I am so pleased you decided to fly to New York," he said. "Where were you, was it Europe?"

"No. Peru," answered Nicholas quickly without batting an eyelash..

"Ah yes, Machu Piccu," Malachi smiled. *What a damnable liar*, he thought. "I didn't like it there. A filthy, disgusting place. My office building is more impressive that that overrated pile of rocks."

"I've never heard it described quite that way," responded Nicholas. "We enjoyed it very much and thought it was quite impressive."

Malachi grimaced and quickly changed the subject. "Here, take a look at some of these blueprints and pictures, Nicholas. I was looking them over when you arrived. This is some of the architecture I had commissioned for my global offices. Later, if there's time, I'll give you a quick tour of the first forty floors my company occupies."

"These are impressive, Malachi," said Nicholas as he studied them.

"Do you think so? I'm a frustrated architect," lamented Malachi. "Alas, there is not enough time in the day or in one's life. But at least I can hire great talent to execute my visions." He smiled. "Can I offer you a cigar? The fire marshal tells me it's illegal to smoke in this building. Screw them, I say. This is America, not Red China for God's sake! I own this damn building! I will smoke in my office anytime I please." The financier chuckled and lifted the top of his humidor to reveal a row of cigars. "Try one," he urged. Nicholas declined.

The pleasantries wound down to their inevitable conclusion as the two men looked out over Central Park, talking about travel, the weather, and the qualities of modern art. Malachi finally waved Nicholas to a large comfortable leather sofa. Once both men were seated Nicholas began outlining his thoughts about the presentation.

Malachi nodded in agreement. "I'd love to read your completed draft," he offered. "I'm good at proofreading, and if there are any logical fallacies in it, I'll find them and you can fix them."

"That's nice of you, thanks."

Pleased to have settled that point, Malachi shifted direction. "Now, I'd like for you to meet my colleague, Mika Hunter. You'll be working with her at some length on the details for the conference."

He pushed a button. "Mika? Would you please come and join us in my office? Dr. Shepard is here." Nicholas rose politely and straightened his tie. He was curious to meet the woman his brother had found to be such a formidable associate.

Instead of coming through the private door between the two offices, Mika walked around through the lobby to enter through the big double doors. Steeling herself to greet her former lover's twin, she pushed the doors open and pasted a welcoming smile on her face. Unbidden, Alex's name came to her lips and she felt the room swirl around her. She lightly touched the thick doorframe and silently caught her breath as she stared at the tall handsome man gazing at her with a bewildered look on his face. She could not take her eyes off of him.

Malachi cleared his throat. His face was a mask of disapproval and puzzlement. "Mika—Mika!" he said sharply, snapping her into focus.

"Dr. Shepard," she smiled warmly as she shook his hand. "What a pleasure it is to meet you at last. You will forgive me, Dr. Shepard, for my entrance. I rose quickly from my desk and I became dizzy for a moment."

She bowed and shook his hand. Nicholas bent his head to study her face, but she did not raise her eyes to meet his.

"I am sure we will be speaking again," she said softly. "I am afraid I have a conference call and you must excuse me." She gave Malachi a brief nod of apology and turned quickly to leave.

Malachi frowned. Her behavior lately had been one bewildering at best. But, for now, he finally had Nicholas in his office.

Chapter 47

Were she a ship cresting the ocean waves, the London Savoy Hotel would be the *Queen Elizabeth*. Crowning the end of a small street off the Strand—the only street in England where one can drive on the right—she stands proudly, honoring the medieval Savoy palace with every architectural embellishment designers in the year 1889 could imbue her with. However, the lobby was modernized one too many times, and did not sit comfortably in its high Victorian station.

Cassandra had been to the hotel several times because of her work on a project with the Royal Academy of Arts. Galen, however, had never been to England. His excitement abated somewhat when they were shown to their two-bedroom suite overlooking the river and the London Eye. He stood in the center of the room, smiling but looking out of place and very uncomfortable.

"What's the matter, Galen?" she asked as the obvious struck her. "I hope you're not embarrassed to share a suite with me? Nicholas thought it would be safer."

With a sweep of his arm, Galen bowed in the style of an Elizabethan courtier. "Indeed, madam, I would protect you with my life." He walked over to the window and continued in a more serious tone. "I'm used to the simple life, Cassandra. Ninety-nine percent of the people I deal with don't even know places like Paris, Rome, and London exist. They have a different, more basic reality—one that often can't rise above abuse and addiction."

He stared down at the river that had brought civilization to this island two thousand years earlier. "Of course, I daresay that there are as many broken people in this city as in any other. They just don't have rooms in the Savoy." He turned back to Cassandra and tried to smile. "I guess this Texas priest just feels a little out of his element."

They had never considered the priest's reaction. She smiled warmly. "I tell you what, Galen," she said with a wink. "How about a nice cup of tea?" A surprised look swept across his face. "Come on," she laughed, "it's true! There is nothing a good hot cup of tea can't cure."

Galen chuckled in spite of himself, settled his Stetson on his head, and grinned. "I'm game. Let's go!"

When they entered the Thames Foyer, Galen froze. The soft piano music and the array of sandwiches, delicate pastries, teacakes, and scones with clotted cream and strawberry preserves, enchanted the tourists; they horrified him.

"Cassandra," he whispered, "I may be a man of the cloth, but I am still a man. No little cakes and cucumber sandwiches for me, thank you." He took her by the arm and escorted her out the front door and across the street to a corner pub, where he ordered two dark ale drafts as he ambled past the bar and steered Cassandra to one of the dark mahogany booths.

"Now," he said with a satisfied smile as they snuggled into their booth, "there is nothing a tall mug of good beer can't cure." They picked up their heavy glasses and gently clattered the rims together.

Cassandra smiled happily and licked the thick foam from her top lip. "Would the people you counsel be better off if they could see how other people in the world live?" she asked. "Just seeing life differently might offer a better perspective for the way they live their lives."

"No." He shook his head. "Cassandra, you are talking about a world that you appreciate because you know its historical and cultural background. Seeing this reality and appreciating its beauty requires a spiritual clarity most people I work with can't even approach. Some of them would see it as oppressed and oppressor, the haves and have-nots. Others might be driven into a frenzy of covetousness. Still others might settle into bitter resentment."

He took a long pull of the room-temperature ale before continuing. "Furthermore, not many would be able to connect this world you're talking about to its spiritual source—which brings me up against our favorite topic of conversation these days: our mysterious Egyptian symbol. I've been doing a lot of thinking about these warrior monks from the era of the Crusades who seem to have had something to do with the cartouche."

She leaned forward expectantly. "Yes?"

"The Knights Templar saw us all as just souls on the same journey to Jerusalem. Their money might allow them luxuries, but they realized these things ultimately belonged to God and not to them. After all, man could not have created all of these works of art, architecture, music, rich furnishings, and other extravagances had it not been for God's gifts. These Knights knew that everything is a spiritual issue." He paused and assumed a pensive look. "I am growing to appreciate these people very much. I have much to learn from them."

Cassandra's high regard for Galen ticked up a few notches. "I know now why Nicholas and Alex admire you so much. I have never heard truth spoken so plainly." She gulped another mouthful of ale, enjoyed its smooth rich taste, and swallowed. "Ok, so you're saying that these Knights, and those that followed them, the Hospitallers, worked in faith, doing good works and living in grace? So, the implication is there is no evil behind any of this?"

Galen sipped his beer with his large hands wrapped completely around the mug. "Yes to that first part, but of course our story doesn't end there. We're examining the goodness, but there is also evil in some of the people behind this cartouche. There is no doubt about that, Cassandra. Like anything else, people use or abuse power." He looked down at his mug and continued softly. "If Alex was murdered by people who want to keep the power of the box to themselves, it is possible that even now there may be a battle taking place between good and evil."

Cassandra gulped, feeling as if she was sliding into a movie script.

"Tell me, where does the Rosslyn Chapel you want to visit fit into all this?" he asked.

"The Knights Templar built the Rosslyn Chapel, as well as other much larger and grander cathedrals, hospitals, and buildings. They were responsible for Chartres, Notre Dame de Paris, Mont Ste. Michele and many others. But this particular building has so much mystery and legend attached to it that I'm confident we'll find some of our missing links there. We also need to look at the British banking systems. It was here the American stock market was born, you know."

Galen nodded in agreement. "Not to change the subject, but didn't Dan Brown go to Rosslyn Chapel in that book he wrote?"

"*The DaVinci Code*? Yes, he did. But he wasn't after banking information. He was more interested in the goddess. By the way, he should have called it *The Leonardo Code*. Any art historian will tell you that Leonardo was his name. Otherwise, you're just saying, 'of Vinci,' which is where he was born."

Galen thought about that and slouched back in the booth, stretching out his long frame with a sort of growl. "All right, I stand corrected. I didn't read the book cover-to-cover, so correct me if I am wrong. Wasn't *The Da Vinci Code* wrapped up in conspiracy theories?"

"Yes," Cassandra responded. "Don't forget, that book is a work of historical fiction—and a darn good one. But we're actually living our journey, *and we have the box*! Brown can have the romance," she joked, tipping her mug dry.

They finished their beer and left the pub for a stroll through Covent Garden before splitting up. Cassandra left to shop for a few things she needed, and Galen went to look at St. Paul's Church, which comforted him with its plainness and honesty. Inigo Jones designed it in 1633 along with a huge piazza, but of the original design only the church is left. Inside, he prayed at some length for more clarity regarding their search, letting the airy, uncomplicated architecture seep into his bones. He left what money he had in the alms basin and went off to find Cassandra.

He found her toting shopping bags, the contents of which she felt compelled to justify. "I didn't buy any accessories in Cuers," she said. "Things are unbelievably inexpensive at the flea market they have here once a week. I bought this sensational jewelry for nothing compared to prices in the States, and I found a sterling silver mirror for twenty Euros that is surely worth three or four hundred dollars at home."

When Galen regarded her with a cocked eyebrow, she apologized; "I'm afraid it's going to take me a lifetime to become as spiritual as you are."

He disagreed. "You don't have to be monastic to be spiritual. It's all there inside you. You have a wonderful sense of history, and a deep knowledge and enjoyment of art and architecture. I can really feel history live and breathe when I'm around you. That's important, and it's something I personally lack."

ℬ

Back in the hotel, Cassandra powered up her laptop and reviewed her notes to be sure of what they would be looking for the next day. Galen was at his computer as well, communicating with his counseling centers back in the States and answering the several hundred e-mails he had neglected over the past several days.

In her own mailbox was a message from Nicholas telling her about his meeting with Malachi—and with Mika Hunter. "Remember, Alex knew her? When Malachi offered me the job and Alex said he didn't want her anywhere near our discovery? It was a strange meeting. When she walked in and saw me she nearly fainted. Maybe she didn't know Alex and I were twins? I wonder if there was something deeper than just a working relationship between them?"

The last line brought Cassandra up short. She tried to recall when Alex and Mika might have been working together. Surely that was before he met Francesca? Funny, he had never mentioned her before all of this. She frowned and continued reading Nicholas' e-mail. "She looks like a real ice queen, so I don't think I will be asking her about Alex. Anyway, I'm hard at work on my speech. Malachi has offered to review it for me before the conference. Not sure I am comfortable with that. What do you think?"

She wasn't comfortable with it, either. Nicholas could handle Malachi, she thought, so she kept her misgivings to herself: "Since Malachi is paying for the whole event, he probably deserves a sneak peek," she typed.

ℬ

The following day, Galen and Cassandra grabbed a flight to Edinburgh, Scotland, and rented a car. They flipped a coin to see who would drive, an honor neither of them wanted. Galen called "heads" and lost the toss. "Guess I drive," he groaned.

"Well, it's only right since you are left-handed," she laughed back.

Map in hand, she directed him towards the A720 and cringed as the traffic whizzed by them on her side. Galen turned south onto the A703, which was a bit less crowded. A steady drizzle of rain began to fall and they nearly missed the sign to the town of Roslin. Perched at the edge of a steep wooded gorge, the valley of the North Esk, Roslin was a tiny village with no more than a single street of small houses, shops, and two pubs at the end. They would have to drive seven more miles to reach what was formally known as the Templar Preceptory of Balantrodoch.

The last stretch of the journey through the gorge was under a canopy of twisted trees. There wasn't another car in sight. *This is creepy*, thought Cassandra, who nearly jumped into Galen's lap when she saw what looked like a wild pagan head carved into a rock outcropping. They passed a waterfall with a cave behind it, and then another huge head seemed to take shape beside them.

Galen at last summoned his rational faculties. "We're anthropomorphizing."

"I can see why," Cassandra responded. "This is spooky as hell. Look at that."

They passed a cliff face into which someone had carved perfect stone windows. As they would later discover, behind those windows was a warren of tunnels extending far into the cliff face. Legend had it that the famous Scotsman Robert the Bruce took refuge there, and that it had secret entrances accessible only through a well. The ruined stone buildings dotting the landscape added a touch of loneliness to the haunting countryside. Desolate and bewitched, particularly in the rain, Scotland gave Cassandra the shivers. She pulled her sweater tightly around her.

Galen saw the chapel first. The eerie miniature cathedral, decked out in the tallest Gothic architecture either of them had ever witnessed, completely commanded the gorge. "That is without a doubt the most eccentric building I have ever seen," she said admiringly. Galen turned into the short driveway and turned the key to the "off" position. They sat still for a few minutes, studying the architectural detail. The façade, with its magnificently carved entrance, was a huge wall much wider than the chapel itself.

"What's this big wall doing with that little chapel?" Galen asked.

"Apparently, they originally designed it as a Lady Chapel for a much bigger building," she replied, flipping through her notes. She pointed her finger. "See those huge stone blocks jutting out from the wall? That's where the construction came to an end. They ran out of money in 1486 after about forty years of construction. Sir William Sinclair—or St. Claire, or St. Clare, take your pick; the name varies according to whose research you read—began building it. His son, Oliver, never got around to finishing it. Not too many years later, Henry VIII turned the country to Protestantism, and the Knights Templar went underground for a few centuries. They reemerged as Masons, which is something I have not yet looked into. They're next, though, when we take a time trip through Threadneedle Street."

"This is time trip enough," muttered Galen, getting out of the car and putting up his umbrella. He couldn't take his eyes off the flying buttresses and the comical gargoyles adorning every nook and pinnacle. Cassandra stepped out and popped her own umbrella against the rain, and together they entered the building through a 25-foot-tall door.

"I feel like a Lilliputian," she noted, stepping lightly across the threshold.

The interior was adorned with every embellishment known at the time of its construction. Pillars and arches covered with intricately carved leaves, fruits, animals, and other figures competed with bas-reliefs of great Biblical stories. Even the ceiling was festooned with a jumble of carvings. Cassandra and Galen had no idea where to begin.

"Can I help you?" queried a voice from somewhere in the gloom. A very tall, very thin, pleasant-looking fellow appeared from behind a column with a roll of drawings in his hand. They stared as him as though one of the figures carved in the walls had suddenly sprung to life. He laughed. "I'm John Ritchie, spokesman for the Knights Templar."

Cassandra could not believe her ears. She cleared her throat and asked incredulously, "Today's Templars?"

"Indeed, yes," he laughed again. "We are Masons now, technically," he replied in a thick Scottish brogue, "and have become quite popular thanks to some of you Americans." When their mouths did not respond and their eyes remained unblinking, Ritchie shook his head and closed his eyes for a moment, chuckling the whole time. "You're still staring at me. I assure you I am no ghost, and Indiana Jones is not going to appear from the vestry. And neither will Robert Langdon," he added. "We would, in fact, like to dispel some of the mysteries and mistakes that have been perpetuated about us. We have been getting thousands of people here recently with all sorts of notions about this place. And here are two more. Now, what can I help you with?"

By this time Galen was grinning from ear to ear. Here was just the man they needed—a de-mythologizer! "People often assume rumor has truth in it. My name is Father Galen, and this is my good friend Cassandra Shepard." They shook Ritchie's hand and exchanged pleasantries for a minute or two. "Please, call me John," said Ritchie.

"John it is then," replied Galen. He lifted his eyes and looked around at the myriad symbols covering the walls. "About the only thing missing on these walls are Egyptian symbols."

"Don't bet your last communion wine money on that, Father. We have quite a few Egyptian hieroglyphs and carvings," Richie replied.

"You're kidding. Really?" asked Cassandra, playing along with Galen's line of inquiry. "We both love Egyptian art."

"Well then, over there is a small pyramid," he said, pointing to one wall, "and there, just to the right of it, are some hieroglyphs." He walked them along the wall several yards studying the richly decorated surface.

"Are there any cartouches in this cathedral?" asked Cassandra. He gave her a blank look. "A cartouche is an oval or oblong figure in ancient Egyptian hieroglyphics that encloses—"

"I know what a cartouche is, Ms. Shepard," Ritchie answered. "I am just surprised you are inquiring about something so . . . so specific. Follow me."

He led them to a far wall and lifted his arm with a flourish. "As you can see, cartouches cover many of the decorations. Above you are several Moorish-inspired versions. The Templars learned many, many things from the Saracens. This particular cartouche," he continued, pointing to one carved deeply into a Moorish trefoil, "appears most often."

Cassandra and Galen looked at each other and then back at the wall. A shiver slid through Cassandra's legs. They had found what they were looking for. "That is really unique and lovely, John. You don't happen to know what the cartouche means, do you?"

"What it means? No. Do you?" he asked, pursing his lips as he looked at her curiously. "Please don't tell me you are another writer. We don't need yet another mystery!"

"No! I am not a writer, and there is no mystery here," she laughed. "We are just tracking down some family genealogy. Oddly enough, a few of the limbs on the old family tree seem to be connected to this symbol somehow."

"I see," he said nodding. "Would you like to see what our project is all about here?" He unrolled the roll of drawings he had been carrying with him the whole time, both proud and anxious to show off his work. "There are so many rumors and legends swirling around this place. Some believe it is the repository of the Holy Grail, or that we are protecting the Ark of the Covenant, and even the writings of Christ!"

Galen smiled. "So we have heard and read."

Ritchie did not miss a beat. "We have a trust set up to collect funds for the chapel's conservation, and to use technology to 'see' nearly twenty feet beneath the ground, into the vaults sealed by Cromwell. We have raised more than 700,000 pounds! We discovered a mammoth room extending more than ninety feet in length; apparently, it was to have been used as a nave. We're going to get a team of archaeologists with high-tech ultrasound equipment to do a noninvasive search of the walls and grounds. It's a very exciting time for us." Galen and Cassandra agreed.

They examined the drawings illustrating some of the famous legends, such as that of the Apprentice Column, which was supposed to hold a lead casket with the Holy Grail in it. Ritchie took them to a small office at the rear of the building full of books about the chapel written by scholars and scientists. "We need to establish what is true about this place," he said, "and preserve both truth and mystery. Is that not the foundation of faith?"

Galen clapped the curator on the shoulder with a grin. "Enough gloom and doom," he boomed. "The truth will set us free!"

Ritchie spent two hours with them showing off carvings, telling stories, and luring them deeply into the medieval world so they could better see through the eyes of those who had done this work with all the love and skill they possessed. When at last the hour grew late, the Americans took their leave.

On the way out Cassandra dropped a check into the alms basin, which Ritchie found only after seeing them off. He dashed to the door, but they had vanished.

"How very curious," he muttered. "A 'Mrs. Kamen' left me a check signed by 'Cassandra Shepard'. I hope it will cash!"

ß

Once they got back to their rooms in London, Cassandra e-mailed Nicholas to tell him they were now funding part of the scientific exploration of Rosslyn Chapel. "Of more importance is that we found the cartouche in several places. This seems to confirm that the box came across the channel with the Templars," she wrote. "Tomorrow we'll be looking into the history of Threadneedle Street and the banking industry."

The rain socked them in, so they took a late supper in the grill. Impeccable service, crisply grilled salmon, crushed new potatoes with lobster and chervil, and leeks braised with thyme rejuvenated them. They ate with leisure, made friends with the waiters, and lingered over after-dinner drinks. Cassandra was pleased to see the priest relaxing. He did so much for other people. She hoped this little taste of luxury rejuvenated him and his soul.

It was late when Cassandra opened up her mail to find that Nicholas was having a grand time being wined and dined by Malachi and his colleagues. He had not had much contact with the ice queen woman, she noticed, but did manage a reunion with Lev and Felicia. According to Nicholas, Lev was being groomed for a leadership position in Malachi's global business network. *And what are they grooming Felicia for?* she wondered uncharitably.

I'm so glad not to be there, she thought with an inward shudder. She clicked out a long loving note, adding that the next day that she planned "to track down handwriting samples of one John Castaing, who practically invented the Bank of England in 1694."

Galen and Cassandra rose and left early the next morning for a trip to Threadneedle Street, where the Bank of England had set up shop 350 years earlier. They were in a taxi when Cassandra suddenly yelled "Stop!" Perplexed, the driver pulled over and she jumped out, pulling Galen with her. "Come on!" she shouted, handing enough cab fare through the window to cover the tip. They were on Victoria Street, where a display of archaeological finds was displayed not far from the sidewalk.

"Look!" she exclaimed. "It's Mithras, the ancient god!"

"So 'tis," he said, wishing he had drunk more coffee. If he were fully awake, maybe he would be able to recall who Mithras was.

"This is really strange," said Cassandra, standing on the early morning street with her hands on her hips as she pondered the Roman deity. "A temple of Mithras was right here in Roman London, Galen! Do you know what that means?" When he shook his head, she continued. "That means Egyptian mystery cults can't be far behind!"

"Oh, I remember now," he said. "That's the cult everybody thought would overtake Christianity, with its secret rites and so forth."

"Yes! It means the mystery cults existed right here in London. It says so right here." According to a sign she pointed to, a Nazi bomb hit the area during the war and exposed the ancient temple. Her hand gripped Galen's forearm. "If the Mithraists were here, and the Templars were here—there's a church near here where some of them are buried—it seems likely that the box spent some time here, too."

They caught another taxi and continued to the Bank of England museum on Bartholemew Lane, which skirts the Bank of London. Once inside the museum, they split up to look for the several documents

Cassandra believed would be there. After some digging she found a biography of Castaing. She sat down at a table and began flipping through its musty pages. According to the book, Castaing married into the Weishaupt family in Germany and was also connected to Jewish banking families in Amsterdam.

"Excuse me," she said to a museum docent walking past with a stack of books in her hands. "Do you have any letters or other documents from or relating to, John Castaing?"

"Yes," she answered. "We have several file drawers of materials that are not currently on display, but along that wall in the display case," she said, pointing in the corner, "are several of his letters."

Cassandra thanked her and scurried over to take a look. Unsure whether she could take pictures, and figuring it would be better to ask for forgiveness than permission, she nervously eased a digital camera from her purse and took as many photos as she could without anyone noticing.

She found Galen in another room sitting at a large oak table, his hands covered with thin white cotton gloves, the type used by archivists to avoid contaminating or injuring artifacts or old documents. Someone had delivered several folders of letters to him, and he was carefully studying them when she entered.

"What do you have there?" she asked, leaning over his shoulder.

"Letters written by Adrien da Wignacourt and Ramon Perellos y Roccaful, the sixty-third and sixty-fourth, respectively, former Grandmasters of The Sovereign Military and Hospitaller, Order of St. John of Jerusalem of Rhodes and of Malta," he gasped, taking a breath. "That is quite a mouthful. I have letters from them to officers at the bank between 1694 and 1720. Take a look," he encouraged, pointing a white finger at the corner of first one, and then another. Each bore a faint but clearly discernable cartouche. Cassandra patted him on the shoulder, glanced around the room, and snapped several more photos.

"This is our lucky day, eh?" she said in the taxi back to the Savoy. "It's all coming together." They grabbed a quick lunch at the grill.

"I'm going to stay for one more ale and meet you back at the room," said Galen.

When she arrived at the suite, the telephone light was blinking. Cassandra called the desk. "You have a message for me?"

"One moment," said a pleasant voice. He returned a few seconds later. "A Francesca Shepard called an hour ago. She needs to talk with you, and told me to tell you it was urgent."

Cassandra hung up the phone. He stomach knotted as she placed the call.

Francesca answered the telephone. "It's gone," she said desperately. "The box is gone!"

Chapter 48

Cassandra went cold as she stood up and ran her hand through her hair. "Francesca, calm down," she said firmly. "What happened?"

Francesca took a deep breath and exhaled. "I noticed the bed skirting was folded under, and thought maybe the kids had been playing near the bed, so I decided to check inside the suitcase just to make sure. It was just not there!" she wailed.

"The suitcase is gone?" asked Cassandra. "Maybe the kids are playing with it?"

"No! The box and documents inside are missing!" cried Francesca. "I've checked for the suitcase nearly every day, but only this minute opened it, so I don't know when the box disappeared." She was crying now, and Cassandra didn't know whether to try to comfort her or hang up and call Nicholas. She opted for comfort first.

"Maybe one of the kids found it. Did you check with them?"

"Of course! I asked everyone. It has just vanished. What are we going to do?"

"Galen and I are done here, Francesca. We can come straight back to Siena on the first plane we can catch. Does Nicholas know yet?" She privately hoped not. That was all he needed while being fêted by Malachi in New York.

"No, I haven't spoken to Nicholas," answered Francesca. She seemed a bit calmer.

"Ok, I need to call Nicholas," said Cassandra. "He told me he doesn't really need the box any more, but it was important as evidence to support the technology," she explained, *and also to establish a motive for Alex's death*. Cassandra bit her lip and did not voice her thoughts to the young widow.

When she finally hung up, Cassandra collapsed on the bed. *How am I going to break this news to Nicholas?* "I guess I better just tell him," she said out loud as she picked up her cell phone, took a deep breath, and dialed his number.

He answered after the second ring. "Hello? Cassandra? I'm in a meeting. What's up?" She told him the news. Several seconds of silence followed. When he finally spoke, his voice was remarkably calm. "I'll get right back to you."

She waited for his call, tapping her foot and uncharacteristically channel surfing on the plasma television. She flashed right by Nicholas' face on CNN, did a double-take, and flipped back. Rhonda Schaffler was conducting an interview with him—asking him about his keynote address. Nicholas dropped small hints about his economic discovery, but gave nothing away. Cassandra marveled that he could make it sound so fascinating. *No wonder your students love you*, she thought. *And you're a handsome dude, too!* She smiled at his image. Her phone rang, and she answered it with a start. "I'm watching you on television! I assume it was pre-recorded."

Nicholas cut her off. "What the hell happened? Where is the box!"

"I don't know. Galen and I are flying back to Italy tomorrow to see what we can find out."

"Is Francesca alright? Is the family in danger there? You need to assess that, Cassandra. Explain that to Galen. Listen, I have about thirty seconds free. I have to go, but I will e-mail you. Let's handle this by e-mail alone." He hung up.

ɸ

Cassandra and Galen spent the evening packing and trying to find decent seats on a flight to Florence. After Galen went to bed, Cassandra stayed up working with the newest photos, attempting to match the handwriting on documents with the cartouche to the handwriting on those without it. After nearly three hours without any luck, she finally gave up. When she finally fell into bed she slept fitfully, a myriad of names and cartouches and symbols swirling through her head.

Galen, of course, slept like a baby and took charge of the trip to Italy, which allowed Cassandra to get at least a little rest en route. They arrived in Siena late in the day after a mercifully uneventful flight. Cassandra made a quick call to Nicholas to let him know they had arrived and that she would call again in the morning. Then she collapsed into bed.

It was the middle of the next day when Francesca finally woke her up with a tray full of breakfast. She pulled herself up, arranged the pillows behind her back, and took a sip of the delicious hot coffee. "Now I can finally think," she smiled wanly at her friend. "How are you doing? Are you ok?"

"I simply came apart, Cassandra. Everything seemed to cave in on me at once, and I lost it. Galen helped a lot. He talked to me until late last night, and I got some good sleep," she said, helping herself to some *biscotti* on the tray.

"We can't figure out what happened. The house is always open, of course, so I guess somebody came in and just took it, but nothing else is missing, and we know and trust everyone who lives or works within miles of here. I understand that there are people out there who want it, but how in the world would anyone know it was here—much less exactly where it was hidden?" She paused and then asked the question she had obviously been avoiding. "How did Nicholas take it?"

"That's a good question," answered Cassandra, knitting her brows together and biting her lip. "He seemed upset when I talked to him, but he also calmed down pretty quickly. I'll check my e-mail in case he wrote, if you don't mind bringing me my laptop while I freshen up."

"In a heartbeat." Francesca hurried downstairs and Cassandra walked over to the window, studying the puffy white clouds making a *chiaroscuro* of the Tuscan landscape. She ate the baked eggs in cream, ham, and grilled wild mushrooms slowly, feeling her body beginning to re-energize. Francesca returned with the computer and set it up next to the breakfast tray.

Cassandra turned it on. "Here's an e-mail. I'll just read it aloud:

> Honey, Sorry if I seemed a bear on the phone. I know you're working hard, and I miss you so much. Malachi keeps pushing me to be more specific with my draft. He wants enough detailed analysis to support the magnitude of the discovery. He has also been pushing the ice queen on me. Mika keeps asking pointed questions about the phase inversions. In the vast scheme of things, I wouldn't

think that was so important—at least compared to the accuracy of the longer-term monthly and yearly trends. I keep thinking about what Alex said about her, and I don't trust her. My gut feeling is that I need to remove the phase-inversion solution from my speech, and from accompanying documents, just as a precaution. And besides, I'll have enough explaining to do just convincing the world that gravity seems to control at least some human emotions. There are still a few more days until the symposium, so I have plenty of time to make changes.

Cassandra looked up at her sister-in-law. "God, I can't imagine the pressure he's under." She continued with his e-mail: "I'm meeting some incredible people—leaders from all over the world will also be at the symposium, and some major economists. It's very exciting—but I would trade it all to be in Siena with all of you now."

Cassandra looked up at Francesca, and both women blinked back their tears. Francesca patted Cassandra's shoulder. "I remember Alex talking about this Mika," she said with a shake of her head. "She certainly sounded like a witch."

"Is that what Alex called her?"

"Oh, no." Francesca laughed. "You know Alex. He tried to give everyone the benefit of the doubt. I remember him talking about how frustrating it was to work with someone who was so competitive."

Cassandra's heart froze and she managed a weak smile. "When was that, exactly?"

"That was just after Rosemary was born. I remember because he had to make a lot of business trips and he felt so bad that he kept bringing back lovely little gifts for me or the baby." Francesca smiled at the memory and picked up the empty breakfast tray. "Better let you get dressed. See you downstairs."

Cassandra sat there for a long moment, thinking about Alex and the ice queen. *Was it possible?* No! She shook her head, angry with herself for her suspicions. What does it matter now, anyway? Alex is gone and if something happened between them, it was none of her business anyway. *However,* she thought, biting her lip, *could it present a problem for Nicholas?* She quickly hit the "reply" button and typed out a return e-mail. "If you are uncomfortable with Mika, follow your instincts. This discovery belongs to you and Alex, so you are right to feel protective." She frowned. Did that sound innocuous enough? Could she come right out and tell him that she thought Mika would steal the discovery if she could, just like she tried to steal Francesca's husband? She added a few more lines of a personal nature and signed off.

With the help of Francesca's parents, Galen talked again to the children, the nanny, and several farm hands living on the property, but he failed to turn up any additional information. Cassandra's intuition told her that somebody was lying and covering it up pretty well.

Galen suggested they wait and watch, but inconspicuously. "Somebody might make a mistake," he said. "Especially if they think we've given up." Cassandra agreed. What other option did they have?

For the next two days they pretended to take it easy, enjoying Francesca's cooking and waiting for something to happen. Nothing happened. They assumed whoever had stolen the box was now long gone, but the mystery lingered. How did someone slip into the house unseen and know exactly where to find it?

$$\wp$$

Days later they were no closer to finding the box, but the search had to be put on hold; it was time to meet Nicholas in Paris for the symposium. Galen, Cassandra, and Francesca landed at Orly, where a limousine picked them up and delivered them at the hotel hosting the symposium. It was bad enough to be chauffeured there in a limo, thought Galen, whose chagrin was compounded when he found out their destination was the Ritz. Cassandra had to poke him hard in the ribs to get him inside the long black Mercedes. The priest rolled his eyes heavenward and muttered a prayer as he doffed his Stetson and tucked himself inside.

When Nicholas had arrived a few hours earlier, he was ushered into the F. Scott Fitzgerald suite with the same reverence usually accorded visiting heads of state. Sitting on the red brocade Louis XVI sofa, he marveled at the suite's beauty. *Cassandra will love this*, he thought. He laughed out loud, recalling that Fitzgerald had tried hard to gain acceptance in European social circles, but had failed miserably. He never achieved the social status he so desperately sought. *A subtle message for me there?* Nicholas wondered wryly.

A knock interrupted his reverie. He cracked open the door to find his beautiful Cassandra, followed by a porter with the luggage. Nicholas couldn't tip him fast enough, and as soon as the door closed behind him they rushed into each other's arms. Neither spoke for some time.

Francesca and Galen had been assigned adjoining suites on the floor below, where they had a view of the gardens. They had about twenty-four hours to gear up for the event, so Francesca began the painstaking process of deciding what to wear. *Galen can wear black with a collar,* she thought as she surveyed her opulent surroundings, *but I didn't come as prepared for this as I should have.* A quick call to the concierge secured the name of two establishments where she would be treated royally for un-royal prices.

At 6:00 p.m., Francesca and Galen met Nicholas and Cassandra at L'Espadon for dinner. Seated in a curved red velvet tufted banquette, they relished the view of the Vendome gardens, cool and fresh in the early evening light. Francesca glanced around her. At this hour, they had the place almost to themselves. "Nicholas, are you still traveling under your assumed name?"

"No, not with all the publicity surrounding this symposium," he answered. "All I want now is to get it over with quickly. My hope is that once I make the information public, there'll no longer be any reason for anybody to hurt us. The cat will be out of the bag."

"Where is Malachi?" Cassandra wanted to know.

"In meetings, I think," replied Nicholas. "He wants us to come and meet him for after-dinner drinks in the Hemingway Bar. Mika is supposed to show up in a while and give us the details." He grinned. "You will get to meet the ice queen soon enough."

Cassandra managed not to choke as she took a long sip of her wine. *This ought to be interesting,* she thought gloomily.

Sure enough, between the pan-sautéed Dublin Bay prawns and the sole with morel mushrooms in a puff pastry with asparagus, Mika made her appearance. She had abandoned her customary black for a hot pink

Chanel suit with a lime-green silk shirt. To Cassandra, it seemed obvious she was paying particular attention to Francesca, though no one else seemed to notice. The two women had similar tastes. Francesca was wearing a sage-green floor-length skirt and an apricot, off-the-shoulder, gauzy linen blouse.

Mika held Francesca's hand for several seconds longer than necessary, and the widow invited her to join them. Cassandra wanted to scream, but pasted a smile on her face and bit her tongue instead. An outburst now would be both unprofessional and risk damaging the business Mika was conducting with her husband. While Mika paused to consider Francesca's offer, Nicholas gripped his wine goblet tightly and exchanged knowing glances with Cassandra. Mika caught the interplay, offered everyone a small bow, and excused herself. "Malachi will be joining you in the bar at eight sharp." Cassandra watched in relief as the woman walked away.

"Was it something I said?" asked Francesca. "She seemed very nice, Nicholas, and not at all cold as you described her. And I love her taste in clothes."

"Nothing you said, Francesca, and give that woman half a chance and she'll open an artery," Nicholas replied.

Galen had been watching everyone and everything carefully. He wasn't sure what was going on with Nicholas and Cassandra, but he could see right through Malachi's assistant. "That is one hard-working *nouveau* Japanese woman who is totally conflicted over her heritage," he observed out loud.

"Conflicted? How?" asked Cassandra in disbelief. She preferred the malevolent ice queen image.

Nicholas looked at Galen and frowned in an effort to discourage this line of discussion. He didn't want to know any more about her than he already did. Galen seemed not to notice.

"Did you notice the very smart, contemporary clothes with the traditional Japanese manners and Geisha-style hair? Those are two completely different worlds, and worlds apart. Even her name combines two traditions. *Mika* means "new moon" in Japanese. *Hunter* is, of course, American." The look on Francesca's face interrupted his train of thought. "What's wrong?"

Francesca had stopped eating. "I don't know. Something about the Geisha image. I hadn't noticed it until you mentioned it, but now I'm getting a weird feeling."

Cassandra quickly interceded. "Let's skip all this psycho-babble," she suggested with a forced laugh and a pat on the priest's arm. "I think Galen just misses his work. I am more interested in the dessert tray than I am the ice queen's hair!"

"Ok," answered Galen. Something *was* going on with Nicholas and Cassandra, and it had to do with the Japanese woman.

When the coffee arrived, Nicholas began explaining tomorrow evening's main event. "It's all rather thrilling," he said, barely able to contain his excitement. "Malachi asked the Ritz to squeeze two hundred people into the Louis XV salon for dinner. Some may spill over into the *Salon d'Été*. I went to look at it. It's just like Versailles. World leaders have signed treaties there. Meetings of global importance take place there all the time. You won't believe how splendid it is. People like the Prince of Denmark and Margaret Thatcher will be here, along with President Clinton. There'll be Nobel Laureates, not to mention most of my colleagues at Harvard and Yale."

"My God, Nicholas, you must be petrified!" said Francesca.

"I'm at the point where I just want it to be over with. Malachi suggested I tease the financial press with the discovery beforehand, which I did a bit, but not a word of the speech has leaked out to anyone as far as I know. He warned me to be ready for some tough questions, but I'm as prepared as I can be."

Everyone except Galen, who had had enough of opulence and corporate intrigue, was looking forward to moving to the Hemingway Bar. The priest finished his coffee and stood up, excusing himself on the grounds of prayer and meditation. "You'll need those tomorrow, my friends," he said, sauntering off toward his room.

Malachi turned toward them as they entered the bar and waved them over. Cassandra was awed to be shaking hands with a former Secretary of Defense and several former members of Parliament, but got through the introductions with more aplomb than she thought possible. Mustering up the courage, she asked the Secretary about our Iraq foreign policy when he had been in office. The Secretary smiled with enough charm to melt a rattlesnake's heart and totally ignored her question.

"Come join us!" Malachi called out, motioning to a current member of the United Nations General Assembly. Smiling, the diplomat left his leather armchair and joined the group. For the next hour Cassandra participated in a spirited and occasionally contentious, discussion of world politics that amazed both her husband and her sister-in-law. The only thing these diverse leaders had in common—at least as Nicholas saw it—was a commitment to world prosperity. By the time he retired for the night he was confident that he was in the right place at the right time. Nicholas slept more soundly that night than he had in weeks.

Cassandra and Francesca left the next morning to buy their dresses. When they returned, they found the hotel bristling with secret service agents and security people. Everyone had to show identification before even walking in the door and every personal item carried into the event room was opened and pawed over by security.

"Versace doesn't do bombs," Francesca told one of them who insisted on digging endlessly through her small purse. Cassandra hid a grin with her hand. The security checker, humorless to the end, finally waved them through.

Nicholas was going over his speech when Cassandra entered their suite. "I think this is the best I can do," he sighed. "This is about the hundredth draft. Would you like to read it? Or hear it? Should I just stop obsessing?" She voted for the latter.

An hour later they answered a knock at the door. Francesca wore a Versace gown in lime-sherbet green, strapless and tightly wrapped half way to her knees, where it stopped in front and spread to the floor in back in grand taffeta wings. She walked into the room and twirled around, her long auburn ringlets shimmered in the light.

"You look gorgeous!" Nicholas exclaimed, giving her a tender hug.

"Just keep her away from the chefs," Cassandra quipped warmly, kissing her sister-in-law on the cheek. Her own dress was a vintage rose chiffon by Elsa Schiaparelli from the 1920s. It dripped with heavy beading and draped over her shoulders in front and in back. The generous skirt was made in many layers, each one different, so that the dress seemed to float. "It was made for dancing," she said, and took a spin with Nicholas to show off how it moved.

Nicholas answered the door a second time and found Galen standing stiffly in the hallway, looking as though he would rather be anywhere than where he was. His black suit fit him nicely, but instead of a bow tie he was wearing his clerical collar.

"You look sharp, Galen," Cassandra said, squeezing his arm. "Now let's go see what the ice queen is wearing!"

℘

The walk to the elevator was pleasant and full of light-hearted moments. Once they stepped inside, however, the laughter died away, replaced with a more sober, self-conscious air. The hour had finally arrived, and soon everyone would know the truth. And Alex was not here to share the moment.

As they walked into the Salon, Cassandra gasped when she spotted Mika. *Who could miss her?* she thought in shock. The woman was not wearing much of anything at all. She had on a strapless Ungaro charmeuse slip dress in Chinese vermilion, lined in turquoise and cut up to the hipbone on one side and down to her ankles on the other.

A string quartet was playing a Mozart concerto as Nicholas and Cassandra were being shown to their seats at the head table. Francesca, holding onto Galen's ample extended arm, was escorted a short distance to a different table near the front of the room. Each table was festooned with fresh floral arrangements and bottles of expensive cold champagne. Liveried waiters served tournedos covered with foie gras, baked in puff pastry and topped with a black truffle sauce.

Even Francesca was impressed. *She looks simply delightful,* thought Galen. Rivaling a Versace runway model, and with brains to boot, she prodded, listened, and argued, enlivening the dinner conversation with an engaging honesty everyone found refreshing. *I didn't know she had it in her*, Galen thought admiringly. *I thought she only spoke recipe.*

The hum of conversation and excitement filled the room. Cassandra's stomach began turning somersaults as she met dozens of smiles and chatted her way through dinner. Nicholas said barely a word, and she noticed he picked at the food without eating much.

At last, Malachi Foust rose to introduce the keynote speaker. After a few minutes of perfunctory remarks sprinkled with levity, he cleared his throat and got down to the business of the evening.

"Ladies and gentlemen, esteemed colleagues, allow me to introduce you to an economist who has not only distinguished himself in his own field, but also among the scientific community. Dr. Nicholas Shepard will share with us tonight a profound and amazing theory that stands to change the way we view and use the markets in today's economies. In my own humble opinion, it has global applications and represents a paradigm shift of seismic magnitude."

Malachi smiled broadly and scanned the crowd of dignitaries from around the world. "As early as tomorrow morning, we may all be looking at the world's financial markets with an entirely new understanding."

Malachi went on to outline some of Nicholas' accomplishments and academic accolades, and then gestured for him to rise and take the podium.

Chapter 49

"Thank you, Malachi," answered a nervous Nicholas once he reached the podium. "Colleagues, fellow economists and esteemed guests, I thank you for this privilege to address you at the inaugural International Symposium on Economics. I hope to present to you this evening a theory that will immediately and forever change the way you perceive financial markets.

"Indeed; what I am about to share with you is a *new paradigm*, a sea change, if you will, perhaps comparable even to the scientific discoveries of Galileo, Kepler, and Newton. My hope is that you will be impressed with what I believe is a far-reaching discovery concerning the effect of gravity in the analysis and forecasting of economic time series data related to human-influenced phenomena such as those found in publicly auctioned financial markets."

A light chatter filled the room for a few seconds, and Nicholas took the opportunity to reach for his glass of water, drink quickly, and set it back down again. "Let me add immediately that some of you are quite familiar with past attempts to understand such phenomena on the basis of closed-system models, presumably guided by wishful thinking in imitating the great scientific accomplishments of classical physics. This evening I will detail my discoveries in such a manner that you will be taken not only by the freshness of the ideas, but by their common sense.

"Let me begin with what I call Xybernomics. Human behavior is the foundation of all economics, according to every observation made by students of economy throughout the ages. Human behavior is manipulated by an exogenous driver created by depressions in the spatial membrane, connecting the separations between all matter, which encompasses the entire known universe. It is these depressions in the spatial membrane, caused by particles of matter in space, that creates *gravity*."

He swallowed and took a deep breath. *This is it*, he thought. "My discovery, essentially, is this: The financial markets' expansion and contraction is qualitatively in direct correlation to the increases and decreases in gravitational fluctuations experienced at the human level. The increases in market price are in direct response to decreases in gravitational forces and the decreases in market price are in direct response to the increases in gravitational forces."

The low but steady murmur that rippled across the salon was accompanied by dozens of shaking heads and skeptical faces. Nicholas had expected as much. "To accept this statement would be, of course, a quantum leap for most of us. I only ask for your patience, for I must explain this in terms of natural physics." Nicholas threw his audience a winning smile. "I shall endeavor to describe this phenomenon as simply as I can.

"To understand how gravity affects human behavior, we must first revisit Newton's law which, in layman's terms, is this: the strength of the gravitational attraction between two bodies depends on the size of each body and the distance between them. Newton's theory of gravity provided guidelines for using gravity in other physical calculations."

The audience seems to be paying close attention, he thought with relief. He continued, speaking slowly, but making sure he did not come across as patronizing.

"Newton's instructions are used by aerospace engineers to plot the course of rockets. Astronomers and physicists use them to predict lunar eclipses, the motions of other heavenly bodies, and countless other applications. However, Newton speculated many theories to explain what exactly gravity *was*. To Newton, however, the reality of gravity was truly a mystery."

Nicholas paused again to take a drink of water. "It was Einstein's discovery of general relativity that offered the answer. According to Einstein, 'gravity is the fabric of the cosmos.' Einstein deduced that space was not just a vacuum, but a solid membrane, a latticework connecting the separations between all matter. Each particle in the solar systems, the galaxies and including the universe, has an effect on all other particles by means of the connection by this solid membrane. The greater the mass of an object, the larger the depression it makes in the solid membrane, and the greater the gravitational forces produced by the depression."

Nicholas took note as several guests raised their eyebrows and looked at their neighbors in bewilderment. He could read their minds: *Where is this man going with this? Be patient*, he thought. *Be patient.*

"For example," he continued, "the sun is the largest mass in our solar system, and it holds in place not only the planets, but all smaller particles including gases, asteroids, and dust in their orbital paths of least resistance to the sun's gravitational pull. Similar to the sun's gravitational pull, the Earth's gravitational pull holds in place the moon during its orbit around the Earth. To put it simply: the gravitational forces of the moon and the sun affect everything on earth. The combination of the earth orbiting the sun, and the moon orbiting the earth, causes increases and decreases in gravitational forces felt by human beings."

Now that he had fully set the background, he repeated his opening bombshell: "From these facts I make a simple deduction: *Increases in market price are in direct response to decreases in gravitational forces*; and, *decreases in market price are in direct response to the increases in gravitational forces.*"

This time a loud chorus of voices swept the room, punctuated by bursts of outright laughter. Dozens of smiles of indulgence—or was it embarrassment?—were glued onto the faces of his listeners.

Had he already lost them? Well, of course he had.

He had just told the world's greatest economists that none of their theories, studies, or knowledge in general, had any real association with general economic conditions. He had just suggested, indirectly, that the esteemed economics professors might as well resign their positions. He had just told this room of the world's leading financial experts, world leaders, and consultants that they were no longer needed to manage the global economy.

An inkling of what Galileo must have felt when he faced the wrath of the Church swept through Nicholas. He knew he was right, but he was telling every man and woman sitting in front of him that they were completely *wrong*. His adrenaline surged. He had given a lot of great lectures in his day. This one would have to top them all.

He gulped a breath of air, smiled, and continued. "The effect of the motion of the moon relative to the earth has long been known to affect human physiology; witness the human female menstrual cycle and gestation period. From time immemorial, 'lunacy' has been associated with the full moon."

Another burst of laughter threatened for a few seconds to turn into a contagion, but thankfully died away. Nicholas understood the laughter—his theory appeared "loony." He smiled gamely and persevered.

"Recently, serious research papers as well as books by psychiatrists, psychologists, and statistically oriented sociologists have provided overwhelming evidence of an extraordinary correlation between phases of the moon and maximal episodes of violent behavior in mental wards. There is undeniable proof that cyclical changes impact general human violence, such as homicides, suicides, and fatal automobile accidents.

"My brother Alex and I discovered an undeniable— *undeniable*— correlation between prices in public auction markets, such as in the Dow Jones Industrial Average and the S&P 500 Index, and the relative positions of the sun, earth, and moon. Scientists have known for many centuries, in the highly developed field of tidal predictions, from dynamical astronomy, fluid mechanics, and geophysics, how to predict the daily fluctuations of tidal levels at any point on earth, with great precision, for millennia into the future. Using commercially available nautical software to predict the tidal fluctuations, we discovered that an identifiable sequence of times have an extraordinary correlation with times of maximal likelihood of change of the smoothed plot of equities price-action from upwards concavity to convexity, or downwards, and vice-versa. Using standard statistical procedures pertaining to the auto-correlation and cross-correlation of time series, we produced a forecasting methodology, the successes of which would, in the Middle Ages, have led to our being burned for witchcraft."

He looked up and smiled at his audience. Few actually met his gaze. "We hope that in our own more enlightened times, this discovery would lead us to a far different reward!" There was some polite laughter, but not as much as he had expected. He shot a glance at Cassandra, who looked directly into his eyes with a confident smile accompanied by a small nod. He swept his eyes back toward the audience and saw Francesca's glowing smile. Galen, however, appeared more concerned. When he noticed Nicholas looking at him, he nodded and encouraged him to continue.

"We used the well-established engineering discipline of LTI (Linear Time Invariant) System Identification via ARX technology, or autoregression, on an exogenous input, as in the MATLAB System ID Toolbox of L. Ljung, combined with the standard technology of Kalman-Bucy Filtering. This filter extracts signals from noise in estimating the state-vector of a state-space model of a time series, as advocated by M. A. Aoki and his school of econometrics.

"We spent literally hundreds of hours comparing the correlation between intra-day trading records as well as daily records with cyclical physical phenomena, such as weekly, monthly, and yearly cycles, after which the relative positions of earth, sun, and moon repeat."

He looked up and made direct eye contact with his audience. "We found that yearly gravitational cycles correlate with the yearly stock market cycles *100 percent of the time*. That is *100 percent*."

Nicholas watched as several guests turned to look at one another. "That's impossible!" mouthed one of them to a woman seated next to him. They were listening again—carefully.

"The monthly gravitational cycles correlate with the monthly stock market cycles at 99.7 percent. The weekly gravitational cycles correlate with the weekly stock market cycles 82.7 percent of the time.

"I realize that the science I just outlined may be confusing to many of you. I'll leave it to the science writers to sort that out for you. But be assured it is because of these remarkable empirical results that I am standing here in front of you. It would be unthinkable for me to conceal this amazing discovery from the world. If my brother were alive today, he would be standing here alongside me. I have in front of me Alex's papers describing his findings, including descriptions of his software programs that make the incredible predictions. I would like to share them with you.

"It appeared intrinsically impossible to make highly accurate long-term forecasts based upon Linear Time Invariant techniques, because the hypothesis of *constant* coefficients should become less and less plausible the farther into the future one attempts to compute a forecast. But by using fluid dynamic algorithms, we were able to calculate, with great precision, a precise schematic for producing long-term forecasts that are not subject to stability problems, and offer extreme utility.

"Of course, there can be, upon isolated occasions, an external veritable 'shock' applied to any economic time-series. An example might be an announcement by the Federal Reserve of interest-rate decisions or, for individual stocks, unexpected earnings announcements. In the present context, this is like a 'hammer blow', which discontinuously knocks the state-vector to a new position in its n-dimensional state-space.

"Econometricians refer to the visible effects of such external shocks as 'anomalies'. No forecasting system can anticipate every anomaly, and therefore the presently outlined forecasting methodology may be affected by significant anomalies in the case of weekly forecasts. However, it is *never* affected for the longer-term forecasts, whether monthly or yearly.

"One major obstacle we encountered concerns the phenomenon which we call the 'occasional phase-inversion effect'. Normally, the upward or downward—concavity/convexity—of the forecast turns out to be precisely that of the actual data, when known. However, on occasion, the concavity/convexity of the forecast is precisely *opposite* of what actually happened! This is not a symptom of a poorly performing forecast, but an objectively real phenomenon that we eventually solved."

As Nicholas paused to take a sip of water, Galen's attention was drawn to Malachi and Mika. Both had leaned forward simultaneously when Nicholas mentioned the phase-inversion problem. It was like watching two feral cats eyeing their prey. Just as a smile of triumph began to appear on Malachi's lips, Nicholas skirted the answer.

"In short," continued Nicholas, "Alex made a remarkable discovery regarding equities markets, contrary to all wisdom, and effectively reduced it to practice via a suite of MATLAB-language computer programs."

Galen locked his eyes on Malachi, whose face had reverted to its former stony composure. He couldn't see the financier's fist clenched beneath the table in frustration. To anyone watching, Foust appeared calm and collected. Only Mika knew the rage churning inside him.

"Although we made our discovery completely independently, I would like to point out that the objective merit of our discovery is strengthened by regarding noteworthy prior similar conceptions, albeit seen only 'as through a glass, darkly,' as *enhancements* of our fundamental plausibility, rather than simply as potential *detractions* from our priority.

"Leonardo da Vinci designed a toy helicopter five hundred years before Sikorsky built and flew the first helicopter piloted by a man. Galileo created a paradigm when he realized that the earth was not the center of the universe. Kepler defined planetary alignments. Newton and Einstein created a methodology that quantified gravitation, which enabled us to unravel a mystery that will be studied throughout the next millennium.

"Accordingly, if our discovery is an objective reality, we expect that prior students of equities price-action would have published discoveries that can, *in hindsight,* be marshaled to buttress the solidity of our findings. As you all know, the two approaches to the study of equities prices are *fundamental*, based upon such information as studied by accountants in a corporation's annual report, and *technical*, popularly called 'charting'. Until quite recently, prevailing academic opinion has regarded 'technical market analysis' as sheer lunacy—pun intended—but for obvious reasons, and in view of the burgeoning sea-change encompassed here, we restrict our attention to gravitational fluctuations as the only true *leading indicator* and as a guiding light to future market action.

"Finally, we make the *utility* of our discovery manifest by the remarkable success of our unique market-data processing algorithms and procedures, and the magnitude of the answers provided by simple astronomical measurements.

"In conclusion, the discovery we share with you this evening, possesses each of the three desiderata of *novelty*, *utility* and *non-obviousness* to a high degree. I've fully elaborated this in a technical essay and technical appendix, which is available upon your request. In addition, I've included listings of computer programs used in our research.

"Our discovery is in a field where thousands of highly motivated and talented investigators have labored diligently without ultimate success. Accordingly, the present disclosure constitutes an *enabling disclosure*, as the term is used in intellectual property law. Or, in other words, the discovery of *Shepard's Law* is an excellent example of what one Supreme Court patent decision called a 'result long sought, seldom approached, and never attained.' Thank you."

For a full five seconds the room was utterly silent. When the applause began, it was light and polite, but nothing more. It died out within a few seconds.

The silence stunned Nicholas, who drank deeply from his water glass, cleared his throat, and stated, "I will now entertain questions from the floor."

A colleague from Yale he recognized stood up. He had a visible smirk on his face. "Dr. Shepard, it sounds like you're telling us that the moon is responsible for the movement of the stock market. Certainly a man of your credentials doesn't take such a thing seriously?"

A round of snickers swept through the room, and Nicholas felt his face reddening from embarrassment. "That is not what I am saying. I am stating positively that *gravity* is responsible for changes in human emotional behavior, and this behavior can be correlated between the stock market price-action and astronomical measurements."

The Yale economist broke into an outright laugh at this, and his ample girth shook like Jell-O. "Astronomy?" he jeered. "Sounds more like astrology to me!" Raucous hoots echoed inside the ballroom, leaving Nicholas stunned and wishing he could sink into the floor and disappear. Even Lev, seated at the head table with his now-fiancée, Felicia Theobald, was laughing.

A man with bushy black hair and big thick glasses that would have looked stylish in the 1970s was standing in the back of the room, waving his hand wildly in the air. Nicholas nodded in his direction and pointed.

"Sam Griffin, *New York Times*," he said loudly. The press had been deliberately relegated to tables in the salon d'Été where they couldn't hear easily. Griffin, however, had slipped into the larger salon and spent most of the evening slouched against the mirrored walls listening with keen interest. "Dr. Shepard, you spoke of aero-space system identification and a lot of things most people know absolutely nothing about. What does any of this have to do with this symposium and the future of stabilized economies?"

Malachi seethed with anger. *How did that bastard Griffin get in here?* He had specifically ordered security to keep him out. He turned to look at Mika, who merely shrugged and shook her head. A badger of a reporter, Griffin had a habit of wanting to know more than was good for him. Nicholas, however, breathed a sigh of relief—a good solid question he could hit out of the park. Before he had a chance to address the journalist, however, a subtle signal from Malachi brought another question from the rear of the room.

"So you're saying the stock market moves up and down with the tides? Maybe we should all move to the beach."

The whole room erupted now, and it was all Nicholas could do to keep from throwing his hands up in frustration. Such unprofessional behavior was the last thing he expected from this audience. He tried to smile at the joke and answer the question. "Maybe we should," he said. "But all I'm saying is that market price fluctuations correlate exactly with changes in the gravitational forces that also create tidal fluctuations in the oceans and seas—as well as people. Human bodies are more than 75 percent water, and you could say that we as small bodies of water are influenced by gravitational forces just like tides in large bodies of water."

Nicholas could feel his fingers clenching the podium. He thought about Alex. His brother would not have stood up here and absorbed these blows without fighting back. Nicholas gritted his teeth. This was the opportunity of a lifetime, and it was time to take the glove off. He forced a smile.

"Next question!"

Everybody wanted a shot at him, but Griffin was now up on his feet and waving his pen in the air, yelling the loudest. "Dr. Shepard, this is such a radical departure from traditional economics. Does this mean that econometricians have been wrong all along?" Even Malachi enjoyed that question, since it invited Nicholas to continue hanging himself.

"Economics as we know it today, can only give us half the answers we are looking for," Nicholas replied. "Before Alex and I made this discovery, every economist, financial engineer and financial advisor only guessed as to what the future would bring—and I am sure no one in this room will disagree with that."

Nicholas waited, looking out across the sea of unfriendly faces. He was determined to take charge of this presentation. "I didn't think so. Well, as we all also know, often those guesses weren't very accurate." Two or three people actually booed at this knock against traditional economics, but Nicholas swatted it away with a gesture of his hand.

"What I am presenting here today is the other half of the picture. I am presenting the future: known and *predictable* market fluctuations. Until a few months ago, no one knew for sure which way, and for how long, the market would move. We now have the ability to know the direction and duration in advance, which will give us the ability to manage the economies of the world in such a way as to ensure global stability. That, as I see it, will be the true legacy of Shepard's Law."

Griffin walked toward the podium, talking all the while. Several security officers stiffened and took a few steps toward him, but Nicholas waved them away. "When you say half of the picture," the reporter asked, "do you still think traditional economics has an important role to play in your discovery?"

"Absolutely," Nicholas answered. "This discovery gives us the means of knowing only the direction and duration of market movements—but not how far it will fall or how high it will rise. It will take the collective efforts of all economists to determine what properties are present in the market influencing how deep or how high the market will move." The assembled honored guests were suddenly calmer now, and seemed fixed on Nicholas' every word.

"When you say 'properties,' Dr. Shepard, what exactly do you mean?" continued Griffin.

"There are many lagging indicators economists use to make value judgments about what the future might bring. Knowledge, such as the sums of money available for investing in the stock market, is a true indicator. Understanding market sentiments, whether it is bearish or bullish, for example, determines the shift of money from safe investments like bonds or cash, to stocks, and vise-versa. What our discovery will give economists is the understanding of when recessions will begin and end, when depressions are likely and how long they will last, and when bull and bear markets will occur."

I never thought this would be so frustrating, Nicholas thought, as he laid it on the line as plainly as he could. "In truth, there is only one real leading indicator—Shepherd's Law. Everything else is speculation."

Malachi and Mika exchanged glances. Did Nicholas realize that he had just asserted to the entire forum that all of their economic theories were inconsequential? Surely he had not intended to insult anyone, but Nicholas' confidence had the unbelievable ring of conceit.

Professor Shepard has just buried himself, along with his reputation. A perfect note to end on, Malachi thought. Having succeeded beyond his wildest hopes, Malachi stepped to the podium to bring the proceedings to a close. He nodded and smiled lightly in Nicholas' direction, and then gently eased him away from the podium.

"Ladies and gentlemen, it is now time to adjourn. Dr. Shepard will be available for questions on an individual basis. Thank you for coming, and for your . . . attention."

Beneath considerable merriment not even a faint ripple of applause could be heard. Most of the audience looked thoroughly entertained and amused, though several looked outright angry. Not a single person, if Nicholas was any judge, had believed a word he said.

As they made their way from the head table into the milling throng, Cassandra hugged him tight and whispered in his ear, "You were brilliant, and I smell a rat." He smiled appreciatively and turned right into Griffin, who had apparently been waiting to introduce himself.

"I'd love to meet with you next time you're in New York," the reporter proposed.

Malachi, close by but surrounded by fawning admirers, couldn't hear what Griffin and Nicholas were saying, but whatever it was, he knew he wouldn't like it. Griffin was a scavenger, with way too much interest in Malachi's business ventures. Both he and Mika went to a lot of trouble to keep the man at arm's length.

"If you're right," Griffin told him, "the world is in for a hell of a shock. I'd really like to hear more. Do you have time later this evening?"

With his adrenaline sinking like a stone, Nicholas was beginning to feel like a deflated balloon. Except for this lone journalist, everyone else was avoiding him like the West Nile Virus. One out of two hundred people. "I can't this evening," he mumbled to Griffin, but if you will give me your card, I will be in touch."

Malachi beamed in spite of himself. He was delighted. The symposium had dealt a deathblow not only to Nicholas' 'discovery' but probably to his career. The thirty-year ascendancy of the "random walk" theory—which claimed the market was utterly unpredictable— remained without a serious challenger.

Precious few people knew the trouble to which his family had gone to ensure that theory was enshrined in its place of preeminence. Even fewer knew about the deal his father, Bernard Foust, had struck with the heads of Princeton University thirty-five years earlier—the fabulous scam that had brought the greatest econo-physicists in the world to that campus to take up the challenge of finding a method to predict the stock market. Eleven scientists spent an exhausting six weeks working day and night— only to conclude that the stock market was a quasi-periodic *sine* wave that could not be predicted. None of the scientists knew, of course, about the huge sum of money Malachi's father had paid the university to make sure that Princeton's own team of researchers manipulated the data. The eleven scientists all believed they had done their best, and they were further reassured of their findings when Princeton economics professor Burton Malkiel published his best-selling *A Random Walk Down Wall Street*, a book that solidified the "random walk" theory as unassailable.

Just as his father had done more than three decades earlier, Malachi had taken the steps necessary to protect the family's legacy.

Chapter 50

Nicholas plowed his way through the crowd while Galen followed as closely as possible. The priest had been too absorbed in his own specialty—people—to pay much attention to Nicholas' speech. Galen's place near the front of the room had afforded him a nearly 180-degree view of the players on the stage, and he had studied them intently.

When the speech began, Malachi had focused exclusively on Nicholas. It was the polite thing to do in a setting like this, but it was more likely he did so because he wanted to make sure he stuck to the script. Although Lev and Felicia were seated next to him, Malachi paid them no attention whatsoever. This didn't appear to bother Lev, who was obviously showing off Felicia to the world's power brokers.

Sitting next to Malachi and apparently on call, if needed, Mika sat throughout the speech without registering any outward emotion. The only time she looked even remotely interested was during the brief discussion on phase-inversion. Indeed, she had barely lifted her head during dinner, which seemed curious to Galen. At the cocktail party before the event, she had held court in the Salon d'Été, surrounded by Japanese men. Even when people were laughing at Nicholas' ideas, Mika stared into space or at her coffee cup. *Why?*

What amazed Galen more than anything else was the question and answer session, if you could call it that. By all rights it should have been an engaging and lengthy give-and-take between some of the greatest economic minds on the globe. Instead, only one intelligent question had been asked by a reporter. *One question.* The same man had approached Nicholas after the affair broke up. *He is an interesting character*, thought Galen, *and the only person in attendance not wearing a tuxedo.*

The reporter and Nicholas were talking, but the crowd noise was too loud for him to catch any of it. As Galen eased his way forward, he spotted Malachi barreling his way through the throng of attendees. He had a smile on his face and was nodding or chatting to everyone he passed, but he dripped pure displeasure. When he reached Nicholas, Malachi grabbed his arm, leaned over and said something to the reporter, and led his featured speaker away.

Galen followed discreetly behind the throng as Malachi ordered everyone to head for the Ritz Club for a round of after-dinner drinks. With a studied look of indifference, the priest ambled a few steps behind Malachi, Lev, Felicia and Mika, listening as they chatted happily about the success of the symposium. Galen found the conversation both curious and a little disturbing. From the audience's reaction, it was obvious no one had given the least bit of credence to Nicholas' theories, and many had openly scoffed at them. A prominent Georgia politician had sworn he would see to it that Nicholas never taught another class at Emory University. *How was it that Malachi did not understand all this?*

As the throng of people moved toward the paneled clubrooms, Nicholas caught sight of Galen, excused himself, and waited for his friend to catch up. He wanted to talk to the priest without being overheard. Nicholas needed to tell Galen about his meeting with Griffin.

"To tell you the truth, that guy was the only bright spot in the whole deal," Nicholas admitted with obvious dejection.

Galen sighed. "I know it did not go as you had hoped, Nicholas." He hesitated, looking over both shoulders before continuing. "I just overheard Malachi and his people chattering on about the symposium's great success. You were too far away to hear it."

"Success? They said that?" asked Nicholas with shock written across his face.

"Yes. Given all the money and prestige Malachi expended on this evening, and the hostile reception you received, it is a rather odd thing to say, don't you think? Oh, I almost forgot. Lev and Mika clearly agreed with him."

Nicholas' shock turned to puzzlement. "I don't get it," he finally replied. "Maybe Malachi was just saying that to save face. What did you think of him?"

"Of Malachi?" Galen stopped before an antique tapestry, ostensibly to study it. "I think he's Alexander VI reincarnated."

"The Borgia pope?" Nicholas answered. "Why would you think that?"

"That man is a king full of rage. He has no boundaries or scruples, and no sense of honor. I think he is a man who will do anything to secure and enlarge his empire. Now that I think about it, he's more of a Machiavelli, really. I could not heal him or help him."

Nicholas regarded his friend with disbelief. "I have never heard you condemn a human being like that."

"I'm just offering you an honest evaluation, Nicholas," answered Galen slowly. "It's not up to me to judge or condemn. That's God's prerogative. But there seems a presence of—I use this word cautiously, lest you think I speak of the devil—of *evil* about him. My advice to you is not to sell your soul to avenge your brother's death."

"It's odd you should say that just now," said Nicholas, looking at Galen closely for his reaction. "He has been pushing me to come back to New York. When I told him I believed Alex was murdered, he said he would help me find whoever was responsible. He also wants to finance further research into gravity and human behavior."

Galen placed one of his large hands on Nicholas' shoulders and gripped it gently, but firmly. "I don't mean to sound harsh, my old friend, but why should he care about Alex? He barely knows you and he never set eyes on your brother. I don't think you need Malachi Foust to lead you to whoever was behind Alex's death. As for your research, wouldn't you feel more comfortable doing that in an academic setting, free of any outside influence?"

Nicholas sighed softly and nodded. "That occurred to me as well, Galen, but I guess I want to know what he has to offer. Maybe I can take some of his help, and continue on my own."

That's a bit naive, thought the priest. "I seriously doubt Malachi would offer you half a loaf of anything, let you eat it, get up from the table, and leave without paying him back—with interest." He looked his friend straight in the eye. "Think deeply about your decision, Nicholas. I don't trust that man, and neither should you."

When they entered the bar where Malachi was holding court, images of the Borgia popes swept through Galen's mind. Malachi would have fit quite easily into that royal household. To Galen's dismay, the modern day money-counter stood up and headed in his direction.

℞

Malachi honed in on the priest as he slid across the room. *That man has very little to say, but he is a confidant of the Shepards,* thought the financier, who was curious to see what was going on behind the enigmatic countenance of the tall priest.

"What did you think of my little evening, Father?" he asked, motioning Galen, Nicholas, and their female companions to join them. Everyone sat except for Malachi and Galen, who remained standing at the end of the table.

Cassandra noticed that Lev, Felicia, and Mika were seated one table away, where they were quickly joined by a couple of Mika's Japanese admirers. Her first inclination was to sit with her back to them, but she decided that it might be better to keep her eye on the odd little group. She sat facing them; Nicholas dropped down next to her.

Foust's steely blue eyes and sly smile made Galen momentarily uncomfortable. *His little evening?* he thought. Galen did not return the smile. "It was one of the most interesting evenings I have ever experienced, Mr. Foust," he replied honestly. "But I lead a simple life. I own no stocks and never will. I'm just here for moral support." He caught and held Malachi's gaze, wondering how the great financier would respond.

Malachi bared his teeth. It might have been a smile, but to Galen it looked downright predatory. "Father, call me Malachi. I like your clarity, your straightforward way of speaking." The financier lowered his voice, passed his glass of brandy to his left hand, and gripped Galen's shoulder with his right. "So please take no offense at my own forward response, Father. I have never understood attitudes like yours. If the world was filled with people like you, think of how dull it would be! None of the finer things in life—and worse yet, no competition! Which means there would be no people like . . . me." Malachi bared his teeth again. They glistened in the soft light. "The world's civilizations would still be tribal. Where would that get us?"

"Into heaven, possibly," Galen replied softly, looking him squarely in the eye. Malachi scowled and his grip loosened immediately as he let go of the priest's shoulder. "The world will always have people like us, Mr. Foust. It's all about checks and balances."

Malachi's eyes narrowed. *He had underestimated this man.* "I like all the checks coming to me, and I'll balance the books. Make no mistake on that score. Father."

Galen imagined the man pulling gloves over claws. *Was he actually trying to pick a moral fight with a priest? Make no mistake about what? Was he threatening me? Trying to corrupt me?*

Just then, a member of the U.S. Senate stopped by the table to congratulate Malachi on the success of the symposium. The financier turned away from Galen, for which the priest was profoundly thankful. Cassandra called to him to sit down and have a drink with them.

Galen pulled up a chair as Nicholas redirected the discussion to the ongoing Senate investment scandal. A group of ex-senators playing the market had beaten the indexes by 12 percent per year between 1993 and 1999—an even better return than CEOs buying their own stocks. The scandal had come to light just a few months earlier, and financial and political pundits were still buzzing about it.

"It seems nearly impossible that they could produce that sort of return, year in and year out," someone observed.

"I need to hire them as consultants!" laughed Malachi, returning to his seat. The truth, of course, was the other way around. He was *their* consultant; it was his way of buying political influence. His people were busy at that very moment trying to quash any further investigation, particularly by Sam Griffin. Galen excused himself at this turn of the conversation; Cassandra and Francesca followed suit as soon as protocol allowed. Nicholas remained behind, speaking about his lecture and discovery to a pair of Malachi's friends.

They gathered in the Shepards' suite, where Cassandra kicked off her shoes with a groan of relief and fell into a *chaise*. Francesca did likewise. "What did you say to that man, Galen?" asked Cassandra. "I watched you two conversing and I thought for a minute Malachi was going to eat you alive."

The priest lowered himself into the one of the damask chairs and sighed. "I confronted him with a happy, healthy person who has no need of him. He can't buy, bribe, or influence me, but it doesn't mean he won't try." Galen shook his head sadly. "I have been thinking about it. Malachi tries very hard to conceal his anger with a smile, smooth talk, and all that forced geniality. I've been reading a new translation of the *Iliad* by Robert Fagles: 'Even if he can swallow down his rage today, still he will nurse the burning in his chest until, sooner or later, he sends it bursting forth'. Homer was writing about King Agamemnon. Only the name has changed."

"That is the best description I've heard yet," declared Cassandra. "I think he is just plain creepy, and his son is a chip off the old block."

Francesca slipped off the four-inch heeled sandals that had made her seem six-foot-two. "I thought Nicholas did a fantastic job, Cassandra, even if the room was full of some of the snobbiest and rudest people I have ever spent an evening with! Nicholas got stronger and stronger as he went on—I could feel Alex's presence from beginning to end, urging his twin along." Her friends nodded, and Cassandra was thankful for the kind words.

"And now, ladies, I propose we move onto more important issues," exclaimed Galen as he rose to tower above them. "Let's see what they have in the mini-bar."

All three laughed deeply as Galen strode to the small refrigerator and opened the door. As he poked and prodded through the selection, Cassandra and Francesca debated the merits of the menu and ordered room service for Nicholas, who was going to be famished by the time he made it upstairs. The 'morrow would bring sadness with it, for the party was about to split up again. Galen needed to get back to the States, and Cassandra needed to return to London to finish her research on the documents. She was more determined than ever to determine the box's lineage through the ages and, by doing so, track down the most recent owners of the box. Gabe had told her that his father had no idea who owned anything in that room, but it seemed likely that whoever had a hand in stealing the box from the Gamba's house also had once owned it—or knew who did.

℘

It was nearly midnight by the time Nicholas returned to the suite. Galen and Francesca had long since turned in. After filling Cassandra in on the conversation at the Ritz Club, Nicholas offered a cursory dissection of his lecture and its disastrous aftermath.

"I told you earlier I smelled a rat, and I still do!" Cassandra seethed. "You were set up to fail, Nicholas."

Her husband sighed and shook his head. "I am so tired right now I can't think straight. Maybe you're right, who knows?"

When the subject turned to the immediate future, Cassandra's insistence on traveling alone to London created a small late-night firestorm. "I don't want you traveling by yourself, Cassandra. Why don't you at least take Francesca with you?"

"Nicholas, for God's sake, her children need her right now! I should only be gone a few days, and then I will join you in New York," she replied firmly, turning away so he could not see her face. Alex's murder, the burning of the Beaudrot's house, the theft of the box in Siena— she couldn't deny that she was frightened, but this would never end unless she could discover who was behind it. She turned back to him and put her hands on either side of his face. "Please, let me do this Nicholas. We have to know the answers, and I promise I will be extra careful."

"Ok," he finally answered with great reluctance. "I know you will be careful." Cassandra was right. They had to find the answers, and she was the one best suited to continue digging through the historical paper trail. But that didn't mean he had to like the idea.

℘

Downstairs in the Hemingway Bar, the guests were trickling away. Malachi had already returned to business as usual, fielding a midnight cell call.

"You have it? *Bella.* Take it to Florence. I will send a private jet for it. Tell Customs it is merely an antiquity. We will take care of them. And the documents? Good. Send them along as well." He clicked his phone shut and nodded to Mika, who took out her phone and began arranging the pick-up.

To give her some privacy, Malachi invited the Japanese investors at her table to join him. They had been drinking Suntory whiskey for the past two hours, and were hoping to find some women to host them for the rest of the night. Malachi didn't give a tinker's damn about their physical needs. It was time to talk business.

"Gentlemen, I want to propose a toast. You have seen your stock market rise some 42 percent since last March, thanks to the efforts of the Bilderberg Group. Now, do you believe my Group can restore your markets to prosperity?"

Words of praise and thanks spilled from their lips as the members of the Japanese delegation raised their glasses in unison. Malachi raised his above theirs.

℘

It was a somber group that packed its bags the next morning. They had all seen the "CNN Today" report that had poked fun at the symposium. The running joke had to do with tides washing over the Manhattan markets. Nicholas went out and brought back a few newspapers. On its front page, *Paris Match* ran a composite photo of Nicholas with a fishing rod and a hat full of lures beneath a banner headline—*Poisson Marches*. "World's leading economist believes tides cause market movements," ran the sub-title. Cassandra translated the article until Nicholas finally groaned, "Enough!"

Francesca and Galen rummaged through other papers looking for something positive to share with Nicholas. Francesca found it first.

"Hey, look at this. It's the *New York Times*, with a by-line from Paris by Sam Griffin. Wasn't that the man you were talking to last night?" she asked. Nicholas nodded. "It's on the financial page, and just says 'Gravity Moving Markets?' for a headline."

She handed the paper to Nicholas, who skimmed through Griffin's summary of his speech. At Cassandra's urging, he explained to the others what it said. "It ends with Griffin writing this: 'Truth is often overlooked, ignored, and rejected until it proves itself beyond the shadow of a doubt. Dr. Shepard's science will need testing. Like any stock, his theory must be evaluated by how it performs over time. He proposes empirical proof that the financial markets are predictable—a radical notion to say the least. This reporter, however, sees the possibility of a new truth, a paradigm shift, a world-changing discovery that might lead to global prosperity. We must hope Dr. Shepard is given time and support for further research, and welcome him as possibly this millennium's Galileo.' That's it," sighed Nicholas.

Francesca looked up at his gloomy face. "I hope this doesn't mean that they will place you under house arrest until you recant your wicked theories!" She laughed out loud, but laughed alone.

Cassandra offered a weak smile as if to say 'thanks,' but Nicholas' sense of humor had long since abandoned him. "It's worse than that," he said quietly. "Except for that one man, I might as well be locked away. My reputation is in ruins, and I've become a laughing stock." His elbows were resting on splayed knees, his head hanging low between them.

"Right now, Nicholas, nothing any of us can say or do will make you feel any better," Galen said delicately, rubbing his hand on his friend's shoulder. "Despite my low opinion of that man, you might have to go back to New York and work with Malachi Foust."

At that, Nicholas raised his head and looked at Galen in surprise. "What? That is exactly the opposite of what you were just telling me last night!"

Galen nodded slowly. "I know. But I have been thinking deeply about this much of the night and this morning. Foust is the only one who can restore your reputation, and for an academician, your reputation is everything. I despise it, but I cannot ignore the fact that the man has the power to help you and the means to make it happen. If he really believes the symposium was a great success, his success came at your expense. In other words, he used you, Nicholas." Galen waited a few seconds to let the words sink in. "Maybe it is time to return the favor."

Nicholas sat up. "Manipulate the manipulator?" Cassandra and Francesca stood by, their mouths open and their ears locked into the conversation.

Galen tightened his lips. "This is not the sort of advice I normally give, but people like Foust are so arrogant they don't realize when they are being used. They are like crocodiles on their own sandbank; it's their territory and they think they are in charge. But if you know a reptile's habits, you can easily control it. It's the same thing with salespeople. They'll buy anything."

Nicholas smiled and began to rub his temples as he contemplated Galen's words. It would never have occurred to him to turn the tables on Malachi, but his friend's advice and intuition was always sound.

Besides, it was the only viable option left.

Chapter 51

After a very long goodbye, Cassandra returned without incident to the Savoy in London, one of her suitcases bulging with printouts of documents. She had reserved a smaller suite on the same floor so that she could look out over the historic Thames. In an odd way, it was nice to be alone. She wanted to take some time to gather her thoughts and get organized. She longed to return to their normal lives, but knew that wasn't going to happen as long as they lived in fear.

Once inside her hotel room, Cassandra began by making a list of all the lists she had compiled. Once that was done, she began moving names from one list to another, linking them to other names belonging to the same period. Beginning with the Knights Templar, she worked her way forward until she reached the late 16th century, when the name John Dee appeared.

What do I know about that man?

She turned to her laptop and began searching for information. A simple Google search returned a tremendous amount of data, much of it from a group calling itself The John Dee Society. Dee was one of Elizabethan England's most fascinating characters. He had dabbled in all the popular mystic arts of the time, practiced alchemy, the occult, and astrology, and claimed to speak to angels. Nothing seemed to be too exotic for the man. Oddly enough, even though he was a cabalist and soothsayer, he was also a man of science. Dee designed navigational instruments using Euclid's geometry, translated Euclid into other languages, and applied his mathematical studies to scientific theories. Dee built a personal library of more than 4,000 volumes. When he became a confidant of Queen Elizabeth I, he provided her with astrological readings and convinced her it was her legal right to colonize North America.

Cassandra's eyes widened as she continued reading. Dee based this premise on the legend of Madoc, a Welsh Prince who established the first colony in New England in the Middle Ages. These settlers, according to this website, intermarried with the Indians and therefore left no proof of their existence. *Yeah, right,* she thought. It was Dee who coined the word "Britannia," and he was a driving force behind Elizabeth's Navy, which (according to the information Cassandra was reading) defeated the Spanish Armada after Dee put a hex on the enemy fleet and it sailed into bad weather. Another Dee admirer was playwright William Shakespeare, who developed the characters Prospero and King Lear after the court favorite. Dee is also commonly recognized as one of the founders of the Rosicrucian order.

While much of Dee's resumé was impressive, there was one thing on his list of accomplishments that stood out above all others. Cassandra put her finger on the screen and read the words out loud.

"Dee sold the mysterious Voynich Manuscript, a cipher yet to be deciphered—'the Everest of cipher studies'—to the Holy Roman Emperor Rudolph II, for a fortune in gold. This manuscript today resides at Yale University in the Beineke Library. To this day, no one has been able to translate this medieval artifact."

The Voynich Manuscript?

Cassandra sat back and stared at the screen. "Where there's a fortune in gold . . ." she whispered aloud, scrolling through the Internet to learn more about it. The more she read, the more inquisitive she became.

The manuscript is considered by many scholars and students of history to be "the most mysterious manuscript in the world," largely because no one can agree what it is or what it says. "It is either an ingenious hoax or an unbreakable cipher," claims one historian. Its name comes from its discoverer Wilfrid M. Voynich, an American antiquarian book collector. In 1912, Voynich stumbled across the manuscript buried inside a collection of ancient manuscripts housed in a villa outside Rome. The 325-page vellum manuscript, which is copiously illustrated with seemingly scientific drawings, measures seven by ten inches. Unfortunately, it is written in an unknown calligraphic script, and no other example of the script has ever been found. Who wrote it, where it was created, or what it says, has never been determined. Most experts believe it is European in origin, written sometime between 1400 and 1600 A.D. According to a scrap of parchment that was attached to the manuscript, it once belonged to the private library of "Petrus Beckx S. J.," the 22nd general of the Society of Jesus.

This is one fascinating mystery, thought Cassandra. She typed in a new search string, pressed 'enter,' and scrolled down the results. An entry in an ancient manuscripts forum utilized by scholars looked particularly intriguing, and she clicked on it: "*Dee stated in his diary that he had 630 ducats in October 1586 (Keynes, 1931), and his son remembered that while in Bohemia, his father owned a booke containing nothing but Hieroglyphicks, which booke his father bestowed much time upon: but I could not heare that hee could make it out' (Browne, in Keynes, 1931).*"

When she learned a copy of the Voynich Manuscript was housed at Hatfield House, where Elizabeth I was raised until she became queen, Cassandra decided it was worth the twenty-mile train ride to have a look.

She rubbed her eyes and yawned. *No wonder I am tired and hungry,* she thought after looking at her watch. She had burned several hours reading up on John Dee and the mysterious manuscript. After freshening up, Cassandra went downstairs and ate dinner alone in the American Bar. She couldn't resist the temptation to stay and listen to the Brent Runnels Trio, a jazz band from Atlanta. It was a mistake. The cool Georgia jazz only made her homesick and miss Nicholas all the more.

The next morning, Cassandra walked to Waterloo Station and caught the train to Ware to visit Hatfield House. The sixth Marques, Robert, and his wife Marjorie Wyndam-Quin had spent many years lovingly restoring the Jacobean manor house and grounds. The day was bright and sunny, and Cassandra found herself surrounded by a handful of tourists admiring the renovation and the beautiful gardens. Once inside, a 12-year-old American boy became terribly upset when he spotted animal heads mounted in the library. "Back then," his mother assured him, "people didn't know about animal rights." Cassandra rolled her eyes and bit her lip to keep silent.

When the small tourist group ambled down the hall, Cassandra took the opportunity to step quickly into the first large parlor. The original wooden floor was magnificent, and she could almost imagine a young Elizabeth dashing across the polished boards. *That poor child,* she thought. Elizabeth had been sent away because she was born a girl which, in Henry VIII's opinion, made her useless to the crown. Mary, Elizabeth's older half-sister, had also been stashed in this house for a time. Cassandra picked up the tour group as it moved to the sumptuous public apartments and then up to the archives, where there was a treasure trove of documents, including the legal proceedings justifying the beheading of Anne Boleyn.

Cassandra recalled the first time she had visited the Tower of London and stood where two of Henry's wives, Anne Boleyn and Catherine Howard, had lost their heads to the royal axe. An icy hand took told of her heart as she leaned over the glass and examined the crude revisions and crossed-out sentences. *All that horrible effort just to legalize and legitimize the beheading of one innocent woman.*

At last she came to a copy of the Voynich Manuscript. It was everything she imagined, and more. The pages were a sumptuous feast of graphs, charts, fine script, and hand-colored drawings. It was obviously a scientific book of some sort. Some of the drawings even looked like cells glimpsed through a microscope!

Cassandra's mouth flew open as she steadied herself against the display. *At the bottom of one of the pages filled with numbers, symbols, and graphs, was the cartouche.*

She exhaled slowly and made her way over to a small desk, where the archive's curator was sitting. "Excuse me, do you think I might have a closer look at the Voynich Manuscript? The glare through the glass is quite terrible, really, and my eyesight is not good to begin with."

The old man, whose seventieth birthday looked to be well behind him, blinked in surprise. Apparently no one had ever asked him that question. "I have been quite fascinated with this document for some time, and have come all the way from America," pleaded Cassandra. She put on her best smile. "Please?"

For a moment she was afraid he would say no. The old man brushed back a thin lock of white hair that grew from the top of his otherwise bald head. "Well, since it's only a copy, I suppose it'll be all right," he answered slowly. "You came such a long way, I would hate for you to return disappointed."

"Thank you," answered Cassandra as she followed him to the case. The curator felt his way through a ring of keys, found the one he was searching for, and unlocked the sliding door. Reaching in, he grasped the manuscript gently in his aging hands and carried it to a small table by the window.

"There you are, miss," he said with a small bow. He reached into his pockets and pulled out a pair of thin white cotton gloves. "Even though it is only a copy, I would feel better if you would wear these if you plan to touch it. Don't want oils or dirt on the pages, now do we?" His smile revealed a mouthful of crooked teeth, yellowed from decades of tea-drinking and smoking. "My name is Ian. Please let me know how else I may be of service to you."

Cassandra smiled her thanks and sat down at the table. Slipping on the small gloves, she began slowly turning the pages. Except for the cartouche and another symbol she recalled from her recent research, an odd, rose-colored cross, she could make little sense of anything. After thirty minutes of paging through the brightly colored pages, she called Ian over, turned in the book, and left for London. The manuscript was utterly perplexing. Certainly she had found something that directly related to her search, but what did it mean?

Back in her room, she returned to her lists. Every spare moment for the past several weeks, Cassandra had been creating a database to link names with the various cartouches they had uncovered. It was difficult and frustrating work. Sometimes the cartouche appeared in a document, but other times it was part of a building or structure. She stopped when she reached the name John Valentin Andrea, whose letter to Cromwell she had earlier found. The letter mentioned the Rosicrucians. Stunned, she pawed through the pile beside it until she found the list she made yesterday afternoon.

John Dee again! He founded the Rosicrucians as a Protestant alternative to the Jesuits.

She pondered this for a moment, recalling Oliver Cromwell's campaign against King Charles I and the Church of England. It was the "Divine Right" claimed by the Crown that upset Cromwell and his puritan Roundheads the most. It was bad enough that the King had dissolved Parliament, but when he began recklessly emptying the kingdom's coffers in the name of God, and continued persecuting puritans, civil war broke out. In 1649, Charles I lost his head and for eleven years Britain was governed as a republic. It seemed obvious to Cassandra that King Charles I didn't have access to the box or he would not have found it necessary to loot the English treasury. But what about the Rosicrucians?

As she quickly learned, the Rosicrucians arose out of the Egyptian mystery cults, blended with the Gnostics, reappeared with the Knights Templar and the Hospitallers, and then merged again with the Freemasons. Her fingers flew over the keyboard, matching names with organizations. Every name she keyed in appeared in the lists of Grand Masters of each organization. *Oh my God*, she thought. *There are connections everywhere!*

The trail of Freemasons led straight to the United States, and she jumped in and quickly followed it. Beginning with George Washington, more than half of the nation's presidents had been members of the organization. She found Freemasons among the country's wealthy: Rockefeller, Busch, Pabst, Miller, and Astor, along with German immigrant Weyerhauser.

Her inquiry thus far had uncovered clear links from Europe to the New World. But as fascinating as the investigation was, she had no idea that a few more keystrokes would break everything wide open.

ℬ

Nicholas was sitting in one of Malachi's boardrooms, across from the financier, Mika, and Lev. Malachi's son and protégé had spent most of the meeting in silence, watching and listening as his father peppered

Nicholas with questions. Nicholas glanced occasionally at Lev's expressionless face and wondered fleetingly what their personal relationship was like. There were a lot of things about Malachi he found elusive. He wished Galen were with him.

Unfortunately, even Galen could not have begun to fathom the things they didn't want Nicholas to discover. He had no way of knowing that Mika had been administrating the buy and sell signals for the Japanese markets for more than a year now, all based on the same technology Alex and Nicholas had identified. Nor was he aware that their present endeavor to incorporate Nicholas' "discovery" into the firm's planned Asian expansion was just a ploy that Malachi had improvised to extract the final piece of the puzzle he so desperate craved.

"What I'm saying," explained Nicholas, "is that whatever happens in our markets will be followed soon thereafter across the Pacific." He was theorizing that his technology would be every bit as valid in Asian financial markets as it was in America.

"What should we do about the phase inversions?" asked Mika, and not for the first time.

Malachi, Mika, and Lev looked at Nicholas expectantly. He shook his head dismissively and responded exactly as he had several times already. "We won't have to worry about the phase inversions for a while. I'll let you know well in advance when it's going to happen, and you'll have plenty of time to adjust." He wasn't sure how long he could keep his cards so close to the vest. As instructed, Mika didn't force the issue. Instead, she lowered her eyes in acknowledgment.

Malachi, however, was losing his patience. "Why not tell us now?" rasped the financier. "The sooner we integrate your entire technology into our systems, the better it will be for the bottom line. And of course, your fees will reflect that improvement." He raised his eyebrows and looked long and deeply at Nicholas, his bright blue eyes bracketing a large hooked nose and sallow cheeks.

"I'm sorry," shrugged Nicholas with studied indifference. "It was Alex's discovery, and it will take me some time to work through his notes and programs to figure out the best way to incorporate it into your system. It is very complex, as you might imagine." Nicholas was beginning to enjoy his role. He stiffened his backbone and looked into Malachi's icy eyes. "And quite frankly, Malachi, I'm a lot more interested right now in trying to solve who killed Alex than digging into the phase inversion issue. So is my family."

For a moment Nicholas thought Malachi was going to jump across the table and wrap his skeletal fingers around his throat. A passion burned in the old man's eyes like no other Nicholas had ever witnessed. Instead, the financier cracked a smile and nodded as if he understood fully. Emboldened, Nicholas continued. "You mentioned in Paris that you might be able to help me out with finding my brother's killer, Malachi. That's one of the reasons I'm here."

"Agh . . ." Malachi crushed out his cigar in a crystal ashtray and stood with a sigh. He walked slowly to the window where, with his hands folded behind his back, he stared out at the city he largely owned. The room was deathly still.

Two full minutes later he turned back to face Nicholas. "I placed a call to the Charleston police yesterday to see what I could find out. The detective in charge assured me that he had concluded the investigation. He told me the car was totally incinerated, and that they had found no evidence of any device like the one you mentioned attached to the front bumper. I am quite confident your little niece was just imagining things. After all, her father had just died."

Is this all the help Malachi is going to offer me? thought Nicholas. *What about his vast information network? Hell, I could call the police station and ask a couple questions just as easily as Malachi. On the other hand, maybe the case was closed for good reason. Maybe Rosemary had been mistaken. Maybe there was really nothing Malachi or anyone else could point to or help with. But what about the fire at the Beaudrot's house, and the theft of the box at Siena?* Nicholas' gut told him that if he stuck with this and held his cards close, matters would sort themselves out.

He gave the group a look of resignation. "Perhaps you're right, Malachi. Rosemary seemed convincing, but she is young, her father had just died, and she has quite an imagination." Inwardly, he groaned when Malachi offered him a knowing nod of assurance.

"Sometimes you have to just let these things go. Perhaps it is for the best," Lev suggested, speaking out for the first time.

Nicholas had a sudden urge to reach across the table and slap the young man. *How in the world would he know what was best?* It was time to put Galen's plan into action.

He took a deep breath and began. "I've made arrangements for a colleague of mine to cover my classes at Emory until the end of the semester, and I have asked for a sabbatical for the following semester. In the meantime," he continued, "I would enjoy being your consultant. The technology I have is proprietary information, and I'll make it exclusively available to you, as we agreed."

For a brief moment Malachi looked as if he was ready to jump up and dance a jig on the table. The flash of emotion faded just as quickly and he offered nothing more than a firm bob of the head. Malachi turned to look at Mika as if he expected her to speak.

"I'm glad you're aboard," pronounced his assistant with the merest hint of a smile. "You'll be a tremendously valuable member of the Group"—she glanced at Nicholas' face for the briefest second—"especially if you trust us."

What an odd thing to say, thought Nicholas. "Trust takes performance over time," he responded. "I agree there hasn't been enough of it."

Malachi sighed with relief. "All right, let's move on. Mika, run some numbers on his predictions and do a couple of days worth of testing. Lev, I want you to come with me after lunch for a meeting with one of the Group's European executives. Nicholas, let's . . ."

"Sorry, Malachi, but I have plans for lunch," his new consultant interrupted, rising from the table to the astonished looks of all three of his new colleagues. "I can't be reached by cell because my battery went dead a few hours ago, but I plan to pick up a new one later this afternoon."

Malachi's mouth fell open as the brazen economics professor turned and walked out of the room.

℗

Cassandra stopped typing, stopped reading, and for a few seconds, stopped breathing entirely. When she finally filled her lungs with air, it came in several great gasps, large and fast at first, and then shallower and slower until her breathing returned to normal.

She had stumbled upon an obscure site linking investment strategies to modern Freemasons. Her scalp tingled as her eyes poured over the pixilated text. Before her was a scanned memorandum regarding Joe Kennedy and J. P. Morgan. The words strongly suggested that the knowledge these men used to monopolize financial decision-making was based on market timing—not luck, or insider knowledge, or even a careful reading of the balance sheets, but *market timing*.

The author of the memorandum was Leviticus Foust.

Cassandra sat in shocked silence and gripped the table to keep it from spinning. She closed her eyes tightly, held them shut for several seconds, and then opened them slowly, as if by doing so the name on the screen would somehow change.

Foust.

It was the one name that pulled all the threads together and bound them tightly in significance. Her instincts had been right from the beginning. Foust.

"Damn!" she shouted, pounding her open palms on the desktop. "Of course!"

The fact that corruption and Joe Kennedy were mentioned in the same breath was nothing new. But who was Leviticus Foust? Malachi's father? His grandfather?

Sucked into the story, she read on as if afraid to pull her eyes away for fear the text would disappear forever. According to Leviticus, Kennedy became part of a cabal of Irish-American investors, all of whom had been instructed by Leviticus Foust on the timing of their investments. Kennedy was part of what became known as the infamous 'pool operations,' a system of taking advantage of the group's insider timing information and, necessarily, the public's lack thereof. It was quite simple, really. Foust would bribe newspaper journalists to plant fake financial stories, and the targeted stocks would then rise or fall as Foust desired. Kennedy and others in his group would then buy or sell, as directed by Foust. The result was that fortunes were made—many times over. Just as shocking to Cassandra was a note from Leviticus instructing Kennedy to cash out of the stock market *just before the crash of 1929*. As the market began its free fall, he vigorously shifted gears, shorting stocks as it fell further.

Cassandra continued reading, unable to tear herself away from the shocking disclosures. According to Leviticus Foust, Joe Kennedy helped FDR reach the presidency. With Randolph Foust's encouragement, Kennedy contributed $50,000 of his own money to FDR's campaign, with an additional $200,000 directly from Foust himself. She stopped for a moment and thought deeply. *Randolph Foust? Leviticus Foust?* She kept turning the names over and over in her mind.

Randolph Foust negotiated with Roosevelt after the election to have Kennedy appointed as the first commissioner of the Securities and Exchange Commission. When Roosevelt was accused of selling out to Wall Street, he argued that Kennedy was the right choice because of his personal experience with the very practices that the SEC was set up to avert. In Roosevelt's own words, "It was a classic case of the fox guarding the hen house."

Dumfounded, Cassandra read on, growing increasingly astonished and dismayed. The notes outlined how Kennedy used threats, favors, money, and influence—always backed by Randolph Foust—to manipulate the media. Kennedy apparently threatened to destroy certain publishers if they printed negative stories about his son, John F. Kennedy. After Randolph Foust made interest-free loans to various publishers, they endorsed Kennedy's son in the 1952 Massachusetts Senate race. Foust paid an enormous amount of money to get John F. Kennedy's picture on *Time* magazine's cover just before the 1958 Massachusetts Senate contest.

Why? Foust was positioning JFK for a run at the presidency in 1960.

Incredible, thought Cassandra as she got up and walked to the mini-bar to uncork a bottle of 1998 French Burgundy. *This lengthy memorandum implicates just about every powerful person in the country.* Unable to find a suitable wine glass, she poured the liquid into a water glass and drank half of it in one gulp. The question confronting her was obvious: how did the Fousts manage to get so powerful? Knowing what she knew, the answer fairly jumped from the memorandum: *the Foust family had the box!* Now all she had to do was find the connection.

She refilled her glass and sat back down, marveling at the magnitude of the power and corruption generated by the Foust family. She didn't have any concrete proof that they were connected to the box, but there had to be a trail linking them. *When did the Fousts enter into all of this?* she wondered.

Cassandra returned to the keyboard and repeatedly clicked the "back" button in the browser window. "Could it be possible?" she said out loud, excited by the possibility. She examined each page carefully.

Nothing.

She was about to take a break when she found a digital reproduction of the note Leviticus Foust had written to Joseph Kennedy instructing him to cash out of the market just before the 1929 crash. Cassandra scrolled her eyes down through the paragraphs to the bottom. Just below Leviticus' signature was a round embossed stamp. At first glance it resembled a presidential seal. That's why she had missed it the first time.

In the center was the Egyptian cartouche.

And then it all made sense to her. The cartouche itself was the connection that linked the Foust family. It had served as their coat of arms through the ages, the calling card to those who knew its meaning, its distinction . . . its power.

Malachi! . . . Nicholas!

A feeling of dread coursed through her veins and she jumped up, knocking over her chair and spilling her wine at the same time. She tugged at her collar as though a rope were tightening around her throat. Grabbing her purse, she hurriedly dug out her cell phone, punched in Nicholas' number, and waited as the phone rang.

"Nicholas!" She shouted. "Pick up the phone!"

And rang.

"Answer it, please!"

And rang. "Hi this is Nicholas Shepard . . ." She hung up.

"Ok, what do I do, what do I do?" she asked herself as she paced in small circles. "Think Cassandra, think! Is it safe to leave a message on his voicemail?" It took her several minutes before she settled on a plan. First, she called the front desk to arrange for an overnight package to be shipped to the States. Moving quickly, she gathered up the documents and addressed them to Galen. Her hands were shaking so badly she dropped them on the floor. *I just need to get to Nicholas,* she thought frantically as she gathered them up and packed them for the journey.

She picked up the phone to make flight reservations to New York. She found a seat on a plane that was leaving in less than two hours! When the agent asked her for her name, she decided that after the publicity of the symposium, Cassandra Shepard would do just fine. She put her false identity papers in with the documents and wrote a short note to Galen telling him to put all the papers in the safety deposit box.

When she was through she called Nicholas again. This time she left a voice message informing him of her hasty return, the flight number, and asked that he meet her at the airport. She tried again every ten minutes for the rest of the evening, but he never answered.

After she e-mailed him her flight schedule, just to be sure, she poured another glass of wine and sat beside the window, watching a huge Ferris wheel spin brightly in the gathering dusk. Emotionally exhausted, she floated off into a fitful sleep as a deep chill stole into her bones. Cassandra knew she was drifting off, but was unable to wake herself, even as her forehead pressed up against the cool window glass.

Where was her husband? As the gauzy clouds of sleep sucked her in, she imagined herself walking along a razor's edge; on both sides a sinister, bottomless, darkness awaited.

∅

Even before Nicholas reached the elevator Malachi was on the phone. Nicholas wasn't about to have any lunch plans—or breakfast plans, or dinner plans—without Malachi knowing about them.

After stopping by a drug store for a new phone battery, Nicholas hailed a cab. "Two ninety-nine West 43rd," he told the cab driver, who bore a startling resemblance to Danny de Vito. Nicholas leaned back and closed his eyes, thinking about what he was getting into with Sam Griffin. He felt a twinge of guilt about doing this on the sly.

"What is it you Wall Street guys got I don't got?"

Nicholas raised his eyebrows and looked at the driver. "Pardon?"

"The wife and me. We both work hard and still struggle to pay the mortgage. We got a kid in college, the first time in our families!" He paused for congratulations, but Nicholas managed little more than a grunt. "But our parents, they worked like dogs, saved a little money for their retirement, which they gave to a broker, who lost it when the market bubble busted. They had to sell their houses. My wife's parents spend their time visiting their kids in other parts of the country. They're homeless, for Christ's sake! My parents live in a low-rent apartment now down in the Bronx. But you guys! You make money coming and going. The rest of us suckers just lose. It's disgusting. It outta be illegal."

The statement was the last thing Nicholas expected to hear in a cab. "I'm sorry about your parents, but I don't work on Wall Street."

"No?" said the de Vito lookalike. "Well, you sure look like you do. Anyway, something ain't right, ya know?"

"I do know," mumbled Nicholas as he focused his attention out the window and watched as the buildings merged together in a blur of gray and glass. He held his phone to his ear to check for messages. The only voicemail was from Cassandra. "Today!" he said out loud. He looked at his watch. He only had a few hours before her flight arrived.

"Today what?" asked the driver suspiciously.

"Nothing," answered Nicholas. "I was talking to myself.

When then reached the *New York Times* building the cabbie said, "I don't expect no tip," he said.

Nicholas leaned through the front passenger window and handed him a hundred-dollar bill. "If things go the way I want them to," he told the driver, "you'll be seeing a lot more of these."

"I don't take no charity," the cabbie shot back, at the same time checking the bill closely to make sure it wasn't a fake.

"It's not charity. It's a down payment." He patted the cab door and started toward the door. Griffin was coming out of the building.

"Dr. Shepard! Let's head down to the West Bank Café," he said, steering Nicholas by the elbow toward West 42nd Street. The reporter spent so much time looking over his shoulder during the short walk that Nicholas finally asked if he thought they were being followed. "Nah," he replied. "I'm just paranoid."

In the mood for comfort food, Nicholas ordered smoked salmon pasta while Griffin opted for linguine with shrimp. The waiter placed small, laminated placards on the table with photographs of their orders. "Not all of our personnel speak English," said Griffin. "These show them what goes where."

Griffin got right down to business. "Thanks for agreeing to meet with me, Dr. Shepard. I have looked up your credentials, spoken with precisely four of your colleagues at Emory University, and have read several of your peer-reviewed articles. I believe that you truly believe in what you are saying, and I know a man like you would not jump off a cliff voluntarily without making sure you have a parachute on. I also notice I seem to be the only one who believes that."

Nicholas smiled softly. Unbeknownst to the journalist, he had also made a few calls to check on the reporter's background. "Well, that's refreshing to hear, Sam. I think Malachi Foust also believes in my theory. At least, he seems eager enough to incorporate my discovery into his investment strategies. He's also extremely anxious to get his hands on Alex's phase-inversion solution, which I've decided to keep secret. Once I hand that over, I have the feeling he'll drop me in a heartbeat."

"Phase inversion? I'm sorry I don't understand," Griffin replied, sipping from a tall glass of Pepsi.

"Oh, that's something Alex figured out during his research. It is rather complicated and it's the one thing that I've not fully explained to Malachi." Nicholas lowered his voice when a man at a nearby table turned his head and stared in his direction. "It appears the inversion sequence means a lot to Malachi, though. He isn't particularly happy about me holding back the information."

"Well, if Foust believes in your discovery," replied Griffin, his eyebrows pushed together in thought, "he sure didn't show it much the other night. I don't recall him coming to your defense or asking questions to help get you back on track after others knocked you down a few times. Odd way for someone who believes in you to act, don't you think?"

Nicholas' reply was barely audible, and Griffin had to lean forward several inches to hear him. "I can't explain it. But it was a disastrous evening for my career. Potentially career-ending."

Griffin was about to respond when Nicholas again found his voice and his determination. "To tell you the truth, Sam, my immediate goal is to use Malachi to restore my reputation."

"Using Foust?" The journalist chortled. "Now that's a switch. And don't feel bad about it!"

The waiter brought the plates of pasta and arranged them on the table. When he left, Griffin studied his food for a few seconds before speaking. "Look, Dr. Shepard, I'm going to be honest with you. I've been after Malachi for many years. He's just no good, and I think he is as crooked as hell. Every time I get close, though, someone gets bought off. I can't get anyone to go on record. When I do, papers disappear. It's always something. The few times I've gotten one of his companies before a judge, the court rules in his favor. I admit it has become something of an obsession, but this is one story I am determined to put to bed."

Nicholas took a bite of his pasta and washed it down with a mouthful of Italian red wine. He wiped his mouth carefully with his red cloth napkin. "You wouldn't be pretending to believe my theories just so you can get to Foust, would you?"

Griffin regarded him with some surprise. "I wouldn't have thought you'd be so suspicious. Malachi has that effect on people, doesn't he? But to answer your question, no. It is serendipitous that you turned up in his camp. See, if your theory is correct, I genuinely believe you could be this millennium's Galileo. I don't go that far out on limbs in print unless I believe what I'm writing."

Deep in thought, Nicholas twirled pasta around his fork, left it in the bowl, and leaned back in his chair. "I'm going to level with you, but it has to be off the record until I say it is on the record—understood?"

"Absolutely. And so you know, I'm not taping our conversation."

Nicholas looked carefully around the restaurant before settling his eyes back on the reporter. "I believe someone . . . or a group of people, maybe . . .have the same information my brother and I discovered."

Griffin's eyes widened. "Whoa. I'm all ears."

"Somebody who didn't want to share this information. Somebody who killed my brother to stop us from using this information."

Griffin nearly choked on his Pepsi. "Killed your brother? Did you say killed your brother?"

Nicholas looked embarrassed. "They were after me. It was my car that exploded, but Alex—my identical twin—was driving. Then there was an attempted robbery, the arson, and the Siena theft."

"Hold on!" Griffin was pulling out his notebook. He held it in one hand and a pencil in the other. "May I?"

Nicholas took a gulp of water and finally nodded. His hands were starting to sweat. "We've been all over Europe trying to figure out who is involved and doing what to whom. My wife is flying in from London this afternoon—hopefully with some answers."

With thirty years of chasing stories under his belt, Griffin knew a good one when he heard it. This was what his editor called a "holy shit story." He leaned forward and somehow managed to keep his voice low and easy: "Why don't you tell me everything that has happened. Start from the beginning and take your time. I have all day."

Nicholas took a deep breath and did just that. He described how they found the box and documents, how they discovered how the box worked, and how they adapted it to the stock market. Griffin wrote like a fiend, looking up now and again to shoot Nicholas a "you have got to be kidding me!" glance. The more Nicholas explained, the more furiously the reporter captured the story on paper. Nicholas told him how much money they had made and eventually got around to Alex's mysterious murder. Griffin's eyes grew wider by the minute. When Nicholas' cell phone rang, the reporter nearly jumped out of his seat.

It was Galen. "You have what? Why would she do that? She must have figured something out. Thanks. I'll be in touch."

He closed his phone and looked at the reporter. "That's weird. Cassandra overnighted her documents and notes from London to our friend Galen—he's a priest." When he realized he was getting ahead of himself, Nicholas began filling Griffin in on the rest of the story.

The reporter continued scribbling for all he was worth while Nicholas talked. When Nicholas finished, Griffin rubbed his chin for a moment. "What about Ernest von Stuyvesant? It seems like he would be the obvious link. After all, he owns the Biltmore Estate, right? Wouldn't you simply assume he was the last owner of the box?"

"Yes," Nicholas replied, "But Gabe's father told him he didn't know who owned the items, and they had been there for many years. Besides, the von Stuyvesant assets have been helping us track down our clues. Believe me, that wouldn't be happening if the old man had anything to do with this. Besides, when we found the box initially, von Stuyvesant seemed not to care about it at all—if he even knew what it was."

Griffin nodded, satisfied by the answer. He pulled off his glasses and began cleaning them with the corner of his shirt. "Listen. I have an idea. I want you to provide me with documentation on the gravitational ups and downs over the last, say, twenty years, and correlate that against the stock market. Once I am completely confident about all this, I'm going to send a copy of your speech, along with a copy of your scientific documents I picked up at the Symposium, to Nathaniel Stevenson, the Federal Reserve Chairman. I've known him for many years, and I'm positive he will be interested in your theories. Then, I think it's time to do a series on the financial page about how your system works, and what the possibilities are. Does that sound like a plan?"

Nicholas hesitated. "I don't know what Cassandra may have discovered in England. You may want to look at it that first." He gazed out the window at the passers-by. So many people heading somewhere, oblivious to what was going on around them. "But . . . sure, that's a plan. It's time to get this information out there where it can do some good."

"So you'll help me write some of these columns, or at least review them?" asked Griffin with growing enthusiasm. "I'm sure there's a book in here somewhere, but we'll talk about that later." He paused and shot Nicholas a genuinely concerned look. "I'm not going to ask you to spy on Malachi, Dr. Shepard. That could get dangerous, and you don't have the investigative skills anyway. But if you see something that bothers you, let me know and I'll do my best to look into it."

Nicholas sat back in his chair. He was aware that journalists weren't always the most selfless people in the world, and he had to wonder what Griffin's true motivation was. Nicholas had already decided how he was going to proceed. "Just know that spying on Malachi isn't my top priority, but if you help me, I'll help you."

Griffin nodded and glanced at his watch. "We've been here for a long time. Traffic is going to get heavy, so you'd better get to the airport."

On the sidewalk Nicholas pulled a thin CD case out of his pocket. "This CD contains Alex's programs, his notes, the phase inversion solution, and a back-up of some of the documents I spoke of." He held it up to the reporter and their eyes met for a moment. He realized Griffin might be the only person who could, or would, help him.

Nicholas turned to hail a cab and then back again to shake his hand. "I'm not sure exactly why, but do you realize that I'm trusting you with our lives? Don't let me down."

"I know, and I won't," said Griffin, slightly unnerved by Nicholas' confidence. "I promise." After looking right, left, and behind him, Griffin began walking back to his office.

ȸ

Ten minutes later a messenger with a package appeared outside Malachi's office. Mika gave the young man a generous tip and then interrupted her boss. Malachi watched as she popped the tape into the machine on his desk and pressed 'play.'

"Not all of our personnel speak English. These show them what goes where. . . . Thanks for agreeing to meet with me, Dr. Shepard. I have looked up your credentials . . ."

The recording had been surreptitiously made by a waiter at the West Bank Café. As Nicholas headed toward the airport, Malachi listened to the exchange with growing anger.

Even before it ended he turned and shouted spoke to Mika through clenched teeth. "Get me my Customs man at JFK."

Chapter 52

Cassandra checked out of the Savoy early in the morning to catch a train for Gatwick. She moved stiffly, as though suddenly afflicted with arthritis. It was tension, and nothing she could think or say would dispel it. More concerned for Nicholas' safety than her own, she was determined to communicate with him before it was too late.

The morning's events, however, conspired against her. The taxi was deathly slow, the traffic creeping forward at a nightmarishly sluggish place. Cassandra's stress was only increased by a late-arriving plane, followed by a one-hour delay on the tarmac. She was already exhausted before the long trans-Atlantic flight, during which she found herself unable to read, listen to music, watch a movie, or even sleep. When a mug of herbal tea prepared by an especially thoughtful flight attendant failed to relax her, Cassandra finally took an antihistamine.

By the time the plane landed she was still groggy from the drug, but no less worried about her husband. Thankfully her luggage all arrived with her. When she got to customs, one of the attendants drew her aside and asked to search her bag. "Fine," she snapped. "Just make it fast." As he dug through her suitcase, Cassandra stepped to the side and pulled out her cell phone. Five missed messages from Nicholas. She rang him.

"Nicholas! Thank God you're okay! Are you on your way here?"

"Yes, sorry I am late, honey . . . maybe twenty minutes out."

"Please hurry. I'm so anxious and nervous. And Customs has pulled me aside and is pawing through my luggage. Listen, I have tracked the box, Nicholas. It . . . Hello? Nicholas?" Her connection dropped. "Ah, damn!"

She was in the process of calling him back when the custom's officer closed the suitcase and shot her a wary look. "You will need to come with me, ma'am. And I'll take the cell phone."

Cassandra was indignant. "What? You can't take my phone!" She was wrong. He could and he did.

Furious, she followed him to a small office well off the concourse, where two other officials joined them. Sitting in a chair, she was now beyond sensibility and in a cold fury. "Why aren't you out looking for real terrorists?" she demanded.

Two of the guards suddenly leaned over and held her firmly in place while the third grabbed her by the arm. Cassandra tried screaming, but a cold, clammy hand sealed her mouth shut. Her eyes opened wide when she saw the Custom's officer uncap a syringe. She felt the prick of the needle and a few seconds later tumbled into blackness.

∅

By 5:00 p.m. Nicholas knew something was wrong. Cassandra's plane had landed more than an hour earlier, and except for a straggler or two, the passengers on her flight had all claimed their luggage and left. When he asked the Customs office if they knew his wife's whereabouts, no one could help him. His wife had been spot-checked and released, someone recalled, but so had a half-dozen other passengers. Cassandra didn't answer her cell phone, and she wasn't at the hotel.

Nicholas took a deep breath and held it. *This was not like Cassandra,* he thought, exhaling loudly while turning in circles in a vain effort to spot her somewhere in the airport. *The last thing she would do is vanish from here knowing I was on the way to pick her up.*

When he tried to fill out a missing person's report, the police told him his wife had to be missing for twenty-four hours. By now Nicholas was growing desperate, running from one official to another until security advised him to leave the premises. Worried sick, frightened, and furious, he caught a cab back to the Plaza Hotel.

"Galen?" he said, when his friend answered the phone. "I'm in the back of a taxi on the way to the Plaza. Cassandra is missing." He filled him in on the details.

The priest was more disturbed than he wanted Nicholas to know, but he managed to keep his voice calm. "Nicholas, I don't know what is happening, but if Cassandra is really missing and not just off on an errand, then I want you to check out of the hotel. We will need Gabriel's help. Go straight to the von Stuyvesant's private airfield. I'll e-mail directions in a few minutes. Don't tell anybody where you're going—nobody! What about that Griffin fellow you were talking to?"

Exciting the cab, Nicholas pushed his way through the revolving door in the lobby of the Plaza, his cell phone glued to his ear. "I can trust him, Galen. I'll call him as soon as I figure out something. But I can't leave New York! Cassandra's plane has landed and she called me, so I know she made the flight ok. She could walk through the door any minute! Don't you think I better stay here, in case she shows up?" As he breezed past the desk, the clerk handed him a stack of mail as he made his way toward the elevator.

"Those are good points, Nicholas. But if Cassandra is missing you are in danger as well. You cannot stay at the Plaza."

Nicholas did not hear a thing Galen had said. He fell back against the marble wall outside his room and his legs buckled, sending him sliding to the floor in a heap. In his hand was a piece of expensive stationary. Nicholas had just ripped open the hand-addressed envelope embossed with a fancy wax seal.

"Nicholas, are you there?" asked the priest. When he heard a soft moan, he asked again, sharply and loudly. "Nicholas?"

The voice he heard was quiet, halting, and terrified. "It's a ransom note, Galen. I just opened it. Cassandra has been kidnapped."

Galen closed his eyes and willed his friend to stay calm. "Read me the note, Nicholas. Can you do that?"

"Yes. It says: 'Dear Professor Shepard: We have invited your wife, Cassandra, to be our guest until you return what belongs to us. Take the box, the original documents, and any other information concerning the documents' histories, along with your brother's complete solution to the phase-inversion problem, and FedEx the items for general delivery to the Manhattan 14th Street Mailbox Express. Address the delivery in care of Masako Kagawa. Please do not notify the authorities. Your loved one's health and well-being are at stake. We will expect immediate communication from you.' There's an email address here, Galen."

Nicholas bit his lip to keep from crying out, but he was unable to prevent the hot tears from coursing down his cheeks. He felt as though he was standing on the edge of an abyss, and any way he turned he would fall off. "What should I do?" asked Nicholas. His voice trembling badly despite his best efforts to stifle his emotions.

Before Galen had a chance to answer, Nicholas picked up the torn envelope. "Wait a second." The wax seal had fallen off nearly intact. He picked it up and held it in his palm, staring at it in disbelief. "It's the cartouche, Galen! The letter was sealed with a wax cartouche!"

The priest remained silent. He was no stranger to kidnapping cases, most the product of a deranged spouse absconding his or her children in domestic disputes. It was a serious and sometimes deadly crime, regardless of who was perpetrating it. This situation, however, had an evil to it that was beyond anything he had ever experienced.

He cleared his throat. "We might have to go to the police in spite of what they said, Nicholas. How would they find out?"

"Galen, everything I do is being watched!" Nicholas said, a low level of hysteria obvious in his voice. "They could be monitoring this cell conversation."

"Yes, that's true," the priest agreed somberly. "I'm going to send you an encrypted message on your computer, Nicholas. The password is the name of your first puppy spelled backward."

After he hung up, Nicholas collected the bits and pieces of the envelope, entered his hotel room, and turned on his laptop to wait for the e-mail. When it arrived a few minutes later he entered the name backward, downloaded the file, and unplugged the Internet connection.

My Dear Nicholas,

Be strong. Cassandra needs you now like never before. With God's help we shall persevere and all will be well.

We must use our brains and think our way logically through this. Why would someone take Cassandra? I think it has something to do with her research in England. Why did she feel compelled to overnight her documents to me? We need a safe place to meet and study them. I have a hunch she stumbled upon something big—that has to be why she sent them to me in the first place. We have another problem, perhaps. Whoever is behind her disappearance may have already traced the documents from England to me.

We have to move as quickly as possible. There's an abbey just outside the city. I'll ask Gabe to fly me to Hartford, and we'll come pick you up in the city. Take the subway up to the Cloisters. We'll look for you in the museum tomorrow shortly before noon.

The letter you received requires a response. I suggest you e-mail and say that the box is overseas in one location and the documents in another foreign location. Tell them that it will take you several days to collect everything. Ask for some proof that Cassandra's okay—a phone call would be best, but at least a video e-mail.

Nicholas leaned back with his head in his hands. *How could this be happening?* He took the risk of calling Galen back rather than e-mailing. "Wouldn't a video be better proof that she hasn't been hurt?"

"I don't think so," replied Galen. "A video could have been made earlier, and you wouldn't know for sure she was still all right. Actually talking to her would be best. Otherwise, the video will have to do. Set up a guest address on your computer for them to send it to. In the meantime, don't check out of the hotel. Pay for the room for another week to throw off whoever might be monitoring you. See you tomorrow."

Nicholas began implementing Galen's suggestions, but felt as though he was moving under water with his feet mired in deep mud. It was already early evening. Once he had called Malachi's office to report that urgent personal business had prevented him from returning that afternoon, he set up a new e-mail account and sent his answer, and his request, to Cassandra's abductors.

There was nothing to do now but wait. He lay on the bed, stiff with tension, hands clenched by his sides. Never had he felt so utterly helpless and useless. A violent rainstorm slashed against his window. Somewhere close by, engines raced to confront fires the sudden electric storm had ignited. In a macabre way, the shrill sirens were fit accompaniment for the inferno raging in his heart and mind.

He might have slept for a minute. He might not have.

℘

Cassandra awoke in complete darkness. Carefully lifting her hand, she touched her face to make sure she was actually there, *somewhere*, and slowly extended a toe from beneath what turned out to be a scratchy wool blanket. When it touched a cold metal rail, she quickly brought it back under the blanket.

Well, at least I'm not dead, she thought. *But where am I and what happened?*

Her head throbbed with a migraine-like headache, and even blinking her eyes made her temples throb. She lay curled in a fetal position, dressed in a cotton shift. She listened for any sounds that might help her understand where she was, but there was nothing to hear but her own beating heart and soft breathing. Slowly, she stretched out and looked around. It took fully thirty seconds before her eyes grew accustomed to the darkness. She could make out the fuzzy outline of what looked to be a covered window near the ceiling. There was also a wooden door, arched to a point at the top. She reached out cautiously and felt metal bed rails and a small table next to the bed, which she now realized was a narrow cot.

The room was cold. She pulled a thin blanket from the side of the cot around her shoulders and rubbed her arms. Who had kidnapped her? Terrorists? Malachi? Other people associated with the box and documents? The same people who had killed Alex? *I could be anywhere, from Baghdad to Buffalo*, she thought. She was fairly certain she hadn't been raped, but someone had undressed her and put her in this gown. She shivered again and moved her toes around on the bare floor, trying to locate her shoes.

A soft knock at the door startled her. She wrapped the blanket tighter. "Yes. . . ?" The wooden door creaked open and to Cassandra's infinite surprise, revealed an older woman in a nun's habit standing silhouetted in the doorway. Cassandra threw her hand up to shield her eyes against the glare of the light and shrank away further when the nun switched on an overhead bulb in the room.

"My name is Sister Elizabeth Justin, Mother Superior. You are our guest here." The nun moved into the small room and sat down on a solid wooden chair next to the table.

Flabbergasted at this turn of events, Cassandra simply stared at the woman. None of it made any sense. "Guest? Sister, I don't wish to be a guest here. Where am I, and where is my husband?"

"I can honestly say I don't know where your husband is, my dear, and I am not at liberty to tell you where you are. I only hope that during your stay you won't cause us any problems." Sister Elizabeth's voice was soft, but firm and uncompromising. Cassandra thought she detected a tiny bit of concern in her brown eyes.

"What do you mean, during my stay?" answered Cassandra, sticking out her chin defiantly as she sat up on the cot.

"I am afraid I cannot tell you how long you will be with us," the abbess replied. "But you must follow my instructions in order to assure your safety. We are a silent order, and we say nothing, either to each other or to anyone coming into the convent."

Cassandra's eyes widened in fear and disbelief. "But you are speaking to me and I have come into the convent—against my will!"

"There are exceptions to every rule."

The nightmare made no sense. "I want to go home." She began crying softly.

"That is a request I cannot grant," said Sister Elizabeth coldly. "I am sure your husband is doing everything he can to alleviate this situation. In the meantime, you will follow my orders. Beyond that, I suggest prayer and contemplation." She stood up in a swirl of black habit. "You will come with me now. Your husband wishes to be assured of your health and safety. I need you to speak to a camera, which will send your image and voice to his e-mail. You will say nothing except a greeting, and tell him that you are safe and well."

"I am not safe, and I don't feel well," shot back Cassandra, rising unsteadily to her feet. She was mad that she had broken down for a few seconds and revealed such weakness.

"Come." Mother Superior handed Cassandra a pair of leather slippers and waited for her at the door.

The floor was made of large rough-cut cold stones, as was the hallway. There were no windows. *Are we underground?* Cassandra wondered as she looked about in a vain effort to catch any clues she could to determine her whereabouts. She walked two paces behind the sister, soaking in every detail of her surroundings. How to escape was the sole focus of her thoughts. They passed a number of doors similar to her own before reaching the end of the passageway, where a stone stairway wound its way up to the next floor.

She looked at the nun who motioned with her head. "Up."

Cassandra climbed the roughly hewn steps slowly, holding onto a well-worn rail. They emerged into another hallway, this one lit by Tudor-style leaded windows opening onto a courtyard with kitchen gardens. Several women were tending some of the smaller plots clothed in the same coarse cotton gowns with long sleeves she was wearing. Sister Elizabeth showed her into a small office with brick-and-stone walls. A bookcase full of Bibles and other religious works lined one wall, and a laptop computer looked out of place, sitting on a simple wooden desk.

A tiny camera was perched on top of the laptop screen. Cassandra sat as directed on a low bench in front of the bookcase, her knees clenched, one foot over the other, and her hands clasped tightly in her lap. Sister Elizabeth tapped at the keyboard, turned the monitor and camera toward her, and nodded for her to begin.

Cassandra took a deep breath. "Nicholas? Oh, darling." She broke down into a heaving sob and caught herself just as quickly. "I'm okay. I love you. I love you. Please . . . ."

Sister Elizabeth turned off the camera and Cassandra dissolved into tears. The sister pushed a box of Kleenex toward her and looked away, waiting for the storm to subside. The young woman's tears moved her more than she was allowed to show. Only rarely had she been asked to hold people against their will, and she fervently prayed the situation would end quickly. Sister Elizabeth regretted having ever acquiesced to the Group's wishes in the first place. *It makes me as trapped as this woman*, she thought, *and more of a sinner.*

But the time for saying 'no' to the Group was long past.

ø

Nicholas waited through a sleepless night for the e-mail video to arrive. When it finally appeared, the brief seven-second clip enraged more than consoled him. He picked up the laptop and was about to smash it against the wall when his better judgment kicked in. Instead, he paced the beautiful room, a lion in a gilded cage, until it was nearly time to leave.

The cold shower he endured did little more than shake off the edge of his terrible fatigue, and he cut himself several times shaving with hands that trembled in both rage and frustration. When he finally left the Plaza at 10:00 a.m., he had on a nice suit and carried his laptop—the very image of a businessman on the way to work or a meeting. But instead of heading down to the main lobby and out the door for Malachi's office, he disappeared into a stairwell and left the hotel via a little-used side door. After walking two blocks he hailed a taxi, jumped out at the subway station, and caught the A train north to the Cloisters.

He had arrived two hours ahead of his scheduled meeting with Gabriel and Galen, so he wandered, wearing a distracted gaze, through the vast holdings of the Metropolitan Museum's Medieval Art collection. Built to resemble a medieval monastery, the building evoked memories of Europe and happier times, which made the present a bitter pill to swallow. He was sitting on a hard bench, withdrawn and silent when his friends finally arrived— accompanied by a small reddish-blonde woman Gabriel introduced as Phoebe.

Nicholas was surprised he would bring someone else into their spreading web of danger, and his expression showed it. "We thought we might need another female—maybe as a diversion," he explained. "She's quite resourceful."

Galen didn't comment but Nicholas took note of his face. Concern for Cassandra was written all over it. He fervently hoped his faith would hold firm and see him through. They left the museum and climbed into Gabriel's Lexus SUV. "It's a family car," he explained. "We keep them at airports that we use frequently."

Nicholas told them about the e-mail video from Cassandra as Gabriel filled in the blanks for Phoebe, who nodded but asked few questions. When she did, she surprised Nicholas with her mountain drawl and less-than-perfect usc of English. He remembered her now from that evening so long ago in the Biltmore Mansion. *Curious*, he thought. *She is far removed the young New York debutantes Gabe usually goes for.*

"I'm afraid that we can't go to the monastery like Galen planned," announced Gabriel as he drove them south of the city. He glanced over at Phoebe with a small smile, "Women are not allowed. I think we will be safe in Intercourse." Nicholas winced at his friend's bad joke; Galen's mouth actually dropped open in shock.

"Intercourse is the name of a village deep in the heart of Amish country," Gabriel quickly explained. "Believe it or not, the old man set up a compound there in the event of some kind of catastrophe—civil unrest or something geo-political—in case he couldn't evacuate New York by plane. It's equipped with state-of-the-art communications, safe lines, and best of all no one will suspect us there. The place is as secret as a missile silo. It will take about three hours to get there."

It was the longest three hours of Nicholas' life. At last, they turned off on exit 298 and made their way into the rolling farmland owned by some of America's most reserved people—people who care nothing for the material world. They do, however, tolerate millions of tourists each year in their towns peering at their antique customs. The Lexus passed Amish families walking along the roads or riding in horse-drawn carriages, and prosperous-looking farms with neat, beautifully tended yards. Every mile seemed to take them further back in time, until Gabriel turned onto a twisting road that led down to a valley. At its bottom, nestled near a winding stream, was a 17th-century farmhouse and large stone barn. Gabriel turned into the drive and the heavy hinged wooden doors slid open. The car pulled inside, he pushed a button, and the doors slid shut. They were closed in, safe from the outside world.

They got out and followed Gabriel into an abandoned horse stall that still smelled of mildewed hay. "Where in the world are we going, Gabe?" asked Phoebe. Gabriel smiled as the stall's plank wall opened to reveal a wide steel door.

"I bid you enter," he said, motioning with his arm. Once inside, Gabriel turned on a battery of halogen lights, which illuminated a command center equipped with computer monitors and assorted electronics installed in engineered compartments. "Welcome to Mission Control," he announced. "You'll find a fully equipped—and fully stocked—kitchen to the right and bedrooms to the left behind the computer room. The communications are satellite-based, so there won't be any tracking of our calls."

Galen clapped Nicholas on his shoulder. "Let's get to work, my friend. Cassandra sent us these papers and documents for a reason, and now her life probably depends on us." He turned to look at their host and held out a briefcase full of paperwork. "Gabriel, I believe this is your field."

Chapter 53

Malachi sat at his desk with the fingertips of his hands pressed firmly together, as if he were praying. The box was before him, undamaged by its journeys. Many of the documents were missing, but at the moment they seemed insignificant compared to his current project. He hadn't seen the box in decades. It brought back flashes of memories, most of them unpleasant.

His father had been a brilliant and shrewd businessman, but he was anything but a good father. He had been often moody and usually cruel. Today they would have diagnosed him with some designer psychiatric disease, although any diagnosis would not have excused him from his mistreatment of Malachi's sister Gwendolyn. Malachi closed his eyes tightly and conjured up her image in happier times.

He heard the connecting door open and his eyelids snapped apart as Mika entered. She was back to her traditional expensive black garb, and at the moment she reminded him of a raven with red lips. She sat down primly in a chair in front of the desk. Her face betrayed no emotion. Her hands held a stack of notes and a newspaper. A wall had come down between them both.

"I can't wait to see how he's going to explain the disappearance of the box and the documents." Malachi could not keep the smugness out of his voice. "What do you have to report?"

Mika looked up from her notes. "He called in late yesterday to say he had personal business to attend to, and wouldn't be in."

Malachi hooted at this information. "I do love a plan when it works."

"I set up an e-mail account in the name of "cartouche" for us to use to communicate with him," continued Mika. "He already replied to our ransom request—also late yesterday. He says the box is overseas and the documents are in different locations, so it will take him several days to collect everything. He also wanted to speak with Cassandra to confirm her safety, but this morning I e-mailed a short video from his beloved instead. Security says he left the hotel this morning at ten and caught a train to the Cloisters, where he met two men and a woman."

Malachi furrowed his brow and picked at his earlobe with a claw of one finger. "Send him another e-mail," he directed, "just to let him know that we know he's not at the hotel any more."

Mika made a note and continued. "They drove away in a Lexus SUV. The license number is registered to Ernest von Stuyvesant." She paused and looked up. "I think we can safely assume the son is part of this drama."

Malachi stood and began pacing behind his desk. "Most likely. Check the von Stuyvesant's real estate holdings to try to get some idea where this group might be going. Somewhere in upstate New York would be my best guess. I assume we've arranged for homing devices on all of von Stuyvesant's vehicles?"

Mika cleared her throat. "It was disabled."

"What? They have someone with them who is actually that clever? Who are the other people?"

"One is Father Galen, the priest with the Stetson hat and cowboy boots. The other is a frizzy-haired little blonde. We are working on her now."

"That damn Father Abbott, that's who it is!" spat Malachi. *God, I dislike pompous fools, especially those with a religious streak*, he thought. "Do we have a tail on them?"

Mika looked at the floor. "We assumed the homing device was operational."

Malachi's hands gripped the back of his chair until his fingers turned white and his thin skin displayed the veins coursing beneath. The look he gave Mika was more petrifying than Medusa's.

"There's worse news," she said steadily, dropping the newspaper on the corner of his desk. It was open to the *New York Times* financial section and a long column by Sam Griffin about the discovery Nicholas and Alex had made. Malachi swept up the paper and dropped into his chair all in the same motion, his eyes locked onto the page. The lengthy positive article included two paragraphs about the critical importance of Alex's phase-inversion solution in forecasting short-term financial trends. Griffin concluded by arguing that the future of the U.S economy—and ultimately the global economy—depended on the prompt sharing of "Shepard's Law" with the Federal Reserve Board of Governors.

Instead of exploding with rage, as Mika anticipated, she witnessed something she had never seen before. Malachi slumped forward as if he had taken a blow to the solar plexus. His thin blue-veined hands squeezed the sides of the arms of his chair and his face turned several shades of red. If he had not been sitting down, he would have fallen over.

"Malachi, are you alright?" asked Mika, thinking he might be having a heart attack.

"I thought we had the son of a bitch." He was shaking his head slowly, as if resigned to defeat. "I thought he was in our camp. Even after the damn tape we heard, I thought I could explain everything to him, talk to him." The great financier's voice grew fainter. "And now he's gone and given the secret to the enemy. He has no idea what he has just done."

Malachi tried to stand but, unable to do so, reached back for the arms of his chair and dropped into his seat. His eyes were cold and lusterless. "You know, Mika," he said with an odd calmness, "I really, really hate it when I'm wrong. Please find someone who will rid the planet of this reporter. And please find that someone now, before any more damage is done."

℘

Cassandra sat with her hands folded on the edge of a table looking into a bowl of split pea soup. A dozen other women—some dressed in habits, others clothed like her—ate in silence. Keeping her eyes lowered, she studied the younger women.

Most looked Asian, though two she thought were Latino. When they finished eating, they took their bowls and utensils back to the kitchen, where several other novitiates had kitchen duty. Sister Elizabeth was nowhere to be seen. Stepping out of the kitchen, Cassandra eased her way toward the hallway to see what was beyond. One of the older nuns took her by the shoulder and pointed to a list on the door. She was now a number: seven. And number seven had specific gardening duties. The nun led her to the rear of the kitchen and out the door.

Cassandra gulped the fresh early-summer air thankfully, all the more so since being outside was a step closer to freedom than being locked inside a room. She studied her surroundings carefully. There was little to see. All around her was a tall brick-and-stone wall. Beyond was the low buzz of occasional traffic, but there seemed to be no way to scale the wall to get to the road. Other novices were tending tomato cages and wiring string between beanpoles for the plants to follow. Cassandra's chore was to weed the carrot bed, then the peas, and then the broccoli.

Kneeling down, she began pulling weeds by hand, watching her beautiful French polish disappear by the minute. After thirty minutes of backbreaking work, she headed toward the kitchen to see if she could find a trowel. There seemed no other way out of the garden except for the door into the kitchen. Inside, she was directed to a closet where tools awaited. She picked out a trowel, a hand rake, and a cotton bag for the weeds. On the way back to the carrot bed, however, she spied a small gate in the wall. She had missed it entirely before because it was nearly covered by scuppernong vines.

Cassandra threw herself into her work. After a few minutes, when no one seemed to be watching her, she began weeding her way in that direction. As soon as she gathered enough weeds to fill the bag, she stood up with it as though to return to the kitchen door. When she came abreast of the gate, however, she quickly darted toward it and reached for the latch. An electric current shot through her body and threw her flat on her back on the gravel path.

ß

Nicholas carefully unwrapped the bundle of papers his wife had sent to Galen. Cassandra had arranged the documents chronologically, beginning with the 11th century, and tabbed each century with different colored sticky notes. Her detailed lists were on top of the stack. Each name had been matched with an original document bearing the cartouche, and she had inserted cryptic abbreviations next to each name—EG, KT, KT/H, H, I, F, R, B.

Galen looked up, perplexed. "What do these initials mean?"

Nicholas studied them for a few moments. "Well, I am pretty sure 'KT' stands for 'Knights Templar.'"

Gabriel stood suddenly, as though jerked up by an invisible string. He leaned over Nicholas' shoulder and deciphered most of the abbreviations: "Egyptian Gnostics, Hospitallers, Illuminati, Freemasons, and Rosicrucians. I haven't a clue what the B stands for."

"Who are those people?" asked Phoebe, puzzled by his reaction.

Gabe offered her a thumbnail sketch: "Secret organizations that have controlled a good deal of wealth and power throughout the history of Western civilization—sometimes for better, sometimes for worse. The Rosicrucians are probably the most unsavory. They oversee satanic cults and get the blame for a lot of the evil in the world. I've never had much interest in the occult, though, so I don't know that much about them."

Her face went pale. "Satanic?"

"Practicing witchcraft and actually possessing the power are two different things," Galen replied, trying to reassure her.

She didn't look convinced, but Galen ignored her as he sifted through the stacks. "A lot of these documents list contributions to charities, and it looks like, for centuries, the Poor Clares have been one of the most frequent recipients. I'm not sure how I feel about that. A lot of my counseling centers are in their facilities, and it kind of bothers me to think of some of these groups funding the order." Galen's mouth opened and his face blanched before he tightened his eyes shut and shook his head as if embarrassed.

"What's the matter, Galen?" asked Nicholas.

"Rosemary and Harrison's nanny is a Poor Clare."

Nicholas and Gabriel stared at him for a few seconds before both cried out at the same time, "She took the box!" It struck the group like a flash of summer lightning. "She's the one on the inside who lied," continued Nicholas. "Francesca's parents would never have done it, despite the fact that they never wanted the box in their house."

"If I was a betting man, that's where I would lay down my sawbuck," nodded the priest.

"Let's assume for a moment that's true," Gabriel interrupted. "She takes the box, but who does she give it to? We should also assume she overheard everything you said in Italy, so she probably passed all that information on, along with the box. That means Francesca might be in danger. I think we'd better call her—now!"

Nicholas jumped for one of Gabriel's secure phones. "Francesca! Are you okay? How are the kids? Really?" Nicholas turned to the others: "The nanny left a couple of days ago to take care of a sick family member. They haven't heard from her since. The children are heartsick, and . . ." he turned back to the receiver. "What? No, don't do that, Francesca. Well, because we're pretty sure she took the box." Nicholas explained what they had just discovered. "Okay, let me put Galen on the phone." He handed the phone to the priest. "She wants to talk to you."

Galen covered the mouthpiece. "Should I say anything about Cassandra?" he whispered. Nicholas shook his head.

"I know, I know," Galen responded to Francesca. "It just seems like it's never going to end, and every new thing that happens brings all the old things up to bite you. Try to just think of this as nothing except having lost a nanny, and find another one who's not a Poor Clare, okay? No, we're all fine here. Fine." Galen looked heavenward and folded his hands in prayer while cradling the phone on his shoulder. "Okay. Talk to you later," he said and hung up.

"What number is that, I wonder?" asked the priest. "I haven't lied so much since I went to parochial school. God forgive me! At any rate, it seems clear now that all they want is the box and the information. It looks as though Francesca is safe. How are you communicating with Cassandra's kidnappers?"

"Remember, they gave me an e-mail address to use."

"Ah, yes." Galen rubbed his chin and looked at Nicholas. "Why do you suppose they are asking for the box if they already have it back? Is there something else they're after?"

"I'm not following you," replied Nicholas.

"I wonder if you need to tell them the truth about the box and the documents, Nicholas—that you no longer have them."

Nicholas stood up and walked back and forth across the small room. He was approaching the far wall when he stopped suddenly and turned toward Galen with an astonished look on his face. "It's the phase-inversion, Galen. That's what their after. After all, it was one of their requests." Nicholas frowned.

"You mentioned it in your speech in Paris," said Galen, "and Malachi has known about it for some time. You might tell them all you really have to offer is an answer to a problem they probably haven't thought of yet: the invaluable phase-inversion solution. Are you ready to give that up?"

"Of course!" Nicholas exclaimed. "They can have the damn programs! All I want is my wife back!"

"Then maybe you should arrange the deal."

Nicholas nodded and opened his laptop. When he accessed his e-mail, a letter was waiting from him. "This is cute," he said with an angry tone in his voice. "An e-mail from someone with the user name 'cartouche.' It says, 'We must hear from you immediately.'" He began typing a reply.

"Hold on," suggested Galen. "Let's make sure we're taking the right step."

Nicholas stopped typing and looked across the screen at the priest. "I'm just going to tell them that they can have everything I've got, and that I'll send it to that Mailbox Express address." He paused. "But how do I know they'll give Cassandra back to me?"

"Let's consider that," suggested the priest. "While you have your laptop on, can I see Cassandra's message to you?"

Nicholas called up the brief video clip and turned the screen toward Galen. "I don't want to see it again," he said, getting up and heading toward a leather sofa at the other end of the room. He was about halfway across when he heard Galen shout out, "Hallelujah!"

Nicholas turned and hurried back to his laptop. "What, Galen? What is it?"

"Nicholas, she is being held at a Poor Clare convent!" Galen happy countenance quickly assumed a stormy look. "But how can this be?" he asked, rubbing his cheek with one hand and looking up toward the ceiling as if seeking Divine guidance. Nicholas had never seen Galen so visibly upset. "I've spent half my life ministering to the Poor Clares and the people they've brought to me. I've been betrayed! I've been a complete fool!"

"How do you know that's where she is?" asked Gabriel as he leaned toward the screen. It just looked like someone's office to him.

"Cassandra is wearing what the novitiates wear during their service years. They sew the clothes themselves out of cotton—simple, collarless, floor-length, long-sleeve shifts. Plus, I'm positive I've seen that wall behind Cassandra before. I just can't recall where." Galen racked his brain trying to remember. "I'll figure this out. I know it's here in the States," he said, the confidence rising in his voice. "We might even be able to rescue Cassandra. You may not have to give up anything, Nicholas."

Nicholas stared at his friend. "Cassandra's in a convent and we have no idea where, but if you can figure it out, Galen, I'm up for anything."

"I'd make a good nun," offered Phoebe.

"You would not!" Gabriel said, shocked that she would even consider it.

"Yes, she would," Galen argued. "If I can figure out where this place is, I can take Phoebe there as a potential novitiate. Some of my witness protection people are Poor Clares. That makes an interesting mix, doesn't it? Lord, what have I done!"

She was in a convent! Nicholas exhaled and felt a small sense of relief. At least Cassandra was not on a slave ship heading for the Middle East or Asia, or locked in a cold damp cellar in the hands of a murderous lunatic. The terrible images that had been swirling about in his mind receded. "So assuming we discover where she is being held," he said slowly, "the plan is to get Phoebe in there, find Cassandra, and they just leave the property while we wait outside?"

"I'm sure it will have to be much more complicated than that," sighed Galen. "But we have to find the place first!" He evidenced his frustration by vigorously shaking his head. "How about writing back to Mr. Cartouche? Tell him you'll turn over everything he wants, but you need to be assured of seeing your wife again. Ask them how they want to make the swap."

Nicholas agreed and replied to the e-mail. The response came back almost immediately. He read it out loud: "FedEx all the requested items to the Mailbox Express address. When we receive the package, your wife will be in the Plaza lobby waiting for you."

"Hmm," said Gabe. "That means she's somewhere around New York City, or they wouldn't be able to produce her that fast. Assuming he is telling the truth."

"I am going to write back and tell them no deal—that I have to see her before I hand over the information," replied Nicholas.

"I think that is wise," said Galen slowly. "That'll buy us some time. Ask them to reply tomorrow. Tell them you need the time to gather up the documentation they want."

"What documentation?" When Galen merely smiled in response, an elated Nicholas nearly shouted out, "You remember!"

"Yep. I know exactly where we can find it." The big priest slapped his Stetson firmly on his head and grinned. "Next stop, St. Mary's, Pennsylvania."

Chapter 54

Sam Griffin took off his glasses and rubbed his eyes with his fists. It was just past 10:30 p.m., and he was putting the final touches on the next day's installment in his series on the Shepard brothers' discovery. He yawned as he stretched, stood up, and contemplated his cubicle.

The small space looked as though the wrath of God had been visited upon him. Old newspapers, empty French fry containers, books, and miscellaneous papers and documents littered the desk and fell into what he liked to call his "floor files." Management had long since given up on changing his habits, and had instead moved him into an out-of-the-way cubicle where visitors were unlikely to stray. That suited Griffin just fine; he liked working alone.

The reporter tucked his shirt in and started stuffing papers into a battered briefcase when he thought better of it. He was too tired to get anything else done tonight. After adjusting the photographs of his two college-age daughters he threw his suit jacket over his shoulders and headed for the exit. The room buzzed with the activity of night reporters working away at their stories. He waved goodnight, gave the cleaning man a conspiratorial wink, and climbed into the elevator.

The reporter leaned back and relaxed against the wall of the elevator, enjoying how its smooth cold surface felt against his aching shoulders. It was easy to calm down and loosen up inside the protective box. But once he left the security of the elevator, his antenna shot up and his nerves began to rattle. His therapist had reassured him that his constant edginess was just free-floating anxiety, a natural reaction to a divorce he hadn't wanted or expected. It was just a reaction to change, he was told, to living alone in middle age.

Griffin took the subway to Queens and pounded the pavement a few blocks to his second-floor walk-up. The building was run down and his apartment was no better, but he hadn't cared much about setting up house after the divorce. By now he was used to the few pieces of dilapidated furniture and lamps rummaged from a Goodwill store. What did he care? Most of his waking hours were spent working at a giant, walnut, roll-top desk that had belonged to his father. It was the only thing besides the Eames chair that he had kept when his wife had broken the news that their marriage was over.

He had spent the last eight years walking around in a fog, and the Shepard story was his ticket back. He knew his co-workers thought he was a strange duck, his editor merely tolerated him, and the owners had talked more than once about canning him. For eight years he had been living on his past work. That was about to end. Nicholas Shepard was his savior and he was finally going to nail that bastard Malachi Foust. The scent of a Pulitzer Prize lingered in the air.

He looked about his dreary apartment. "Ah, screw it," he said out loud, turned around, and walked back out. Griffin trotted down the steps and hiked quickly one block to Tootie's Bar. The hole-in-the-wall bar-pub was as familiar to him as his wretched apartment, and smelled nearly as bad. But at least it wasn't lonely. He settled down two stools in from the corner, as he always did, and gazed at the sport banners, movie posters, campaign buttons, and license plates that littered the walls. There was even a pair of prosthetic limbs hanging just above an autographed *The Fugitive* movie poster. He nodded to the familiar faces.

"Hey, Sam," said Fred Barczyk. "Long time no see. How's it going?" The bartender had been greeting him the same way for years. Sam nodded his hello while grabbing a plastic bowl full of peanuts.

"How about a Heineken and a fried pastrami sandwich, Fred."

"You need a wife," groaned the bartender. "Then I wouldn't have to cook sandwiches at eleven o'clock at night." He had been saying that for six years, too. Fred drew the beer and fired up the grill while Sam watched some middle-aged women dancing to a country song. Girls' night out, he thought with a smile.

It was easy to tell who was new to the place because years ago some joker had super-glued a couple of silver dollars to the dance floor. Sam never tired of watching the newcomers bend over to pick them up. Three young girls who had been hustling some of the guys at the billiards table disappeared into the bathroom. When they were gone, Fred rang the bell over the middle of the bar, turned down the music, and told everyone to be quiet. Sam knew what was coming next.

The girls were from Jersey, their accents thick enough to cut with a butcher's knife. "Ohhhh, he's so hot. He makes me shiver just lookin' at him." The voice poured over the loudspeaker, which was piped into the main bar from the ladies' room.

"You can't have that one. He's mine," laughed another.

"What? You's gonna leave me with dat midget dufflehead?" complained the third girl. "No way!"

Two of the boys at the pool table hooted at their shorter companion while the girls in the bathroom continued their drunken argument. Now they were flipping a coin to decide who got stuck with which guy, but none of them was sober enough to catch it. By this time their profane buffoonery had the patrons in the bar in hysterics. When it became obvious they were about to come out, Fred whisked the three boys into a back room. By the time the girls stumbled out of the john the music was playing again and Fred was earnestly polishing the bar. Everything was normal except their quarry had disappeared.

"Hey, Mac," asked the ringleader, "what happened to the guys who was playing pool?"

Fred looked up nonchalantly. "Oh, them nice boys? They left with some girls from Queens. You know, class types."

The girls stormed out and the boys came back in, high-fiving Fred as he drew them fresh beers on the house. Sam played a few games of pool with the boys, had a couple more beers, and was feeling no pain when he stumbled out two hours later. His usual anxiety was gone, and for once he was looking forward to going to work the next day.

Whistling softly, Sam was nearly to his door when someone reached out of the darkness and grabbed him from behind. "Jesus Christ!" he yelled as a rough hand was clasped over his mouth. *Damn!* he thought. *I am being mugged on my own street!*

Before he could think of what to do he felt something cold race across his neck from left to right. He gasped in pain, choking and wheezing as a hot rush of blood sprayed out and ran up his throat to fill his mouth and gush over his lips. It took Griffin a few seconds to realize someone had slit his throat. He was dying.

Not fair. I got a "holy shit story" and . . . this is . . . not . . . fair.

Sam Griffin lay still on the sidewalk as a pair of men stood over him. The bigger, beefier one was breathing heavily in excitement, just as he always did when he had a job to do up close and personal. He wiped his knife on the reporter's pants, examined it closely, and wiped it again. Satisfied, he put it in his coat pocket. The other man leaned over the body and removed Sam's wallet and keys. "I hate this wet work shit, and this guy bled like a stuck pig. Come on," he grunted.

It was well after 1:00 a.m. and no one was awake to see them slip into Griffin's apartment. They searched through every drawer quickly and quietly, disturbing nothing. The killer watched as the other man turned on the computer and inserted every disk and CD he could find. After thirty minutes he gave up.

"Ah, fuck this!" he hissed. "The CD we want ain't here." He took out a cell phone and punched in a number. "The apartment is clean" he told the voice on the other end. He hung up and turned to his companion. "Let's get out of here."

A moment later a cell phone rang in Griffin's office. The janitor answered his phone, listened and acknowledged the message, and went back to his work. When the newsroom was finally empty, he searched his way through Sam's mess. One hour later he called in his report: the CD wasn't in Sam's office, either.

Chapter 55

"St. Mary's is home to about 15,000 souls," explained Galen, "nearly two-thirds of whom work in the powdered metal factories. It was founded in 1842 by German Bavarian Catholics, so it has quite a history. Decker's Chapel, America's smallest church, is there. There's a little brewery, too—Straub's—that puts out about 40,000 barrels a year. Not a bad beer, as I recall."

They were on their way to a small town in the Allegheny mountain district, about 125 miles from Pittsburgh. Gabriel was behind the wheel of his Lexus SUV, driving well above the speed limit but using his sophisticated radar equipment to watch out for the Highway Patrol.

"We'll need to go to the downtown section, the historic district, to scope out the convent," Galen went on. "We can camp out at the local Best Western across the street from the Wal-Mart." Gabriel and Nicholas shot the priest a skeptical look and appealed for better quarters. "What do you want? This is a tiny industrial town in the Allegheny foothills. The Ritz would go broke here. It's also the most obscure place in the world to hide a hostage. Give me a phone, please."

Gabriel handed his phone to Phoebe, who passed it to Galen in the back seat. Nicholas just stared at the priest. Galen had always been a take-action sort of guy, but this . . . this was straight out of the Old West, and he felt like he was traveling with Wyatt Earp! He smiled to himself and looked out the window for a few moments. Alex would have loved this.

Galen dialed information and asked for the Poor Clare Convent in St. Mary's. "Sister Elizabeth? This is Father Galen Abbott. Yes, it's good to hear your voice, too. I know it has been such a long time. I'm calling because I have a young woman with me who I would love to place in your care. I'm in the area, and can swing through this afternoon. To tell you the truth, we are on our way there now. I've . . . well, let's just say I have taken her out of a rough domestic situation, and she needs some nurturing. She's from Pittsburgh . . . by way of Asheville, North Carolina." Despite all his recent practice, Galen still wasn't accustomed to lying. "She has been very devout since she was a child. How old is she?" He turned and looked at Phoebe, who whispered, "Twenty-eight." He made an appointment for after lunch and hung up.

"You have one hour to turn yourself into a devout Catholic maiden," he said with smile. "We need to figure out our strategy, too."

"No kidding!" interrupted Nicholas. "What's she going to do once she's inside?"

"The Poor Clares is a silent order, so she won't be allowed to speak. We'll have to resort to notes. Here," he said, handing Phoebe a small pad of sticky notes and a short pencil. "Hide these in your underwear."

She raised her eyebrows. "Excuse me, Father?"

"Sorry," answered Galen, "but it's not like you're going to be able to walk around with a purse and cell phone. This is a very strict order—one of only a handful like it anywhere. If Cassandra is still there, you will have to find her and get a note to her, tell her who you are, and that Nicholas and Gabriel are close by."

"Galen, if it's a convent, why can't we just walk in there and get her?" asked Nicholas, running a nervous hand through his hair.

"You could try that," nodded the priest. "And then I will bail you out of jail for trespassing on private property and assaulting nuns." Galen shot Nicholas an empathetic look. "If we have to break in, my friend, we will do so. But I hope it won't come to that. I'd love to know whether Sister Elizabeth is in on this, or whether the cartouche people are somehow twisting her arm. We are dealing with very clever, very ruthless, and very experienced people. They could easily have someone keeping an eye on the convent—just in case people like us try something."

Nicholas pushed his case. "Ok, let's assume Cassandra is there, and Phoebe contacts her. Then what?"

Everyone was silent and looked at Galen. "I guess we'll have to fly by the seat of our collective pants," Galen said at last. "It depends on many things."

"No offense, Galen, but I think I have a better plan," offered Nicholas. "Instead of just leaving Phoebe inside there, let's tell the Mother Superior that you've got business back in Pittsburgh for a couple of days and would like to check in on her tomorrow just to see how she's doing. Okay?"

"That's good," replied Galen slowly. "Phoebe will have a chance to let us know what she has found. Hopefully, Cassandra has already scoped out the place. Maybe we'll be able to get her out tomorrow. We just have to be careful not to set off any alarms."

When Gabriel pulled off at an exit to refuel the SUV, Phoebe excused herself to use the restroom. Nicholas picked up a six-pack of cold Peach Snapple inside and walked back to the car, handing one through the window to his friend. Nicholas leaned against the outside of the door and twisted the top off, listening to the familiar vacuum pop as the lid came free in his hand. "Galen, we got sidetracked earlier. You never did tell us why you are so damn positive Cassandra is inside this convent."

Galen popped the top of his bottle of flavored tea and grinned, setting the lid down before reaching up to tap the side of his nose. "Ah, by deduction my dear Dr. Watson."

"That is the worst British accent I have ever heard," said Gabriel as he climbed into the driver's seat. "But, I am curious. Deduction of what?"

"You remember that wall in the video behind Cassandra? There was a bookcase in the corner. On it was probably the one thing you'd least expect to see in a convent, sitting right there in plain view."

"What?" asked Nicholas, his eyes wide open with expectancy.

"A set of dog tags," Galen replied. "Sister Elizabeth's brother was killed in Vietnam in 1967. She keeps the tags there as a permanent reminder of him. I asked her about them the first time I met her, and she told me the whole story. Anyway, we know now that Cassandra *was* there, and we have to hope she's *still* there. These people might not keep her in any one place too long. You think we can stall them for two more days?"

Phoebe returned and set off on the road again. "What if I e-mail and say I'll have the phase-inversion materials at the Plaza hotel lobby the day after tomorrow?" answered Nicholas, continuing the conversation where they left off "I'll also go ahead and tell them the box and documents were stolen from where we were keeping them in Italy."

"I think that would be wise," answered Galen. "Whup, Gabe! You're driving past the hotel."

Gabriel groaned as he looked over his shoulder. "That's the hotel?" He turned the vehicle around in the entrance to the Wal-Mart and drove up to the cement block-and-stucco hotel, where they took adjoining rooms. They agreed to meet back at the SUV in fifteen minutes. Phoebe wanted to take some time to wash her face and comb her hair.

"I don't know how I'm going to explain this swanky vehicle to the good sisters," Galen mused, standing next to the car. "Maybe I won't have to. The convent only faces the street by a door next to the church. I'll let you boys out in town and drive to the other side of the church with Phoebe."

An anxious silence prevailed as they neared their destination. So much depended now on Phoebe's intuition and common sense. She reached over and took Gabriel's hand.

The "historic" district of St. Mary's consisted of a main street divided by an island surrounded by parking places, each with its own parking meter. It had experienced its last renovation in 1955, when the 19th-century shops received plate-glass fronts, parking meters were erected up and down main thoroughfare, and a new combined fire and police station was built at the head of the street. The convent and its attendant gray stone church occupied the crest of a small hill a little more than a mile away.

Galen pulled up to one of the parking meters. It was after lunch, and the street was virtually deserted. Gabriel released Phoebe's hand reluctantly and he and Nicholas climbed out of the SUV. They had noticed a library on the way in, and they headed there now. It seemed like an inconspicuous place to spend some time.

Gabriel was trying to convince himself Phoebe would be okay. "She's smart," he said to Nicholas. "Street smart." The depth of his concern quickly bubbled to the surface. "She's the best thing that ever happened to me. If something should go wrong…"

"Plenty could go wrong," said Nicholas honestly. He had his own worries. "We'll do the best we can, and if this doesn't work, I'll give the information to the cartouche people and pray they'll let Cassandra go. But Phoebe'll be okay. I mean, these people are nuns, for heaven's sake. They aren't murderers."

Gabriel's look told Nicholas exactly what he was thinking: anyone could be a murderer and he was not going to stop worrying about it. "You're right," said Nicholas softly. "I have no idea what they are."

The men entered the little library and took up vigil in dusty vinyl chairs in the periodicals section. Each grabbed a magazine and pretended to read it. They weren't fooling each other at all.

&

As they drew up to the convent, Galen asked Phoebe if she was afraid.

"No," she replied, shaking her head. "Gabe wouldn't let me do anything dangerous. It's not a den of lions, after all." She looked up at the big priest and smiled.

"Good answer, my dear. By the way, what is your faith?"

"I'm an Anglican; an Episcopalian," she answered. "Catholic light."

Galen chuckled. "Close enough. You'll be able to understand what they're talking about. Here we are."

He parked a short distance down the street and walked quickly to the convent. It had been cloudy all morning, and now rain seemed imminent. The day was gloomy enough without all the gray stone. Galen lifted one of his large hands, formed a fist, and knocked on the heavy Gothic door. He was about to knock a second time when a small elderly nun opened it.

"Welcome, my dear," she said to Phoebe. "Sister Elizabeth would like to see you right away. Good afternoon, Father. I will be unable to communicate with you any further."

The old nun closed her mouth, offered a slight bow and smiled, leading them with a skittering walk down a stone hallway to the cloister. She ushered them in to the Mother Superior's office and disappeared without a sound.

Sister Elizabeth rose to greet them, paying close attention to Phoebe. Galen examined the wall and bookcase, relieved to see the dog tags still hanging in place. *Thank You for those dog tags*, he said silently. *And thank You for allowing me to recall them.*

He described Phoebe's "situation," drawing upon hundreds of similar cases he knew only too well. Phoebe, as she had been instructed, kept her eyes cast down and only looked up when addressed. "Is the reason you wish to join the order only to escape your domestic situation?" Sister Elizabeth asked.

Phoebe shook her head emphatically and spoke in a low voice. "I have wanted to do this since I was a little girl. I started catechism at six, and prayed rosaries every day to our lady." Phoebe hoped this sounded plausible. She had seen *The Sound of Music* a hundred times, but beyond that. . . . As if to demonstrate, she knelt in prayerful contemplation.

"Rise, young woman," said Sister Elizabeth gently. "Your faith makes you whole. Welcome." Real tears of relief ran down Phoebe's cheeks as she rose, taking Galen's hand. "Thank you, Father," she whispered.

He gave her a tiny wink and squeezed her hand. "Go with God," he managed to choke out.

Sister Elizabeth rang a small bell on her desk and the elderly nun returned as though she had been listening outside the door. Phoebe left with her. Galen watched her go with a sinking heart. *What have I done?*

Sister Elizabeth offered him some refreshment, but Galen wasn't sure how long he could keep up the charade. *I have to leave before I find myself in a web of lies I can no longer lie my way out of*, he thought frantically. He assured her he would return the next day to check on Phoebe and left quickly.

ᛒ

Tossing aside their magazines, Nicholas and Gabriel walked out of the library and down the street. It was raining now, and they huddled under a canopy until Galen pulled up in front of them and unlocked the door. "It went well," he said, filling them in on every detail. "Phoebe's up to the task. It is all in God's hands now."

They gathered in Nicholas' room, where he flipped on the television and flopped back on the bed. Mayor Bloomberg was addressing the increase in violence in New York City. He was convening a task force, he said, and in the meantime hiring more police officers. Nicholas was about to change the channel when he heard the news anchor say, "For those of you just tuning in to this breaking story, respected *New York Times* financial reporter Sam Griffin was found murdered early this morning near his home in Queens. We're going to join our correspondent Tom Burns at Tootie's Bar, where Griffin was seen late last night."

"Oh, no!" wailed Nicholas. Galen and Gabriel sat with open mouths, staring at the television.

The bartender was on camera, his hands wringing a white bar towel as he kept repeating. "So sad . . . so senseless."

The anchor asked reporter about a motive. "Tom, do we know whether there was anything Griffin was working on that could account for his death?"

"The police are pretty tight lipped right now," declared Burns. "Our sources claim Mr. Griffin's wallet was missing, and the Police seem to be hinting that this is just another random, pointless, New York-style mugging turned bad. According to a witness who found the body, however, the reporter's throat was slit, which is not consistent for even a mugging gone awry."

"Thanks, Tom," said the anchor. "In other news. . . ."

Nicholas switched off the set, his face pale as a sheet in the lamplight. He rose and ran into the bathroom, where his friends could hear him vomiting into the toilet. They looked at one another in stunned silence.

When Nicholas returned, he was wiping his face with a towel. "That reporter is dead because of me. What's next?" he rasped. "Everyone I know . . . ." He clenched the towel. "Even you guys are in danger."

Gabriel started to speak but Nicholas cut him off. "Damn it!" he shouted, throwing the towel at the television. "Don't you see? It was the end game. Sam was my ticket to legitimacy. What am I going to do now?"

"How about we rescue Cassandra," Galen fought to remain calm.

Nicholas' glare revealed the depth of his frustration. "You don't understand. This isn't just my career. I gave Sam a disk with all of Alex's information on it, including the phase-inversion documentation. I don't have anything to negotiate with any more. What the hell do I do now?"

"Let me say it again," Galen replied quietly, but with a firm resolve. "We'd better stick to the task at hand. Cassandra is our only concern now."

℘

Phoebe gave Father Abbott one last look and followed the elderly nun out of the room. A group of nuns where waiting for them. Only one spoke, to help orient her to the protocols of her new life. They showed her to a small room identical to Cassandra's on the basement floor, where she found the standard clothing, two coarse towels and a face cloth, and basic toiletries. The tour proceeded to the dining room, the kitchen, the garden, the washing and sewing rooms, before ending in the chapel with the late-afternoon prayer.

When Mother Superior announced the presence of the new novitiate, Phoebe stood at the rail so the others could see her. Cassandra sat in the group of nuns, nodding her greetings like the rest. *That frizzy hair*, she thought. *It looks oddly familiar.* Fleeting glimpses of surreptitious smiles flickered in her memory. *Why were images of the Biltmore and Gabriel coming to mind?* Cassandra focused on the new novitiate's facial features. *I have seen this woman before. But where?*

And then she knew. Gabriel. The Biltmore. Forbidden love.

Her name was Phoebe, and she was Gabriel's girlfriend. *Nicholas! Nicholas must be close by!*

Cassandra stifled a gasp as she cast furtive glances to see if anyone noticed she had recognized the novitiate. No one paid her the slightest attention. She kept her head up, hoping Phoebe would recognize her face. Only once did her eyes pass by Cassandra, and there was no sign she recognized her.

During dinner that evening, which consisted of boiled meat and vegetables from the garden, Cassandra maneuvered herself to sit next to the new nun-in-training. Phoebe nodded once in her direction, but there was not a flicker of recognition in her eyes. A few minutes later while adjusting her napkin Phoebe dropped a folded sticky note into Cassandra's lap. Elated, Cassandra tucked it up her sleeve, frantic with anticipation. Neither woman looked at the other.

When the evening chores and prayers were over, the novitiates filed down to their basement rooms. Cassandra's hopes soared when she saw that Phoebe's room was next to her own.

As soon as the door shut behind her, Cassandra pulled out the note. "G, N, and G here," it said. "Tomorrow night they will come to get us. Need information. Wait until lights out."

In one corner was a kneeler below a shelf of votive candles. On the wall above was a plain wooden cross. Cassandra lit a votive and burned the note. She had already searched the room for video and audio surveillance, and was fairly certain the room was not bugged.

Thirty minutes after lights-out, Cassandra gripped the knob on her door and turned it clockwise. It was unlocked. She eased it open and quietly ventured into the hall with a sleepy look on her face, pretending to head for the bathroom. Knowing that freedom was possible made her all the more petrified that something might go wrong and ruin her only chance to escape. She brushed the door to the room next to hers and knocked softly. Phoebe opened it quickly and pulled her inside, where the two women hugged as if they had been friends all their lives.

"Galen needs to know if there's anybody watching you who might be armed," Phoebe whispered.

"Other than the nuns, I haven't seen anybody except the monk who handles all the heavy work around here," answered Cassandra. "But I don't know how they're going to get in here. Every night they lock the hall door that leads to these rooms."

Cassandra could no longer contain herself. It was Nicholas' safety that drove her to distraction. "Phoebe, listen," she hissed, grabbing the woman's arm just above the wrist and squeezing it tightly. "This is critically important. Nicholas needs to know that the man behind the cartouche is Malachi Foust. It's his family crest! Has he figured that out yet? That's why I sent the documents home. I thought I left a clear trail, but I was afraid to simply scrawl the answer on a page because I was unsure who might intercept the package."

"I don't think they got that far," Phoebe replied with a small frown and a shake of her frizzled head. "They have been too busy trying to figure out how to rescue you. I don't remember anyone mentioning that name. I'll tell Galen tomorrow. He's coming back here to check up on me and find out what he can about you."

Cassandra exhaled loudly. "Good. Well, let's concentrate on getting out of here first. The best way to get in is through the little door in the garden wall. But it's protected by an electric fence. My nerves are still jiggling from trying to escape through it!"

"Can we sneak through the halls to the chapel in the middle of the night?"

"No. Like I said, they lock the door into this hallway every night. But somebody always keeps an all-night vigil in the chapel, or at least that is what I gather from the list posted in the vestry doorway. Maybe you could volunteer? Right now that's the only thing I can think of."

ℬ

After dinner at one of the local restaurants, the trio headed to Wal-Mart, where Nicholas and Galen followed Gabriel as he pushed his cart through the hardware section. He picked out rope, cables, wire cutters, hammers, screwdrivers, a small battery-operated drill—even a ladder, which he drafted Nicholas to carry. "You never know what you're going to need when you're breaking and entering a convent," joked the priest as he elbowed Nicholas.

Their last stop was in the clothing section, where Gabriel picked out black jeans and a black turtleneck. "You, too, Nicholas," he advised. "Galen can go like he is—without the Stetson."

Galen's mind was turning quickly. "I wonder where we could get some chloroform?" Under any other circumstances Nicholas would have started laughing. The image of knocking out nuns with chloroformed handkerchiefs seemed so ridiculous.

Back at the motel they talked late, speculating on all the possibilities. Their primary concern was whether a guard had been posted to watch Cassandra. Gabriel suggested they cut the power and phone lines, a plan his companions found to their liking. Midnight seemed like a propitious hour, so they decided on that, too.

Galen sketched out a rough map of the convent. They would go in through the church, where they would have to wait until midnight without arousing suspicion. There was an entry into the convent chapel behind the altar, and Galen thought he might be able to get Phoebe to make sure it remained unlocked. That was as far as they could plan until Galen had had a chance to speak with Phoebe.

Exhausted with worry, Nicholas stared at the ceiling for a long time. When sleep finally came, it was blessedly deep and refreshing. The next morning he e-mailed "cartouche" that he would be in the Plaza hotel lobby at 3:00 p.m. the following day, ready to hand over the phase-inversion solution. The box and the documents, he explained, had been stolen in Italy. Five minutes later he had his reply: "This arrangement is acceptable."

"They bought it!" Nicholas shouted while still looking down at his laptop. *We still may still have a chance*, he thought.

℘

"Excellent!" declared Malachi.

Mika had just reported the e-mail exchange, and the financier could not have been more pleased. "There is a lesson to be learned here," he explained to her. "Don't pussy-foot around when you can just eliminate the problem right away."

He threw her a generous smile. The momentum had shifted strongly toward Malachi, and he was enjoying the game more now than ever. "I would like you to have a car sent to the convent tonight. Let's bring Mrs. Shepard here for a little visit."

Chapter 56

According to the list on the vestry door the next morning, Number Three was scheduled for the all-night vigil. Both Cassandra and Phoebe had a sudden, and unsettling, awareness of the feebleness of their plan.

Phoebe wasn't Number Three, and it was obvious Cassandra wouldn't get the duty, either.

When Galen arrived that afternoon, Phoebe was escorted to Sister Elizabeth's office.

"May I talk with her privately, Sister Elizabeth?" Galen asked. It has to do with a matter unrelated to her duties here."

After hesitating a moment, Sister Elizabeth acquiesced. "You may stay here or walk about freely, but please Father, keep your conversation as quiet as possible."

Phoebe and the priest walked out into the hallway and closed the door behind them. She quickly advised Galen that the plan they had come up with would have to be changed because another novitiate had pulled chapel duty that night.

"So how can we get to you and Cassandra?" he asked. "Can you leave your room at night?"

"Yes, but just to go to the communal bathroom at the end of the hall. The only door to the dorm area is locked after the lights are turned out." She explained where the hallway door was, and then asked anxiously, "Do you think you can rescue us?"

"Don't worry," Galen said with more confidence than he felt. "We'll see you tonight at midnight. One more thing, though. Before you settle in for prayer this evening, try to get to the chapel door and unlock it. I plan on being in the church, doing prayer and meditation, but we'll need to get from the church into the chapel."

Phoebe nodded her understanding and left as Galen returned to the office. Sister Elizabeth was on the phone. "Yes, I understand. Tonight. Yes, I will follow your instructions." Her voice was shaking as she hung up the phone with one hand, and used the other to cover and squeeze her eyes.

Galen poked his head inside the door and cleared his throat. "She seems very happy here, sister," he told her. "I think it will be a good fit." The nun looked distracted and did not speak. He noticed that her hand was still resting on the receiver. "Sister, is everything alright?"

"Funding," she managed to say with a weak smile. "Always such stress." It took her a few breaths to recover her equipoise. "Well, I'm so glad your young friend is happy here," she said as she stood behind her desk. He was being dismissed.

Galen took the hint. "Thank you for all you have done," he said as he left. *If that call was about funding,* he thought to himself, *then my hat is not suitable for a Texas priest.* That Sister Elizabeth was involved somehow now seemed beyond dispute. *Tonight.* Would their midnight rescue operation come in time to save Phoebe and Cassandra?

When he returned to the hotel, he found Gabriel cleaning a .45 automatic. "Whoa there a minute!" began the priest.

Nicholas cut him off. "Did you see Cassandra? Is she all right? Couldn't you have just taken her out while you were there?"

"No, yes, and no," Galen answered, his hands raised palms-out in an attempt to calm Nicholas down. "I didn't see Cassandra, but I talked to Phoebe and she says Cassandra is fine."

"Thank God!" Nicholas and Gabriel said together.

"How's Phoebe holding up?" asked Gabriel.

"Phoebe is great. Don't worry about her. She'll go the distance. We have two problems, though. First, the chapel will be watched by one of the other novitiates tonight. So we'll have to deal with that young woman before we can get to Cassandra and Phoebe."

"And the second problem?"

"The door that leads to their rooms stays locked at night, so we're going to have to figure out how to break through." *If, God willing, we still have time.* He decided not to share the phone call and his subsequent concerns with Nicholas and Gabe. They both had enough to worry about.

"Now tell me about the gun, Gabe," instructed Galen his gaze settled on the .45.

"I always carry it with me in the SUV, and I have a license to do so," Gabriel answered. "And you never know." He held up a small bottle. "Chloroform. I forgot I had some in a kit I keep in the car. Great solvent for fatty oils on gun handles," he smiled, "and for making novitiates faint dead away."

"You keep a gun in your car? Where do you hide it?"

"In a secret compartment below the front passenger seat. My old man can get pretty paranoid. It goes back to the Cold War. He was convinced one day we would have to defend the country on our own soil. Then with all the rich-bashing going on, he was afraid the liberals would turn on him in the streets." He grinned at Galen. "That's a joke."

Galen sat down as far from the gun as possible. "You really know how to use that?" he asked. Gabriel nodded. "OK," Galen exhaled. "Nicholas can tend to cutting off the power and telephones. I don't think they have cell phones there yet. I know Phoebe doesn't have one. How about Cassandra?"

"They would have confiscated it," answered Nicholas. "My guess is that whoever kidnapped her took it, but if it's in the convent and the Mother Superior wakes up with the phone line cut, she might be tempted to use it."

"We'll have to risk it," replied Galen with a wave of his hand. "In fact, we've got to hope that Sister Elizabeth sleeps right through the whole thing. Who's going to be in charge of knocking out the novitiate, just in case?"

Nicholas and Gabriel looked at the priest. Gabriel shrugged. "You can get close. Who would suspect a priest?"

Galen lifted his eyes heavenward. "Oh Lord. How much penance am I going to have to do for this?" He turned to Gabriel. "How do I use the chloroform?

"Father Galen," winked Gabriel, "don't you watch old spy movies?" All three laughed. "I don't really have a clue, because I have never tried it before. I guess pour a decent amount on a wash cloth, hold it against her nose, and wait until her knees buckle."

Since they had better information now, they decided to abandon the garden gate plan. The convent chapel was connected to the church by a short hallway. All they had to do was get into the chapel and work their way to the dorm area. Everyone admitted that the plan was half-baked, and they would need a lot of luck. Galen made Gabriel promise to keep the gun in his pocket.

At 7:30 p.m. they headed for town, somber but focused. The last service at the church was the 7:00 p.m. mass, and Galen decided to turn up at the door for late prayer. He knew the priest would leave a fellow man of the cloth there alone as long as he needed to pray, and his plans were to pray until midnight, when Nicholas cut the power. He didn't say anything out loud, but he figured that they could use a few extra prayers. They dropped Galen off at the church and returned to the hotel to wait.

At 11:15 p.m., Gabriel and Nicholas climbed into the SUV. Neither man said a word.

Chapter 57

Nicholas was checking off the items they had with them: ropes, wire cutters, flashlights, stepladder, power drill . . .

"Clothes! We don't have anything to dress the women in once they get out."

"Hmm. That, my friend, will be the least of our worries should we actually get them out tonight." Gabriel stopped the SUV up the street from the church and cut his headlights. "Good luck."

Nicholas nodded and quietly climbed out with the wire cutters, a small ladder, and a large clamp. Thankfully it was a dark night, damp and overcast. Gabriel rolled down his window and watched as Nicholas crept along the wall of the convent, located the phone line leading inside, and cut it.

"That was easier than I thought it would be," muttered Nicholas to himself as he set up the ladder so he could reach the metal pegs sticking out from a utility pole. Checking it for stability, he climbed it as quickly as he could, secured his footing on the permanent bolts, and ascended the pole.

It was so dark Gabriel lost sight of him completely. Fifteen minutes later he heard him before he could see him when Nicholas dropped one end of the metal stepladder with a clatter onto the sidewalk. Gabriel grimaced and slid lower in the driver's seat, holding his breath. Nicholas scurried up to the SUV, slid in the equipment, and climbed into the passenger seat.

"Jesus, I am way too old for this," he exclaimed, breathing heavily. "My heart was beating so fast I thought I was going to have a heart attack!" When Gabriel shot him an inquisitive look, he nodded as he tried to slow his labored breathing to an acceptable rate. "I disconnected the transformer circuit breaker connecting the building to its power supply. So far, so good."

Inside the church, meanwhile, Galen was quietly reading a Bible. *"And Moses was not able to enter into the tent of the congregation, because the cloud abode thereon, and the glory of the Lord filled the tabernacle. . . ."*

The only thing that filled the church was darkness, sudden and heavy. Galen smiled, rose quietly, and opened the door for Gabriel, who handed him a small flashlight with a precise, non-peripheral beam. Without speaking a word they made their way to the door leading into the rear of the chapel. *God I hope Phoebe managed to unlock it,* prayed the priest. Breaking the lock was a last resort, and one that would surely alarm the novitiate on duty. Galen held his breath and turned the ancient brass knob. The door clicked open.

Kneeling in the candlelight inside the chapel was the young novitiate, sound asleep with her arms crossed on the altar rail. Galen motioned for Gabriel to follow him. Soundlessly they crept into the hallway—and stopped dead in their tracks. Flickering light spilled out from beneath Sister Elizabeth's office door. She must have lit candles when the power went out.

Gabriel turned slowly to move down the dark hall and stumbled against a tall, unwieldy candelabrum, which fell against the stone floor with enough noise to wake the dead. Galen, his hands all thumbs, fumbled and pulled at the cloth with one hand and the chloroform with the other. He was dumping the liquid into the thirsty cotton when Sister Elizabeth opened her door.

"You're here already!" Sister Elizabeth said into the blackness beyond her door. "I'm sure Cassandra's asleep. I thought you were going to call . . . ." The nun took a step forward into the dark hallway and turned to the right. "Hello?"

Galen saw his opening and stepped forward quickly, grabbing her from behind and pressing the saturated cloth over her mouth and nose. She was stronger than he thought, and for a few seconds kicked and thrashed about wildly until her legs and arms suddenly turned to jelly and she collapsed in his arms. Grimacing at his behavior, he carried the nun into her office and laid her down gently in the corner on the stone floor.

The two men ran quickly downstairs to the hall entrance door. "This one!" said Galen, pointing to a door. "That's supposed to be Cassandra's room." Gabriel wedged a pry bar between the doorframe and the latch, and one quick pull broke the door open. Cassandra and Phoebe were already standing there, ready to flee. The noise of a breaking door was impossible to mask, and within seconds several other doors up and down the hallway cracked open, the young faces of the novitiates peering out in alarm.

Without even trying to provide an explanation, Galen led the other three back up the stairs toward the chapel. Phoebe gasped when she saw Sister Elizabeth lying in her office, the soft glow of candles illuminating her corpse-like appearance. Gabriel whispered reassurances and the party continued its exodus, running through the chapel and past the novitiate, who somehow was still asleep on the altar rail. Ahead of them was the church, and beyond that, after what seemed an eternity, they reached the door and spilled outside into the cool damp night. An elated Nicholas had the SUV's doors open. "Hurry!" he shouted.

They were still piling in—Cassandra in front; Galen, Phoebe, and Gabriel in back—when a black Chevy Suburban screeched to a halt behind them. Its doors flew open and two men leaped out and began running toward the SUV.

"Hold on!" screamed Nicholas as he floored the Lexus. He looked in the rearview mirror and could just make out the two men climbing back into their suburban, which wheeled around to give chase. Nicholas turned down one street after another, but couldn't lose them.

He shot a look at his wife. "Are you ok?" he yelled.

She smiled back and nodded. "I'm fine and I love you! But keep your eyes on the road!"

As the Lexus screeched back onto Main Street, a crazy idea into popped Nicholas' head. "Hang on to something!" he hollered, barreling toward the "modern" 1955-era police station with its plate-glass front. He laid on the horn as a warning to anyone inside, and stamped on the brakes just before impact. The Lexus smashed through the large window, sending the officers on night duty diving under their desks as cloud of glass shards, paperwork, and plaster dust rained down around them. The black suburban slowed down but never stopped.

Nicholas had handled the crash so expertly the air bags had not even engaged. The five passengers climbed out slowly, unsure why they had just experienced a drive through a police station window. When the policemen emerged from behind their desks, they did so with guns drawn. "We need to be arrested and jailed," said Nicholas evenly, his hands in the air like everyone else. "We . . ."

"Not a problem," stuttered the police sergeant, the gun in his hand shaking so much it threatened to fall to the floor. "You're definitely under arrest!" He looked them over carefully, finally calming down enough to think clearly. "Now why would two convent novitiates, a priest, and two men dressed in black crash into my office in the middle of the night? You have some explaining to do." He turned to the other officer. "Danny," he ordered his deputy, "lock 'em up."

The man called Danny, a young graduate of a local criminal justice program, had suddenly found himself in the middle of the most exciting night of his life. He escorted the prisoners to the rear of the building, where he put the two women in one cell and the three men in another. Each was furnished with a double-decker bed and a toilet in plain view. Danny pulled a cot from a closet and slid it into the men's cell. "That was just like a movie!" he said, obviously impressed by the event. "You guys trying to escape from mobsters or something?"

"Danny!" they all heard the sergeant shout. "Get back up here and take some pictures of this vehicle and the damage!"

As soon as Danny left, the men and women tried to enjoy their reunion in the relative safety of the jailhouse. An aisle separated their cells, so they couldn't touch, but Nicholas and Cassandra let their tears express their joy at being together again. Gabriel couldn't quit staring at Phoebe. Her tenacity and bravery amazed him. None of this would have been possible without her help.

Galen, meanwhile, was trying to figure out what to do next. "Looks like we might be here for who knows how long," he yawned. "But how are we going to make bail?"

"My old man can get us out of anything," offered Gabriel. "Of course, he'd probably rather see me rot in jail."

Galen fell back onto the cot and groaned in exhaustion. "I say we congratulate ourselves on a job well done and try to relax," yawning a second time. "For the time being, we're safe." The priest settled his Stetson over his face and stretched out his feet over the end of the cot. He was snoring a few seconds later.

The others tried to follow suit, but the noise from the lobby of crunching glass and a revving SUV engine, where Danny was busy trying to back the Lexus out of the building and clean up the place, kept them awake for the next hour.

"Up and at 'em," hollered the young officer the next morning. "Time to go. Your bail's been made."

Rolling out of their uncomfortable beds, the inmates looked haggard and dirty as they followed him to the lobby. The sergeant eyed them closely, especially Galen. "I don't know what your story is, Father. Right now I guess I don't much care. I called the convent and was assured by the Mother Superior that she had no interest in pressing charges."

Galen nodded, as if he had been expecting such an outcome. "I did not know our bail had been set, and we did not call anyone about our, ah, predicament," he answered. "So who posted the money?"

The sergeant shrugged. "I double as a magistrate and I set your bail. A man came in a few minutes ago, paid it, *and* covered our expenses for the damage done here. There are no charges, and there is nothing for you to reimburse us for." The phone rang. As he reached for it, he tilted his head toward the door. "You're free to go."

Galen shot a look at Nicholas and the two men bolted toward the shattered front window and looked out. The others followed close behind. They watched as a large man in a dark suit climbed into a black Chevy Suburban parked half a block away, backed out of a parking space, and drove off.

"It's a trap," muttered Cassandra. "He wouldn't just let us go."

"He who?" asked her husband, turning slowly to look at her in surprise. When he saw her face he lowered his voice to a whisper. The others crowded closer. "You *know* who did this?"

Cassandra's mouth dropped slowly open as she twisted her head to look at Phoebe. "Oops." The younger woman covered her mouth, "I forgot to tell Galen."

Cassandra looked at the puzzled faces and smiled slowly. "That's alright, Phoebe. I think we had other things on our mind last night. I guess you guys didn't have an opportunity to look at the documents and lists I sent Galen?"

"Barely. Why?" asked Nicholas.

Cassandra shook her head. "Have I got a story for you! But I think we should get out of here fast, maybe get some coffee and get on the road. Galen?"

"We can't stay here forever, and now is as good a time as any to vamoose," agreed the priest. "Let's go."

Danny watched as the five strangers walked outside and climbed into the SUV, which had rather miraculously emerged from the accident with a few dents, a crooked front bumper, and a small crack on the front windshield. He watched them drive away. "What do you reckon was going on?" he said to the sergeant, who grunted in reply.

"Who cares? They weren't wanted for anything, no charges were made, and the window was paid for. Just rich folks down from New York City, I guess."

"I was sure this was my big chance," he muttered. Ever since a North Carolina friend had discovered suspected pipe-bomber Eric Robert Rudolph rummaging through a dumpster, Danny had dreamed of a similar day for himself.

"My shift's over," he told the sergeant. "See you later." The sergeant waved without looking up from his paperwork.

Danny stepped through the empty window and climbed into his cruiser. "Bet they're mobbed up," he said to himself as he backed out.

℘

Once in the SUV, Gabriel turned the key and they drove slowly down Main Street. "I think we should head back to North Carolina," he suggested. "We can regroup at my house and try to figure out our next move. Probably safer if we drive all the way instead of catching a plane." Everyone agreed. "Cassandra, hold your explanation for a few minutes. Let's pull in here and get some coffee first. I need to wake up. I already know what each of you drink."

As he maneuvered the Lexus into a parking spot, Cassandra lightly punched him in the shoulder. "You of all people!" she laughed. "How could you miss my trail?"

"Hey, I'm driving here!" he laughed back, putting the SUV into park. "Seriously, Cassandra, we were digging through your lists, but then we were distracted by the small matter of arranging your liberation." He opened the door to get out. Phoebe joined him.

"That was my fault," Galen said to Cassandra from the third seat. "I spotted something in the video e-mail that helped us identify where you were."

He was explaining what he saw and how they figured it out when Gabriel and Phoebe returned with five cups of coffee, three black and two with cream. He started the engine but did not put the Lexus into drive. "So what is it that we were supposed to discover?"

Cassandra cleared her throat and turned around to look back at Nicholas. "It's all Malachi," she said slowly, knowing how betrayed her husband would feel.

Nicholas brought his hands up, covered his face, and groaned. "What an idiot I am! I was in the nest of vipers all along," he said with a mirthless laugh. "Giving them the information they wanted, being played for a patsy. How stupid can I be? How did you find out it was Malachi?"

Galen patted him on the shoulder. "We were all taken in, my friend. I'm the one who should have been more forceful about my suspicions."

"What do you mean?" Nicholas asked.

"The way Malachi reacted during your speech. When you mentioned the phase inversion issue but didn't provide the answer or any real details, Malachi nearly came out of his seat! He was *waiting* for that information, Nicholas. And then when the questions from the attendants started to get out of hand, he did absolutely *nothing* to save you or your reputation. Nothing!" Galen stopped and pursed his lips in a sour look. "And to think I'm the one who sent you back to New York."

"We don't have to worry about all that now," Cassandra offered with calming assurance. "Let me answer your last question, Nicholas. By the middle of the twentieth century, parts of all those groups—from the Egyptian mystery cults up to the Freemasons and Rosicrucians—fed into the formation of the Bilderberg Group. Didn't you see my 'B' next to the mid-century documents? 'B' was for Bilderberg!"

"That's incredible, I can't believe you managed to make all those connections," replied Nicholas. "But how does this directly tie into Malachi, other than that he is a member of that group?"

"It all came together when I found a scan of an old memorandum that talked about timing the market. The author was someone named Leviticus Foust." The rest of them stared at her in disbelief. Nicholas shook his head again in disgust. Cassandra spent the next ten minutes filling them in on everything, including the fact that the memo had been sealed with the Egyptian cartouche.

"Well, it all makes perfect sense now," sighed Galen as Gabriel put the SUV into gear and eased out of the parking spot. He stopped at a red light, waited for it to turn green, and continued.

"Oh, no!" Gabriel exposed his front teeth and sucked in his breath as if he had just experienced a sudden toothache. He was looking in the rearview mirror and pressing the accelerator at the same time. Nicholas followed his eyes and turned his head to look behind the Lexus. The black suburban had just pulled out of a small alley and was barreling down the street after them.

"I told you he wasn't going to just let us walk away," said Cassandra.

℘

Danny's adrenaline surged when he saw the suburban run through the red light. "Yes!" he shouted, switching on his blue lights and sirens. *This could be my first car chase!* To his dismay, the suburban slowed down and pulled over to the shoulder. "Ah, damn," he muttered as he pulled up behind it. "I just can't catch a break."

∅

"I don't believe it!" shouted a relieved Gabriel after driving on for a couple minutes. The road behind them was empty. "They actually pulled over."

"I think the last thing they want is to make this a high-profile matter," suggested Galen. "But we better make haste, Gabriel."

"I agree," he replied, glancing back over his shoulder at his equally relieved passengers. "Let's put the hammer down and see what this machine will do."

"Gabe!" screamed Phoebe, the only one to see the old yellow dog meander out into the road.

Gabriel swerved to miss the animal and the SUV went into a sideways skid on the wet pavement. He expertly turned the wheel back to pull out of the slide and nearly had the car back under control when the right front tire hit a soft patch on the shoulder and wrenched the vehicle down into the roadside ditch, where it began to roll. The occupants saw nothing else except for a blast of white as the airbags inflated and threw them backward into their seats. The SUV rolled once before landing upright.

"Is everyone all right?" asked Galen. The airbags and a good design had done their job. No one was injured but everyone was badly shaken up. Gabriel opened his door and climbed up to the road. The suburban was nowhere to be seen.

The others exited the car and watched as Gabriel slid back down into the ditch, walked around to the front of the car, and reached below the front bumper. "Phoebe, pull that little red lever underneath the steering column, would you? Nicholas, give me a hand here."

Gabriel un-spooled a heavy wire cable from beneath the bumper. "Damn, Gabe," muttered an admiring Nicholas. "This car really does have everything."

"I'm telling you," he laughed, "we need to give thanks to Dad's paranoia." He looked around for a sturdy tree that would afford the right angle to winch them out of the ditch.

He located one quickly and a minute later the SUV was half-way out of the ditch. He was about to say something to Nicholas when he caught sight of the suburban closing fast and barely a quarter-mile away. "It's them!" he shouted. "Get down behind the car!"

Gabriel ran for the front seat and grabbed his .45 before diving next to the front wheel to cover Nicholas, who had tripped and fallen between the road and the SUV. "Get down! Get down, Nicholas!" he screamed again.

As the suburban slowed, Gabriel watched the tinted passenger window slide down. It was as if everything was happening in slow motion. A hand with a pistol rigged with a silencer appeared. Whoever was holding it was aiming at Nicholas.

"Hey!" screamed Gabriel, jumping from behind the car. The arm jerked in his direction and a pair of shots, muffled and dull, rang out. He collapsed to the ground, clutching his side.

"Gabe! No!" screamed Phoebe, who was physically restrained by Galen from running to his aid.

Clenching his chest in pain, Gabriel lifted his .45 and squeezed the trigger. The noise was deafening, but the bullet sailed wide of the mark. He fell back and exhaled, feeling the warm blood seeping through his black sweater. *Jesus, don't let me die like this!* he thought as he propped himself up on one elbow to try and fire again.

The sound of a police siren reached his ears just as a small clump of ground exploded next to his head. The arm hanging out the window withdrew and he watched as the suburban sped away. A police car blew by a few seconds later.

The others scrambled out from behind the Lexus as a terrified Phoebe ran to Gabriel and fell down beside him, sobbing hysterically. Nicholas frantically punched 9-1-1 into his cell, only to discover his battery was dead. Galen's cell did not have reception.

Cassandra tore off the end of Gabriel's shirt. "Here, let me make a tourniquet," she said.

Gabriel looked up at her and laughed in spite of the pain. "Where are you going to put it, Cassandra, around my neck? Besides, what's with you people? Every time I'm around you I get shot." He grimaced in pain.

This time, however, the injury was no flesh wound. Cassandra and Phoebe worked on stanching the blood while Galen and Nicholas finished winching the car out of the ditch. Working together, all four carefully picked up Gabriel and eased him into the folded-down back seat of the SUV.

Nicholas was climbing into the driver's seat when Danny blew a quick siren and skidded to a halt next to them. The young officer jumped out of the car and ran to the driver's side of the SUV. "They got away," he said. "Are you folks okay?"

"No. Our friend has been shot and we need to get him to a hospital," shouted Nicholas. "He's fading in and out of consciousness!"

"Got it. Follow me!" Danny fired up the siren once more and radioed the Elk Regional Healthcare facility to prepare for a gunshot victim. With his patrol car in the lead, he provided a speedy escort to safety. "I was right!" he kept telling himself all the way to the hospital. *Something big was going on here!*

He couldn't wait to tell his buddy in North Carolina.

Chapter 58

"Take the Suburban to our parts shop in Pittsburgh," Mika said into the telephone, tapping her long fingernails on her desk and trying hard not to shriek at the imbecile on the other end of the line. "Shred your identification documents and make sure the VIN number on the vehicle is eradicated." She hung up, scribbled a few notes, and went to see Malachi.

"You seem unconcerned," she said when she walked in and found him seated at his desk, looking as though all was right with the world. Mika perched, as usual, on the edge of the chair across from him.

"I am, completely," answered Malachi as he blew a puff of smoke into the air. "The Shepards will re-surface. When they do, we'll deal with them at our leisure."

Mika raised her eyebrows. "And Gabriel von Stuyvesant?"

"Ah yes, that worthless S.O.B. son Ernest produced from his loins." Malachi leaned back and shrugged lightly. "He could present a problem. We don't know how much he knows, but I think Ernest will be able to control him. Whether Ernest knows it or not, he has a soft spot in his heart for that little bastard, and I plan to leverage it to keep him quiet—at least long enough so that anything that might happen to him won't be connected to the Shepards."

Malachi gnawed softly on the end of his Don Alejandro before inhaling deeply. He blew out the smoke and shook his head. "I have to admit, when I got the early report I hoped he wouldn't survive. But if he does, I will bide my time and see what his old man comes up with." He glanced up sharply at Mika. "What about the bullet that hit him?"

"It came from a gun manufactured by one of our Swiss companies. It was unregistered, of course, and it's very unlikely it can be traced, but I can make plans to jettison it over the Atlantic if you would prefer."

"I *would* prefer. Put it in with the other materials scheduled for the next drop. The Bermuda Trench isn't deep enough for some of it. What about the deputy?"

"He either stopped following the suburban at the county line or lost it, and radioed an APB to his dispatcher. We scrambled the transmission. It never went out."

Malachi smiled. "And what about Sister Elizabeth?"

"She's requesting a transfer to another Poor Clare convent. I am certain she can keep what she knows a secret. And she doesn't really know that much. She has performed well in the past. She will be helpful again in the future."

"She knows too much now. Get rid of her. Accident or illness. Your choice."

Mika nodded, her expression hard and cold. "I'll take care of it."

She rose to leave as Malachi picked up the phone to call Ernest von Stuyvesant. She had always thought that Gabriel's father was a spineless fool. Perhaps his time was also at hand.

℘

Gabriel woke in a sunny white room. Phoebe was asleep in a chair next to the bed, curled under a light blanket. He tried to reach over to stroke her hair, but the pain was too intense and he only managed to move his arm a few inches. An anesthetic drip was stuck into the back of his hand, but it didn't seem to be doing a whole lot of good. A pint of blood, nearly empty, fed his body on the other side.

"Phoebe?" he croaked.

Phoebe stirred and sat up, her eyes brightening. "Gabe! "I'm so glad you are awake. You look better."

"What day is it? How long have I been here? Where is here?" He groaned softly and licked his dry lips. "My head feels like it is ready to explode."

"I guess for you it's tomorrow," she smiled, smoothing his hair down and kissing his mouth lightly. "We are at the Elk Regional hospital. Would you like some water?"

"Do they have any whiskey?" he coughed once and winced as he did so.

She laughed. "I don't think you want to mix that with all the other stuff they're pumping through you." Phoebe cranked his bed up a few inches and helped him negotiate a small cup of water.

"Sister, you look different." Gabriel had noticed she was wearing a periwinkle-blue pin-tucked shirt and a long slit skirt to match.

"Nicholas and Cassandra went into town and bought me some clothes. Kind of Cassandra's taste, don't you think?"

"I think you look wonderful," he said, his eyes resting upon her beautiful happy face. He tried to listen as she caught him up on yesterday's events.

"So where's everybody now?" Gabriel asked.

"They left early this morning after the doctor assured them you would be fine," she said. "They didn't want to leave, but Galen said they should keep moving." Phoebe sat carefully on the edge of the bed so as not to jostle him. "You gave us a rough time for awhile."

"If I had any choice, I wouldn't have." Gabe looked up at her. "You didn't want to go with them?"

"You know I only want to be with you."

"And so you shall. You're going to marry me, and never leave my side again."

"I am? *I am!*" she cried happily. She leaned over to kiss him and pressed against his side.

"Ow!" he hollered. Phoebe started laughing, and Gabe would have, but his ribs felt like they were cracking. "How bad am I?"

"The bullet ricocheted off a rib and broke it, but missed everything important. The doctor said that if it had missed the rib, it would have killed you for sure. Someone up there is looking after you, Galen says." Phoebe smoothed back a wide lock of her frizzy hair, which kept dropping in front of her eyes.

"Is there a phone in here?" he asked. Phoebe picked up a white phone from the stand and shifted it to the bed next to him. He took the receiver and gave her a number to dial for him.

"Dad? How are you? Yeah? That's good. I'm . . . well, I'm in the hospital in St. Mary's Pennsylvania. No, I mean, I'm okay now. Listen, we need to talk."

Phoebe sat still and listened as Gabriel told his father everything. He started with the box and admitted that the Shepards had figured it out. He told him about Alex's murder, his friends' adventures in Europe and what happened the previous night at the convent. He paused, looked at Phoebe, smiled, and then told Ernest von Stuyvesant that they knew all about Malachi Foust.

Phoebe watched his face for several minutes as Gabriel listened to his father. Finally, he answered, "Okay, I'm ready." He hung up and gave her a weary smile. "They'll be here in an hour."

"An hour?" she answered, puzzled. "Don't your parents live in New York? How can they get here that fast?"

"He has a helicopter. Ever gotten engaged and met the parents on the same day?"

Phoebe's eyes widened in panic and she ran to the bathroom to look in the mirror. "I've never been engaged at all," she said, combing her fingers through the tight curls encircling her head. "I look terrible!"

"You look lovely. Come here." Gabriel slowly held out his arms. Despite the pain, he just wanted to hold her. "I love you. You are the love of my life. The hell with what anybody else thinks. And while we're at it, the hell with the stupidity I've been guilty of, too."

Sure enough, exactly sixty nervous minutes later they heard a helicopter circling overhead. It landed on a nearby football field. Five minutes later Gabriel's parents were standing in the doorway with the doctor beside them. Ernest handed his coat to Phoebe, who took it and moved out of the way as they took up possessive parental positions on each side of the bed. The old man looked tired as he rested a hand on his son's shoulder. Gabriel's mother stared down at him as though seeing him for the first time.

"We've made arrangements to fly you to the family clinic in New York City," Ernest finally announced. He turned to the doctor. "Not that you didn't save his life. We just want him to be near us." The doctor nodded that he understood.

Gabriel smiled weakly up at his father. "Been a long time since I've heard those words."

After the doctor left to see about the paperwork, Lilly von Stuyvesant finally realized that the person standing in the middle of the room was not a nurse. "Who is this?" she asked her son with a nod of her head.

"This is Phoebe Snow, soon to be Mrs. Gabriel von Stuyvesant." A small gasp escaped Lilly's lips as both parents turned to look at Phoebe and then back at their son. "It's a done deal," he added with conviction. "We're officially engaged."

Lilly gazed thoughtfully at Phoebe for a long while. When she finally spoke, the soft words eased out slowly, but with a genuine air about them. "I . . . don't know you, or who your family is," she said, "but something tells me you do love my son. And that's enough for me." She lifted her eyes to her husband. "How about you, Gabby?"

Ernest had never let go of Gabriel's shoulder. Now he squeezed it very gently, a wordless signal of approval. *I must be dreaming,* thought Gabriel. *This cannot be happening.*

Lilly slipped off her three-carat, brilliant-cut blue diamond that had belonged to Gabriel's grandmother and laid it in the palm of her hand. "I've waited a long time to do this," she said. "Will this do?"

Gabriel looked at her incredulously. He started to say he would buy Phoebe her own diamond, but caught himself before ruining the moment. "It's beautiful, mother," he said. "It's just overwhelming."

Ernest walked slowly to the other side of the bed and joined Lilly, leaving space for Phoebe to move up and take his place. Gabriel could only use one hand, so she helped him slip the brilliant ring on her finger. An equally radiant smile creased her face as she reached across the bed and shook hands with her future in-laws. "I'm so glad to finally meet both of you," she said. "Yes, I love your son very much."

Ernest nodded politely, his voice raspy with emotion. "Congratulations, my son."

Gabriel looked at his parents. Between them was a chasm filled with years of disagreement, isolation, and bitter feelings. It seemed a miracle that they were here at all. Could that wide gulf really narrow so quickly? For the first time in a long time he realized just how much they had aged since his rebellious student days. "Dad, we've burned quite a few bridges, haven't we," he said, not apologizing exactly, but offering his father an opening.

Ernest's eyes lit up. "That's what construction companies are for, son, and I think I own a few. To build bridges—fireproof bridges." He paused and decided to continued. "Age, and deep contemplation, usually brings about a different set of priorities."

Lilly reached out and touched his arm. "Gabby . . ."

"No, it's alright," Ernest replied. "For a long time I looked at your work—funding every do-gooder organization that stepped up to the trough—as sheer rebellion against the system that supplied you the funds."

"That's where it started," admitted Gabriel. "But after a while I realized I was actually making a dent."

"Well, maybe you were just ahead of your time," replied his father. "Your work will be recognized, probably sooner rather than later. Even before what you told me today, your mother and I had been talking—hell, we have been talking and arguing since you and your friends found that damn box! And we are now in agreement. For nearly a century, we've let that god-damned Foust family control our financial operations. Well, sir, that's over!"

Gabriel gave his father the widest smile he could muster. "What can we do to help?"

"Let's get you well first. We'll take both of you back to the city and start making plans when you're feeling up to the task."

On the way out to the helicopter two hours later, Ernest stopped at the desk and asked how much the bill was. "We don't know yet," said the office manager. "But normally we would bill his insurance company."

Ernest wrote out a check for $5,000,000 and handed it to her. "This should take care of it," he said. "Name the wing after my son."

He walked out the building whistling.

Chapter 59

"Mr. Foust, you have a call on line four. It is Ernest von Stuyvesant."

Malachi smiled and picked up the phone. "Good morning, Ernest . . .What? . . . How is he? . . . Oh, thank God! Is there anything I can do?"

Ernest's answer nearly knocked the wind out of Malachi. "What! That's completely absurd, Ernest, have you lost your mind?" Malachi clenched his jaws and listened as von Stuyvesant explained what he had in mind.

"How can you possibly think such a thing?" Malachi interjected, only to be cut off. "Yes, of course, as soon as you can get here. I'll cancel everything else on my calendar."

Malachi felt his stomach tighten as he carefully and gently set the receiver down in its cradle. He rubbed his face and leaned back in his chair. *The game was getting complicated and had taken an unexpected twist.* "So the Shepards have figured out the final piece of the puzzle," he whispered softly, shaking his head in a mixture of amazement and admiration. "But then they had to go and share it with their friend Gabriel von Stuyvesant. Damn it!" He should have gotten rid of the whole lot of them long ago.

Malachi rose somewhat unsteadily and walked to the bar, where he poured two fingers of bourbon and tossed it back.

It didn't do to start worrying about the past. What was done was done. Besides, it had been working. He was certain the phase-inversion solution had been within his grasp. He poured another shot and held the glass up to study the deep amber color. A smile spread across his face. *I need to find the Shepards and that damn priest and deal with them once and for all.*

He downed his second bourbon and leaned on the bar. For now, his immediate problem was Ernest von Stuyvesant, to whom Ernest's no-longer-out-of-favor son had apparently told everything. Malachi laughed out loud at the situation.

What a time for the great father-son reconciliation!

Malachi's and Ernest's fathers had been colleagues, partners, close friends. But not the sons. Where Malachi excelled, Ernest fell flat, proving quickly that he had no head for finance, and worse, no strategic vision. Malachi had long ago dismissed Ernest as weak and contemptible. His own gift was dealing in real estate, and Malachi had not minded taking full advantage of that gift. He knew how to get the best return on Ernest's money, and Ernest gave him free rein to do so. The result was hundreds of millions in profit—and enough information for either man to have the other hanged in any court in the world.

Of course, there was also the matter of the box. Ernest's family had been given possession of the damn thing, but only Malachi knew how to use it—a deal struck by their fathers that Malachi had come to despise. It was supposed to guarantee prosperity for both families. Ernest let down his end of the bargain when he allowed the box to be taken from its hiding place at the Biltmore Estate.

Malachi walked to the window and looked out at the New York skyline. *Such a shame it didn't work out,* he thought with a fiendish grin. Leviticus would never have let such traitorous deeds go unpunished.

Malachi pushed his intercom button. "Mika! I need you in my office."

Chapter 60

After they knew that Gabriel was going to recover from his surgery, Cassandra, Nicholas, and Galen rented a car and headed out of town. "I hate to leave Gabe, but he will be safe once he talks with his parents," Nicholas said, handing his wife a map.

"Where are we going?" Galen asked from the back.

Cassandra opened the Rand McNally atlas and smiled. "Let's go to Bluefield, West Virginia. I have some distant relatives there."

"You seem to have relations all over the world!" Galen laughed, trying to lighten the mood. So much had happened in the last twenty-four hours they all felt numb. They drove for hours, with long gaps in the conversation.

"Do you think we will ever be happy again?" asked Cassandra at one point.

"You two have been through a lot," Galen assured her, "from the loss of Alex to the kidnapping, and whatever awaits us around the next corner. You have a right to feel depressed."

"So what's the remedy?" Nicholas asked. "Positive thinking?"

"No, Lord, that just puts it off," answered the priest. "Two things will cure you. Time, and accepting your own feelings. Don't fight them, just feel them and accept the sadness. Accept your mistakes. Accept what you cannot change. You might even work on forgiving Malachi."

"What?" Nicholas cried out. "Sorry, never."

With that the trio looked out at the most beautiful poverty in America. They were driving on State Highway 19, bypassing Charleston, the capital of West Virginia, and heading for the little town of Bluefield, on the Virginia border and less than a day's drive from Washington D.C. This part of the Appalachians had once been a thriving center of the coal mining district, but was essentially abandoned once the coal ran out. West Virginia wasn't just suffering the wave of unemployment currently sweeping over the whole country; it had been crushed under it for decades. The abject poverty visible all around them seemed incongruous in a state so close to the nation's capital.

Bluestone County buckles and folds before rising sharply at East River Mountain, the smooth 3,000-foot wall separating the two states. It designates the division between Valley and Ridge Provinces. To the south, across Virginia, run the Blue Ridge Mountains, Appalachia's easternmost range. The trio felt truly hidden here, ducking between mountain ranges far from any shout of home. But they knew they were not safe. Malachi was a many-headed Hydra, and no matter what they did or where they fled, he would eventually find them.

From the front passenger seat, Cassandra gazed out at green forests that almost rivaled Ireland's in their luminescence. "Here we come," she said, "into Bluefield. They used to call it 'Nature's Air conditioned City.'"

Indeed, at 2,655 feet above sea level, the title was an apt one. They drove past abandoned rail warehouses and started following the four-mile gravity-switching yard that veteran trainmen used to call "the hump." Its construction was seen as a model of efficiency in the 1920s, and it was widely imitated. Above it ran "The Avenue," once the center of a town that boasted 25,000 people. Only half that population lived there now, but efforts were underway to revitalize the old business district with the charming attraction of local crafts and antiques. Tourists were walking the streets with shopping bags in their hands—always a good sign.

"We're going to 2109 Jefferson Street, to the Dian-Lee Bed and Breakfast. A niece of my great-grandfather bought it in 1995 and restored it." Nicholas nodded and followed her directions. When he turned onto John Nash Boulevard, she added, "This street's named after a famous son. He's the guy in *A Beautiful Mind*."

"Hmmm," said Galen a moment later as they rolled up to the beautiful old Victorian. "I hope they don't serve tea at this place."

Cassandra laughed, recalling how Galen practically dragged her out of the Savoy and over to the pub for a pint of ale. "You and Nicholas can go to the bars downtown. I'll have my tea in the morning room."

Their spirits began to lift as they disembarked from a long day in the car. Sandra, the Inn's owner, welcomed them warmly, though she had never met Cassandra before and was in fact surprised to learn that she had North Carolina relatives. Since the two women had a century to catch up on, the men decided to catch naps instead. It was thus with groggy consternation that Nicholas pulled himself out of a deep sleep to answer his cell phone. It was Gabriel.

Five minutes later Nicholas bounded down the Victorian staircase to tell Cassandra about Gabriel's engagement and reconciliation with his parents. She took Nicholas' cell phone onto the porch, settled into a rocker, and punched in Gabriel's number. She was calling to congratulate him, but Gabriel had other matters in mind.

"Listen, Cassandra. I want you to put all the documents in chronological order," he instructed, "with the latest on top, and going back to the earliest."

"Latest to earliest, rather than the other way around. Ok . . ." she said, holding the last syllable. Nicholas tapped her arm and gave her a quizzical look, but she waved him off and turned around to concentrate on his instructions.

"We nearly missed the whole damn thing when you started with the eleventh century."

Cassandra scrunched her face in bewilderment. "Missed what? What are you talking about?"

"I . . . we're not quite sure yet, but I really don't want to speculate on the phone." Gabriel hesitated. "Something really big is up, but all the pieces aren't in place yet. Just be ready to travel in the next couple of days."

She told him they would be ready and that after a couple of days in Bluefield they would be bored anyway. In reality, she was wishing they could hide away in these mountains forever. She hung up and explained his call to Nicholas, who was just as puzzled as she was.

After supper with the other guests, Nicholas, Cassandra, and Galen returned to their rooms. They had taken the family suite so that Galen could have a connecting room and the three could work together in the common area. With a sigh of frustration, Cassandra dropped her stack of documents on a coffee table. "I wish it would somehow re-sort itself. I am getting rather sick of these damn documents."

"As are the rest of us," agreed Nicholas. "It looks as though if you had arranged them before as Gabe suggested, we would have known who we were up against."

The remark was innocently offered, but it nudged Cassandra over to the defensive. "Would it really have mattered?" she retorted. "One bad guy is just as bad as the next."

Neither of the men agreed with her. "The difference is that the one alive today had Alex killed, had you kidnapped, and would now no doubt like to do away with all of us," Galen explained with Nicholas sitting next to him nodding in agreement.

"Ok, I see what you mean," Cassandra conceded. "You've got a point." As she began separating the stack, her interest in the papers slowly rekindled. "You know, this really explains a lot of things," she continued. "Now we know why a guy who looked just like Malachi appears in the Veronese painting—it was his ancestor!"

"And," Galen jumped in, "it explains why the cartouche so enigmatically showed up in all those strange places—Malachi's family probably owned or financed them all, including, evidently, that Paris restaurant."

"Good God," exclaimed Nicholas when he arrived at the more modern 20th-century documents. "They're all here! Rothschilds, Rockefellers, Mellons, Kennedys, Vanderbilts. Every one of them is attached, one way or another, to this cartouche. Why didn't we see that before?"

"Well, part of it is because we were working forward in time," said Cassandra. "We just did not have the ability to start yesterday and move backward. It would have been impossible. And don't forget," she added, "modern-day families were a lot more diligent about concealing things."

Cassandra sighed deeply. "If we were doing this on a movie set we might be gifted with second sight, but sometimes it's hard to see the big picture from all these little pieces. I don't know what Gabe has in mind, but I hope it's a way to string Malachi up by his eyelashes and leave him twisting in the wind." She turned to Galen and smiled sweetly. "What am I going to do with all this anger, Father?"

He smiled at the joke. "Somehow you'll find a way to deal with your anger, Cassandra, but Gabe might have something different to worry about."

"What do you mean?" she asked.

"The documents mention the Vanderbilts. Do you think Ernest is involved with Malachi in all this?"

"I admit the thought has crossed my mind," began Cassandra slowly, "but I have come to doubt it. Gabe and Ernest might have a difficult relationship, but I can't imagine that having your own son shot— twice!—is standard business practice." When Galen merely looked at her and raised his eyebrows in reply, she realized what he was implying. "Oh my God, Galen! You think the reconciliation with his son is phony— some sort of grand scheme with Malachi?"

"I don't know, frankly," answered the priest honestly. "But the last few months have taught me that little is what it seems, and powerful people have powerful motives to keep it that way."

Nicholas and Cassandra looked at each other. The same icy deep chill coursed through them both.

ß

Two days passed before Nicholas' cell phone rang again. The trio was wandering around the coal museum. Nicholas paused before a reproduction of a vein of "black gold" to pull the phone out of his pocket.

"Yes, this is Dr. Shepard, who is this?. . . . Who? Oh, yes, sir! Thank you, I appreciate you calling me, Mr. Chairman." He listened at length, his smile widening with each passing second. "Thank you. No, I had no idea Sam had already sent it to you. I'm grateful for your interest. Yes, we do have additional documents. Certainly. Tomorrow, then."

He closed his phone and turned wide-eyed to Cassandra and Galen, who had been listening with interest. "You are not going to believe this! We're off to Washington to meet with Nathaniel Stevenson."

"What?" she asked. "The Federal Reserve chairman? Nicholas, that is wonderful!"

"I think so, to. He's interested in our discovery. Sam Griffin sent him the information I gave him. He must have mailed the CD just before he was killed. Stevenson told me he is putting together a meeting of financial governor-types from all over the world."

Cassandra couldn't help but be wary. "And we're to assume, I suppose, that none of these people are linked to Malachi?"

Galen interjected. "We should assume some of them *are* associates of Malachi, don't you think?"

"I don't know exactly what to think," replied Nicholas, his enthusiasm dampened somewhat. "I guess we'll find out tomorrow."

They found a little restaurant out in the country and celebrated that evening with pan-fried mountain trout and corn chowder made with butternut squash and goat-cheese croutons. Washed down with a dry, crisp Napa Chardonnay, the meal completed their restoration. All they needed now was a few hours of sleep.

Up early, they set out for Washington at 4:30 the next morning. They approached the nation's capitol with guarded optimism. "This is what I should have done a long time ago," Nicholas confessed. He was certain the Fed chief was exactly the right person with whom to share his discovery, and he silently thanked Griffin for making it possible.

They negotiated the beltway and found the Federal Reserve building without incident. Inside, Secret Service agents whisked each of them to private rooms for a thorough search. Galen thought they were going to tear his Stetson apart, never mind his rattlesnake boots. "Priests don't wear these clothes in Washington?" he asked the agent, unable to penetrate the agent's humorless demeanor.

Thirty minutes later all three were escorted into the anteroom of a conference chamber. The double mahogany doors opened and the men around the table rose to greet them. One of them stood up and walked toward them with his hands extended beyond his thin black-draped frame.

"Welcome!" boomed Malachi. "It's wonderful to see you again."

"What did I tell you?" whispered Cassandra as the trio stopped and instinctively backed away—straight into the hands of waiting Secret Service agents.

Chapter 61

"Wait!" commanded Malachi, gliding forward, quickly with both arms outstretched in supplication. "Turn them loose! They aren't going anywhere." His voice softened. "Nicholas, welcome! I told you I would help you reclaim your reputation. And that's what we're doing here."

The Federal Chairman stepped around the conference table and introduced himself, first to Nicholas and then to Cassandra and Galen. He showed Nicholas to a chair next to him at the table; Cassandra and Galen were offered seats on the side of the room. One chair at the table remained empty. Chairman Stevenson motioned for the agents to fill it with the last guest.

An older man, with a medium build and slight paunch, walked in. Nicholas studied him. He looked vaguely familiar. Stevenson turned to face the latest arrival. "Gentlemen, for those of you who do not know him, I would like to introduce Ernest von Stuyvesant."

Nicholas set his jaw and watched Malachi closely as he shook hands with Gabriel's father. Both men smiled and seemed perfectly at ease. His hopes began to dim. *It looks like Galen was right,* he thought.

Nicholas studied the faces of the men around him. He recognized only one other person, a balding middle-aged man sitting on Stevenson's right. The man attended the failed Paris symposium, and was one of the few who actually congratulated him on both his presentation and accomplishments. Nicholas stretched to recall his name. *Michael Rosenthal*, he suddenly remembered. *Federal Reserve Board of Governors and widely considered to be next in line to succeed Stevenson.*

Everyone but the Chairman sat down. He began by acknowledging the quick response from overseas members of the group, and then came quickly to the point. "I would like to begin with a bit of historical context. All of us have been operating all of our professional lives under the same notion—confirmed over the years by academics, economists, and scientists—that the stock market simply cannot be predicted, that indeed it is a 'random walk.' I was one of the many who subscribed to that belief."

This sounds rather upbeat and in my favor, thought Nicholas.

"We here at the Federal Reserve have been charged with shoring up economies, not only in the United States, but the entire world. I don't think anyone here would deny that statement. The principal mission we share is to make every effort to establish universal harmony among *all* financial markets, including stocks, interest rates, bonds, and currencies. We have researched and tested every available means of doing so. Many times we have responded too late. Many times we misjudged what the effects of our policies would be. But regardless of our accomplishments and failures, we have always endeavored to do what we can to create a stable environment in which the free enterprise system can flourish. I am pleased to be in this company," he extended his hand to encompass them all. "A league of responsible commissioners, each a representative of his own country, to accomplish our collective goal, which is to find the truth."

Stevenson offered a faint smile and looked down briefly at Nicholas. "Today, we welcome a man who has stepped forward to help us reach that goal—Dr. Nicholas Shepard. Nicholas Shepard has put his family and his reputation on the line in order to share with the world the incredible discovery he and his brother made. Indeed, Nicholas and his family have suffered the ultimate sacrifice—the tragic loss of his brother, Dr. Alex Shepard. Before Alex's death, Nicholas and Alex made the remarkable, paradigm-shifting discovery that world economies can be directly correlated with the fluctuations of gravity. Alex took this basic concept and incorporated the astronomical measurements into a mathematical platform, and then produced software programs that do, in fact, predict the future trends of financial markets."

Nicholas was stunned by what he was hearing. He shot a glance at his wife and Galen; both seemed equally incredulous by the words pouring out of the Fed chairman's mouth.

"Incredibly," continued Stevenson, "the Shepards were able to predict long-term yearly cycles with 100 percent accuracy, mid-term monthly cycles with 99.7 percent accuracy, and weekly cycles—which are especially bombarded with anomalies, such as earnings reports, unemployment reports, CPI, PPI, consumer confidence, and whatever geopolitical news, and this includes announcements from us, the Federal Reserve Board—with 82.7 percent accuracy."

He smiled at his own little joke and continued. "I know this seems extraordinary to all of you, but we must look at the opportunity presented to us. The science bears out this discovery, gentlemen. I have run the numbers, looked at the charts, and evaluated the program. It is indeed real."

Murmurs of surprise rippled around the table in a wave, as translators in another room spoke through earphones to those attendees who did not speak English. Nicholas blinked twice—hard. Rosenthal leaned forward, caught his eye, and offered what appeared to be genuine smile, followed by a "nice work" wink. Nicholas shifted his gaze to Malachi, who face remained a mask of stone.

"We will know in advance when a recession or depression is in the making, or when a bull or bear market approaches," droned on Stevenson in his monotone voice. "This discovery gives us the tools to be proactive with fiscal policy. We will know when to raise or lower interest rates to offset extraordinary spikes and gaps in the markets. We will know when to fluctuate currencies to maintain a healthy balance in world exports and imports. Each world leader will be able to focus on diplomacy, rather than economic stability. In other words, we can do our jobs better."

The Chairman, looking pleased with himself, sipped from a glass of water and held up his hand for quiet. "Yes, it is an astonishing discovery, but please understand one thing. I must reemphasize something I said earlier: I have had my analysts working on this information for several days, and we can vouch for its revolutionary authenticity. We are here today to make sure that all of us"—Nicholas saw Stevenson's eyes glance pointedly at Malachi—"agree on what this paradigm shift will mean. By no means do we forsake the free enterprise system, but this discovery gives us the means to manage world economies so that every nation benefits, to ensure not just personal, but *global* prosperity."

As the meeting continued, Malachi's initial delight turned quickly into outright suspicion. *What the hell is happening here?* he fumed to himself. He was doing his best to keep his face expressionless, but he could feel the heat rising in his cheeks and knew they were turning red. His eyes dulled and assumed an even colder appearance than usual.

Malachi thought back over how the meeting came about in the first place. Stevenson had initiated it, apparently after analyzing the CD Griffin had sent him. The Chairman had called Malachi to invite him to address a distinguished group of world financial governors, to be on hand so he could explain how the Bilderberg Group could help them improve their economies. When the Chairman mentioned that Nicholas Shepard would also be there to share his remarkable discovery, Malachi had rubbed his hands in glee. *Like leading the lamb to slaughter*, he had told Mika. No one had mentioned that Ernest von Stuyvesant would also be in attendance. Indeed, his entrance had caught Malachi flat-footed.

"It has come to my attention in recent days," the Chairman continued, "that certain individuals and groups are more interested in their own power than in global prosperity. I have been shown evidence that economies are being manipulated by these individuals—not just for years or even decades, *but for centuries*."

When the translated words reached the headphones, the financial governors turned to look at one another in surprise. For centuries? What was the Federal Chairman talking about?

Stevenson looked at the puzzled faces and answered the question most of them were thinking. "Mr. Rosenthal, whom all of you know, has been gathering and studying this information, and I would now like to call on him to share these findings with you in detail."

As Rosenthal rose to speak, Nicholas watched Malachi like Hamlet observed his Uncle Claudius. *The play within the play*, he thought.

"I was present in Paris for the International Symposium on Economics," Rosenthal began, adjusting his glasses and giving his notes a final shuffle. "When I got back, I spent some time briefing the Chairman, emphasizing how fresh and exciting Dr. Shepard's ideas were—provided they could be verified. Then, just a few days ago, my old friend Ernest von Stuyvesant called me. We met in Washington, and von

Stuyvesant told me a most bizarre story which, in retrospect, probably should not have surprised me as much as it did."

When Ernest's name was mentioned, Malachi lowered his head a few inches and his eyes glowed colder, like a cat evaluating its chances against a larger prey. His hands were beginning to fidget, Nicholas noticed.

"Here is the bottom line," continued Rosenthal. "The Bilderberg Group, with which I'm sure all of you are familiar, owns the majority of the national debt of the United States Government through various treasury purchases. Let me add that there is nothing illegal about entities, whether personal, corporate, or foreign, buying U.S. treasuries.

"The Bilderberg Group, however, has invested trillions of dollars with little or no tax consequences. Mr. Foust, who happens to be president of the Group, owns a firm that has recently come under our scrutiny. The Atlantic Trade Partnership takes income from its corporate holdings, both foreign and here in the US, including securities, futures, and options trading off-shore, as well as the interest earned, and buys United States Treasury bonds, bills, and notes that support government spending. They also buy general-obligation municipal bonds from every state in the U.S., all insured by the good faith of each individual state."

Rosenthal paused and looked over his glasses at Malachi, who matched his gaze. "The states, of course, have the ability to levy additional taxes on their taxpayers in the event the economy goes bad, which would be used to cover the bond interest payments and principal. By and large, this money is federal and state tax-free earnings. These proceeds are then distributed to the members of the Group to use as they see fit. Mr. Foust maintains the bulk of the income and principal in his own family holdings. There's no telling how much money he has placed in bank accounts around the world or controls to one degree or another, but we are estimating trillions."

Malachi rose with remarkable calm as several of the members talked among themselves and shot accusatory stares at the financier. Malachi's demeanor was not unlike that of a bemused grandfather who was more than ready to turn his grandchildren back to the custody of their parents. "Mr. Chairman." His voice was clear, calm, and faintly smug. "I fail to see the relevance of my business practices to the proceedings here today."

"Perhaps you will in due course, Mr. Foust. Proceed, Mr. Rosenthal," Stevenson directed.

Rosenthal cleared his throat and continued. "In addition, Mr. Foust produced an incredible annual income for the Bilderberg Group by using a sophisticated forecasting technology—exactly the same one Dr. Shepard and his brother replicated. How Mr. Foust happened already to have the same technology the Shepards subsequently discovered will be explained shortly. In the meantime, suffice it to say that while Nicholas Shepard has been kind enough to share this discovery with the world, the Bilderberg Group members had no such intention, deciding instead to keep it for their private advantage. Indeed, the vast sums that have flowed into Mr. Foust's and his Group's accounts now offer Mr. Foust what he has long sought—world financial domination."

Malachi rose again and leaned forward across the conference table, his face drained of color. "Mr. Chairman!" he said in a controlled snarl but with substantially less equanimity. "This is preposterous! Had I known that the purpose of this convention was to indict me and the Bilderberg Group, I would never have agreed to this charade. I had no idea that among *friends*," he emphasized with a sweep of a hand, "I needed to bring my attorneys with me." He narrowed his eyes and drilled them into the Chairman. "You may be sure that both you *and* Mr. Rosenthal will pay dearly for this defamation."

Stevenson listened politely until Malachi finished, and then motioned him back to his chair. "No one has charged you with any crimes, Mr. Foust. We are merely setting forth facts that you, better than anyone, know to be true. Please sit down!"

To Nicholas' surprise, Malachi noisily reseated himself. *He can't leave now*, thought Nicholas. *He has to see where this is leading.*

Rosenthal continued: "For a clearer picture of the operations of Mr. Foust and his Group, I would like to call upon . . . Ernest von Stuyvesant." Malachi's eyes nearly jumped from his skull and he turned in a huff to stare at his childhood friend.

As he stood to speak, Ernest didn't bat an eye or even look at Malachi. Instead, he kept his eyes on a point somewhere outside the large plate glass window and, in an unsteady voice, began his tale. "I must explain how the operation worked internally. The Bilderberg Group owns majority interest in most of the largest brokerage houses in the world. The families belonging to the Group, including my own—something I freely admit—have large investments in various overseas accounts, all managed by Malachi. The money is invested in instruments such as U.S. Bonds, major indices from every country that has an exchange, and futures and options markets on the Globe-X exchange. All of this is managed offshore, legally, through international brokers. The profits and interest on these investments are U.S. tax free, and internationally tax-free. If any money is transferred back into this country, then only *that* money is taxable. But of course, it never appears here in that format."

Malachi shut his eyes and did not reopen them. His breathing became more rapid, and his blood pressure began building.

"Mr. Rosenthal mentioned that the Bilderberg Group owns the U.S. debt. You may ask how. What the Bilderberg Group did in the beginning, at Randolph Foust's and then Bernard Foust's direction, was to buy U.S. savings bonds from an international exchange. This was the earliest and first of many methods to launder profits from investments and interest earned by the Group. Of course, now there are instruments available that make savings bonds look like a kid's piggy bank, but the savings bond investments were the first step into the international money-laundering business. The Group could earn tax-free returns internationally and invest tax-free or tax-deferred in these bonds. Again, this was just the beginning."

Ernest knew he would stumble if he looked into Malachi's ice-blue eyes, but he didn't make that mistake. "Since the advent of the Treasury Direct Bonds—from thirty- to ten- and five-year bonds and bills, all the way down to three-month notes—Malachi has been buying huge amounts of these instruments ever since they've become available. Profits are primarily tax free, and the interest earned goes directly to the members of the Bilderberg Group. They pay their fair share of taxes on this income, but the principal was invested tax free—which eventually makes the income grow exponentially. The Group is now earning thousands of percent a year on their principal—tax-free money—all at the expense of the U.S. government's legitimate taxpayers."

Ernest paused for a drink of water, providing Rosenthal the opportunity to hurry him along to the main course. "Excuse me for one moment," Rosenthal interrupted. "I want to say that I have long been a student of techniques for the regulation of markets. I have closely followed the work of leading scientists in the field of economic time series forecasting—men like Masanao Aoki, J. M. Hurst, Dr. Claude E. Cleeton, Dr. Arnold Lieber, and Nobel Laureate Clive W. J. Granger. I have never given up on the idea of a predictable market. So you can imagine how fascinated I was to have Ernest von Stuyvesant tell me that the Foust family had manipulated financial markets for generations. How had they done it? What did they know that the rest of us didn't? I advise all of you to listen closely to his story. Mr. von Stuyvesant?"

Cassandra could hardly contain herself throughout this unforeseen turn of events. Their hour had arrived—and in a most peculiar fashion. Finally, all those months of mining through Europe's archives, digging into the catacombs of Paris, researching in libraries and online, and the conclusions they had drawn from it, were about to be corroborated by Gabriel's father!

Ernest's hand shook as he returned the glass to the table, but his voice had steadied. "For more generations than I'm aware of, the Foust family has been in control of a most peculiar . . . box. An ancient box, which somehow—I am still not sure how, exactly—measures the force of gravity. Malachi and his ancestors many hundreds of years ago came to understand how to use and, more recently, computerize, the information gleaned from the box to predict the movement of financial markets of all kinds. Once Malachi's experts had computerized the technology, the box itself was no longer needed, and we agreed to hide it away in a secret room at the Biltmore Estate, seal it up, and never speak of it again. Dr. Shepard," Ernest said, nodded at Nicholas as he cleared his throat, "found the box."

Malachi leaned forward and hissed. "He *stole* the box, and he should be arrested!"

Ernest finally looked down on his friend and held his gaze until their eyes locked tightly. "My son Gabriel *gave* Dr. Shepard the box when I, in an effort to conceal its significance, told him it wasn't worth anything and didn't even know who owned it. In reality, it was not worth anything to Malachi, and I have just explained why. My hope was that Gabriel would think it a curious antique and simply put it on a shelf at home, dust it twice a year, and forget about it. That did not happen. Instead, Nicholas and Alex Shepard quickly rediscovered its remarkable usefulness—and then put it to use in the financial markets."

Malachi slumped back in his chair and exhaled. He was being thrashed in the presence of his peers, and was at a loss as to how to reverse the tide of a game that had turned terribly against him.

"But back to the point," Ernest continued. "Malachi and his Group leveraged this technology to reap financial gains never imagined before. Although he never solved the one glitch in the technology—the occasional 'phase inversions,' when the markets would move contrary to their predictions—Malachi could now generally predict the long-, moderate-, and short-term trends of all types of financial markets. The information brought not only money, but power, and he used it to buy immense political influence while managing money for the richest and most prestigious families in the world."

The members in attendance were stunned beyond belief at what they were hearing, and each leaned forward so as not to miss a single word. Ernest went on to outline the history and lineage of the box, insofar as he knew it—how its power had been used to make or break nations, kingdoms, and empires. "Coups, revolutions, and wars have all been nothing but profit streams for the individuals and organizations that have been in control of the box." He went on to explain how the Bilderberg Group had been manipulating the Japanese economy for the last thirteen years, and outlined the Group's plan to take over the Asian economy over the next few months.

Ernest paused for a last deep breath. "In my opinion, Malachi Foust is the most dangerous individual in the world, and he would resort to any means to achieve his ends." Ernest turned to face Nathaniel Stevenson. "I understand that when Malachi's operations fully come to light, I myself may be implicated. But as of now, my conscience at least is clear. All connections between the von Stuyvesant family businesses and the Foust financial firm have been completely and permanently severed."

"Thank you my old, old friend," snarled Malachi with a vicious smile. "I'll see you in court. Afterward, I'll visit you in prison."

"Yes, well, that remains to be seen," interjected Stevenson, looking around at the astonished faces of his colleagues. "In the meantime, I believe that Cassandra Shepard, Dr. Shepard's wife, has some documentation to share with us. Mrs. Shepard?"

With her stomach churning wildly, Cassandra gripped her overstuffed briefcase and approached the conference table. Malachi's intimidating presence shook her, but she steeled herself with the knowledge that she was among friends. She thought back to when she had asked Galen what she should do with all her anger. *Well, this is what!* she thought as she laid her fat packet of documents on the mahogany table.

Cassandra untied the bundle and began to speak, softly but with more authority than she had thought possible. "These documents link Malachi and his family to any number of interesting events in world financial history. The most recent, from the middle 1950s, document the formation of the Bilderberg Group and its leadership by Malachi's own father. Those from a few years earlier reveal the part Malachi's grandfather, Leviticus Foust, played in the stock market crash of 1929."

"You have *copies* of documents," Malachi asserted coolly. "Papers that can be replicated on a throw-away printer with some cheap graphic software? I assure you that no one is impressed." In fact, everyone was impressed, and the financier knew it.

Cassandra looked directly at Stevenson and smiled. She confidently continued. "I have nearly all the original documents in a safe deposit box. I believe even Mr. Foust will find them impressive." She gave Malachi a triumphant smile and returned to her seat. Nicholas and Galen beamed.

Into the stunned silence that fell over the room, Chairman Stevenson rose to speak. "Malachi Foust, I will be turning these document copies, along with the testimony we've heard today, over to the Justice Department. I fully expect you to be investigated for fraud, conspiracy, obstruction of justice, any number of illegal financial practices, and possibly murder for the deaths of Alex Shepard and Sam Griffin. I will strongly recommend to Justice that you be stripped of any licenses under which you do business, and that if you are found guilty, your firm be closed or, at the least, substantially restricted pending a full investigation of its internal operations."

Stevenson glanced around at the people he had assembled while a chorus of whispers coursed through the room. "I am aware that what you have heard today has come as a shock. Perhaps you consider yourselves as constituting an odd forum for such disclosures. My purpose in having you here today is so that the worldwide influence of the Bilderberg Group can be curtailed as speedily as possible."

As he listened impassively to the Fed Chairman's pronouncement, Malachi carefully withdrew his Blackberry from his suit coat pocket and typed in two simple words: "Clean Sweep."

Once the device was back in his pocket, Malachi stood slowly and, with his hands pulling his suit jacket tight, smiled at Cassandra and Nicholas, and then spoke directly to Stevenson. "I'm sorry you have been so misguided. The accusations against me are ridiculous, each and every one of them. That you have brought me before this distinguished panel of colleagues only to subject me to such slander is an insult I won't ever forget." With that, Malachi turned and walked past the security officers and out through the double doors.

"Can he just walk out the door like that?" asked Nicholas, rising from his seat.

"Yes, I am afraid he can," answered the Chairman. "Until the SEC and the Justice Department bring charges, assuming they are able to do so, there's nothing more to be done. Everyone is innocent until proven guilty—even Malachi Foust."

ø

Mika looked down at her Blackberry, only somewhat surprised by what appeared on the screen. Though always prepared for this day, she ever really expected it to take place. Mika had a set of carefully detailed, unambiguous plans from Malachi to deal with the current situation. The first stage of the plan had been implemented years ago, during the construction phase of their 80-floor building.

Mika picked up her attaché case and laptop and walked to the door. When she reached it she remembered the single red rose on the desk, and turned to retrieve it. Her heels clicked on the marble floor as she strode purposefully down the hallway and across the lobby to the elevator. The door was open and she stepped lightly inside.

The digital display assured Mika that she was on the fortieth floor. A small grin creased the corners of her mouth. She inserted a key into the control panel, turned it counter-clockwise, and pushed the round button with the glowing "40" outlined in red. The elevator moved up one floor and stopped—on the fortieth floor.

When the doors opened, Mika stepped into a lobby identical to the lobby one floor below. She waited until the elevator doors closed before making her way down the same hallway, her heels clicking on the same cut marble, past the same artwork, and into an office exactly like her own.

The entire floor was an exact replica of the "other" fortieth floor. Only she and Malachi knew of its existence. Once inside, she set her laptop and attaché down on the desk and placed the beautiful rose in a small ceramic vase and carried it into her private bathroom. She filled the container with tap water and returned it to her desk.

For longer than she realized, Mika stood at the window and gazed out across New York City.

Chapter 62

The Northern Lights were spectacular—curtains and bands and arcs and rays of light roiling across the sky, all mixed in a palette of greens and yellows and dark reds. Cassandra and Nicholas had never seen anything like it, and even though the night air was frigid, they stood outside the hall, mesmerized by the swirling, fantastic light show.

An event organizer tapped Nicholas on the shoulder. "They are ready for you, sir."

"Thank you," he answered, guiding a mink-bundled Cassandra back into the glittering hall. They returned to their table to rejoin Francesca, Galen, Gabriel, Phoebe, the elder von Stuyvesants, and other selected dignitaries. Members of the Royal Swedish Academy of Sciences, the Swedish Academy, the Nobel Prize selection committee, and the National Bank of Sweden filled nearby tables.

A representative of the National Bank of Sweden, which sponsors the Nobel Prize in Economics, waited for the noise to subside before introducing Nicholas. The applause was deafening. Nicholas gave Cassandra a soft kiss on the cheek and walked to the podium. He never thought he'd be addressing such a distinguished body, and especially so quickly. The implications of the twins' discovery was so extraordinary, however, that it completely dwarfed all other potential nominations.

"Thank you. Thank you," he began as the room quieted. "I am deeply grateful for this honor. I want to thank the Swedish Nobel Committee and the National Bank of Sweden, in particular, for bestowing upon me the Nobel Memorial Prize in Economics. I would like to especially thank my wife, Cassandra, and my dearest friends sitting with her, for standing by me during the difficult days leading up to this occasion. I also must accept this award on behalf of my brother Alex who, regrettably, cannot be here to join me this evening on this special occasion. This honor is not mine alone, but belongs also to those who suffered to bring this discovery to light; I accept it on their behalf as well."

Cassandra and Francesca both felt the tears welling up and took each other's hands as the members in attendance broke out in applause.

"Your Majesties, members of the Swedish Nobel Committee, Excellencies, Ladies, and Gentlemen: from a certain perspective, history can be read as a sad record of mankind's resistance to change. Conventional wisdom, by which so much of our life is guided, sometimes seems indestructible and immutable. Our human nature makes us insecure, makes us embrace the familiar and fear the unknown. Time and again down through the centuries, those in authority have persecuted and sometimes put to death great philosophers and scientists who believed that perhaps truth is not set in stone, but is rather evolving, limitless, ever-changing. When evidence of a new truth becomes overwhelming, world leaders, both secular and religious, are dragged kicking and screaming into an age of enlightenment. Some people still believe the eighteenth century represented the pinnacle—that the Age of Reason discovered all that was yet to be known.

"But scientists and intellectuals continue to ask questions, and the body of truth continues to change its shape. New technologies and discoveries in the biosciences and medicine made the twentieth century as distant from the nineteenth as the nineteenth was from the first. The answers to eternal questions are being re-asked today in light of ongoing discoveries in fields such as quantum physics, stem cell research, genomics, and cloning.

"During the course of my long journey to this podium, my brother and I discovered how dangerous it can be to share new knowledge with the world. Indeed, my brother was assassinated by powerful individuals who believed that advancements in economics were not meant to be *shared*, but instead *exploited* for their own use.

"But I am here to tell you tonight that a paradigm shift has occurred in conventional economics. I can tell you this because we have shed the superstition of alchemy for the hard light of science. We now know beyond doubt that we behave according to the effects produced by the physical law of gravity, and that our monetary polices reflect those effects. I can tell you we know now how to use our discovery for the benefit of every nation's economy, not just for a small group of powerful people. And I can say with absolute certainty that yesterday's beliefs, yesterday's 'random walk,' will forever be laid aside to make room for today's technological breakthrough.

"Through new research stemming from our discovery, we will begin answering questions asked over the centuries, involving many different fields of science. To offer just one example, I was notified recently that a physician in New York is administering chemotherapy to his patients during the times of highest gravitational effects. He has found that none of his patients suffer nausea during or after the treatment when administered during this time. Other studies are showing that the incidence of homicides, traffic accidents, and still births markedly increase during periods of high gravitational effects. I believe that gravity is one of the prime drivers of human behavior, and that the sciences that study behavior—psychology, sociology, criminology, even the sciences of nutrition and kinesiology—will benefit tremendously from extended research into this very young discovery of this very old natural law. I believe we have entered a new paradigm, one which will resolve questions we never thought possible."

Galen stood first to applaud, followed rapidly by Cassandra, Francesca, the rest of the table, and then the rest of the hall. It was a thunderous standing ovation. Three more times Nicholas was interrupted by applause before he reached the conclusion of his speech.

"The Book of Revelation in the Bible speaks of the new Jerusalem," he said at last. "The pages burn with images of fire. I can tell you tonight that as we stumble toward this new Economic Paradigm, there will be more fires to douse, more rivers to cross, more mountains to climb. But ladies and gentlemen, like Moses standing on the edge of the promised land, we can see in this new discovery a land of milk and honey for every man, woman, and child in our world. We can see peace and prosperity on our horizons now, the result of stabilized economies across the world. I intend to spend the rest of my life working toward that New Paradigm. I hope science and all mankind will join me. Thank you."

The applause shook the dazzling chandeliers and reverberated through Nicholas' heart as he accepted the award. "This is for you, Alex," he whispered to himself.

As soon as he descended from the dais, he embraced Cassandra and kissed her as though they were alone. His family and friends cheered and hugged him as he returned to the table, and he basked in the love and approval of those who mattered most.

ß

They had much to celebrate. Francesca had returned to Charleston the previous fall and put the children in school. The grand opening of her new restaurant, *Mia Mama*, was reserved to host Gabriel's and Phoebe's wedding reception. To the surprise of no one, the wedding would be held at the Biltmore Estate. Lilly von Stuyvesant was planning it, an arrangement Gabriel objected to until Phoebe sensibly explained, "It's not *our* wedding. It's your mother's. Let her do what she needs to do." Galen agreed to officiate, and Cassandra was asked to be Matron of Honor. Francesca volunteered to serve as the "Matron of Cooking," and persuaded Lilly that Tuscan food would be perfectly appropriate.

The friends were noisily toasting these happy moments when a man dressed in a crisp black suit and tie walked up to the group and asked Nicholas if he could speak with him privately. Nicholas, reluctantly, let go of Cassandra's hand and followed the man through the glass doors into an adjoining foyer.

"Dr. Shepard, my name is Steven Wright," the man began. "I'm an agent for the National Security Administration." He flashed his credentials.

"NSA," said Nicholas slowly, studying the ID. His eyes narrowed. "What's this about?"

"First, congratulations on your award. It's quite an accomplishment. Second, I would like to apologize for interrupting you at such a special moment, but I was ordered to find you and relay a message from the Justice Department. Malachi Foust has been absolved of any responsibility for your brother's death."

Thinking he had heard him wrong, Nicholas asked him to repeat it. He did. The impact felt like a sucker-punch into the solar-plexus. "That's impossible," Nicholas spat out through clenched teeth. "He had the motive, the means—all the evidence points to him!"

"Dr Shepard, if I may explain. The NSA works closely with the Central Intelligence Agency, and we have been presented with some very disturbing information. We have conclusive intelligence your brother was killed by a group financed by Saudi oil interests."

"What?" Nicholas gasped. That was the last thing he had expected to hear. "What are you talking about? What group?"

"A member of JAMA'AT."

Nicholas held his hand to his forehead. Everything that had finally fallen so neatly into place was starting to slip away, as if the floor had opened up to swallow him. "I . . .I don't understand." He wanted to shake this man until his teeth rattled. "That's a terrorist organization. Why would terrorists want to kill my brother?"

Wright wore an expression of infinite patience and solicitude. "Dr. Shepard, are you aware that your brother was working on an alternative energy device?"

Nicholas caught his breath, remembering the information he had found on Alex's laptop. "Yes . . . well, sort of. So what?"

"For the last three years, Alex researched and developed a device that produces 'over unity' energy. Every academic institution and industrial lab that measured this device found it produced more energy than it used. Seven times more energy, to be exact."

"I still don't understand," said Nicholas . "This a reason for *terrorists* to kill my brother?"

Wright sighed as he began to feel sorry for the poor fellow. His voice softened as he explained. "Dr. Shepard. your brother's molecular generator has the potential to meet and exceed the world's energy demands—and eventually eliminate the need for all fossil fuels."

Nicholas studied him carefully. "That, of course, would end the world's dependence on Middle Eastern oil."

"Yes sir, I think you understand now."

"How did they do it? How did they make the car crash?"

"It was quite ingenious," answered the agent. "They used an explosive device inside the front bumper, but the trigger that detonated it was new to us. They used a small plunger filled with carbonated fluid. After Alex had been driving long enough, the vibration from the car caused the liquid to expand."

"Like shaking a soda can," Nicholas said quietly.

"Yes, a good analogy. The expanded fluid pushed the plunger and triggered the explosives. The air bag hit him so quickly that he had no chance to react before hitting the seawall."

"What about what happened to Francesca after my brother's wake? The guy on the bicycle?"

"We investigated that, too, and found it to be just a coincidence. The vial of fluid the man had on his bike was a drug—liquid LSD. We eventually tracked down the owner of the bike. He was under the influence when he ran into your sister-in-law." Wright continued, anticipating Nicholas' next question. "The fire at the Beaudrot's home in France, according to the French authorities, was simply part of a wave of random hooliganism that has recently plagued that part of the Parisian suburbs. Frankly, our relationship with French authorities is not very productive these days, so we simply have to take their word for that one."

Nicholas laughed and shook his head in absolute disbelief. "You're not going to tell me that my wife wasn't kidnapped, are you? And that Gabriel von Stuyvesant wasn't shot in the process of rescuing her?"

"No. She was kidnapped and he was indeed shot," Agent Wright answered with a shrug. "But we have no evidence to connect anyone to these incidents. Even with the help of the FBI and local police agencies, we have simply run into a wall. We have no idea who kidnapped your wife, and the men who shot Mr. von Stuyvesant have yet to be found. Even the Mother Superior at the convent in St. Mary's, Sister Elizabeth, I believe her name is, has vanished. It's as if she never existed."

Nicholas frowned as the agent laid his hand lightly on his shoulder. "I'm afraid I have even worse news," he said. "According to our best intelligence, the JAMA'AT terrorists assume you had or currently *have* access to the computer programs your brother used to develop his generator. You and your family are probably in great danger."

Nicholas didn't know what to say, so he just shook his head slowly as the agent apologized for breaking the news to him. "This is why you told me tonight. You think the danger could be that great—that imminent?"

Wright looked him squarely in the eyes. "Yes. If you don't mind, we would like you to meet with NSA agents tomorrow. We have a lot to discuss. Meanwhile, we have you under surveillance and you and your family and friends are safe. For now."

Nicholas thanked the agent and agreed to the meeting. "I need to get back to them."

By the time Nicholas returned to the banquet hall, the champagne flush of happiness had drained from his face. He dropped into his seat and took Cassandra's hand. Every eye at the table was on him, waiting.

What do I say? he asked himself.

He looked from face to face—from Ernest and Lilly von Stuyvesant, to Gabriel and Phoebe, to Galen, to Francesca, and finally back to his beautiful wife. He hated pulling them into the abyss, but they were going to need one another, again. Soon.

"What was that all about?" asked Galen.

"Oh, we have a small problem," Nicholas answered, squeezing his wife's hand while preparing for the explosion sure to come. "Malachi won't be convicted of Alex's death, because he didn't do it."

Everyone started speaking at once. "Is that what that man told you?"

"That's nuts."

"Who was he?"

"Yes . . . it's not . . . he's a National Security agent," Nicholas replied.

"Did he tell you who did do it?" Gabriel asked.

Cassandra interrupted. "We still have to worry about Malachi?"

"I'm not exactly sure, but let me try and explain," he said, taking a sip of champagne. It was warm now, and he pushed it away. He told them everything Agent Wright had said. Francesca held her hand to her mouth and listened without saying a word.

"Alex was working on some revolutionary alternative energy device the oil cartel never wanted in production, because it would destroy the world's oil markets." Before he could say another word, the ringing of his cell phone interrupted him.

"Oh for God's sake, Nicholas. Don't answer it now!" begged Cassandra.

Nicholas pulled the small phone out of his pocket and checked who was calling: the caller ID was blocked. He punched the button to open the line. "Hello?"

"Nicholas, my boy! Malachi Foust here. Congratulations on your wonderful prize. I couldn't be more proud," he said while caressing the granite lid of the ancient Egyptian box resting on the desk in front of him. "However, if my timing is right, your happy evening has been spoiled by a most unpleasant message from the NSA. Very regrettable. Those JAMA'AT terrorists are a nasty bunch. They rank right up there with al Qaeda. Maiming and torture are their stock in trade. I suggest you come to New York, where I can look after your family's safety." Malachi drew a sharp breath as he ran his fingers under the box's lid. The serrated edge was missing. "What the—"

Nicholas snapped the phone closed and set it on the table. He reached out and took Cassandra's hand gently into his own. There was no need to recount the phone conversation to anyone when one word sufficed: "Malachi."

ɞ

Mika kneeled in front of the shrine inside her Dakota apartment. In her hands was an article about Alex's death and the award of his posthumous Nobel Prize. With a small bow she held it over one of the votive candles, where curls of orange flames licked its edges before blurring the ink and turning it to ash. She bowed low, her lips moving in prayers, as was her custom. A small tear ran down her cheek. She quickly wiped it away.

When the candle exhausted its life, Mika leaned over and removed the gold-covered wooden tray holding the incense burner. Reaching inside and past the ornate Buddha, she opened two panels at the back of the shrine. Using both hands, she carefully slid out the Egyptian box. Mika moved her fingers sensually across the granite lid. As she caressed the serrated edge along the bottom, the first genuine smile in months broke across her face.

Introduction to *The Taylor Effect*

The core of any serious work explores two ideas on various levels. What is *true*, exactly? And what is *the truth*, exactly?

It is *true* that this book is a work of fiction, and the *truth* is that, encapsulated within the text of this fiction, is a real scientific discovery. It is based on the *true* fact that leading financial experts and scientist believe the stock market to be unpredictable, i.e., a "random walk."

But, the *truth* is that the stock market is 100% predictable.

ৱ

Hidden in *Paradigm* is an endowment, or what scholars refer to as "The Genuine Article." It is exciting, revolutionary, and flies against prevailing "knowledge." Many of you will use my discovery to your advantage. I have faith in human curiosity, in the inclination of everyday people to conceptualize abstract notions. For those of you who look closely, your lives could become profoundly richer.

In *Paradigm*, I propose and prove a theory that will immediately— and forever—change the way we perceive financial markets. You will be quite surprised and, I hope, very much impressed by a glimpse at this far-reaching discovery concerning the effect of *gravity* in the analysis and forecasting of economic time series data related to human-influenced phenomena, such as those found in publicly auctioned financial markets.

My discovery is this:

> The financial market's expansion and contraction is quantitatively in direct correlation to the increases and decreases in gravitational fluctuations experienced at the human level. Increases in market price are in direct response to decreases in gravitational forces; and, decreases in market price are in direct response to the increases in gravitational forces.

Perhaps for many, *gravity* doesn't *need* to be understood; it is simply a force that exists. Its presence is a *truth*. But science is compelled to know what exactly is *true* about *gravity*, and how it affects human behavior. That has been the course of my studies for a decade and longer. Since I am merely a student of science, it is difficult—if not impossible—for my theory to be accepted by the scientific community. Scientists have a tendency to protect their own fields, and an outsider's views are seldom welcomed.

As an outsider, I am not constrained by traditionally accepted theories. I can draw from many disciplines, testing and postulating from many angles.

My studies range from quantum physics, mathematics, astronomy, and astrophysics, to biology and other medical disciplines. I discovered long ago that human behavior is influenced by *gravitational fluctuations*, and have taken this piece of the *truth* on a long scientific exploration. You hold the result in your hands—a scientific truth wrapped in a work of fiction. I used this vehicle because I wanted the broadest possible audience to learn about, about hopefully benefit from, my discovery.

The following pages include a scientific essay called *The Taylor Effect,* followed by a *Technical Appendix*. Both are included for scientific review. Each document was prepared according to the strictest scientific methods.

I am not be the first to postulate a new theory deemed unacceptable by reigning authorities or skeptics who inevitably try to ferret out a version of their own truth. History is filled with characters who endured ridicule, imprisonment, and even death because they discovered things we know today with absolute certainty to be *true*. Momentous discoveries often require not only thinking outside the box, but thinking *from* outside the box. For example:

— *Leonardo da Vinci* experimented with different designs for human powered flying machines;

— *Galileo* made momentous strides in the study of planetary motion. His passion for the *truth* brought him before the Church. He encountered house imprisonment for the remainder of his life;

— *Benjamin Franklin* was many things, including a scientist who just happened to comprehend the power which drives today's planet— electricity;

—*Alfred Nobel* invented dynamite. The *truth* of his discovery contains deep irony, given the fulfillment of his lifetime interests in the pursuit of explosives becoming the Nobel Peace Prize;

— *Thomas Edison,* one of America's most productive inventors, obtained more than1,000 patents. Advocates of the "If it wasn't invented here, it couldn't possibly work" theory were silenced for a long while;

— *The Wright Brothers*, Wilbur and Orville, are credited with the first human flight. Their theories proved empirically correct, even facing the winds of hard logic and skepticism;

— *Guglielmo Marconi* is the "Father of Radio." No one imagined they would ever witness the wireless transmission of sound, but Marconi proved even the most enlightened thinkers utterly wrong;

— *Henry Ford, II* turned his grandfather's floundering automobile company into the second largest industrial corporation the world had ever known;

— William H. Gates, III, instead of being prized as an industry leader, is often ridiculed for his competitive ability to dominate the computer software business. If Bill Gates had been born Japanese, he would be a national hero.

These discoverers and inventors have much in common. Each received his fair share of skepticism from the reigning authorities of their age, though each had discovered the *truth*. I would also point out that the other common theme shared by these forward-thinking gentlemen is the *absence* of any advanced degrees.

It is important to remember that what you believe you know to be *true* could be a logical fallacy. Thirty years ago, Burton Malkiel wrote the best-selling book *A Random Walk Down Wall Street,* which discussed in detail the apparently random behavior of the American stock markets. He did not *prove* market behavior was random. Rather, he simply deduced that because we cannot discern a pattern, the behavior *must* be random. Malkiel's mistake falls under the category of "fallacies of irrelevant evidence." It is an example of *argumentum ad igoratium,* or the "appeal to ignorance." No one can prove the random walk theory incorrect; therefore, it must be correct. This also exemplifies the *argumentum ad verecundiam,* or the "appeal to prestige."

The fact that learned voices sing does not make their song the *truth*. My research proves there *is* a predictable pattern to the movement of the stock markets—which is revealed to you in the pages of *Paradigm*.

Robert D. Taylor

The Taylor Effect

Drs. R. W. Bass, G. W. Masters, Jr.
and Robert D. Taylor

*"There is a tide in the affairs of men
Which, taken at the flood, leads on to fortune . . ."*

—*Shakespeare*

Abstract

The effect of the motion of the Moon relative to the Earth has long been known to affect human physiology, as in the human female menstrual cycle and gestation period. From time immemorial, 'lunacy' has been associated with the Full Moon. Recently serious research papers and books[4], [13] by psychiatrists, psychologists, and statistically-oriented sociologists have provided overwhelming evidence of an extraordinary correlation between phases of the Moon and maximal episodes of violent behavior in mental wards, as well as cyclical increases in general human violence, such as in homicides, suicides, and fatal automobile accidents.

After years of research on the human circadian rhythm and the psychological aspects of human behavior in such fields as effectiveness of individual salespersons on different days of the lunar month, Robert D.

Taylor discovered in 1987 that there is an undeniable correlation between local maxima and minima of prices in public auction markets (such as in the Dow Jones Industrial Averages [DJIA] or the S&P500 Index) and indicia of the relative positions of the Sun, Earth and Moon. It has been known for literally centuries, in the highly developed field of Tidal Predictions[1], from Dynamical Astronomy, Fluid Mechanics, and Geophysics how to predict the daily fluctuations of tidal levels at any point on earth, with great precision, for millennia into the future. Using commercially available Nautical Software to predict the tidal fluctuations, Taylor discovered that an identifiable sequence of times, which he calls **Pivot Points**, have an extraordinary correlation with times of Maximal Likelihood of change of the smoothed plot of equities price-action from (upwards) **concavity** to **convexity** (or downwards *vice versa*). The Pivot Points occur at variable times, but never more frequently than 4 days apart, nor longer than 10 days apart, so that in any 10-day interval of calendar time there are always at least two Pivot Points. Taking any Pivot Point, Taylor has shown how to Forecast the concavity or convexity of the [smoothed] price-action to the next Pivot Point with extraordinary accuracy. Using standard Statistical Procedures pertaining to the auto-correlation and cross-correlation of Time Series,[11] such as in the well-established engineering discipline of LTI System Identification via ARX technology (Autoregression on an Exogenous Input), as in the MATLAB System ID Toolbox of L. Ljung, combined with the standard technology of Kalman-Bucy Filtering([5], [12]) for extraction of signals from noise in estimating the State-Vector of a **State-Space Model** of a Time Series (as advocated by M.A. Aoki and his school of econometrics,([6], [14]) Taylor has produced a Forecasting Methodology whose successes would in the Middle Ages have led to calls for his being burned for Witchcraft, though we surmise that in our own more enlightened times he will be nominated for a Nobel Prize in Economics!

Cracking the Circadian Code

According to the cover-jacket synopsis of Robert Taylor's 1994 book[10] on Optimum Performance Scheduling (OPS), the author has made a breakthrough in the secret to perfect timing for success: "After studying human behavioral patterns for several years, he has discovered the secret to predicting when everyone's peak and sub-par performance times will be. The system, known as . . . [OPS], is keyed to the biological clocks that regulate all animals, plants, and people, making the patterns of productivity universally predictable on an hour-by-hour basis. . . . With OPS you can know when customers are more likely to buy, a meeting will be most productive, your athletic ability will be at its highest, and the stock market will rise and fall."

In 1994 Taylor was the owner of one of the largest construction companies of its kind in the Southeast, and a careful observer of the times at which his employees were most successful in sales presentations, which appeared to fluctuate cyclically.

Taylor researched the 1960s-inaugurated field of *chronobiology*, and found that people isolated from sunlight and solar time-keeping cues have an internal clock which runs on a 25-hour day, and therefore gradually gets out of phase with the standard 24-hour solar day! But is this internal pendulum synchronized to some perceptible influence independent of the standard solar clock? There are published studies suggesting that living creatures can sense changes in the gravitational field in which they are immersed. For example, it has been claimed that cockroaches caged in an opaque box will all gather to one side if a large spherical lead mass is positioned outside the cage. Using state-government gathered statistical data to augment his own studies based upon statistics gathered from both friends and employees, Taylor found that human emotional and physical intensity fluctuates several times per solar day, not unlike the coastal tidal levels, which have maxima and minima 4 times on most days, but as a result of gradual phase-shifting have extrema only 3 times on certain days, at least two of which will be found in any 10-day period.

Watson & Crick received a Nobel Prize for unraveling the spiral-helix structure of the DNA molecule, which led to "cracking the code of life." When Taylor disclosed his discovery to a physician, Dr. Ted Abernathy, this specialist in pediatric and adolescent medicine wrote: " . . . the more I studied, the evidence of some great pattern connecting the ticking of all the clocks became overwhelming. Now you have cracked the code."

The original draft of Taylor's 1994 book on OPStime[TM] contained a chapter entitled "The Ups and the Dows," but Taylor withdrew this chapter just before publication, and the book[10] as available now [ISBN 1-56352-187-3] contains only a sprinkling of hints of the applicability of the OPStime technology to forecasting market fluctuations, a mere suggestion for any motivated reader to follow up further on his own if so inclined.

But continuing to pursue this facet of chronobiology privately during 1987-1999, Taylor spent literally thousands of hours of his own time in comparing correlations between intra-day trading records (every 5 minutes, or 79 ticks per trading day) and daily records (every half-hour, or 14 ticks per trading day) with cyclical physical phenomena, such as the famous *saros* (6585.32 days [about 18 years], after which the relative positions of Earth, Sun and Moon repeat), which was known to the ancient Babylonian and Mayan astronomers and to the builders of Stonehenge, who discovered that an eclipse in one *saros* occurs about 8 hours later and falls nearly 120 degrees of longitude further west in the next cycle.

Taylor's most remarkable discovery came from plotting tidal heights (either 79 ticks or 14 ticks per 6.5-hour trading day) and noticing **Pivot Points** which characterize the days on which such plots switch from (downwards) convex to concave (or upwards *vice versa*). Such a day can be discerned at a local maximum of successive local minima, or a local minimum of successive local maxima. It is well-known[6, 14] that if the cross-correlation and auto-correlation series of two finite time-series define, for a given number n of lags, a Hankel matrix of rank n, then there is an LTI (Linear Time Invariant) state-space model of the ARX type, of state-dimension n, under which one of the series is "caused" by the other series in the sense that when the LTI system model is excited by the exogenous input series, the other series is reproduced as the system's output.

For definiteness, consider the case of data recorded every half-hour per trading day, i.e. 14 ticks per day. Thus the raw data consist of a finite economic time-series of discrete-time type, wherein the total length N of the series is 14 times the number of days under consideration.

If one takes, for example, 30 days (i.e. $N = 420$ ticks) of historical data, then a use of the MATLAB *System Identification* Toolbox's highly-developed matrix-manipulation programs will produce an n-dimensional "black-box" model of the DJIA as the *output* of the LTI dynamics assumed to reside inside the box, when the *input* to the box is the tidal-height series taken as the known exogenous input.

But this exogenous input can be computed for millennia in advance! So, if one knows the final n-dimensional state-vector at the end of the historical data, then one can attempt to forecast the future evolution of this vector (and so its scalar-valued projection defined to be the DJIA output), by running the model, say, 10 days into the future, using the predictably-"known" future exogenous input as the (putative) causative driving agent.

In the over-idealized version of this scheme, wherein there is neither "measurement noise" (affecting the state-vector's projection into the DJIA) nor "process noise" (affecting the assumed exogenous input), an excellent forecast will be obtained up until the future time at which the *non-stationarity* of the actual system begins to become important, i.e. until the LTI assumption begins to degrade (in that the computed "constant" coefficients of the identified model start to change).

So it is intrinsically impossible to make highly accurate long-term forecasts based upon LTI techniques, because the hypothesis of *constant* coefficients becomes less and less plausible the farther into the future one attempts to compute a forecast.

Worse yet, the actual empirical data is self-evidently from a noisy rather than a smoothly-varying source. If there were no noise, then the final state of the system would be the last known historical datum of the DJIA, together with its immediately-preceding (−1) lagged values. But use of these *n*-values as the initial *n*-dimensional state-vector defining the forecast is problematic because of the great differences in forecasts based upon relatively "nearby-seeming" initial states.

Fortunately, the powerful technique[5], [12] for extraction of signals from noise known as Kalman-Bucy Filtering (and readily available from the MATLAB Control System and Robust Control Toolboxes) enables this difficulty to be circumvented. The KBF technology, when run through the historical data, produces a "smoothed" estimate of the DJIA whose final *n* values define a terminal state-vector suitable for use as an initial state-vector in computing often-reliable forecasts.

The Kalman-Bucy Filter is a generalization of the Wiener Filter, and in honor of Wiener (who coined the term Cybernetics), the present approach is called *Xybernomics*. The X, or symbol of the unknown (namely the *unknown* LTI-system model to be identified), has a dual function; it is used also to remind the user that one is not merely using an autonomous XID methodology, but rather an XID**x** methodology, which incorporates the presence of a known *exogenous* input. (When allowed to choose his own auto license plates, Taylor selected ***XOG***.)

Of course, there can be upon isolated occasions an external veritable "shock" applied to any economic time-series (such as an announcement by the Federal Reserve of interest-rate decisions, or, for individual stocks, unexpected earnings announcements). In the present context, this is like a "hammer blow" which discontinuously knocks the state-vector to a new position in its *n*-dimensional state-space. Econometricians refer to the visible effects of such external shocks as 'anomalies.' No forecasting system can anticipate all anomalies, and therefore the presently outlined forecasting methodology may be affected temporarily during significant anomalies.

Only two theoretical questions remain; discussion of the second (and most vexing) will be postponed until later below.

The theorem which says that *n* is the rank of the Hankel matrix defined by the autocorrelation of the input series and the cross-correlation of the input & output series is true only in the ideal, noiseless case. Because of the noise, *every* singular value of the Hankel matrix will be typically non-zero, and it is a vexing theoretical and practical question to determine the true rank of a numerically defined Hankel matrix when the data contain even very small amounts of noise. One may clean the noise out of a Hankel matrix, it has been proved rigorously by one of us, by taking its Singular Value Decomposition (SVD), inspecting all of the singular values, noting where they essentially level off at a very small value, and then setting all of the small values to zero, while subtracting the mean value of the small values from each of the larger ones, and subsequently inverting the SVD procedure to reconstitute a matrix which is then demonstrably an optimal estimate of what the Hankel matrix would have been if there had never been any noise. Thus the rank of the Hankel matrix, and so the sought-for dimension n, is the number of non-zero singular values of this "cleaned up" Hankel matrix. To some extent, this works in numerical practice, but there is no objective test for how small a singular value should be before one decides to set it to zero, and one is reduced to guessing based upon experience. This is the most correct approach *theoretically*, but we cannot see how to render it meaningfully objective.

Taylor has elected to use instead an obvious "pragmatic" approach to the determination of n, which in practice works quite well. In the example being discussed, he takes 75% of the historical data (i.e. $N = 420$, so $N\_pseud\text{-}hist = 315$ ticks) and designates this data to be all that is known. The above-described XIDx-plus-Filtering technology is then applied to make a forecast of the remaining 25% of the historical data (i.e. $N\_pseud\text{-}fut = 105$ ticks), while assuming that this data is actually "out of sample" or truly unknown data. But under the circumstances, the quality of this pseudo-forecast can be "graded" by taking the rms error between the forecast and the actual truth (preferably multiplied by the *Akaike Information Criterion* weighting factor $AIC = \{ (N+n)/(N-n) \}$ in order to penalize taking the dimension n so high as to "fit the noise" rather than the underlying signal). Taylor then simply tries every n, in sequence, between say $n = 2$ and $n = 32$ by using his "pragdim" program. This program chooses automatically the best estimate of n that had worked the best in this automatically-evaluated, numerically-graded pragmatic test.

Taylor's major discovery, based upon countless thousands of hours of experiments, is that use of the preceding forecasting technique often works wonderfully well when the beginning of a 10-day forecast (based upon the preceding 30 days of historical data) is taken to be a Pivot Point, and then the reliability of the forecast is discounted at any time after the next succeeding Pivot Point.

Taylor's best results have been achieved when the preceding forecasting technique has been applied to a future interval defined to be EXACTLY from one Pivot Point to the next. However, since there will always be a second Pivot Point in any 10-day interval, for programming convenience he has elected to continue to make 10-day forecasts, but to have them displayed via a graph in which the second Pivot Point is manifested by a vertical Red Line which serves to flag the viewer's attention to the limited size of the actual optimal span rather than the full displayed span.

The final difficulty concerns the phenomenon, discovered by Taylor, which he calls the "occasional phase-flip effect."

Normally, the (upward or downward) concavity/convexity of the forecast turns out to be precisely that of the actual data (when known).

But, upon occasion, the concavity/convexity of the forecast is the precise opposite of what actually happened! That is, if the forecast had been printed on translucent paper, and then turned upside down and placed with its face against an outdoor window, and the forecast traced in black ink on the back of the page, another "wonderfully accurate" forecast would have been obtained. In electrical engineering terminology, somehow the model has suffered an anomaly which has put the signal "180 degrees out of phase." That this is not merely an excuse for a poorly-performing forecast, but an objectively real phenomenon, will be discussed later below. Suffice it to say that Taylor's presently-preferred "work-around" circumvention of this phenomenon is to be more skeptical of the determination of n, and to apply more refined tests than the automated "pragdim" test mentioned above. For example, instead of letting n be decided automatically as described above, Taylor will inspect visually the quality of the grading of the pseudo-forecast *within* the known recent historical data as n ranges from 2 to 32. If none of the forecasts, for any n, is strikingly excellent, then Taylor assumes that some unmodeled effect is at work, and elects to "stand aside" instead of paying attention to the automatically-produced forecast based upon a supposedly "optimal" choice of n. Using this more stringent version of "pragdim", Taylor has reduced the percentage of "bad forecasts that would have been acted upon" between August 1998 and January 2000 to a mere 14%!

In short, Robert Taylor has made a remarkable discovery regarding equities markets, contrary to all received wisdom, and effectively reduced it to practice via the suite of MATLAB-language computer programs.

Prior Partial Anticipations

Although Taylor made his discoveries completely independently, when he disclosed them privately to us, we immediately pointed out that the objective merit of his discovery is strengthened by regarding noteworthy prior similar conceptions, albeit seen only "as through a glass, darkly", as *enhancements* of Taylor's fundamental plausibility (rather than simply as potential *detractions* from his priority).

Leonardo da Vinci designed a toy helicopter 500 years before the first man-carrying helicopter was built and flown by Sikorsky.

Accordingly, if the Taylor Effect is an objective reality, it is only to be expected that prior students of equities price-action would have published discoveries that can *in hindsight* be marshaled to buttress the solidity of Taylor's findings. The two approaches to study of equities prices are *fundamental*, based upon such information as studied by Accountants in a corporation's Annual Report, and *technical* (popularly called "charting"). Until quite recently, prevailing academic opinion has regarded "technical [market] analysis" as sheer lunacy [pun intended!], but for obvious reasons and in view of a visibly-burgeoning sea-change[5], [6], [9], [11], [12], [14]) we restrict attention only to technical analysts.

In particular, we have called to Taylor's attention the earlier work of J. M. Hurst,[2], 1970) of Dr. Claude E. Cleeton,[3], 1976) of Dr. Arnold Lieber,[4], 1978) and of Jim Sloman & Welles Wilder,[7], 1983-1991) which will now be reviewed. [For titles of their books, see the References below.]

J. M. Hurst

Hurst was a physicist who took up electronics and communications (including radar) engineering before and during World War II and worked in the aerospace industry for 25 years prior to retirement from Douglas Aircraft in Santa Monica in 1960. He spent the next decade (by his own account, some 20,000 hours of full-time work) analyzing economic time-series with the tools (numerical spectral analysis and large-scale computing) with which he had become familiar in his career in radar and signal-processing R&D.

Hurst discovered that the DJIA could be represented as the sum of 3 signals of distinctly different characteristics. About 75% of the amplitude was a smooth, relatively slowly-varying, long-term underlying trend-signal of no apparent causation, and the remaining 25% consisted of two radically different components. Some 23% consisted of the sum of up to 10 or 11 semi-predictable curves, similar to modulated sine waves, of slowly-varying amplitudes, frequencies and phases. (Each of these curves looks like a "slowly pulsing," somewhat distorted but recognizable sine wave, say

$$y(t) = A(t).sine(\omega (t).t + \phi(t)),$$

where the amplitude $A(t)$, frequency $\omega (t)$ and phase $\phi(t)$ remain nearly constant, but slowly "tremble" about their mean values.) The final 2% consisted of truly random "white noise," added to the underlying smooth 98% like a jagged fringe.

This white-noise fringe had misled many people into believing that equities prices are simply random walks (i.e. Brownian motion, or integrated white noise).

Oskar Morgenstern (co-author with von Neumann of *The Theory of Games and Economics Behavior*) of the Princeton Institute for Advanced Study and his collaborator, mathematical economist Clive Granger, had published monographs allegedly demonstrating the random character of both stock prices and commodities prices. They had taken the *differences* between successive prices (after first replacing the prices by their logarithms), and sought to demonstrate "Gaussian normality" of these stochastic processes. However, they had sufficient intellectual honesty to admit in the middle of their works that their numerical techniques were insufficient to detect the presence of an additive component of the series of the type $y(t) = A.sine(\omega .t + \phi)$, $0 < \omega < 1$; this of course constitutes a loophole in the random walk theory big enough to drive a tank through, which is exactly what Hurst did. In a personal conversation with Granger in 1980 one of us mentioned the possibility of identifying a "colored noise" model by means of standard electrical-engineering "ARX System-ID" and "Kalman-Filtering" techniques such as those now exploited by Taylor, referring to NASA-Ames's mainframe computer program called **MMLE3** (now available as a MATLAB system-ID Toolbox) which had been used to identify the aerodynamic derivatives of the Space Shuttle during its test flights—without knowing that Granger had already outgrown the random walk theory and had in 1978 co-authored a book on bilinear time-series predictive models!

Unfortunately, Princeton economics professor Burton Malkiel had written a best-selling book, *A Random Walk Down Wall Street*, citing Granger *et al*, that had convinced virtually the entire economics profession that the random-walk theory had been demonstrated to be correct beyond a reasonable doubt. So that the reader will not blame Granger for this lamentable development, we hasten to add that in 1992 Granger served with distinction as the economics advisor to the Santa Fe Institute's Time-Series Prediction Contest and contributed an excellent paper, *Forecasting in Economics* [cf. Sect. IV of [9]] which is perfectly compatible with the (LTI, system ID) methodologies mentioned hereinabove, and which specifically mentions "Kalman filter, state-space formulations" as often providing "superior forecasts" when used in their time-varying versions in cases wherein nonlinearity or nonstationarity renders the simpler LTI modeling inadequate.

Granger's evolution from Random-Walker to Forecaster supports our position that Hurst's 2% white-noise fringe is not of great importance.

Also, it appears that Harry S. Dent, Jr. has largely explained Hurst's 75% trend component. Dent[15] deserves the mantle of a prophet because nearly all of the highly specific yet radically contrarian predictions regarding the late '90s which he published in 1993[8] have startled everyone by coming true! In one stunning revelation, Dent[8] showed that by adding the birth-rate 46 years ago (weighted by 0.75) to the birth-rate 25 years ago (weighted by 0.25), one gets a profile whose long-term identity with the S&P500 is uncannily accurate! Dent's explanation is that the economy is largely consumer-driven, and that people begin to purchase major durable goods when starting families at age 25 and then reach their peak spending years by age 46 (sending children to college, buying final houses, etc.)

This leaves unexplained Hurst's all-important "semi-predictable" 23%. Designing 22 "comb filters" or narrow-bandpass filters whose overlapping bandpass intervals span the frequency range from 0 to 0.5 [the normalized anti-aliasing Nyquist frequency], and passing the DJIA through each comb in turn, and then subtracting the result from the DJIA and repeating with the next comb, Hurst decomposed 23% of the DJIA into the 10 or 11 oscillatory signals mentioned above. By identifying each of these 10 or 11 undulating, trembling sine-waves, and then "freezing" its amplitude A, period $2\pi/\omega$, and phase ϕ at its mean value, Hurst extrapolated each of these cycles into the future, with an aggregate stunningly effective result. (Our only reservation about this procedure is that when we tried it the results resembled simply assuming that the recent past would repeat itself almost exactly in the near future—the so-called *Adam Theory* of Sloman & Wilder.[7]) Hurst sold the coefficients of a bank of "optimal" comb filters to one of his fans, Ray Frechette, for $350,000 and in their heyday, prior to Hurst's disappearance [!], they developed a large following who made money consistently by acting upon their forecasts.

In his book,[2] Hurst recounts a 30-day experiment done with the aid of friends, in which they proved that, even using crude hand-calculator and graphical methods, Hurst's principles while paper trading sufficed to make a 9% profit every 9 days!

Alas, non-stationarity was to be the Achilles' heel of Hurst's approach. In the late 70s the *constant* weighting coefficients which Hurst had optimized for earlier market conditions gradually became less and less effective. Frechette finally sent a pathetic letter to his subscribers saying that he was abandoning the methodology and pleading for someone to suggest a better approach! (If they had had PCs, and if the Hurst approach had been automated to be updated regularly, this debacle might not have occurred.)

Like Taylor, Hurst had discovered the phase-inversion phenomenon. His basic tool was a weighted moving average (or digital filter in today's terminology), and he used the frequency-response plot's possibility of a negative gain (at inappropriately high frequencies [low periods]) to illustrate phase-inversion. Hurst stated: "Similarly, slightly higher frequencies (than that of cutoff) come through attenuated and 180 degrees out of phase. . . . In using moving averages to help define turning points of price-motion model components, one is now aware of the potential for high-frequency 'creep through'—either in-phase or 180 degrees out of phase. Such knowledge permits identification of these unwanted residuals, so that they do not mislead conclusions." Hurst's insightful remedy was to augment the standard moving average by an "inverse centered moving average," whose frequency response is *always* positive and therefore cannot affect phase. Phase inversion in the standard centered moving average can be detected by simultaneously plotting the inverse centered moving average; any phase discrepancy between the two shows that the former has produced, as a mere artifact of processing, a *false* phase inversion!

We believe that a test of whether or not, in a particular modeling-forecast, Taylor's procedures have introduced an artifactual phase-flip, can be developed along the lines of Hurst's just-cited solution to the problem. Specifically, the dominant two periodic terms in the exogenous input (tide-height[1]) can be represented as the real part of the sum of two complex phasors. Then the complex frequency response can be computed for all frequencies between zero and the Nyquist frequency, and known methods from communications engineering for computing the "complex envelope" of the output can be employed. If the absolute value of this envelope becomes zero at any frequency, then a phase-flip occurs in passing (from below) through that frequency. We have made a preliminary effort to implement this test in Taylor's forecasting procedure, but in all cases tried, the envelope's magnitude stayed bounded away from zero. If this were universally true, then the phase-flips encountered by Taylor could not be artifacts but must have some more fundamental cause, such as another unmodeled exogenous input.

Note that Hurst's model was autonomous, although, as we shall see, he speculated that in fact there must be an UNKNOWN exogenous factor, which he called **"X motivation,"** that was actually driving the cyclicity. Hurst's approach was kinematic rather than dynamic. Just as Kepler found that the orbits of planets *are* conic sections (parabolas, hyperbolas, or ellipses), while Newton explained that gravitational dynamics *caused* motion to evolve into such orbits, so Robert Taylor has taken the Hurst cycles and provided the causal dynamics which produces them.

The big question in Hurst's mind was, of course, what is the cause of this identifiable, semi-predictable cyclicity? He stated: "The conclusion is unavoidable that the cyclic regularities noted must be due to the lumped sum of all other possible contributions to the human decision processes—or to what we have called '**X**' motivation."

Hurst continues: "And this is the concept that is difficult to accept. To do so, we must admit the possibility that something causes millions of investors operating from widely differing locations, making countless buy and sell decisions, at varying points in time, to behave more or less alike—and to do so consistently and persistently! How can this be? The answer to this is not known, although reasonable theories can be formulated."

Then Hurst came awesomely close to discovering the Taylor Effect: "Recent experimental evidence tends to show that such intangibles as fatigue and frame of mind are influenced by the presence or absence of physical force fields. [He cites experiments on U-2 pilots artificially shielded from the Earth's magnetic field.] Now all of us exist in an environment that is simply riddled with force fields—gravitational, electrostatic, etc. If such fields can influence *some* physical and mental functions, might they not influence *others*—perhaps causing masses of humans to feel simultaneously bullish or bearish in the market, for example? Conjecture, but a possibility. . . . Seeing how it *might* come about helps us to accept the evidence of our own eyes and analyses, even when the results seem irrational by past experience."

In summary, Hurst concluded: "The unknowns in the [decision-making] process probably mask the true cause of price-motion cyclicality. . . . Although the cause of cyclicality is unknown, the nature of the effect is certain. . . . The implications of cyclicality include possible external influences of the decision processes of masses of investors more or less simultaneously. If this is fact, you must guard yourself carefully against the same influences. . . . Cyclicality is probably not related to rational decision factors. . . . . The extent of non-random cyclicality precludes any major contribution to price action by random events. . . . All price fluctuations about smooth long-term trends in the market . . . are due to manifestations of cyclicality."

The twin achievements of Robert Taylor are to have discovered the true nature of Hurst's "external motivation **X**"—which, Hurst speculated, might result from the effects upon human emotions of "gravitational fields"[!]—and to have utilized that knowledge in successfully forecasting market fluctuations in a manner automatically adaptive to changing conditions.

Dr. Claud E. Cleeton

Dr. Cleeton, for many years prior to his retirement, was Director of Electronics Research at the Naval Research Laboratory. He mastered everything in Hurst's book and built upon it. In particular he (like Taylor and Hurst) noted[3] the phase-flip problem, which he calls the "out-of-phase problem." Cleeton's solution is to utilize two different centered moving averages of different spans. In his book[3] Cleeton states: "Figure 7-3 illustrates the distortion in a moving average when the amplitude error is negative. . . . The 30-day and 60-day moving averages crisscross to show a cyclic component in the DJI average. The period of the cyclic component is such that large-amplitude errors are introduced in the moving average and further the 60-day average is moving out of phase with the price data." In summarizing, Cleeton concludes: "For periods less than the span length, the output of the moving average may be 180° out of phase with the data. This distortion shows up in the charts and may be corrected."

In the Taylor procedure, the analog of the Cleeton test for phase-flips would be to make the forecast for several different choices of n and plot them on the same graph. If one or more is out of phase with another, then at least one of the dimensions n is unacceptable. Taylor had independently discovered this idea in his own experiments, and notes that as the hypothetical state-space dimension n runs from 2 to 32, there may be several forecasts at adjacent dimensions which dramatically disagree owing to a clearly visible phase-flip. Taylor has concluded that "at least one of the trial-dimensions n nearly ALWAYS provides a correct forecast; the main difficulty is to select *which* dimension n to accept and which values of n to discard." The difficulty is not so much that of discrimination when the analyst has time to examine all plots visually; the difficulty is to develop a reliable method of selecting the optimal dimension n strictly automatically, without subjective human intervention.

Cleeton told one of us in the early '80s that, in the early and mid '70s, that is, during the 7 years between the appearance of Hurst's book[2] and that of Cleeton,[3] this virtuoso technical analyst had amazed his friends by mailing out Christmas cards for 7 consecutive years which predicted the DJIA for the next 12 months, and being consistently awesomely correct! In his book,[3] Cleeton explains step-by-step and in great detail exactly how he did it. The only complaint we have about Cleeton's methods is that they involve too much painstaking manual labor, refitting, trial-and-error, and customization to be acceptable to anyone except a retired post-doctoral expert in numerical analysis who was willing to spend literally months on a single (one-year) forecast for a single time-series.

Busy twenty-first century investors want to consider many different stocks rather than just one index, and they want their analysis procedures fully automated so that they can be updated daily and/or weekly, rather than just annually. In this sense, with all due respect to their pioneering brilliance, a fair comparison between the final results of Hurst & Cleeton and of Taylor would be that between da Vinci's conceptual toy-helicopter design and Sikorsky's operational man-carrying vehicle.

Jim Sloman & Welles Wilder

Welles Wilder, originally trained as a mechanical engineer, was widely regarded as the USA's premier "technical" market-analyst when in September 1983 he received an unexpected phone call from Jim Sloman. According to Wilder, young Sloman had placed among the top high-school students in the USA in a national exam given to all senior math students, and subsequently had been awarded a National Merit Scholarship to Princeton University where he studied math and physics in special advanced classes.

Wilder paid Sloman "a very large sum of money" to learn the rationale of the results which Sloman showed him. Later Wilder printed 100 copies of his book *The Delta Phenomenon* and, in conjunction with a two-day private tutoring seminar for each purchaser, sold nearly all 100 copies for $35,000 cash each to new members of the secret Delta Society International.

Some years later one of the members broke his contract of confidentiality and a book was offered for public sale that was obviously a clone of Wilder's book. By threatening legal action, Wilder got the book withdrawn, but he knew that the secret was out. With agreement from all of the members, he then sold about 1000 new copies of the book for $3,500 each and gave the original purchasers three-quarters of the profits.

Quite recently, Wilder saw the 1996 reprint[13] of Dr. Arnold Lieber's 1978 book,[4] which he had not known about. Realizing that further secrecy was futile, the members agreed to mass-market the book and it has now been offered to hundreds of thousands of potential buyers for less than $200/copy.

After college Sloman had tried several careers, including stock-broker and commodity trader, but decided that he lacked the right temperament for it.

Sloman began[7]: "Where my house is on the beach, when the tide is out there is a nice sandy beach, but when the tide is in, the water comes all the way to the rocks at the sea wall. [In order to run on the beach, one uses] TIDE CHARTS to know when the tide will be out. . . . A tide chart is a picture of an end result of the interaction of the sun, the moon, and the earth! . . . How long would it be until a day occurred that was identical to the current day? Would this not present one complete interaction of the sun, the moon, and the earth?"

Sloman's theory of "Short Term Delta" (STD) is that markets repeat directly or inversely [phase-flipped] "every 4 days." [Taylor's independently discovered theory of Pivot Points says that the basic period varies *between* 4 to 9 days.]

Sloman's theory of "Intermediate Term Delta" (ITD) is that markets repeat directly or inversely "every 4 lunar months."

Sloman's theory of 'Medium Term Delta" (MTD) is that markets will repeat directly or inversely every 12 lunar months. Also stated: "Markets repeat directly or inversely every lunar year."

The word "*inversely*" is there (in STD, ITD, MTD) because Sloman & Wilder also discovered the *phase-inversion* problem that had earlier plagued Hurst and Cleeton, and was soon to plague Taylor.

Sloman further defined "Long Term Delta" (LTD) as every 4 calendar years and "Super Long Term Delta" (SLTD) as every 19 years and 5 hours. (In the *saros*, the period is 18.02 years; in the modern theory of tidal heights,[1] the period is 18.6 years; where they get 19 years and 5 hours, we do not know.) However, interestingly, Wilder claims that in studying hundreds of years of data he has *never* seen a phase-inversion in either LTD or SLTD!

The LTD is a well-established phenomenon of cyclicality in the DJIA. One of us in the late '70s asked the famous technical analyst, Joe Granville, at a public address to thousands of his fans, "why does the DJIA have a 4-year cycle?" Granville (who had come on stage carrying a live goose) replied, "How would I know? Why do the lemmings march into the sea every 4 years?"

We omit further discussion of the Sloman-Wilder discovery, because their method is not amenable to automated analysis; to decide whether or

PARADIGM 601

not to expect a phase-inversion at the end of one cycle, several highly subjective decisions have to be made while studying long-term historical charts. Wilder admits that a few of the original Delta Society members never could quite get the hang of it!

We mention the Sloman-Wilder discovery, however, because no reader of their beautifully-printed, multi-colored chart-illustrated, and breathlessly excitedly-written book can close it and still doubt that the Taylor Effect is an objectively real phenomenon. If Wilder had been trained in digital signal processing (DSP) and electrical engineering rather than mechanical engineering, and if he had been able to do his own programming rather than being limited to hiring a programmer, he might have succeeded in not only getting an understanding of the nature of the problem and its central difficulty but in truly "solving" it and reducing its solution to practice, as has Taylor.

But Wilder admits that his "turning points" only have a 51% probability of occurring within a few days of when they are expected

So with all due respect to Sloman's flash of genius, and to Wilder's informed appreciation of the awesome magnitude of Sloman's insight, they have not (in the sense of intellectual property law) truly reduced their ideas to practice as yet.

Conclusion

The several prior partial, yet incompletely practiced, anticipations of Hurst,[2] Cleeton,[3] Sloman & Wilder,[7] together with the unrelated but relevant psychiatric research of Lieber,[[4],[13]] provide overwhelming evidence of the validity of Taylor's discovery without in the slightest detracting from his *priority* as the first person to both make the discovery and then to reduce the discovery to a practically useful form.

References

1. Paul Schurman, *Manual of Harmonic Analysis*, 1940, U.S. Dept. of Commerce, Coast & Geodetic Survey, Special Publication No. 98.

2. J. M. Hurst, *The Profit Magic of Stock Transaction Timing*, 1970, Prentice-Hall.

3. Claud E. Cleeton, Ph.D., *The Art of Independent Investing: A Handbook of Mathematics, Formulas and Technical Tools for Successful Market Analysis and Stock Selection*, 1976, Prentice-Hall.

4. Arnold Lieber, M.D., *The Lunar Effect: Biological Tides and Human Emotions*, 1978, Doubleday & Co.

5. Andrew C. Harvey, *Forecasting, structural time series models and the Kalman filter*, 1989, Cambridge University Press.

6. Masanao Aoki, *State Space Modeling of Time Series*, 1990, Springer-Verlag.

7. Welles Wilder, *The Delta Phenomenon, or The Hidden Order in All Markets*, 1991, The Delta Society Int'l.

8. Harry S. Dent, Jr., *The Great Boom Ahead*, 1993, Hyperion.

9. Andreas S. Weigand & Neil A. Gershenfeld, *Time Series Prediction: Forecasting the Future and Understanding the Past*, 1993, Addison-Wesley.

10. Robert D. Taylor, *OPS* time: The Secret to Perfect Timing for Success* [Optimum Performance Schedule], 1994, Longstreet Press, Atlanta, GA.

11. D. R. Cox et al, eds., *Time Series Models: In econometrics, finance and other fields*, 1996, Chapman & Hall. [*cf.* particularly Ch.3 on Forecasting]

12. Curt Wells, *The Kalman Filter in Finance*, 1996, Kluwer Academic.

13. Arnold Lieber, M.D., *How the Moon Affects You*, 1996, Hastings House.

14. Masanao Aoki & Arthur M. Havener, eds., *Applications of Computer Aided Time Series Modeling*, 1997, Springer-Verlag.

15. Harry S. Dent, Jr., *The Roaring 2000s*, 1998, Simon & Schuster.

See also, Brian Greene, *The Elegant Universe*, 1999, Vintage Books; Lee Smolin, *Three Roads to Quantum Gravity*, 2001, Basic Books.

Technical Appendix

1. What pre-processing is required to put market data into a form suitable for use in the Xybernomics program?

While historical values of actual trading data are available for only 6.5 hours per trading day, and not at all on weekends and holidays, data for the exogenous input are available on a continuous basis. If samples of actual trading data are taken every half-hour, from 09:30 a.m. to 4:00 p.m., with the 09:30 value assumed to be identical to that at the close of the preceding day, there are 14 values per day available for processing. The exogenous data can, of course, be synchronously sampled at those same times.

There are several methods by which the data segments can be connected or linked to form a continuous stream of data. One such method is simply to ignore the gaps in the data, placing the segments side-by-side. Such a method disrupts the time base and ignores the time-continuity of the dynamics of both the market and the effect of the exogenous input on the market; this will affect the accuracy of the market modeling and, therefore, the prediction.

Another method of linking the data segments is to fill in the gaps with constant values equal to the last known value of the variable. While this method preserves the time base, it injects dynamically unrealistic values of the variable into the record and will, therefore, create prediction errors. A third method of linking the data segments is to linearly interpolate between the variable values on either side of the gap. That method preserves the time base and improves the continuity of the values indicated by the actual record, but ignores the dynamics both of the exogenous input and the trading market.

A fourth method of linking the data segments is to utilize an interpolator based upon a dynamic model of the market derived during the immediately preceding interval, during which actual data were available. If sufficient data are available during the preceding interval to generate the dynamic model, this theoretically more advanced method will preserve both the time base and the dynamics of the variables involved.

A final adjustment can be made to match the filled-in data to the actual data at the end points. The only prediction errors introduced by this method are those caused by inaccuracies in the short-term model used for interpolation.

All of these methods of linking discontinuous data segments have been investigated and found to be viable. The method employed in obtaining the results related herein is that of filling in the data gaps with constant values equal to the latest known sample during non-trading days, and then taking each "day" to have only 14 ticks, as shown above. The resulting input-output series are then piecewise composed of 14 consecutive ticks, followed by a jump of $17 \times 2 = 34$ ignored ticks, each day, but during non-trading days, the market data is held constant at its last value. The obviously problematic nature of this discontinuity is discussed below in Item 4.

2. What mathematical model is employed for the market, and how are the model parameters determined?

The market model employed is that of a linear, time-invariant (over a reasonably short period of time) dynamical system driven by inputs which, except for unpredictable anomalies, are dominated in the short term by an exogenous input identified by one of our group, Robert Taylor. The model is derived from a financial time series, $\{ y(k) \}$, with bias removed, assumed to be (in the language of the MATLAB System Identification Toolbox) the output of an ARX(p,q) x(t) process with measurement noise, represented by the equations:

$$x(k) = a(1) x(k\text{-}1) + ... + a(p) x(k\text{-}p) + b(1) u(k\text{-}1) + ... + b(q) u(k\text{-}q) + w(k),$$
$$y(k) = x(k) + v(k)$$

where the w(k) and v(k) are zero-bias, random input noise and measurement error, respectively; and where the input noise includes that part of the series not attributable to the ARX(p,q) process.

3. How are the order (p,q) and the p+q parameters, c=[a' b']', of the ARX(p,q) process model determined?

The ARX x(k) is taken as the market history series, y(k), in the regression method of estimating the parameters of an ARX model under the assumption that p = q. The order p is chosen by the use of AIC. Specifically, the estimate of the model parameter vector, c, for a given p and q, is done by stacking the ARX equations, with the measurements, y, for all values of k, and finding the OLS estimates of the c's. The linear regression equation resulting from stacking the ARX equations is: $y = [Y\ U]\ c + noise$. The OLS estimate of c, $c^\wedge$, is given by: $c^\wedge = [X'X]\backslash X'\ y$, where the matrix $X = [Y\ U]$, and $[X'X]\backslash$ denotes the left inverse of $[X'X]$, and X' denotes the transpose of X.

If the choice of $p = q$ were to be questioned, there are several very good answers. In the first place, it is necessary to take $q < (p+1)$, for otherwise [as can be seen most easily by introducing the z-transform and replacing the above system by a model defined by a z-transform *transfer function* from the input to the output] we would be allowing for a constant multiplier of the input to be an additive component of the output, which is *a priori* absurd. Secondly, this transfer function can be regarded as a ratio of polynomials in z, of which the numerator has degree q and the denominator has degree $(p+1)$, where, as mentioned, it is necessary for plausibility that $q < (p+1)$. But there is no loss of generality by taking $q = p$, for if the actual degree of the numerator were of lesser degree, then the coefficients of the higher-order terms in z would be zero. We have tested this on artificially-constructed numerical examples wherein the answer was known because the data was generated by a system with $q < p$, and the presently disclosed algorithms worked sufficiently well that the higher-order coefficients were "identified" as equal to zero to better than 17 decimal places. Finally, the Ho-Kalman Lemma mentioned in Item 7 below implies that the system should be modeled via the state-space model (F,G,H) specified in item 5 below, wherein the model is isomorphic to any model obtained by a linear change of variables on the state-variables, which is equivalent to replacement of (F,G,H) by (inv(T) F T, inv(T) G, H T), where $abs(det(T)) > 0$, which allows us to take F in companion-matrix form [i.e. to introduce "phase variables"], which then leads automatically to the ARX(p,p) model-form chosen above.

4. How do you justify deleting 17 ½ hours of the exogenous input per trading day and setting the trade history series value to a constant for 24 hours on each no-trade day?

These practices are based upon the tacit assumptions that the market is dormant during non-trading hours, that the model of the market is stationary, and that the errors introduced into the model are acceptable. The exogenous input is a physical variable which, with respect to physical, chronological time, runs 24-hours/day, 7 days/week, continuously, and is known to be a multiply-periodic function of time with 31 independent frequencies, so omitting the weekends would introduce fallacious dynamics into the exogenous input more severe than the errors introduced by assuming that the exogenous input drives market activity only when the market is open. In the future the equities markets will probably be open continuously and then the daily discontinuity noted in the present methodology will disappear. But until then, the ultimate justification for our present practices is that these practices have been shown to produce useful market forecasts. (See Item 1 above.)

5. How are the variances q and r of w(t) and v(t) estimated?

The estimates of both q and r are set equal to the square of the following expression: std(yd) / [abs(ym) + max(abs(yd))], where ym = mean(y), yd = debiased(y), std = standard deviation, abs = absolute value, and max = maximum value. The values of both q and r are deliberately determined in a manner calculated to desensitize the Kalman filter's stability to variability in (F,G,H,q,r), i.e. to enhance its "robustness" to modeling errors. More accurate estimates of q and r are obtainable using the MSE of

$y^\wedge(k) - a(1)\, y^\wedge(k-1) - \ldots\, -a(p)\, y^\wedge(k-p)$, and using the MSE of $y(k) - y^\wedge(k)$, where $y^\wedge(k) = a(1)y(k-1) - \ldots\, - a(p)\, y(k-p)$.

The extent to which the improvement in forecast accuracy, possibly attainable by using these more complicated but more precise estimates for q and r, would justify the additional programming complexity is under investigation, but the question remains open because the "tradeoff" involved is more subjective than objective. In fact, from the point of view of desiring the Kalman Filter to be as "robust" as possible, it is not necessarily advantageous to take q and r to be realistic; in his published theory of "*Rho*bust" filter design via "*Rho*-synthesis", R.W. Bass has shown that filter robustification can be maximized by taking completely artificial choices of q and r, selected entirely to make the filter robust irrespective of what the theoretically correct choices of q and r may be. This is legitimate because the Kalman-Bucy Filter has *proved* optimality only when the model parameters are exactly correct; indeed, as Kalman himself pointed out in his exposition of the Bass theory of *asympotic state-estimators* [see the book by Kalman, Falb, and Arbib], if the process noise and measurement noise are actually merely unknown wave-form disturbances [as in C.D. Johnson's theory of Disturbance-Accommodating Control] rather than stochastic processes, then the filter's estimate of the system's state-vector will converge (with a small residual error) in a manner more dependent upon the filter's stability and "structural-stability" [robustness] than upon the choice of a filter gain matrix via the Ricatti Equation defined by exact values of q and r.

(In aerospace engineering, the values of q and r are adjusted by trial-and-error purely empirically; this is called "tuning the Kalman filter.") The present methodology includes an adaptive feature in which q and r are adjusted, if necessary, until the Kalman filter is found to be stable, although in practice we have found that only in very unusual markets does this adaptivity-feature get exercised.

6. How is the Kalman-Bucy Filter used to determine the initial state for predicting the future?

The ARX-in-measurements model discussed in Item 3 is defined by the standard state-space-model equations:

$$X(k) = F X(k-1) + G U(k-1) + G w(k) , y(k) = H X(k) + v(k),$$

where $X(k) = [x(k-p+1), ... , x(k)]'$ and F, G, H, and the covariances q and r of w and v can be determined easily as specified in Item 5 above, and, without loss of generality, it may be assumed that F is in companion-matrix form. Applying the Kalman-Bucy Filter for this state-space model to a market data series of selected length up to the immediate past, we obtain an estimate of the state vector, $X(t)$. This estimate is the initial state then used for running the ARX model to predict future values.

7. How do you justify a system model identifying the state variables, x(k) with the sequential measurements, y(k)?

A system model that identifies the state vector, $x(k)$, with sequential measurements of the output, $y(k)$ is one of many valid models for a single-output system. There is a published theorem by Packard, Farmer *et al* (*Phys.Rev.Lett.*, 1980) concerning "geometry from a time-series" in which it was demonstrated that collecting the lagged values of the series, with an optimal choice of the number of lags, defines a state-space which is differentiably homeomorphic to the actual state-space in case the time-series had been generated by projection from a state-space dynamical system. In the case of an unknown system excited by a known input, the assumptions of linearity, stationarity, and finite-dimensionality, require, in the noiseless case, via the fundamental Ho-Kalman Lemma, that matrices (F,G,H) exist which define the type of state-space model that was specified in Item 6 above — which leads automatically to the use of lagged outputs as a state-vector when one makes a linear transformation that puts the matrix F into companion- matrix form. It may be objected that both the Packard-Farmer Theorem and the Ho-Kalman Lemma depend upon assumptions which may not be realized perfectly in the case of economic time-series modeling. The only reply to that objection is to note that the empirical demonstration of our remarkably reliable market forecasts is the ultimate practical validation of our modeling choice.

8. Do you estimate the error covariance of the estimates of the system parameters?

No. The error covariance is not used here. If it were, an estimate of it would be the inverse of X'X / s where s = y' [(I-X (X'X\X')^2] y .

9. How is the ARX modeling procedure used to forecast the market?

It is used to make relatively short-term forecasts between two consecutive predictable anomalies observable in the exogenous input, which can be called *inflection points*; previously, Robert Taylor had termed them Pivot Points, although inflection points appears to be more precise geometrically. Note that, in predicting future market trends, the needed values of the exogenous input are known but the future values of the market data are not known and must be predicted by the ARX process itself. The absolute values of the predicted market values are generally not in good agreement with those of the actual values. However, the market trends indicated by those predictions are, generally, in good agreement with the actual market trends. Since inflection points are known to interfere with the prediction of market trends, it is important to flag these points. These inflection points are clearly provided by the methodology employed in our process. The market trends indicated by the market forecast plots, in conjunction with the inflection point flags provided, have proved to be a remarkably good indicator of the actual market trends to be expected over that interval.

10. How are the inflection points identified?

Linking together the 14-sample segments of the exogenous input produces "cusps" in the resulting series, when displayed graphically. These "cusps" in the resulting curve point upward for a number of segments, and then flip over and point downward for about the same number of segments. An inflection point can be recognized visually as the point in the composite exogenous series at which the cusps change direction. Robert Taylor presently renders more numerically-precise his selection of inflection points by choosing either the maximum of a sequence of local minima, or the minimum of a sequence of local maxima, which generally occur at points at which the visible "cusp-flip" from a row similar to UUU. . . to a row of upside-down U's can be seen, but which he finds to be a less subjective decision than picking the point of visible "flip" by visual inspection of a graphical display. Earlier, Taylor had selected inflection points as those days on a Calendar of Daily Tides at which 3 rather than the normal 4 daily extrema occurred; but although this discovery had great heuristic value, and generally selects inflection points within a day of two of the two other methods discussed, it involves additional subjective complications which Taylor was relieved to discard when he discovered the more mechanical/numerical procedure specified above.

11. How do you explain the high rate of success of the procedure in forecasting trends in the market?

The exogenous input is a very important consistent driving factor for any financial time series, driving the series in upward or downward fluctuations. This is the essence of the "Taylor Effect".

To be patentable, an invention or discovery must be demonstrated to possess novelty, utility, and non-obviousness.

Novelty is demonstrated here by the fact that although Hurst and Cleeton recognized that *some* exogenous input was driving the "quasi-predictable" quasi-periodic fluctuations which they exploited, and though Hurst speculated that "gravitational" or electrostatic or magnetic or electromagnetic fields might be involved, neither Hurst nor Cleeton [nor *any* predecessor] was able to derive a valid exogenous-input model.

Non-obviousness is demonstrated by the fact that although Sloman and Wilder correctly identified the exogenous input as the influence of the lunar gravitational field on human biological/emotional rhythms (as in psychiatrist Lieber's "biological tides" effect), and got a rough estimate of the periodicity of the inflection points (which they specified as "every four days" in comparison to Taylor's more accurate *adaptive* specification of "every four to nine-days depending upon the particular recent history of the exogenous input"), they were unable to reduce their discovery to useful algorithmic practice, despite tremendously diligent efforts over several years.

Finally, *utility* of the Taylor Effect is made manifest by the remarkable success of our unique market-data processing algorithms and procedure.

Conclusion

We have demonstrated that the discovery documented in the preceding technical essay and the present Technical Appendix, as reduced to practice in the computer program *Xyber9*, possesses each of the three desiderata of *novelty*, *utility* and *non-obviousness* to a high-degree, in a field which has been studied diligently by thousands of highly-motivated and talented investigators, without prior complete success. Accordingly, the present disclosure constitutes an *enabling disclosure* in the sense of intellectual property law. Moreover, the Taylor Effect is an excellent example of what one Supreme Court Patent decision called a "result long sought, seldom approached, and never attained."

Author's Note

How did Nicholas and Alex do it?

Please refer to the pair of spreadsheets that follow this section. One represents dates in time where you can anticipate the "highs" in the stock market, while the other represents the "lows" in the stock market.

I have used the DOW (Dow Jones Industrial Average, symbol INDU) for my examples, although the S&P500, NASDAQ, and other stock market indexes follow the same predictable patterns. Individual stocks will typically follow the same cycles as the indexes, but vary in amplitudes due to other factors, as discussed in the book and my essay *The Taylor Effect*.

Note that the attached Dow Jones Industrial Average charts exhibit the predicted yearly lows and highs based on the nautical data presented in the following two spreadsheets.

Yearly trends are easily attainable by using this relatively simple process. The monthly and daily trends are another matter. By using Nobletec's nautical program, you can produce and observe monthly and weekly fluctuations similar to those in yearly trends.

As Nicholas and Alex discovered, you might realize somewhat of a problem deciphering the monthly charts. Many of the months exhibit the same values, thus leaving the researcher to guess which month is the actual low or high. The same applies to the daily and weekly charts. Filtering the monthly and daily charts works to some extent by applying smaller time frames, such as hours and minutes, but this is not as effective as it is with years.

In *Paradigm*, Alex solved this problem by writing *Xyber9*, an Aerospace System Identification program. The *truth* is that I personally developed *Xyber9* and I use it daily.

Besides identifying highs and lows in the market, *Xyber9* filters noise or anomalies, such as a shock in the market that can cause other problems. During the duration of the expected monthly or shorter-term weekly trend, an anomaly can interfere with the known market direction and cause unexpected results. Anomalies that affect shorter term trends include earnings reports, the PPI, the CPI, unemployment reports, the Michigan Sentiment, Consumers Confidence, interest rate announcements, and just about anything in the news that affects human emotions.

With yearly forecasts, when an anomaly shocks the market the trends are typically long enough in duration and the amplitudes so great that the anomaly doesn't have enough of an effect on the market to cause an incorrect prediction. This includes geopolitical events, wars, recessions, assassinations, or any other traumatic social event.

My studies have spanned more than 85 years of historical stock market data and eighteen years of real-time experience. I was fortunate to work with world-renowned scientists in the field of Control Theory and Systems Identification software. This experience brought me great insight and, more importantly, the program *Xyber9*. *Xyber9* uses nautical data and incorporates stock market data to produce highly accurate monthly and weekly forecasts.

You can find detailed information about the *Xyber9* program inside *Paradigm*, or visit the website www.paradigmbook.com for more details.

Empirical Proof

As most of you have likely already discovered, *Paradigm* is actually two books in one. It is both a scientific and historical thriller, as well as a scientific essay. In an effort to avoid bogging down the novelized portion of the book with the technical details, I decided instead to outline the practical applications in an addendum. This allows the reader to actually retrace the steps that Nicholas and Alex took to become millionaires.

I invite all interested readers (and especially skeptics) to investigate for your own satisfaction the same procedures I used to create the results found in the pages of *Paradigm*. These are the exact procedures I continue to use and take advantage of for my own personal financial gains. This is a simple way for you to plot out the true correlation between gravitational fluctuations measured by tidal undulation patterns, and that of the stock market. You will also discover the pivotal years of change and future direction of the stock market, as far into the future as you wish to go. In *Paradigm*, I provided forecasts all the way to the year 2020.

Still skeptical? Even if you decide not to follow my step-by-step instructions, I encourage you to turn to the final few pages of this book and review the spreadsheets and the results, which were drawn on samplings of the DOW historical data.

ॐ

The nautical software program I use is commercially sold over the Internet by a company called Nobeltec. Its Web address is www.nobeltec.com. Under "Products," click on "Tides & Currents" and locate the "Tides & Currents SRP for North America," East and West edition. The software sells for $129. Follow the directions to order.

Once you receive and install the Nobeltec software, just follow the simple instructions below:

Finding the HIGHS in the market.

Click on "File," and then click on "New Tide Window."

Click on the "Name Search" button on the bottom the page and type in the name "Reedy Point." Click "OK." This opens the correct tide window.

Go up to the top of the page and click on "Search," and then "Event Search."

In the "Search for Event" window, go to the "Search For: Section," click the down arrow, and select "High Tides."

Go to the next down arrow, click and select with the "Greatest" value.

Go to the next down arrow, click and select for each year.

Go to the "Date Range: section." In the "Start" box, change the date to 1/1/1920. In the box below, marked "End," change the date to 12/31/2020.

Click the "Specify Time of Day" box. Change the Start time to 9:30 a.m. and in the End time box change the time to 4:00 p.m.

Click the "Specify Day of Week" box. Then click on "Monday," "Tuesday," "Wednesday," "Thursday," and "Friday."

Finally, click the "Search" button and print the results when you are finished.

The increases in market price are in direct response to decreases in gravitational forces.

Once you have printed the spreadsheet, follow the "Value" column down and mark the tidal values with the lowest number as a "HIGH." The years with the lowest high tide values represent the lowest gravitational forces. You will find some consecutive years with the same value. Mark each with a "High." I have provided a spreadsheet with those dates marked correctly.

As I described in the text of *Paradigm*, the nautical program rounds off numbers, which accounts for similar values in consecutive years. Looking closely at the data in time segments such as days, hours, and even minutes, constitutes the exact date by deducing the number of same value occurrences during the month.

৯

Finding the "LOWS" in the market

Remember: you already have the proper tide window open. Just follow these simple instructions:

Go up to the top of the page and click on "Search then Event Search."

In the "Search for Event" window, go to the "Search For: section," click the down arrow and select "Low Tides."

Go to the next down arrow, click and select with the "SMALLEST" value.

Go to the next down arrow, click and select for each year.

Go to the "Date Range: section." In the "Start" box, change the date to 1/1/1920. In the box below marked "End," change the date to 12/31/2020.

Deselect the "Specify Time of the Day" button and the "Specify Day of the Week" button.

Finally, click the "Search" button and print the results when finished.

The decreases in market price are in direct response to the increases in gravitational forces.

Once you have printed the spreadsheet, follow the "Value" column down and mark the tidal values with the lowest number as a "LOW." The years with the lowest low tide values represent the highest gravitational forces.

You will find some consecutive years have the same value. Mark each as a "Low." I have provided a spreadsheet with those dates marked correctly. As I described in the text of *Paradigm*, the nautical program rounds off numbers, which accounts for similar values in consecutive years. Looking closely at the data in time segments such as days, hours, and even minutes, constitutes the exact date by deducing the number of same value occurrences during the month.

ॐ

You have now successfully produced two spreadsheets *totally unrelated to financial markets*. You will now be able to compare these results to real-time data. I use TradeStation as my real-time data provider. However, you can use any daily historical data that charts the DOW history back to 1920.

In order to make a direct comparison use the following provision:

> The lowest price in a year marked with a "Low" will be below the highest price in the preceding year marked with a "High." The "Highest" price in a year marked with a "High" will be above the lowest price in the preceding year marked with a "Low."

Search For Event at: Tides, REEDY POINT

High Tides with the Greatest Values, 9:30 a.m. To 4:00 p.m., M-F

Event Year	Value			Event Year	Value	
1920	6.5	High		1971	6.8	
1921	6.7			1972	6.7	
1922	6.8			1973	6.5	High
1923	6.8			1974	6.7	
1924	6.6			1975	6.9	
1925	6.4	High		1976	6.8	
1926	6.7			1977	6.6	
1927	6.8			1978	6.5	High
1928	6.7			1979	6.6	
1929	6.4	High		1980	6.8	
1930	6.6			1981	6.7	
1931	6.8			1982	6.5	High
1932	6.8			1983	6.6	
1933	6.5	High		1984	6.8	
1934	6.6			1985	6.8	
1935	6.7			1986	6.6	
1936	6.8			1987	6.5	High
1937	6.7			1988	6.7	
1938	6.4	High		1989	6.8	
1939	6.8			1990	6.6	
1940	6.8			1991	6.5	High
1941	6.8			1992	6.7	
1942	6.6	High		1993	6.8	
1943	6.6			1994	6.8	
1944	6.7			1995	6.6	

Search For Event at: Tides, REEDY POINT (cont)

High Tides with the Greatest Values, 9:30 a.m. To 4:00 p.m., M-F

Event Year	Value			Event Year	Value	
1945	6.8			1996	6.6	High
1946	6.6			1997	6.8	
1947	6.4	High		1998	6.8	
1948	6.7			1999	6.7	
1949	6.7			2000	6.4	High
1950	6.7			2001	6.6	
1951	6.5	High		2002	6.8	
1952	6.6			2003	6.8	
1953	6.8			2004	6.4	High
1954	6.8			2005	6.6	
1955	6.6	High		2006	6.8	
1956	6.6			2007	6.8	
1957	6.8			2008	6.6	
1958	6.9			2009	6.5	High
1959	6.7			2010	6.8	
1960	6.4	High		2011	6.8	
1961	6.6			2012	6.8	
1962	6.8			2013	6.8	High
1963	6.6			2014	6.8	
1964	6.6			2015	6.8	
1965	6.5			2016	6.8	
1966	6.7			2017	6.8	
1967	6.8			2018	6.8	High
1968	6.7			2019	6.8	
1969	6.4	High		2020	6.8	
1970	6.7					

Search For Event at: Tides, REEDY POINT

Low Tides with the Smallest Value

Event Year	Value			Event Year	Value	
1920	-0.9			1971	-0.7	
1921	-1	Low		1972	-0.5	
1922	-0.9			1973	-0.8	
1923	-0.7			1974	-0.9	Low
1924	-0.8			1975	-0.9	
1925	-0.9			1976	-0.8	
1926	-0.9	Low		1977	-0.8	
1927	-0.7			1978	-0.9	
1928	-0.6			1979	-1	Low
1929	-0.7			1980	-0.8	
1930	-0.8			1981	-0.6	
1931	-0.8	Low		1982	-0.8	
1932	-0.6			1983	-0.9	Low
1933	-0.6			1984	-0.8	
1934	-0.8			1985	-0.6	
1935	-0.9	Low		1986	-0.5	
1936	-0.7			1987	-0.8	
1937	-0.7			1988	-0.8	Low
1938	-0.9			1989	-0.7	
1939	-1	Low		1990	-0.5	
1940	-0.9			1991	-0.8	
1941	-0.8			1992	-0.9	Low
1942	-0.9	Low		1993	-0.9	
1943	-0.9			1994	-0.7	
1944	-0.9			1995	-0.8	

Search For Event at: Tides, REEDY POINT (cont)

Low Tides with the Smallest Value

Event Year	Value			Event Year	Value	
1945	-0.7			1996	-1	
1946	-0.6			1997	-1	Low
1947	-0.7			1998	-0.8	
1948	-0.8	Low		1999	-0.8	
1949	-0.7			2000	-0.8	
1950	-0.5			2001	-0.9	Low
1951	-0.6			2002	-0.8	
1952	-0.9	Low		2003	-0.6	
1953	-0.8			2004	-0.6	
1954	-0.6			2005	-0.8	
1955	-0.7			2006	-0.8	Low
1956	-0.9			2007	-0.6	
1957	-0.9	Low		2008	-0.6	
1958	-0.8			2009	-0.8	
1959	-0.8			2010	-0.9	Low
1960	-0.9			2011	-0.8	
1961	-1	Low		2012	-0.7	
1962	-0.9			2013	-0.9	
1963	-0.7			2014	-1	Low
1964	-0.7			2015	-0.9	
1965	-0.8			2016	-0.7	
1966	-0.8	Low		2017	-0.8	
1967	-0.7			2018	-0.9	
1968	-0.5			2019	-0.9	Low
1969	-0.7			2020	-0.7	
1970	-0.9	Low				

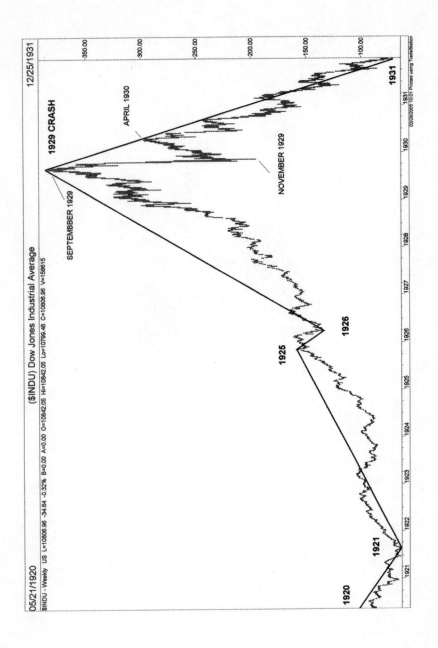

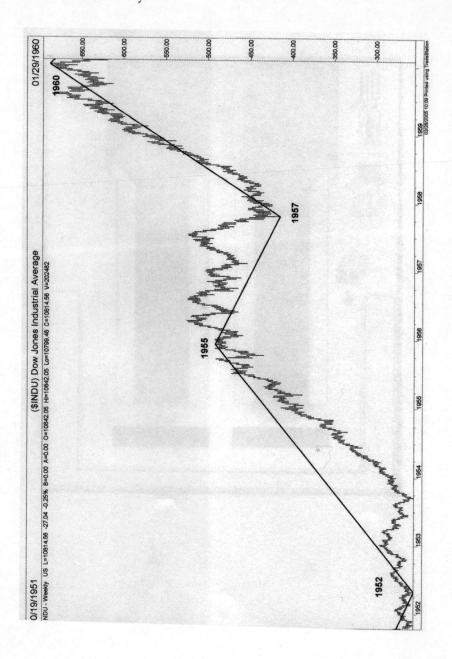

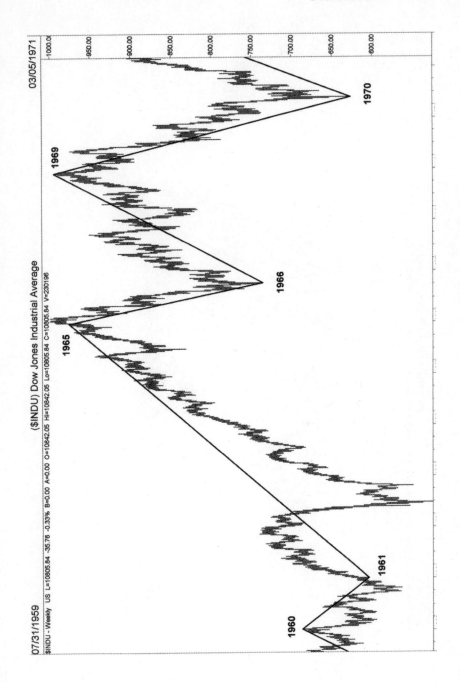

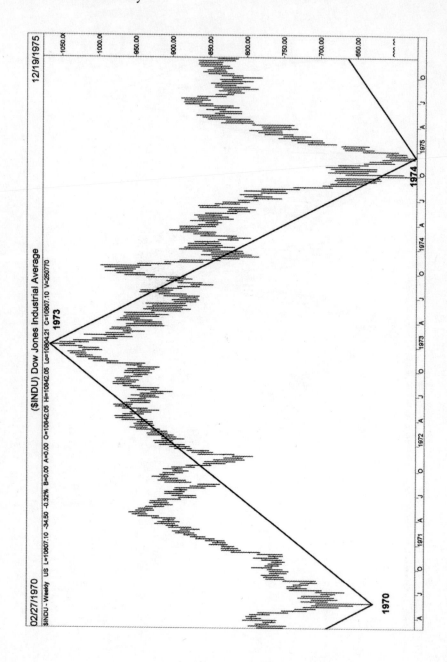

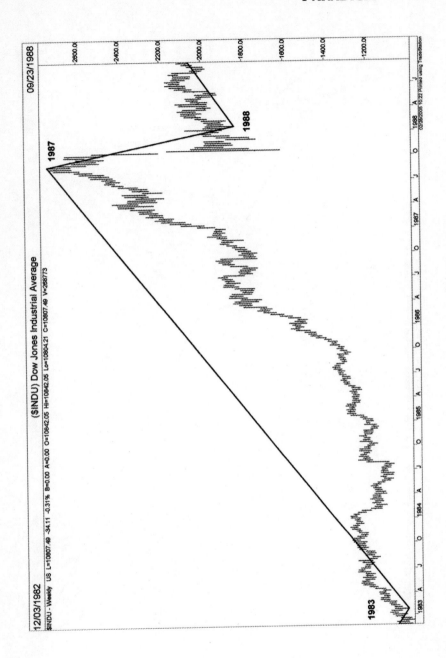

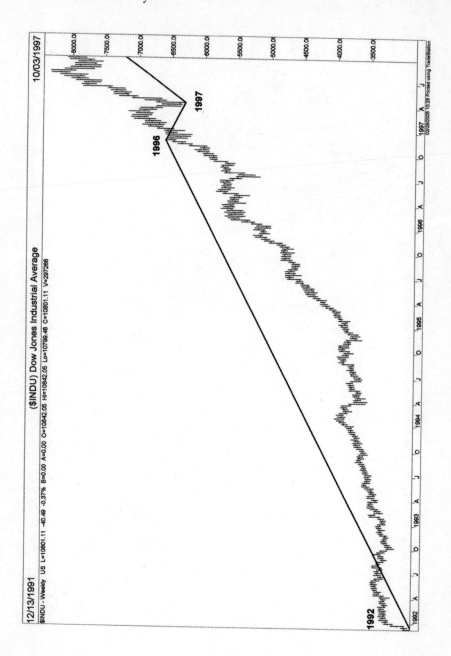

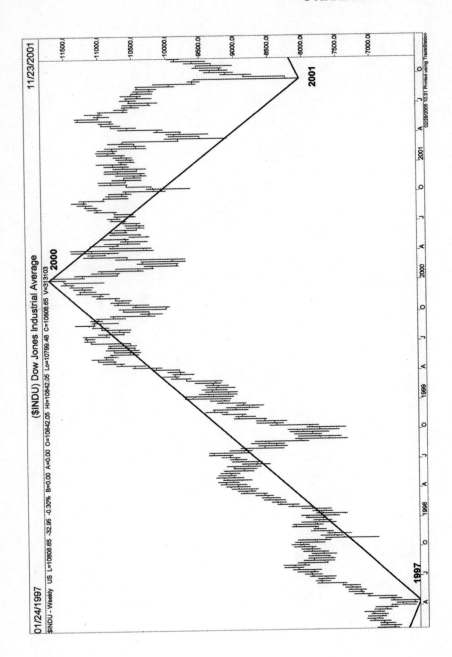

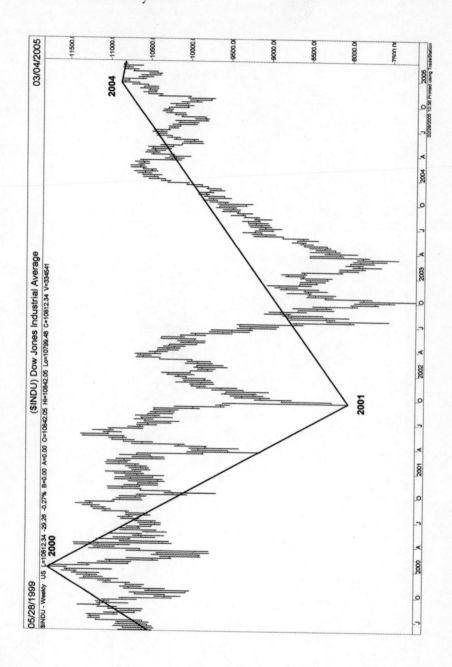